Sirena fought his embrace, her struggles useless against his powerful arms. Ignoring her protests, he siezed her and began to remove her gown. His lips found hers again, and lost in the moment, Sirena could only surrender to the feelings which engulfed her. All was forgotten and she was again in the cabin of her ship surrounded by the isolating fog. Then she remembered the wicked scar on her arm.

"Stop!" she cried hoarsely, pushing him from her as she strained to escape. He said nothing, but his eyes said it all. He meant to have her.

In spite of herself, Sirena was aware of a building response. She closed her eyes, and like the sea, felt her resistance ebb to be replaced by a surging tide of passion. . . .

By Fern Michaels
(published by The Random House Publishing Group)

ALL SHE CAN BE
CINDERS TO SATIN
DESPERATE MEASURES
FOR ALL THEIR LIVES
FREE SPIRIT
SEASONS OF HER LIFE
SERENDIPITY
TENDER WARRIOR
TO HAVE AND TO HOLD
TO TASTE THE WINE
VALENTINA
VIXEN IN VELVET

The Captive series
CAPTIVE PASSIONS
CAPTIVE EMBRACES
CAPTIVE SPLENDORS
CAPTIVE INNOCENCE
CAPTIVE SECRETS

The Texas series
TEXAS HEAT
TEXAS RICH
TEXAS FURY
TEXAS SUNRISE

The Sins series
SINS OF OMISSION
SINS OF THE FLESH

CAPTIVE PASSIONS
&
CAPTIVE EMBRACES

TWO NOVELS

FERN MICHAELS

BALLANTINE BOOKS • NEW YORK

2006 Ballantine Books Mass Market Edition

Published in the United States by Ballantine Books, an imprint of The Random House Publishing Group, a division of Random House, Inc., New York.

BALLANTINE and colophon are registered trademarks of Random House, Inc.

ISBN 0-345-49567-5

Printed in the United States of America

www.ballantinebooks.com

OPM 9 8 7 6 5 4 3 2 1

CAPTIVE PASSIONS

To my husband

Prologue

Java, A.D. 1623

Tropical night breezes, fragrant with oleander and cloves, cooled by a gently ebbing sea, filtered through lacy, silk draperies into a softly lit bedroom of deep rose and pale beige. The candles in their brass sconces cast wavering shadows onto the low, wide bed. Pale pink satin coverlets rustled, the only sound in the hushed, sultry atmosphere.

Gretchen trailed long, tapered fingers across his glistening, sun-bronzed skin. "Take me, Regan," she breathed, as she raked her fingers across his chest, etching tiny red rivulets.

He grabbed her, crushing her softness in his hands. She moaned with the sounds of his passion and dug her nails into the hard muscles of his back. The moistness of drawn blood quickened her breathing as she became a wild jungle animal in the instinctive, abandoned throes of passion.

"Damn you, Regan," she panted as she struggled to free her breasts from his imprisoning grasp. "Stop playing with me! Don't make me wait any longer!" His answer was to slide his hands to her groin, never breaking the rhythm of his movements. He sought for and found the soft indentation where her thighs ended.

Thrusting, the giant astride her brought his hands downwards, crushing her arched body flat against the bed. A wild shriek tore through the room as Gretchen moved against the pressure of the man atop her.

Spent, Gretchen lay still, her breathing ragged. She spoke harshly: "I've seen you perform better, Regan. I've bedded schoolboys that could do what you just did. Where's the expertise the Javanese women credit you with?" she asked mockingly.

Regan van der Rhys leaned on one elbow and looked into her changeling, hazel eyes; at her splendiferous pale gold hair as smooth and glossy as the satin pillows. Her passion satisfied—for the moment—she resembled a sleepy-eyed tigress. "Javanese women don't demand these . . . these little cruelties you like to inflict. There are other ways to satisfy passion."

His tone was light and easy, and Gretchen was chagrined that her sharp criticisms had little effect on him. He was so completely certain of his magnetism, so entirely confident of his prowess, he vexed her. Regan's cool, phlegmatic composure constantly infuriated her. That he remained unaffected by her scathing remarks was testimony to his superficial feelings for her. It rankled that she meant so little to him. Her full, pouting lips curled in frustration, her chameleon-like eyes darkening to a hazy brown.

"Bah! You men are all alike! Let it suffice to say you enjoyed it. Must we constantly play these games?" She smiled fetchingly, even teeth flashing against her reddened, kiss-bruised lips. "The women of Java know nothing of sensuous delights. Where is the passion? They lay like slugs for men like you; and men like you come to women like myself to satisfy what they really want. Why lie, Regan?" she taunted.

"A bitch in heat," Regan muttered coldly, his handsome features stony and enigmatic.

"Bitch in heat, am I? How many times, Mynheer van der Rhys, have you mounted me when at the end we were both smeared with blood?" she asked derisively. "It was you who sought me! I'm your only release for whatever drives you! This inner burning, this intangible compulsion of yours! You come to me to exorcise yourself. But I don't mind," she said, stretching luxuriously, her eyes on the golden hair on Regan's chest. "Tell me," she coaxed, as her slender hands caressed her full, round breasts, "what would you do without me?"

She moved so that her taut bosom touched his nakedness. Narrowing his eyes, Regan grasped the soft flesh of her haunches and twisted it, pinching viciously.

Gretchen drew in her breath and writhed sensuously, her body glistening with a veil of perspiration. Pressing Regan back onto the mound of satin pillows, she straddled him. Clutching a handful of his hair, she shook his head wildly. "Love me, Regan, love me!"

He reached behind her, seized her round, white buttocks, and savagely brought her to him.

Lust blazed as their bodies sought to quench the flames engulfing them.

Gretchen watched Regan as he dressed, enjoying his unhurried, fluid movements. He was masculinely graceful, like an athlete. Wide broad chest, muscular arms, proud leonine head—all tapering to a flat stomach and slim hips atop long, well-developed legs. His handsome, sun-darkened face; his piercing blue eyes, cold and aloof one moment, igniting to the sharp glare of a lynx the next. A sheaf of white-blond hair fell crisply over his wide and intelligent forehead. But it was his sinewy, muscular body that made her pulses throb.

He swung about to face her as he finished buttoning his lawn shirt, his cold, chiseled features expressionless.

"What are you thinking, Regan? I can never see behind your mask."

"I was wondering what you'll do for diversion, Gretchen. Our being together won't be so frequent after a certain ship arrives from Spain."

"Why not?" she pouted, eyes darkening, betraying her posed indifference.

"I've a bride arriving," he stated simply, enjoying the fleeting pain in her eyes.

"Your humor is in poor taste, Regan. I don't appreciate it!"

"I'm speaking the truth. The wedding will take place shortly after Señorita Córdez arrives." He flashed her a winning, boyish smile, mischievous but tinged with embarrassment. Seeing no trace of mockery behind it, Gretchen became alarmed. It was true!

"Córdez? A Spaniard? A Dutchman marrying a Spaniard!" she laughed shrilly. "Don't tease, Regan."

He saw she was verging on hysterics but ignored this. He had chosen tonight to tell her, so she wouldn't do or say anything intentionally insulting when Señorita Córdez arrived. He hoped by that time Gretchen would be over the shock and at least try to act like a lady. Society, being quite limited here in Batavia, would soon throw her into company with the newly married couple.

Gretchen Lindenreich, a widow now, had been brought to Java in 1606 by her husband, a German sea captain; she had been but twenty years old. The Hamburg mercantile company for which Captain Peter Lindenreich sailed had encouraged him to take his brash and amoral new wife out of Saxony, to where her deviltry and disconcerting behavior would not reflect on the trading organization. Lindenreich, in love and beguiled by young Gretchen's beauty, readily agreed. And did more. He relinquished his German captaincy and accepted a new—and stationary—position with the recently formed Dutch East India Company, for he had long had friends in Holland. He was glad they were to be sent to the Spice Islands, for he too wanted his passionate wife away from the temptations of Hamburg society, and believed and hoped that in a more isolated environment she would settle into placidity and perhaps bless his old age with children.

Gretchen had no choice but to accompany her sixtyish husband. But the renunciation of his captaincy greatly depleted his earnings. Captains received a healthy share of cargo profits, but as a D.E.I. official in Java Peter merely earned a yearly salary with a promise of pension. Five years later, having showered Gretchen with as many luxuries of the rich

East Indian trade as he could afford, Peter Lindenreich died poor and childless. He never knew of the three times his wife had visited an old native crone who used witchcraft and herbs to abort her.

Although free of Peter, Gretchen could not leave Java. She would receive her husband's East India Company pension only if she stayed on the island. This she accepted in a conciliatory manner, for she had by then met Regan van der Rhys and meant one day to marry him, when he should be free.

Regan had, unfortunately for Gretchen, cast his eyes on the youngest daughter of a Javanese tribal chief some three years following his arrival in the islands in 1607, and had married her. Tita's soft, quiet manner and brown-skinned beauty had fully captured his fancy; and their marriage had been in addition a diplomatic coup for the Dutch in their rivalry with mercantile competitors—and predecessors—in the Spice Islands: the Portuguese and Spanish, united at the time under one crown, that of Philip III of Spain. The marriage had furthermore been a feather in the cap of Regan's father, Vincent van der Rhys, D.E.I. Chief Pensioner since his coming to Java in 1603.

"I'm not teasing, Gretchen. It's been arranged and I'm going through with it. I'm marrying Señorita Córdez!"

"I stood by once before and watched you marry that mincing tribal virgin! If she were still alive she'd be fat and toothless by now!"

Gretchen gasped as she saw Regan stiffen. The words had burst from her and now she realized she must suffer the consequences.

Their eyes locked, cold chills danced up her spine. She almost wished he would strike her—anything instead of this frigid fury.

"Whatever her appearance, she would have remained a good and faithful wife, a loving mother to my son. Now she'll always be beautiful and young in my memory." His eyes bored into Gretchen's. "How old are you, my dear? Thirty-six? Thirty-seven? It won't be many years before I see *you* become a toothless hag."

"I'm no such age, Regan, and you know it. I'm

years younger than you—" He turned his back on her, cutting her words off as with the sharp edge of a knife. Goaded by frustration, she attacked again. "And just where did you meet this Spaniard? On a pirate ship? In Spanish prison? In a Lisbon or Cádiz brothel?"

"No," he answered, his back still turned. "My father arranged the marriage a little more than three years ago, before my return. I've, well, not set eyes on her."

"Now I know you're lying! No father makes a marriage contract for a grown son, and one that's a widower besides! Do you take me for a complete fool?"

"Think what you like! It was a condition of my release from Spain—and one you doubtless did not know!" A shadow crossed Regan's eyes at the thought of this unwanted marriage, and his brows drew downwards like thick, golden hoods.

"I find it hard to believe your father would have been so presumptuous as to arrange this," Gretchen persisted angrily. "I won't stand by and let you do this! When you married Tita, Peter was still alive. We're both free now. There's been nothing to stop us, these past three years. You've led me to believe we would eventually be mar—"

"Married?" he finished for her coldly. "There was never a mention of marriage. And, I won't betray my father's honor, though he has been dead these twelve months and more. When Señorita Córdez arrives in Batavia our wedding will take place." The serious, scolding tone of his voice lifted, and he mocked, "You *will* come, won't you?" His eyes slid over the expanse of her creamy skin.

"I'll kill you!" Gretchen shrieked as she sprang from the bed, heedless of her nakedness. She raised her clenched fists and pounded his chest, her breasts heaving with outrage.

Savagely, Regan seized her to him and brought his mouth cruelly down upon hers. Her anger melted and she moaned in renewed desire. Brutally, he shoved her backwards onto the satin pillows. She sprawled grotesquely, hair spilling across her face.

"Bitch in heat!" Regan snarled.

Her initial shock abated, Gretchen straightened herself on the silken coverlet and slightly parted her legs. She had never met a man with a greater capacity for brutality than this one. It always caused her some surprise, for she knew he wasn't that way with the Javanese women, nor had he been with Tita, his native wife. Only with Gretchen, and she loved it! She shivered—but not with fear.

She smiled, vulture-like. "We shall see, Mynheer van der Rhys, if you come back to me after a few nights with the Spaniard. I understand they say a rosary during lovemaking." Sensuously moving her legs on the coverlet, her quivering breasts small mountains of white cream, she stretched her arms above her head.

Regan moved to the elegantly appointed bed with its silken hangings and threw down a pouch of gold coins. Gretchen eyed the pouch and spat on it. "There isn't enough gold to buy me, Regan. But then you aren't buying me, are you? You're paying me off! Bring me her rosary, that will be all the payment I need!" she laughed as he quietly left the room, softly closing the door behind him.

Gretchen sprawled over onto her stomach, the pouch of gold held tightly in her hand. Regan belonged to her and no Spanish slut would take him away! After all the planning and . . . She would have to speak to Chaezar. Did he know of Regan's little Spanish bride? Not likely; Chaezar told her everything. When he discovered what an adept pupil she was in the use of the whip, she had been able to glean any and all kinds of information from him—confidences that were soon forgotten in the throes of his passion.

Chaezar would help her as he had before. Her eyes turned murky as she remembered. If Regan ever discovered . . . he would kill her!

But first, she knew, he would see her suffer.

Regan mounted his horse and rode out of the cobblestoned courtyard. He was troubled. Gretchen had accepted the gold and given in too easily. She would play fast and loose and the Devil take all! He almost felt sorry for Señorita Córdez. Señorita Córdez . . .

He didn't even know her first name. He recalled the terms of the marriage agreement: ". . . that Regan van der Rhys, widowed these several years, shall take to wife, on my death or when she shall reach twenty years of age, my eldest daughter."

The contract itself had puzzled him, these three years since his return to Batavia. Why should Don Antonio Córdez y Savar, of Cádiz, have wished to marry his daughter not only to a Dutchman but to a Protestant—and a man he had never seen—as the condition for obtaining Regan's release from the Spanish prison? She was probably a snaggle-toothed, pockmarked shrew.

He wanted this marriage even less than Gretchen did—if that was possible. He had never had much use for the Spanish. Furthermore, Gretchen's words now came back to taunt him. He too had heard of the piety of Spanish women, that they hung a rosary about their necks and prayed constantly to God to see them through their wifely "duty." Would this one do that? Then perhaps it would be just as well if she were as homely as he suspected. She would doubtless smell of an unwashed body beneath her many layers of clothing and more than likely reek of garlic. Perhaps her father had merely wanted her out of his sight . . .

As his horse cantered along toward home, Regan turned his thoughts to the Javanese women he found so entrancing. Their comely looks, the clean and fresh scent of the sea hanging about them like an aura . . . *They* at least appreciated a man. They sought his favors and actually thanked him for "honoring" them.

Ha. He knew that it was mainly because they felt it to be good luck to sleep with a white man; nevertheless, they were so uncomplicated . . . so refreshing . . .

Like Tita . . .

He decided he would not bed the Spanish woman if he didn't like her looks. He would lock her away in the chapel and forget about her. Then it immediately dawned upon him that he did not have a chapel. He must see that one was built immediately!

What a far cry from Gretchen Señorita Córdez was sure to be. Brutal, fiery Gretchen, who had long wanted to marry him. As if he would marry her! She amused him, pleasured him, but he would never take her to wife. She was useful when his pent-up frustrations and hatreds began to get the better of him. Gretchen could take it, and could mete out some furies of her own! He laughed at himself as his horse quickened its pace, instinctively knowing it was nearing home.

He ought to pack off Señorita Córdez to Chaezar Alvarez, he thought. To that damned Spaniard!

Chaezar Alvarez held much the same position for the Spanish-Portuguese Crown in the Indies as Vincent van der Rhys had once held for the Dutch East India Company. Now Regan occupied that position. Based in Batavia, both men were responsible for the trade of their respective nations among the vast archipelago—Sumatra, Celebes, Borneo, Timor, Bali, New Guinea, and thousands of smaller islands, as well as Java—sometimes called the Spice Islands. Theirs were positions of great responsibility: charting courses, warehousing cargoes, cataloging every yard of silk and pound of spice . . . in addition to keeping diplomatic channels open with the many inland chiefs and sultans.

Before Regan's father had come to take up his post on Java some twenty years before, the Dutch had not been faring well against the Spanish and Portuguese. The Netherlanders were too businesslike and aggressive to suit the gentle ways of the natives, whereas the Hispanic traders, educated by more than a century of world exploration, took the time to bring gifts and make friends with the tribes of the various islands. But the Dutch were determined to beat the Spanish and Portuguese at their own game. The efficient but personable Vincent van der Rhys, an established D.E.I. official in Amsterdam for some years, was sent out to manage the East Indian trade. A highly popular man and a born adapter, he succeeded marvelously well in his new post.

But Vincent van der Rhys's early days on Java had been lonely ones. Not only had his only child, Regan, been left behind with an aunt in Amsterdam in order to complete his education, but Irish-born Maureen, Vincent's ailing wife, had died en route to the islands. The middle-aged Dutchman was left only with his task of diplomat/trader. Nevertheless, a few years after his arrival in Java it became clear to all that the Dutch dominated the Spice Island trade at last.

Seventeen-year-old Regan van der Rhys sailed into what was later to be known as Batavia four years after his father, and set himself to the task of learning the business. At about that time a slick, sophisticated Spaniard only a few years older than Regan arrived in the harbor: Chaezar Alvarez, son of an impoverished Malágan don.

Regan had never liked the darkly handsome Chaezar, but the ratio of Europeans to native islanders in Batavia was so low that it behooved the small trading colony—officials of the two Crowns, sea captains, and merchants, and their wives—to band together, if not for safety, at least for social commerce and friendship in this island paradise so far from their homelands. Such friendships as did develop, however, did not begin until after business hours, for the days were spent in an aggressive competition for trade.

Regan's distaste for Chaezar Alvarez was based less on his Dutch dislike of the Spaniard's affected grandeur and suave pretense than on the iniquitous role Alvarez had played in ruining Vincent van der Rhys . . .

In 1615, when Regan's son was four years old, he embarked with the child and his wife, Tita, on a voyage home—to the Netherlands. It was to be a sentimental journey as well as one made for business reasons of his father's; it was to be a voyage of discovery and enlightenment for Tita and their child. But it was never to be completed. Before their ship, the *Tita*, captained by an old friend of Vincent van der Rhys, reached Capetown for reprovisioning, it was attacked by a shipful of Spanish-speaking pirates. Tita was murdered before Regan's own eyes, by the quick thrust of a Spanish broadsword, and the last time he saw his son—before he himself was prostrated by the butt of a Hispanic musket—the screaming boy's chubby hands were gripping the ship's wheel as a filthy bandanaed heathen lifted him to his battle-bloodied shoulders. Regan's memories of those scenes were indelible. As indelible as his enduring puzzlement that he, of all the crew, should have been singled out for survival—provided, indeed, with food and drink and set adrift in the ship's dinghy while the other passengers and the captain, dead or dying, were pitched overboard mercilessly. Someday, perhaps, he would learn the reason.

Two days later, or three—for his memory of the hours adrift was unclear now, eight long years after—Regan had the good fortune to be spotted by a brigantine, again Spanish, but one of the merchant ships out of Java and bound for Cádiz. His good fortune lasted only until he was aboardships. Accused of being one of the crew of a recently demolished Dutch pirateer which had preyed on Portuguese and Spanish vessels approaching the African coast, he was manacled, impressed in the gallows of the ship, and taken to Spain—where, imprisoned without trial, he spent almost six years in a hellhole of a dungeon in Seville.

For nearly five years, the grief-stricken D.E.I. Chief Pensioner had given his son up for dead—butchered along with Tita and his grandson. Until, one day, a merchant ship out of Rotterdam reached Batavia with the news that a Dutchman of Regan's description was an inmate at one of Philip III's infamous prisons in Seville or Cádiz—he was not certain which.

The news, however vague, aroused the elder van der Rhys. Further inquiries, made warily by one of his captains who, anchored at Cádiz for imaginary repairs and unnecessary reprovisioning, elucidated that a "Vanderrí," as the contact called him, was prisoner in Seville. And that, yes, the man was probably twenty-eight or -nine and blond-headed.

On receipt of this further information, Vincent van der Rhys made an unpleasant but necessary visit to the offices of the Spanish Crown in Batavia.

Yes, Chaezar Alvarez said, he would do all that he could; he was only too happy to know that his competitor's son still lived. But, he went on, inviting the aging Dutchman to a velvet-upholstered chair, there would be expenses . . . strings to pull . . . And, what was more, he confided to van der Rhys, Spanish trade had been hurt substantially over the past few years by the competence and persistence of the Dutch, and he, Chaezar, would welcome some of that trade. Or some of the profit from that trade. It would enhance his own position with his masters in Spain, might earn him a promotion, a return to the homeland . . .

Hundreds of thousands of gold sovereigns and a good portion of the Dutch trade later (Dutch ships were delayed by van der Rhys and reached their rendezvous with island chieftains later than the Spanish and Portuguese merchants), Chaezar Alvarez sent a letter to his godfather, Don Antonio Córdez, in Cádiz, in the hope that the old statesman and shipbuilder might sway Philip . . .

Now, four years later, Regan had repaired his father's losses, his personal fortune, and had reestablished the Dutch East India Company as leader in the Indies—all the while concealing his father's shady dealings with the Spaniard, Alvarez. But the strain had been too much for the older man. His son regained, his honor and name untarnished, Vincent van der Rhys died.

"Alvarez!" Regan muttered, almost as an oath, as he reached his front gate. He knew Gretchen had amused herself with the slick Spaniard while he sat rotting in that Spanish jail! Alvarez . . . Regan's jaw contracted into tight knots just thinking of that Spanish swine.

Chapter One

The sleek, three-masted frigate seemed to scrape the late afternoon heavens of the South Pacific with her topsail, as she skipped and frolicked before the playful persuasion of the easterly trade winds. With flair and grace the pride of the Córdez Shipbuilding Line was skillfully demonstrating her prowess in this her maiden voyage, to the proud pleasure of her owner, the young and vivacious Sirena Córdez. Named for the Greek goddess of the sea, the *Rana* sported fresh decks scrupulously scoured with holy stones and a stern castle whose varnish had not yet dulled from the salt spray.

Sirena impatiently paced the deck, her bottle-green eyes on the sails. "If *I* were skippering the *Rana* I'd steer her two points into the wind. The sail would draw fuller! What do you think, Tio Juan?" Sirena turned to her uncle, a tall, graying, elegant gentleman of the Spanish aristocracy.

He knew this impetuous niece of his had no need for his opinion; she was a better sailor than he would ever be. She was deferring to his age and experience out of love and respect. "What do I think? That you'd better allow the captain to sail this ship! He's complained to me of how you interfere with his orders. I wouldn't care to have a mutinous captain on my hands, Sirena."

"Spare me, Tio," Sirena laughed, her chin lifting with a hint of her stubbornness and headstrong character. "If I hadn't taken some matters into my own hands, we would have lost days! Didn't I tell you it was best to sacrifice cargo for speed? I've no doubt we'll set a new record for the distance between Spain and Java."

"Sirena," Don Juan Córdez said in an indulgent tone, "has it ever occurred to you the empty cargo holds are the reason behind Captain López's black moods? He's a hard businessman and has no time for dalliance. Yet you insisted your *Rana* carry little cargo. That cuts his profits from this journey in half."

"He's being compensated," Sirena answered hotly, her full mouth forming a pout. "This is my ship! The captain is a grog-soaked drunk! I'll never understand why you commissioned him to sail my ship in the first place. And his ablebodied seamen! Straight from the dregs of Hell! They're poor beasts who have been press-ganged from the worst ports on earth. They handle my ship roughly and I won't have it!" Sirena stamped her narrow-booted foot for emphasis. "The *Rana* is mine and I intend to get her to port in one piece, even if I have to throw the crew overboard!"

Juan Córdez watched his niece with an expression that contained equal amounts of admiration and awe. Her wide green eyes glittered fiercely when she spoke of the *Rana;* her dark, unruly hair now billowed free of its pins.

"It was unwise of your father to take you with him on his sea voyages. And to teach you the art of the cutlass and rapier!" He hesitated, throwing his long, slim arms up in a gesture of hopelessness. "Sirena, you should be thinking of marriage and children. You're past eighteen, you should be settling down . . ." He shook his iron-gray aristocratic head forlornly. "I only want what's best for you, child."

"As you know, Tio Juan, the good sisters at the convent adored Isabel, but despaired of me," Sirena laughed, a glimmer of remembered mischief lighting her eyes, "and father felt that only he could guide my youthful energy."

"And now you're going to tell me about wise old de Silva, your late father's master-at-arms, who took such a motherly interest in you, seeing to your studies in geography, science, Dutch, English, French, and Latin, sitting up with you when you had the croup, and"—he pierced her with a disapproving stare—"teaching you to use of the cutlass, the rapier, the scabbard—"

With lynx-like grace she spun about. Quicker than the eye could see, she had Juan's scabbard in her hand, the point pressed firmly against his ribs, Her head thrown back, revealing the long, graceful arch of her throat, her hair spilling down her back, she laughed again—the silvery, tinkling tones dancing over the waves. "De Silva was the best damn teacher in all of Spain and you know it, Tio Juan!"

Córdez pretended shock as he looked at her reprovingly. "And that's not all de Silva taught you. Your speech is as salty and briny as his own. Am I doomed to watch you become a sinewy old spinster, who for want of a cool nature and a sweet tongue loses all chance for marriage and children?"

"Why do you chastise me, Tio? Is it perhaps because you're jealous of my talents?" she teased lightly, her eyes softening as she gazed fondly at the man who had assumed responsibility for herself and her sister, Isabel, on Don Antonio's death not quite a year ago.

"It's true, Sirena, that you have an expertise few men possess, but it's not a sport for a gentlewoman."

"Then I am the first! Please Tio Juan, I've heard this all before. That I'm a woman and although I do possess some talent in the art of fencing I overestimate myself—I'd be useless opposing a man who really meant me harm." She sighed with repressed vexation. "As for marriage, I've yet to meet a man I would prefer to my ship. I've only to look at Isabel and how she dreads this ridiculous marriage our father arranged before his death. She wants only to join a convent. She has a genuine calling for the order and you know it, Tio. Perhaps when we reach Java you'll speak to Señor van der Rhys and tell him Isabel wants only to be left to her prayers." Sirena grasped his arm earnestly. "Say that you'll speak to him, try to buy him off, anything!"

"Child, you speak of our family honor! Your sister has been promised to Regan van der Rhys and it will not be changed! Isabel hasn't your verve and resilience but she's strong in a way you could never be. She accepts life, and endures."

"You may think I am obsessed with my sister. I'm

not, I assure you, but I know her better than you do. I love her and it saddens me to know she's being denied what she wants most, to become a nun. She wants to be close to God! Can you deny her that?"

"Your protection of Isabel is most admirable, but quite unnecessary."

Sirena accepted his gentle admonishment quietly. Great green eyes brightened by tears looked up at him. "I shall never understand why Father promised her to anyone—much less a Dutchman and Protestant."

"I am as uncertain of Don Antonio's motives as you are, my dear, although I know Regan van der Rhys's mother was a Catholic. Perhaps one day we shall discover them. Though, with the elder van der Rhys dead, I have little reason to believe we shall."

"The Dutch nations breeds milky-skinned barbarians. And this van der Rhys is with the East India Company, a competitor of the Spanish Crown! How could Father do such a thing?"

"You make your father sound like a criminal, Sirena. And I will not have that! Sirena, your father was more than a Spanish grandee, he was above all a man of business—with a sound head for it. You, more than anyone, know to what extent he succeeded, since it is to you he left the bulk of his fortune and all of his shipyards and vessels. Perhaps—and I am but guessing—his mind worked this way: he had two daughters, one of them independent-minded, the other pliable if over-religious. He had little hope of ensuring *your* future by marriage; your husband will be of your own choosing, when and if you will. He therefore left his wealth to you. Isabel he knew he could marry—and doubtless *wanted* to marry, for he had little belief that convent life would make his elder daughter happy, regardless of what you seem to think. The favor he did for Chaezar Alvarez afforded Don Antonio the opportunity of arranging a prosperous marriage for Isabel, *and* of sending her far from our Inquisition-hounded Spain, with its cloisters and black gowns!"

Usually a man of few words, Don Juan Córdez exhibited his pent-up exasperation with Sirena through this long dissertation.

Sirena wanted to remain on good terms with her uncle. Together they enjoyed an open, loving relationship. She also knew him to be a man of strong convictions and a deep sense of duty. At the moment, he saw it as his duty to marry Isabel to Mynheer van der Rhys. She knew it irked him that he would probably never be able to arrange a marriage for herself—her energy and independence were an embarassment to him. Quickly, Sirena stood on tiptoe, kissed Juan's leathery cheek, and fled down the deck to the sterncastle, where she and her sister shared quarters.

The red glow of the setting sun reflected off the calm, azure sea through the sterncastle's mullioned window. Isabel was utilizing the last light of day to read her prayer book. Upon Sirena's entrance, she dropped her slim hands to her lap and glanced up, her liquid-brown eyes gentle and doe-like.

Isabel's composure irritated Sirena, who would have much preferred to find her sister spent from crying, eyes red and swollen with tears. Uncle Juan had been correct in his remarks about twenty-year-old Isabel's inner strength. At times Sirena believed that she was more upset about Isabel's thwarted vocation than Isabel was.

It seemed to her that Isabel had always been destined to join the Order. When the girls' mother had died in childbirth with Sirena, Don Antonio, having no close female relative to see to their upbringing, placed one-year-old Isabel with the holy sisters and had one of his young servant maids midwife the infant Sirena before confiding her in turn to the sisters a few months later. Isabel fit very well, from the first, into the quiet and restricted life of the convent, while Sirena, from the time she first walked, was into one kind of mischief or another. By the age of ten she was incorrigible—demanding, to the sisters' astonishment, to know why girls must either join a convent or marry and have babies, whereas boys were encouraged to seek exciting lives as warriors, explorers, and sailors. Having no answer to Sirena's demanding questions, the piqued Mother Superior immediately sent word to Don Antonio Córdez, pleading with him to come and take away his inquisitive daughter.

Córdez first cajoled, then pleaded, and finally begged the Mother Superior to revoke her decision. The sister, nevertheless, held out. So that at last, with a wary glance at his exuberant daughter—sitting curiously inactive and composed across the dark-walled visitor's room of the convent—he found himself not merely a wealthy shipbuilder and a father, but also a mother.

In addition to his shipyards, Don Antonio possessed a tidy fleet of trading vessels that sailed between West Africa and Cádiz. On one of three ships, retired from active service to become the don's private pleasure boat, Isabel rejoined her sister for several weeks each summer. Although the older girl appeared to enjoy these excursions along Spain's Atlantic coast and in the Mediterranean, her behavior was always so proper and decorous that it sometimes prompted Sirena to pull at Isabel's hair and tease her unmercifully. Isabel endured all this, saying, "I shall pray for you, Sirena."

"What has Captain López done this time, Sirena?" As was everything else about her, Isabel Córdez's voice was gently modulated and unhurried.

"Nothing. If you must know, it's you! Why don't you put up a fight? You don't want this marriage and you've resigned yourself to it! If you'd only kick and scream, I know Tio Juan would listen. But no, here you sit while I'm on deck pleading your case with Tio Juan." Swiftly, she dropped to her knees and buried her head in her sister's lap. "Isabel, I don't want you out on the edge of nowhere, dependent on the whims of a barbaric Dutchman!"

Isabel lightly touched Sirena's lustrous dark hair. "You silly! Don't torment yourself so. We have no reason to suspect Señor—er, Mynheer van der Rhys is a barbarian. Besides, even if I did not marry him we wouldn't be together any longer. It was my intention to join a cloistered order. Sirena, it's time to put childhood behind us!"

The younger girl jumped to her feet. Were she a

cat, Isabel could have imagined her snarling and baring her claws. Her words came fast and furious. "Is that what you think? That I want to prolong our childhood? That I want us to cling together like a pair of marmoset monkeys? Isabel, it would benefit you to hear me well! I don't give one twit how you spend the rest of your days as long as it's of your own choosing! If you want to be a nun, then you should *be* one. If you want to be a whore, then so should you be! What I object to is your being forced into a life you don't want. You can't fool me, Isabel, I hear you crying in the night. I see the aversion in your eyes when one of the crew looks at you the way men will look at a comely woman. Do you really expect me to believe you're so strong that you could sleep with a man and let him have his way with you night after night, and not go crazy?"

"I like men . . . well enough, Sirena. I love Tio Juan," Isabel protested.

"I've no doubt of that, Isabel," Sirena went on, her voice calmer, softer. It was unbearable to hurt her sister this way, but it must be done. "But I also have no doubt that you have already committed yourself body and soul to God! In a way only one who seeks the religious order can understand. Please, Isabel, go to Tio and make him understand. If God has truly sent you the calling, perhaps He wants you to protest this marriage and He will grant you Divine Intervention."

"Sirena dear, I know that I hear the call to become a nun. It is true, what you have said. And," she sighed, smiling contentedly, "my faith in God is so strong that I know He will intervene somehow . . . and that this marriage will never come to pass."

Isabel had spoken softly, her piquant face glowing with an inner faith. Sirena's eyes lit up happily. So . . . Isabel had *not* given in to their father's whim after all. She hoped to be saved from the approaching marriage.

Impetuously, Sirena hugged her sister tightly—not yet knowing that her sister's words about God's intervention would haunt her till the end of her days.

"Sail ho!" a loud cry rang out from high in the ship's rigging. "Sail ho!"

"Where away?" the captain shouted.

Sirena, excitement heightening her vivid coloring, released Isabel from her embrace and ran out the door and up on to the deck.

A cry in the rigging answered the captain. "Directly astern, sir!"

"What flag does she fly?"

"No flag, Captain."

Sirena swiveled about to face the stern, her hands to her forehead in order to shield her eyes. A brigantine was approaching them from the north, the crimson light of sunset giving it a black, spectral appearance. A chill penetrated Sirena as she peered into the distance.

Slipping up beside Juan Córdez, she said, "I don't like her looks, Tio. Captain López! Loosen sail and full speed away," Sirena shouted. "I see her sail and she gains on us!"

The captain shot her a disapproving look and ignored her command. "Swing those yardarms. Look lively, men. Heave to!"

"How dare you!" Sirena exploded. "This is my ship! Can't you see she flies no flag? Do as I say! Full speed ahead!"

"Send Señorita Córdez to her quarters, Senor Córdez, or I'll not be responsible for the men's actions." The captain's voice was thick with warning—and, Sirena thought furiously, with grog.

"Sirena, you heard the captain. Go below with Isabel."

"I won't! The *Rana* is mine! Isabel is fine." Turning again to face the captain, she commanded, "I won't warn you again, Captain López. Full speed ahead!"

"She flies a distress flag on her foretopmast!" came the clear call of the Caleb, the young cabin boy, who had climbed into the rigging for a look at the vessel.

"It's a trick, I tell you!" Sirena implored her uncle. "She doesn't appear to be in distress, her speed is too great. She gains on us by the minute and that fool of a captain won't listen!"

"Sirena, I insist you join your sister." The determination in Juan's eyes pierced her. Nimbly but sulkily, she stepped over a coil of rigging and headed for the sterncastle.

Isabel was sitting quietly, her hands folded in prayer, eyes downcast. Noticing Sirena's presence, she crossed herself and looked up. "What's all the shouting? Is something wrong?"

Sirena forced a smile in order to abate the alarm that widened her sister's dark, long-lashed eyes, flushed her pale olive complexion and accentuated her still girlish heart-shaped face. "Everything is fine," Sirena said, her hand going to Isabel's gleaming black hair. "Go back to your prayers."

An eternity crawled by as Sirena compelled herself to sit on her ornate but narrow bed listening intently for sounds out on deck. She felt the *Rana's* slow pace; she was merely drifting. She heard the sounds of the crew slowing her ship and the angry shouts of Captain López. Then, finally, the bump and scrape of a second ship nestling up to *Rana*.

Startled, Isabel looked up at her sister, a questioning expression arching her brows. Sirena was unable to be still any longer.

"Stay here and don't come out on deck!"

She reached for her rapier, which hung near the bed. Encumbered by her long skirts, she stumbled. With the rapier, Sirena tore the hem of her gown, then ripped upward to the level of her knees and crosswise, until she had made a short, tattered skirt. It allowed her free movement.

Cautiously and quietly, she closed the door behind her and moved up the steps toward the open deck, anger constricting her breast. Distress! In a pig's eye! she thought. Wasn't she her father's daughter and hadn't he schooled her well? And to think this stupid wretch of a captain had ignored her orders and allowed an assault on her *Rana*. There was no room for fear, only white-hot anger. If her father had been aboard he would have seen through the ruse. Now it must be left to her. She stood barely breathing, listening to the shouts on the mid-deck.

Creeping out further, to see what was happening, her heart pounded fiercely in surprise—the second ship was lashed slackly to her *Rana.* What was that in its rigging . . . A glint? God! she screamed silently. Her father had told her of marauding ships and of the harquebusiers who stood in their riggings sniping at the crew of their victim ships. She knew that first they would pick off the captain and then down the crew one by one.

Sirena, herself, had never seen it done, but instinct told her this was the situation. The square-rigged sails hid the marksmen from view; it would be as easy as shooting unsuspecting birds.

The ship was broadside to the *Rana,* and Sirena could see its captain standing on deck. Naked to the waist, his broad, deep chest was covered with a mat of thick brown hair. Cupping his hands to his mouth, he shouted, "Do you have a man versed in medicine aboard? I have wounded men! We were attacked by pirates at sunup!"

The man spoke in English! Sirena noted with surprise. That cursed language of those old enemies of Spain, and the aiders and abettors of the Dutch in their war to gain independence from the Spanish.

Seeing that López did not understand him, the man began to use Spanish—but a garbled Spanish it was.

"We carry none!" came Captain López's reply. He was unsteady on his feet and Sirena guessed that he was well on the way to intoxication—again! "How many wounded? Can your ship make port?"

From her position Sirena could see the crew of the brigantine. They had gathered behind their captain, evil sneers marking their faces. Cannons were jutting from the ship's ports. What did they want? Couldn't they see how high her *Rana* rode the waves? They must know she carried in her holds little more than what was necessary for the journey.

Anger blazed in Sirena's eyes as the brigantine's crew abruptly, and without warning, threw grappling hooks across the *Rana*'s deck rails. The result was instant chaos.

The *Rana* rocked from the force of a burst of cannon shot from her enemy while her crew hacked frantically with short-handled axes at the lines attached to the hooks embedded in their deck rails. The marauder's crew now scrambled aboard the *Rana* and as Sirena raised her eyes she saw that she had been frighteningly correct. There were men in the brigantine's rigging, their flintlock pistols aimed directly below. The *Rana* was outnumbered and outmaneuvered; her beautiful frigate would be totally disarmed within minutes.

Panic seized her, choking off all reason. She wouldn't allow this, she couldn't! She must fight for her ship, for her life!

Sirena moved out onto the deck, her rapier in hand. Taking a moment to orient herself, she ran to her uncle's aid. He was fighting for his life, but was no match for the near-naked crewman of the brigantine, whose cutlass was swinging so widely and wickedly.

She advanced a step, and her eyes spewed flames as she thrust her sword at the surprised crewman, bringing up the weapon wth a forceful motion to knock the attacker's arm awry, and bringing it down again with such force that the quarterdeck rail received a gash an inch deep. In that second the crewman lost his advantage and Juan pierced the man's chest with his cutlass. Blood spurted from the wound and streamed from his open, gaping mouth.

Averting her eyes from the gore, Sirena swung about. Where was her crew? Hiding below decks, she would wager. "All hands to repel boarders!" she shouted, her voice ringing over the waters. "Fight, damn your eyes!" she yelled as she directed a high-flying swing at one of the pirates. Taken by surprise by a woman bent on cutting him down, he was sent off his stride.

Sirena's arm flashed in the twilight, her unruly, sable hair billowing out behind her. "You dare to assault my *Rana!* I'll *kill* you first!" Her rapier flashed and jabbed, feinting to the right with a lithe movement, slashing at the pirate's arm. Wildly, in frantic defense of her ship, she parried his advances. Unbridled savageness raging within her, she forgot the rules of the polite art of fencing: she had become a tumultuous barbarian defending herself and her own. When with one final slash she saw the pirate's arm roll along the deck, instead of shock she felt herself near to elation. Could she have gone mad? Was this Sirena Córdez laughing cruelly at the bewildered, wounded pirate and calling, "Pick up your arm, dog."

As he lay howling on the deck, Sirena snatched up his cutlass, which lay near the severed arm. Then she swung about—a blade now in each hand—to see how young Caleb was faring; she'd heard his voice a moment before. The half-grown lad had abandoned an English ship some months ago in Cádiz and had signed on to sail with Sirena's small fleet of merchant vessels. She'd taken a great liking to the boy.

Within seconds, she found herself back to back with the boy—facing a new opponent. With a lunge and a jab, Sirena quickly had the man pinned to the ship's rail, however, and without further ado she wiped the wet, crimson blade of her cutlass on her short, ragged-edged skirt.

Turning, she saw that Caleb was fighting far more valiantly than any twelve-year-old could be expected to do. But he was no match for his brawny attacker. Her head thrown back and her long legs apart, she shouted in order to be heard above the bedlam around her. "Caleb, push off the bow! If they fire into us again they'll smash us to pieces! I'll take this man for you."

The boy gone, she attacked the man with her rapier, shrieking, "You had no right to board my ship! Now you'll fight and die! I'll not ask for quarter, nor do I give any!"

"I'll cut your heart out and hang it from the topsail," the pirate spat. "But first I'll have my way with you, same as every man aboard this ship."

For answer, Sirena brought up her cutlass.

The man was jarred from his feet as it caught his arm. Clumsily, he tried to regain his footing, but Sirena was too quick for him. In a lightning motion she struck once, then twice, forcing the pirate backwards. A fierce left jab—and he was pinned to a mast, his nostrils quivering in fear.

In a last frantic effort, he lashed out at her. For defense she plunged forward with the cutlass, sinking it in his chest but at the same time feeling a stinging sensation down her left arm. In surprise she saw red soaking through the sleeve of her tattered gown. Gasping with pain, she turned about, only to see her Uncle Juan's body topple to the deck. The frigate's crewmen were lying about now like slaughtered cattle. Rivers of blood ran everywhere.

"Quarter! Quarter!" the *Rana*'s crew were shouting. They fell silent, backing away, as the pirates picked their way among the dead bodies and came to stand before them awaiting their captain's orders.

"Throw the stinking flesh overboard!" he roared in English. His command was instantly obeyed. Jeering obscenely, the pirate's crew fell to their task. The sound of the dead and the half-dead hitting the water rang hideously in Sirena's ears. Fighting back hot tears, she stood mute near the sterncastle, her shaking hand cupping the elbow of her injured arm.

"Spare *one,*" the pirate captain growled loudly. "The pretty one there by the sterncastle! I'll have plans for her later," he chortled, leering lewdly in Sirena's direction. "But tie her hands. That young woman is too handy with a weapon!"

"Pray God they don't find Isabel! Not alive . . ." Sirena whispered as two tall brigands strode towards her.

The pirate captain then set his crew to the task of emptying the hold. Within a half-hour nearly everything of real value was transferred to the brigantine, save food and water. Evidently they were not going to destroy the ship . . . *her* ship, Sirena mused as she stood, hands tied behind her, near the foremast.

The cruel shock of the twilight attack on the *Rana,* her *Rana,* had begun to wear off, however. Now Sirena trembled uncontrollably, her thoughts only on her sister Isabel's fate. She grieved, too, for her uncle—he who had protected her for the past year. But he had died like a man; of that she was glad. Then her thoughts turned to her own part in the defense of the ship. Had that fighting, shrieking animal really been Sirena Córdez? Could she had been so merciless, so barbaric? But she had been compelled to it—to defend her ship and her family. It *had* to be done! She had been taught the art of self-defense, and to have done any less would have been idiocy. She had been like a tigress who defends her cubs, but she had not enjoyed taking men's lives . . .

A hoarse shout suddenly broke the air as one of the pirates dragged Isabel Córdez onto the deck. "The prize! See the prize! And she *prays!* What do you think, men, does she pray for salvation or does she pray for—"

"Pig!" Sirena shouted, her eyes spitting fire. "Leave her alone! She is promised to God, she's to join a convent!"

Raucous shouts of laughter greeted her statement. "A convent! When we finish with her, there's not a convent that'll have her!"

The pirate leader called for order. "Take her below and let the men have their sport. Look lively now, we've many leagues to travel. *This* wench," he said, roughly pulling Sirena against his sweating, hairy chest, "is mine. Only when I'm done with her is she yours!"

Outrage seized Sirena, fear gripped her innards. "Isabel! Isabel!" she screamed.

This couldn't be happening! But it was, and the reality was paralyzing. Isabel, her sweet, gentle sister, who wanted only to be a bride of Christ, was writhing, struggling to be free of the brawny monster who pawed her roughly, intimately, heedless of her gasping sounds of protest, pitiful pleadings, and pale, terror-stricken face.

Laughing and sneering derisively, the lusty captain untied Sirena's hands, dragged her across the frigate's blood-slick deck, and threw her down near her sister. She struggled to get up, and kicked—her long legs aiming to strike a vulnerable mark. She screamed in protest, obscene oaths she hadn't realized she knew, torn from her throat along with low, heart-wracked sobs for mercy for Isabel and herself. She wrestled laboriously beneath the captain's brute strength, her fingers stretching into curving, talon-like claws and punctuating her screams with swift, violent slashes at her attacker's amused and jeering face.

He straddled her, his bulk pressing her back against the deck. Writhing and fighting, Sirena yet struggled to escape him. Suddenly, her hand made contact with the knife stuck in his wide belt. Clutching its handle, she whipped it forth, a murderous intent contributing to her strength and agility. But for all his bulk, the pirate was a nimble warrior. He adroitly dodged the swift slash of the knife and retaliated by delivering a stunning blow to the side of Sirena's head. The amusement disappeared from his coarse features; in its stead was a dark, malicious, purposeful light.

He called to one of his men, who now knelt near Sirena's head and stretched her arms above her, holding them fast to the deck. The captain, still straddling her legs, retrieved his fallen weapon and cut and tore her clothing from her body. His hands touched her shrinking flesh, his weight pressed her downward. Her breath came in painful rasps.

Sirena's head ached from the blow he had dealt her. Her wounded arm felt leaden and numb. She fought against the dim shadow of blessed unconsciousness, the sweet oblivion that could take her away from this horror and blanket her in sheltering, dark folds.

Isabel's pleadings brought her back from the edge of night.

Clenching her teeth, Sirena compelled herself to fight the beckoning blackness, determined to remain alert for any opportunity to escape.

She was naked now, exposed to the pirates' salacious stares, and her knees were forced apart and the captain fell upon her. Heedless of her virginity, he thrust himself forcefully upon the girl again and again, enjoying her screams of outrage and pain. Again and again he tore his way through her unwilling, recoiling body.

Hoarse animal shrieks spilled from her lips, paroxysms of burning anguish.

Isabel's screams echoed Sirena's as a pirate drove his way into her with animal brutality. The crew had ignored their captain and had not taken her below. They were raping her alongside her sister!

Sometime during the attack, her resolve weakened and Sirena momentarily lost consciousness. When she was roughly slapped to her senses she looked for Isabel. It was almost with relief that she heard her sister's screams. She lived! Thank God, she lived!

But another of the pirates was upon Sirena, his shoulders blocking Isabel from her view. Shock and humiliation flooded her senses, bringing a kind of detachment. Everything seemed to be happening in slow motion and she viewed the man a-top her as though through heavy gauze. Then an alarming cry from Isabel commanded her attention. Fuzzily, Sirena saw a pirate with a hook for a hand throw himself upon her sister's naked body. As he was raping her, he placed his hook at the base of the girl's throat and scored her tender, naked flesh, drawing the hook down the length of her torso and leaving in its wake a scarlet ribbon of torn flesh and oozing blood. Deformed and depraved, he laughed sadistically, the sight of Isabel's bleeding intensfying his lust.

Sirena's conscious mind rebelled and she swooned, only to be slapped awake again after what must have been eons of time. Almost immediately Sirena saw that Isabel was no longer on deck—the girl's terrified screams were coming from below. The ordeal was evidently not over, for as soon as one man was done with her another took his place. At some point, however, Sirena realized that Isabel's screams had long since ended.

When the men were done with Sirena, they left her shivering, naked, exposed to the chill night air. She lay on the deck, staring blindly up at the stars; then she painfully pulled her battered body up to a sitting position, as her eyes searched for something to cover her nakedness. It was the boy Caleb who brought her a torn and dirty shirt.—Compassion for her humiliation shone from his dark eyes. For a fleeting moment, she was ashamed for Caleb to see her condition, but his pained expression was so mature in its understanding that her embarrassment abated.

The ship was curiously quiet now, with only a few drunken pirates softly singing, aloft near the ship's vessel. The *Rana* was like a ghost ship; yet the marauder's brigantine still clutched the frigate's sides.

Buttoning the front of the shirt, which came only halfway to her knees, she stumbled toward the hatch that led below. "Isabel, I must see Isabel!" she whispered hoarsely.

Caleb, his eye on the open hatch, quickly spun Sirena around. "Don't look," he pleaded. "Please, Señorita Córdez, don't look!"

Alarmed, she struggled free of his grasp, in time to see two of the pirates carry her sister's slim, battered body up through the open hatchway.

"Isabel!" the cry ripped from her, bringing with it all the pain and torment that had welled up inside her. Frantic, she pushed her way forward, her eyes straining to look upon her sister's face. But the long, red gash running the length of her body was all she could comprehend, all her eyes would focus on . . .

The men carrying Isabel swore at Sirena and brutally shoved her away, fighting off her groping hands. As she collapsed, sprawling on the deck, horror choking her, she watched them hoist Isabel's body over the rail and drop it into the greedy arms of the sea.

Caleb came to her side and helped her to stand. "She was dead, Señorita. I heard them say so as they came above. She was dead long before they stopped—" He caught himself, his black eyes mournful.

But it was too late. Sirena had heard his last words. "Oh my God! Isabel! Isabel! *Isabel!*" she sobbed. Then, heaving, she leaned weakly over the ship's rail and retched.

Chapter Two

It was nearly a week now since the pirates had commandeered the *Rana* and began sailing it with a skeleton crew under their captain, Dick Blackheart —he who had so cruelly raped Sirena. The pirate brigantine sailed close by, in the wake of the frigate.

Tonight Sirena lay in the hold of the rocking, pitching ship and was numbly thankful for the storm that raged about them. All hands were needed to secure the frigate, and there would be no time for any of the brigands to ravage her yet again.

"Dear God," she moaned miserably, "how much more can I take?"

Weakly, Sirena turned over on her side and looked with vague interest as the raw, festering wound on her left arm. A greenish pus already oozed from it. She would probably lose the arm, she thought with alarm, the first emotion she had felt since seeing Isabel's poor ravaged corpse thrown into the sea.

She held her throbbing arm carefully and attempted to gain her feet, but the pitching and rolling of the *Rana* drove her back to her knees, causing her to knock her injured arm against a sack of rice. Pain shot through her body, doubling her over. Her head felt fuzzy, her eyes wouldn't focus. She knew she was burning with fever.

Suddenly, she heard the cover of the hatch open. "Please God, no!" she whimpered. "Not again!"

Her latest ordeal was still all too clear in her muddled head. She had been clearing the rough plank table in the galley after the evening meal. The boatswain was cursing at her for being slow and clumsy. With a savage sweep of his arm, he cleared the table, threw her upon it, and ravished her while the others shouted their encouragement. One after the other they had mounted her as their shipmates offered their loud and leering approval. When they were done with her, they had knocked her to the floor and jeered obscenities and curses. Somehow she had managed to get to the hold, where she had collapsed onto a pile of dirty sacks.

A scratching sound now reached her ears. She held her breath in fear. Was that a whispered word she heard? Painfully, she inched toward the door and pressed her ear close.

"Senorita Córdez . . ." It was Caleb.

"Caleb, how did you get here?" Sirena gasped. "You must go above decks. If they find you here you'll be beaten. Go! I don't want *you* on my conscience, you can't help me."

"Listen to me," Caleb pleaded, his boy's voice urgent. "I've a few minutes. It's storming so fiercely they won't miss me. I found a medicine chest and some powders for your arm. When you serve the morning meal, I'll try and get them to you."

Surprised, she tried the door latch. It did not move. So, they had locked her in!

"It's hopeless, Caleb. My arm is so swollen and festered that powders can't help me now. Go away," she muttered dejectedly. "I've a fever and my head aches so."

"Señorita Córdez, if we could find a way to get free could you manage?"

"I'm afraid not, Caleb. I don't think I can ever manage again. How could I hold my head up, after what's been done to me? I wish I could join Isabel and Tio Juan. But *you* must save yourself, Caleb. Forget about *me*."

"Never!" Caleb said in a tear-choked whisper. "I won't leave you! Your uncle shouted to me as he fell that I should watch over you and your sister. I failed once"—a sob broke his voice—"but I won't fail again!" His boy's tone was determined. "I don't know how . . . but there must be something! Perhaps when the crew is full of ale."

Sirena gave no response, and her silence inspired Caleb to ask anxiously, "Señorita, are you all right? Can you hear me?"

After a moment, she answered lifelessly. "Yes."

Caleb breathed a sigh. He knew, now, that he must do something to help her. He had never seen the señorita like this. Usually she was full of vinegar and salt and had the tongue of a viper. But now all the will and vitality was gone from her. He shook his dark brown head. What could he do? Nevertheless . . . Sirena Córdez knew her ship like the back of her hand. She knew the sea and could captain the *Rana*. If only there were some way to make her come alive again, so that if he could devise some miraculous escape she would have the stamina to follow through.

"Someone's coming," Caleb warned as he skittered to his feet. "I'll be back if I can."

"What kind of god are you?" she screamed, raising her tormented eyes heavenward. "He's but a boy!"

Her crawl to the door and the forced scream had drained the last of her strength. Sirena lay beaten and defeated. Perhaps tomorrow she could find a way to get to the ship's rail and go over. "If you *are* my God," she gasped, "then let me die. Let me die in peace!" The fever raged within her and she slept.

Hours later, Sirena found herself being hoisted to her feet. Swaying as she determined to focus her eyes, she recognized the captain.

"On your feet, my pretty," Blackheart commanded. "Fix food and drink—and it would be best if you remember to move quickly. The men have complained about you."

His swarthy face and bushy, brown beard repelled Sirena, and the stench of his rotting teeth made her turn her face away. But he grasped her injured arm and dragged her to the ladder leading out of the hold. Sirena cried out in pain and received a sharp blow on the side of her head.

"None of your dramatics, señorita! Your cries will go unheeded. My men are not about to forget that you brought death to some of their shipmates."

Clenching her teeth, she staggered up the ladder, not caring that the filthy shirt she wore afforded the captain a spectacular view of her long, tawny legs as he followed her and pushed her into the galley.

Shaking her head in an effort to clear her clouded vision, Sirena numbly sank to her knees. "I can't," she whimpered. "I don't have the strength to stand. Let them run me through. I don't care!"

"You'll care if I tell the crew you're feeling lonely!" Blackheart growled. "They'll all come running to keep you company. Now, get to work!" he commanded, slamming the door behind him as he left the galley.

"Please don't do that . . ." Sirena sobbed, too weak to notice the captain had left. "I couldn't go through that again. Please don't!"

Caleb had quietly entered the galley and now dropped down beside the weeping girl. Quickly he withdrew the packets of powder he'd located earlier and sprinkled them liberally on the oozing wound. Next, he uncorked a small bottle and with gentle hands raised it to her lips. The smoky, amber liquid dribbled into her mouth—until she gagged.

Apprehensively, Caleb wondered if he had given her too much or too little. Whatever the case, he thought fearfully, she was so sick she would probably die no matter what he did.

"I *thought* you were up to something!" came the captain's gruff voice. "What've you got there? Answer me, damn your eyes!"

"Medicine," Caleb answered defiantly.

"Medicine, is it? And where did the likes of *you* get medicine? In my cabin, I'll wager!" His bullish face was red with anger, the cords in his thick neck swollen with rage.

"In the Señorita's cabin. It's *her* medicine—just as this is her ship!" the boy replied as he got to his feet. "She's sick, and someone has to help her or she'll die."

Sirena, hearing their voices, struggled to attention. "Leave the boy, captain. He was only trying to help me. Please," she begged, grabbing hold of his trouser leg. "Please . . ."

Dick Blackheart looked down at the girl. How prettily she begged. Skin flushed with fever, eyes bright with tears . . . but she had cost him the services of some of his best men.

With his booted foot he kicked her away and grasped Caleb by the neck. "You'll get ten lashes, and the girl five. If she survives, you may minister to her. If you're able!" he laughed cruelly. "The señorita first. We'll lash her to the mizzenmast on deck —but you'll strip her down first!"

"I won't do it!" Caleb rebelled.

"You'll do it or go over the side. Then what would become of her? What would she do without your tender care?"

"Do as he says, Caleb. I'm ordering you. Quickly now," Sirena whispered.

Out on deck the wind was fresh and clean in a sudden break in the storm. Before the mizzenmast, Caleb shyly removed the coarse shirt and lashed Sirena to the mast, securing her tightly for he feared she would slip to the deck.

"Fear not, pretty señorita," Blackheart shouted. "I'm a well-practiced hand with the whip. I'll venture to say I won't draw blood to scar your long, exotic back."

Calling for one of his men to fetch him his whip, the pirate chief took the opportunity to study Sirena's arm. The boy was right, she'd probably be dead in a day or two. He would be sorry to toss this pretty morsel over the rail.

Caleb watched as the captain brought down the whip across Sirena's back in five quick, successive strokes. Her body swayed and jerked with the force of the blows, yet she uttered not a sound.

Pray God *I* can be so brave, the boy cried silently.

Dressed again in her shirt—though the scratchy material on her back was almost more than she could bear—Sirena watched with pain-wracked eyes as Caleb's body jerked beneath the whip. But again the captain displayed his skill. Although he raised angry welts, he did not break the skin. Caleb would have no scars to mark him as a mutineer. She was puzzled by the captain's gentleness.

As the boy turned his head, ready for the eighth blow, she saw his brave, stoic expression and the quivering of his lower lip. He appeared younger than his twelve years, his round smooth cheeks crimson against the white circle of fear that was his mouth. He was manly for his years. What kind of god was it who protected only these pigs, their captors?

You're not *my* god! Sirena cried inwardly. You couldn't have been Isabel's either! Her god was merciful and kind. From this moment on, I *have* no god!

But as Blackheart laid on the tenth blow, a determination and a will to live coursed through Sirena.

Using every scrap of strength left in her, she hefted herself to her feet. She stood erect and directed a pointed stare at the captain. *"There will be a time and a place,"* she said with chilling certainty, *"when I will come upon you! I will sever your manhood and force it down your throat for what you have done to this boy and to me.* You will die choking on your own blood and flesh. And if you should die before this comes to pass, I'll wreak havoc on every Dutchman from here to Capetown! There won't be one of you left alive to—"

Hearing her threat to his manhood, Blackheart brought up his hand and struck her across the face. "You're a raving lunatic," he shouted. "My men have a need for food. Crawl into the galley and see to it!"

"No!" Sirena screamed back defiantly.

"A few more lashes and we'll see if it's still 'no,'" the captain menaced.

"Whip me till I die. I do nothing more for you."

Grinning at the deadly calm in her voice, Blackheart turned on his heel and left the deck.

Sirena quickly unlashed Caleb from the mizzenmast. Gathering the shreds of her dignity about her, she gently led the boy back to the galley and sat him in its sole chair.

Caleb forced a smile. "Aye, but it was good to hear you speak so to him!" His dark eyes clouded with pain. "But what will happen now? What will he do?"

Sirena shrugged. "In truth, Caleb, what more could they do to us? We're beaten, aren't we? What can we do, where can we go? Though . . . we should be nearing a port soon. It's been seven days since we were captured. Does their brigantine still sail alongside the *Rana?*"

"No. When the captain noticed the approaching storm, he ordered full sail and we left the brigantine behind."

"Hmm. He wouldn't have done so if we had not been nearing his port. He would never chance sailing a small ship like the *Rana* without protection. If we're to do anything, we must decide now!"

The boy's breathing was ragged as he tried to speak. "I've wanted to tell you before, but didn't have the chance. The captain found maps in Señorita Isabel's trunks. I heard him talking to the first mate."

"In Isabel's trunks? Oh, if only I could think!" Sirena said softly, lightly touching her temples. "I can't remember any maps . . ." Caleb changed his position, wincing with pain. "Poor Caleb," Sirena crooned, "how do you feel?"

"I've been flogged before," he gulped. "Has the medicine stopped the throbbing in your arm?"

"A little," Sirena lied. "My eyesight has cleared a little also."

"Your arm must be lanced so it can drain," the boy muttered. "I think I can do it . . . if you can take the pain."

"I can take it."

Sirena, in her exhaustion, sank to the floor. Caleb secured a galley knife from the wall, and forcing his hand to be steady, with a quick motion lanced the festering wound.

"I'll have to squeeze it," he warned through tight, white lips. "It's going to hurt like the devil."

"Don't talk, do it!"

But Sirena fainted with the first pressure the boy exerted. When she revived, her arm was neatly bound in a piece of galley toweling.

"You did well, Caleb," she sighed. Then: "Listen, the storm! It will vent its wrath on us this day."

"It's not the worst I've seen. And the *Rana* rides the sea well, doesn't she, señorita?"

"If only I were at the wheel. How I love this ship, Caleb. It's all I have left. How could I have let them overtake her? It's all my fault," she wept, remembering . . .

"No, it was that drunken Captain López. But in truth your uncle didn't know what a sot the man was. Señorita, why did you curse the *Dutch* to Captain Blackheart?"

"Why? Because of the appearance of his brigantine, for one reason. She's Dutch-built, I'd stake my life on it: her lines are low and narrow. And the flintlock pistols for another—a Dutch invention!"

"These things mean nothing, señorita. Flintlock pistols are available to everyone. And the brigantine could have been a captured ship, like the *Rana*. Even Blackheart is English, not Dutch."

"I don't care what you say, Caleb. There are only two powers in the East Indies, the Dutch and the Spanish. I tell you the brigantine sails for Dutch interests! If she sailed for Spain, do you think she would have taken the *Rana?* We were sporting Spain's flag. If she'd been a Spanish pirateer, she'd at least have spared our lives—and taken only our valuables. But even though the captain is English, you and I know that means nothing. Except that he may be all the more a friend to the Dutch!"

Caleb interrupted with fearful, whispered urgency: "Shh! Someone's coming. Get down on the floor and stay quiet!"

Dick Blackheart entered the galley, some of his crew of degenerates behind him.

"To show you I'm a man of mercy, I'll free you from your duties for today, girl. Toss the girl in the hold and secure her there," he instructed his first mate. "Take the boy to my cabin!"

Sirena lay undisturbed, except by the continuing storm, for the remainder of the evening. She slept. But by midnight she woke and realized her fever was gone.

Slowly, she flexed her arm; some of the pain seemed to have disappeared. Her back was stiff and painful, but she knew now that in a few days she would heal. The only scars she would bear from the lashing were the marks on her soul—and these would be small compared to the damages done to her on the day Blackheart took over her ship . . . small compared to her sorrow for the deaths of her beloved Isabel and Tio Juan.

Sometime toward dawn, Caleb swung open the door to the hold, a ring of keys clanking in his hands. "I'm to take you to the galley and we're to see to the morning meal. The crew hasn't eaten since the storm began yesterday. Hurry, Señorita."

As they mounted the ladder, Caleb murmured low, "I have a plan. I'll tell you about it in the galley."

Sirena smiled. This little sea urchin with his strange, flashing black eyes and tumble of mahogany hair had assumed the position of her protector. Little more than a baby, he displayed a sense of responsibility far beyond his years. Following him up the ladder, Sirena noticed that he, like herself, avoided extending his arms. She, who had received only five lashes, could imagine how his young back pained him from the ten.

The *Rana* rolled still, but the storm had abated and the rains ceased as Sirena cut thick yellow cheese into slices and arranged them alongside chunks of hard brown bread. Caleb was soon browning slabs of salt pork over the galley's black iron stove.

"Señorita, I was able to steal sleeping draughts from the ship's medicine chest. If we put them in the crew's ale . . ."

"And what, Caleb? Think! When they awoke, it would go worse for us. And there are no bolts for us to slide on this galley door! They would kill us! . . . Still, it may be—a good idea. Hmm. If we put the draughts into the ale—yes—and served it to them up on deck, then when they went under the drug we could easily toss them overboard . . . But I have to think," Sirena said, knowing that whatever they chose to do it would give them a chance to escape.

As they went about preparing the food, Sirena asked curiously, "What did that brute of a Blackheart want with you in his cabin?"

"I don't know . . ." Caleb said, puzzled. "He asked me where I came from and who I've sailed with. I told him the truth," Caleb said, his face downcast.

"You did exactly right, Caleb. Now tell me how you managed to get the sleeping draughts."

Caleb's eyes brightened and he enthusiastically launched into his story. "While he was asking me questions, he was swilling ale. Because he hadn't eaten, the ale worked quickly and he fell asleep. That was when I took the draughts and more medicine for your arm. I hid it out on deck. Then I lay down and slept, myself. He woke me up this morning and told me to get you and prepare breakfast."

"They're coming now, Caleb. Stay out of their way. We'll sit here in the corner and eat."

As Caleb and Sirena ate in the far corner of the galley, they listened to the conversation among the cursing crewmen, at the central table. The seamen spoke of the storm's intensity, and of how it may have driven them far off their course—which, to Sirena's surprise and delight, appeared to be Java.

"It's hard to tell, Hans," Blackheart yelled at his first mate. "We'll have to check with the stars. We may be farther to the south than you think. I'll wager we've not gone far off course!"

Later, clearing off the plank table, Sirena was smiling. "Caleb, I've been thinking. How many draughts did you steal?"

"Enough, I believe, to put the crew asleep for days."

"Good! We'll put it in their coffee and take it out on deck. Now that the sea has calmed considerably and the sun's appeared again, the men will be glad for the fresh air. They've, most of them, been confined these past two days and will willingly come on deck at our suggestion. You're sure the brigantine is nowhere near?"

"Aye. It hasn't been in sight for three days. But what happens afterward, Señorita? Neither of us is fit to handle the ship."

"We'll drift with the trade winds for a time. And we can sit on the deck and heal our wounds. It will be simple to find our course again."

Caleb watched her skeptically. Though the Señorita spoke confidently, he had noticed a fleeting, tortured expression in her jade-green eyes. Did she truly believe her physical and spiritual wounds would heal, or did she speak with such confidence only for his sake? How would she explain what had happened aboard the *Rana?* What would become of her when it was discovered that she was a used woman? Could she face the derision? And, did she really expect that the two of them could bring the ship into port alone?

The boy was shaken from these thoughts by the entrance of Captain Blackheart, who sat down at the rough table and called for more coffee. Caleb replenished his thick mug.

The pirate's voice was a low growl in the quiet galley. "We'll make port by tomorrow, at nightfall. I'll set the boy ashore, but you'll stay aboard. I'll quarter you in my cabin. The men will leave you alone from now on."

"I'm to be your whore, is that it?" Sirena demanded coldly, tossing her wealth of dark brown curls.

"And a fetching one you make!" Blackheart retorted, his voice surprisingly gentle. Though a rough man of the sea, he could appreciate Sirena's beauty. He looked at the perfect oval of her face. He had been wondering how that full, sensuous mouth would taste if offered willingly in a kiss. Her body had the slim, carved beauty of a ship's figurehead: high, full breasts and low, narrow hips. But it was her legs—tawny-skinned, slender, and supple, muscularly chiseled and far longer than a woman had a right to possess—that had fascinated him.

Sirena was sickened by the lust she saw in his face. The foul stench from his mouth carried across to where she sat, and she found the animal stink of his body vile and offensive. Furthermore, she did not think she could cope with one more attack on her bruised body.

"Finish up now. Just leave the food on the table for the midday meal. The boy will then bring you to my cabin—the first mate will see to it that you arrive safely. Now that the storm is spent, the men begin to think of other pastimes."

Sirena watched Blackheart leave the galley, and hatred was alive and running rampant in her. Dear God, not again! It was then that she remembered she had renounced her god.

Seeing the beaten expression on Caleb's face, she hastened to reassure him. "Once more, little one, then we'll follow your plan. He can't hurt me anymore. You'll place all the sleeping powders in the bucket of coffee you take to the crew. Most of them will be on deck now. Call down to the others to come up. Be sure you see them drink it. Lace the coffee with rum. That way, it won't be refused."

"Aye, you can rely on me, Señorita. I . . . I'd better take you to Captain Blackheart now. I'll lay out the meal. It'll go easier with you if he's not angry."

Sirena, dreading the ordeal, moistened her parched lips. "Caleb, you're a good friend, the best I've ever had. Do you think you can call me Sirena? It would make me happy if you would."

Caleb's young face fell into lines of sorrow. "You call me friend . . . yet I must take you to the captain."

She hesitated a moment at the anguish she read in the boy's eyes. "There are worse things in life than having someone abuse your body. I'll be all right, truly I will! Just the thought that soon we'll be free will give me strength. One day we'll find them, you and I, and it'll be a different tune they sing. I give you my word on it! The day will come for us—believe me!"

The oak-paneled cabin with its sparse furnishings was quiet and still. The captain had not yet arrived. Irresistibly, Sirena's eyes fell on a chair near the mullioned windows. In it Isabel had sat reading or reciting her prayers; it had been brought here from the sterncastle. Pulling her gaze away, Sirena swallowed bitter tears. "I won't cry! I won't!" Her brave words to Caleb seemed empty now. Instead, something her sister had said on the day of her death swelled within Sirena and resounded in her head. "I know God will intervene somehow and that this marriage will never come to pass." Isabel had been so serene, so hopeful when she'd said those words.

"You spoke the truth, sweet Isabel. Something did happen . . . And now you are dead. But I'll find a way to avenge you—or the Devil take my soul! After I've dealt with this animal crew I'll find the others, on the brigantine, and deal with them. But that pirate who wears a hook will receive a special fate for using you so brutally." The long red gash that had scored Isabel's body swam before Sirena's eyes and her determination to punish her sister's sadistic attacker was revitalized.

Heavy footsteps outside the cabin door announced the pirate captain's arrival. The low, narrow, oak door swung open and he ducked his shaggy black head, stepped inside, and crashed the door closed behind him. He threw the bolt.

Sirena knew that her presence was noted, yet he did not even glance in her direction. He moved to one of the narrow bunks, sat down, and began to remove his boots. His disregard of her was more shattering to her nerves than if he had immediately attacked her.

She remained standing near the windows, her heart beating rapidly, her breath ragged in anticipation of the ordeal. When at last he chose to notice her, he had discarded his shirt and belt. The sight of his muscular chest with its mat of chocolate-colored hair reminded her of the first time she had seen him, on that fateful day when the brigantine had accosted the *Rana.*

He spoke, his voice a deep basso growl. "You're frightened, señorita. I will not hurt you, so why do you stand there cowering?"

"You ask why? After the humiliation and degradation I've suffered at your hands and those of your crew?" Her words were hot with anger, her eyes flashed like shattered emeralds.

"That's all past," he said, coming toward her. "You're mine now. The crew won't come near you again."

Sirena backed away, dreading the touch of his paw-like, callused hands. But there was no escaping his long arm, which reached out and pulled her toward him, crushing her. Savagely, he wound his fingers in her sable curls and yanked her head back until she thought her neck would snap. His thick, wet mouth burned her throat where he kissed her, nipping at her tender flesh, making her recoil.

She writhed to escape his grasp, but when she was almost free he caught her again and flung her onto the bunk. He stood over her, a lustful glitter in his eyes, his tongue moistening his viscous mouth. She cowered on the bunk, apprehensive of his next move.

Dick Blackheart appraised the woman on his bed; a temptress, enticingly seductive, full pouting lips parted, showing her straight and glistening white teeth. Her olive skin flushed pink, heightening the green of her eyes.

He threw himself on her, his weight pushing her down into the bedding. But his intimate touches to her stiff, unyielding flesh were light, seductive in their intent. His kisses to her unwilling mouth, throat, and breasts, however, were fraught with suppressed frenzy.

Sirena could not allow him to do this to her without

a struggle. This attempt at arousing her was almost worse than the attacks she had suffered previously. At those times they had used her, expected nothing of her, merely demanding that she be a receptacle for their lusty cravings. But this! This blatant attempt to elicit a willing response from her. It was an admission that she was alive, real, capable of choice. That this barbarian should assume that she could be enticed by his advances was adding outrage to her already wounded dignity. She couldn't—she *wouldn't*—allow him to assume she would respond like a seductive wanton to his insidious caresses.

"Get your filthy English hands off me! Leave me alone!" she spat out, pushing him away and wriggling from under him.

The shock on his grizzly face was almost comical.

Sirena wrestled to her feet, her eyes flying to the door and its bolt. The helplessness of her situation nearly rendered her insensible. Even if she could make her escape from this animal, where could she run? Over the rail into the waiting sea? Then what would become of Caleb? She could not leave him to face Blackheart's wrath! And what of their plan to regain control of the *Rana?* How could she dash the young boy's hopes, and her own?

In that moment of indecision the captain was upon her.

Well . . . if she must be raped by this animal, it wouldn't be without a fight. She lashed out blindly, her nails gouging the flesh over his cheekbones. He cuffed her on the back of the head, then pinioned her arms to her sides. Her struggles were the minuscule protests of a flea biting a dog.

"So! There's spirit in you yet!" he crowed exultantly.

Forcing her to the floor, he held her wrists above her head with one powerful hand. She spit and snarled, twisting her head, trying to sink her teeth into his capturing arm. He struck her on the face, smashing her lower lip against her teeth. Her mouth was suddenly full of blood and she found it difficult to breathe because her nose had received a glance from his blow and was bleeding profusely too.

His knee was forcing her legs apart, his free hand

was touching her breasts, her stomach, between her thighs. His face was directly above hers now, grinning salaciously down. She sprayed his beast's face with spittle and blood.

With that, his free hand flew to her throat and made it impossible to breathe. She choked, grappling for air till she felt her lungs would burst. Then slowly, gradually, her struggles abated and she felt herself slipping into sweet oblivion . . .

Imperceptibly, Sirena began to realize it was easier to breathe, Blackheart's pressing weight was gone. Her eyelids fluttered open slowly, as if weighted. Hazily she watched him pour himself a tankard of ale. Swallowing, he uttered a grunt of satisfaction and collapsed drowsily in a chair.

"Now, Señorita," he smiled almost benignly, "you are mine!"

"You can take me morning, noon, and night"—she spat out her words, disgust and repulsion vivid on her face—"but I'll never be yours. Never!"

Sirena emerged from the cabin raw and bruised. Hatred spilled from her like honey from a comb. If it was the last thing she ever did, she would get her revenge!

Standing outside the cabin door, she suddenly realized how calmly the *Rana* rode. The storm seemed to have run its course. Had Caleb done his work? Somehow she would have to force some of the coffee into the captain, but no—not for all the gold in the world would she ever set foot in that cabin again while he was in it. But he mustn't be allowed to come on deck and find his crew asleep. Caleb would have to do it. Soon it would be over.

Sunlight had begun to peep shyly out from the cloud cover. The storm spent, the sea was beautiful, surging gracefully beneath the ship's hull.

Raking her gaze down the length of the forward deck, she saw the crew drowsily hanging onto rigging or sprawling contentedly on the deck. Those who were still able to notice her made no move to stop her as she began to search for Caleb. Not finding him, Sirena panicked and called out his name. When he didn't answer, she ran lightly down the length of the deck. She heaved a sigh when she saw him emerge from the captain's cabin. He winked slyly as he passed her, his bucket swingly loosely at his side.

"One more cup for the lot and the *Rana* will again be yours, Sirena," he smiled.

The men swilled second cups of the steaming coffee, thankful for its warmth and the liberal lacing of rum.

"You go to the galley and rest a bit, Sirena," the boy said to her when he'd served the crew. "You'll need your strength for what we're about to do."

"I could be dying and I'd find the strength," Sirena responded grimly, her face full of hate. "Have no fear, little one, I'll do you credit." Her voice was weary and a feverish brightness was returning to her eyes.

"Sirena, your fever is returning. Have you looked at your arm?"

"No," she answered woodenly. "In truth I'm afraid to look, for I can't think of myself going through life with only one."

"Now would be a good time to dress your wound. It will be a time yet before the captain and his crew are well under the drug."

"All right, but let's hurry! The sooner the *Rana* is ours, the better I'll feel."

Caleb returned a moment later with clean dressing. When he uncovered her arm, they both gasped at the angry, swollen wound. "I'll have to lance it again," he said fearfully.

"I know. Do it!"

Sirena clenched her teeth as the knife found its mark. A whoop of pain escaped the weary girl as Caleb drained the wound. Rubbing some foul dark salve into it, and sprinkling it liberally with a healing powder, he sighed and began to wrap a clean cloth about Sirena's arm while the girl sat groaning on the foredeck.

Working diligently for over an hour, they hefted the seamen into the ship's small jolly-boat with the aid of a rope and winch. Only once had they spoken during their task. This was when, at the start, Sirena ordered him to throw the men over the side.

"But, Sirena, these are shark waters. They'll die."

"And you think I care if they're ripped to shreds, is that it? Well, I don't care! Toss them over!"

Caleb peered deeply into her burning eyes. While her voice demanded their death, her eyes were saying something else.

"Sirena, there's nothing I would not do for you, but I can't do this. It would be murder! I'll lower them in the jolly-boat and let them take their chances. You said there would be a time and a place when the reckoning would come. Please hold to that!"

"Your heart is made of jelly, young Caleb. Do what you will," she said as she swayed against the rigging.

Caleb's eyes were sick as he looked at her. As soon as the captain went over the side into the boat, Caleb released the lines, freeing the dinghy. The wind caught the sails of the *Rana* and spurred the frigate away from the drifting dinghy.

Sirena was weaving unsteadily and her eyes were glazed and feverish. Caleb was frightened, not only for himself but for Sirena. What would he do now if she died . . . ?

Chapter Three

For five days and nights Sirena lay in a delirium. She had exhausted her last reserves of strength in helping Caleb lower the crew and captain into the jolly-boat and had fallen into what was, at first, a death-like sleep. From time to time, however, she cried out in pain, and at other moments she would shout hoarsely for Isabel. In between, she cursed the Dutch and all they stood for.

Caleb wanted to cry, but there was nothing for him

to do but watch her. His youth and inexperience made him angry with himself. He believed that if he were older he would know how to help her. For a time he thought the sea-water baths were helping her arm, but the next day, when he changed the bandage once more, the wound looked angrier than before. The medicinal powder was almost gone and he had nothing to use in its place. Dejectedly, he sat down next to her and continued applying cold compresses to her head. Sirena Córdez had always seemed impervious to pain—and now she was so vulnerable to it. And Caleb could do nothing but sit and watch her suffering.

Five days after the sending off of the pirates, it was time to change the dressing again. He would use the last packet of powder.

Dreading to see the wound, he closed his eyes as he untied the bandage. Merciful God! He blinked disbelievingly. The greenish-yellow pus was gone. A slight scab was forming over the gash and there was no drainage. He rolled his tearful eyes heavenward and sprinkled on the powder, replacing the soiled bandage with a clean one.

Timidly, he reached out to touch Sirena's brow, and was not surprised to find it cooler. An idea sprung into his head. Reaching the captain's quarters, he searched for the jug of rum. His feet were sure and steady on the rolling deck as he ran back to Sirena.

Holding her head in the crook of his arm, he poured some of the rum down her throat. She gagged and sputtered.

"Caleb—are you—trying to kill me?" Sirena smiled weakly.

Caleb, overjoyed to have her conscious again, burst into a fit of laughter. "Your death is exactly what I'm trying to avoid, Sirena."

Caleb didn't know if she had heard him. Sirena had closed her eyes and was falling into the first natural sleep she'd had in five days.

She slept most of the afternoon and, when she awoke, Caleb had a tray ready with hot soup and black bread.

"So, I live after all . . ." She pierced the boy with a

steady eye. "Why didn't you let me die? What good am I to anyone now?"

Refusing to listen to her, he began to tell her of their situation. "The *Rana* is drifting south, I believe, and I've not seen another ship."

"That's good. Why do you look troubled?"

"You were very sick and you said many strange things." His closed face and averted eyes resisted any further questioning.

Nursing Sirena back to health, Caleb was cheerful and helpful, anticipating her every need. A few days later Sirena again questioned him about what was on his mind. He described her delirium but again refused to answer any further questions.

At length, Sirena began to tell him something of herself, and of Isabel, and why the two sisters had been on their way to Java. As she spoke, an idea was born in her mind and she began to tell it to Caleb . . .

"Caleb, Mynheer van der Rhys is expecting a bride to arrive . . . and I wouldn't want to see him disappointed. I've told you of the marriage contract concerning Isabel. What would you say . . . if I told you I intend to take her place?"

Caleb was incredulous, his black eyes sparkled quizzically.

"Don't look at me that way," Sirena laughed, liking her idea more by the moment. "Regan van der Rhys, as representative of the Dutch Crown in these isles, is doubtless responsible for the attack on the *Rana,* I'd stake my life on it! He must have a score of privateers in his employ, if only to protect his shipping. And they would not be averse to attacking Spanish and Portuguese ships—with or without his orders. I'm puzzled—but angrier than words can tell—that he gave no orders to his marauders to let pass the Spanish vessel in which his intended bride was arriving! He is, therefore, ultimately responsible for Isabel's and Tio Juan's deaths! I want to see him pay for what he did to us!"

"But how will you do *that?*" Caleb asked, not liking the determined look in her eye.

"I don't know . . . yet. But as his wife I would soon

find ways. The brigantine that attacked us was Dutch-built—and under the orders of the Dutch East India Company, I'd wager. Perhaps I can discover a way to undermine the Dutch hold on these waters. Destroy their business, destroy their power—and the Dutch economy will be ruined, leaving a wide perch for the Spanish to sit on!"

She smiled maliciously. "What do you think, Caleb, will it work? Will you join me in this little adventure? I'll say you're my brother, and that way we can stay together. We'll concoct some story to tell the Dutchman that will satisfy him. Now run and get me the maps and charts. I want to see if I can calculate where we are."

The young boy was delighted to have his señorita once again interested in living—even if her plans did seem wild. "I swear you my allegiance, Captain Sirena. I'll do as you say!" His round, handsome face was so serious that Sirena laughed for the first time since the brigantine had attacked her *Rana*.

Caleb brought the maps and charts to her from the deserted captain's quarters. "These are mostly Captain López's, and your uncle's. But these soiled maps, I think, are Captain Blackheart's. They were in a separate pile."

Sirena reached for the pirate's maps. "Why, they're done in great detail, and show the inlets, shoals, reefs, and straits around Java, Bali, and southern Sumatra!" she exclaimed, her knowledge of geography coming back to her as she pointed out the island to Caleb. She was grateful to Don Antonio Córdez and de Silva, his master-at-arms, for not neglecting this aspect of her education. "This is very curious. Generally, pirates have only more simple maps—and poorly drawn ones at that! These—these greatly detailed types are usually made for traders, not for marauders. And, look—these words at the sides and near the bottom! They're in Dutch, not Spanish! This makes me believe, even more surely, that Blackheart and his men were in Dutch employ. And, who controls Dutch shipping—and, doubtless, Dutch marauding on Spanish ships—in this region? Mynheer Regan van der Rhys, of course!"

She pored over the maps, and the effort made her poor head swim.

"Let's wait until this evening, when I can take a reading from the stars," she said. "I think we're not far off the south coast of Java. Perhaps another three days and we'll make port."

Caleb sighed. Sirena had had a look in her eye when she spoke of van der Rhys that boded ill for the Dutchman. Yes, Caleb would place his purse on Sirena if it came to a wager. He almost felt sorry for the Dutchman. Still, if he were responsible—even indirectly—for the attack on the *Rana* then he deserved whatever it was she would do.

Two more days had passed and Sirena was rapidly regaining her strength. The dressing had been removed and the sun was now allowed to caress the angry wound.

"It itches," she complained.

"That's good. It means it heals inside as well as out," Caleb chided her.

"How do you know so much about medicine and doctoring?"

"I don't, but I'm learning!"

Now that Sirena felt so much better, she decided to rummage through her trunks and find something more suitable to wear than the long, tattered—and now rather filthy—shirt Caleb had tossed her immediately after her ordeal with the pirates. But her long, full-skirted gowns, with their stiffly starched crinolines, would never do—though she could use her bright crimson silk scarf to tie about her head to keep her hair from blowing into her eyes. And her mid-calf-high boots of glove-soft leather could be worn; they would permit her firmer footing than the thin, light slippers she had been wearing.

In desperation she turned to her Uncle Juan's trunk. Although some of the contents had been taken by the pirates, she did find a pair of black trousers. Don Juan Córdez y Savar had been a tall and slender man but his trousers would fit snugly over her wider, femininely rounded hips. Yet Sirena needed movement, and the wide lower parts of the trouser legs would prevent this. To remedy the situation she slashed at the material with her knife and threw the cuttings away. Slipping the shortened trousers on and pulling them up over her hips, she regretted her impatience: they were very short—barely covering her lithe, muscled haunches.

Discarding the ragged shirt in disgust, she sorted through more of Juan's wardrobe and selected a blouse of bright scarlet. Hastily, she tore away the lower parts of the sleeves and donned it, tying the shirt's tails tightly into a knot high on her ribs beneath her full breasts. Adjusting the scarf about her head and lacing the black boots, she dashed over to the shiny polished-metal mirror hanging behind the cabin door.

She studied herself with amazement. A woman long of limb and torso, dark hair haloing her proud head, then cascading from the scarlet bandana. But her expression belied the amazement. Lips parted to show fine white teeth, she exuded a brazen aura of feline grace—an animal beauty, wild and untamable.

What she saw pleased her. The costume befitted a lady pirate.

But wait! Something was missing. Swiftly, she ran and reached into the trunk and drew from it a black leather belt, then fastened it low on her hips. Slipping her knife under it, she again appraised her reflection and laughingly approved.

The *Rana* kept her course for two more days and, with the passing of each, Sirena's strength increased. She stood at the ship's wheel, exhilarated by the sun and wind and rolling sea.

Young Caleb came out on deck and Sirena was once again struck by his youthful beauty. Dark, thick, tousled hair fell over his smooth brow to accentuate the startling blackness of his eyes and his long, sooty lashes. His sturdy young body held a promise of tall, broad-shouldered manhood. His remarkable strength of character had helped Sirena through an agonizing ordeal.

Sirena smiled fondly at him. "By sunup we'll sight Java. Have you got our story straight?"

"Aye!" He returned her smile. Caleb loved to see her this way, laughing and happy, ready to face life with the same verve with which she turned her beautiful face into the wind. "I know what to say. All hands lost at sea. Everything went overboard to lighten the ship. You are betrothed to Mynheer van der Rhys and I'm your brother. Thank the Lord I've learned some Spanish—*and* a smattering of Dutch—during my travels on the *Lord Raleigh* and with your own fleet these past months. The trunks containing my belongings were lost at sea; fortunately yours were saved. No mention of pirates or what they did to us." A touch of impatience tinged his words. Sirena had rehearsed him so many times since she first devised her plan.

"That's the straight of it, Caleb. Remember, our uncle went overboard with the crew and we're in mourning. There mustn't be any hint of Isabel, however. And give Mynheer van der Rhys no hint that we intend to discover whether it was indeed his marauders, English-speaking or not, who did us harm."

"I can remember, Sirena." Caleb assured her.

His boy's heart hardened with resolution. He would die before he let her down. Caleb's mind still held the memory of her eyes, brilliant with determination to "discover" van der Rhys, and the deadly calm with which she had said, "Power is the life's blood to men like van der Rhys! I'll *ruin him* and see him grovel—a broken man—for what he did to us!"

"Caleb"—Sirena's voice brought him back to the present—"bring the maps out here to me. There's no sense struggling to read them by lamplight in the cabin."

"Aye, Sirena." He knew she had an aversion to the cabin since Dick Blackheart had occupied it.

On the boy's return, moments later, they sat near the ship's wheel, poring over the charts. When Sirena had estimated their bearings as being just hours off the southern coast of Java, she began rerolling the maps and slipping them back into their protective leather pouches.

"I also found *this* in the cabin, Sirena." Caleb held out a long, cylindrical black leather pouch bearing the Córdez crest. "I believe Blackheart took it from your uncle's belongings."

Accepting the pouch from Caleb's outstretched hand, Sirena remembered seeing her Uncle Juan carefully place it deep between layers of his clothing. When she had asked him what it was, he had answered simply that it was a wedding gift for Mynheer van der Rhys.

Curious, she opened the leather thong drawstring and withdrew a thin, fine-grained animal skin—possibly goat skin, she thought. It had been tanned and was soft and pliant in her hands. It was a map. In the lower right-hand corner of the irregularly shaped hide was the map's legend, and from its style she deemed it to be several hundred years old, if not more. On saying so to Caleb, he asked how she could know this, and she explained to him that her uncle was a collector of ancient shipping charts and had shared his interest with her.

"It's an old map of the Indies, Caleb. Look, here's Borneo, there's New Guinea." She pointed. "Sumatra, Java . . . Although they're labeled in what looks like Arabic, or perhaps even Persian."

Caleb broke in excitedly, "In the islands they speak of Moslem kings—sultans—who sailed the seas with their navies here long ago. Legend has it that they looted the islands and killed many natives in search of gemstones and gold."

When the top of the map was unrolled completely, a delicate slip of paper slithered out and fell to the deck. Sirena picked it up and read the few short words. It was addressed to Regan van der Rhys; it was a note of congratulation on the wedding between the Córdez family and the van der Rhys. Sirena frowned.

Caleb was quite obviously fascinated with the map. Sirena explained to him what she knew of the early European explorations among these, the Spice Islands, telling him how, as early as 1525, the Dutch—blast them—followed the routes established by the Portuguese to the Indies and the Far East. When they arrived on the marshy shores of the Spice Islands, they felt almost at home among the network of waterways, which were indeed almost like a tropical "Holland."

The Dutch felt they could offer the Portuguese stiff competition for the commercial conquest of the East. Just forty years before, in 1583, the burgesses of Amsterdam had founded the predecessor of the Dutch East India Company. They called it the "Company of Far Countries," and they had commissioned heavily armed ships to follow the Portuguese routes as far as possible beyond the Cape of Good Hope to the Kingdom of Spices. Because of a royal marriage, however, Spain and Portugal became in effect one kingdom and banded their forces together, the Spanish now sending out ships from their Far Eastern "capital" of Manila, in the Philippines, to aid the Portuguese in the Indies, to the south. The Dutch soon found themselves harassed at every turn. And soon the Spanish were as firmly entrenched in the Spice Islands as were the Portuguese. Only in this new century had the Dutch frequently gained the upper hand in trading.

Caleb's eyes returned to the old map, which, though it might not be as accurate as López's or Uncle Juan's or Dick Blackheart's soiled maps of the straits, inlets, and various islands of the Indies, gave interesting details of its own. "Look at these drawings of volcanos! Look, Sirena! See, here on Sumatra! I've seen them with my own eyes. And here, these on Java! I've seen some of them, too. Just sitting up out of the blue like some angry gods! But I had no idea there were so many of them!"

"What do you think these funny little drawings are next to the islands?" Sirena inquired, puzzled.

"Why, they're trees. Look. Cinnamon! Bay!" His finger darted across the unfurled skin. "Nutmeg, cloves, peppercorns . . . ginger, mace, aloes! The old map shows each area and what treasure is to be found there!"

Sirena and Caleb studied the old chart for some time and, heads spinning and eyes aching from deciphering the fine old writing, they at last began to curl the chart in order to replace it in its case. It was then that Sirena noticed a drawing of Java alone —in enlarged detail—on the back side of the skin.

Upon examination of the drawing, Caleb appeared to be surprised.

"What is it, boy?" Sirena asked.

"This river, Sirena. This river some short distance from Batavia. It must be the one that lies to the west of the town, beyond one of two volcanos that stand one on each side of its mouth . . ."

"Well?"

"You notice the drawings of ships passing up the river, and inland? I'm puzzled. You see, the natives of Java call it the River of Death, because it's impassable. The mouth of the river is wide—as it is drawn here. But there are rapids not far upstream, and the shallows at the mouth are treacherous. Only native proas enter and leave its mouth. The European merchants neither enter it or ever anchor there. Of course they've little need to use it, for the Java chieftains send down to Batavia all their spices by native carriers. And look," he continued, "there appears to be a cove, upstream some distance—and the mapmaker has drawn in two vessels, which appear to be anchored there!"

Sirena's eyes indicated that she was deeply considering something. Caleb went on.

"I've seen the River of Death when I was here aboard the *Lord Raleigh* a year ago. We bought some spices from the Dutch and Spanish in Batavia, and then traveled west, past the river and its two volcanos. Not far off, upriver, we could see a waterfall—perhaps less than three miles away, for the river is not a long one."

Almost with reverence Sirena picked up the skin. If what the map showed of the River of Death were true . . . perhaps, in later times, some eruption had shallowed and partly blocked the mouth of the river and earned it its cruel name. But maybe there was still a way to cross those shallows. That cove, upstream, offered possibilities . . .

Caleb noted Sirena's glittering eyes and shivered involuntarily. Nevertheless, whatever she did, he was behind her all the way; he had sworn her his allegiance and he would abide by it. He knew instinctively that the map was a wedding present Regan van der Rhys would never receive.

Chapter Four

Sirena's first sight of Java—its westernmost tip—left her breathless. Green . . . green . . . green was the only word she could find to describe the high-rising jewel that stood over the horizon at the first light of day.

Entering the Sunda Strait, which separated the island from its larger neighbor, Sumatra, the *Rana* drew in toward the shore and Sirena saw two volcanos in the near-distance, the masts of some ships and what looked like a town a bit farther east. She and Caleb managed to bring the frigate in toward Java, and approached the River of Death.

They watched the current of the river enter the sea, its frothy backwash swelling and churning.

"See, I told you"—Caleb pulled on her arm—"there's no way up that river. Even the current's against it!"

Sirena lifted her eyes to the topsail and squinted against the sun. "We're going to try it," she said in a quiet and solemn voice.

"Sirena, we can't! We'll be dashed on the rocks!" His words went unnoticed, which added to his fears. Her mouth was set in determination and she had already begun to steer the *Rana* toward the river's mouth. Then, appealing to the sailor in her: "Sirena, we've no crew. Just the two of us can't get the *Rana* up that deadly river!"

"I think we can! Look at the flag on the topsail. See the way it's blowing? Now look ahead. See? We've caught a westerly wind. There are rocks visible in its mouth there, on the right. But look to the other side, where there appears to be a clear channel. We'll sail right on up the river in that crevasse as if we were out in open water."

Caleb saw the logic behind her thinking and had to agree that it might not be a problem, but he protested again. "But even a frigate draws too much water."

"Perhaps . . ." Sirena muttered, "but I say we can do it!"

It was clear to Caleb that Sirena would not attempt it without his agreement—but she was like a dog with a bone. She would worry the subject until she wore him down and dragged a Yes out of him. Deciding to save time and nerves, Caleb shrugged his shoulders and agreed. "Let's do it, then. *I've* nothing to lose and *you've* only the *Rana* at stake. If you can bear to lose her . . ." He shrugged again.

"I won't lose her! Never! Now, please, go to the cabin and get me the chart. I want to find that cove in the river."

As the *Rana* sailed closer to the river mouth, they saw that, to the right, the fresh river waters churned over the slick, glossy-black rocks and mixed, foaming, with the blue of the sea. Under Sirena's orders, Caleb struggled to lower all but the mizzen sail. Sirena strained at the wheel, keeping to the left of the rocks in what, indeed, was a sort of channel in the river mouth.

The *Rana* rose and fell in the swell of waves, her bow nosing valiantly, majestically out of the surf. Sirena held her breath and squeezed her eyes shut, praying she would not hear the crash and splintering of her beloved ship's hull against unseen, submerged boulders.

Minutes passed, but the wind lifted the *Rana* and drove her deftly through the channel past the rocks at the river's mouth!

Caleb shouted, "We made it! We did it!"

Daring to open her eyes, Sirena saw that they had indeed made it. The ship had skittered beyond the rocks and was now holding her own, with the aid of the prevailing westerly wind, against a swift but manageable river current.

Though rapid, the river flowed through a low, flat

valley flanked on either side by the steep heights of the volcanos Sirena had seen on the ancient map—and also on one of Dick Blackheart's maps. In the distance, she spied the waterfall Caleb had described, and closer, the rapids he'd mentioned. But, suddenly, to her left—in the direction of Batavia—was a huge cove of calm deep water. Deeper water than that of the river itself, Sirena judged. And the cove was concealed behind the steep slopes of the easternmost volcano, which smoked high above them.

With Caleb's quick help, she turned the *Rana* at a ninety-degree angle and sailed into the placid waters of the cove.

The emerald-green foliage that surrounded the cove was thick with flowers. Birds called out in strange warblings that broke the eerie silence. Slowly, the *Rana* nestled into the steep cliff that formed one side of the cove.

A marvelous anchoring place! Sirena and Caleb were delighted with their victory over the River of Death, and with this haven for the *Rana*. Weighing anchor, they felt giddy with their success.

"Come, Caleb," Sirena challenged, posing bootless atop the rail of the ship. "I'll race you to the shore!" She dove into the deep waters and swam toward a miniature shoreline behind which the Javanese jungle rose steeply.

Following Caleb's direction, she could just barely see the red-tiled roof of D.E.I. Chief Pensioner Mynheer Regan van der Rhys's house. Caleb assured her it was the most splendid on the island—a sprawling two-story building built in Portuguese fashion with thick masonry walls to keep out the heat of the tropical sun. The estate was huge, encompassing thousands of acres of clove and cinnamon trees. But Sirena was unimpressed by van der Rhys's wealth and her possible share in it. With a calculating eye she measured the distance from the top of the rise where she stood to the van der Rhys mansion; just above two miles, she guessed. The cover where the *Rana* was anchored lay back through the jungle and down the opposite side of the rise, nearly equally distant from her.

"Caleb, the *Rana* needs a crew. Where are we to find one for her?"

"A crew . . . ? But why?"

"To carry out my plan against the Dutchman, of course! Now, think! Where can we get a crew? I want good men, mind you! No scurvy lot will man my ship!"

Caleb was obviously rattled by this extreme change in her mood. Only moments ago Sirena was placid, tranquil; she had allowed the green lushness of the jungle to work its spirit-healing ways. Now she was tightly strung again, boiling with determination, the fire of vengeance blazing in her thickly lashed eyes.

"Sirena, I know of some men—stout and hearty men, too—who live in a tiny fishing village, Teatoa, we passed before we sailed up the river. The village lies west of Batavia. Those men are fishers these days, but once were sailors on one of the finest ships of the Dutch East India fleet!"

"Dutchmen! Caleb, where are your wits? Dutchmen on my *Rana?* How much use do you think *they* would be to me? They would never strike a blow to their own countrymen!"

"Working for the Dutch East India Company does not make a man a Dutchman. In fact, two of the men I'm thinking of are Malayans who signed on with the company. But the others are Dutch with a very bitter taste now for the company."

"Bitter? How so?"

"Bitter because of forced retirement. The D.E.I. pays them a pitifully small pension and has declared them unfit for service. They are survivors of the plague that once riddled the ship they sailed. They were, as are all plague victims, denied readmittance to Holland—to their home and their families! Instead, they fish to feed their bellies and hate the Dutch East India Company to nourish their souls! I talked with them at length when the *Lord Raleigh* was at anchor here."

"And you think they would sign on the *Rana* even if they knew I intended to sail her against the Dutch?"

"They would sign on the *Rana* just to feel like men again! To be useful and to feel the sea rolling beneath the decks."

Sirena considered Caleb's words for a moment and the risk she would be taking in revealing herself and her hiding place to these banished Dutchmen. She spoke softly, barely audibly. "Then, Caleb . . . you must bring me these men to me."

While Caleb trod the long path back over the hills behind the waterfall to the fishing village, Sirena busied herself aboard the frigate. Above decks and below, she went over every inch of the ship to be certain no evidence of the pirate attack remained for her new crew to see. Perhaps later she would decide to tell them what had happened, but for the time being she preferred to keep it her secret and Caleb's.

She hesitated outside the cabin which Dick Blackheart had occupied—the scene of her final humiliating experience. Pushing thoughts of that degradation from her mind, she opened the door and stepped inside. Quickly, she crossed the distance to the wide, mullioned windows that made up the back wall of the room and threw aside the heavy draperies. Light streamed into the square cabin, illuminating millions of dancing dust motes.

Sirena wrinkled her nose at the musty smell mixed with the scent of stale sweat and sour ale, and tried not to think of Isabel.

A timid knock sounded on the cabin door. Sirena lifted her dark head from the maps she was intent upon. "Come," she called quietly.

"Sirena, this is Jan, one of the men I spoke of."

The woman straightened to her full height and authoritatively extended her hand. "I am Sirena Córdez, captain of this ship," she said quietly, looking deep into the man's eyes. He was returning her handshake with a grip as firm as her own.

"Jan Verhooch, Señorita. The boy has spoken of you and this ship you . . . captain. Forgive me, too, if I seem surprised; I thought I knew the island, but

I must confess my ignorance of this cove. How did you find your way into it?"

"I found it on the advice of ancient kings," Sirena laughed lightly. She had no wish to share the secret of the Persian charts.

Seeing he would not receive a direct answer to his inquiry, Jan asked, "What is it you want of me and the men in our small village?"

"I am searching for a crew to man this ship. Reliable, honest men who will do my bidding with no questions asked."

"You ask this and will tell me nothing in return?"

"I need a crew," Sirena repeated, her tone firm.

"There is no captain—be she man *or* woman—whom I would sail for on mere blind faith. Tell me what it is you want, and I will give you my decision. It is a fair request."

"Aye, fair it is." So, she thought, I'm forced already to tell my story. Yet perhaps it's for the best. "Very well, Jan. Several weeks ago I boarded this ship—my own—with my uncle, my sister, and young Caleb. We were approaching Java, where we were bringing my sister, Isabel, to marry Mynheer van der Rhys, when we were attacked by pirates. My sister was raped and killed—gored from neck to navel by a pirate who carried a hook for a hand. I, myself, suffered at their hands . . ." Her lowered eyes conveyed her meaning. "Caleb managed to aid me and we made our escape." She explained the drugging of the captain and the ship's crew. "I carry a memento of the—" quickly, she rolled up the sleeve of her shirt to reveal the scar that ran the length of her upper arm. She smiled at the man's indrawn breath. "I see you have not seen many such wounds."

"Aye, it's true. Rarely have I seen a wound such as that."

"Regan van der Rhys was, I am certain, responsible for what happened to my sister and myself and my uncle. The brigantine was Dutch-built, English-captained, and I found Dutch trader's maps. Now he will have to pay—and pay dearly—for what he has cost me in honor and family. I plan to assume my sister's purpose and marry Mynheer van der Rhys. I will lead two lives: one, the demure wife; the other, a witch of the seas. I plan to ruin him as he ruined me. To do this I need a crew and a loyal one . . . You may keep whatever cargo you wish, when we board ship, and divide it among the men. But, also, I will pay a fair wage for all. You must swear your allegiance to me and obey me as if I were a man. Can you do this?" she demanded.

Pale blue eyes searched the depth of the green ones opposite. "The boy tells me you command this frigate better than any man."

"Yes, Jan, I command this frigate. I think it would be safe to say that I can do it . . . *as well as* any man. I brought the ship through the mouth of the river—which, I'm told by Caleb, is called by the natives the River of Death. Perhaps that will help to convince you of my abilities."

"The boy has already told me of this. Very well . . . Capitana," he said, bowing low, "I will sign aboard this ship, as will the other men. This day I swear my loyalty and allegiance to you and you only."

"I plan to keep the *Rana* berthed in this cove. You and the crew you provide me with, since you come from a village west of the river and Batavia lies to the east, will easily be able to come aboard unseen and unsuspected by the Dutch or Spanish trading companies in the town. You will be able to prepare the ship, while awaiting my arrival, so that we shall be ready to sail. Until that time comes, however—and you will know, by a message I send with Caleb to the village—I will employ you, a bit . . . For I want the frigate painted black and her sails dyed to match. Also, her name must be obliterated," Sirena added haltingly, overcoming a catch in her throat. "As far as the world is concerned, the *Rana* lies at the ocean's bottom. Ready the ship and lay in stores soon, for I may want to set sail sooner that I now believe."

"I will take care of all this," Jan said quietly.

"One more thing, Jan. Mynheer van der Rhys will have to be informed of my arrival. Go to him, tell him you and your crew were fishing as usual and happened to see the storm-tossed, invalid *Rana* off the Java coast. The seas we weathered a few days ago are common knowledge in every port of these islands. He'll believe you when you tell him the frigate was half underwater when you found her. But he may be surprised when he learns she contained no crew but me and Caleb—whom, you must explain to him, is my brother! He will doubtless be forced to conclude that one of his private marauders—knowing nothing of the expected arrival of his intended, *by his forgetting to tell them*—had murdered her Spanish crew and set her adrift with her brother. He knew, by letter, that his bride was to be en route for Java, but did not know that her sister accompanied her—so we are safe there. Nevertheless, he will expect that she had some companionship in addition to her brother; tell him of my Uncle Juan, and let him think that his privateers killed that worthy gentleman. For I must be in mourning! It is a part of my plan. Finally, tell Mynheer van der Rhys that Señorita Córdez and her brother are in your village and will be arriving at his home late this afternoon."

"It's as good as done," Jan said, smiling conspiratorially.

"Would you care for a glass of wine before you leave, Jan? We shall drink to a long, profitable relationship," Sirena said, pouring some port into elegant goblets that she withdrew from their hiding place beneath Captan López's bunk.

"To Mynheer van der Rhys's downfall," Jan shouted.

The goblets clicked against each other and Sirena found herself smiling into the Dutch eyes of her first mate, noting ironically that this Dutchman would help her bring one of his countrymen down!

"To you, Capitana," he continued.

It was a moment before Sirena realized that Jan had coined a new word. She decided she liked it, it sat well on her. As the crew's "capitana" she would lead them on a course to destroy their common enemy, the Dutch East India Company, *and* Regan van der Rhys.

Chapter Five

Regan van der Rhys, tall and sun-gilded and with a neat white-blond thatch of hair, strode up and down his opulently appointed library, a fragrant cigar clenched between his perfect white teeth. Suddenly, and angrily, he took the slim black smoking stub from his mouth and crushed it into a pulpy mound in the glass tray on his teak desk. Hands clenched, he paced the room like a caged lion.

The last thing in this world Regan wanted was to marry again: a wife simply did not fit into his scheme of things. Now that she had actually arrived, he had learned that she brought with her a variety of problems. For one, her uncle had died and she would be in mourning.

"Damn!" Regan exclaimed. "This means that one of my privateers—those I use only to protect my traders from the Spanish—has run amuck and attacked the Señorita's ship! My warnings to those devil-may-care buccaneers should have been more explicit. Thank God they spared the lady and her brother! But for her uncle's death, I may be held responsible—and rightly so. Still, the lady may not be so quick-witted as to make the connection . . ."

Regan considered himself knowledgeable on the mourning practices of Spanish ladies: heavy black gowns with high, choking collars and long, tight sleeves held aloft by dozens of horsehair crinolines; downcast features half hidden by a lace mantilla; fingers working feverishly over a chain of rosary beads.

A thought glimmered in his head. Perhaps propriety would be better served if he postponed his wedding until after the mourning period was over, but even as he thought it he negated the idea. The women on the island had wagging tongues. Merchants' wives, the agents' wives—all of them decreed the morals of the island. What they themselves did secretly behind the closed doors of their musk-scented boudiors was another matter. But Regan knew he must marry the mournful señorita and preserve her reputation. No one would believe that Señorita Córdez could live beneath his roof and be safe from his advances.

Regan grinned wickedly as he thought of the rumors that peppered the drawing rooms of every captain, agent, and grower from the Sundra Strait to the China Sea. The men called him a rake—though they respected his expertise with his ships as well as with a woman, provided the woman wasn't one of their wives. Smiling at his reflection in the looking glass on the cedar-paneled wall, Regan decided he was flattered by the general consensus about the extent of his amours, though he knew the gossip to be greatly exaggerated.

Then his thoughts raced back to his intended. What would she look like? Probably a scarecrow of a woman, all bones and angles to prick a man in his bed. She would no doubt be as ugly as sin, and have teeth like a horse. He had personally seen the results of some of these arranged marriages. He would give the girl his name and a roof over her head. More than that he would not promise. "Damnation!" Regan roared, forcefully driving the fist of one hand into the palm of the other. He would take his pleasure where he found it and not rely on a skinny, narrow-eyed Spaniard's resentful submission to *his* lovemaking.

The van der Rhys wagon had come for Sirena and Caleb. It was driven by a small, loose-jointed man with shiny yellow skin and inquisitive, slanted eyes, who explained in halting Dutch that his name was Ling Fu and that the Mynheer had, he believed, sent the wagon to save the Juffrouw from the prying eyes of the townspeople. Although the trip through the jungles and hills was hotter and longer than traveling in a native proa, by skirting the shoreline the Juffrouw would be on display for all curious eyes in the port to see. Mynheer felt that the Juffrouw would not care to expose herself to this until she was rested from her ordeal.

His almond eyes cast downward in apology, Ling Fu shuffled his bare feet in the dust as he spoke.

To Sirena the meaning was clear: Mynheer van der Rhys did not want his bride to be seen until he himself had an opportunity to see what he was getting. Her first impulse was to feign exhaustion and demand to be taken by proa. But, although she didn't care to admit it, Sirena herself was not ready to meet those curious eyes. Yes, she and Caleb would ride to the Mynheer's estate in the wagon, skirting the town, and avoiding the possibility of meeting any of the Mynheer's friends.

Her trunks were loaded on the back of the wagon and Caleb climbed in after them. The single jounce seat in which Ling Fu sat made it necessary for Sirena to follow Caleb into the wagon and sit wearily amongst her trunks and belongings.

The heat of the day was stifling, though a gentle breeze blew in off the village quay. As the wagon bounced inland along the rutted, dusty road, the closer the air became and the more noticeable the humidity. Sirena found herself wishing for the fresh, brisk wind of the sea, the tang of the salt air, the domain of her *Rana*.

Sitting atop one of the trunks, she was able to catch a glimpse of the village, laid out along its tiny waterfront. Many of the gabled rooftops were tiled and others were just thatched, but there was a sense of permanence about it. This village—crowded between jungle and water—seemed to have been there always, unobtrusive in its surroundings. Then, the village disappeared from view, and without its diversion Sirena became more conscious of the broiling sun and red dust spewing up from the wagon's wheels. The hair on the nape of her neck stuck to her skin. Her armpits felt uncomfortably damp and her black and brown bombazine gown—one of the few of her sister Isabel's habits that the pirates had not carried off—was becoming stained with perspiration beneath her breasts and between her shoulder blades. She longed for the cool, abbreviated costume she had devised aboard the *Rana*.

Her eyes fell on Caleb, who had fallen asleep on the floor of the wagon. Poor Caleb! He had been running about all morning, first to fetch Jan to the *Rana* and, later, when he and Sirena had gone back to the village with the Dutch fisherman to help the latter brief his fellow-fishers on the care and painting and dyeing of the ship's sails. He deserved this short catnap before the ordeal of facing Mynheer van der Rhys.

"Mynheer van der Rhys"—even as she thought of his name, her spine stiffened with apprehension. She was on her way to meet the enemy!

Gretchen Lindenreich adjusted the short, sleeveless jacket that barely covered her full pink-and-white breast and left her midriff bare down to the long, brightly colored sarong skirt that rode low on her slim hips. Like so many women on the island, Gretchen had adopted the native Malayan costume to keep cool through the worst heat of the day, when any Western woman with a brain in her head stayed home and bathed her wrists in cologne. Unlike the native women's, Gretchen's brightly colored raw silk costume was cut to reveal as much of her body as she could allow in front of her servants.

Through the long gauze-covered glass doors leading to the garden, a movement caught her eye. Stepping closer for a better look, a blur of orange silk disappeared behind an ornamental persimmon bush.

"That damn Sudi!" Gretchen swore, a surly pout on her petulant mouth. "What does she care if my gowns hang in tatters!"

In the sultry damp of the tropics, the bane of every woman's existence was the preservation of her wardrobe. Mildew ate even beneath closet doors to wreak destruction in the folds of the garments, rotting and shredding the fabrics. More than once, a lady was embarrassed by the sudden tearing away of a sleeve or bodice while she was in public. Although Gretchen could afford cheap labor and inexpensive yard goods constantly to replace her Western gowns and underpinnings, she was fiercely possessive of her belongings and would not part with them either as gifts to her babo, or handmaiden, as was the custom, *or* to the ravages of the damp. Therefore it was Sudi's chore to take the long gowns and nightdresses, one by one, out of their protective paper wrappings and press them over with a warm flatiron. Hour after hour, day after day, Sudi stood at the padded board in one of the spare chambers, heating the heavy irons on the glowing brazier which, in turn, heated the closed room to a point beyond sweltering. Gretchen would not allow the doors leading to the garden to be opened, for she claimed this defeated the purpose of ironing the damp out of the garments.

Now, seeing the orange blur of Sudi's sari in the garden incensed Gretchen. She had been warned that these Hindu girls made unreliable servants unless kept under strict supervision. This was not the first time Gretchen had caught the toast-colored fifteen-year-old sneaking away from her duties to meet the young djongo or houseboy, who worked for the Daans.

Crossing the room and reaching into her closet, Gretchen groped for the familiar feel of her leather riding crop. Panting with the force of her rage, she stepped out into the heat of the day. Her small slippered feet silent on the cobblestones, she crossed the verandah, determined to find the rebellious Sudi and her lover and teach them both a stinging lesson.

Gretchen followed the path to the edge of the garden. Already a small trickle of perspiration ran between her breasts and down the small of her back. Cursing the interminable heat under her breath, she scanned the sky and noticed with some small relief the gathering of the dark clouds of the daily late-afternoon thundershower which added to the humidity yet did bring with it a dousing of the heat.

When, in her search for Sudi and her lover, she approached the tall yew hedge that separated her garden from the seldom-used country road that approached Batavia from the west, her ears caught the sound of horse hooves and wagon wheels plodding up the dusty byway. Her first thought was of Regan, who often accompanied his wagons full of nutmegs into town to supervise the loading of them aboard his ships. Her heart fluttered in her breast at the thought of seeing him again. She had not seen him for weeks, not since the night he told her of the expected arrival of his Spanish bride and had left her on a bitter note. Her eyes were hungry for the sight of him, her hands greedy to touch him, her mouth ached for his kisses.

Peering through the thick yew branches, Gretchen could see the wagon coming down the road. Her breath caught in her throat. It was Regan's wagon, yes, and there was that crafty-looking Ling Fu driving it. However, there was no sign of van der Rhys. Hope still flowered, and Gretchen remained where she stood, expecting to see Regan following the wagon at a distance, where the clouding dust would not bite into his face and sting his nostrils.

A movement in the back of the wagon attracted Gretchen's attention. There, perched atop a trunk, was a tall, black-garbed figure mopping her sweat-streaked and dust-filmed face. Dark hair tumbled from its knot down her back. The heavy black bombazine gown looked asphixiating in the heat.

Comprehension washed over her. So this was Regan's Spanish bride! No wonder he'd sent the wagon to fetch her instead of bringing her by proa through the cool lagoons and harbor. Look at her!

Laughter bubbled up in Gretchen and burst forth in a raucous cackle.

Sirena heard the sound of laughter breaking the heavy air. How long had it been since she had heard the sound of laughter—or laughed herself? But there was a derisive note in the sound. Was it scornful and contemptuous? Was that why her skin prickled?

Boldly, Gretchen parted the thick branches of the hedge and, heedless of the scratching growth, stuck her head through the opening to laugh directly up into Sirena's face.

The women's eyes locked, and the laughter died with a gurgle in Gretchen's throat. Instead of the misery and humiliation she had expected to see in the Spaniard's face, there was a cold, chilling regality, a positive power of confidence and poise. Sirena's back stiffened rigidly, her chin climbed several inches, the bright bottle-green eyes flashed in challenge. For a full moment the two women stared at each other, until Ling Fu took the wagon around the next bend, leaving Gretchen standing in a cloud of red dust.

Pulling herself back into her garden, Gretchen was silent, Sirena's expression having paralyzed her. Then slowly she moved toward the house, and the ridiculousness of the confrontation washed over her. The sight of Regan's Spanish bride covered with road dust and perspiration, rumpled and inappropriately dressed for this heat, once again amused her. Regan, she thought, it won't be long before you search out my cool blondness and white skin. If your grubby Spanish bride smells as bad as she looks, all the fragrances of the Orient won't improve her!

Slowly and surely, her laughter resumed until she was shaking under its force. Stumbling into her bedroom, she threw herself down onto the cool silk coverlet and indulged herself in howls of glee.

The echo of the blonde's derisive cackling resounded in Sirena's ears. Vainly she tried to brush away some of the clinging red dust from her skirt. The woman's laughter mingled with the remembered jeers of Blackheart's pirates and hate overwhelmed her. She had dealt with the lot aboard the *Rana* and she would somehow deal with that near-naked woman who had been cruel enough to mock her so openly.

Ling Fu drove the wagon up the cobblestone drive leading to the van der Rhys courtyard. Seeing the European-style cobbles, Sirena recalled that because ships returning to the Indies had scant cargos they carried heavy cobbles for ballast. The enterprising settlers on Java and the surrounding islands therefore used the cobblestones to pave their drives and their streets. This helped to combat the inevitable mud that was left behind after the daily rains.

The clatter of the wagon's wheels against the cobbles woke Caleb. Drowsily, he sat up in his nest in the wagon, face flushed from the heat, eyes bright. Sirena reached out a gentle hand to smooth his dark-chocolate hair. With a pang, she realized how infrequently over the past weeks she had thought of Caleb as a child, for with her he had witnessed things no child should witness. He had been her only friend in a time of need and she relied on his good common sense and his strength of character. What's more, Caleb had proved he possessed the heart of a lion. When she referred to him as "little brother" in rehearsing the plot they were executing against van der Rhys, Sirena realized how meaningful the words were, after all. She loved the boy and to her mind he could not have been more her brother than if they had shared the same parentage.

Within her breast welled a fierce protectiveness toward him, the likes of which she had not felt since Caleb had suffered the lashing at the hands of Dick Blackheart aboard the *Rana*. Caleb's young back had been lashed because of his determination to help her, to tend her wounds, and to revive in her a will to live. And to repay him for his devotion to her, she was involving him in a plot against Mynheer van der Rhys—a plot that could place him in a dangerous position. Perhaps it would be better to admit her true identity, go to Mynheer van der Rhys and tell him of Isabel's fate and her uncle's and beg his assistance in helping her to return to Spain. Caleb would then be safe. She could take him back with her and give him all the advantages a young man could desire.

An audible gasp escaped her. What was she thinking? Go to Regan van der Rhys and beg his assistance? For a moment she had forgotten that it was Regan who was responsible for the pirate attack on the *Rana* and for the subsequent deaths of Isabel and Tio Juan.

Regan van der Rhys might even have engineered the attack on her ship. He might have decided he wouldn't care to marry a Spaniard and while Isabel lived he was honor-bound to do so. The thought of the dowry, too, those chests of gold coins had been too tempting. So he had ordered them accosted at sea, all aboard murdered, and the gold and the ship gained for himself.

How he must have felt thwarted when he realized that Señorita Córdez and her brother had been found

—alive!—aboard the fast-sinking Rana. Sirena smiled as she guessed at the Mynheer's puzzlement. He would be wondering what had happened to Blackheart and his crew. How had the English pirate failed in his mission? Where was Blackheart now? How had the two Córdezes manages to escape death?

She would enjoy seeing the surprise on his pasty-white ferret features—as she imagined all Dutchmen must have.

The wagon slowed as it neared the front entrance of the two-story, white-pillared verandah and the massive, intricately carved mahogany double doors. The grounds about the house were meticulously kept. Even now several gardeners went about their chores of pruning and weeding along the brightly colored flower beds. The scent of spices and flowers permeated the air, and exotic wild birds called raucously to one another. The house, the grounds—everything—showed evidence of pride of ownership. Many years and much labor had gone into the acquisition of the van der Rhys mansion. The deep red stone from which the front steps were chiseled she recognized as the precious "pink marble" from the foothills of the China mountains. In Europe jewelry was carved from it and statues of great beauty. Here on Java, a wily agent for the Dutch East India Company used it for his front steps!

Caleb and Ling Fu assisted her descent from the wagon. When the Chinese turned to unload the trunks and baggage, Caleb made a move to assist him, but Sirena placed a restraining hand on his arm. "No, little brother," she whispered, "you are no longer a paid cabin boy. You are Caleb Córdez of the shipbuilding Córdezes. Remember to leave the servants to their own duties."

Caleb flushed slightly. Not even inside the van der Rhys house and he had almost made his first mistake! He would have to be more alert, he promised himself, but he still felt uneasy about the role he was to play. How does the son of a wealthy shipbuilder behave? he questioned himself silently.

With a sigh and a shrug, he stepped closer to Sirena as they waited in the comparative cool shade of the verandah for someone to answer the Señorita's calculatedly timid knock on the impressive door.

Although Sirena did not let Caleb know it by either word or action, she felt indignant at this apparently intentional inauspicious welcome. It was as if she were a peddler begging for a sale! At any moment now, these ostentatious doors would swing open and an imperious servant would look down her long nose at her and insist that all beggars and peddlers were received at the back entrance.

She extended her arm, about to knock a second time, when the door swung wide. A young, harried-looking girl of about seventeen stood glancing back and forth from Sirena to Caleb with a frightened, shocked look on her face. The loose printed smock which hung from her shoulders fluttered from the force of the girl's trembling. Then, seeming to regain her senses, she turned on her heel and ran down the hall, calling, "Juffrouw, Juffrouw is here!" Caleb and Sirena heard a great commotion in the room at the end of the hall and, lastly, the sound of a sharp slap and a choked sob.

A tall and stately woman with a coronet of salt-and-pepper braids wrapped about her head stepped into the hall and moved swiftly toward them, a look of consternation about her tightly pinched mouth.

"Welcome, welcome, Juffrouw," she smiled, her florid complexion offsetting strong white teeth and a square jaw. "Come in out of the heat, please. Come in! I am Frau Holtz, Mynheer's housekeeper. Come in!" she repeated in a thick German accent.

Sirena and Caleb stepped into the cool hallway. Frau Holtz quickly stepped behind them and quietly closed the heavy doors. "We wish to keep out the heat," she stated simply, as if Sirena and Caleb were ignorant schoolchildren who didn't know enough to keep the doors closed against the elements.

An assemblage of servants now appeared in the wide, stone-floored hall, including the tearful young girl who had answered the door.

Frau Holtz explained, in clipped tones, "This stupid girl will be dismissed, Juffrouw. It is because of her that you rode all the way from the village in the baggage wagon. She is incapable of delivering a message correctly! As if the new lady of the house would be made to ride in a baggage wagon! There was a proa at the Batavia quay sent to meet you purposely. This idiot," she said, pointing a finger at the trembling girl, "mixed everything up. Even now Mynheer is at the landing, where he was ready to greet you. Ach! These lazy servants! Be sure, Juffrouw, this girl will be dismissed as soon as the Mynheer learns what trouble she has caused."

Sirena glanced at the young honey-colored servant and experienced a pang of pity for her. Besides, she didn't care for Frau Holtz's imperious attitude. It was clear that the van der Rhys house was the woman's domain. She had probably managed the household for years and years and secretly resented the intrusion of a new "Mevrouw" to answer to. More to be perverse than to assert her rights, Sirena said, "I do not want the girl dismissed. The message concerning my arrival should never have been entrusted to a child to begin with, Frau Holtz. You should have seen to it yourself."

The housekeeper's jaw slackened and she stammered for words, but Sirena spoke before the woman could answer:

"I'd like to be taken to my rooms now. Also, my brother will need quarters and a fresh change of clothing until a new wardrobe can be made for him."

"*Ja,* Juffrouw, I shall see to it myself." Frau Holtz motioned toward the wide, gracefully curving stairway.

"That won't be necessary, Frau Holtz," Sirena said coolly. "The girl whom you find so offensive will do very nicely. I believe I will even have her for my personal maid. I should think she'd be easy to train, once she is given kinder treatment!"

Frau Holtz stepped back from the staircase to allow Sirena and Caleb to pass in front of her. As they mounted the stairs, they heard the housekeeper's voice. She spoke coldly to the girl. "Do not stand there, Juli, the Juffrouw wants you for her servant. Now, show her to her rooms—and the young señor also. Pieter will be up in a moment to see to his needs."

Frau Holtz's tone was so clipped and cold that

Sirena regretted overruling the housekeeper's authority. Juli, as she had heard Frau Holtz call her, had made a terrible bungle in delivering the message incorrectly and justly deserved the housekeeper's scorn. Now that Sirena had come to the girl's defense, it would go very hard with her.

Just as Juli lifted the hem of her long, colorful, sack-like garment to climb the stairs, Frau Holtz spoke again; this time her tone was softer and not unkind. "Juli, the Juffrouw has found the kindness to forgive your blunder, which must have caused her great discomfort. You are to serve her well and be helpful and loyal."

Turning to look at Frau Holtz, Sirena was surprised to see that the expression in the woman's eye matched the softness in her tone. Juli's expression brightened, her ink-dark eyes glistened with happiness as she smiled at the woman. Sirena felt instantly contrite for her misjudgment of Frau Holtz. In spite of the woman's overbearing manner, it was evident that she was fair and just to the servants. Frau Holtz would consider herself above petty grievances, and Juli and the other servants apparently knew this and respected her for it.

Sirena turned to climb the stairs.

"Juffrouw, it is much cooler in here," Juli said as they entered the suite of rooms set aside for Sirena.

The room was draped, all around, in silk gauze embroidered with gold threads depicting pomegranates and birds with glorious plumage. Fresh pale blues deepening to indigo were woven into the thick carpeting. The window hangings were sheer, of a pale blue silk, and the light streaming through them gave Sirena the impression that the whole room was a soft, pale blue cloud.

"Would you like a bath?" Juli asked as she stood behind Sirena undoing the buttons of the black bombazine gown.

"Yes, Juli, a bath is just what I need. But before you go to prepare it, tell me where my brother's room is to be."

"Down the hall, I believe, Juffrouw, to the left. But I'll see to the bath now. Mynheer will want to see you soon." Juli's eyes dropped. "I have shamed Mynheer before his wife-to-be, he will be most angry with me."

"And well he should be!" Sirena chastised her, reinforcing Frau Holtz's position in the matter. "But I'm sure that if you promise to serve me well, he will deal fairly with you. Now hurry my bath water!"

"Yes, I will get the water. Then you can rest. Mynheer will want to have dinner with the Juffrouw. I heard him order a very special dinner!"

Sirena paled visibly as a knock sounded on the door. What if it was Mynheer van der Rhys! She couldn't possibly meet him now! Not in this condition!

Juli opened the door cautiously to admit Frau Holtz.

"I came to see if you needed . . ." Sirena's blanched face alarmed Frau Holtz. She bustled into the room and immediately took command. "Juli! A cool cloth for the Juffrouw's brow! There, there, sit here, my lady. Hurry with the cloth, Juli!"

By Frau Holtz and Juli's ministerings, Sirena's normal color returned.

"Frau Holtz, when Mynheer returns to the house, you are to go to him and explain that I can't see anyone in my condition. Not for several days at least. I am prostrate with grief, and only my brother is to be admitted." Although Sirena's voice was quiet and soft, there was a ring of iron to her words.

The Frau stayed with Sirena and saw to the placement of the trunks that the djongo had brought up from the verandah. Juli now returned once more, leading two djongos, who toted large pewter urns of steaming water and poured it into a gilt hip bath which Juli revealed by the removal of a lacquered Chinese screen. Several urns of cool water were added to the steaming wetness to bring it to a comfortable tepid temperature.

After the djongos had gone, Sirena addressed Frau Holtz. "I wish to have a bolt on my door! Please arrange to have this done as soon as possible. No one is to enter my room without my permission! I am in mourning. I hope I am understood?"

"Yes, Juffrouw," Juli and Frau Holtz chorused.

The housekeeper considered Sirena's instructions peculiar but said nothing. God only knew what strange ways these olive-skinned Spaniards practiced!

Frau Holtz impatiently bided her time until Regan returned to the house. Marching to the library, on his instructions, to answer his inquiries concerning the señorita, she closed the teak doors discreetly behind her and promptly explained the mix-up concerning his bride's arrival.

"She is not . . . receiving anyone," the housekeeper said, lifting her eyebrows. "She knows you expect her for dinner, but she claims she is prostrate with grief. She also requests a bolt to be put on her door and that no one—no one," she repeated—"was to enter unless she admitted him!"

Regan suppressed a grin. It was so rare that Frau Holtz felt displaced, and he was enjoying it. The elderly and imperious housekeeper prided herself on her proprietorial rights due to long years of service first to his father and now to himself.

Acquiescing to the anger he knew Frau Holtz expected of him, he raised a shaggy brow. With what he hoped was an angry tone, he said, "I'll go and speak to the Juffrouw immediately." He wanted to meet this woman who could so effectively rattle the unflappable Frau Holtz!

The Frau smiled her satisfaction and dismissed herself. As she left, Regan noticed the thick salt-and-pepper hair at the back of her head creeping out from its heavy coronet of braids. Now Regan was even *more* eager to meet his Spanish bride, for the last time he had seen a mussed hair on the housekeeper's head was when, as a boy, he gave the dictatorial lady a few healthy shocks.

Regan strode down the hall and up the stairs and stopped at the door of his intended. He grasped the ornate door handle and hesitated, but only for a second, before he swung open the door.

Sirena, bathed, with her thick dark hair in a tight, discreet knot on the nape of her neck, and dressed in a loose-flowing blue wrapper, turned with a gasp as he burst into her room. Maddened by the sudden intrusion that was precisely against her request, her first impulse was to vent her anger; but she held herself in check, conforming to the pattern of a well-bred Spanish lady in bereavement—which after all, was true.

"I told Frau Holtz I was not receiving anyone. I am in mourning," she choked out, lowering her lids over dangerously glittering eyes.

Angered by her abrupt statement, Regan explained hotly, "I came to wish you welcome to your new home and to apologize for the confusion which caused you to ride in the baggage wagon." A vision of this aristocratic Spanish lady riding along the hot, dusty roads in the back of the wagon floated before his eyes and he fought to suppress a smile. He continued, striving for a note of sympathy in his voice: "Ever since Jan Verhooch told me how he and his crew rescued you and your young brother from the sinking frigate and brought you here to Batavia . . ."

"Your apology is well offered, Mynheer," Sirena interrupted as she turned away from him to look out over the gardens.

Regan noticed that she had not really accepted his stumbling apology, but he decided not to press the issue. He was momentarily stunned by the picture she created standing before the long windows through which the late-afternoon sun filtered—outlining her slim, softly rounded body. Pulling his eyes away from the shadowy outline of her full, round breasts to her exquisitely molded oval-shaped face, he was conscious of his good fortune. Other men could have searched a lifetime for a bride of such beauty. Her gleaming dark hair offset the slight ocher tint of her flawless skin; her features were delicate: high cheekbones, wide-set eyes fringed with thick, lush, black lashes . . . When she had spoken to him, he had seen a flash of straight white teeth behind her full, promising lips. She was exquisite!

Regan van der Rhys was a man accustomed to culling an unintentional envy among his associates. Immediately, he recognized the advantage of having a beautiful woman to grace his table and drawing room. He owned the most opulent home, the most productive groves, held the highest position with the Dutch East India Company in the islands—and now he would have the most stunning wife on Java. A white wife, who was not a "company daughter": one of that heartlessly exploited group of girls, instruments of one of the company's schemes to keep their agents contented and useful, and sent out East for the purpose of ensuring the continuance of the white race in the East Indies. "Company daughters" were mostly girls of poor or unknown beginnings, some of them rescued from the gutters and alleyways of Holland's port cities; they were given some formal education, a bit of the social graces, and then were exported like any other product—to marry any planter, agent, merchant, or clerk who had failed to secure a white wife for himself. Since not many "proper" girls cared to leave behind family and homeland for the uncertainty of a tropical island and a never-before-seen husband, the company's scheme worked exceedingly well and initiated many happy marriages.

If the *only* criterion for a wife was being white, Gretchen Lindenreich would have been a logical choice. But Gretchen's reputation certainly would not have enhanced Regan's prestige on the island.

Regan was still not reconciled to marrying *anyone*, but since he should marry, this Spanish señorita held both a promise of delight and auspicious possibilities . . .

The jolt of his good fortune registered on Regan's handsome features, and Sirena took his expression to mean he was surprised to find she had escaped the ravages of his pirates apparently unscathed. Her gaze flicked over him steadily now for the first time, and as she took him in her shamrock-green eyes widened with the impact of his appearance. Instead of an aging, fat, milk-skinned barbarian, there stood before her this tall, muscular sun god whose rugged features were offset by a crop of hair as pale as the moonlight shining on a still, black sea.

Raising her ire with an amused twinkle in his

agate-blue eyes, he spoke softly in thickly accented Spanish: "We will settle this matter now, so you may be left to your mourning," he scoffed. "Our marriage was arranged by our fathers—an agreement which we will fulfill as soon as it can be done."

Sirena lowered her eyes, her thoughts racing. She had not been prepared for this handsome, virile man—one who would never allow his wife to play a chaste, prayer-filled "nun." Not this man! Heart thumping wildly, Sirena looked up, forcing her face into lines of placidity.

"I beg of you, Mynheer, to respect my year of mourning. I have many prayers to be said. And I must see to my small brother . . ."

"Our marriage will take place one month from today. That should give you ample time to recover from your ordeal. You'll find that although Java is far removed from the courts of Europe, propriety must be served."

Regan assumed that the wild ray of disbelief that lit her eyes was because he was insisting upon an early wedding date. In fact, Sirena was finding it almost impossible to keep from lashing out at him and demanding to know exactly what part he had played in the "ordeal" of which he spoke so lightly.

Regan hoping to smooth the lines of dismay from her lovely, cameo-like features, amended his previous dictum: "Señorita, it is only to protect you that our marriage must take place in what seems such a short length of time. I will not expect you to share my bed until your mourning period is over."

How magnanimous of him, Sirena thought spitefully, but she quietly murmured, "Thank you, Mynheer," and clasped her hands before her to prevent their trembling.

What had come over her? No man had ever made her tremble, except her father—and then only when she was guilty of something and knew she deserved his wrath. Not even the pirate captain, as he wielded the lash against her naked back, had had this effect on her.

Regan stepped closer, his height intimidating her.

"Señorita . . ." he began, then hesitated, "I cannot always refer to you as *Señorita* Córdez, can I?"

"No, Mynheer. In view of our relationship it would be absurd." Lifting her eyes and challenging him with her voice, she blurted out, "You must call me Sirena."

"Sirena. Your name suits you. Quiet, poised . . ." he continued with his gallant flattery.

All the while Sirena's mind screamed: You cur! You son of a viper! Hijo de puta—son of a whore! Not to realize that the girl you were to marry was named Isabel and that *she* was, in truth, all you are saying of *me!*

Regan saw her lower her lids and sensed her withdrawal, and he was angered by it. "Look at me!" he commanded softly.

Sirena raised her eyes to meet his and was once again impressed by his height. There were few men she had to look up to, for, tall herself, she met most men at eye level. Standing close to Regan, she realized she only stood as tall as his shoulder and noted he was deeply tanned from the sun. Did he also love the freedom of the seas, the tangy salt spray stinging his face? Sirena looked at his hands. Yes, she answered her own question: he would know how to hoist a sail, and captain a ship. There were rough calluses on the palms of his capable angular hands. She wondered what it would be like to have those hands stroke her . . . Blushing, she again lowered her eyes.

Noticing the riot of color that now stained her cheeks, Regan smiled. There was something about the girl. Was it in the eyes? He couldn't be sure, she seemed so timid and generally avoided looking directly at him. Was it possible that he somehow offended her delicate sensibilities? Rot! He preferred women with spirit and vivacity. A woman who would answer his caresses in bed. Bah! This frightened girl would lay like a newborn calf, mewing for homeland and mother. He would have to find his pleasures elsewhere. The Spaniard could grace his table and he would give her the considerations due a wife.

He would feed and clothe her and her brother, and in her spare time she could pray for his soul!

Suddenly, he reached out and grasped her face in his callused hands. His grasp was firm, yet gentle. Cool green eyes returned his mocking stare. Regan was perplexed for a moment. Was he mistaken? Something stirred in him as Sirena continued her now-bold scrutiny. Regan was the first to look away in confusion.

"I will expect you to keep your word, Mynheer, that I won't be expected to consummate the marriage until my mourning is over."

Once again her emerald eyes sparkled dangerously. Regan drew in his breath. Perhaps he had been hasty. A *spirited* newborn calf, perhaps. With the proper . . . Stunned, he found himself a moment later in the dim, cool hallway, and not quite sure how he got there.

Sirena collapsed on the edge of the blue-and-white bed, consciously attempting to control her quaking and trembling. Regan van der Rhys would be a formidable opponent. She realized that he was not a man who could be easily fooled. His keen intelligence was mirrored in his cold, agate-blue eyes. His stubbornness was evident in his lean, square jaw. With great accuracy of thought, however, she also realized it was not his strength as an adversary that troubled her—it was the man himself, his animal magnetism.

Would he keep his word and not demand his rights as a husband? And did she want him to?

Chapter Six

Dappled sunshine wove a lacy pattern on the cobbled walk beneath Sirena's feet as she strolled the paths through the lush tropical gardens surrounding the van der Rhys house. Her eyes were sharp and alert as she gauged the distance from where she stood at the rear of the mansion to the cove where the *Rana* was secretly berthed. Regan's property lay on the western edge of the town of Batavia, rather isolated from other houses and mansions—as befitted the position of the D.E.I. Chief Pensioner. Then her attention was drawn away from the ship to the splendid array of brilliant, multicolored flowers. From her window she had seen Oriental gardeners painstakingly weeding and pruning the lush flower beds. They had transformed the wild jungle into a paradise of scents, color, and landscaping. Stooping near a row of particularly bright blooms, her fingers picked a crimson blossom from its stem. Sniffing experimentally, Sirena was disappointed to find it without scent.

"That particular bloom, Sirena, has no scent, although it does possess other interesting properties," Regan said quietly, startling her as he approached. She wondered how long he had been observing her.

"I'd arrange to have a bouquet of them sent to your room, but I'm afraid it would never do. It wouldn't be wise to arouse speculation among the servants," he said snidely.

Ignoring his attitude, Sirena inquired, curious, "But why *can't* I have them in my room? How could this gorgeous blossom offend anyone?" she asked quietly and modestly. She must remain the mourning Spanish lady!

"Offensive isn't exactly the word I would use. Actually, in many parts of the world they're very much in demand," he explained guardedly.

"It looks very much like a poppy," she said, bewilderment sharpening her tone. "I think it's beautiful, and I . . . would like to have some in my room. I'll get one of the gardeners to cut them for me," she said coolly and stubbornly with averted eyes.

Regan looked aghast and Sirena enjoyed this. Now he would probably tell her some trite superstition that made the flowers unlucky.

"Since you persist, I'll see to it myself. In fact, I shall have your room festooned with them. I'll have your balcony hung with garlands of them. I'll drop their petals in your wine. Everywhere you go their bright color will greet you—along with the quizzical expressions on the faces of the islanders." By this time Regan had worked himself into a subtle rage.

Delighting in his anger, Sirena said, with great control, "Do that, Mynheer. Immediately will not be too soon." Her fingers caressed the blossom langourously.

Regan's eyes narrowed, "Your wish is my command." He bristled. "But first there's something you should know. This particular variety of blossom has a unique usage among the natives. To be more specific, its stamens and seeds are ground into a fine powder which amorous lovers apply to a particular part of their anatomy. Upon the penetration of their partner, the powder causes the sex organs to enlarge and swell. I've heard of couples being locked together for hours and—"

Sirena blanched. "I see, Mynheer . . ." she said as her gaze perused the thick, lush beds of the infamous flowers. "And you keep yourself well supplied." As she spoke, she casually let the petals slip through her fingers; then, walking away, her foot ground the blossom to a dark, bloody pulp.

Regan was stunned by her quick recovery. He hadn't meant to tell her the history of the flower, but when she became so coolly imperious he could not help himself. "I'll be damned!" he muttered, feeling like a little boy caught with his fingers in the jam pot.

"I think you've taxed your poor head enough today, Caleb," Sirena grinned. Seeing the lost look on the boy's face, she widened her smile. "You did well today, little brother. Don't be in such a hurry. It took me years to learn what I'm teaching you. Navigation is an art. You must learn it thoroughly. A mistake could be deadly. But I don't want you to despair," she said, rolling up the charts and sliding them under the bed.

"Let's pray that Frau Holtz doesn't take it into her head to clean this room. I'll have to find a better hiding place for your charts." His tone was light but his eyes revealed some secret disappointment.

"What's troubling you, Caleb?"

The boy stood scuffing his feet on the thickly carpeted floor. "You promised to teach me to fence," he blurted out.

"So I did—and I will. Tomorrow I shall give you your first fencing lesson. I've noticed a secluded area in the garden. But I tell you, the navigation lessons must come first. Patience, Caleb," she sighed.

Since their arrival in Batavia, Sirena's mode of living and behavior had conformed not only to her mourning pose and to her position in the van der Rhys household as mistress-to-be, but also to the weather—and she and Caleb were both restless. During the cool mornings, she busied herself with seeing to the completion of Caleb's wardrobe. The heat of the afternoons and the daily thunderstorms—which lasted sometimes an hour—forced her to take life slowly then, either napping or giving Caleb lessons on navigation. The evenings were sultry, but the nights cool for sleeping. To all outward appearances, Sirena seemed reserved and contented. Inwardly, she constantly battled to control her energies and her impatience to learn enough about the van der Rhys trading business to implement her revenge plot.

"Aye, Sirena, you're right as usual," Caleb was saying. "it's just that I want to learn to protect you. Perhaps the time will come when you'll need my help."

"Little brother, why don't you go outside or down

to the quay. The rains are over for the day. Possibly you can pick up some information useful to us."

"I'll do my best, Sirena."

"I myself have an appointment with Frau Holtz to go over some of my wedding plans," Sirena said bitterly. For she had not been able to convince Regan to postpone the wedding. "I fear she'll find me sadly lacking in enthusiasm. Despite her politeness, the woman resents me, Caleb. She jealously guards the position she has established for herself over the years, and is fearful that her authority will all too soon be usurped by me. As for my feelings toward her . . ." Sirena continued, "I find her overbearing. '*Ja!* You may have your breakfast now, Juffrouw!' " Sirena mimicked Frau Holtz, making Caleb laugh. "Really! She acts as though the courtesies and luxuries of this house flowed merely from her beneficence!"

"But she means well, Sirena. It's perhaps just the way the German language sounds."

"And that's another thing! When we first arrived here, I couldn't bear the way she stumbled over the Spanish language. So I told her I'd been schooled in several languages and that German was one of them. So now she speaks to me in German and I answer her in kind . . ."

"I know, I know," Caleb giggled uncontrollably, "and now *she* rolls up her eyes at *your* terrible *German!*"

"Not only that"—Sirena joined his laughter—"but now she speaks so loudly, enunciating so distinctly, as though I were hard of hearing! I think she feels me an idiot child and she's going to teach me correct German. I've a confession to make. Caleb," Sirena said, her eyes sparkling with devilment. "Sometimes I purposely mispronounce the words or misuse them—just to get her back up!"

As Sirena finished speaking, a knock sounded on the bedroom door. Putting a finger to her lips as a signal for quiet, she said, "Open the door, Caleb. It must be Frau Holtz."

Caleb ran to the door and, with a flourish, bowed extravagantly low—only to look upon shiny, booted male feet. Flushing, he straightened himself and glanced from Sirena to Regan.

"I've come for Caleb," Regan said in a stilted voice. Then he mused: Could these two somber faces have been responsible for the rollicking laughter I heard coming from behind this door . . . ?

Sirena lowered her eyes, her hands busy in her pocket searching for her rosary. Finding the round beads, she drew them forth and held them in her clenched hand.

"Why is it, Sirena, that every time I see you, you immediately seek your beads? Do I frighten you so much? Enough to make you seek solace in prayer?" Regan's tone was lightly sarcastic, but a muscle in his cheek jumped with suppressed rage.

"Hardly," Sirena said softly, her head half turned. "But I must continue with my prayers, so if you'll excuse me . . ."

"Of course," Regan answered gallantly, taking Caleb by the arm. "But as I've told you before, your period of mourning may be practiced in private and as frequently as you wish. Nevertheless, it is not to interfere with our small social life here on the island."

"Have you no respect for the dead?" Her soft voice rose a trifle as she swung to face the tall man opposite her.

"Very little, I'm afraid," Regan said coldly. "These things are overdone. The dead are dead. What good does all this praying do them? The world is meant to live in. And, tonight you shall live in *my* world. I am arranging a small dinner party, several of my friends are to attend. I insist on presenting you to them. I expect you and Caleb to join me at the table."

"But my mourning—"

"You will carry on your mourning in this room only!" Regan cast his eyes to the window and then lowered his lazy blue gaze on Sirena. "You have *five hours* yet to mourn. I suggest you get on with it and save your strength for this evening's entertainment. Caleb and I will be home before dark."

Sirena narrowed her eyes to slits and glared at him. Caleb noticed the dangerous glitter and hoped that Regan did not.

For a moment Regan was startled by Sirena's stare. Was he mistaken? Was that anger in those cat-green eyes? In his cool, composed Sirena? Not likely, it must have been a trick of the light. Then, having delivered his order, he motioned for Caleb to follow him. At the sound of the door closing behind them, Sirena tossed the prayer beads on the silken coverlet and swore. "How dare he! Who does he think he is? He has actually ordered me to attend his dinner! How dare he?" Anger rose to the surface as she paced the room. Yes, she would have to do as he ordered—but she didn't have to like it!

Once more a knock sounded on her door.

It was probably Frau Holtz, she thought. Quickly dropping to her knees at the side of her bed, she held the rosary beads loosely in her fingers and lowered her eyes. "Come in!" she called.

The housekeeeper took in the picture Sirena created, and grimaced. Did the Spanish have nothing to do but pray? A belief in God was commendable, but this obsessive, continual praying made her want to shake the quiet, secretive girl who kneeled stiff-backed near the bed. Boldly, Frau Holtz strode to the windows and folded her heavy arms across her buxom chest. "I have come to discuss some of the last details concerning your wedding, my lady."

Sirena looked up at the housekeeper. "I think, Frau Holtz, that I can trust you to handle my wedding. Whatever you and Mynheer decide will be acceptable to me."

"Juffrouw, it is not as simple as that . . ."

"And may I ask why not?" Sirena said, raising one perfectly arched brow. Frau Holtz stepped back as she noted the shimmering green eyes. "Mynheer seems to be so authoritative, so discerning, and so in command, one wculd have thought he had this wedding all arranged."

"For the most part it is. He did handle all the arrangements concerning the guests and those who will stay overnight because they live on the out-islands. But there are hundreds of smaller details—" Frau Holtz stammered, "Mynheer thought—"

"Mynheer thought wrong," Sirena said flatly. "Do

what you will. I won't object to anything you decide. I will do as my intended orders. But," she said, holding up a long, slender finger, "I will not help. I am in mourning. Is that understood?"

"Perfectly, Juffrouw," Frau Holtz answered coldly, turning to leave.

"Frau Holtz, there is . . . something else. When I first arrived, I requested a bolt for my door. As yet, I have received none. I am also requesting, now, a new lock with a key only for myself. As I told you before, I don't want any of the servants in this room. Except when I ask them in to tidy and clean. Even Juli knows she is not to disturb me unless I call for her. I wish to be alone, *alone!* There may be times when you will not see me for days. On these occasions, I go into retreat here. My brother, Caleb, joins me on these longer occasions."

"And your meals, Juffrouw?"

"You may leave food outside the door. If we have a need for it, we will eat it. Under no circumstances are you to try to enter this room when I am in retreat here. Even ordinarily when I am in the room, I would like the least disturbance possible. Attend to the bolt and key for the door this afternoon. Oh, and also for my brother's door!"

"This is unheard of! There *are* no rooms locked in this house!"

"You have heard of it now. A bolt and a new lock by sundown! Leave me now. Go and prepare lavishly for my wedding. And don't stint, for I understand Mynheer is quite wealthy. I wouldn't want my wedding to be considered lacking." Sirena suppressed a smile as she watched the horror dance across the housekeeper's face. "Go now!" She said imperiously as she fluttered the prayer beads in the air. "I must get back to my prayers, you have put me behind in my schedule. We Spanish must say many prayers each day—otherwise, how shall we ever get to Heaven? You Protestants may not see the logic, the reason. And I fear for you. We shall surely not see you in Heaven." Quickly, she lowered her head onto prayer-clasped hands. A rich bubble of laughter threatened to erupt from her mouth.

With the sound of the closing door, Sirena doubled over, laughing silently. With Frau Holtz at the helm, she could hardly wait to see what shape her wedding would take.

Regan stood on the quay and considered the youth who was soon to be his brother-in-law. Caleb was shy and quiet, and he could understand the boy's timidity: he'd come to a new land, was living with strange people . . . But there was more to Caleb than met the eye. Regan had not failed to notice the hard, rough calluses on the boy's hands. They were, in fact, like the hands of a seaman; and he wondered what had made them that way. Curiously, too, though both were dark-haired, Caleb and Sirena had little resemblance one to the other. Caleb, indeed, did not look Spanish. But to question the boy would be unfair at this point; Regan wanted to be friends with him.

"How do you like my new ship?" Regan asked quietly.

"She's a beauty!" Caleb said, a light dancing in his eyes. "I'd like to sail her someday."

Regan looked questioningly at the youth. Most young men of noble birth would have said "sail *on* her someday." Caleb sounded like a well-salted old seaman the way he'd spoken.

"It can be arranged," Regan answered. "She makes her first voyage back to Holland carrying a precious cargo of spices and silks on the day after my wedding. Why don't you think of a name for her?"

"I'd like to do that, Mynheer," Caleb said shyly. "I'll think well."

"Why not call me Regan? Soon you'll be my brother-in-law. There's no need for formality. I call you Caleb, and I think it would help if we were to be more informal. We'll be living together until you choose to return to Spain."

The boy seemed flustered and confused. Sensing his discomfort, Regan spoke gently: "If the name Regan doesn't come easily, then continue as before. Whenever you're ready and feel more at ease with me, it will come to you."

Caleb smiled his relief. Caleb liked Regan and at

times it was difficult to think of him as the enemy. Somehow to call the man by his first name would denote a friendship and Caleb wasn't exactly sure whether or not Sirena would feel betrayed by this.

"Come up to the offices with me, Caleb. I want to change out of this damp shirt. There's a meeting of clerks which I must attend this afternoon. And, in my office, I have models of my fleet—and some of my father's. One of the natives carved them for me and I assure you they're works of art!"

In the hot, airless offices of the Dutch East India Company Caleb ran his hands lovingly over the small models. "They *are* beautiful! The man who carved them must have a gentle hand," Caleb marveled.

Regan, naked to the waist, walked over to the boy and held one of the tiny ships in his hand. "This was one of my father's ships: the *Tita,* named for my wife. We sailed on her, my wife and young son. We were going to Europe. She was a native princess, daughter of a Siva high priest, and it would have been her first time away from Java. As we were about to round the Cape of Good Hope into the Atlantic, the *Tita* was attacked by pirates." Regan's eyes clouded. "I saw my wife killed, and my son . . ."

Caleb's eyes were mirrors of compassion. "I was put aboard a jolly-boat. Given food and water, too. I'll never know why. Two or three days later, a Spanish brigantine discovered me and took me aboard. But the captain refused to believe that I and my father owned the ravaged *Tita*—and I knew not whether the *Tita* still floated. When I insisted that we search for her, he informed me that he'd seen the ship sinking into the sea. Then he falsely accused me of being a member of the crew of a Dutch pirate ship that had been preying, at that time, on Spanish and Portuguese vessels near the Cape.

"I never saw my son again," Regan went on with his story. "I don't know if he's alive or dead. The last I saw of the child, he was crying in terror and holding fast to the ship's wheel."

A long moment passed before Regan seemed in sufficient control to complete his story. "I was taken to

Spain as a criminal and thrown into prison, where I rotted for six long years. My father eventually secured my release at a great financial cost. *Your* father, Caleb, was of great assistance to me. He exerted his influence where it did the most good. And I am grateful."

As Regan turned away, Caleb gasped in horror at the deep ridged scars that ran across Regan's muscular back. Regan turned at the sound that escaped the boy.

"A momento of the Spanish prison I resided in for six years," he said cruelly. "And they say the *Dutch* are barbarians!"

"All . . . all Spaniards aren't barbarians," Caleb said hesitantly.

"True," Regan answered coldly. "And all Dutch and Germans are not barbarians, either. Perhaps you could explain that fact to your sister."

His fresh lawn shirt buttoned, Regan lit a cigar and perched on the edge of his massive desk, his leg swinging lightly. "So, young man, what do you think of the East India Company?"

"It's impressive! I respect you, Mynheer, for making it the success it is!"

If Regan noted the formal address he gave no hint as he replied: "It's a devil of a job. Leaves little time for leisure, and now that I'm to marry your sister there'll be even less time. Work, work, work!" he joked.

"Are you wealthy, Mynheer?"

"By some standards, I suppose so. But several ransackings of my own ships at sea by pirates would clean me out. Nearly all my holdings are tied up in my private fleet. Even the plantation would be almost useless to me without the ships to carry my nutmegs back to Holland—I would have to use other Dutch carriers, and the cost would be high!"

"Do you have much trouble with pirates?"

"Not if I can help it. I've spent a small fortune for weapons to outfit the fleet." Regan did not mention the pirateers he sometimes employed to protect not only his own fleet but any D.E.I. ships against the Spanish.

"You spent a fortune? But I thought the ships

belonged to the company, why didn't they spend the money?"

"They do, Caleb. But now I'm speaking of my own ships! I had to provide my fleet with cannons, the newest, largest guns now being made. Shipping becomes more precarious by the day. If one doesn't have an advantage over scourges of the sea, one would find himself out of business!" Regan looked out the window and saw the sun low on the horizon. "I think it's time for you to head back to your sister. By now she should have finished with her prayers. She may be concerned for you," he said cynically.

Caleb obediently made a move to leave.

Regan detained him, his tone softened. "I've told you how your father was instrumental in gaining my release from prison. I've always felt myself in his debt although I've never met the man. Nothing gives me greater pleasure than knowing you, his son." Regan touched the boy's shoulder. "Do you think you can find your way back to the house alone? If not I'll have one of the clerks take you . . ."

"Yes, I can find my way back. I know you have a meeting you must attend."

Regan crushed Caleb's hand in his own. "I enjoyed our time together this afternoon. We'll do it again very soon. Go now so your sister doesn't worry needlessly. I'll see you at dinner."

When Caleb returned to the house, he stopped by Sirena's room before going to his own to prepare for dinner. His young boy's heart was a kettle of boiling emotion and confusion. On one occasion aboard the *Rana*, he professed his doubt that Mynheer van der Rhys was responsible for the attack of Dick Blackheart and his men. Now again he was finding it difficult to believe that Regan was the power behind that attack. How could a man who had suffered so crushing a blow as seeing his wife murdered and losing his only son perpetrate a similar attack on innocent people? Caleb was lost in these thoughts when he heard Sirena bid him enter.

"How did your outing go, little brother? Did you enjoy yourself?"

"Yes, I did. Mynheer showed me his new ship and asked me to name her. He also asked me to call him Regan. He said there's no need for formality. But I didn't call him by name," he hastily volunteered, fearing he would gain her disapproval. He had pledged his allegiance to her and he would keep his word, regardless of his doubts about Regan's guilt.

Quickly, he recounted the afternoon's events. "Did you know he was married before, Sirena, and had a son?"

Sirena's face masked her surprise. "Yes. It was one of the things father told Isabel and me. You like the Mynheer, don't you, Caleb?"

"Yes, I do," he hesitantly admitted. "But don't worry, I didn't tell him anything. He says I don't talk much and he likes that in a man. He says actions speak louder than words."

Caleb related the story of Regan's imprisonment in a hushed voice, though Sirena knew something of this. "You should see his back, Sirena. It's a mass of scars and welts. They're old and healed but nonetheless they're ferocious."

"Held and beaten in a Spanish prison and yet he agreed to marry a Spaniard—or at least agreed to follow his father's instructions . . ." Sirena pursed her mouth in a round of surprise. "If what he told you is true, then he must hold a vengeance for the Spanish. Just as I do for the Dutch because of what happened."

"Mynheer praised your father, Sirena, for helping secure his release from prison."

"And the Mynheer repaid his gratitude by having his scurvy lot of pirates plunder the *Rana* and kill my sister and uncle!" Sirena spat bitterly.

Sirena turned her back on Caleb and went to the long, low windows that led out into the gardens. For a long time she stood there and Caleb suspected she might be crying. But when she once again turned to face him she was dry-eyed.

"It would be wise to bathe and dress now. I have the feeling promptness at the dinner table would be to our advantage. I hate grand entrances!"

"How many guests are expected?" Caleb asked.

"In truth, I don't know and at this point I don't care. I only hope Mynheer will discuss the sailing of his new ship. The one which is to sail on the day after the wedding."

Pulling herself from her thoughts, she realized Caleb was showing signs of apprehension. Thinking it was because of the dinner that night, she said, "I know this is a big step for you, Caleb, your first formal dinner. Everything will be fine. Just watch me at the table and do as I do. You possess a keen sense of courtesy, you can't go wrong. If for some reason you become confused, plead a poor appetite. The Dutch are nothing but barbarians, I doubt they know what good manners are. Just relax and enjoy the meal. We've been confined too long, I'm rapidly tiring of this exile I've placed us in." The look of vexation on her face made Caleb laugh. "All this praying is becoming tiresome!"

Caleb laughed again, tears brightening his dark eyes.

"Why do you laugh at me, Caleb. I know this is all my own doing, but"—she held up a warning finger —"once I put our plan into effect there will be no room for boredom. Only fear that we'll be caught."

"We won't be caught, Sirena, you've planned it well. The plan can't fail." The boy's dark, sultry eyes glistened in anticipation. Returning to the sea, where he felt he belonged, was his wish.

Distant rumblings forced a halt to their conversation. At first it sounded like the very distant roar of a great cannon. The roar grew louder, more persistent, and Sirena and Caleb hurried to her window to study the horizon for the black smudges left by exploded cannonballs. Was it possible that Batavia was under attack from the sea by enterprising pirates? They stood at her balcony, their eyes straining into the distance. Behind them the crystal globes of the lamps on Sirena's dressing table began to vibrate, emitting a tinkling tune. Caleb turned abruptly, relief and understanding smoothing the concerned furrows on his brow.

"It's only the fire mountain," he sighed, "one of the volcanos is just voicing an objection to being ignored." Almost before he finished speaking the tinkling crystal gave up its song and the rumbling in the distance subsided.

Sirena was clearly disconcerted; her fingers were coiled about each other in agitation and her lips were drawn into a thin, nervous line.

"If you're to remain here on Java, Sirena, you must become used to the whims of the fire mountains. Rarely do their rumblings amount to anything. Sometimes rockfalls are caused by the trembling . . ." Immediately Caleb and Sirena had the same thought: the two volcanos guarding the entrance to the cove where the *Rana* was hidden. If enough rocks and boulders fell into the River of Death the *Rana* would be landlocked—or buried! Beads of moisture broke out on Caleb's upper lip.

"Tomorrow, before the rains, after Mynheer leaves for his offices, take a ride over the hills and see how near completion the *Rana* is," Sirena said, hoping to distract Caleb from his apprehension. "Then ride as far as you can down the river and see if the channel is still open to the sea, although I've no doubt that it is." Thinking of the *Rana* was just what the boy needed. His face brightened. If Sirena said the narrow channel was still open then it was. Youthful trust shone brightly in his face.

"Yes, Sirena, I will! It'll be good to see her again!"

It was more evident than ever that Caleb felt out of his element here in this richly appointed house wearing fine cambric shirts and glossy, stiff new boots. It was the open sea and a rolling deck for which he longed.

Sirena prayed that she would be proven correct. If the *Rana* was landlocked it would mean the end of her plans for revenge. If that should happen she would rather be dead.

It was just past sundown and no bolt had been installed. Sirena was furious. Who was at fault, the housekeeper or Regan van der Rhys? If she were to place a wager, the odds would be against Regan. The Frau merely carried out orders after they were issued. Evidently Sirena's order was not sufficient.

Rapping sharply on the stout teak door, Sirena waited patiently. Regan himself opened the door, a goblet in one hand, a fragant cigar in the other. He smiled wickedly at the suppressed fury in Sirena's face.

"You see," he said expansively and a bit drunkenly, "I knew we could be friends. How . . . thoughtful of you to pay me a visit—and without prayer beads." He waved his cigar airily.

Sirena's heart hammered in her chest. Never had she gazed on such a virile man. He exuded a presence, a forcefulness, a maleness that she found eminently exciting and enticing. Forcefully, she brought her mind back to the matter at hand.

"I wish a bolt for my door," she demanded. "A strong heavy bolt made from iron," she said slowly, enunciating clearly to be sure the man opposite her understood her meaning.

The agate eyes narrowed slightly. Regan brought the silver goblet to his lips; he drank slowly, never taking his eyes from Sirena's flushed face. Then, deliberately, he lowered the goblet and brought the cigar to his mouth. An aromatic puff of smoke swam before Sirena.

"It would take more than a bolt made from iron to keep me out of your room—assuming first of course that I wished to enter. Which I don't. Not yet. I want that clearly understood," he said mockingly.

Sirena flinched inwardly, as if she had been slapped. Fighting for control, her unfathomable green eyes darkened till they resembled pools of murky water.

"If," Sirena said quietly, "there were someone in this house who chose to enter my room uninvited, I would be obliged—"

Regan interrupted, his eyes laughing, his voice cool and mocking. "You would be forced to bring out your beads and pray that some magic force would open up the heavens and swallow the . . . intruder. My dear Señorita, let me repeat: Neither iron bolts nor magic prayers said on circles of beads will keep me from a room I wish to enter." The blue eyes fell to the goblet in his hand, as did the emerald ones.

Transfixed, Sirena watched Regan's bronzed hand slowly crush the goblet until both sides met.

She wanted to lash out—scratch, spit, snarl at this man. She wanted to make him feel her real presence, feel her nails raking the length of his handsome face. How dare he think he could intimidate her by a display of strength!

"I find it amusing that you would smash down a door locked against you. I would have thought a man of your character and breeding would be above such an insult. In any case, Mynheer, the bolt and lock would not imply any denial of your marital privileges, but would maintain my solitude from *any* intrusion—yours, or the servants', or Frau Holtz's—when I am praying or in retreat. But this discussion gets us nowhere. Secure the bolt and change the lock by the noon hour tomorrow," Sirena said coolly as she turned to leave, her breath coming in quick, hard gasps. God in Heaven, what was there about the man to make her feel this way?

Her hand on the door pull, Sirena felt herself abruptly being lifted and turned around. Once again she found herself locked in a stare with the Mynheer's hard eyes. Without warning, she felt hard, bruising lips crush her own. Her head reeled with the man's passion, her body trembled from his male nearness. His body scent, clean and masculine, assailed her as she parted her lips automatically in response. Then she felt herself being roughly thrust aside. Regan's eyes were laughing at her bewildered, abashed countenance.

"I always win, Senorita," he said coolly. "Remember that."

Sirena fought to control her humiliation and fury. She matched his tone. "What happens, Mynheer, if the prize you win is worth nothing?"

"Then, Señorita, I shall have won nothing. There are times, such as now, when nothing is better than something." With a slight inclination of his head, he dismissed her. "You shall have your bolt and lock by the noon hour tomorrow. Perhaps we should both pray that it serves your purposes."

Chapter Seven

Once again, Sirena tossed the prayer beads on the bed and flung open the door to the clothes press. She was trying to dispel a vision of the teak door lying in splinters, herself standing at bay in the closet, clutching her beads while Regan advanced on her. Finally the thought fled, and she returned to her perusal of the gowns there.

Frau Holtz had, at Regan's request, obtained Sirena's measurements and bought several new gowns from a dressmaker in the town who had willingly obliged to make them quickly, but these she preferred not to wear. Furthermore, she must wear something long-sleeved in order to hide the unsightly scar on her upper arm—which might arouse questions she was not yet prepared to answer.

Oh, what to wear to this travesty she must attend . . . ?

And then she saw the gown she had salvaged untorn and intact, from what Dick Blackheart's men had left, when they'd gone through Isabel's and her belongings. It was her mourning gown, the one she had worn following her father's death a year before. The wide, low-cut neckline trimmed with jet beads offset her long, slender neck and highlighted her skin to a paler tone of amber. A close, dropped waistline displayed her high, full breasts and accented her flat stomach and low-slung, full hips. She would have Juli dress her dark, gleaming hair in the style she had assumed just before she came to the house of Regan van der Rhys, a sleek, heavy knot tightly drawn back from her face and arranged at the nape of her neck. For the final accessory she would wear a high comb studded with moonstones that peeked through the delicate lace of a black mantilla.

In a flight of fancy she toyed with the idea of wearing her rosary around her neck. She knew she would never do such a thing but thinking about it amused her. She could see herself in the flattering black silk, the rosary about her throat, the cross falling upon her bosom. Every time Regan would glance at her he couldn't help but be reminded that she preferred her solitary prayers to him.

In her imaginings she could almost see Regan set his jaw, gnash his teeth, narrow his eyes, and rip it from her neck. His hands, when he ripped the beads from her, would they . . . ?

She remembered the scene between herself and Regan. "I always win . . ." he had said confidently, his cool, unruffled tone sending icy fingers dancing up her spine. Was it his words or his unbridled passion that she feared? Were those icy fingers of fear she felt, or was it something else? The awakening of an answering response; the tender, teasing touches of her own sensuality.

Shaking her head to clear it of the carnal notions that threatened to invade her, she sat down at the window and directed her thoughts back to young Caleb. Caleb liked Regan, he had made it quite apparent. Sirena had seen Regan look at Caleb in much the same way she herself looked at the boy, with fondness. He had sought Caleb out on two occasions already, to take him riding over the plantation and down to the quay.

Caleb called through the door. Juli, who was putting the final touches to Sirena's hair, set down the silver-backed hairbrush and went to open the door. Sirena had to smile at Caleb, who was struggling with his cravat. "Let me help. There, that's better. You look incredibly handsome. I'll be proud of you this evening."

"All these clothes, all these underthings! How often do I have to dress this way?" he complained.

"You'll become used to them, they look well on you. Mynheer will be impressed."

"You look beautiful, Sirena," Caleb blurted out. "Mynheer will be impressed with you, not me!"

Regan, standing at the foot of the staircase, prepared to light another of his exotic cigars. Sirena followed Caleb down the wide, curving stairs, holding her voluminous skirts up from the toes of her slippers, and affording Regan a glimpse of her slim ankles.

The effect her appearance had on Regan was visible. His hand poised in midair, the flaring taper just touching the end of the cigar. His glance was appreciative, so much so Sirena thought his cigar would drop from his mouth.

Regaining his composure, Regan blew out the taper just as its flare was about to singe his fingertips. Moving to the bottom step, with his arm outstretched, he reached for her hand which she extended toward him.

"You're breathtaking, Señorita."

"You are most gracious, Mynheer," she answered, lowering her eyes modestly. His hands slipped over hers, making her aware of their hard strength. The little game she had played in her room pierced her and she knew her cheeks were burning. His strong, capable hands would find it easy to rip beads from her neck or do anything they wished with her.

"You must call me Regan. Our guests mustn't think we stand on ceremony." His expression of scornful amusement rankled her. Sirena's nails itched to rake the smile from his face.

Instead she smiled sweetly. "Thank you . . . Regan." Her eyes mocked him in return, the light of the lamps bringing them alive. "Who are our guests?"

Her reference to "our guests" did not escape his notice. Her voice was sweet, her smile saintly, but beneath the black, heavy fringe of her lashes there was a glint of something he had seen in Gretchen's eyes. He must be mistaken, it couldn't be triumph!

"Tonight we'll be entertaining Captain Anton Kloss and his wife, Helga; Señor Chaezar Alvarez, the principal authority for the Spanish government in the East Indies; and Frau Lindenreich, the widow of a company captain—a German lady. It is only a small, intimate party, but I'm sure you'll find it enjoyable."

"I'm sure of it Myn—Regan," Sirena smiled demurely, leaving him standing at the foot of the stairs as she walked into the drawing room.

Perplexed by her indifference, he floundered for something to say. Caleb's presence provided him with a remark: "And you, young man. How smartly you're dressed! I'm afraid you'll have to suffer through a dull dinner, but I want my guests to see what a fine little brother I'm gaining as well as a beautiful wife! I'll look into some young friendships for you tomorrow. I want you to be happy here in your new home."

Sirena heard Regan speaking to Caleb. If she wasn't careful he'd woo the boy from her.

"Perhaps later, Mynheer. Right now I prefer my sister's company. At least until she's recovered from her grief."

Good work, little brother, Sirena thought to herself.

"Very well, if it's what you prefer," Regan said, "I won't force you into anything."

A djongo dressed in loose-fitting white pants and a collarless white shirt shuffled in on bare feet. He ushered in a tall, heavyset man with a round, rosy-cheeked woman, both in their late middle years. They wore light clothing and seemed comfortable and at home in the van der Rhys house. It was obvious they were frequent visitors. Regan made the necessary introductions and Sirena murmured graceful replies.

"Señorita, you must call me Helga," the ebullient lady laughed. "Regan, you sly dog, you never said how beautiful your intended was. The island will be in an uproar! Rarely have I seen such clear, glowing skin! Now we have two beauties on Java. Frau Lindenreich will have to watch her rival here, thus far she's held the crown for beauty!" Helga winked slyly in Sirena's direction. "I don't think Gretchen is going to like having someone as lovely as you on the same island with her."

Sirena smiled, liking Mevrouw Kloss. "If I were to put my mind to it I could appear quite ugly."

Regan frowned as the buxom Helga laughed happily at Sirena's joke. Sirena was lovely and Helga was correct. Gretchen wasn't going to like it one bit. He should have waited for Gretchen and Sirena to meet *after* the wedding. It was too late now to reconsider, for the voluptuous, hazel-eyed widow was advancing into the room, the houseboy shuffling at a furious pace to keep up with her.

"Regan, how handsome you look this evening! You quite take my breath away." She smiled sensuously as she raised her luscious mouth for his kiss. Regan silently cursed her and dutifully touched his lips on her pink cheek.

Still smiling, Gretchen slid her arm about Regan's waist. "Captain Kloss and Helga, how nice to see you," she said softly. "And this little creature curled in the chair, don't tell me," she winked roguishly at Captain Kloss, "this must be Regan's bride . . . to-be, that is. What a shy little thing, Regan. Introduce me," she said, jabbing Regan playfully in the ribs.

"Señorita Córdez, Frau Lindenreich." Regan's tone betrayed his misery. Sirena stood and, recognizing Gretchen as the woman who had laughed up at her through the hedge, acknowledged the introduction.

"Does she speak, Regan? Or have you cut out her tongue already?" Gretchen saw the glint of recognition in Sirena's face and silently challenged her to mention it.

Regan glanced from Sirena to Gretchen and then his agate-blue eyes swept to Captain Kloss. The air was charged with conflict.

The captain's watery blue eyes clearly stated that Regan could handle his own affairs. Two beautiful women in one room! A mistake. The evening had hardly begun and he wished he were at sea, basking in the comforting company of the only female he could depend on, his ship! Women! Bah! They meant nothing but trouble and Regan was soon going to find out he had one, large, troublesome handful.

"Well," Gretchen persisted, "does she speak or not?"

Sirena faced Gretchen, the filmy black-lace mantilla casting mysterious shadows on her creamy skin. "I speak when I'm spoken to," she said slowly and carefully, as if she were speaking to a dimwit. "Thus far you have talked around me, as if I weren't here.

Address me and I'll answer you like the civilized person I am." Her tone clearly indicated she didn't think Gretchen civilized.

The hazel eyes sparkled dangerously and Regan laughed loudly. Caleb fidgeted nervously and Helga smiled openly. Sirena remained cool, her lovely eyes on the furious Gretchen.

Recovering her composure, Gretchen forced her facial muscles to smile. "My dear, I meant it as a joke. Of course I knew you could speak. How else could you have accepted Regan's proposal of marriage? You did tell him Yes, didn't you?"

"Regan would not accept No for an answer."

That should settle her, Sirena thought nastily. She must be Regan's whore. Why else would he tolerate such ill manners? Gretchen's proprietary ways were obvious to anyone with half an eye. Well, she can have him! But I'll make her sweat first!

Gretchen seemed as if she'd been slapped, but before she could retort Captain Kloss prodded his wife. Mevrouw Kloss was annoyed. Life could sometimes be very dull on Java—she would have liked to see the Spaniard dress Gretchen down. When Helga saw the pleading in her husband's expression she stepped between the two women. Honestly! she thought to herself. It never ceased to amaze her that men who could show bravery and valor in battle could be reduced to squirming cowards if they witnessed a little showing of claws among women.

"Señorita Córdez, Anton and I have been remiss," Helga stated. "Please accept our sympathies. Regan told us of your recent loss."

"You're very kind, Mevrouw, both of you." Sirena's sad smile encompassed the captain and his wife. Her beauty was not lost on Captain Kloss who, in the early days of his career, had made countless voyages to Spain and had always considered Spanish women intriguing, their reserved manner a foil for their sultry, passionate temperament.

Regan's a lucky man, he thought, beauty and breeding. The girl has the face of a madonna and a nature to match.

"Poor Señorita," Gretchen said, clicking her tongue in sympathy. "I didn't know."

Quickly, Regan related Sirena's story for Gretchen. As he spoke his eyes trailed over her familiarly. She was stunning this evening. She had outdone herself in her choice of gowns, a bright yellow the color of daffodils which offset her pink-and-white skin and silver-blond hair.

"That explains it!" Gretchen cooed.

"Explains what?" Helga asked, and was immediately sorry when she saw Gretchen's eyes change from hazel to deep green.

"It explains why she's dressed like a crow, of course!"

Sirena had to hold herself forcibly in her place. To be insulted by Regan's whore was intolerable. Ooh, she seethed inwardly, wouldn't I just love to snatch her bald-headed!

Regan was speaking: "I find Sirena's dress most refreshing. On a tropical island even the birds wear bright hues, and when women attempt to compete with nature's colors it can be very glaring on a man's eye."

The djongo shuffled into the room again and announced Don Chaezar Alvarez. In his own subservient way, he pointedly looked at the softly ticking clock on the mantlepiece. Sirena could imagine Frau Holtz's storming and bustling back and forth from the kitchens to the dining room, pushing servants out of her way. The last guest, Alvarez, was late in arriving and the Frau's specially prepared dinner was spoiling.

Alvarez entered the room, resplendent in deep-wine knee breeches and rose-colored brocade frock coat which was cut away at the front to reveal a silver-threaded waistcoat and shimmering white ruffles at his throat. His colorful apparel paled Regan's dove-gray costume. Don Alvarez was tall, though not as tall as Regan, and he was well built. His flamboyant clothing might have made another man appear feminine, but his carriage was decidely masculine. He was obviously a dandy, not a mere fop.

Regan quickly made the introductions. Sirena was puzzled by the sudden coolness in Regan's voice. If he didn't care for the Spaniard why had he invited him to this quiet, little dinner?

"You must call me Chaezar, Señorita, society on this godforsaken island is too small to stand on ceremony." He bowed low over Sirena's hand and smiled at her. The effect was startling, lighting his face with a flash of strong, white teeth amid a close-cropped forest of thick black beard trimmed into a point at his chin. His eyes were dark and there were fascinating lights in their depths as he looked at her from beneath thick, steeply arched brows.

Sirena was charmed and very aware of his handsomeness. In Spanish she said to him, "And you may call me Sirena. How comforting to meet a fellow countryman."

"It must be unbearable for you, it took me quite a long time to adjust to these 'Nederlanders' who garble our mellifluous language with their hard, guttural accent. It was so painful to my ears that I returned the compliment and learned to speak Dutch. Now it is their ears which suffer, not mine."

Sirena laughed mirthfully, drawing an annoyed look from Regan. What did she care? Chaezar was witty and handsome and her countryman. Also, it was somewhat comforting when he referred to the Dutch as "they" and included Sirena in "our."

"For tonight, Sirena," Chaezar said, bringing her fingers to his lips, "we will speak Spanish between us." Feeling Regan's contemptuous glance on him, he turned to face his host. "Regan, you've won yourself a prize. The Señorita is quite beautiful, you don't deserve her."

"I see that you're impressed with my intended, Chaezar," Regan answered coldly.

Gretchen seethed as the two men sniped at one another. Like two dogs snapping over a bone, she thought disdainfully, raking a glance over Sirena, and so little meat on the bone! "Behave yourself, Regan, you have other guests who demand your attention!"

Chaezar was amazed by Gretchen's rebuke. The cat was jealous! "Gretchen is correct, Regan. Entertain Captain and Mevrouw Kloss and, of course, Gretchen.

I myself want to become acquainted with my lovely compatriot and her little brother."

"Perhaps later, Chaezar. We've kept dinner waiting too long." Stepping nearer Sirena, he offered her his elbow. "Ladies, gentlemen, shall we go into dinner?"

Sirena's fingers barely touched Regan's sleeve yet she could feel a tension in his arm that matched the tautness of his set mouth. So, the Mynheer had a strong sense of what was his and jealously guarded his rights! I wonder how far he can be pushed? This may be an interesting evening, after all.

A servant opened the double teak doors to the dining room and Regan led Sirena to her seat at the candlelit table.

Regan carried on a low-voice conversation with Captain Kloss while Gretchen was left to talk with Helga, a chore she abhorred. Gretchen's full mouth pouted sulkily and her glances went from Regan to Sirena and Chaezar. I could have stayed home this evening for all the attention I'm getting, she thought. Why in the name of God did Regan invite me? To show me off or to make the Spaniard uncomfortable? He's behaving as if he regretted his decision, whatever the reason.

"You and your young brother, Caleb, must grace my *casa* for lunch and I will have Spanish dishes prepared for you which are fit for the gods."

"I'd like that," Sirena smiled wickedly. "Will you invite me before or after I am married?"

"Before. Then perhaps I can entice you to change your mind. You have no objections, do you, Regan? There are so many things we can discuss about our homeland." Sirena was keenly aware of Chaezar's conspiratorial "our" again. "I haven't had a stimulating conversation in months. All we ever do is discuss trade and our ships. Isn't that right, Regan?" he said, piercing Regan with a fiery gaze.

"True," Regan said coldly and brusquely. What had made him invite the Spanish devil? He must have been out of his mind! Why couldn't Chaezar have paired off with Gretchen? No matter how much Regan blamed his lack of judgment, he still could not have expected the prayer-filled Sirena to be such a scintillating dinner partner.

Sirena perked up her ears as she heard Captain Kloss discuss the *Batavia Queen,* one of Regan's ships. "I keep telling you, Regan, you must travel with a full hold of cargo. Otherwise, the venture is not worthwhile. We spend too long at sea to make it profitable!"

"If you would only hear me out then perhaps you would agree," Regan said authoritatively. "I agree you must travel with a full cargo to port, but that's on your forward journey. On your return I want an empty cargo hold on every second voyage. This will cut your sailing time in half. By my best calculations this would enable you to make four extra trips a year. Besides, we export much more than we import. Why won't you agree? Chaezar has already put the plan to use and it has worked successfully."

"Bah! Empty cargo space! It's a sin! Your father would turn in his grave if he heard you speak like this, Regan."

"My father would have been the first to agree and you know it. You have to move with the times! The Dutch East India Company will sanction my plan."

"Why don't you do something with the pirates and let us sea captains sail our ships!"

"What would you have me do?" Regan demanded. "I've installed extra guns and new heavy weapons with which we'll be better able to defend ourselves." Regan took a breath and modulated his angry tone. "Anton, you force me to say something. I would rather not, but you leave me no other choice. If you don't agree to my plan I'll have to relieve you of your ship. I would hate to do it but the choice is yours."

"Bah! You're infuriating, Regan. I think what you're trying to tell me is I'm too old to captain your ships. If that's what's behind this then just come out and say it!"

"That's not what I'm saying at all and you know it! I merely want an empty hold on every second return voyage."

"Very well," the pompous sea captain agreed. "But you're wrong."

"Wrong! Why, Captain Kloss, Regan is never wrong! He told me himself on more than one occasion," Gretchen broke in. That the occasions were intimate was obvious from the tender look Gretchen bestowed on Regan. Regan scowled at her and she pouted prettily.

Sirena had to bite back her words, so eager was she to voice her opinion on Regan's plan. Inwardly she smiled. If they only knew. Soon the *Rana* would be ready and she would see how great the Dutch expertise was on the sea.

As the evening progressed, Chaezar became more and more openly attentive to Sirena. Caleb watched the dark Spaniard as he amused Sirena with his anecdotes and boastful stories of which he was always the hero. Sirena laughed at his jokes and listened rapturously to his tales of derring-do. During them, her eyes furtively slid across the room to Regan who was smoldering quietly with jealous rancor.

Gretchen made several attempts at conversation with Regan, all unsuccessful. His face a storm cloud of fury, Regan centered his attention on the coquettish Sirena.

Helga Kloss was clearly enjoying herself. Chaezar's discourse on his adventures while in the Spanish Navy was exciting and Sirena's clever repartee was thoroughly entertaining. Helga, too, was aware of Regan's barely suppressed fury, and she secretly applauded the entrancing Spanish señorita who could ignite the tiny flame of misgiving in the self-assured Regan.

Captain Kloss huffed and puffed like an overstuffed walrus. His manner clearly indicated the whole affair was not only in poor taste but spelled trouble.

Once, during a particularly charged lull in the conversation, Helga Kloss addressed Gretchen: "Frau Lindenreich, the little mission is in need of contributions again. If you have any clothing or dress material you no longer want, I can assure you they would be greatly appreciated. Several of the older girls are ready to step out and make their own way by going into service. They can use almost anything you'd care to give. Shoes, dresses. . . ."

"Never!" Gretchen exclaimed with such vehemence all eyes turned to look at her. "I can see it now, one of your little sniveling orphans going into service wearing one of my gowns, cavorting about the island dressed better than the ladies who employ them. You must be daft, Helga, to even entertain the thought that *I* would have anything in my wardrobe befitting a serving girl!"

"I didn't mean to suggest . . ." Helga sputtered. "It's only that the need is so great. Other women on Java are most happy to contribute . . ."

Gretchen was clearly enjoying herself at Helga's distress. Her upper lip curled in what was to pass for a smile. "I was thinking of taking another girl into my household to help Sudi with the laundry and such. Why don't you have one of your little orphans come to see me. I'll look her over."

Helga's lip quivered in agitation. The *last* thing she would ever do was place one of the mission girls with Gretchen. The German's reputation for cruelty toward her bonded servants was notorious. *And* her morals . . . Helga had devoted herself to the little mission on the outskirts of Batavia and the children had captured her heart. Life had been hard enough on most of them without placing them under Gretchen's heavy hand. "I'm sorry, Gretchen . . . but all the girls are placed. Perhaps next year . . ."

"Yes, of course. And perhaps next year I'll have something to donate to your little charity," Gretchen smirked. She knew full well Helga's reasons for not wanting to place one of the girls with her. Sliding her gaze to Sirena, she said in a mock-soothing tone, "Poor, poor Helga. She just wears herself out with those smelly, little native children. It's a wonder she isn't all skin and bones!" Her glinting eyes swept over Helga's ample girth. "Well, I suppose that's the way of it when a woman is past the hope of having a child of her own. Not that you haven't tried, isn't that right, dear Helga? If they had all lived, how many children *would* you have now, dear?"

Sirena gasped. This German bitch was insufferable! Perverse! Helga was white-faced and at a total loss for words. Out of pity, Sirena said, "Mevrouw

Kloss, I consider your obvious interest in this mission most worthy. I'm certain Frau Holtz and myself can contribute to the cause. I'll discuss it with her at the first possible moment."

Helga threw Sirena a look of gratitude and enthusiastically answered the questions Sirena asked concerning the mission and its little inhabitants. All the while both women pointedly excluded Gretchen from their conversation.

As the guests were departing, Gretchen stretched to whisper to Regan. Her face wore a doubtful look as she pressed her luscious mouth to his ear, then assumed an expression of triumph. Throwing Sirena one last scornful look, Gretchen bid her good nights.

With Regan's slight, almost imperceptible nod, Sirena judged he had agreed to meet Gretchen later. She was humiliated as Chaezar smiled knowingly, and his words stung although she gave no hint of her feelings.

"Perhaps Regan's whoring ways will change when you are married. Sometimes it pays to close one's eye to unpleasant things," Chaezar commiserated as he bent to kiss her hand. Sirena's eyes blazed as she returned Regan's cold stare.

Chaezar clapped his host on the back lightly. "A delightful dinner. We must repeat the occasion at my house after you're married. Your intended is charming, I envy you." His dark eyes smoldered as he noticed his host's frost-tipped glare. "Señorita," he said, bowing low and taking his leave.

Sirena's eyes bored into Regan's back as he closed the door. As though her burning eyes were scorching his back, Regan turned and said curtly, "Caleb will take you to your room. It was most generous of you to devote your evening to entertaining Señor Alvarez."

"Yes, Mynheer, the courtesy of my homeland is difficult to abandon. I found Señor Alvarez . . . intoxicating. You must tell me, Mynheer, do you Dutch always make rendezvous with your whores at social functions before the notice of your intended? I only ask so I will know how to act in the future." Her soft voice was an ominous purr and Caleb, standing to the side, gulped as he watched Regan control the fury that boiled within him.

"Somehow I thought you oblivious to my doings this evening. You were so openly . . . intoxicated with one of our guests."

"The word you search for, Mynheer, is polite. I was merely being polite to one of your guests." Her purring tone was fast losing its caress as her eyes bore into the tall, quietly raging man. "You should hurry, Mynheer, it's not polite to keep a lady waiting!" Swiveling abruptly, she took Caleb by the arm and they mounted the stairs.

"Perhaps you misunderstood, Sirena . . ." Regan called, groping for an explanation for his actions. Perhaps Sirena *was* being polite to Chaezar, merely as a compatriot.

"I did not misunderstand. Please, don't insult me further by insinuating I am a fool!"

At the top of the stairs, out of Regan's earshot, Caleb said in a voice that was puzzled and tinged with accusation, "You were occupied with Señor Alvarez all evening. You paid him your complete attention. I noticed the Mynheer didn't like it, he cast murderous glances on the Spaniard. Weren't you doing almost the same thing you accused the Mynheer of doing?" Caleb asked, his face fiery red with embarrassment.

Caleb's spine tingled with the low musical sound of Sirena's strange laughter. "Ah, little brother, it would seem I left something out of your education. There is more to life than charts and maps and fencing. I should have warned you of 'wily women.' True, I was occupied with Señor Alvarez, but for a reason. I was trying to secure information which would help us. In order to accomplish this, I had to make myself attentive. It's not the same as what Regan was doing. He made an appointment with his whore beneath my nose. I find it unforgivable!"

"Did you hear him make the appointment?" Caleb said, defending Regan.

"I didn't have to hear it, it was obvious to everyone. Even Señor Alvarez mentioned it, something a lady should never abide, but I'm sure he only meant to warn me. It's over, we'll forget it for now. You have to trust me, I know what I'm doing. Go to bed now, little brother, tomorrow you must see how our *Rana* progresses."

"Good night, Sirena." Dejectedly, Caleb walked down the carpeted hallway to his room. Wily women! Regan doing that to Sirena! Señor Alvarez kissing Sirena's hand every chance he got! Shaking his head wearily, Caleb quickly shed his constrictive clothes. He liked Regan. He didn't like Señor Alvarez. The woman Gretchen made him feel strange things when he looked at her. Was Sirena right? He had never heard of a "wily woman." Sirena would have to teach him. I like Regan, he muttered to himself. I'd like to be like him when I'm a man. Regan said he would teach me. Would he teach me about men? Was there such a thing as a 'wily man'? What name would they give to Señor Alvarez?

Juli tended Sirena, sleepily brushing her long, thick hair free of its pins. "Don't bother about hanging my gown away, Juli. The morning is soon enough."

Hours later, Sirena found herself lying awake in the low, wide bed, listening for Regan's footsteps. She swallowed a bitter taste that kept rising in her mouth when she didn't hear him. She refused to admit, even to herself, that the bitter taste was unshed tears.

Regan's mood was savage as he mounted his horse in the cobbled yard. His heels dug into the animal's flanks and it shied before taking off in a mad gallop. The temperate breezes were a stimulus to murderous thoughts. Chaezar should see him now, he thought. Riding the beast as if the devils of Hell were on his heels, thinking of that Spanish bitch he had to marry, making cow eyes at the Spaniard all evening!

He rode along the country road that led up into the mountains, then turned back and galloped toward Batavia, reining in at the cobblestones that flanked the steps to Gretchen's front door. Rapping forcefully, he stepped back and waited for the heavy mahogany portal to open.

Her eyes widened in mock-delight, Gretchen herself opened the door. "How nice of you to call, Regan," she said impishly. "To what do I owe the pleasure of this late-evening visit, as if I didn't know."

Regan laughed openly, seeing the humor in the situation. "What would you say if I said I found myself in the vicinity and decided to pay my respects?"

"I'd say I was delighted," Gretchen gurgled. "Sit down, Regan, I'll get some wine to toast your visit."

"It's not wine I have in mind," Regan said harshly.

"No, I didn't think it was. Would you like to talk?"

"That's not what I had in mind, either. On second thought, I will have a glass of wine."

Her eyes dancing with merriment, Gretchen handed him a crystal decanter. She waited as he poured himself a drink.

"So, I'm not a guest, is that what you're trying to tell me?" he asked.

"Anyone who comes to visit me after midnight could hardly consider himself here on a formal basis," Gretchen said. "What is it, Regan; why are you here?"

"No reason. Every reason. Perhaps the horse had a mind of its own. Somehow I found myself on your doorstep," he said, draining the goblet and refilling it. He drained the second glass of wine and immediately poured himself another.

Whenever Gretchen saw Regan like this she knew his thoughts were on the events aboard the *Tita*. Usually a temperate man, Regan only drank heavily when he was wishing he had been killed, too, that day off Africa. Now he was drowning himself in memories and Gretchen's sweet wine, but Gretchen had other plans.

Taking another long drink, Regan eyed the woman over the rim of his goblet. Suddenly, he stood up and lurched to the side, forcing Gretchen to grasp his arm. "I think," he said slowly and distinctly, "I should go outside. Perhaps the night air will restore my wits."

Gretchen smiled to herself; it had been far too long since she had made love under the stars. She stepped with him through the parlor and dining room, and out into the jasmine-scented gardens behind the house. "I think that's a wise decision," she said, helping him to the door. "Your being here will be our little secret," Gretchen said slyly. "We'll lie on the cool grass and make love. That's why you came, isn't it?"

Regan's eyes narrowed and he peered at Gretchen in the bright moonlight. "Yes, that's why I came. Unfortunately," he laughed, "I didn't bring Sirena's prayer beads with me as you instructed."

"I'm forced to forgive you . . . this time," Gretchen laughed. "I don't think either of us needs any beads tonight. Come to me, Regan, let me make love to you as I would have done had you asked *me* to be your wife." Gently, she removed the wine decanter from his grip and tossed it into the shrubbery.

Slowly, she opened the buttons on his shirt and pulled it down over his arms. Loosening his trousers, she instructed him to remove his boots. With one fluid motion, her own garment slid to the ground. Regan reached out to bring her close to him but she nimbly sidestepped him. Cupping her breasts in both hands, she swayed to some unheard music, her movements seductive and tantalizing. Her skin, wet and shimmering with perspiration, gleamed in the moonlight. Her sultry eyes beckoned and teased the mesmerized man who groped for her.

Regan lurched and this time grasped her shoulder, forcing her to him. His feverish mouth sought for and found hers as they tumbled to the ground. She parted her lips and clutched him to her as if to make them one. Their passion was a seething volcano teetering on the brink of eruption.

Spent, Gretchen lay cupping his head to her breast. Why can't you love me as I love you? she questioned silently.

Regan stirred, his head nuzzling the soft suppleness of her breasts. Gently, he brought his mouth to one rosy tip and crushed her body to his. Gretchen writhed beneath him as he aroused her again. Moaning with pleasure, she rolled from beneath him and crouched on her knees, her breathing ragged. She gazed down into his eyes and with a feline movement was atop him. Regan groaned with pleasure and sought her breasts with his groping hands. Wildly rocking, she brought him once again to the heights of passion.

Regan woke to the shrill cries of exotic birds as they fought their way through the lush, tropical foliage. For a brief moment he felt at a loss to explain to himself why he was lying here at dawn on the cool green moss, naked as the day he was born. His eyes searched the locale and came to rest on Gretchen's house. Memories of lust rushed through his body as he recalled his midnight activities. So, this was where he had spent the night! A vision of Sirena in a frilly black nightdress, cap on her head and the beads in her hands danced unbidden into his mind, and suddenly he laughed.

Chapter Eight

Sirena ignored the light, whispery breeze that stirred the gauze draperies as she paced her large, opulently furnished room. She had opened the shutters, allowing the sun to drench her quarters with its light and heat.

Tomorrow was her wedding day, she would marry Regan van der Rhys and there would be no turning back.

Since the first dinner party with Chaezar and Gretchen there had been several others. She had been introduced to the most prominent people on Java and the other islands. Their faces passed before her and they remained nameless. She knew she was considered quite beautiful by the men and charming by their wives. "Regan is a fortunate man, indeed," they had repeated time and again. And why not? she questioned.

Hadn't she made herself pleasing to look at, yet with a restraining hand so as not to be the cause for jealousy among the older, more plain women? Hadn't she sat meekly by, leaving all consequential conversation to the men while her ear was bent with meaningless trifles?

Even Regan seemed approving of her. He was attentive and flattering although once or twice she caught a glimmer of his dismay when he eyed the unrelieved black gowns she wore and her black mantilla. He would have liked to see her wear gay colors and perhaps dress her hair more elegantly, but nevertheless he would allow his gaze to fall on her quite frequently during dinners and afterward when the guests would pair off for card games.

Even when her back was to him she would often feel his eyes on her. The effect was disconcerting, arousing in her contradictory feelings. Mevrouw Kloss, who was a frequent guest, would glance from Regan to Sirena and release a deep romantic sigh. It was evident Helga had formed an opinion that Regan and Sirena were deeply in love. On several occasions Helga tittered excitedly to another of the women and together they looked at Sirena with bright eyes and flushed cheeks.

At times like these Sirena was glad Caleb was excused immediately after dinner to go to his room or walk in the garden. Sirena knew the boy took the opportunity to scale the low foothills on his way to where the *Rana* was hidden and that sometimes he spent nights in the company of the crew. But Caleb was spending far too much time in Regan's company and was coming to respect the man more and more. They had a rapport, a kind of instant understanding. The relationship between them would have been complete if Caleb wasn't always on his guard not to reveal the secret of the *Rana* or Sirena's plan.

Sirena was not offended by Caleb's admiration for Regan. She could understand the boy's feelings. Regan was attentive, sensitive to the moods of others, and he could be very charming. Many times, during the month she had been on Java, she found herself enjoying Regan's company. Waiting expectantly for the end of one of his amusing stories, walking beside him and looking into shops on the busy, planked walkways of Batavia, bumping into Regan's friends and joining them for sherry and tea in their homes.

At first the only way she could bear his company was to push back thoughts of Isabel. Now, and much to her chagrin, there were moments when the *Rana,* Isabel and Uncle Juan seemed to belong to a past life. But it had not happened in a past life, it had happened not long ago! She had seen suffering and she had suffered. The sound of Isabel's screams echoed in her ears, the vision of Uncle Juan's last valiant efforts to defend the ship and his two nieces blurred with the onset of tears. The memory of Caleb's degrading lashing, the spoiling of her innocence never failed to stun her.

No one would make her suffer again! Gone was the girl she had been when she began the journey from Spain. Now she was a woman and she thought as a woman thinks! She had a voice and she would be heard. If they refused to listen, then they would feel the wrath of her actions!

Why should men have all the say?—even the inept, the uninformed, the least of them was put above a world of women! Women must sit meekly by and bend to the wills of men. But not *this* woman! she thought, her blood stirring with the injustice. She had no doubt that, before long, news of a female taking to the seas, captaining her own ship, playing a man's game by men's rules, would create an unbelievable stir. In society's drawing rooms the Capitana would be discussed, condemned. Ladies would raise their eyes heavenward and click their tongues, but every woman who had suffered at the hands of a man merely because she was a woman, and ineffectual in the face of male brutality, would cheer her, applaud her, and whisper silent accolades. She had vowed revenge and she was determined to prove that muscle does not a warrior make!

Her pacing had taken her back and forth before the windows and her last steps left her standing in front of the open clothes press. Sirena's eyes fell on the white gown hanging on the wardrobe door. Wearily, she closed her eyes as her fingers felt the layers of sheer delicate silk. God in Heaven, no woman had less right to wear white! Opening her eyes, forcing herself to scrutinize the blue-white purity of the gown which until now she had avoided looking at, she wailed aloud, "Mother of God, where are the sleeves?"

In a frenzy she turned the gown, examining the bodice. No sleeves! Why hadn't she noticed before? She raced for the door, fumbling with the bolt. "Frau Holtz, Frau Holtz!" she called shrilly, all her frustration and anxiety coming to the surface.

The network of servants brought word to the housekeeper that the Juffrouw was upstairs shouting for her. Frau Holtz mumbled beneath her breath and climbed the stairs, her back held stiffly. Stepping into the hallway and hearing Sirena's frantic call sent chills through her, but the torment in the Señorita's voice twisted her heart. Puffing from the exertion of running up the stairs she flew into the blue-and-white bedroom.

"What's happened, Señorita?"

"Where are the sleeves on the wedding dress? I told you when my measurements were taken that I must have sleeves!"

Relieved her mistress wasn't bitten by a poisonous snake or bug, Frau Holtz was irritated by Sirena's abrasive tone. "Señorita, the climate doesn't call for sleeves . . ."

Sirena whirled on the housekeeper. Her voice was low and dangerous: "I want sleeves on this gown by tomorrow or there will be no wedding. Is that clear? Mynheer van der Rhys will be embarrassed when he stands at the altar *alone!*"

Frau Holtz raised her head haughtily and stared into the glittering green eyes. "The seamstress cannot be recalled. She has left the island."

"Fetch her back," Sirena ordered.

"I'm afraid it's too late. She was going to one of the inner islands. I didn't think to ask which one."

"Then Frau Holtz, it would be wise if you produced a needle and thread and took this gown with you."

"But Señorita, there is no material left. The seamstress did not bring anything but the gown.

"You'll think of something," Sirena said, pulling the gown from its hook on the door and thrusting it into the unwilling arms of the housekeeper.

"Very well, Señorita. What will Mynheer ven der Rhys think when he hears of all this commotion?"

"Who knows?"

Who cares? she muttered under her breath.

Frau Holtz heard, and gaped, her eyes protruding from her head in amazement.

Caleb sat hunched in Regan's chair in the D.E.I. offices. Tomorrow was Sirena's wedding. If only he didn't have to appear at the ceremony. After tomorrow everything would be different . . .

If there was only something he could do. What could he, a boy, do? Nothing. He slouched deeper in the chair and started to doze. Voices startled him to awareness and he listened.

"Where did you come by this information?" It was Regan's voice.

"By way of Michel Rijsen's brother, Jacob, first mate aboard the *Jewel of China.* I spoke with Jacob on Sumbawa; he'd just arrived with his ship, and I was ready to leave with mine, bound back to Batavia. Jacob says that Michel, whose ship is loading sandalwood at Sumba, just east of Sumbawa, has seen the *Tita* in Sumba harbor. She did not plan to stay long. Michel was, you remember, to be first mate aboard the *Tita,* but was taken with the pox the day before the . . . fatal trip you made, and could not go with you."

"The *Java Queen* is being loaded this day for its journey to Capetown the day after my wedding. She'll carry a full cargo. Order the men to unload the ship. I'll take the *Java Queen* myself and recapture the *Tita.* I've long thought her sunk—these past eight years. That lying Spanish son of a whore! Does she carry cargo?"

"Aye, Regan, her hold is full. Spices, rice, and silk."

"Michel is sure it's the *Tita?* He should be surprised —he thought the *Tita* sunk!"

"Aye, it's the *Tita.* Michel told his brother your son's initials are still carved in the quarterdeck. You see, he pretended to be wanting to sign on, and went aboard the *Tita* to speak with its captain. He wanted to be absolutely certain she was the ship he remembered. He said he remembered how you and the boy were laughing when you did it and you told the boy one day the ship would be his and the initials would prove it was. Michel said the boy laughed and started to call it his ship."

"True, Fredrik," Regan said, his eyes glazed with memory of that long-ago happy day. "Who captains the ship and what flag does she fly?"

The man Regan called Fredrik said he didn't know. "Michel told Jacob she's named the *Wanderer.* She sails for Capetown in, let's see . . . three days. Can you overtake her and recapture her? Perhaps," Fredrik said kindly, "you'll find some news of what happened that last, terrible day—though the men aboard cannot be the old crew. All perished, you have told us."

"Finally . . . after all these years . . ." Regan said, his voice husky and low. "Thank you for coming and telling me this, Captain Daan."

"We're friends, Regan. But remember, the *Tita* is only a ship. The . . . boy won't be aboard."

"Ja, I know!" To Caleb the words sounded tortured.

Regan paced the room, never raising his eyes from the floor. Caleb watched him as he paced up and then down, one large fist smacking into the other. Unable to stand it a moment longer, the boy got up from the chair and left the room. Regan didn't raise his eyes, nor did he hear the boy leave.

Returning home, Caleb raced to Sirena's room on trembling legs. Quickly he told her of the conversation he had overheard. "What do you think?" he asked.

"I think we take to the sea as soon as Regan does. I'll study the maps of the eastern isles. Even if we're unlucky enough to be chased when we reach the mouth of the river, we'll disappear around the west tip of Java—as if the sea swallowed us." Sirena looked at the anguish in the boy's eyes. "It's an eye for an eye, Caleb. Yes, I'll take the *Tita,* and yes I know what you say the ship means to him. I remember what Isabel meant to me. *She* was alive! *She* was flesh and blood! The *Tita* is only wood. She's a thing, not a person.

"What will you do to her?"

Sirena eyed the boy across from her. "Ask me when the time comes, not now."

Regan chewed thoughtfully on the butt of a cigar. The initial shock of hearing the *Tita* was still afloat had subsided. There was no action he could take. He would have to bide his time until he could sail the *Java Queen.*

Regan became reflective, his thoughts jumping back over the space of time to the good years with his honey-skinned wife and infant son. Hope sprang anew in his heart. Might there be, perhaps, one member of the crew—one of his Dutch sailors who'd not perished, or even one of the cursed Spanish pirateers who took the ship—who knew of the whereabouts of his son?

Though she undoubtedly knew something of his past from her late father, it was typical of Sirena not to have asked him questions concerning his first marriage and his child. More and more, over the past weeks, he had come to admire the cool, poised Spanish woman with skin the color of ivory and the texture of Chinese silk. How well she fit into his social circle! The men found her beautiful and desirable, constantly called Regan a lucky man. The women seemed to find her sincere and interesting, her beauty admirable yet not a source of envy because Sirena was careful not to flaunt it or use it as a tool to attract their husbands' attention. She was intelligent, fiery when her anger was aroused, and every inch a lady.

When Regan thought of Sirena he could still taste her full, moist, petulant lips. He could almost feel her smooth, warm flesh beneath his hand. Could he wait a year, until her mourning was over, to possess her? Whatever, he told himself, provided he could enjoy her company, see her daily, delight in her friendship, he would wait. In fact Regan was fearful to make an advance toward her. In doing so he might alienate her friendship and possibly destroy any chance of making her completely his.

Suddenly he jumped to his feet and called his manservant. Quickly, Regan scribbled a note to Sirena requesting that she leave her rooms tonight for a quiet, intimate, dinner . . . for two.

Sirena had dressed carefully for dinner. She had never dined alone with Regan, and in spite of herself the idea excited her as she descended the wide, curving staircase and walked to the dining room door.

Regan waited in the richly furnished room busying himself by pouring a sherry at the Chinese red lacquered cabinet decorated with black-and-gold fire-breathing dragons. At a sound behind him he turned.

"May I join you, Regan?" Sirena found herself admiring his cat-like grace as he stepped toward her.

"You are beautiful, as always," he said, kissing her hand.

"And you're a flatterer, as always," she murmured, disconcerted by the warmth of his lips.

Regan had ordered a table set for them on the verandah outside the dining room. The area was hung with netting to ward off mosquitos and the carefully kept gardens just beyond were lit with lamps that created a fantasy scene.

"It's almost like peeking out from a cloud. Thank you, Regan, it's lovely." Her voice was low and sultry, her eyes gleamed brighter than the candlelight.

Through the dinner which was served by a silent djongo, Regan and Sirena were quiet, almost constrained. Each seemed to be lost in private thoughts. When the table was cleared and the claret was served, Regan asked Sirena if he might smoke. Their silence became companionable and Sirena emitted a deep sigh.

Regan enjoyed seeing her like this. He was contented, knowing that in some way he was responsible for her mood. Her head was turned, looking out into the garden, and the night breezes lifted the mantilla from her cheeks to reveal her delicate bone structure and exquisite profile.

Gently, he reached across the small table and touched her fingertips. "Sirena, I'd like to talk to you." Slowly and in detail, he told her the complete story of the *Tita*. She listened, attentively, aware of his carefully held-in-check anguish. She noticed he skirted mention of the Spanish prison, possibly because he didn't want her to think he was criticizing her homeland. He concluded by explaining the visit of Captain Fredrik Dann and the man's information concerning the *Tita*.

"Our wedding is tomorrow, Sirena. I've told you all this so you can understand why I must leave day after tomorrow. I've got to see the *Wanderer* for myself and determine if she's really the *Tita*."

Sirena lifted her eyes to face him, but the thick black fringe of her lashes obscured the triumph glittering in their depths. "I understand, Regan. Of course you must go." Victory fluttered in her breast and brought a slow smile to her lips. Her plan was succeeding! Her display of affectionate friendship and gentle manner were winning him. If he could tell her this—something so close to his heart—he would tell her anything: his shipping routes, the time of departure of his ships laden with precious cargo . . . He would confide in her and she would execute her revenge!

"Regan, what will you do when you find this ship?"

His face hardened into chiseled lines, his eyes smoldered with determination. "I realize that when I find her my son won't be aboard, but I pray the bastard son of a pig the Hook is!"

The hatred that distorted his features practically took her breath away. "Who is this man you hate with such fervor? What has he done?"

Bitterness twisted his mouth, and through clenched teeth he said, "The man is a brutal killer. My wife suffered greatly at his hands, or should I say hook!"

Even by the light of the candles Regan saw Sirena blanch when he mentioned The Hook. The girl had a vivid imagination! He should have kept his own counsel and refrained from upsetting her.

When Regan mentioned the man with the hook and how his wife had suffered, it brought back that misty night on the *Rana* and Isabel's screams. Now she knew she *must* go after the *Wanderer* herself.

"Regan, surely you don't imagine you can comb the seas, stop every ship, to look for this beast with a hook. Why, the man you seek might even be in your own employ!"

"That could well be, Sirena. Seamen are a closed-mouthed lot and there's no way I can be certain. But I will tell you this: If he's out there, I'll find him!" Sirena experienced an emotion close to pity for him. She understood his determination, could sympathize with his bitterness and even share his thirst for revenge. But satisfaction would be denied Regan; his search for The Hook would bear no fruit. If anyone would capture the beast with the hook it would be Sirena Córdez! Her vengeance would be sated—and she would do it without the help of the man responsible for her sister's death. She would best them all!

Chapter Nine

Sirena stood before the long, smoky mirror. Her reflection was that of a tall, white specter in the distortion of the glass. Frau Holtz had done a fair job of setting sleeves into the gown's bodice. Actually they were only elbow-length, but their fullness and modest double layer of silk organdy disguised the wound on the upper arm which had healed leaving a raw, red angry-looking scar she hoped would fade in time.

Carriages had been dropping off their passengers

for more than an hour. Many of the wedding guests had arrived by native proas, drifting up the lagoon that bordered the van der Rhys' property a quarter mile to the north. From the private quay, natives from the plantation compound carried those ladies who did not care to walk the distance to the house along the cobbled path, in tandoes, Javanese sedan chairs.

The hum of conversation had become louder and Juli had breathlessly announced to Sirena that the musicians were tuning their instruments. Caleb appeared shyly at Sirena's door, looking as uncomfortable as could be in his starched white shirtfront and stiff new boots.

A meaningful look passed between the young boy and the girl in her white wedding dress. A look that said there would be no turning back, they were entrapped by vengeance as surely as if they were caught in a whirlpool. The dice were thrown, the deck was dealt, and Sirena and Caleb knew there would be no real winner in the game they played.

The musicians struck a chord below, in the drawing room, and Sirena's spine froze. The moment had come. Solemnly she lifted the translucent veil over her face and stepped forward, taking Caleb's arm.

"Here we go, little brother. Are you with me?"

"Until death, Sirena." His black eyes looked up adoringly although his mouth was ringed with white betraying his fear.

Down the wide stairs they stepped, the strains of music a dirge in Sirena's ears. Seen through the veil, everything about her seemed distant and unreal. There was an expectant hush from the guests who flanked the long, tiled hallway and spacious drawing room, now empty of furniture save the benches seating the ladies in their full, gaily colored gowns. The perimeters of the room were decked with flowers whose lush blooms lent an exotic scent to the air.

Standing before the glass-paned doors leading to the garden, Regan awaited her. A tightness about his mouth and a furrow between his brows betrayed his nervousness. He turned to watch Sirena's progress on Caleb's arm with that infuriating expression of amusement laying about the corners of his flashing blue eyes.

He's actually enjoying all this! Sirena thought, anger flushing her cheeks. He's won! He insisted we be married as soon as possible, regardless of my protests, and he's delighted with his victory. Enjoy it while you may, Mynheer van der Rhys, your victory will be short-lived!

Father Miguel, religious leader of Batavia's Catholic community and missionary, stood before the garden doors, his tall, stately form outlined against the late afternoon sun. He looked out of place away from his church, but the ornate wooden structure had burned to the ground a month before. A worried look creased the Father's forehead, for although Regan had promised that the children—when they were born—would be raised Catholic, the Portuguese priest was well informed about Regan's lack of religion. Even as a Protestant, van der Rhys was not a true believer. Father Miguel feared for the young devout Señorita who was to marry the strong godless man.

Regan took his place next to the priest and turned to watch Sirena's slow, steady approach. She was dazzling; the white of her gown emphasized the rich golden tones of her skin and the black of her hair. Beneath the fine veil, Regan thought he perceived a glimmer of tears in her wide, heavily fringed eyes. She's beautiful, he thought, any man would be proud to take her to wife.

Sirena stood beside Regan, her right hand in his. As Father Miguel commenced the ceremony in his deep, resonant Portuguese-accented Latin, Sirena chanced a glimpse at Regan. Standing beside him this way, she felt so small and vulnerable. As tall as she was, he towered over her. His sheaf of winter-wheat hair reflected the sun rays filtering through the glass. His expression was serious, his blue eyes penetrating, his clean, square jaw set.

Suddenly Sirena felt her knees weaken and the hand resting so lightly in Regan's began to tremble. The enormity of the situation struck her full force. Could she carry it off? Could she actually marry this tall, handsome man next to her? Marry him and swear before God to honor him, to love him, and then wreak havoc upon him? Was this actually necessary—couldn't she have found another way to avenge Isabel and Tio Juan?

It was too late for thoughts such as these, she reminded herself. It was because of this man she could never marry anyone else, for no one would want a ruined, soiled woman. There was no turning back, she had made her decision and now she must live up to it! For Isabel, for Tio Juan and, she admitted, herself!

The trembling of her hand ceased, her back stiffened with renewed determination as she became aware of Father Miguel's rich tones announcing: ". . . before God and these witnesses, I now pronounce you man and wife."

Through the long, exhausting hours of the evening, Regan remained attentively at Sirena's side. Considerate of her needs, introducing her to guests she had not met before, he was the picture of a delighted groom.

Sirena's nerves were strung as tautly as the violin strings on which the musicians played. She felt herself passing through the celebration of her wedding as if through a dream. Nothing seemed real or to have substance. The food was tasteless, the wine flat, the conversation meaningless. During one of the dances she glanced up at the mirror over the mantel and saw herself on Regan's arm. Her cheeks were flushed, her eyes were bright, a becoming smile was on her lips. For a moment she hadn't recognized herself and she found herself thinking, What a pretty girl and she seems so happy, I wonder if she's in love with her dance partner? Startled to realize the glowing girl dancing in the mirror was herself, she missed a step. Regan held her arm and steadied her. "You must be exhausted, Sirena. Come sit here." He led her to a chair. "I'll get you a cool drink."

As she waited for him to return with the punch, once again her eyes gravitated to the mirror. Her image seemed one-dimensional, flat and lifeless. Where was that spark, that fragile thread-like flicker of animation that made her unique unto herself? Had it evaporated, become absorbed into the atmosphere like the puddles on the cobblestones after the rain? Looking across the room, she saw Regan—her husband now—quipping with several guests. He was lively, vital, throwing his head back in laughter. He had stolen her spark and crushed it in his powerful hands by forcing her to play out this farce pretending to be someone she was not. That he was unaware of this travesty was of little consequence to her. It was enough that *because* of him her personality was buried in a sham. Her eyes accused him and found him guilty.

Alone in her room, Sirena prepared for bed. The windows overlooking the gardens were open, allowing the night breezes to carry the sweet, aromatic scents of flowers and spices into the room. She had slipped away from the last lingering guests an hour ago to seek the peace of solitude. Climbing the stairs, she had looked back and her eyes were drawn to Regan. As if her glance were a physical touch, he turned from his conversation and looked up at her and their eyes locked. After a long moment she lifted her chin, turned her back, and proceeded up the stairs.

By the time she reached her room her heart was beating wildly, her pulses throbbing savagely. His one brief glance desired her, coveted her, and was regretting his promise to free her from sharing his bed. She remembered the smile which had played about his lips and in the corners of his eyes. Could it be he had no intention of honoring his promise?

In spite of herself, Sirena took elaborate pains with her toilette. For a final touch, she placed a few precious drops of civet musk on her pulse spots; its heady scent enveloped her in a cloud of sensuality.

Sirena arranged a soft, loose knot atop her proud head, with curly, wispy ringlets feathering her brow and the nape of her neck. Satisfied that she created an alluring picture, she waited.

Over and over she rehearsed the scene in her mind. Regan would tap on the door, seeking entrance. Hesitantly, shyly, she would admit him. His eyes would cover her hotly, their searing passion and need burnishing her soft flesh. She would stand with her back to the dim lamplight, allowing him to discern the voluptuous outline of her body through her thin, lavender nightdress.

He would stand close to her, the musk intoxicating him with desire. His hand would reach out and touch the soft ringlets falling against her cheek, then caress the smooth, silky skin of her neck. Roughly, desperately, he would pull her against his muscular body, his breath would come in light, wine-scented pants. His mouth would seek hers in a long passionate kiss. Drawing away, his eyes would burn into hers, pleading, begging her to release him from his promise.

Sirena smiled wickedly as she imagined his desperation when she allowed him to see that he had aroused her and yet continued to demand that he hold firm to his word. He would concede to her wishes grudgingly, and being the proud man she knew him to be, would never beg his rights as her husband.

Finally, in a modest manner, she would insist he leave. And he would, his head held high, his back straight and tall. And Sirena would know he didn't take her gentle rejection gracefully. His pride would prick him and he would spend a long sleepless night tossing amongst his bed covers . . . alone.

The scene she imagined was so vivid, so real, Sirena felt her first, faint stirrings of desire for a man. That the man was Regan, who she blamed for the tragedy aboard the *Rana*, was a ludicrous affront to her reason. Yet she found it difficult to still this sudden awareness of her sexuality and berated herself for her wanton cravings. The picture of Regan, tall, muscular, sun-gilded, silvery-gold hair dipping low over his broad, intelligent brow, flashed before her, almost taking her breath away. It was only when she remembered his powerful, capable hands and cold, agate-blue eyes that her resolution returned.

Back and forth she paced the room, straining to hear his knock on her door. She heard the departure of the last guests and sounds of Frau Holtz and the djongos securing the house for the night. Still she waited . . .

The long, exhausting day was taking its toll. Sirena eyed her bed longingly. Leaving her lamp burning so Regan would see the light beneath her door and know she was still awake, Sirena removed her slippers and crept beneath the silken coverlet. Deliberately opening the button of her nightdress and posing alluringly, she waited . . .

Once or twice she felt herself drift off into a doze and she shook herself awake. She waited . . .

Suddenly the sound of Regan's boots coming down the hall toward her room shocked her to full attention. Expectantly, she listened as the footsteps came closer and stopped outside her door. Her pulses pounding, her breasts heaving with anticipation, she drew in her breath sharply.

A footfall, then another and another!

He was going right past her room. He hadn't knocked and sought entrance! There would be no gentle touch, no burning kiss, no sweet rejection!

A few minutes later, still awake, she heard his steps pass her door once more, then the sound of his boots on the staircase, and finally the front door open and slam shut. Moments later, hoofbeats sounded their tattoo on the drive and she knew it was Regan. He was leaving, galloping down the country road toward town—the same road that passed Gretchen Lindenreich's house!

Grasping at straws, Sirena willed herself to reason that Regan was making an early start for the *Java Queen*. He had explained to her during their intimate dinner that he would be leaving the morning after the wedding to search for the *Tita*.

That's what he had said, yet no power on earth would convince Sirena that Regan wasn't going to stop at Gretchen's first. Sirena could imagine the Teutonic bitch's triumph to know Regan had left his nuptial bed to fly to his Valkyrie's arms and die a little in the throes of passion as she transported him to Valhalla.

Shamefaced, Sirena buried her head beneath the cover, pummeling her pillows with tightly clenched fists. In place of sweet rejection, she was being raked by the sharp talons of scorn. She had waited and he never came! He had left her for his German whore, denying Sirena even so little as the right of refusal!

She would make him pay, somehow! Unbidden, a plan began to take form in her mind. Regan had deprived her of the satisfaction of turning him away. Now, without a doubt, she would deprive him of something he wanted . . . the *Tita!*

Regan spurred the beast beneath him. He had to get away before he did something he would regret.

The cool fragrant breeze was a balm to his tortured body. Never in his life had he wanted a woman as much as he wanted Sirena. He had seen the light under her door and for one brief moment his step had faltered, but he hadn't stopped. The hour was late, she should have been asleep hours before. Quickly, he reined in the horse. He could go back, he could take what was his, but was that what he wanted? No, his mind rebelled. The unbidden memory of Sirena demanding a bolt and new lock for her door sprang into his mind. A door bolted against him in his own house! She had been beautiful, desirable, exciting him to lose his composure. He had seen the fright in her eyes when he had crushed the silver goblet. What a fool he had been. Instead of intimidating her with a display of strength, he had alienated her further. He had almost felt the sting of her nails across his face. And to make a bad situation worse, he realized he'd made a fool of himself and instead of backing off and allowing her the dubious victory, he had forced himself on her. He had demanded she acknowledge him the victor by surrendering to his embrace. He had been aware of the faint response stirring in her and he had also realized that if that response were allowed to blossom, she, not he, would have become the vanquished. "I always win," he had told her with false bravado to disguise the passion she had roused in him. The taste of her lips, the feel of her lush body crushed against his were as fresh in his memory as if he'd thrust her from him the second before. With a composure which was beyond his belief, she had asked, "What happens if the prize you win is worth nothing?" Regan's instincts became thoughts and he knew that if he had insisted on his marital rights he would have won the battle and lost the war; her words would have become reality. He would have won nothing: her body without her spirit would be meaningless.

What was this sultry Spaniard doing to him? Why did

she make him feel this way? Why, after all his experience with women, should he suddenly care about her spirit, her soul, instead of just the delights and desires of her body? Would she come willingly to his bed?

He needed a drink, needed it badly. With a flick of the reins he spurred the horse down the hard-packed, dusty road toward the D.E.I. offices. There was a bottle of rum waiting there to keep him company through the long, lonely night.

The bend in the road took him past Gretchen's house. A yellow light winked behind gauze draperies. A drink was much closer than the D.E.I offices and Regan turned his mount into Gretchen's drive.

Not bothering to knock on the heavy door, he thrust it open and stared into the brightly lit room. Gretchen stood before him, a goblet in each hand. "You're late, Regan. I expected you an hour ago."

Regan laughed harshly as he downed the wine in a gulp and his free hand drew her to him. He flung his goblet against the wall, as did Gretchen. His mouth crushed hers, his hands ripped the gown from her body. Her creamy breasts became taut as Regan's hands cupped their suppleness. Moaning with desire, Gretchen pressed her body to his as she loosened first his shirt and then his trousers. Locking her arms arround his broad back, she undulated against his nakedness.

Regan brought his arms around her and pushed her onto the bed. A fierce cry of pain escaped her as Regan entered. Frantically, low moans shaking her, her body moving, writhing against him, she clawed his scarred back, her mouth burning beneath his. Tearing her mouth from his she pleaded, "Love me, Regan, love me." With a sudden thrust from Regan the words died in her throat as his lips ground into hers.

Consumed, she relaxed in Regan's arms. Gently she nibbled on his ear lobes. "Sleep," she crooned. Regan sighed heavily and was asleep in seconds.

Gretchen lay with her head on his massive chest. He had come to her on his wedding night. It must mean something, it had to mean something. Did the Spaniard reject him? What had made him come to her? Did he love her? He must, otherwise why would he be lying next to her. "Oh Regan, I love you so," she whispered.

"This should have been our wedding night, yours and mine, our unforgettable wedding night." Regan stirred restlessly beneath her and she whispered softly in his ear. Well, it wasn't her wedding night . . . but she could make it unforgettable. She had the power to make it unforgettable. Gently, she moved away from his naked body and padded over to the chest in the corner of the room. She glanced over her shoulder as she withdrew a small pouch.

Quietly, on tiptoe, she peered down at Regan; he was sleeping soundly, his face was relaxed.

Stealthily, she padded away to the kitchen and sprinkled a little of the powder into a small wooden bowl. She added a few drops of water to the finely ground powder and stirred it with her index finger. She crept back to the bed and knelt down at the side of the bed and gently spread the mixture on Regan's manhood. Touching a bit of the mixture to her own, most intimate parts, she then washed her hands and discarded the bowl.

Gracefully she slid into the bed and lay next to Regan. She pulled the gauze-like coverlet over her legs and lay still a few minutes measuring Regan's quiet breathing, trying to relax her own tortured gasps. What would he say when it was all over? Would he hate her? She stifled a laugh. He'll be so drunk with passion one of the houseboys will have to take him home, she mused.

When she decided enough time had elapsed she began to stroke his body, and dart her tongue over his hard mouth. She moved so that she lay atop him, with her breasts crushing his chest. Bringing her face close to his she forced her passion-seared lips against his. His lips parted and her tongue explored his.

Regan opened his eyes, every muscle in his body twanging to be released as he wrapped his arms around her. His back arched as his legs spread, forcing Gretchen's body to move against him. "You bitch," he groaned, "why did you do it?"

Gretchen, held like a vise in his grasp, sought to elude him, to heighten his desire. With a vicious thrust he pierced her, locking her to him. Animal lust burst forth as both bodies arched and plunged again and again. Gasping, his body glistening with perspiration, Regan flung Gretchen on her back.

"Ride me, Regan," Gretchen screamed. "More, more."

Unable to control himself, Regan plunged again. Wave upon wave of passion ripped through him. His heart hammered in his chest as he sought release, only to find himself once more on the crest of desire.

Gretchen, eyes glazed, body gleaming beneath the titan astride her, rocked her body to meet each wave of passion and cry out demanding still more.

An eternity later, Regan lay, his breathing harsh and ragged to the point of a death rattle, his body limp, his loins raw and burning. "Bitch," he gasped. He wanted to kill her with his bare hands but he couldn't move.

Gretchen, her breathing normal, smiled wickedly. "Regan, I didn't know . . . I swear . . . I thought . . . I just assumed—"

"Damn your soul to Hell, were you trying to kill me?"

"Only with love," she cooed. "Wasn't it magnificent, Regan?"

"What time is it?" Regan croaked.

"An hour before dawn," Gretchen laughed. He gasped in awe. Gretchen laughed again. "A memorable night, wouldn't you say?"

Clenching his teeth in agony, Regan rose from the bed and was forced to grab the bedpost for support.

"How manly you look," Gretchen gurgled as Regan began to dress himself.

His trousers secure, he looked at Gretchen and said quietly, "I'll kill you for this. Not today, not tomorrow, but one day soon—do you understand?"

"But darling Regan, you came to me, and on your wedding night. I only wanted you to have a night you could remember," she said fearfully.

"I'll remember," Regan said, opening the door. "I'll remember."

His ominous words sent a chill over Gretchen's perspiring body. Well, no matter what he said, he enjoyed it, she pouted. What a performance! she sighed sleepily. A night to remember . . .

Chapter Ten

Caleb and Sirena lowered themselves quietly down the trellis beneath Sirena's window. As their feet touched the ground, she breathed deeply with relief. They had been unobserved. What was more, Juli could be trusted to set the food inside her bedroom door, should she and Caleb not return within a day. The handmaid had been puzzled when Sirena first gave her her instructions—and had looked quizzically at the key given over to her. But the girl now loved Sirena, and would certainly not question her mistress. Yes, she would unlock the door, set the food inside—not even opening the door wide enough to see into the room—then reclose and lock it; no, Frau Holtz would not see the key, and yes, she would return it to Sirena on the Mevrouw's return . . .

"Mevrouw"! What strange words the Dutch had, Sirena mused, as she and Caleb made their way across the vast gardens behind the estate. First I was "Juffrouw"—"Miss" or "Señorita." Now I am—and how ugly the term is!—"Mevrouw," or "Mistress." A graduation to true mistress of the household. Let Frau Holtz beware!

Jan Verhooch met them, with horses, at the westernmost end of the gardens, and smiled encouragingly at his "capitana."

"Good evening, Jan," Sirena whispered. "You've not waited long?"

"I would wait much longer for a chance to be back at sea again, Capitana!" he chuckled.

Caleb, who had secretly carried the message to Jan two hours before, now helped Sirena mount the placid roan steed. It and two others had been pastured near the *Rana*'s cove several days before, to be ready whenever they were needed to convey Sirena and Caleb to the ship.

Painting the ship black had been an ingenious idea. Even this close it was difficult to see the ship against the dark night.

Jan leading, for this was the first time Sirena had followed the jungled slope down to the cove at night, they made their way at last to the tiny beach that cupped the cliff-framed cove, and approached the ship. Only one light burned on deck.

"Jan," Sirena whispered as they climbed up the ship's ladder, "tell the night watchman to go below—and any other of the crew who may be on deck. When I call to you and the men, after passing through the channel at the river's mouth, then—and only then—are they to come up on deck. I want them to see how I skirt the rocks at the ocean's edge and triumph over this River of Death!"

In her cabin, Sirena shed her clothing and rummaged in the large battered sea chest for her abbreviated costume. Gleefully, she donned the tight shorts with the tattered bottoms. She buttoned the shirt over her jutting breasts and pulled the tails high on her midriff. The first several buttons refused to remain closed. No matter that the buttons popped open to reveal a deep, full cleavage. She shrugged as she pulled on shiny leather knee boots and folded the tops to above her knee. Her creamy, tawny skin glowed in the dim lamplight. Next she tied a multi-colored striped scarf around her head, its ends hanging loosely over one ear. Suddenly she laughed aloud as she pictured herself standing on the rolling, pitching deck. Perhaps the enemy would die of shock when they saw who captained the frigate.

Carefully, she unrolled the charts that rested next to her bunk and scrutinized them. Satisfied, she dug beneath her bunk and withdrew a cutlass which she fastened to her side. Confident with the weapon next to her, she left the room to meet the crew.

Her hands gripping the wheel, Sirena felt at peace for the first time in weeks. She threw back her head, the warm salt air like a balm to her body. She felt as free as the air.

The frigate had skimmed out of the cove and down the winding river, over the white-capped breakers and—into open water. The sea was rough and Sirena found it took all her strength to hold the frigate steady.

There'll be a storm before the day is over, she muttered to herself, the wind is from the west and it's wild and to be reckoned with. Excitement made her heart beat fast as she pictured herself winning the battle against the elements. But she would always be the victor. The sea would never beat her.

Less than five minutes out to sea, she called for Jan to take the wheel. "Do as I tell you and there will be no problem," Sirena said loudly over the crashing waves as the frigate precariously topped one swell to challenge another. "Remember, at the wheel you are its master."

Picking up the horn that lay next to the wheel, she spoke loudly, her voice carrying over the wildly thundering swell. "All hands to the quarterdeck. Heave to!"

Sirena climbed down from her perch and strode to the deck as the men came out of the ship's hold; she was greeted with loud exclamations of surprise. Instinctively, Sirena reached for the cutlass at her side. Her hand on the hilt, she stood and gazed from one to the other of her crew.

"What say, you men? Speak up now. I'm your captain. Look back ashore. We've passed the rocks at the mouth of the River of Death. Do you not now trust my skill? For Jan has doubtless told you of my sex, and you may not have placed full trust in me. From this moment on you owe allegance to no one save me and this ship. If there's one of you who refuses to obey, then over the side you go for the sharks. I'll play fair with you. I ask the same in return. You'll be given good food and ale. Any booty we secure you may divide among yourselves. Is there any man jack of you that doesn't agree to my terms?"

Sirena stood facing them, legs slightly parted,

hands low on her hips, her wild and night-dark hair streaming behind her.

"Aye, Capitana," came the reply from one and all. Then, from Jan: "We give you our allegiance and our lives while aboard this ship." The others nodded agreement as their eyes met her boldly.

"Very good," Sirena said curtly. "There's one more thing. I'm a woman, and I wish to be respected as a woman first and your captain second. The first of you who makes a move in my direction will find himself cleaning his guts from the deck!" With the agility of a cat, Sirena had the cutlass free of its sheath, advanced a step, and nicked the button from the shirt of the man closest to her. He lowered his eyes to see his naked chest and lifted his head, a surly look on his face.

Sirena backed off a step and narrowed her eyes. "Your name, seaman," she said harshly.

"Wouter . . . Capitana." The surly look was now openly insolent and suggestive. Sirena drew in her breath and brought the tip of the cutlass to the man's throat. Gently, she pressed the tip of the blade against his flesh and smiled. Her words were cold and clipped as she tilted her head to the side to observe the man's bulging eyes.

"A moment ago I read lust in your eyes, your countenance carried hostility and insolence. If I ever," she said slowly and deliberately, "see such a look again, I'll burn your eyes from their sockets. Understand?"

Saliva drooled from the seaman's mouth. If he swallowed the tip of the blade would draw blood. He tried to make a sound only to feel warm wetness drip on his chest. Sirena laughed as she withdrew the blade and carelessly wiped it on the man's trouser leg.

"It's well you fear me, seaman. For a moment I thought your brains were in your loins. Don't ever make that mistake again." The seaman gulped and backed against the quarter rail, the eyes of the crew boring into him.

His dark eyes were thoughtful and crafty as he muttered, "Aye, Capitana."

"The matter is ended. One warning is all I ever give. Who's to serve as cook aboard this ship?"

"Tis me, Capitana," replied a wizened old man with not a tooth in his mouth. "I know me way about the galley."

Sirena smiled. "And your name, cook?"

"Jacobus, Capitana."

"You're the only man besides Jan, my first mate, who has access to my cabin. To anyone else I will consider it an act of mutiny. Is that clear?" she asked, her eyes on Wouter.

"Aye, Capitana," came the chorus of replies. Sirena noticed that Wouter's lips remained compressed. Her eyes narrowed. She would kill him if she had to. His blood on the *Rana*'s deck wouldn't bother her at all.

"Remember, I told you a ship will make better time with the hold empty. Speed is of the essence."

"Aye, Capitana, I remember," said Jan.

"Now I want to study these charts and I have entries to make in the log. This log is for your eyes and mine alone—and Caleb's."

Sirena unrolled the charts and studied them carefully. Her father had taught her well, just as she had been teaching Caleb, who was a promising seaman. If she shortened sail and kept to windward she should be able to outmanuever Regan and reach the rendezvous ahead of him with time to spare, even though she was following a course along the southern shore of Java whereas Regan would doubtless take the northern shore to reach Sumba. She hoped the *Tita,* or *Wanderer,* had not left the sandalwood island yet, for if it had, she knew not which route it would follow. She had one important advantage over Regan. His larger ship wouldn't sail too well in heavy weather. The *Java Queen* wouldn't heave to in a gale under a reefed main topsail.

Sirena looked toward the skies; there would be heavy weather shortly. Her heartbeat quickened at the thought of meeting Regan commanding his ship—perhaps after Bali, the beautiful island off Java's eastern tip, where Regan too would take a southern route. What would he think when he saw her aboard her ship. Would he know she was his wife? Not likely. What could a man know of a woman if he wasn't interested enough in her to sleep with her?

His rejection stung again. How she would love to have reminded him that night of his promise to respect her period of mourning and leave her to her prayers! But her cheeks burned with shame as she remembered her careful toilette, how she had waited for him, even rehearsed what she would say. And then he had denied her the pleasure of the argument, of seeing his desire in those hard eyes. At times, she almost hoped he *would* recognize her! She'd rather have him learn her secret than think of her waiting alone in her room, crying with her need for him. Anything was better than being the object of his ridicule. Still she might not see him at all. If she was clever she could overtake the *Wanderer* and get away quickly. A few moments in some instances could be an eternity. Speed was the answer, it always came down to speed. Once again she studied the charts—and laughed.

Two days now, the *Rana* had been urged on by a strong westerly. She had passed the eastern tip of Java, and Bali, and could see Sumbawa—Sumba's northern, sister isle—off the larboard bow.

"Sail ho!" came the shout from the rigging.

So, we made it after all—I was right, Sirena thought gleefully. I outraced him and I'll outsmart him too! "What flag does she fly, Caleb?"

"None. And she's tightened sail!"

"Good! Caleb, come here! All hands on deck!" Sirena shouted. "Four men to mount the shrouds, four men to the yardarms—they'll slice the *Wanderer*'s rigging. I'll steer her directly astern at full speed and our ram will puncture her stern. Look lively now and tighten sail. When I give the order, fire from the bow as I ram the stern. She won't have time to turn her sail. Heave to, men!" Sirena yelled as she gripped the wheel. "Caleb," Sirena ordered, "raise the red flag on the foretopmast. Speed, Caleb, quickly now. Surprise is our best ally. We cannot lose a minute!"

Caleb climbed into the shrouds with the other men and hung onto the rigging. She was actually going to ram the *Wanderer*. He didn't think she'd have the nerve to try it. From the looks on the crewmen's faces they hadn't thought so either. But if Sirena said she would do it, she would. She handled a ship better than any captain he had served under.

The quarry was dead ahead and Sirena could see the *Wanderer*'s men scrambling on the deck. "Fire on the count of three!" Sirena ordered. "One! . . . Two! . . . Three!"

A loud deafening crash sounded as the cannonball made contact with the renamed *Tita,* splitting a hole in her deck. As the ram punctured her stern large splinters of wood flew in the air. Men toppled overboard as other seamen ran to check the rolling cannon, which was no longer stationary. The crackling and rending of broken wood was deafening.

Sirena shouted the order to board the ship. "Quickly, she'll sink within the hour."

"Lower the flag," Jan ordered one of the men as he swung with his cutlass.

Sirena stood on the bow of the *Rana* and watched as her men fought tooth and nail to overtake the galleon. But the *Wanderer* was old and rotted with teredo worm; the crew was just as rotten.

"Secure the ship!" Sirena shouted from the bow. "Let no man escape!" With an agile move Sirena grasped the rope Caleb swung to her from the rigging and leapt aboard the galleon, her cutlass clanking on the deck as she landed. "How many men, Caleb?" she asked breathlessly.

"Two score if that many and they've no stomach for fighting. Already we've won!"

"Lower the jolly-boats so that we may toss these men into them and let them wait to be rescued. But first," she called out, "is there a man on this ship with a hook for a hand?"

The men stood before her gawking, their mouths hanging open because of her dress and the authority she held over her crew. There was no answer to her inquiry.

"Hold out your hands, the lot of you!" Sirena unsheathed the cutlass and held it in front of her.

Angrily she sliced the air as she watched first one man and then the next hold out his hands.

"It is well for the lot of you there's no such man aboard," she said coldly and cruelly. One of the men, the first mate, shivered slightly at her words.

Suddenly Sirena laughed a gay musical tinkling laugh that raised the hackles on Caleb's neck. Sirena paced threateningly before the *Wanderer*'s crew. The men were lined up against the rail, their complexions oily yellow in the light from the smoky lamp pots. She strode down the line, the heels of her boots clicking a staccato on the wooden deck, and stopped before a tall, heavy man who stood apart from the crew. From his dress and feathered cocked hat she assumed he was the captain. They locked stares. Sirena's upper lip curled in distaste. The man was sweating profusely, his chest heaved, his thick lips trembled with fear.

"You're the captain, aren't you?" she demanded. "Answer me!" she challenged his silence. The man could only shake his head in the affirmative.

"Who does this ship sail for? Who's your superior?" Sirena asked, her tone almost light and conversational; but deep within her she burned with shame, for the enemy crew by and large spoke Spanish. The captain, his eyes riveted on the cutlass she brandished, was quaking in his boots. "Answer me, swine! Who owns this ship?"

Her green eyes glittering dangerously, she advanced on him, and he backed away from her, gasping with fright. Before her disbelieving eyes he toppled over the rail, disappearing into the swells below. The wind was rising, howling about her head, but the captain's scream resounded in her ears. The crew looked down into the turbulent sea muttering: "He's done for . . ." "Never was any good in the water . . ." "Serves 'im right . . . the coward."

Sirena had no stomach to pursue her questioning. Caleb's call came to her over the howl of the wind.

"All cargo is aboard . . ."

"Into the jolly-boats, the lot of you!" The *Wanderer*'s crew were lowered in the ship's jolly-boats, for their galleon was sinking fast. "All hands, back to our ship!" She jumped the widening gap between the two ships with agility. "That's it, Jan, hove away from this scurvy marauder! She'll not last long. Steer before the wind, quickly now!"

The frigate true now on a westward course, Sirena stood at the bow, one hand on the rigging and the other on the hilt of her cutlass, measuring the sea. For the wind, increasing steadily all that day, had now churned up the waves into a fury. It would be a stiff fight to best the wind to westward, where her course now lay, and she might have to veer off the south or north until the gale changed somewhat.

She saw the sail before the cry came from the rigging.

"Sail ho!"

Quickly she turned to Caleb, who stood not far from her. "Go below, little brother. If it is Mynheer van der Rhys, he mustn't see you. And, I pray, he will not recognize his timid señorita!" She had added lip and cheek rouge to her face, and hoped that the new look, plus her costume, would utterly confound him.

Unwillingly, Caleb obeyed.

"Man the guns, but fire only if I give the order," Sirena called back to Jan. "Steer straight on. She's coming to accost us, and if she doesn't veer off we'll ram her as we did the *Wanderer!*"

Hair billowing behind her, Sirena stood, a smile on her lips as she spied the man who commanded the ship that was bearing down on her frigate.

"Have no fear," she shouted to the sweating Jan, "she'll bow to us. If not, the order to ram stands. She's loosening sail, I can see the men in the shrouds. They're furling the sail. She's a brig and she looks topheavy. In a few minutes we'll be almost broadside. Fire only when ordered!"

"Aye, Capitana," came the chorus of shouts from her crew who now trusted her judgment and were exhilarated over their conquest of the galleon.

"Her master stands on the bow, Capitana."

The ships were almost directly broadside. Regan van der Rhys looked with shock at the figure of a woman standing on the bow of the specter-black frigate, her hand on the hilt of a cutlass, wild black hair streaming behind her, a smile of victory on her lips. His eyes went past her to the broken, tilting ship fast sinking some distance behind her. Cold blue eyes narrowed to slits as he watched the nearly naked woman who now made a mocking bow, her cutlass still grasped in her hand.

Regan stared, not seeing her as an adversary but as a woman. She had incredibly long legs, planted slightly apart; her hold on the rigging was secure, as was her grasp on the cutlass—as sure as his own. He glimpsed an angry red scar which ran the length of her upper arm. Her sensuous, reddened lips formed a smile, showing white teeth in her sensuous face. Mesmerized with the sight of her, Regan could only stare in surprise.

"To the victor go the spoils, Captain!" Sirena shouted over the wind.

"Only because I allow it," he returned her shout.

Sirena laughed, the gay musical tinkle that usually raised hackles on Caleb's neck.

"Till we meet again, sultry tigress!"

"And we'll meet again—and again and again," Sirena called in answer. Lithely she swung around to stare at the man as his ship plowed past toward the sinking *Wanderer*.

"A woman pirate!" Regan's crew said in awe.

"She's overtaken the *Tita* and dismantled her."

"Took her booty, no doubt."

Aye, Regan smiled, still thinking of her magnificent limbs, and temptress's face. Like a devil angel! There was no doubt in his mind he could have run her frigate broadside and drilled her with a cannon shot, laying her low and killing every hand aboard. But he was in a charitable mood.

The face of an angel! The tightening in his thighs relaxed and his nether regions again relaxed.

"Shorten sail," Regan called as the *Java Queen* quickly approached the fast-sinking vessel. "And man the rigging! All hands to secure the *Queen,* as we approach. We're in for a real blow!" he yelled to his first mate, who stood at the wheel.

Both ships rose and fell in the heavy waters, and boarding the *Tita* would be dangerous, Regan knew.

But, quickly throwing out ropes to secure her even while she pulled his own ship dangerously atilt, he leaped aboard the galleon and ran to the quarterdeck—where, sure as he knew it must be, were the initials of his lost son. The memory of their carving, and the boy's laughter, clouded his eyes with tears.

But even without the initials, Regan needed no further proof than seeing the familiar old galleon's lines—his father's design—and the arrangment of her rigging. She was like a lost friend—and a dying one now. Remaining no longer, he raced to regain the *Java Queen* and ordered his men to loose the *Tita* . . .

Now she was surely dead and gone; at least she soon would be. He wished the memories she aroused were equally dead.

Sirena took the wheel from Jan's sweating hands. He relinquished his hold on the hard wooden wheel gratefully. Where was she to get the strength to take this ship through the storm? he questioned himself. She was only a woman.

Caleb came to stand at Sirena's side as the Dutchman withdrew to the hold.

"Caleb, help the men secure the ship. Then come back here to relieve me when I tire. Tell the men to go below, I don't want anyone going overboard when I'm in command. Tell them," she smiled slightly, "that I personally guarantee they'll reach port alive and in one piece.'

"Aye, Sirena, I'll tell them," Caleb shouted above the mounting storm.

The wind howled in the rigging as Sirena steered the frigate under her close-reefed sails. She kept her bow pointed as near into the wind as possible, but never dead into the eye of the storm. Gigantic waves, whipped by the gale into curly white combers, rolled continuously from the west. Spindrift flew in flakes, stinging Sirena's face as she fought the wheel.

The holocaust demanded her full concentration. Hands gripping the stout wheel, which was almost as tall as she, Sirena stood erect and brazened the storm. Lightning flashed, illuminating the dark, spectral shapes of clouds scudding across the sky. Rain had not yet begun to pelt the decks, but it was out there before her, waiting for her. Sirena knew the rain was as much her enemy as its sister, the howling wind. She'd heard tales of helmsmen drowning while at the wheel, in the teeming, pouring wet—even though not a single breaker had dashed the decks. The rain could beat the strength out of a man, wearing and draining his vitality bit by bit, sip by sip, like a vampire draining the life's blood. It could choke off a man's air by driving in solid sheets, whipping up the nostrils and down the throat. The rain could pound a helmsman from the wheel and the wind could lure the ship onto a certain course of destruction.

Fearing the worst, Sirena grappled with a long length of sailcloth and lashed herself to the wheel with it. Now if she died, she would die at her post and her crew would know she had done all she could to save them.

Minutes seemed hours and hours seemed eternities. The storm was raging in full fury. Lashed to the wheel, Sirena, blinded by the savage downpour, kept her ship to its heading by instinct. Her body was battered by the elements, her hair beat against her face and twisted about her neck like insistent strangling fingers. When physical strength began to fail, an iron determination to survive became her mainstay.

Suddenly Sirena had a sense of her own magnificence: A woman alone, battling the elements which thundered about her, seeking her destruction. And in that moment of awareness she knew she would win. She was "conquistadora"—the conqueress, the winner, mistress of the seas, She knew herself to be unbeatable. She would survive, no matter what. Nothing, no one, could topple her. Not the rain, nor the storm, nor the sea. Not Dick Blackheart, not The Hook.

A renewed vigor seeped through her as she thought of Blackheart and his men. The sounds of thunder became the roar of the harquebusiers the pirates had fired from the rigging. The flashes of lightning became the quick sparks of rapier against rapier as they boarded the *Rana*. The tenacious pelting of the rain bruising her flesh became the rough, wounding hands of the pirates as they ripped her clothes from her and handled her body intimately. Groping, hurting fingers prodded her, searched her, tearing her flesh as they tore away her dignity. Her legs, her breasts, her most private parts laid bare to leering eyes and persistent fingers. The mournful howl of the wind became Isabel's shrieks of terror. The black hovering clouds were the dark hulking forms of those animals who had violated her, forcing themselves between her thighs as they sweated and grunted, straining for satisfaction.

Sirena bit her lip with remembered agony and tasted the rusty tincture of blood. She thought of other blood she had shed here on the deck of the *Rana:* the blood of her virginity.

The decks heaved with the force of the surf, the masts groaned with the weight of the saturated rigging. Rhythmically, like the rutting movements of her rapists, the *Rana* rose and fell as it rode the angry, swelling sea. Sirena's tears mingled with the rain, but hers were not the tears of the defeated. These were purging tears born of a renewed sense of indomitability. She rode the frigate from the trough to the crest of each swell. For moments she would ride dizzily on the crest, then ride down it steeply into the next trough. Each time she rode up to the next crest she felt buoyant and invincible.

Caleb crept out onto the deck to see how Sirena was faring. The men, experienced sailors all, were voicing their doubts as to how a mere woman, though she be their "capitana," could have the strength needed to ride out such a storm as this. Of the complainers, Wouter was the loudest. Only toothless old Jacobus exhibited complete faith in the Capitana, saying, "She's no mere woman, *that* one! She's driven by the Devil himself. She said she would get us to port, and she will or I'll be a landlubber's mother."

The wind buffeted Caleb against the quarterdeck rail, and only by taking a fast hold on the rigging was he able to pull himself laboriously across the deck to the ship's wheel. He saw Sirena lashed to the wheel.

She was drenched, her raven hair hung in thick slices.

"I came to help," Caleb shouted.

Sirena acknowledged him with a nod of her head, but never took her eyes from the sea swells. Inching his way between Sirena and the wheel, he braced himself against her and placed his hands on the laterals next to hers.

"Take the wheel, Caleb, head her steady onto the seas. An error on your part, allowing her to lay broadside on and broach to, will be the end of her." Tons of water suddenly crashed onto the frigate's decks from abeam, threatening to stove in her hatches. "Steady on, Caleb. Can you do it?"

"Aye, Sirena," he muttered through clenched teeth. He would do it if it killed him. How in God's name had she, a woman, rode this ship with no rest for three hours. Only minutes at the wheel and his arms ached fiercely.

For an hour Caleb steered the frigate with encouragement from Sirena who remained lashed to the wheel supplying him with needed support.

"It's over, calm waters ahead," Sirena shouted happily. "Didn't I tell you there was nothing to fear." Caleb massaged his aching arms and made a valiant attempt to smile. "You did well, little brother," Sirena laughed. "You did well."

Basking in her praise, Caleb went below to tell the men of Sirena's daring run with the ship. The men listened in awe as the boy spoke. Their pride swelled in their Capitana. All save Wouter, who remained silent, his mind racing with furious thoughts of bedding the near-naked witch he served under.

One day later, Sirena ran the frigate before the wind to northeast into the mouth of the Sunda Strait and an hour later between the looming volcanos.

Wearily, Sirena contemplated her first sea voyage as captain. She had done well. There was no doubt of that. The men would have no qualms about sailing with her again. Tired as she was, her thoughts flew to her husband as she remembered him standing on the bow of the ship as she herself had done. He had looked magnificent, all rippling, corded muscle. And when he smiled, her heart had fluttered madly. She had felt strange from the moment she laid eyes on him. He was so sun-bronzed his hair stood out like pure gold and his blue eyes had turned dark and . . . There had been a certain look about him, as if he desired her and wanted her right that very moment. She reveled in the thought and then instantly sobered. What would he think if he knew that she had been ravaged by Dick Blackheart's pirates and that the woman he had really contracted to marry was her dead sister?

Wouter stood on the foredeck and watched Sirena, below, mount the horse the boy held steady for her. The sailor's large, filthy hands caressed his loins as he stared intently till all three horses—the Capitana's, Caleb's and Jan's—were out of sight in the jungle.

Old Jacobus, who stood watching Wouter, remembered Jan's words that first day aboard: "Keep that leering Dutch bastard in sight at all times. He must not get near the Capitana!"

Nor *would* he! the old man vowed.

Chapter Eleven

Tired, yet still exhilarated, Sirena and Caleb dismounted and gave their two horses into the care of Jan Verhooch, who bid them a quiet goodnight in a clump of nutmeg bushes and rode westward, toward the rise, with orders for the men to return to their village and await her further word. They'd best stow away in the jungle—or leave on the ship, temporarily—some of the cargo they'd taken from the *Wanderer;* the villagers might suspect . . . and she wanted no word to leak back to Batavia of her activities. Not yet, at any rate.

She and Caleb walked the remaining distance through the fields of nutmeg and slowly crossed the lush gardens at the back of the mansion. It was a dark night; no one would spot them, she was sure. In minutes, both she and her "brother" had climbed the trellis and were standing in her room. Plates with the remains of food nearly five days' old sat just inside the door.

I must tell Juli to unlock the door to retrieve the plates from time to time, Sirena told herself. But she had done well . . . and can be trusted. "Frau Holtz will be surprised to see us, after our long 'retreat'!" she laughed.

Abruptly, she reached and squeezed the boy to her breast. "We made it, Caleb!"

The boy joined in her laughter. "I—I wonder where your crew think you come from? Only Jan knows for sure."

"They'll know when I want them to. Though they may one day learn—for I've many trips to sea to make, until I ruin Regan van der Rhys and find the man who ravaged poor Isabel with his hook *and* his body. When I come face to face with him . . . !"

Caleb walked tiredly to the door of his room—which adjoined Sirena's suite. "Good night, Sirena," he called back. "Rest well, my sister!"

Before retiring for the night, Sirena collected the dishes and food and hid them in her closet—Juli could dispose of the spoiled food and take the dishes down to the kitchen in the morning.

It seemed only minutes before the sunlight streamed through the windows of the bedroom to awaken her. She had forgotten to draw the shades! A moment later, a knock came at the door. It was to remind her that, outside, her breakfast awaited her—if she wanted it.

Leaping from the bed, refreshed and happy, Sirena surprised Frau Holtz by loudly unbolting and unlocking the door!

The woman stared, unbelieving. These Spanish—

who could stay five days in retreat for somebody long since dead and buried!

With the breakfast tray, the housekeeper handed Sirena a note folded and sealed with the emblem of the Spanish Crown. The Señorita tore it apart as she walked back to her bed, the Frau following her with her morning meal. Sirena turned abruptly, nearly upsetting the tray in the housekeeper's hands.

"I'm having luncheon with Señor Alvarez," Sirena announced.

The housekeeper, surprised, left the tray on a bedside table and left the room.

"Caleb! Caleb, come here!" Sirena called, and a moment later the door to the adjoining room opened and a sleepy-eyed boy appeared in nightclothes. "I'll be out much of the day, and I want you to study these maps of the reefs and shoals at the entrance to the River of Death." She pulled them from the back of the closet, where she'd placed them the night before, on her return from the *Rana*. "You should one day be able to navigate the channel as well as I. Also, study this chart of Java's western tip and the Sunda Strait." Then, suddenly, Sirena changed the subject. "Caleb . . . what do you think of Don Chaezar Alvarez? You've seen him frequently here at dinner or luncheon."

The boy opened his mouth to speak, but Sirena continued: "I find him most charming and gallant. But then all Spaniards are gentlemen. Not like these uncouth Dutch. He carries himself so regally . . . He doesn't stomp and clatter when he walks, and he smokes a most fragrant cigar. Not like Re— I find the Señor charming," Sirena repeated.

"Aye, Sirena, charming." Not for anything would Caleb say he much preferred Regan over the Spaniard. It was true, the Dutchman's words sounded rough and guttural to the boy's ear. But Chaezar Alvarez reminded him of a devil, with that pointed, manicured beard and mustache. Caleb preferred to see all of a man's face. What was the Spaniard hiding behind all that hair? A weak chin perhaps, something that would make him appear less a man?

Sirena gathered up the rolled charts and handed

them to Caleb. "Take these to your own room and be careful no one sees you with them. Remember, Caleb, that perhaps your knowledge of navigation will one day save our lives." At this ominous declaration Caleb left the room and Sirena continued with her toilette.

Sirena sat comfortably in Chaezar Alvarez's library, a glass of wine in her hand.

"May I say how lovely you look, my dear Sirena?"

"You may," Sirena said quietly but impishly.

Black eyes laughing at her reply, Chaezar stroked his pointed beard. Sirena looked at the man's dress. Elegant was hardly the word. He carried his height so regally. Sirena drew in her breath. He was so . . . so masculine.

"I find it . . . amusing that I can see my reflection in your boots," Sirena remarked.

Chaezar smiled, aware of her beauty and appreciating his effect on her. She really was a stunning woman, with remarkable bearing. Ah, he thought, these Teutonic barbarians didn't know how to begin to appreciate a woman like Sirena. They were only stirred by their lusty, Nordic cows with their pale coloring and white skin like the underbelly of a fish. But a woman like Sirena with her dark hair and dark nature could entice a man's imagination, stir him to new heights of passion. He had observed her, studied her, and he was positive that behind that cool, composed mask of good breeding and manners lurked a passionate, fiery nature capable of masterful cruelty. It was her suspected capacity for cruelty that aroused his lust.

"How is Regan these days? Busy as ever, I'll wager."

"To be quite truthful, I really don't know," Sirena replied as she sipped her wine daintily. "He has been away these past five days . . . where, I don't know. But why do you ask, Don Chaezar?"

Sirena listened to his voice which seemed to come from the depths of the man's broad chest. But while deep, it had a soft and crooning, almost soothing quality. Even after so short a time she felt at home in the Spaniard's house. The easy elegance, the soft tone of her native tongue spoken so easily, loosened her taut nerves.

"Yours is such a beautiful name, Sirena. It reminds me of soft, exotic things, rare flower petals, the tip of a bird's wing, a pinch of a cloud."

"How gallant, sir! But . . . you must remember that I am in mourning. My father, my uncle . . . And, I am now Mevrouw van der Rhys," she said softly. But she could just picture the mighty Regan trying to describe her name. He would probably say it was like the name someone would give a stray rooster. Ah, well, Regan wasn't here and Chaezar was.

"Sirena, I asked you here for a reason. And I mean to get right to the point. Where does your allegiance lie? I know that's a foolish question,—once a Spaniard, always a Spaniard—but I must hear it from you. There was no more loyal Spaniard than your father. Because you've married a Dutchman doesn't alter anything, does it?"

"Why . . . no," Sirena stammered. What did the man mean?

"I want to enlist your aid. As . . . allies . . . I feel that we could perhaps strike up a suitable bargain that would benefit both of us."

"Go on . . . Don Chaezar . . ."

"Before I do, let me tell you that I would never have invited you here and would not attempt to ask this alliance with you if I didn't know of the situation at your house— What I mean," he hastened to explain, "is I am aware that yours and Regan's is an arranged marriage. A marriage that he dislikes as much as you must. I am told you each have separate quarters. Regan has his . . . well, affairs . . . servants do talk," he said glibly, "I would assume, and correctly so I hope, that you have little love for the man. If you did, he wouldn't be running with every whore from Java to Sumatra."

"God in Heaven," Sirena murmured to herself. Did the man know what he was saying? Next thing he will offer to partake of my assumed virginity. The thought was so ludicrous that Sirena smiled. Chaezar, taking the smile to mean he should continue, did so.

"Right now, my dear, I find myself in a slightly

precarious situation. As you know I direct the inter-island shipping for Spain. Just as Regan does for the Dutch. For the past several years, the Dutch have attained the major foothold. I must outdo the Dutch, for then I will be able to return to Spain in honor. I would like to return a hero. For I do intend to return in the near future. This island life begins to fatigue me; I yearn for the court at Madrid. And, unfortunately, my life—that is to say, my accomplishments—has gained me thus far little prestige, it has been without *éclat,* if you will . . ." he said suavely.

"Regan and I have our little . . . rivalries. I take a little from him and he takes a little from me. I wound him a little and he wounds me a little. What can I say"—he shrugged his shoulders elegantly—"except that . . . if you could perhaps glean bits of information from him, such as departing ships, alternate routes . . ."

Sirena leaned back in the comfortable chaise and listened to his soft, crooning voice. She was hearing something she did not like. Not that Alvarez's competition with Regan surprised her, nor their schemings against one another. No. It was something else that angered her . . . and she was hard put to contain herself.

Slipping on a dressing gown, Sirena hastened to Caleb's room. She watched him for a moment as he made marks on his slate. His concentration was so great he didn't hear her enter the room. She called his name twice before he lifted his head.

"Caleb, I want you to go to the wharves and find out when Señor Alvarez sends out his next ship. Listen for any information that will be valuable to us. I've decided," she said coldly, "that we will take to the sea and ruin *him,* as well as the Dutchman."

"But—I— What happened to make you decide this?" Caleb asked hesitantly.

"Several things that don't concern you at the moment, little brother. Perhaps some of the fishermen or some of the little children will tell you things that we couldn't find out otherwise. It's close to the dinner hour, so you'll have to hurry."

Caleb looked into the green eyes and a chill ran up his spine. He hadn't seen that look on Sirena's face since those days on the *Rana*—the days she had forbidden him to speak of. He wondered what had happened to bring that look into them.

"Aye, Sirena. What if I should meet Mynheer van der Rhys? How shall I explain what I am doing asking questions about the Spaniard?"

"You'll tell him that since you have noticed how . . . interested I've become in the Spaniard you want to know more of him and his ship. Let the Mynheer believe you are on his side and mean to deter any friendship that might develop between Don Chaezar and myself!" she laughed.

Her recent conversation with Chaezar had both embarrassed and infuriated her. Had Regan actually made it common knowledge that he disliked their marriage? Regardless, Chaezar was assuming too much to repeat it to her! And all his talk about allegiance to home, mother country, forming an alliance . . . this had been only his method to win her over as a conspirator, a spy! He only wanted to use her! Sirena vowed she would never be used again, never put herself in the hands of a man whose only motive was to exploit her, either her body *or* her brain. Chaezar would have her be his instrument to attain his ends. Well, one day soon, he would discover that her sweet smile and gentle compliance were merely a sham.

"Does this," Caleb asked, "is this . . . something to do with . . . 'wily women'?"

Sirena's eyes lighted and she nodded curtly. She tossed Caleb a small bag of coins. "If you have to, give these to the men to loosen their tongues. I'll take the maps and the charts now. Tomorrow we shall again go over them together. Caleb, have you spoken to Regan since he returned today?"

"I passed him in the corridor and he was in such a black mood he did nothing more than nod. I spent time in the library hoping to overhear something, but no one has come near the house. I heard him shout to Frau Holtz not long ago. She appeared to be telling him something he did not want to hear. I couldn't make out the words but I could tell he was terribly angry."

Sirena's green eyes darkened as she stared at some invisible object above the boy's head. She knew well what angered Regan. Suddenly she smiled, much to the boy's discomfort.

He didn't like the look on her face nor did he like her smile. Suddenly he felt sorry for the Spaniard. What had he done to make Sirena turn on him? Whatever it was she wasn't going to confide in him. It was just as well. He already had so many things on his mind his head felt like a beehive. He had difficulty in remembering what he was to say and what he wasn't to say. If only he could go to sea and forget all this—what was the word Sirena had taught him—"intrigue." Intrigue and "wily women". . .

"Hurry, Caleb. When you return, join me in my room for dinner. I intend a ferocious headache and won't be able to bear the thought of dining downstairs with Regan. Report to me as soon as you return."

Back in her room, Sirena pulled a bell cord to summon Juli. She told the girl to serve them dinner in her room. Sirena saw Juli's curious look.

"I feel the ailment coming upon me," Sirena explained. "The one we Spaniards are so susceptible to. I wouldn't want to infect anyone. Once it takes hold, it rages unmercifully. It will be best if perhaps you knock and leave the meals outside the door, as you did these past days. But set them inside the door after a time has passed, and relock the door with your key. The next day, if I'm still not well, and the food is untouched, take the plates back down to the kitchen. Do not let them pile up as you did before. Do you understand, Juli?" The native girl nodded. Sirena raised a slim hand to her face and said wanly: "I feel very ill. You'd better hurry!"

Caleb returned to Sirena's room shortly before the dinnertime in a state of near-hysteria.

"What is it? Has something happened?" Sirena questioned anxiously.

Caleb was finding it difficult to get the words out.

"Aye, Sirena, at the wharf they speak of nothing but the woman who sank the *Wanderer* galleon. Everyone knows Regan wanted her for himself. They say the witch that captained the ship was barely interested in the cargo. All she wanted was to destroy the ship. Regan is in a fit of anger. The Spaniard smiles and says the Dutch are going to have a run of bad luck. The old fishermen say the black ship with the black sails was mystical. Regan's sailors are telling everyone how that, once he picked up the crew of the galleon, he pursued the black ship through the storm. It seems that they had just glimpsed the top of our sails when we disappeared off the face of the earth. They say you're an avenging angel."

"Disappeared off the face of the earth, did we?" Sirena cried jubilantly. "That must have been when we entered the mouth of the river!'

"Captain Kloss was boasting that Regan could have run you through and dismantled you in minutes if he had so desired. They say that he was in a charitable mood and smitten by your beauty."

"Never!" Sirena snorted. "Regan only said that to save face. What else was mentioned?"

"The Spaniard has sent two ships out to sea. They left less than an hour ago for Capetown. Both travel with a full cargo. The second galleon is escorted."

"What does she carry?"

"Silk and cloves. Very costly at this time of year."

"And Regan, what of . . . *him*—Regan?"

"The *Java Queen* leaves at dawn tomorrow. She'll be loaded to the top of the hold. She carries cinnamon, nutmegs, and cloves."

"To which port?"

"Straight through to Amsterdam, except for stopping at Enggano, off Sumatra, where Regan will disembark and return home in a fishing sloop. His plan is to see the *Java Queen* out of the waters where the female pirate lurks. And I heard Regan say the *Queen* comes back with an empty hold."

Quickly Sirena pulled the charts from the back of the closet. "If the tides are right we can leave the cove and river less than two hours from now. The *Rana* is light—and swift. We'll catch up with the Spaniard's ships, heavy as they are, not far beyond the Sunda Strait. This time we sail west, little brother! And after we attack and dismantle his ships, we can reverse course, and attack the Dutchman on our way home. It will be a tight schedule, but if the winds are in our favor it should work out well."

A knock sounded on the door and Sirena quickly thrust the charts and maps beneath the bed. "Who is it?" she called.

"It's your dinner," Frau Holtz called through the door.

"Very well, leave it. If I get hungry I'll bring it in. Leave me now, please, for I feel rather ill."

"Very well, Mevrouw."

There followed a loud clatter and much muttering. Sirena smiled at Caleb who was grinning openly. Just the thought of going out to sea again was enough to make him happy.

Suddenly Sirena unlocked and pulled open the door. "Frau Holtz," she said, holding her hand to her forehead in a weary gesture.

"*Ja,* Mevrouw," the housekeeper acknowledged, straightening her back from placing the heavily loaded tray on the floor outside the door.

"I have just spoken to my brother and he has agreed that we shall go into another retreat starting immediately. We've also decided to fast so there will be no need for you or Juli to bring food as often. The fasting will break this devilish ailment that has overtaken me. Don't concern yourself over my health. It's happened before and a few days of light fasting has always cured it. My brother will see to my needs. I also want to thank you for this sturdy bolt that was placed on my door. Remember, if you should knock there will be no answer. When we are in retreat we do not speak. It would defeat the purpose of the prayers. Do you understand me, Frau Holtz?"

"*Ja,* Mevrouw," Frau Holtz answered, her expression stating she didn't and never would.

"We'll eat now. This meal will sustain us till the end of the retreat. God go with you," Sirena sighed languidly.

Frau Holtz turned and left abruptly. "Heathen

ways," she muttered on her way down to the kitchen. But, then, what did she care? For all she cared the Mevrouw could retreat till the moon was again full. Her room could gather dust and mildew till it was rank with it. If Mynheer didn't care, why should she? Such a marriage! Never in her life had she heard of such a thing! She stomped her way into the kitchen and bit her tongue to keep from offering her complaints to the cook. Frau Holtz was not given to gossip concerning her employers.

I must inform the master, Frau Holtz thought, unable to keep still any longer. God knows what he'll say when he hears!

The housekeeper entered the offices occupied by Regan on the first floor of the house and spoke hesitantly: "The Mevrouw . . . has gone into a . . . retreat. She wants no food and she's bolted the door. Mevrouw said she will not answer any knock. Is she allowed to do this?"

"Is she allowed to do this?" Regan parroted her. "Of course she is allowed to do this! The Spanish do things differently. If Mervrouw wants to stay locked in her room to pray, then allow her to do so. What seems to be the problem, Frau Holtz?"

"Why—I—I—just thought that you should—"

"Know what is going on? My dear lady," Regan said coolly, "this will mean less work for the servants. You will obey my wife's wishes and leave her and her brother to their prayers. Just because we do not believe as they do doesn't mean we can't respect their wishes. I wish to hear no more about the matter."

"But, Mynheer, I worry about the bolt on the door."

"Perhaps she is afraid of you, Frau Holtz. And this is her way of keeping you out of her eyesight. Have you thought of that?" he teased.

"Why—I—"

"You are not to concern yourself with my wife's activities, is that clear," Regan said, his voice firm and controlled.

"Yes, I understand perfectly. Thank you, Mynheer."

Regan watched the housekeeper's retreating back, a smile on his face. She was disturbed. Perhaps it would do her good. Too long she had reigned over his domain like a dowager queen.

But a thought occurred to him. Who was Sirena keeping out of her room—Frau Holtz or himself? She need not fear him, he had other fish in the ocean. He would be charitable and leave her to her prayers. With luck she would pray for his soul. And perhaps for a safe journey.

His heart quickened momentarily—would he see the sea witch again? What would he do if she attacked his ship? He had never seen a more beautiful woman. The memory of those long, tawny legs haunted him. He drew in his breath at the thought of how she would bed. And there was no doubt in his mind that he would bed her!

Chapter Twelve

Caleb's eyes were apprehensive as he watched Sirena steer the frigate along the river. "At the most, you have a few minutes and the tide will ebb. Can you do it?" he asked anxiously.

"Have no fear, little brother, the *Rana* will make open water—and safely." Then her eyes turned from the wheel to look to the right of the ship—as did those of the men on deck. "One thing worries me, however. Sister Red, as you call her, there to the east. It is she against whose sides the *Rana* nestles, in our cove. Did you notice the warmness of the water surrounding the ship . . . and the red mist that hovers there, near her top, and around the mouth of the river?"

"Aye, the men have been speaking of it. It will make your passing through the channel doubly hazardous, Sirena."

Sirena laughed, the sound bouncing off the jagged

rocks of the red volcano's slopes. "I can see, have no fear. The mist is high."

The boy clenched and unclenched his fists as he watched Sirena, her stance sure on the slow-moving *Rana*. The men in the rigging had as much fear of passing the rocks as he did. But confidence returned as he watched Sirena's face. If she said they would reach the open waters safely, then they would. She had never been wrong before.

Sirena glanced down at the frightened boy beside her. And immediately the feeling returned—the feeling that she'd seen Caleb before, sometime in her past, further back than the time he'd signed on to her merchant fleet in Cádiz. Even his walk, she realized, was familiar; and the sultry eyes haunted her.

"Caleb," she said impulsively, "have you ever traveled in Spain?"

"I've only been in Cádiz, Sirena. Why?"

"It's . . . just that you seem so familiar to me—like someone I'd met before, not in Cádiz, for Father's house was not there but in Seville."

"The only time I've been in Spain is when your uncle so kindly rescued me from the *Lord Raleigh*, when he saw me being whipped aboard the English ship, and encouraged me to sign on with your fleet. I'd never visited your country before that time—though I'd learned enough Spanish through Carlos, the *Raleigh*'s cook."

Caleb threw back his head and laughed. "You seem puzzled, Sirena. I have never seen you in this mood. What is it about me that you don't understand?"

Sirena shuddered. The laugh! She had never heard Caleb laugh in quite that way. The way he threw back his head, and the sound of the laughter itself, was so reminiscent of someone . . . She wanted to reach out and touch the boy, thinking it would come to her. She forced herself to concentrate on the water and the slowly lowering thick reddish mist. "Open water ahead!" she shouted to the men on deck. "And not a minute to spare! Tighten sail."

Caleb breathed a heavy sigh of relief, as did

Sirena, when they had passed through the narrow channel at the rocky mouth of the river.

A shout of pleasure, and admiration, rose from the crew, and Jan came up to speak with her.

"Does the crew fare well?" she asked.

"Aye, Sirena. The booty from the last trip was quite enough for them. They have enough to last them the rest of their lives. As it is they lead a simple life, all their needs are for food and a little ale from time to time! They only want to be regarded as men again, save . . . Wouter," Jan said softly. "The man worries me—and he's ever been something of an outsider, Dutch though he is, and dismissed like all of your crew, from the same ship we once sailed. I would discharge him but I fear his tongue."

"He's not content with his share of the booty?"

"Those are his *words,* but Martin says his eyes say the meaning of the word 'booty' is not . . . 'goods'. He wants *you*, Capitana," Jan said bluntly. Sirena flinched. "Every seaman aboard keeps him within eye range. But he grows more hostile as the days go on."

"I've noticed, Jan. My gut does strange things when I'm forced to look at him. One of these days . . ."

Caleb's face drained as he imagined what "one of these days" might bring.

"But enough! I told them I'd play fair with them. I want no ill feelings among the men."

"Aye, Capitana. That would never happen. They say that you're the best captain they ever sailed under. The fact that you manage the straits almost makes you a sorceress in their eyes!"

Sirena acknowledged the compliment humbly, her eyes straining ahead of her. She turned to Caleb. "Get some rest, little brother. Soon you'll need all of your strength."

Sirena gripped the wheel as Jan left her, with the boy. Her hands were moist and clammy. On coming through the straits she had moments of misgiving. She would never again cut it so close. And of course all the expertise she possessed could not get a ship through those narrow waterways if the tide was low. One day, if in retreat from Regan or Chaezar, she found the river mouth shallow . . . She pushed the thought from her mind. Now the question was: Would she be able to attack and ravage both of the Spaniard's ships? The ship riding as escort with heavy cannon troubled her. She prayed that night would soon fall.

Clouds covered the night sky.

Excellent! Sirena thought. A black ship. The black night. If only we'd been able to depart sooner . . . Where are the Spanish ships?

"Sail ho!" came a muted cry from the rigging of the *Rana*.

Sirena picked up the spyglass and squinted into it. In the dim moonlight that filtered through a sudden break in the cloud cover, she saw them. Dead ahead at five knots, she estimated quickly. She lowered the glass in time to see Caleb poke his head around the wheel.

"Softly, little brother. Remember, your voice will carry across the water as clear as a bell. The brig sails in the second galleon's wake. I do not spy the first galleon, but who cares? We'll cripple the two behind and lower Alvarez's prestige as we lower their sails! But we must fire simultaneously. One shot broadside into each of them and they'll buckle. We'll have time for only the one shot so it must be true on its mark. We'll get no second chance. Pray God that the moon does not decide to peep out before the shots are fired. Now . . . silent as the dead, little brother."

Caleb nodded as he scampered off to give her orders. He was back in moments. "On your count of five we fire," he said softly. "Have no fear, Sirena, the shots will be true on their mark. All hands are on the quarterdeck."

Moments later, whispered orders passed from Sirena to Caleb, and down to Jan and his gunners. On the count of five a double roar split the night as the cannon shots found their mark. Sirena held the glass to her eye and watched men spill into the sea as others ran over the two ships' decks. Hoarse shouts of fear and alarm raged in the night.

The first rays of the moon lighted the night as the *Rana* ran broadside of the broken galleon. The brig was listing to starboard as its men leaned on the rail, not sure yet what had happened. "Take the wheel, Caleb. Steady as she goes."

Sirena raced to the bow, her cutlass hanging loosely in her hand. "Surrender!" she called, her voice high and clear, "and there will be no bloodshed. Shout for quarter and you can take to the jolly-boats!"

"It's the pirate witch," someone shouted. "We give no quarter! We sail with silks to Spain, our mother country."

"Your country's people need food in their bellies, not silks," Sirena shouted. "Silks are only to make fat merchants fatter. I'll count three and if you still call no quarter, you go into the sea. We fire on the count of three."

The heavy cannon fired on Sirena's count of three.

"Fools!" Sirena shouted. "Why didn't you listen? I don't speak to myself and to the open sea. You had your chance!"

The galleon was fast sinking. Sirena ordered her gunners to blast its jolly-boats with shot. Those proud merchantmen would feed the sharks! The men on the brig sent to escort the merchant ship, warriors that they might be, were now shouting, "Quarter! Quarter!"

"Move quickly, you have but minutes," Sirena yelled to the brig's crew as she swung down from the ship's wheel with the aid of the rigging. She raced to the *Rana*'s quarterdeck and leaned over, calling: "Is there a man among you who carries a hook for a hand? Think before you answer or a shot will go into your jolly-boats too, and you'll all be fodder for the sharks!"

"There's no man aboard the brig with a hook for a hand. And none that we know of on the galleon," came the captain's fearful reply.

"You lie!" Sirena hissed. "Show me your hands. I'll cut out your tongues if you're lying to me!"

"There's no hook among us," the man said bravely. "I give me word there's no man with a hook!"

"Tell me, have you ever heard of such a man?

But remember your tongue! A gaping hole in a man's face is nothing to be proud of!"

"I have heard of such a man. They say he killed the Dutchman's wife and may have stolen his son. That was the story years ago. Since that time, I myself have never heard of him." Confident now that his tongue would remain intact, the man boldly asked why she was seeking him out.

"That is *my* business, seaman! If you're fortunate enough to find yourself in a port, tell the story that I look for such a man, as does van der Rhys. I'll sink every ship I meet on the seas till I find the man. He'll be like the teredo worm. He'll emerge or his fellow seamen will kill him and send me his body."

"What if the Dutchman finds him first?" the man asked boldly.

Sirena laughed, the sound tinkling over the water like musical chimes. "Then I'll kill the Dutchman and take the man with the hook from him. The man with the hook belongs to me."

The sudden hush was proof that the men on the brig believed every word the woman said.

"I'm in a charitable mood, so cast off before I change my mind—as we women have a tendency to do!"

The seamen needed no second warning; they set the brig's jolly-boats adrift, pulling frantically at the oars and never looking back.

"Tighten sail and heave to," Caleb called from his stance at the wheel.

A smile played about Sirena's lips, amusement sparkled in her eyes. "Somehow those jolly-boats will get to port and I can imagine the stories that'll be told. No doubt they'll say how well they fought and how a quirk of fate gave me the advantage."

Caleb questioned her with his eyes as she returned to the wheel.

"I've no doubt their tale will fall on Regan's ears and he'll know my plan to comb these waters and sink every ship until I find The Hook! And Señor Alvarez," she grimaced, "when he learns about the sinking of one of the Spanish galleons—and the brig sent to protect her—I can imagine him pulling out his lovely, well-trimmed beard!"

A picture of Chaezar's naked face with a weak, trembling chin made Caleb laugh to the point of tears. After a few moments he asked, "The Mynheer . . . do you plan to attack him, too?"

"Of course!" She noticed the rueful smile Caleb gave her, and remembered his growing affection for Regan. "The Dutchman is expecting us, is he not? We wouldn't want to disappoint him! But we may already have passed Enggano—it is impossible to see in this gloomy night. So we must reverse course, to meet him before he reaches that isle: I want to attack the *Java Queen* while Grand Pensioner van der Rhys is aboard her. And that she's his own ship, rather than simply another Dutch vessel bound for home, will give me double pleasure in sinking her!"

Sirena turned, her eyes seeking her first mate. "Jan!" she called out, "you will come and take the wheel." Then, to Caleb: "You must remain out of sight, should we approach the *Java Queen* suddenly. As for me, I will rest a while out here on deck. The cabin is far too stuffy!"

"How do you fare, Jacobus?"

"Well, Capitana. I compliment you on your seamanship."

Sirena laughed. "And I compliment you on the food.'

The toothless old Netherlander grinned at her praise. "Capitana, a few years ago I served aboard a ship with a man with a hook instead of a hand. He was a villain and a cutthroat. But there is something you should know. He finally had a 'hand' carved for himself by a Chinese artisan. The hook fits into a sheath in the center of the "hand." When he wears a glove, as most seamen do to protect their hands from the rigging, you'd never know it was a wooden hand. I know this, Capitana, I've seen it with my own eyes when I served with him. I tell you this because it seems to be very important to you. When you search for the man with the hook, be certain you see a *bare* hand, not a gloved one."

Sirena gazed at the toothless old man. "Thank you, Jacobus, for telling me this. Someday I shall return the favor."

"There's no need. You already gave me my dearest wish, to feel useful again—and to be at sea. I couldn't ask for more."

"Would you . . . happen to know if the Dutchman knows of the false hand?"

"Mynheer van der Rhys probably does not know of the 'hand.' The attack on the *Tita* came eight years ago, before the villain had the 'hand' made. Though once it was fitted, he seldom showed his hook again. Unless he keeps *pirate* company these days, as he kept merchant company before!"

Sirena winced at the man's words, as memories flooded over her.

"I'm glad you told me this, Jacobus."

"Aye, Capitana."

Dawn showed in the eastern sky.

"Feed the men lightly this morning. No full bellies for what we have to do today," Sirena told the old man.

Once more Sirena lay back on the deck dozing. The rising sun soon caressed her body and a brisk breeze lulled her into a state of calm she hadn't felt for days.

"It is day," Caleb said, shaking her gently. "I gave the order to tighten sail and full speed. If your calculations are right, we'll make our contact with the *Java Queen* before noon."

Sirena was instantly awake and on her feet. "If we're successful, her cargo goes into the sea, remember that. I'll take the wheel from Jan now, till we spot their sail. Stay out of sight, Caleb, that's an order."

"Aye, Sirena."

A feeling of pity washed over him for the unsuspecting Dutchman. Surely she wouldn't kill him. Suddenly it was important to him that she not harm Regan. He wanted to run to her and beg her to show Regan mercy. Instead he remained quiet and fought the anguish that threatened to overtake him. The frigate sailed dead ahead in the rippling water, the ship secure beneath the woman's hands. When the cry of "Sail ho" came, it startled him so that his hands fell to his sides.

Sirena picked up the spyglass. It was the *Java Queen* and Sirena was looking at her broadside, dead ahead.

"She's sighted us. Fire into her stern and her bow. Hurry!"

A deafening roar thundered into the air. The *Rana* rocked and Sirena was thrown off balance. "Fire at once!" she ordered.

"We did, Capitana. See, she flounders. But she got off a shot and hit our bow."

"How much damage have we?" Sirena screamed, outraged that the Dutchman should have hit his mark.

"She can be shored up, Capitana. We take on little water but our progress home will be slow."

"We can't be held up, shore her up now. We're approaching the Sunda Strait, and if we lose time, the tides will shift. We'll not be able to enter the river mouth after our fight with the *Queen* and will be open prey for any ship on the sea. Heave to!" she called out.

Sirena squinted into the glass. Bright orange-red flames danced their way from the Dutch ship's bow to stern.

"There's no way the *Java Queen* can save herself, Capitana," Jan grinned, approaching the wheel. "She'll go into the sea with her cargo. Look! The men go into the jolly-boats!"

"I see . . ." Sirena said softly.

Where was her Regan? Yes, there he was, with the ship's captain, the last to go over the side. And just as he lighted into the ship's second jolly-boat an ear-splitting noise and a great billowing of smoke and flames above him made him look upward. A cannonball from the attacker had hit his ship's powder room! He stood in the small boat, his hands to his eyes—and murderous eyes they must have been, Sirena judged, for she could not see them clearly. This was his new ship's first voyage to Amsterdam and what bitter gall it must be for him to swallow, that she'd been sunk by the sea witch!

Then, all at once, she recalled her own ship's damage. "Bring us broadside," she shouted to Jan, who now took the wheel. With a lithe movement, Sirena ran to the bow of the *Rana* and surveyed the damage to the side of her ship.

"You'll pay for this, Dutchman!" she shouted hoarsely to be heard over the deafening roar of flames from the *Java Queen*. "You'll never again be so fortunate as to land a shot in my direction. I'll hunt you down and sink every vessel you send to sea. My patience is sorely tried at this moment, so answer me quickly: Is there any man aboard your jolly-boats that wears a hook for a hand?"

"If there were," Regan answered, "I'd have run him through long ago. I myself seek The Hook!"

"Which of us will succeed, Captain?" Sirena asked mockingly as she nicked the air with the tip of her cutlass. "I think," she said, driving the point of the cutlass into the deck, "that it will be me! It's said you've searched for three long years and as yet have no clue to his whereabouts. True or false, Dutchman?"

"True!" Regan snarled.

"Then you'd better give up. He's mine! Have your men show me their hands. Quickly now, or I'll order a shot fired into your jolly."

"Obey the 'lady,' " Regan ordered the captain and crew members mockingly. The men held out their hands, looks of fear on their faces.

"You—you—and you!" Sirena roared, pointing the tip of her cutlass at three of the men in the tiny boat below her. "Remove your gloves and roll up your sleeves."

"What's this?" Regan demanded, his eyes narrowed into slits.

"I feel sorry for you, Captain, so I'll tell you a little secret. The man with the hook wears a false hand. He wears a glove to cover his deformity. What say you now, Dutchman? You'll have a long time to think about that on your sail across to Sumatra in the jolly-boat!"

Regan's eyes roved the crew sitting in the jollys. All the faces were fearful yet none uttered a word.

Sirena chuckled. "Let me be the first to console you on the *Java Queen*. It's a pity she didn't reach port. But don't feel badly. This morning at dawn I sunk two Spanish ships, a galleon and a brig. The brig's men are in the same position as you. Perhaps you'll meet them on the way to the island. You'll have much to discuss. Until we meet again, Captain," she said, giving him a low, mocking bow. Her cutlass found its way into the belt at her waist as she grasped the rigging and swung herself to the quarterdeck. "Heave to, men!" she called, "tighten sail and full speed dead ahead. Have a safe journey, Captain!" Her tinkling laugh raced across the waves and came back to grate against Regan's ears.

"Bitch!" he shouted hoarsely, his eyes fiery.

" 'Bitch' am I? Several moments ago you called me 'lady.' Are Dutchmen always so vacillating? Before I'm finished with you you'll have exhausted your vocabulary to aptly describe me." She added strength to her words with a sweeping gesture of her arm that widened the gap of her loosely buttoned shirt and exposed even more of the dark cleft between her full breasts.

Noticing Regan's attention shift from her face to her bosom, Sirena smiled wickedly. Men, she thought disgustedly, could be diverted by the sight of heaving breasts and a shapely thigh, even in the face of losing an empire.

Regan recovered himself and feigned hatred at the lovely sea witch. He had lost his ship at the hands of a woman but his masculine ego shielded him from the full impact of her victory. It was even possible for him to feel a faint amusement. "We'll meet again, and next time *I'll* have *you!*" he boasted.

Sirena's laugh rippled over the water and reached him.

Unconsciously, he stiffened, suppressed rage roaring in his ears.

"Have me, will you? And if you *could* have me, even now, this minute, what would you do, Dutchman! Whisper sweet endearments, caress me with your sea-callused hands"—she shuddered delicately, her eyes sultry, her red lips teasing. "And your mouth, Dutchman, what would you do with your mouth? Swear obscenities at me or kiss me and tantalize me. Would you kiss me here?" She pointed to her neck. "Or here?" Her finger moved to her breasts. "Or here?" Her hand touched her mouth lightly.

Regan turned abruptly to escape her teasing—hating

her, wanting her, and wanting to kill her, yet knowing every word she spoke was true. The hackles rose on the back of his neck; she was laughing again, laughing at *him!*

As the *Rana* pulled away from the sinking *Java Queen,* Sirena felt a bit queasy in her heart. The Sumatra shore, sixty or seventy miles away, was visible only by virtue of the immense mountains that fringed its southwestern shore. She hoped, despite herself, that Regan and his small company would reach the shore in their two craft. Nevertheless, she mused, the sea is calm . . .

"Shore up this bow and heave to, men!" she called out abruptly, leaving her thoughts behind her. "We've taken on too much water as it is. Bastard!" she yelled back at the tiny figure in the jolly-boat, "how did you manage to get off a shot at me?" Then: "Caleb, and Jan, were our gunners at their stations?"

"Aye, Capitana," Jan Verhooch answered. "The *Queen* had time for only one shot and I think it was blind. She didn't have time to do more than merely sight us. It was a lucky shot, I'd say, Capitana."

"I want no more lucky shots!" she growled, then asked soberly, "How much time do you think we have to make it through the strait and to the mouth of our river before the tide turns?"

"We'll have an hour to spare, Capitana," the Dutch first mate replied, cheerful and smiling.

Sirena's mood softened. "Well . . . our men did themselves well, this day. When the ship is secure and we're berthed in the cove, have Jacobus bring the ale on deck. A celebration is in order!"

Sirena left Caleb at the wheel and the crew to their work of shoring up the bow of the *Rana.* She went to her cabin to quell the trembling which was threatening to overtake her. She threw herself on her bunk and tried to renew the feelings of jubilance over her victory. Instead a dread seeped into her bones, the dread of discovery. She had met Regan twice on the seas and twice she had cost him dearly. Neither time had he shown any recognition of her identity. But in this last meeting he had had a closer look at her, and they had argued. Had she given herself away? Or would recognition dawn on him the next time he met with her as his shy, introspective bride? If he did comprehend her identity what would he do? A vision of strong, capable sun-darkened hands flashed before her. She gagged, so vivid was the illusion of those hands closing about her throat.

Chapter Thirteen

Safe in her room late that same morning, the charts in their hiding place beneath the bed, Sirena breathed a sigh of relief. "Go to your room, Caleb. Our retreat and fasting is over."

The boy walked to the door, his shoulders slumped. "What is it, Caleb? Something is bothering you. Tell me now so I can relieve your mind."

"Regan in the jolly-boat. What if a storm comes up? What will happen to him?"

"There will be no storm. What kind of seaman are you that you couldn't tell by the winds."

"Perhaps a squall?"

"The jolly-boat could ride out a squall and you know it. Rest easy, little brother, Regan will be home by this time tomorrow. He was on a well-traveled route."

"There'll be no living with him when he returns," Caleb muttered.

"You speak the truth. Are you worried?"

"For myself, no. What if he should take his vengeance upon you?'

"Why me? I have been locked safely in my room. Rest, little brother, you're as tired as I am. Tomorrow is another day."

Sirena bolted the door, lay down on the bed, and was instantly asleep. She dreamed of a sun god smiling at her mockingly.

She awoke to a knock at the door. "Who is it?" she called.

"Frau Holtz, I have your breakfast tray." The housekeeper was surprised to receive an answer to her knock.

Sirena remembered the condition of her hair and the spray of the spindrift on her skin. "Leave it, please. I wish to bathe first. Have one of the girls bring water. Then I will breakfast."

"Very well, Mevrouw." Frau Holtz hastened below to order Juli to carry water to the Mevrouw's chambers.

The little maid soon trudged down the corridor, the pails grasped tightly in her hand. Once inside the room, she glanced at her mistress. Juli was shocked at Sirena's condition. The wild unruly hair cascaded down her back and white flecks glistened on her face. Was this the ailment? To Juli it looked like the spindrift that settled on one's skin when one was out at sea. How could the Mevrouw's hair have become so matted and straggly just sitting in her room? What kind of ailment was it? Fearfully she backed from the room, the pails knocking against each other.

"Bring more water! Have someone help you. You're much too small to be carrying those heavy pails. I need at least six more. I wish to wash my hair."

"Six?" bleated the little maid.

"Six," Sirena said firmly. "The ailment has to be washed away so I do not get reinfected."

Juli was skeptical as she scurried off. Back in the kitchen, she repeated the happenings and the Mevrouw's orders to a fellow servant. Unknown to her, Frau Holtz stood quietly listening.

". . . It looked like the spray of spindrift. Her hair was matted and tangled. It must be a fearsome ailment. Who'll help me with the water? She says I am too little," Juli prattled on to the alert cook.

The housekeeper now stepped from behind the door that led to the dining room, where she had hidden to overhear anything Juli might say.

"Get a djongo to carry the rest of the water! You stay here in the kitchen. You can start by peeling the potatoes and then slice cabbage," Frau Holtz ordered, interrupting the intolerable gossip.

Frau Holtz stood outside the door of Sirena's room when the djongo left with his empty pails. She waited till he closed the door before she spoke.

"Is it true the Mevrouw's skin is covered with a substance much like spindrift?" she asked craftily.

The houseboy shook his head. "I heard it said below that she suffers from some rare Spanish ailment," the boy replied, eager to please the stern housekeeper.

"And is her hair in disarray?"

The boy nodded.

Frau Holtz was in deep thought. She must speak to the doctor when he next visited the house. Surely he would know of this strange ailment. *If* it was an ailment!

The days dragged on and Regan had not yet returned. Caleb went to the quay every day to see if there was news of him. The wharves buzzed, for many knew that Mynheer van der Rhys had intended to leave his ship at Enggano and soon return home to Batavia. The crews, especially those loading and unloading the Dutch ships, were alive with worry. Each day Caleb would return to Sirena, dark questions in his eyes.

Sirena found it hard to comfort the boy. "And the Spanish crew, has there been news of them?"

"No, and I couldn't ask questions for fear I would give us away. What do *you* think happened?"

"I have no idea. But rest assured, little brother, Regan would never let the sea get the better of him. I would imagine he washed up in some cove or inlet on Sumatra and is waiting there for a ship of rescue."

The boy seemed dissatisfied with her obvious confidence and lack of concern.

"I see by the look in your eye that your next question is: Why don't I take the *Rana* to sea and pick him up." Sirena laughed.

"Don't tease me, Sirena. I would have never thought to ask you that."

"Then I won't have to refuse you. Regan will return, have no fear."

Two days later at the noon meal, Sirena heard the furious pounding of horse hooves. She looked out the wide windows in time to see Regan dismount from his horse. Turning, she smiled at the expression on Caleb's face. The boy's relief was unrestrained. He rushed out of her room and down the wide staircase, Sirena fast on his heels.

Regan stood framed in the doorway. He had a week's growth of beard and his blue eyes stood out starkly in his coppery face. His clothing was tattered, his shirt hanging in strips from his titan shoulders. The golden hair on his broad chest matched the stubble on his chin. A magnificent figure of a man, a very angry man, Sirena thought.

"Frau Holtz!" he thundered.

The housekeeper emerged into the front hallway, a look of fright and awe on her face.

"Bring water up to my quarters and food. Caleb," he said, piercing the boy with a steady stare, "follow me. I have an errand for you. With your permission, Sirena," he said, disregarding her shocked expression.

Sirena nodded and the boy followed Regan without a backward glance.

"What—what happened that you look like this, Mynheer?" Caleb questioned in a quivering voice.

"If I told you I doubt if you would believe me. Remember the promise I made you that I would let you sail on the *Java Queen?*"

"Yes."

"I must break that promise to you. The *Queen* was sunk, by . . . she was sunk! I won't bore you with the details, they aren't pretty. I want you to go to town and leave messages for those that I tell you. You'll tell them they are to come here for dinner this evening. We shall have a party to celebrate the loss of the *Java Queen* and her cargo," he said bitterly, once in his room, as he ripped the rags from his back. "I have a feeling in my gut that this is only the first of many ships that I'll lose."

"Who . . . was it a pirate ship or just some wild marauder?"

"It was a pirate all right, the likes of which I've never seen," Regan said grimly. "I don't understand why it happened. The *Java Queen* was destroyed, her cargo lost into the seas. There was no reason for it. Not only did I lose the *Queen,* Don Chaezar Alvarez, I . . . learned, lost two ships also by the same . . . pirate!" A knock sounded on the door, interrupting him.

A maid and one of the boys carried steaming pails of water and carefully poured them into a large tub in the corner. "Fetch twice as much," Regan ordered. "It will take hours to wash away the filth and the stench."

"Caleb, go to my offices. On the desk is a list. You will go to each of the persons inscribed on the list and ask them to come here for dinner. Tell them I will not take no for an answer. Before you do that tell Frau Holtz that there will be sixteen at table. Tell Sirena I wish her, of course, to attend and to act as my hostess. Speak to me when you return."

Caleb scampered away to do Regan's bidding. He found Sirena and quickly explained his errand. A chill ran up his spine at the smile she gave him.

"Then go now and do the master's bidding. I will tell Frau Holtz about the dinner. *I* wish a full report, too, on your return," she said in a voice ringing with steel.

"You'll have it, Sirena," the boy said, taking his leave.

Sirena found the housekeeper in the pantry. "There will be sixteen guests for dinner, Frau Holtz. Have the cook prepare a full-course dinner." And she said ominously, "I want no sour cabbage served at the table. I think perhaps . . . some rice, properly spiced of course, and . . . a whitefish baked in cream sauce. I'll leave the choice of vegetables to you. For a sweet, I think perhaps some dates and figs in a thick syrup with some heavy cream.

"But . . . Mynheer . . . prefers the sour—"

"I have just told you what to prepare. You'll see to it immediately. And from now on if you cook your sour cabbage for my husband, do *not* make a portion for my brother and myself. In Spain we feed it only to the swine. In a while, I myself will come into the kitchens to inspect the cook's progress. I would hate to see any last-minute disasters. One other thing: you will have the cook serve a fruit-flavored wine."

When Sirena left her, Frau Holtz's face was a purplish red. The housekeeper made her way to the kitchen and, in a voice choked with venom, she gave the cook the order to prepare the food Mevrouw had ordered. Grimacing, the cook accepted the change in menu and ordered a sack of rice to be brought upstairs from the pantry.

"The . . . Mevrouw . . . wants spices and herbs in the rice."

"Then she shall have spices and herbs," the cook said calmly, and Frau Holtz was aware of the woman's satisfaction. For years Mella, a Malayan, had rebelled against the bland German food she was made to prepare. Tonight, thanks to the Mevrouw, she would have an opportunity to display her true creativity.

Sirena returned to her room, where she patiently waited for Caleb. When, hours later, Caleb burst into her room, his face was wreathed in smiles.

"I did just what Mynheer said. Every person is coming to dinner. Even Frau Lindenreich is attending—with Señor Alvarez. She was at his house when I went there and she pouted so that the Señor said he would bring her."

"Is there any talk at the wharf?"

"I don't know. I heard nothing myself. There was no time for me to stand around and ask questions."

"Did you come to me first or have you reported to Regan?" Sirena asked, her voice nonchalant.

"I came to you first, Sirena. I must go now and tell Regan what I accomplished."

"You did well! Go to Regan so I can go to the kitchens and see how my evening meal is progressing. I have a surprise for you tonight."

"What?" Caleb asked, his eyes lighting inquisitively.

"There will be no sour cabbage tonight."

The boy sighed. "I am glad! Boiled meat, boiled

vegetables, boiled cabbage! Ugh! As bad as the food aboard the *Lord Raleigh!*"

Sirena followed the boy's departure and descended to the kitchen. Her entrance caused a stir and the servants stopped what they were doing, looking at her in awe.

"Continue as before, I merely wish to see how the meal progresses." She sniffed delicately as the cook stirred first one pot and then another. Sirena nodded her approval as she walked around the kitchen. "And the fish, have you boned it?"

"Yes Mevrouw. I myself boned the filets," Mella answered. "I added a few herbs and some butter—along with a touch of lemon."

"My mouth waters. I wish to thank you for following my directions."

"Mevrouw, you've only to ask and I'll prepare anything you wish. I added some cloves and cinnamon to the dates and figs." Sirena smiled her thanks at the cook.

"You seem pleased with yourself, Mella. Something tells me you'd rather cook like this than boiled cabbage." The roly-poly Malayan cook smiled brightly, white teeth sparkling in her nut-brown face. "Perhaps you'd like to cook especially for my brother and myself every night. If you've the time . . . we'd greatly appreciate it."

The cook's delight was evident in the way she went about her business, a watchful, victorious eye out for the door—and Frau Holtz.

"I'll make you anything! In the morning have Frau Holtz send Juli with your breakfast orders, and I will prepare it for you."

Sirena nodded and left the kitchens. The cook looked up to see Frau Holtz standing in the doorway.

"You have enough work cooking for the Mynheer," the grim housekeeper said. "Where do you expect to gain the time to prepare another set of meals. You will forget what she has just said and do as I tell you."

"But—the—Mevrouw—"

"*I* give the orders in this kitchen! You will do as I say, and only as I say. Is that understood?"

Sirena, her back against the wall outside the kitchen door, quietly opened the door and stood, her hands on her hips, her green eyes glittering angrily.

"You take it upon yourself to countermand an order that I have given? How dare you? *I'm* mistress of this house! You will do as *I* say. And I say you will follow me to my husband's quarters and we shall straighten this matter out immediately. You too, Mella, I want you to hear what my husband has to say."

No sooner were the words out of her mouth than she regretted them. This certainly wasn't the time to confront Regan, when his mind was no doubt occupied with the pirate woman! Especially after their last meeting at sea! Pulling the lacy mantilla closer about her cheeks, Sirena made a conscious effort to control her anger against Frau Holtz. Regan must not see any resemblance between his saintly wife and the bold, fire-breathing piratess.

Down the hall they marched, three women at odds. Standing outside his study door, Sirena gulped a deep breath and willed her voice to a sedate tone free of the anger knotted in her breast. Then, before she could change her mind, she rapped sharply on the door and was told to enter.

"I have a problem," Sirena said coolly, "I'm afraid only you can solve it, Mynheer. Am I mistress of this house or is Frau Holtz mistress?" Her voice was softly modulated, her eyes lowered in humility.

Regan stood up from his seat next to the window, his eye narrowed. "You're mistress, of course. What is the problem?"

"I issued orders to the cook and Frau Holtz countermanded my orders."

"What sort of orders?" Regan asked testily.

"I asked the cook to prepare separate meals for Caleb and myself. But," she added, "only if she had the time to do it. Cook answered that she would be glad to prepare such meals for us."

Regan's eyes clearly stated he wished himself elsewhere. "Cook has agreed, then why do you come to me?"

Sirena's heart fluttered madly. Regan was looking straight at her, a glimmer of admiration behind his penetrating, blue stare. To her relief there was no hint of recognition.

Confidence restored, Sirena went on, more boldly. "We came to you because . . . Frau Holtz told the cook not to prepare our meals. She told Mella there was enough to do without cooking for my brother and myself. Please settle the matter for us, Mynheer," she said softly, her voice controlled.

"You defied the Mevrouw," Regan said to the German housekeeper, his face a mask of fury. "Why," he shouted angrily, "why in God's name does this have to come up now, when I've other things on my mind? . . . Well, are you going to answer me?"

"I did not think, I— It seemed to me the cook had plenty to do with three meals a day without making extra work for her."

Regan pierced the Malayan with a cool eye. "And what do *you* have to say? Do you mind the extra work? Will this cause you any problem in the kitchen?"

The cook shook her round head, her lips betraying a smile. "Mynheer, I told the Mevrouw I'd be glad to cook for her. She asked me first if it would be too much trouble. I told her no."

"The matter is settled then. You will prepare whatever my wife wants."

The cook and the housekeeper left the room, Sirena in their wake. She was almost at the door when Regan spoke: "I've heard it said that the Spanish are effusive in their thanks when a favor is granted them." Sirena watched him, her eyes cool and aloof. She said nothing. "Well?" he continued, prodding.

"That was a favor . . ." Sirena raised an eyebrow, making the statement a question. "I don't consider it a favor, Mynheer. Frau Holtz should have been told, much earlier, that I was mistress and she was to obey me. You did me no 'favor.' Had you denied my claim, however, I would have found ways to have myself and my brother invited to Don Chaezar Alvarez's house to dine."

"You would have done that?"

"Of course. I wish no tension in this house. Since

you're the master I would think you would control the servants—not the other way around."

"What is that supposed to mean?" Regan shouted.

"I apologize. In Spain we do things differently," Sirena said softly, bowing her head so that the mantilla hid her face in a shadow. "I must constantly remind myself where I am." She couldn't resist adding impishly as she turned, "I wonder how it feels to have a paid servant issue orders and have them obeyed by the master."

"No such thing happens in my house," Regan said briskly as Sirena closed the door.

Or does it? he raged within himself. His last encounter with Frau Holtz vivid in his mind, he flushed as he rang the bell to summon her once more to him.

Regan stood at the woman's entrance. "Listen to me carefully, Frau Holtz, for I shall not repeat this again. You will do as the Mevrouw says. She is mistress of this house. I told you once before that you take much upon yourself. Things are different now that I'm married. I don't wish to be bothered with the household management. If there are any problems you will go to the Mevrouw. I want none of this backbiting and tattling. If this should happen again I will have to discharge you. I wouldn't like to do that as you have given my family loyal and efficient service over the years. The matter is ended."

"Very well, Mynheer."

Sirena dressed carefully for the dinner party, choosing a new—and sedate—black gown.

Caleb knocked and entered, his face a big smile. "I can hardly wait to eat!"

"Tell me, what sort of mood was Regan in when you returned to him."

"Angry, I've never seen an angrier man. He wouldn't tell me who sunk the *Java Queen,* he just said it was jettisoned along with her cargo. But I know he can't make any sense of it! He also said he had a feeling in his gut that this is only the first of many ships that he'll lose. Then he said the Spaniard, Alvarez, lost *two* ships. What do you suppose will happen at dinner? Why this last-minute party?"

"There will be only one topic of conversation this night. I actually feel sorry for Frau Lindenreich and the other ladies! They won't get much attention. The men will be preoccupied with the fortunes they've lost and those they might lose in the future. It will be hard to keep a straight face." Sirena laughed. "Be sure you don't correct any mistakes they may make."

Sirena came downstairs just as the first guests arrived.

In the drawing room, moments later, glasses of wine were served and small sweets. Sirena declined both and settled herself next to the loquacious Helga. They spoke of the good lady's charges at the mission and the warm, balmy weather.

Sirena leaned closer to Helga after a few minutes and asked softly, "Why are the men in such a state this evening? My husband tells me nothing of business affairs. I assume it is business they discuss."

"I don't know. The invitation, or should I say 'summons,'" Helga amended, "came this afternoon. It must be serious—whatever it is. Regan rarely invites anyone at the last minute like this. But I see that Frau Lindenreich is here. Perhaps I'm wrong and this is just a social gathering after all."

"She's the guest of Don Chaezar Alvarez. Since the Señor is unmarried he supplies his own partner."

"Quite, quite," Helga replied as she marveled at the deep cleavage exposed by Gretchen's shimmering red gown. The vast expanses of creamy skin drew more than one man's eyes in her direction.

Sirena's hot, Latin temper raised her temperature several degrees and Gretchen's chameleon-like eyes swept over toward her several times, the corners of her mouth curved into a smirk. Sirena knew Gretchen felt she surpassed the Spaniard in the drab, black gown. When Gretchen clawed at Sirena with her glance, the blonde's eyes would afterward sweep over Regan in a caress. Only the memory of the flaming desire burning in Regan's eyes for the long-legged scantily clad piratess kept Sirena from slapping the smirk from Gretchen's too-red mouth. Furthermore, the handsome widow was receiving too much attention as it was. And if the wanton German moved too suddenly the shimmering red gown would slip even lower and reveal *all* of the cow's udders!

Dinner was announced. In the dining room Sirena was pleased to note large silver bowls of flowers at each end of the table, the candlelight reflected in the mirror surface of the metal. There was much scraping of chairs and appreciative low-voiced comments as the djongos began to serve the meal.

Sirena looked at Caleb, who was holding his breath in eager anticipation as a servant filled his plate. It was all Sirena could do to contain her mirth at the hunger in the boy's eyes. After the first course of consommé the tempting rice and baked fish were served. The vegetable was to be served next. What had Frau Holtz decided upon? The emerald eyes were pinpoints of flame as they sought out the housekeeper standing aloof in the corner, her eyes on the servants. Cabbage! How dare she?

Sirena spoke softly to the servant ladling out the cabbage. "There has been a mistake in the kitchen," she apologized to the guests. "Remove the cabbage and bring the other vegetable."

Regan watched Sirena's eyes seek out those of Frau Holtz. He was amazed to see the anger emanate from the housekeeper and from his wife as well.

The cook must have been intuitive, for within minutes a large steaming bowl of peas with onions was being served.

"An excellent dinner, Señora." Chaezar smiled. He looked around at the assembled guests and they added their approval. Even Regan had emptied his plate and seemed satisfied.

The meal over, the ladies settled themselves in one corner of the drawing room and the men in the other. At a signal from Sirena, Caleb joined the group of men.

Sirena tried to keep up her end of the conversation but found it difficult as she strained with one ear to hear the men's discussion. Her eyes traveled from time to time to the voluptuous Gretchen. She was a beautiful woman and was fully aware of her effect on the men as well as the women. Feeling Sirena's eyes on her, she turned and spoke. "How do you like our island by now?"

"I find it quite beautiful, Frau Lindenreich," Sirena replied graciously, her voice low and controlled.

"And our men, Mevrouw, what do you think of these tall virile Dutchmen?" Her eyes fell possessively on Regan.

Sirena pondered the question a moment as all the ladies' eyes swung in her direction.

"I really haven't had time to meet any of these . . . virile men you speak of save my . . . husband. I do however find Señor Alvarez enchanting." Her voice was a rich purr as Sirena met Gretchen's glare.

Helga raised merry eyes to Sirena and laughed. "I understand that Señor Alvarez plans a ball in a few weeks' time. Every one on the island will be invited. Even those merchants from the inner islands."

"I doubt Chaezar will hold the ball now," Gretchen said coolly.

"Why is that?" Helga asked.

"Don't tell me you're not aware of what's happened! Chaezar told me on the drive here that there's a woman pirate who has been robbing and plundering his ships. Regan's, too! I hardly think anyone will be in a festive mood for a time. Nor will Chaezar be able to afford a lavish party, considering the loss of his cargo."

"What else has he said, Gretchen?" Helga demanded, her eyes dancing.

"Chaezar lost two ships. A galleon and a brig which rode as escort. He himself wasn't aboard, but Regan *was* on his *Java Queen*. This devil of a woman blasted his ships fore and aft and left the cargo to sink into the sea. She told Regan she searches every ship she meets till she finds someone she is searching for. A man with a hook for a hand."

Sirena lowered her gaze to her folded hands. "And the men, Frau Lindenreich, why didn't the men fight back? I find it a mystery that a woman could prevail against our formidable seamen."

"Chaezar says his men said they hadn't a chance. She captains a ship whose hull and sails are as black as the night. She attacked under cover of darkness. And," Gretchen said, her voice rising, "this female buccaneer disappeared as if the ocean swallowed her up near the Sisters of Fire."

"The Sisters of Fire?" Sirena asked, lowering her lids to hide the excitement dancing in her eyes.

"That's what the natives call them. Actually they're two volcanos. Surely you've seen them from the garden. Their purple peaks are as bleak and ominous as shrouds."

A few of the ladies gave involuntary shudders, their complexions paling perceptibly. Earth tremor had increased in the past weeks and there were reports of sulphurous gases. Volcanos were a very unpopular topic on Java.

"Don't pay any attention to them, Sirena," Helga clucked. "Not in anyone's memory have the Sisters erupted. It's just a lot of silly prattle the natives drum up. Though it seems"—she scolded her neighbors—"that many otherwise sensible colonists' wives believe it!" She cast a scornful glance in the direction of the frightened ladies. "And, I'll admit, mention of the volcanos is enough to shock even some of our brave men into silence. The most the Sisters have ever given us, however, is some earth tremor and a hearty pelting of hot stones. We've never suffered the devastation and the spewing of lava that Krakatoa wreaks, out there on the southern tip of Sumatra where she sits like some angry god! . . . Well, we Netherlanders—as well as you Spanish—are a stubborn lot! No sooner have the Sisters sighed their last angry rumble, than the debris and stones are cleared away and whatever was damaged or burned is restored. But enough about the fiery Sisters! Gretchen, what else do you know of this adventuress?"

Gretchen, annoyed with Helga's interruption, was glad to be the center of attention again. "Regan said she headed for the straits after she came upon his ship and sank it. But she allowed him and his captain and men to go into the jolly-boats. Regan said he got off a shot into her bow, first, but her seamen shored the frigate up and she made her getaway. Regan said she's like no other woman he's ever seen, and," Gretchen lowered her voice conspiratorially, "the piratess captains her ship nearly naked. She wears rags and her breasts are nearly exposed and her legs are part bare! One of Chaezar's men says she has a wicked scar that runs along her arm. A scar, vicious-looking and cruel!"

"Don't you . . . exaggerate, Frau Lindenreich?" Sirena asked skeptically.

"When the men join us, ask for yourself. Listen: It's all they can speak of. Chaezar said Regan is mesmerized by the woman and has given her a name. He calls her the Sea Siren!" Gretchen's tone was malicious as she pierced Sirena with a cold, haughty look.

"I've never heard of such a thing! A woman! How can a woman captain a ship and do all these things without being caught?" Helga argued.

"She's like a devil. She attacks at night and, as I said, her ship and sails are as black as midnight."

"Does anyone know why she searches out this man with a hook?" Helga asked.

Gretchen shook her head. "Regan, himself, searches for such a man. *As* we all know . . ." she said, her eyes dark and fathomless. "He holds the swine responsible for his wife's death." Thoughts of The Hook brought the *Tita* to mind, and Gretchen hastened to continue. "You all know the story of the *Tita,* and Regan's feelings for the vessel, and how little more than a week ago she was sighted in harbor at Sumba. Regan set out with the *Java Queen* to find the old ship and met the Sea Siren instead! She'd beat him there and sank the *Tita* before his eyes! What do you say to that?"

The ladies had heard much of the tale before, but the telling of it once more added enjoyment—and a certain fear—to their evening at the van der Rhys home. They shook their heads, clucking their tongues. However, their eyes revealed their satisfaction that a woman, a mere woman, could wreak such havoc.

"I wonder why this . . . Sea Siren, as you call her, would seek a man with a hook? It must be very important to her if it provokes her to attack innocent men," Sirena said, her voice just above a whisper.

"Who knows? But she'll never find him! Regan has

searched for him for three long years," Gretchen said confidently.

Sirena spoke again. "It would seem to me that Regan and Chaezar should redouble their efforts to find this man, perhaps put bounty on his head to increase the effort. This way, once the man is caught the . . . Sea Siren might cease and desist."

"That makes sense!" Helga said excitedly. "If the men haven't thought of it, then perhaps we should mention it. Sometimes we women come up with an answer that completely eludes them. We're stronger than men give us credit for being. The Sea Siren has only proved my point: the piratess wants something—and fights like a man among men to get it. I'd like to ride her ship!" the loquacious Helga bubbled.

"And I . . . I too would like to join her," Sirena smiled. "I find it admirable that a woman can do these things." The other ladies nodded their agreement with some hesitation. Not so, Gretchen.

"I don't believe what I hear," Gretchen sniffed. "You! Ride the seas like a wild wanton!"

"What makes you think she's . . . wanton?" Sirena queried.

Gretchen snipped, "If she's not a slut now she'll arrive at it eventually. How can a woman with any respect for herself carry on like that?"

"You're only . . . well, speculating, Frau Lindenreich," Sirena said softly. "Personally, I applaud her aggressiveness."

The hazel eyes sparkled dangerously. "Would you favor her valor if your husband bedded the slut?"

Sirena pulled her mantilla modestly across her face, and spoke delicately. "I . . . I should imagine that, here alone these past three years, Mynheer van der Rhys will have . . . will have patronized many 'sluts.' Don't you think so, Frau Lindenreich?" she asked sweetly.

Gretchen's shocked face boded ill for Sirena, but the beautiful widow's comeback was cut off by Regan's crossing the room.

"I think we're ready for our coffee now," he said, the pleasant host.

"All this talk of a Sea Siren has made my mouth dry," Anton Kloss said from across the room.

"Dear, is all the talk of a Sea Siren true?" Helga questioned her husband.

"Unfortunately, yes. She appears bent on destroying the Dutch fleet—along with the Spanish. Any ship! It is not a laughing matter!" Captain Kloss admonished his smiling wife.

"Sirena has said something I think you should hear," Helga announced to him and the other men, stifling an even wider grin.

"What is that, Helga?" Captain Kloss cast her a stern eye.

"Sirena said you should all band together to seek out the man with the hook and put a bounty on his head. That may be all the Sea Siren wants. If she's successful in capturing that man, she'll stop her plundering and then all our ships will be safe."

Anton Kloss looked at Sirena with admiration. "We've already decided this matter. Regan, as you know, seeks the same man. We've agreed to send out word about him, perhaps even some of our smaller ships—to go out among the nearer islands—beginning at dawn tomorrow."

Sirena sought Caleb's eyes and was amused by the twinkle in them.

"What will happen when you find him?" Gretchen asked hesitantly. "Will you run him through or will you turn him over to this . . . Sea Siren?"

"I will run him through," Regan said brutally.

"But, Regan," Helga interrupted, "the Sea Siren . . . *wants* him. If *you* succeed in finding him and she hears of it she may seek revenge."

"Yes, Mynheer, what if that happens?" Chaezar asked, as he stroked his beard thoughtfully. "That in itself could pose even more problems. I think we should decide now that if we do find him we hand him over to the piratess."

"Never!" Regan shouted. "I bear him too great a personal grudge."

"But, Mynheer, what we do has to be what is best for *all!* Forget your vengeance, my friend. How many more ships do you think you can afford to lose?"

"She is only a woman! You all talk like scared rabbits. I shall refuse to turn him over to her if my men or myself capture him."

Sirena saw the fear mount in Gretchen's eyes, yet the woman's voice was calm when she spoke: "It's a mistake, Regan. Let the Siren run him through, it will be less blood on your conscience. For that matter, the man could be dead, washed overboard in a storm or run through by some other cutthroat. Do you plan to spend the rest of your days tracking down a ghost!"

"Quite simply, I'll never allow a woman to dictate to me," Regan said harshly. "I am not speaking of you, Mevrouw, but of this female buccaneer!"

Anton Kloss broke in: "Even at the cost of your fleet? From what I hear, the woman has as much . . . well, expertise as any of our captains. And," Kloss added ominously, "I fear that if it is put to a vote, Regan, you will lose. Change your mind, old friend."

"Never!" Regan thundered.

"You're a fool, Regan." Don Chaezar Alvarez's voice was arrogant in his disdain. "It's not just a question of *your* survival, it's all of us. How can you be so blind?"

"You have my answer. I'll not change it. Do what you will, but if I come across the man first I'll run him through!"

"And let the rest of us lose our ships!"

"If it comes to that, yes. It's every man for himself."

"Bravo," Sirena murmured to herself. Almost shyly, she spoke: "Regan what will you do if this . . . Sea Siren learns what you've decided? What if she takes a double vengeance?"

"Such as?"

"It is said she doesn't kill unless necessary, that she . . . lets the men go into the jolly-boats. What if she decides to retaliate and starts to run men through? From what's been said, that would seem to be her vengeance. Speaking from a woman's point of view, I would say that if she's gone this far, nothing on this earth will deter her from her mission in finding . . . The Hook." She shivered delicately. "Perhaps you had better give it some thought?"

"I agree," Helga Kloss said, her eyes snapping. "A woman who has gone to these lengths to do what she's done will never bend to you."

"Nor will I bend either!" Regan stated, as adamant as before.

"You sound so determined, Regan. Almost as if you hate the Sea Siren," Don Chaezar said softly. "It's difficult to believe you commissioned a figurehead in her likeness!"

It was as if a shockwave had passed through the room, almost as if the Sisters of Fire had grumbled and sent tremors through the group assembled in the van der Rhys drawing room. Sirena's eyes expressed pure shock—and then delight—and she pulled the mantilla close around her face. Gretchen's face turned beet-red with fury, though she dared not speak. Helga and the other ladies in the room lowered their eyes to the kerchiefs they held in their hands.

Regan strode, somewhat embarrassed despite his determination not to lose face, toward the wide window that looked out on the verandah.

After a momentary silence among the men, they began talking once more as the houseboys entered to serve them coffee. Was Regan enamored of the Sea Siren? they wondered. Did he really *want* to see her again?

"Let me put it to you another way!" Don Chaezar said quietly. "Let's just suppose for a moment that what Mevrouw van der Rhys has said comes to pass and the Sea Siren begins to show no quarter. Will you then agree?"

Regan let his eyes travel the length of the room. He did not like the look of hostility on his guests' faces. "Very well," he acquiesced.

Sirena's eyes sought those of Gretchen and she was surprised to see them full of relief. What had Gretchen been afraid of?

Chapter Fourteen

The next morning Gretchen rode over to the estate of Don Chaezar. She found him sipping his morning coffee in his study. Always the gentleman, he rose to greet her and promptly offered to order her some breakfast. Gretchen refused his offer and dropped wearily onto the settee opposite the windows overlooking the garden.

It was obvious to Chaezar that Gretchen had come to his home for a specific reason and he hoped she would get to the point quickly. Women on the edge of hysteria—which certainly described Gretchen this morning—bored him.

"How did you find the dinner last evening?" he asked the pensive blonde next to him.

"It gave me much to think about, Chaezar. What—do you think will—happen now?" A hint of fear made her voice quaver.

"God only knows. Regan is like a madman! I shudder to think what will happen if and when he finds our friend with the hook. If Regan merely kills him I'd have no complaints. However, if he gives him a chance to talk, then it will be another matter. If that gruesome thought should come to pass I intend to be reclining under a Spanish sky. And you, Gretchen, where will you be?"

"You make it sound as if it's already a fact. If Regan has not succeeded in three long years, what makes you think he can find our friend now? Be realistic, Chaezar!"

"I *am* being realistic, Gretchen. When Regan searched before, there was no bounty on The Hook's head. And, too, there was no Sea Siren on his trail!"

"The money we paid him should have made him

content for the rest of his life," Gretchen pouted. "He promised to go to one of the inner islands—Borneo—or Celebes—and retire. What in the name of God could have gone wrong? Why did he take to sailing again?"

"It won't do either of us any good to question it now. We have to find him ourselves and turn him over to the Sea Siren. If it comes right down to it and Regan somehow manages to find him, his hate will never allow him to hand the man over to the pirate woman! If I were in his position I wouldn't either."

"There must be some way to find him! A word here and there. Offer your own reward. You have to do something!" Gretchen screeched, panic disfiguring her beautiful face.

"Why do *I* have to do something? I'm sorry I ever allowed you to talk me into the affair in the beginning. You convinced me that Regan would marry you if Tita was done away with. You've had three long years now to capture him!"

"I would have had *eight*, and he'd surely be mine by now, if Pedro Gomez—instead of your own ship—hadn't picked Regan up in his dinghy and carted him off to Spain to rot in a Spanish prison. A fine outcome our schemes had for me!"

"I deeply regret the scheme now. It was a mistake," Chaezar said wistfully.

"A mistake? You got an unexpected benefit out of it—if the benefit *was* unexpected. When Vincent van der Rhys heard, later, of his son's imprisonment, he paid you well and aided Spain to regain some of the trade privileges she'd lost to the Dutch those past years. But, Chaezar," Gretchen sputtered, "you helped me once, and you must help me again! I should say 'help *us*'! For if Regan van der Rhys learns from The Hook what happened to his son—and our part in it—he'll kill us both! Both, do you hear me?"

"That's where you are wrong, my dear. Regan could never prove a thing against me. Now you," he said thoughtfully, "are another matter. He'll believe the story—the true one—that you wanted Tita killed so he could marry you. I think he could understand your kind of jealousy and hatred—although he would never forgive you. What he won't understand is the boy! I told you *that* was a mistake. But you said you wanted 'no reminders of his marriage' and that the boy had to go, too! Where did you send him, Gretchen, when The Hook returned from Capetown with the boy? I'd washed my hands of the affair by then, and let you have your way. If you want my help, you'll have to tell me where—"

"To Mindanao, in the Philippines—Spanish territory, where the Dutch do not trade." Gretchen hesitated, as if thinking. Finally, she said, "I've been thinking, Chaezar. Since last night. Do you suppose if we went there, or sent a ship up, we could somehow manage to reclaim the boy and get him back here? Tell Regan we'd heard rumors of his whereabouts and sent out to find the boy? Out of pleasure at his son's return, Regan might forget his anger against The Hook—and let the Sea Siren have the man, if and when he's found . . ."

"How would you prevent Regan from suspecting we'd had some part in the boy's abduction—*and* his mother's murder—"

"We could have one of your marauders 'discover' the boy—at our command—and play no part in his return at all."

"And on his return, it would be interesting to see whether or not the boy tells some interesting details about his capture and his being sent away—by you, no less, for he saw you here when The Hook brought him back—to Mindanao. He's no doubt about twelve years old now, but he was an alert four-year-old at the time of his mother's death."

Gretchen was speechless for a moment, and trembling visibly. "Or perhaps a letter could be posted to Regan telling him where we think the boy is, but not giving our names . . . anonymous." She pursed her tremulous lips.

"For the first time I see you're truly afraid. Do you love Regan as much as all that? And fear for his life at the Siren's hands?"

"Love has nothing to do with it," Gretchen sobbed. "Regan is married now. And I would wager before long Sirena will make him happy, and they'll begin to raise healthy, happy babies."

"Then she'll grow fat and ugly!" Gretchen spat.

"What difference will that make? She'll still be married to him!"

"Please Chaezar . . . you must help me."

"And if I do? What will be my reward?" the Spaniard asked softly, his dark glance falling on her sulky mouth and coming to rest on her bosom.

"Name it, and it's yours," Gretchen whispered.

This would be easier than she thought. She'd known that his assistance would require some sort of payment and she had been momentarily fearful that he would demand several pieces of her jewelry. Most of her jewels were merely costume baubles, but several gentlemen admirers had gifted her with exquisite and valuable pieces. Gretchen was both amused and relieved that Chaezar obviously would be satisfied with an hour's dalliance.

From the fervid gleam in his eye she knew that his appetites ran to the exotic today. Chaezar gripped her wrist with a feverish hand and led her to his chamber. She followed him willingly, eager to meet his demands so that she could leave early enough to keep an appointment with her dressmaker.

Chaezar, on the other hand, attributed Gretchen's willingness to eager anticipation and, as was his way, he stripped off his clothes without a word. He preferred not to engage in any conversation at these times —as Gretchen well knew; she supposed it was because he wanted nothing to divert his concentration on his role.

Gretchen knew the rules by which Chaezar insisted this game be played. She stood coolly in the center of the room and waited.

Each time Chaezar played this exotic game that was about to begin, Gretchen was amazed at the transfiguration of the man. She knew, from other experience with him, that the Spaniard could be a dynamic, vigorous lover, completely at ease and fully masculine. But this was one of those "other" times. Gone now was the forceful yet urbane gentleman sure of his every move. Before her stood a simpering, mincing, cowering minion—it was a fantasy, of course, or so she hoped—intent on pleasing a cruel, flint-hearted mistress . . . and trembling with the knowledge that she would be impossible to please. The Mistress was a role Gretchen herself had no trouble playing.

Reverently his hands went to the buttons at the back of her gown. Carefully, he undid them one by one, his fingers barely grazing the silky flesh beneath her gown. Layers of clothing were removed until all she wore was her satin corset, frilly lace drawers, black silk stockings, and high-heeled slippers. Deliberately, yet feverishly, he snapped her garter and immediately recoiled in terror.

Gretchen knew her cue. "Clumsy oaf!" she said sternly. "See how you've bruised your ladyship's thigh!" She extended her silky limb, pointing to where the garter had snapped against her creamy leg. "Kiss it!" she ordered him harshly.

Chaezar dropped to his knees before her and pressed ardent lips to the imaginary wound. Gretchen was pleased to notice how aroused he was: a little while longer and she would be free to leave.

"You realize you must be punished for your clumsiness," she said with great authority.

Chaezar's answer was to grovel pitifully at her feet, kissing her insteps, her ankles; his whole attitude was that of a panic-stricken animal.

"Get the whip!" she ordered. Chaezar cowered close to her legs, whimpering. "Get the whip, I tell you! Now!"

Chaezar hesitantly pulled away from her and dragged himself to his feet. His eyes were black pools of anguish, his lips quivered with fear. From his face and posture anyone would have believed him to be the badly used servant of a monstrously brutal master. Only his loins betrayed his pose. Alive and erect, his phallus betrayed the true object of his desires.

From the top of his clothes press, he withdrew a long, evil-looking whip. The handle was heavy carved wood, ornate in design. At one end of the handle were large, round opalines, and when one looked closely one could see that the shaft of the handle and the placement of the opalines represented the male sex organ. The tails of the whip, while cruel-looking, black, and knotted, were actually braided silk, designed to sting the flesh yet not cut or tear it or even raise a welt.

Humbly, Chaezar offered the instrument to Gretchen. Chaezar worshipped the whip in a way he could never adore a woman's body. While fascinated by its uniqueness, she therefore abhorred its significance to him. In some twisted way the whip represented a rival to her. To know that Chaezar could be sexually satisfied by three long cords of braided silk was an affront to her self-esteem. That she cared nothing for the man—in fact didn't even like him, only used him as a means to an end—mattered not at all. She was a woman who recognized her own desirability and she demanded that a man, any man, appreciate her qualities.

Gretchen accepted the heavy-handled whip noting the slavish, fanatical light in Chaezar's eyes. He was ready. He had goaded himself to fever pitch. The muscles in his back and thighs quivered in anticipation. The dark curling hairs on his chest and belly were practically standing on end. His breathing was ragged; small flecks of saliva danced on his beard.

Gretchen brought up the whip and spun the long, trailing braids in wide circles about her head. Chaezar held his breath and watched, mesmerized, waiting for the curling ends to strike his flesh. His eyes never left the whirling braids. At last, Gretchen brought down the adored instrument of torture. Again and again she lashed him about the back and chest. Again and again the long, trailing tails would glance off his buttocks and thighs. Chaezar moaned in ecstasy, his body trembling with paroxysms of passion.

At last he fell to his knees gasping for air, until his convulsive excitement abated. He crawled across the floor until he reached her, tears of gratitude shining in his eyes. Like a dog at his master's knee, he pressed his dark head against her thigh, small sobs catching in his throat.

Now was the time for the cruel mistress to become the magnanimous benefactor. She petted his head and held him against her, soothing his pain and humiliation. Mutely moving closer, Chaezar began to kiss her hand, her thigh, begged her forgiveness. His face was moist with saliva and tears, staining her skin with silvery wetness.

He kissed her fervently and she cradled him in her arms and led him to the bed. Soothing him with soft tones and maternal gestures, she dried his tears and held him close. With narrowed eyes she estimated the length of time she must stay with him until, still sobbing heartbrokenly, he would fall asleep.

This was the part of Chaezar's little play that really repelled her. She didn't mind beating him with the whip—she enjoyed seeing him pay her homage and groveling at her feet. It was when she was obliged to forgive him that he disgusted her by crying all over her, his wet mouth and cheeks pressed against her skin.

Chaezar's grip on her was slackening now. Soon he would be asleep and she could leave and the events of the past hour would never be mentioned by either of them.

She *must* have a bath before she went to the dressmaker's!

Chapter Fifteen

"Sirena," Caleb fretted, "Regan and Don Chaezar Alvarez are gone looking for The Hook! Why aren't we chasing them?"

"Remember what I told you about 'wily women?' Regan and Chaezar *expect* the Sea Siren to be out there. Never do the expected. Have no fear, little brother. The Hook will have gone into hiding as soon as word spreads he's being hunted. He'll wait, as we do. You must always be one league ahead of your adversary. This time we'll let the men chase themselves. What they're doing is sailing blind. Before long they'll all be frustrated and losing money, for nearly all Dutch and Spanish shipping will have ceased for the time being."

"How do you know this?"

"Because, if you'll forgive me, little brother, men think with their loins. If they used their brains they'd never act so foolishly. I tell you, they sail blind. At best they'll find some wild marauder and get their ships damaged—perhaps get themselves killed for their effort! I'll give them ten days and they'll be home, half-crazed with rage. Just in time for Chaezar's party." Sirena's tone was light, her expression amused.

"Perhaps there won't be a party."

"There'll be a party. The invitation came today from Chaezar."

"It should prove interesting?" Caleb smiled.

"*Very* interesting," Sirena agreed.

One day ran into the next as Sirena and Caleb awaited Regan's return. Every day the boy went to the wharf, but there was no news. On the ninth day he was sitting on the edge of the quay when he spotted the first sail. Waving excitedly, he raced to the end of the quay and waited.

The minutes seemed like hours to Caleb, as the ship approached. Then, finally it was at anchor.

Regan was the first to disembark. His face was a mask of cold fury. "No sight of the long-legged bitch *or* of the man with the hook, Caleb. The scurve must have his ear to the wind and is hiding out. Either that or he is on a lengthy voyage. We came upon one small pirate ship, smaller than our own vessel, that would have run from us. But I signaled that we had peaceful intentions toward the tiny, flagless frigate, and they approached. They said they'd come across him in recent months, but none of them knew now of his whereabouts. One cutthroat is much like another—but I'm sure they told the truth. The bounty on the bastard's head is too attractive. And we inquired among the ports of Borneo, Celebes, Bali, with no luck. We'd have gone farther—to the Moluccas and New Guinea—but have left such long trips till later."

"Perhaps the Sea Siren has given up too!" Caleb said hesitantly.

Regan clapped his arm around the boy's shoulders as they walked into the D.E.I. offices. "I think not. I believe, however, she learned of our voyage. She's probably, right now, this very minute, laughing her head off at our stupidity. I admit it was ridiculous going to sea like that. When a man's fortunes are at stake he is apt to do many foolish things. She's won again."

"How could she 'win' if she didn't go after you?" Caleb asked, puzzled.

"She made fools of the lot of us!" Regan closed the door to his office and sat down on his leather-backed chair. "Fetch me a cigar, will you, boy?"

Caleb looked around the small office then went to the heavy-laden shelves. He let his eyes wander over the array of objects on the many tiers and finally bent down and reached for a square leather humidor; but he hesitated and reached instead for a small wooden box. He grasped it in both hands and handed it to Regan.

Regan's eyes blazed and the skin pulled back over his teeth suddenly like a snarling dog. "How did you know what was in that box?" he demanded harshly.

Frightened by the man's intensity, Caleb drew back, clutching the box to his chest. "But—you—said—to fetch you a—cigar."

"I know what I said. How is it you knew where they were?"

"I . . . I don't know. I must have seen you get them the—the last time I was here with you. Did I do something wrong? Is something in this box that you don't care to have me see? I'm sorry, Mynheer!"

Regan perceived Caleb's fright and his tone calmed immediately. "I'm sorry, Caleb, it's just that my own son used to get my cigars for me. I used to keep them in the big leather humidor, but, being less than five years old, he couldn't lift it. I moved them to the box you're holding now. When you bent over like that, it just reminded me of those long-ago days. I'm sorry if I upset you—I guess I've been out to sea too long. Sometimes I get caught up in the past and can't forget."

"You must have loved your son very much," Caleb said hesitantly.

"Very much," Regan said gently. "But you'd better get home now. I'll see you at dinner. Tell your sister I've arrived, safe and sound—if she should inquire, that is."

"I'll deliver the message, Mynheer," Caleb said as he closed the door behind him.

Regan paced the small room, his mind in a turmoil. He was positive he had never taken a cigar from the wooden box when Caleb was in the office. As a matter of fact, Regan preferred the brand of cheroot he kept at home and always carried several in his shirtfront. Lately, he'd kept the cigars in the office only for visiting merchants. His heart pounded wildly in his chest at the thoughts that invaded his mind.

Chinese paper lanterns swayed lazily in the timid breeze that floated in from Batavia's harbor. From the distance they resembled hundreds of fireflies dancing among the tropical shrubbery surrounding Don Alvarez's palatial home. Situated on the elite Avenue of the Lion, within the walls of the city, Don Chaezar's home surpassed any of the city's dwellings in its charm and grace.

Music spilled out the verandah doors into the dark garden. The lavish ball was a huge success. His guests tipped their fragile, long-stemmed wine glasses to smiling lips, toasting his generosity. Everyone on his long guest list had come—Spanish, Dutch, and Portuguese alike. Even some English and French merchants were here.

Sirena and Regan had arrived nearly an hour late, owing to last-minute business Regan was forced to conduct in his office on the wharf. Whatever business it was that detained Regan, Sirena noted that it had left him in a black humor. His heavy brows were drawn together in a scowl, the muscles in his jaw were knotted beneath his lean, clean-shaven flesh. His eyes were bright, the black pupils narrowed to pinpoints glowering with barely suppressed menace.

Prior to their arrival at Chaezar's, Sirena had timidly asked Regan what was wrong. She had even gone so far as to suggest that perhaps he didn't care to attend Chaezar's ball. If that were the case, she would understand and stay home with him. His answer had been to laugh. A great, booming, angry sound of derision. "Stay home?" he had exclaimed "Never! I'm going, even if I have to crawl!" Perplexed, Sirena had stepped into the carriage and held her skirts to make room for Regan on the seat next to her. They drove to Chaezar's in silence, the Mynheer puffing angrily on the cheroot he held between tightly clenched teeth.

Now, standing at the entrance to the ballroom, the blazing candlelight turning his pale blond hair to silver, Regan's eyes raked the room in more than just a curious perusal of the party. Sirena knew he was looking for something . . . or someone.

Sirena noticed Gretchen's approach before Regan. As the blonde moved across the room, all heads turned to watch her. And why? Gretchen's gown was infamous! Sirena saw. Made of incandescent blue silk studded with crystals across the bosom and pelvis, it clung seductively to her figure, revealing the fact that she wore absolutely nothing beneath it. As form-fitting as a snake's skin, the dress molded itself to her every curve, revealing quite plainly the separation between her buttocks and the sensuous indentation of her navel. Nevertheless, while her scantiness of clothing was shocking, she carried herself with dignity and grace, giving the effect of a mythical goddess instead of a brazen whore. The women were scandalized, the men delighted.

A mocking smile spread slowly across Regan's face. Sirena knew from the appreciative way he appraised Gretchen that the hillocks and valleys of her body were familiar territory.

Sirena felt dowdy and outmoded alongside the German temptress. The blue of the scanty silk gown turned Gretchen's hair to a pale shade of silver which almost matched Regan's. Sparkling gems glimmered from her curls, their brilliance matching the sparkle in the widow's eyes.

It was Don Chaezar who rescued Sirena from the embarrassing spectacle of the charged glances between Regan and Gretchen. Bowing low over Sirena's hand to plant a delicate kiss on her fingertips, he swept her away to introduce her to several guests from outlying islands. Faces swayed before her and names became garbled in her mind. The jealousy she had felt at the gleam in Regan's eyes when he looked at Gretchen left her seething with rage. It was only with a concentrated effort that she was able to prevent herself from turning around to follow their movements.

Alvarez, the perfect gentlemen, never left her unattended. He was a genial host and had planned his party with consideration for his guests' enjoyment. The music was gay, the wines superb, the tables laden with tempting food of every variety. Once, when Chaezar left her for a moment to instruct his servants on the serving of the wine, Helga Kloss hurriedly approached Sirena.

"You must share the secret with me, Sirena," she gasped breathlessly. Her little, round eyes shone with excitement. "Surely Don Chaezar has told *you* what the surprise is! You *must* tell me! I shall faint with suspense if you don't!"

"I've no idea what surprise you speak of, Mevrouw," Sirena laughed. "Unless, of course, you meant Frau Lindenreich's surprising attire."

Helga Kloss's face went blank for a moment before understanding flushed her round, pink cheeks. "Oh yes, did you see her? Of course, you must have," she tittered. "Captain Kloss is simply scandalized! Whenever she's within sight, the poor man doesn't know where to look. But no, Gretchen is not what Don Chaezar has planned for this evening. It's something else. He's been hinting at it for most of the evening, hadn't you noticed?"

Helga cast Sirena a quizzical eye. What was wrong with the girl? Helga had always considered her quite clever. What was Sirena thinking of all evening if she hadn't heard mention of Don Chaezar's secret "spectacular"!

After Helga ran out of gossip to impart to Sirena and she had secured a promise to "come to tea very soon," she departed in search of her husband, leaving Sirena blessedly alone. The number of people, the music, and the sight of brightly colored, bobbing and dipping skirts had become a trifle overwhelming. Sirena looked for an opportunity to be alone with her thoughts and saw the perfect answer: the doors leading onto the verandah.

The cool night air felt fresh against her cheeks, the strains of the music seemed sweeter out here in the moonlight.

After a few quiet moments, Sirena became aware that she was not alone. From behind some large shrubs near the verandah the sound of a woman's light laughter was wafted by the evening breeze. She was about to go inside when something about the pitch of the woman's voice struck her as familiar. The slight intonation of derision, the lilting quality—husky yet girlish. Gretchen!

Suddenly Sirena remembered riding on the back of the baggage wagon along a hot dusty road, the sun baking the black bombazine dress into the flesh of her back, heavy black hair falling awry, sticking to her damp, perspiring neck. And the sound of the laughter—taunting and scornful. Followed by the sight of a beautifully coiffed head peeking out through the hedge, a laughing face looking up into hers, enjoying Sirena's misery.

Sharp stabs of hatred shot through her, an icy resolve to slap that snickering mouth until its full ripe lips were swollen and bloody.

Without further thought, Sirena pushed her way through the shrubs and found just what she had expected: Gretchen and Regan holding each other in a tight embrace.

For a full moment she went unnoticed as her rage mounted and all reason was swept from her. She only half saw Regan's lips pressed against Gretchen's, one arm around her back, his hand caressing the firm, round flesh of her buttocks, the other hand pushed down into the wide deep neckline of the iridescent blue gown.

In one sweeping motion, Sirena was upon them, tearing them from each other's arms. Like a spitting, snarling cat, she turned on Gretchen in unleashed violence. "Since you seem bent on exposing yourself, Frau Lindenreich," she hissed, "why allow a slip of dress fabric to stand between you and my husband!" With a claw-like hand Sirena reached out, grasped the neckline of Gretchen's gown, and ripped it nearly to the hem.

Gretchen rose to Sirena's attack with surprise but with bared teeth and a show of sharp nails. Cursing with rage, she reached for Sirena's hair, but Sirena dodged her flailing arm. Like two spitting cats the women faced each other, each seeking the destruction of the other.

"I've wanted to slap that snickering smile from your face for some time," Sirena continued. "Now I intend to scratch your eyes out, too!"

Her tone was low, yet held such menace that Regan was taken aback. He'd have never thought his composed Sirena capable of such violent speech. More to get a closer look at Sirena than to protect Gretchen, he stepped between them. Immediately, his action was misinterpreted by both women.

"Stand aside, Regan. *You've* had *your* lark with this German whore! Now I intend to have mine!" Her eyes flashed with venom; she poised, lithe as a cat, to resume her attack on the German. "If you insist on protecting her, be warned: I'll cut you down to get to her!"

Fear now began to take hold of Gretchen. Sirena had said she would scratch out her eyes and Gretchen had no doubt whatsoever that the Spanish cat meant to do it. So, when Regan placed himself between the women, Gretchen allowed herself the luxury of hysterics. Her mind now ran to the actual damage done to her. "My gown!" she wailed. "Look what she's done to it! It can never be repaired!" She took a step closer to Regan's back, enjoying its protection. Something crunched beneath her foot.

"The crystals! They've been torn off! Regan, help me find them, they cost a fortune!" Crawling about on her hands and knees, she sought out the tiny beads which had been sewn onto her gown.

Sirena glanced down at Gretchen crawling about searching for the lost beads and saw Frau Lindenreich's breasts fall unbecomingly out of the shredded bodice. The woman's hair had come undone and was falling in an untidy mass down her back.

Regan, too, glanced down and saw the ridiculousness of Gretchen's position. He burst into a great peal of laughter. Then, seeing the murderous looks the woman cast him, his mirthful sounds froze in his throat.

A shuffle of feet and the appearance of Don Chaezar standing just outside the verandah immediately cooled the charged atmosphere.

"Chaezar!" Gretchen sobbed, jumping to her feet, "see what she's done to me!"

"I see . . . Gretchen," the Spaniard soothed her. "And how magnificently she's done it!"

Gretchen, stupefied by his remark and wide-eyed with surprise, was about to return the insult, when she noticed Chaezar's eyes fall on Sirena. Gretchen thought she saw a light of admiration in his black gaze.

Turning to Gretchen, however, he said, "You may go around the verandah to my chambers. Take one of my dressing gowns to wear home. I'll have my coachman bring the trap around to the back. You can leave from there and no one will see you. I assume you don't want to be seen in the state you're in."

"I don't give a damn who sees me!" Gretchen spat.

"But *I* do," Chaezar said threateningly. "I won't allow you to make an even greater spectacle of yourself in my house, and before my guests."

Regan and Sirena were amazed at how quickly Gretchen's temper quelled in the face of Don Chaezar's authority. They watched her sulk around to the back of the house, silently prepared to follow Chaezar's orders.

Both Regan and Chaezar now viewed Sirena with bewildered expressions. They were clearly wondering how she could have been a seething spitfire only a moment before and now appear to be in complete control of herself, composed and unruffled.

In a courtly and solicitous manner, the Spaniard flashed Sirena a dazzling smile and offered her his arm. "You must put all this behind you, *querida*. Don't let anything spoil your evening." His eyes were quick to note, however, that rather than spoiling his country-woman's evening, Sirena's fray with Gretchen had been the highlight of it. "Now, you must both come back into the ballroom. I am ready to unveil my little surprise—my 'spectacular,' as everyone prefers to call it."

Sirena saw that Regan was scowling at the easy manner Don Chaezar had with her. And, her eyes glued on her husband, she had noticed the sudden alertness about Regan when Chaezar mentioned to them his "surprise."

"Yes, Alvarez," Regan was saying, a biting edge to his voice, "I'm most interested in this little 'surprise' of yours. Let's go with him, Sirena. We wouldn't want him to keep us guessing any longer than necessary." Muscles knotted in Regan's jaw, the thick column of his neck was corded with fury.

So this is what Regan was angry about on our way here, Sirena thought with amusement. Whatever Chaezar's little surprise is, Regan knows—and doesn't like it. She was curious to see what was going to happen.

As the three entered the ballroom, all eyes turned to watch them expectantly. The musicians had stopped their playing and all the guests milled about a tall, shrouded shape which stood in the center of the ballroom. As Sirena and the two men stepped into the center of the throng, she heard Helga Kloss call out, "Hurry, Chaezar! The suspense is making me feel faint. But I can guess what it is, you rake. You've imported one of those statues from Greece, haven't you? The ones that hardly have anything on . . ." Helga's voice ended in a muffled giggle.

A small titter of laughter broke out from around the Dutch captain's wife. Smiling, Sirena guessed that Anton Kloss had put an end to his wife's speculations.

Chaezar left Sirena and Regan standing on the

inside perimeter of the circle of guests. With great aplomb he stepped up to the tall shrouded object. Clearing his throat importantly, he began to speak: "As is well known by all of you, the islands of the East Indies are recently under seige by the most ruthless marauder of the seas that we have ever known. There are those among us who have been fortunate enough to have glimpsed this notorious piratess on her own domain, the sea. There is even one among us who, having confronted this sea witch, has become so infatuated with her that he commissioned the construction of her likeness."

Standing next to Regan, Sirena felt him stiffen. His hand, which had been resting lightly on her arm, gripped her flesh painfully.

"Without further ado, my honored guests, I give you the Sea Siren!"

Chaezar pulled lightly on a silken cord, and the draperies fell away. There on a podium which had been especially constructed was Regan's figurehead.

Gasps and oohs of delight filled the ballroom. It was magnificent. Carved with loving hands, the figure was nearly life-sized. What Sirena saw when she looked at it was a startlingly close resemblance to herself, her flowing hair sculpted to appear as though the wind were sweeping it back from its beautifully molded face. The arms were fashioned close to the body; the breasts were high and full, and accurately displayed beneath the illusion of a short body-hugging blouse tied high over the ribs. The long satiny torso was smooth and rounded into the swells of its hips. The figure was astoundingly correct—even to the dramatic headband tied about the forehead of its finely chiseled face.

Fearfully, Sirena looked about the room to see if anyone had noticed the astonishing resemblance to herself. Finally having the courage to glance at Regan, she watched him as he studied the work he had commissioned. She wondered nervously how he had remembered the Sea Siren so . . . so accurately? As Regan gazed upon the figurehead of the Sea Siren she saw in his eyes the same hunger and desire she had seen when he looked at her as she stood defiantly on the deck of the *Rana*.

As the guests gathered around the figurehead—some to stare, others to touch the satiny teak—Sirena backed off, her stomach muscles knotted in apprehension. She accepted a glass of wine, keeping her face in profile to the guests as she sipped the crimson liquid.

Turning back toward the crowd of guests a moment later, for she dared not be too obvious in her lack of interest in the figurehead, she saw something in the Spaniard's eyes she'd dreaded since she had first heard of the construction of the image of the Sea Siren: recognition.

Don Chaezar watched Sirena bring the fragile wineglass to her lips once more; then an expression of consternation, of infinite surprise, stole across his features.

Regan turned away, finally, from the figurehead. As he did so, he saw the look on the Spaniard's face. Quickly he glanced back at the representation of the Sea Siren; then he shifted his gaze to his wife—he too as intent as Don Chaezar.

Then Regan's piercing blue eyes met Chaezar's black ones. "If," said the Dutchman, "your purpose was to embarrass me this evening, you've fallen short of your victory, Don Chaezar Alvarez. The figurehead's beauty far outshines its scandalousness! And, we shall see who is so cocky when you yourself mount my figurehead on my ship tomorrow—at the end of my sword-point!"

The tip of Chaezar's tongue wet his dry lips. The Dutchman's rapier was a thing not to be taken lightly.

Chapter Sixteen

Shortly after eleven o'clock on a cool, balmy night several days after the ball, Sirena crept into Caleb's room and shook him awake. The entire household had retired earlier than usual, and Sirena was certain that all were asleep.

"Dress little brother, we take to the sea," she whispered.

Caleb was instantly awake and reaching for his trousers.

"I'll wait for you in my room. It's down again, by way of the trellis, for both of us. Hurry now! After dinner as I passed the kitchen door, I heard Frau Holtz say that one of the Mynheer's ships was to set sail late tonight. She's doubtless gone by now, but we may be able to overtake her. Quickly now!"

"But the men! The crew! I've taken Jan no message to have them aboard ship."

"I sent Ling Fu to Teatoa with a sealed message. You needed some sleep. The old Chinaman's not one to puzzle out the whys and wherefores, he'll suspect nothing, and he's probably asleep in the servants' quarters once more by now. It's been nigh on two hours; the men should long since have left the village and reached the *Rana*.

A few hours later, the first hints of dawn streaked the sky. Sirena, Caleb, and Jan stood near the wheel, the Señorita's hands clasping it professionally.

"It won't be long now," Sirena purred. "Order all hands on deck, Jan."

"Aye, Capitana."

"You'll take the wheel, as usual, when I speak to

the enemy. And, Caleb, you'll go below as soon as we've approached them. I want none of our Dutch traders to recognize you. You're too well known in Batavia now, little brother!"

"Sirena," Caleb asked softly, "will you . . . send the enemy into the sea this time without the jolly-boats?"

"No. Not as I did with the Spanish trader's men. But, remember, even then I gave them fair warning."

Only minutes later came the cry: "Sail ho!"

Sirena called down the deck, to Jan: "Get her in your sights and fire when ready. Blow her stern first, then her bow!"

"She's too far away, Capitana," Jan called back.

"True, Jan. And only one of our shots may make its mark. But by surprising them, we may get in another shot before they've readied themselves."

"Why do you gamble like this?" Caleb asked anxiously.

"Because we don't have the cover of darkness."

The *Rana*'s deck rocked with the blast of two of her cannons.

"Good!" Sirena called to her men, lifting the spyglass. "Yes, one of our shots has hit the Dutchman's bow. I told Mynheer van der Rhys that no Dutch ship—his or any of the Dutch East India Company's—would strike mine again!"

A cannonball from the Dutch trader exploded from her port side but fell far short of the black-rigged *Rana*.

"She fires, you see, Caleb—but in blind panic! Now, boy, out of sight below!"

Jan Verhooch ran up to take the wheel from Sirena as the ship approached the burning Dutch brig.

"Call for quarter and I'll allow you to go into the jolly-boats," Sirena shouted in order to be heard over the melee.

"Quarter!" came the high-pitched shout.

"Do you see the heavy cannon she carries?" Sirena yelled up to Jan.

"Aye, Capitana. For all the good it did her," he grinned.

"If her shot *had* found its mark, we wouldn't be

standing here now. She might have hit us straight on if she hadn't panicked."

A hiss of steam pierced the air as the brig now listed sharply to starboard. Before long she would settle into her new home fathoms deep.

"All hands on the Dutchman!" Sirena shouted. "Do you carry a man aboard who has a hook for a hand?"

"No, there's no such man aboard!" came the reply.

"Hold out your hands and remove your gloves." Her order was instantly obeyed and Sirena lifted the glass to her eyes. Satisfied, she nodded. "On your return to Batavia—*when* you get there—" she laughed, "give Mynheer van der Rhys a message for me. Tell him I've heard he refuses to turn The Hook over to me if he finds the man first. I give only one warning and this is it: The next time I capture a Dutch ship, woe be it to the man who tells me the Grand Pensioner hasn't gone back on his plan to keep The Hook from me!" She dug the point of her cutlass into the *Rana*'s rail and stood peering down at the brig's crew. "What was it you carried in your hold today?" she asked.

"Cloves and nutmeg and peppercorns."

"The price of spices in Europe will soar," Sirena laughed, her voice high and melodious.

The captain, a brash and outspoken man in well-pressed, perfectly tailored clothes, stood up in one of the jolly-boats as it was being lowered and shook his fist menacingly at Sirena. "If the Dutch East India Company is hurt by this loss, you won't take all the credit, Sea Siren! You'll owe some Spaniard your thanks for doing his damnedest to help you!"

"How is that?" Sirena shouted her question.

"Native gossip has it that unlimed nutmegs have been cached somewhere on the island of Java. The slaves who lime the nutmeg seeds have loose mouths —thank God for that!—and report that bushels of the seeds often fail to reach them. No Dutchman would do a thing like that. Only a Spaniard! To break the hold we Netherlanders have on the majority of the trade! The cursed Iberian will be wanting to start a plantation near the shores of Europe, that's what!"

The Dutchman's complaints were cut short.

"Sail ho," came a cry from the *Rana*'s rigging.

"What's that? Another ship?" Sirena called up to her man aloft.

"A mile or two to starboard, Capitana. By the shape of her, she's Spanish or Portuguese."

"Loosen sail!" Sirena ordered her crew. "I want to be behind her stern."

A quarter-hour later, the Dutch brig in her watery grave and her jolly-boats bobbing in the distance, Sirena's frigate approached a Spanish brigantine lately out of Batavia.

Behind Jan at the *Rana*'s wheel, Sirena spoke calmly: "Don't fire unless I give the order. We won't touch this ship. She goes free."

At the first mate's puzzled expression, Sirena smiled; Jan, she remembered, was a Dutchman after all.

"What if she fires at us, Capitana?" he asked his commander.

"In that case, we ram her. But only on my order. You see, Jan, she's Spanish, and if I let her go free—after sinking the Dutch ship—well, Mynheer van der Rhys will be at Don Chaezar's throat at once, for he'll suspect I've made a bargain with the Spaniard. For a time, then, the Mynheer will be too busy watching the Spaniard to give much thought to The Hook.

"Here, Jan, take the wheel. And give me the glass." Sirena raised the glass to her eyes and read the name of the Spanish brigantine. It was the *Crimson Fire*.

Picking up the ship's horn, for the two vessels were still at some distance from one another, she called out: "Hear me well, *Crimson Fire!* I see that your men are at their guns, so be aware of who I am—the Sea Siren! One shot and all aboard are dead men. However . . . I will be kind," she laughed through the horn. "Captain," she said, addressing the black-bearded figure near the *Crimson Fire*'s wheel, "remove your men from their positions at the guns and lay down all arms, and I will allow you to sail on." She waited for a moment. "Well," she shouted through the horn, "do I have an answer?"

As a response, a cannonball exploded from the

Crimson Fire's flanks and cut through the *Rana*'s foremast sail. But no other shot followed. Raising her spyglass, Sirena quickly sent her men to their gunner's positions.

Through the glass she saw that the Spanish captain was smiling—his shot was a challenge to battle, he thought he could quickly best the black frigate, ill-captained as he deemed she was.

The *Rana*'s guns burst in rapid succession and raked the brigantine's decks and rigging. Turning about, to provide only a narrow profile to the Spaniard's guns, the *Rana* continued to fire and, under Sirena's keen direction, was preparing to ram the larger vessel.

As the two ships neared one another, the captain of the *Crimson Fire* raised his ship's horn and called out in haste: "Quarter! We ask quarter!" Then, throwing his cutlass to the deck, he called out, "We surrender! We surrender!"

Few of the Spaniard's missiles had struck the *Rana*, and those had caused little damage. Nevertheless, Sirena was not of a mind to spare the crew of the offending trader until Jan reminded her that since she had not been able to let the Spanish ship sail on—and bring the D.E.I. Chief Pensioner to suspect her allegiance to the Spanish Crown—she ought, at least, to spare the *Crimson Fire*'s crew as she had the Dutch brig's. "Why stir up Alvarez's suspicions of a Dutch alliance?" he said.

"You're right, Jan," the Capitana replied. "We'll take her cargo this time, however—to share among the men." Sirena laughed heartily. "We'll get the Spaniards into their jolly-boats, check their hands for any sign of The Hook—and off they may go, paddling away, home to Java! Unless they want to try for Spain!" she roared. "Two ships in one day!" Sirena smiled. "And I only sought one!"

A cheer rang out from her men for the gallant Capitana.

Sirena stood on the captured trader's decks, musing, and grinning as she did. In the distance she could see the *Crimson Fire*'s jolly-boats rowing wearily back toward the Sunda Strait—on the heels of the Dutch trader's two tiny craft. What a sight the four would make, limping into Batavia harbor late that night or the next morning!

Her crew, ransacking the brigantine's hold, had brought up silks and other Javanese handicrafts and left the nutmegs, peppercorns, and other spices below. What need had they of *those*? They lived in the Spice Islands! But their wives, back in Teatoa, would put the other cargo to good use. And the Spaniards had, they discovered, also carried kegs of a type of Javanese whiskey that could be transferred to the *Rana*'s stores.

"Make haste, men!" Sirena cried out finally. "We've the tide with us yet, and we want to reach the river by midday. We'll want to pass those four cursed dinghies long before they see us turn into the River of Death!"

She turned on her heel as she heard a heavy puffing behind her. It was Jacobus, the *Rana*'s cook.

"What have you there, old man?"

"An interesting chest, Capitana—which I found in the captain's cabin . . . and," he chuckled wickedly, "which I just happened to open with my handy blade." Dramatically lifting the lid of the chest, he displayed to Sirena myriad shining pieces of eight, as well as a rainbow of gemstones.

Sirena toyed with the gems, and pocketed a few. Then she called to her men. "Here, my hearties, a pleasant booty Jacobus has discovered for you! But fast, men, we must away. And we still must gut this proud brig!"

The sleek black frigate skimmed the calm sea, several miles away now from the slowly sinking *Crimson Fire*. Caleb stood, once more, next to Sirena as she held the ship's wheel.

"What do you think will happen when the four jolly-boats get back to Batavia?" he asked.

"Don Chaezar Alvarez will throw a beastly fit—and Mynheer van der Rhys will charge around his office like a bull!"

Caleb laughed, but Sirena's expression turned thoughtful. Mention of Chaezar had brought to mind the startling information the Dutch captain had passed on earlier . . . "Unlimed nutmegs"—what were they? What did the expression mean?

Her musings were interrupted a moment later.

Jacobus, the toothless old cook, came out on deck carrying a mug of strong, fragrant coffee for his "capitana."

Accepting the mug from him, she asked, "Jacobus, you were on the deck, were you not, when we took the Dutchman's ship?" He nodded. "What did he mean when he spoke of 'unlimed nutmegs' and how some Spaniard, he thought, might be intending to start a nutmeg plantation nearer Europe?"

From his surprised look, it was evident to Sirena that Jacobus was amazed to find she was ignorant of the most stringent rule of the Indies—and the single most important precaution upon which the Indies trade, both Dutch *and* Spanish, was based. "Capitana, no fertile nutmegs are allowed to be shipped out of the islands. All the merchants—Dutch and Spanish alike, as well as any incoming ships of other nations—abide by the rule. For only if the Indies holds the monopoly for the spice trade are the Dutch and Spanish fortunes secure. We want no other plantations established in, say, the Caribbees or Africa by, say, the French or English or Austrians, or anyone else."

Sirena noticed that Caleb was evidently embarrassed at her ignorance. The boy must know the rule, too, and had obviously thought she was aware of it . . .

Jacobus continued speaking: "Every planter has his slaves pick the ripe nuts, and then certain of the slaves immediately steep the nuts in a bath of lime—which makes them infertile, though when they're cleaned they can of course be used without fear." A sharp gleam burned in Jacobus's watery, pale-colored eyes. "As for the common seaman like me—well, he'd never be able to get his hands on the fertile nuts, but"—the old cook shook a warning finger—"our persons and gear are frequently checked anyway. And, Capitana, anyone caught smuggling fertile nutmegs out of the Indies can expect the death penalty!"

Later, alone at the rail of the frigate, Sirena thought over Jacobus's words. And the Dutch captain's, whose ship she had gutted. Who among the Spanish—if indeed it was the Spanish—could be foreswearing the agreement made between the two nations and stealing great hordes of fertile nutmeg seeds? It would have to be a person of some power. And . . . only with difficulty and a great deal of bribing could it be a merchant or trader, for he would have only tenuous contact with the plantations. The most likely suspect would be a plantation owner, or someone who dealt directly with the island chieftains whose people grew the nutmegs. Someone like Regan . . . or—Don Chaezar Alvarez! The man's vainglorious personality, his desire for luxuries, his wish to return to Spain an honored and wealthy man . . . all these things came immediately to mind, though Sirena cursed herself that she should accuse, even mentally, a proud Iberian, a man of her own race. But . . . *could* Don Chaezar be removing the nutmegs from the island—hiding them somewhere beyond the seas, or even on a neighboring island? Or perhaps simply secreting them somewhere on Java, ready to abscond with them to his beloved Spain when the opportunity presented itself? But, then, where would he grow them in the homeland? Spain was far too dry, too rainless . . .

The wind blew Sirena's hair back from her face, the salt spray misted her eyes. Her heart lay heavy in her chest. Mournfully she remembered Jacobus's words: "Anyone caught smuggling fertile nutmegs out of the Indies can expect the death penalty." She was so mesmerized by her own thoughts that she failed to hear the soft, padding footsteps behind her. And then, suddenly, an uneasy feeling settled between her shoulders. The ship was too quiet. Where were all the men? Oh, yes, she remembered, she had told them to go below for ale. Perhaps she should join them—she had been "distant" for far too long.

She swung around from the rail—

And stared into the lustful eyes of the seaman Wouter.

She stood as if rooted to the deck, her mind spinning back in time to the moment when she stood like a trapped animal, staring into Dick Blackheart's eyes. Panic stunned her, but she willed her body into movement. Stumbling, she backed off one step, then two steps, her eyes glazed with fear. Step for step, Wouter stalked her—till he had her backed into the doorway of her cabin. Sirena knew she had to do something, but the fear coursing through her veins rendered her immobile. Her cutlass! She had to get her cutlass. Where was it? God in heaven! It was resting on a coil of rigging, where she had stood at the rail. But she had to do something. Anything! Her indecision cost her dearly, for Wouter forced her into the room and slammed the door shut.

No words were spoken as the seaman forced her backwards . . . backwards . . . till she collapsed on the narrow bunk, her eyes dilated with fear. Merciful God, not again! Not ever again!

A blood-curdling, high-pitched scream ripped from her throat just as Caleb burst into the room. Fearlessly, the boy brandished his rapier, and his voice was high and shrill as he demanded Sirena's release.

"Get out of here before I kill you, you whelp," Wouter shouted. "That puny blade is no threat to me. Now get your carcass out of here!" the seaman said, bringing up his cutlass.

Caleb, beside himself with fury at the torment in Sirena's eyes, shouted, "En garde!" and advanced a step aiming the rapier low and bringing it up with a lightning-quick movement. He noted the surprise in the hooded eyes of the seaman—for Caleb brought his blade straight up and then down with such force that the man's trousers ripped from groin to ankle. Clumsily, the seaman swung the heavy cutlass, missing the boy and slicing the air, and agile and quick-footed as a cat, Caleb leaped and parried with expertise.

Sirena knew that she must summon aid: the boy was not yet fully trained in the art of swordsmanship. And he would soon tire. On trembling legs she sidled out the door and shouted, with all her strength, "Jan! Jacobus! Anyone!"

The two men, accompanied by another seaman, Willem, and quickly followed by several more, arrived on the run, their cutlasses drawn.

"Nothing must happen to the boy! Nothing must happen to my brother!" Sirena screamed, gripping Jan's arm.

"He appears to have the battle in hand," Jan grinned. "That scurve Wouter is so full of ale he can barely see straight! The boy will finish him off in another minute."

"No, no, Jan, Caleb mustn't kill! Somehow you must intervene. The boy is too young to have blood on his hands!"

Jan looked with compassion at the Capitana. He nodded, waiting for an opportune moment. Caleb parried each thrust of the seaman's cutlass with wide purposeful lunges. Twice he drew blood from the drunken sailor. And both times he seemed to regain his stamina at the sight of his opponent's spouting blood.

"End it!" Jan shouted. "Let him go, Caleb, or kill him!"

The youth turned at the sound of the first mate's words and lost his advantage. Quickly Jan sliced the air between the seaman and Caleb, thrusting the boy out of harm's way.

"Open your drunken eyes now and fight like a man," Jan said brutally as he sliced at the man's legs. "No man on this ship swears his allegiance to the Capitana and then turns mutineer. You deserve to die like the vermin you are!"

"Bah," Wouter spat. "She's a piece of flesh, just like all women! She has one use and I claim her as mine!"

Wouter's hooded eyes were those of a vulture as he swung his cutlass, missing Jan's head by a wide margin. The first mate thrust again and again, forcing Wouter against the wall and knocking the cutlass from his hand. Then Jan drew back and swept the cutlass between the rebel seaman's ribs.

A fountain of blood gushed from Wouter's chest; his eyes went wide and disbelieving as he fell forward, his hand grasping for Sirena's booted foot. "You're—just a—piece—of flesh," he managed to gasp out in a froth of blood as his body slumped to the plank floor.

Chapter Seventeen

Sirena bided her time with short strolls around the vast van der Rhys gardens and frequent excursions into the kitchen to talk with Mella about the tasty new dishes the cook was now preparing for her mistress and young Caleb. Sirena had a growing affection for the kindly Malayan woman, who was enjoying her work immensely now.

At the back of Sirena's mind, however, the question still nagged: Was it truly Don Chaezar Alvarez who was hiding vast quantities of unlimed nutmegs somewhere on the island, or sending them off to a cache in Africa, India, or some Caribbean isle, She hoped, out of pride for her country's honor, that it was not he—not a Spaniard. But, she told herself, I must discover whether or not he is the offender. And discover it I will! If only to clear the name of the Spanish Crown!!

Today Sirena had been sewing in the shade of a luxuriant, wide-leaved shrub in the corner of the gardens farthest from the house. Abruptly laying aside her needlework, she stretched her arms wide and gazed around at the beautiful flowers that met the eye on all sides. Graceful breadfruit trees swayed and dipped in the light easterly breeze. Soon it would rain and then she would have to go indoors. With an anxious eye to the light fluffy clouds that were rapidly changing color, she noticed Caleb catapulting himself over the garden gate.

"Sirena!" he gasped, out of breath. "What a story I have to tell you! I had taken a walk—to the east side—of Batavia harbor," he stammered.

"Slow down, Caleb, or I won't be able to understand a word you say," Sirena ordered him, breathless in anticipation herself. Somehow she knew that what he had to tell her had something to do with the mystery of the unlimed nutmegs.

"Well, I was lying, out of the sun, in a clump of mangroves near the edge of the water. There are only a few small fishing boats at that end of the harbor, and almost nobody goes there. I was falling asleep when—when I heard him, and another man!"

"Heard who, little brother?"

"Señor Alvarez!"

Caleb took a deep breath and sank to his knees at her side. His breathing more normal, he hastened to explain: "I heard the Señor tell a man—and a cutthroat he was from the tone of his voice—that he was to help him tomorrow at dawn to move some nutmegs to a safer hiding place. That's what he said, Sirena, a safer hiding place. The other man was angry and called the Señor a 'worrying old woman.' And he said he had no intention of breaking his back a *fourth* time! He said he'd moved the nutmegs in their heavy casks three times already. He called Señor Alvarez many names and told him all the money in the Indies wouldn't make him move them again."

"What was Chaezar's answer to this?"

"The Señor told the man this was the last time they would be moved. He said one more trip and he would be ready to go to his 'kingdom'—whatever that means. And I know where he's going to move them, Sirena!"

"Where?" Sirena asked excitedly. This was what she'd been waiting for!

Caleb frowned. "To the southwestern tip of the island, fairly far from where he has them stored now. Now they are not far from Teatoa, where our crew live. "I think," he said, continuing to frown, "that if . . . if *we* were to go there, however"—his eyes sought Sirena's and she nodded to go on—"it would be best to go by land, and on horseback. The Señor intends mainly to go by sea and the lagoons, in a small launch with his man."

"You are right, Caleb. We could not risk attacking his tiny boat with the *Rana*, for we would be too close to shore, and would be seen."

Caleb continued: "I remember from my study of the maps, Sirena, that the cove where the Señor must berth his ship is small and narrow—and is the only suitable landing place on that part of the island; the other coves nearby are full of coral reefs. It is logical that he must take the nutmegs by boat, for carrying them overland would take more time and would be dangerous. Natives, or even white traders, might see him and his man. But you and I, and perhaps Jan and some of the crew, could go overland without too much suspicion."

"It certainly would be a novelty to have the Sea Siren attack by horseback. "Yes, little brother, horseback it is." He smiled as she continued: "Did the Señor say, more specifically, where near the cove he plans to store the nutmegs?"

Caleb laughed. "He was most explicit when he told his man where to place them. He said he wouldn't have to carry the casks far inland and that he had no need to worry about a strained back. Actually they are to be placed in a cave in plain view of the cove. Mangroves are to be cut and thrown over the entrance when the casks will be secured."

"You did well, little brother. When does he sail, did he say?"

"At mid-evening, Sirena."

"Do you think it would be wise for us to travel tonight by horseback and wait near the cove, or let them secure the nutmegs and set out tomorrow night?"

Caleb's eyes danced with excitement. "Speaking for myself, I'd rather go tonight. I'm tired of sitting about with nothing to do. I'd best set off immediately to alert Jan, and maybe Willem, to meet us as usual with the horses." Then, as was his custom when he became bored, he harked back to his favorite subject. "When are we going to have another fencing lesson, Sirena?"

Ever since the day he had confronted Wouter and had failed to finish the job himself, Caleb had insisted on doubling his fencing lessons. More than once

Sirena had been tempted to tell him that Jan had only intervened on her orders. The boy had taken a wide leap toward manhood when he challenged Wouter to defend Sirena, and his expertise with the rapier had been formidable. Indeed, he could have finished off the lustful seaman. But Sirena had not wanted the youth's hands to be tainted with blood—not yet. And, she had told herself several times since the encounter aboard the *Rana,* too much confidence—if he had in fact killed Wouter—might be the death of the boy.

Nevertheless, Caleb believed that Jan had intervened because he had not had the skill to fight Wouter to the death. And this belief nagged at him, hurt him.

"We could practice tonight, Sirena. After my return from the village, and before we follow Señor Alvarez and his man."

"On our return from the cove, little brother. On our return. You've enough to test your strength before our departure! Now—off you go to Teatoa!'

Caleb's eyes swung overhead to the daily gathering of dark clouds as Sirena picked up her needlework and headed for the house.

Because of a dense fog that hid him and Willem, Jan Verhooch brought the horses from their jungle pasture and stable near the river directly to the edge of the van der Rhys gardens. Sirena put her finger to her lips in a gesture to be silent as she and Caleb approached the two seamen. And only when the four were at a safe distance from the house, crossing the vast plantation and headed up into the foothills that lay inland, to the south of Batavia, did she speak a word.

"Caleb has studied the maps carefully, Jan. But we'll all have to be alert if we're to cross the island and not lose ourselves in these forested foothills or in the jungle we're sure to meet as we descend toward the sea on the south side of the island." Turning to Caleb, she asked, "What would be your guess as to when the Spaniard and his accomplice will arrive?"

At the word "accomplice," Jan's and Willem's faces

became grim masks: as Dutchmen they realized fully the treachery in which Don Chaezar Alvarez was engaged.

"The Señor travels with a full hold. But the breeze is fresh. If he sails the launch with a half-furled sail he should arrive at Rara Cove—that's what it's called on the maps—within three hours. He had, of course, perhaps an hour or two's start on us. However . . . if the fog moves out to sea before long, he may be delayed."

"Aye," said Willem, turning to look back down toward the plantation and the town. "See how it curls like wisps of smoke and how it moves toward the sea's edge."

On reaching the highest hills in the spine of low mountains that separated Batavia and the island's north shore from the less populated southern coast, Sirena ordered the two men and Caleb to a halt.

"I've brought some fruit and cheese and wine. We'll rest now, and eat!"

As they tethered their horses, Caleb asked Sirena, "Will you attack the Spaniard, once he's beached the launch? And will you destroy the nutmegs?"

Jan and Willem were all ears.

"Too many questions at once, little brother. I'll do neither. Though we've Jan and Willem with us, there's no need to attack Don Chaezar. And as for the nutmegs, I have what I believe is an interesting plan. We'll move the nutmegs to another hiding place! And leave evidence that will let him know he's been robbed of them! What a surprise for our elegant representative of the Spanish Crown when he next looks in the cave!" Then, turning to the men: "We'll rest a while, Jan. We've the time. Will either of you or Willem keep watch, and let us not sleep too long?"

Willem responded, "I'll do the duty, Capitana, if you and Jan agree. He's had a busy day today, what with the fishing. Busier than mine, I'll wager—for I caught none!"

Chuckling, Sirena finished a small slab of cheese and wrapped her heavy cloak about her, for here in the highlands the temperature was chill. The thick fog swirling about her gave her a lonely feeling despite the company she had with her. She dozed from time to time, and woke an hour later at Willem's nudging.

The small party descended the slopes toward Java's southern coast.

Sirena, Caleb, Jan, and Willem crouched in a clump of palms and mangrove bushes some fifty feet from the eastern bank of narrow Rara Cove. Caleb's map study had brought them to their goal half an hour before.

All four came suddenly to alert attention at the sound of oars hitting against the sides of a small boat. They had not seen the launch approach!

Within minutes, they saw a bobbing light through the fog and heard the scrape of the boat's hull on the sand at the end of the cove. Soon the sound of voices —two men's, they judged—reached them. They heard muttering, labored breathing, cursing, as well as what was evidently Don Chaezar's voice peremptorily ordering his man to more speed. "More foot power—" and curses. From time to time there was a thump, as of a wooden cask being let fall from the edge of the launch onto the sand below; then followed the heaving breathing of a man who must be lifting it to his shoulders. This last sound was repeated, Sirena noted, twenty-five times.

"Traitor!" Sirena murmured half to herself. "That traitor Alvarez—who would break his country's word to gain wealth for himself alone!"

Abruptly now, words reached the four clearly for the first time.

"Well . . . that's the last of them. An easy night's work, wouldn't you say?" The elegant tones of Don Chaezar Alvarez rankled Sirena.

"If all I'd had to do was hoist the casks to the launch's rail and drop them to the sand—yes! But lugging them to the cave—some forty yards away—that's a different story! My back will be bent out of shape tomorrow. And, I tell ye, I want double the amount you promised me!"

"I'm paying you precisely what the work was

worth. Greed," Alvarez sneered, "is not an admirable trait."

His accomplice's answer was a harsh and guttural cry—and Sirena heard the man spit. "I'll have twice the amount or—"

Chaezar broke in: "You leave me no other choice, José." Then, in a softer tone: "Sooner or later I knew it would come to this."

"But—I didn't mean— No! No!" And then they heard a gurgling sound, and no more words.

Sirena placed a restraining arm on Jan's as he began to rise.

The sound of oars reached their ears once more, and through the fog the yellow launch light bobbed as the boat moved away, out of the cove, toward the lagoons it would follow back around the island's western tip on its return to Batavia.

When she was certain the launch had raised its sails and was safely out of the cove, Sirena rose and, followed by the men, crossed down the sand to the spot from whence the voices had come.

As she stumbled on something soft and unmoving, she fell to her knees. "Here he is, Jan!" She put her ear close to the man's chest. "No signs of life. Will you—Jan and Willem—do what you can to bury him?"

Caleb touched Sirena's arm. "Sirena," he said, "the fog is still thick here—but inland it will not be so. Shall I search out a new hiding place for the nutmegs?"

"Yes, little brother. But first let me light this oil lamp. By it, you'll see where we stand."

As her two seamen dragged the unfortunate José's body back into the bushes, Sirena, another lamp in her hand, made her way toward where she thought the cave must be. Caleb disappeared into the jungle.

Through the lifting fog, Sirena spied Caleb, clambering through some mangroves and onto the beach.

"I found another cave—and it's not far from here!" he cried exultantly.

"Good lad!" shouted Jan.

"Aye, aye!" Willem yelled.

"We have our work cut out for us, men!" Sirena sighed. "But I want to scatter the contents of one cask in his cave, for I want him to think he's been robbed."

"You'll not lift a cask, Capitana!" Jan smiled. "Not if I have anything to say about it!"

"But you don't." And Sirena pitched in to help.

Within minutes, the first of the twenty-five casks had been transported up a slope behind the cave to what appeared to be a screen of impenetrable bamboo. Behind the stalks of thick bamboo, however, lay the low and narrow entrance to a tiny cave. So low was the cave roof that only Caleb could stand inside. It was he who, for the next hour and a half, rolled the casks as they arrived—sometimes carried by Jan and Willem, sometimes by Jan and Sirena, sometimes by Willem and the Capitana—back into the depths of this lucky hole he had found.

"Now let Señor Alvarez wonder what has become of his treasure!" Sirena exclaimed, somewhat breathless, as the last of the kegs was pushed by Caleb to the dark extremities of the cave. "He'll have to begin again, if he wants nutmegs for his 'kingdom'! And, what's more, I doubt that there's another man on Java whom he'll trust with his secret from this day on!"

Riding slowly upward through the foothills, through the forests which the sun barely penetrated, Sirena's horse—as well as the mounts of the other three—began to shy nervously.

"There, there . . ." she soothed the roan, "what's troubling you, my beauty?" Petting the horse's sweat-slick neck, she continued to coo to him, persuading him to keep steady in his pace.

Caleb, his mount in control after a moment of fright, scanned upward toward the highest slopes for some sign of what had made the horses skittish. Exchanging glances with Jan and Willem, he rode on watchfully, leading the small party.

As they entered a clearing at the top of the final slope, the group halted, alarmed. The sunlight, not an hour old, for they'd wanted to reach Batavia before the day was much spent, appeared suddenly to dissolve behind a gray, ashen sky that was ominous with pale yellow streaks darting toward the horizon. A noxious odor of sulphur struck their nostrils and made them smart. Then, without further warning, the earth beneath them volleyed and trembled, and the trees about them swayed as if pummeled by a silent wind.

The horses neighed and whinnied now in panic, pawing the air with their forelegs and nearly throwing the four riders from their backs.

Jumping down from his saddle, Jan warned, "It's the Sisters of Fire!" A white ring of fear circled his mouth, his eyes were bright with anxiety.

Quickly following his example, the others dismounted and attempted to calm their frightened horses. The sky had now almost completely darkened, and was peppered with a glowing red ash that began to rain down on them, though the Sisters were many miles away.

Pulling the horses behind them, the four ran for cover beneath a dense clump of breadfruit trees. There, safe from most of the singeing and stinging ash, they soothed the nervous beasts. Gratefully, Sirena's roan nuzzled his velvety nose against her, nickering softly.

Then, abruptly, the still trees were shaken by a second tremor and another gush of sulphurous gasses reached the noses of the four hidden among the trees.

"Capitana, have you heard the legend about the Sisters?" Willem asked Sirena.

She shook her head.

"Native stories have it that the Sisters are angry at some proud and sinful woman, and that one day they will destroy her."

" 'Tis true, Capitana, what Willem says," Jan put in. "All the Javanese who trade with our fishing village—so near one of the Sisters—confirm the legend. Lately, though the Sisters have been quiet, a story has gone about that they are nearly ready to render judgment on the woman." Jan laughed softly, as if he disbelieved what the natives thought true.

But Sirena was wondering who the "proud and sinful woman" might be . . .

Chapter Eighteen

"Are you ready, Sirena? Regan is waiting for us downstairs," Caleb exclaimed breathlessly as he burst into Sirena's room.

She was seated before the silver-framed mirror that hung over her dressing table. "Let him wait!" she grumbled as she impatiently tugged at a tendril of hair that had escaped the sleek knot at the nape of her neck. She had adjusted her black lace mantilla for the fourth time and was still dissatisfied with the effect.

Caleb watched her, questioning her disgruntled mood. Sirena read his expression in the reflection of her looking glass. "I didn't mean to snap at you, Caleb. It's just that I'm so sick and tired of wearing the same black gowns and hiding behind this lace curtain. I always look the same!" She was thinking of Gretchen and the myriad of colors she wore. "And now I can't get this comb to stay where I put it! Go tell Regan I'm not going to the wedding. Tell him I've got a headache! Tell him anything—but I'm not going!"

"Sirena, you must go. The bride is the daughter of a Javanese chieftain, a very important man. Regan's the head of the Dutch East India Company, and as his wife you'd insult the man if you didn't go. This could stir up trouble: insult the chief and you insult every Javanese on the island. All the native servants would refuse to work, the sailors, the fishermen . . ."

"You've made your point, Caleb. I've stirred up enough trouble, is that it?" When he didn't answer she turned around and gave him a sharp look. "The least you could do, little brother, is *pretend* that isn't what you meant!" Still, when no excuse or answer was forthcoming, Sirena conceded: "Very well, go tell Regan I'll be a few moments yet. There's no help for it, I'll have to go to the wedding dressed like a nun!" She turned back to the mirror and picked up the mantilla.

"No you don't! Wait a minute, Sirena, don't do anything, I'll be right back!" Caleb ran out of the room as quickly as he had entered it. Within minutes he was back again, holding several camellia-like blooms in his hand. "Try these instead of your comb."

"Caleb! They're—they're just the thing!"

Sirena arranged three of the waxy-white flowers on the crown of her head, their paleness making a striking contrast with her raven hair. She arranged the mantilla over them, allowing the flowers to peek through the fine web of scalloped lace. For effect, she placed an unopened bud in the bodice of her gown between her breasts.

"There, how do you like it?'

She needed no answer. Caleb was wearing an expression of admiration on his boy's face.

"You're a genius, Caleb. Well, don't just stand there. Do you want to make us late?" She picked up her skirts and breezed out of the room.

Sirena rode between Regan and Caleb in the carriage on the way to the Javanese village. Sirena remembered it was called Djatumi, a village in the mountains southeast of Batavia. Regan's eyes kept sliding covertly to the bud Sirena had placed between her breasts. The delicate white of the flower perfectly offset the silky texture and the buffed ivory tone of her skin.

Feeling Regan's eyes on her, Sirena was annoyed that it should excite her so. She almost wanted to tear the flowers from her hair and rip the bud from her gown. Then she thought of the almost-dressed Gretchen at Don Chaezar's ball and the way Regan's eyes drank her in. Let him look, she thought, a smile of mischief playing about her lips. Looking wasn't touching.

From her seat in the carriage she could hear their baggage thump behind them each time the wheels hit a rut in the road. The actual wedding ceremony would not take place until the next day. But Caleb had explained to her that he'd learned that the day before the wedding was, to the Javanese, almost as important as the actual ceremony. There were rituals to which every bride must conform, and Sirena—as Regan's wife and therefore a most honored guest—would be privileged to witness these solemn preparations. She and Regan would sleep in the village compound tonight as a further honor to the bride and groom.

Until this moment Sirena had not realized the implications of staying away for the night with Regan. She chanced a worried look at her husband.

As if reading her thoughts, Regan said, "Don't worry, Sirena, you'll be left to your prayers." His eyes then lighted with a mocking look. "It's against local custom for men and their wives to cohabit until after the bride and groom are married. The men and women will occupy separate quarters. Kalava, the chief, will have had separate huts prepared for us."

Regan laughed aloud when he saw he had been correct in guessing her thoughts, for the tiny frown between Sirena's finely arched brows faded. "As a matter of fact, once we get to the village the women will sweep you away and Caleb and I will go on to the groom's house."

For more than an hour they rode through the lush, green foothills. Then, in a clearing just below the cliff-like slopes of the first full-sized mountain they had encountered on their trip thus far, sat the tiny town of Djatumi. The village was festooned with flowers and garlands. In its center, over a wide open pit, several old women were roasting a wild boar and baking little round loaves of bread on flat rocks near the fire. There were no men in the town, Sirena saw at a glance.

When the women saw Regan's carriage drive into the clearing, they dropped what they were doing and ran to greet their guests, calling to other women inside the huts. Regan jumped down from the trap and courteously helped Sirena from the high carriage step to the dusty ground. From over Regan's shoulder Sirena now saw a lovely young brown-skinned girl come running out of a large hut. Several women were chasing after her in squealing protest. As Regan turned, the girl threw herself into his arms in joyous greeting.

"Telaga! How you've grown!" he roared.

The women who had been chasing the maiden had caught up with her, but stood a respectful distance away from Regan and Sirena. The Mynheer continued his conversation with the young girl in Javanese dialect. A moment later, he greeted an older woman who was looking sternfaced at the impetuous girl. It must be some joke, Sirena guessed, for the woman covered her mouth with her hand, tittering in delight. Sirena speculated the woman must be the girl's mother—who was very perturbed that her daughter should break custom and show herself—before her wedding—to a man. But Regan, with his charming ways, had cajoled her into a better temper.

With great ceremony, Regan now introduced Sirena and Caleb. Several of the native women hurried forth and picked up Sirena's trunk which Ling Fu had lifted out of the baggage compartment. Others crowded around Sirena and she was glad to hear one of them address her in Spanish.

"I am Nalu, Mevrouw," she said, her voice high and delicate-sounding. "The bride is my cousin, Telaga. Please forgive the naughty girl, but she could not help herself—Mynheer van der Rhys has been a family friend for many years. He knows Telaga since she was only a little girl. I speak Spanish very good, *sí?* I will stay with you, Mevrouw—or would you rather have me call you Señora?" Sirena nodded; she so detested the awful-sounding "Mevrouw." "You will please come with me?"

Just as Sirena was about to follow Nalu and the other women, Regan stepped up to her and made a courtly bow. "Until tomorrow, my dear."

Taking advantage of her inability to protest without making a fool of herself, he put his arms around her and kissed her tenderly on the mouth. Before he released her, he plucked the bud from between her breasts, looked mockingly into her eyes, and kissed its pearly petals.

The Javanese women nearly swooned with the implied sexuality of his gesture. Sirena felt her cheeks grow warm and her temper flare. How dare he do this to her when she was a helpless prisoner of propriety? How she would love to scratch that smile from his face!

Regaining her composure, she turned to say good-bye to Caleb, whose reddened cheeks betrayed that he had witnessed Regan's intimate gesture.

It was then that she felt something else, as though a spear of ice had been thrust into her back, chilling her to the bone. Her glance fell on Telaga, whose black eyes were staring into her, through her, with shocking hatred! Telaga's mother also noted her daughter's distorted features and hurried the girl away, making a hasty good-bye to Regan and Caleb.

Nalu, who had also seen the undisguised hatred in Telaga's eyes, led Sirena toward the huts. "Please, do not pay attention to my ungrateful cousin. She is a spoiled and willful creature. Mynheer van der Rhys has been almost an . . . uncle to her since she was only a child. She always had grand ideas and imagined that someday she would be his wife. Not that the Mynheer ever gave her reason to hope for such an unlikely event," Nalu hastened to add, her embarrassment suffusing her brown cheeks with pink. "Mynheer has been like an . . . uncle."

Sirena followed Nalu into one of two new-looking huts that were separate from the other buildings in the village. "Our chieftain, my uncle, had these huts erected especially for the Mevrouw and Mynheer," Nalu explained. "As you know, all husbands and wives in the village must remain apart until after the wedding ceremony. I know this is a great hardship on the Mynheer. Everyone in the village could see how much he loves his Mevrouw."

Nalu giggled and Sirena knew she was referring to that tender kiss Regan had given her before he left her in the woman's hands.

When Sirena made no comment, Nalu was afraid she had spoken out of turn. These Europeans had such strange attitudes concerning love and passion . . . They were so tight-lipped about love, easily embarrassed and secretive. So unlike the easy free-living Javanese.

"Has the Señora ever attended a Javanese kawin—that is to say, wedding?" Sirena shook her head. "Not to worry, Señora, Nalu will explain everything to you and you will do everything exactly correct." The plump, smiling native beamed at Sirena confidently. Her smile was so infectious and friendly that Sirena found she was liking Nalu more each minute.

"We will have to hurry, Señora. You must change into this humble garment. All women attending the pre-nuptial pageant must wear them."

Nalu held up a kaftan of sheer, cool, gauze-like material richly embroidered around the neck and sleeves with the most exquisite handwork Sirena had ever seen. Humble indeed! Quickly Nalu helped her make the change. Her dark, heavy, and unsuitable gown was exchanged for the cool kaftan. By suddenly calling Nalu's attention to the lace mantilla's proper storage, Sirena was able to conceal her scarred arm. When the native woman had returned to her side, Sirena's hair was unloosed and allowed to fall in a heavy cascade down her back. A circlet of flowers was placed on her head. On her feet she wore the soft, calfskin sandals common to the natives.

"It is a disgrace for the Señora to dress like a Javanese servant," Nalu sighed, fingering the rich material of Sirena's black gown. "But it is the custom that all the women be dressed alike."

Sirena noted that although the style of her costume was similar to what the others wore, great pains had been taken with its embroidery to make it worthy of the honored Chief Pensioner's wife.

"Come, Señora, it is time for the dilalar and Telaga is a bad-humored girl when kept waiting."

Sirena followed Nalu out of the hut into the sunshine of the village clearing. Across the space, in the shade of the trees, all the women were gathered expectantly. Apparently they had been waiting for Sirena, for when they saw her approach they all welcomed her in light, musical voices and turned their attentions at once to the pageant.

Telaga was sitting on a grass mat in the middle of the circle formed by the women. Sirena was not expected to sit cross-legged on the little cushions strewn over the ground; Nalu led her instead to a comfortable-looking little chair upholstered in soft, shimmering satin.

Telaga cast Sirena a momentary stinging look and then turned her attentions back to the ongoing events. Immediately several village matrons stepped out of the circle and went to the girl. They stripped her of her clothing, leaving her body bare to the afternoon sun now filtering through the trees. Sirena saw that Telaga was breathtakingly beautiful! Her heavy jet-black hair was tied in a knot atop her head, lending grace to her long, slim neck. Her body was slim and delicate. Small but full breasts rested high on her torso. Her legs were long, and gracefully tapered to tiny, narrow feet. Her skin was the color of honey—tan with rich golden depths that heightened the whiteness of her teeth and the blackness of her eyes.

With great dignity, Telaga now lay face down on the mat. Three village matrons dipped their hands into pots of a coarse-looking powder and began to massage Telaga's body with it until the honey skin turned pink. While the massage was taking place the other women in the circle clapped their hands and sang songs. Telaga's mother bit her lips and held back tears of pride and sympathy at this, the first step toward her only daughter's marriage.

"The powder they use is called lalar, Señora," Nalu explained, "It is made of temoe and ketan leaves ground together."

Whatever it was, Sirena noticed that it seemed to be quite abrasive. Telaga's skin was now a deep and angry shade of red. When the matrons turned the girl onto her back, Sirena could see she was biting her lips to control tears of pain. But with seemingly no pity, the women continued to rub her with the coarse powder from head to toe—until not an inch of her body was left undone. Then they helped her to her feet and sat her in a large tub of water, washing away the dull gray powder and cooling her stinging flesh. After they had dried her off, they led her back to the grass mat.

Over the voices of the chanting women, Nalu explained: "Now they will rub her with bedak wida. This is not so bad, Señora. It is ground very fine and smells good." Nalu also explained that the recipes for the lalar and bedak wida are strictly adhered to and that every Javanese girl must submit to the massage according to custom. Working diligently, not an inch of flesh escaping their notice, the women rubbed Telaga with a mixture of the bedak wida and rendered fat. It had indeed a pungent smell, filling the air with a scent of herbs and leaves reminiscent, to Sirena, of spice and woodlands. Telaga's body glowed pink and fresh.

Moments later, Telaga was bathed again in fresh water and returned once more to the mat.

"Now, Senora, now is the time Telaga must show great courage. You will see. If she utters one sound during this ceremony her mother will be obliged to beat her. To cry now would be proof that Telaga is not a virgin."

With great pomp and circumstance six matrons surrounded Telaga's supine form. The bride's mother stood just outside the circle of crouching women, holding a long switch cut from a tree. Her expression was solemn. The singing halted abruptly and the air was still with expectation.

The six matrons immediately attacked the bride's body from the neck down, plucking the hairs from her! Telaga displayed her virtue by not uttering a sound.

When the women had plucked every hair from her arms and legs, a woven, circular grass screen was placed between Telaga and the audience to protect her modesty. Only Telaga's mother was allowed to witness the completion of the depilation ceremony.

When at last the screen was removed, Telaga was standing on the grass mat, her body completely denuded of hair, her expression triumphant. She had undergone the Test of the Virgin with tremendous success! The mother of the bride beamed with pride.

Another bath, another massage with soothing oil . . . and Telaga's body shone with a soft, supple glow. Her hair was now loosened from its topknot and her mother washed it and rinsed it with coconut milk; it was then smoked over a fire of sweet-scented wood to give it a pleasant odor. The ritual was at last ended by Telaga's being anointed with exotic oils called tapel.

Nalu's eyes were misted with tears. "How beautiful she is! I remember when *I* was prepared for my husband . . ." she sighed wistfully.

The singing began again, but instead of the cheerful, high-spirited songs of before, the new tunes were sensual and almost mournful. Several of the older women, who Nalu told Sirena were Telaga's aunts, began keening and wailing. They were crying for the lost flower of Telaga's youth. They had seen her through the ritual of readying herself for her husband and were joyful for the exciting night of love Telaga would experience, but they were mourning for the loss of her carefree youth. Soon would come the pain of childbirth, the responsibilities of maturity, the sadness of growing older . . .

Telaga's mother finally stepped forward and draped her daughter with a fine kaftan edged with pale blue flowers. Telaga stood tall, her slim and graceful body held erect, her demeanor prideful and even haughty, for she was certain of her beauty. A crown of flowers was placed on her head and smaller garlands were fitted to her wrists and ankles. The girl had been prepared for her groom, her skin shone like sleek satin, she was the essence of femininity and desirability, pampered and petted for a night of erotic love.

Telaga's dark, insolent gaze met Sirena's. In that one glance Sirena understood with infallible womanly intuition that it was Regan, however, for whom Telaga yearned. She wanted Regan alone to enjoy the delights of her body, to smell her sweet, wood-scented hair, to caress her silky, anointed skin. Sirena wondered if Regan's first wife, Tita, had undergone this difficult ritual and if it had, indeed, made her more desirable to the Mynheer.

The women now swarmed about Telaga to congratulate her, and the girl glowed with pride. Huge platters of food were quickly brought forth and the women ate with gusto. As did Sirena, who had seldom tasted more delicious fare.

When the last of the rich, spicy food was eaten and everyone was sated, the platters were cleared away and a stirring of excitement ran through the gathering. Night had come with its velvety softness. In a few hours the men of the village would be returning and the women's festivities must come to an end. Nalu told Sirena that the time had now come for the women to present their gifts to the bride.

Sirena hurried back to her hut and brought out her gift, which was wrapped in rice paper. Regan had given it to her to present to Telaga, but Sirena had seen the present and admired it. It was a length of fine Chinese silk dyed a jewel-toned emerald.

When Telaga opened the rice paper and withdrew the length of silk, gasps of appreciation escaped the retinue of onlookers. Telaga, too, was seemingly impressed with the gift, for she smiled at Sirena and thanked her. Then, with a graceful flourish, she wrapped the silk about herself, looking quite smug and satisfied.

The gifts that followed Sirena's overwhelmed her by their diversity—and practicality: household items of every sort . . . grass mats . . . lengths of cloth . . . the necessary carven images of Javanese gods. Then, after what had seemed, to Sirena, like hours, the village women once again surrounded the bride-to-be. With native-crafted knives they snipped an inch or so from Telaga's luxuriant length of hair; the snippings were divided among the girl's relatives.

Once again Nalu came to Sirena and explained the custom. "Her relatives are each to place their lock of hair into the shell of a young coconut and toss it into the sea. This is to insure that Telaga will bear many healthy children."

Telaga was finally led to a hut constructed of palm leaves and thatch, which she entered alone. Before her daughter could step inside, Telaga's mother hurried up to her to embrace her solemnly and issue directions for her behavior during the night to come.

Huge tears stained the cheeks of the woman as they walked away, leaving Telaga in the palm hut.

"She's to spend the night in contemplation," said Nalu. "She is to think seriously of the life before her as a married woman. All night she will sit, among pots of flowers, with nothing but the Klapagading to keep her company. Oh, this is a bowl of bananas, betel-nut, and two yellow coconuts on one of which is a drawing of the god Ardjoeno and on the other of Soembadja, his wife."

From the forest nearby, masculine shouts of revelry abruptly broke the solemn silence and Nalu cautioned Sirena, "Hurry, Señora, to your hut! It is unlucky for the bride if the men gaze upon even one of us. Hurry, my lady!"

Sirena dashed into the hut with Nalu close behind. As the noisy men marched into the village Nalu peeked out from behind the palm leaves which made up the walls of the hut.

"Nalu, I thought it was unlucky for Telaga if one of the men sees the women!" Sirena called to her.

"Yes, surely, Señora, the most horrible things will befall the marriage! Telaga's hair will fall out, she will be unable to bear children, her husband will take a lover and bring the woman to Telaga's house for Telaga to tend her and wait on her . . . Terrible things! Bad luck, Señora!"

"Then why are you peeking out at the men?" Sirena demanded.

"It is not bad luck for the women to see the men, Señora," Nalu said with incomprehensible native logic. "You can believe me that each woman here looks out to see how much rum her husband has drunk so she can plague the poor man and make his life miserable if it was more than to his wife's liking."

Sirena heard Regan's booming voice singing loudly above the other men's. It came closer and closer and Nalu noticed Sirena stiffen with apprehension. "Do not worry, Señora, the Mynheer will not come in here. He knows the custom, he would not want to bring bad luck on Telaga," Nalu whispered. "His hut is next to this one, he goes there. The Señora's brother will sleep with the other village boys tonight."

Regan's roaring voice could be heard clearly as he entered the hut that had been erected not ten feet away from Sirena's. His singing continued for a moment or so, then stopped.

"The Mynheer will sleep well tonight—as will all the men. So much rum drowns their need for a woman. Good night, Señora, until the morning."

"Good night, Nalu," Sirena answered politely. But her thoughts were on the man in the next hut.

Having changed from her kaftan to a nightdress, Sirena lay on the low mat bed, taking care to drop the fine mosquito netting into place around her. She closed her eyes, ready for sleep. Her last waking thoughts were of Telaga sitting alone in the darkened hut, with pots of flowers, fruits, nuts, and two coconuts for company.

The night was hot, the humidity oppressive. Sirena awoke with her nightdress clinging uncomfortably to her perspiring body. She was aware of the sound of wind blowing through the treetops, though no air stirred within the hut's palm-leaved walls. She sat up, pulled the wispy mosquito netting away impatiently, and slipped her feet into the calfskin sandals Nalu had given her.

Stepping outside her door, she saw a faint glimmer of light in the eastern sky; it must be near dawn, she mused. Sirena stretched out her arms to the breeze, which caught her damp nightdress, cooling and refreshing her. Then suddenly a sound fell on her ears and quickly she stepped back into the doorway of her hut, realizing that according to village custom she should not have been out, beyond the enclosure of her hut. If one of the men had seen her, she would be accused of wishing to bring bad luck on Telaga. The sound was closer now, the sound of stealthy footsteps!

A cloud crossed the waning moon and, from her hiding place just inside the doorway, Sirena could see little. Then, peering out cautiously, she saw a figure nearing the hut next to hers. As the steps halted, she heard a scratching noise. A moment later, the door to Regan van der Rhys's hut opened, the light from a candle outlining the man in its flickering yellow light—

And casting a golden glow on the girl Telaga!

She wore a sarong made of the emerald-colored silk Sirena had given her as a wedding gift!

Sirena gasped and involuntarily took a step outside her own hut. The two—caught at their moment of meeting—turned to see her. Telaga's eyes gleamed triumphantly and a wicked smile distorted her pretty mouth. After an instant's surprise, Regan's full mouth opened wide in a mocking grin; his eyelids, reflecting the golden light of the candle, were heavy with the effects of rum.

Sirena froze immediately in her tracks as her husband stepped gallantly aside, allowing Telaga entrance to his lodging. Red-faced with embarrassment, yet quaking with fury, Sirena rushed inside her stifling, airless hut and flung herself down on the mat bed.

Minutes passed as she lay listening, imagining her husband caressing the Javanese girl—only a few feet away—though not a sound from the neighboring hut reached her ears. Only the wind, rising now as morning dawned over the village, blotted out the sound of her tormented sobs.

Chapter Nineteen

Days raced into months as the Sea Siren plundered the Java seas at sporadic intervals, generally sparing neither Dutch nor Spanish ships in her search for The Hook. Her laugh rang across the water following each victory, making the men in their bobbing jolly-boats tremble with fear not only of the sea they faced in such small vessels but of the "sea witch" herself! Some now called her the "devil witch," too. Many were her names. Her own crew were more and more proud to serve under her—not only because of her expertise but because she refused to gut any ship that asked for quarter, letting it pass by unharmed after inspecting the hands of its seamen.

One particular star-filled evening, when Sirena and Caleb stole out of the house to ride with Jan to the secret cove where the *Rana* was berthed, she was welcomed with cheers from the crew. Old Jacobus, the cook, seemed especially glad and excited to see her.

"Capitana! Capitana! Come see what we've done!"

Solemnly the crew led her to the bow of the black frigate. Willem held high a lantern. There on the frigate tip, painted in bold white letters, was the name *Sea Siren.* Once, Caleb had explained to her that the superstitious crew were uneasy about serving on a now-nameless ship, for when the ship had been repainted black the name *Rana* had been obliterated.

Sirena was touched, the crew proud. Jan cracked a keg of ale, Jacobus opened a wheel of cheese, and the crew and their capitana spent the evening telling tales of derring-do—all the while singing seafaring songs. Sirena played the guitar she always kept in her cabin, and sang love ballads. Some of the older men, remembering their youth—in Amsterdam, Rotterdam, The Hague, Delft, and other cities of the Low Countries, so far away—cried shamelessly at the sound of her lovely voice and the sad music.

Riding home, near dawn, after finding no quarry that night, Sirena was quiet and thoughtful. "What's worrying you, Sirena?" Caleb asked.

Jan merely rode along silently.

"Our many absences from the house. Have you noticed how Frau Holtz watches us?"

"Aye, she makes me nervous. She almost seems to play cat-and-mouse."

"Not cat-and-mouse. Rat-and-mouse! I think our story of taking these frequent retreats is becoming weak. Soon she will go to Regan and then there will be trouble. I have a feeling she suspects, now, that we leave the house."

"Perhaps she should be given a pension and retired to a tiny house somewhere in Batavia," Caleb volunteered.

"She's done nothing to warrant her dismissal, little brother. I would find that difficult to justify to Regan."

"Then if that is the case, the days the *Sea Siren* is being refitted with new riggings will be to our advantage. They will keep us at home!"

"It will help. But we'll think of something, have no fear."

Caleb smiled, and Jan too. "When I'm with you, Sirena, I never quail. I know that you will find the solution, however hard that may be to do."

Sirena stood, her legs slightly parted, hands on her hips, looking toward the upstairs window. Sighing wearily, she lamented, "I don't seem to recall the window being so high, do you?"

"In truth, no. Every time we return it grows higher to my eye, and the trellis longer. You first, big sister. I'll be close behind."

Boy and woman were midway up the stout vines when a shadow crossed the garden beneath them. The figure stood in the darkness of the lush foliage and watched the ascent of the duo as they made their slow progress upward. When a faint, murky glow appeared in the window, indicating that a lamp was lit, the figure crossed the garden and reentered the house.

Caleb made daily journeys to the cove where the *Sea Siren* was berthed and came home each afternoon with a report on the progress the men were making.

"Enough of this lazing about," Sirena muttered to herself as she got to her feet one afternoon. "What sort of life is this?" she questioned herself. "If it weren't for the fact that I take to the sea I'd be a babbling idiot by now! I think I'll pay Don Chaezar Alvarez a visit. I long for some conversation and a little flattery . . . The bastard! Perhaps I can find out, too, what he's up to."

She was descending the wide staricase when Regan emerged from his office. He looked at her coolly and she raised her eyes to meet his. "And where is it you go, Sirena?"

At sight of him, Sirena's eyes narrowed, but she pulled her mantilla modestly across her face. "I . . . I thought, my husband, that I would lunch with your friend Don Chaezar Alvarez. But . . . would you care to join me?" Regan's face made no answer. "No? Well, then, I'll leave you to your duties or pleasures—"

"One moment, Sirena!" His voice had grown stern. "I can't allow this. You are my wife, you are yet in mourning for your uncle, *and* this is not your first luncheon with Don Chaezar!" Regan strode up and down on the hall rug. "You are—well, making me look a fool. There is talk . . . in town . . . that I cannot control my wife."

Sirena ventured a challenge: "Your wife, if I may say so, in name only. As yet." Despite her calm tones, Sirena felt a churning in her stomach when she thought back to the humiliation of her wedding night.

Regan stood rooted to the spot and gazed, curious, at this odd Spanish woman. Why did she bring up the fact that their marriage was one in name only when that was exactly what she herself had wanted! Or was it? The woman was passionate, perhaps, after all?

"Ah, my dear husband," Sirena went on, seeing his bewilderment, "do these same people . . . who say that I am making a fool of you . . . know of our agreement that I shall live a separate life until my year of mourning is over?"

"The matter is ended. If you wish to go for a ride I'll have one of the servants accompany you."

"I need no servant to play nursemaid, Mynheer. I shall, of course, be discreet. I shall not stay long. I need no duenna."

"*I* say you do," Regan replied coldly. "Which is it to be? I have a great deal of work that demands my attention. Decide now, before I lose my patience."

"Very well, send for Juli. I must obey my husband's orders." Though her voice seemed cool, Regan detected the heat in it.

Sirena rode in the open trap next to her handmaid. She smiled upon hearing Juli's indrawn breath when she ordered the trap into Don Chaezar Alvarez's tree-lined drive. "You will wait here," Sirena said to the girl.

"Mevrouw, Mynheer said—"

"And I have said for you to wait here. You may report that to Mynheer upon our return. Amuse yourself with the magnificent view of the wharf."

Chaezar himself opened the door. Grasping her hand and bowing low, he brought it to his lips, his eyes searching hers.

"You're truly a gallant, Chaezar. I want you to know that I have come here at great personal risk to myself. Regan has practically forbidden me to visit you."

The Spaniard shrugged his elegant shoulders. "I see that you are here—and that's all that matters, is it not?"

"Tell me, Chaezar . . . do you miss Spain?" she asked, settling herself in a deep, comfortable chair.

"There are no words to describe the agony my absence from my homeland causes me. One day soon I shall return."

"Then we are compatriots, are we not? I don't think I will ever be able to adjust to this godforsaken island." Then: "Chaezar," Sirena said carefully as she accepted a glass of wine, "why don't you like . . . Regan?"

"Why *should* I like him? I detest him!" Chaezar spat. "At one time Spain and Portugal were supreme in these islands. Now the Spice Islands are referred to as the 'Dutch East Indies'! Regan's father was largely responsible for that. Then, following Regan's imprisonment several years back, it appeared the power might be changing hands again. But Regan returned . . ." Chaezar remembered the important part he himself had played in the young Dutchman's return to the islands, and the resultant losses for Spain as Regan and Vincent van der Rhys managed to steal back their dominance in the spice trade from the Spanish and Portuguese. "Our country plays second fiddle to the barbaric blond Netherlanders—and their greedy efficiency!" Then he recalled, too, the small fortune he had milked out of Vincent van der Rhys for Regan's release, and he smiled. He, at least, was rich himself—and had plans to become richer. If not Spain, then Don Chaezar Alvarez would win in this struggle with the Dutchman!

Sirena saw the smile on Chaezar's lips, and knew he thought of his nutmegs and his plans to establish a "kingdom," as he called it, where he might grow them. And, the proud Spaniard was not poor—indeed, his fine mansion gave adequate proof of that! No doubt he was more interested in his own fortunes than in those of his fatherland.

"What . . . can I do to help you . . . against the Dutch?" she asked.

If he was surprised at her complete willingness to work against her husband, Don Chaezar did not show it. Instead, he surprised Sirena.

"Do? Nothing! Just promise me that when the time is right for me to leave the Indies, you will come with me!" There was a sense of urgency about him as he left his chair and dropped to his knee beside her. "Sirena, *querida,* say you'll come with me and I'll put the world at your feet! Say you agree!"

For answer Sirena allowed him to press his lips to hers in a warm but brief kiss. Chaezar's eyes were soft at what he took for her affirmative answer. Mentally Sirena compared the sultry dark orbs to Regan's blue slits of steel.

"You must give me time . . . to think on the matter. I much prefer to make up my mind in my own surroundings!" Her laugh tinkled in the richly furnished room.

Chaezar stroked his lush beard. Regan was blind. There was no other excuse for it. Couldn't he see past the cool, poised exterior to the fiery she-demon that breathed within this woman? How he longed to make her his mistress.

"What do you know of the . . . Sea Siren?" he asked lightly while watching her face very closely.

"Very little. I've . . . heard of her, naturally," Sirena lied. "It's said that she is the most unbelievable captain. They say she rides the seas like a goddess. She plunders and robs, I'm told—and she must be neither

Dutch nor Spanish, for she robs and kills both. Is it true that cargos the ships carry are seldom of interest to her, and that she throws them overboard? And laughs? Her laugh must carry over the water, making the crews—which she is said to send into their jolly-boats—even more frightened of her. I know she has Regan bewitched. The figurehead is proof of his obsession with the 'water witch.' I also understand, from Helga, that you and Regan have both set trap after trap for her and that she manages to elude you each time."

"Everything you say is true," Chaezar said grimly. "I envy the Mynheer his figurehead. It makes a stunning addition to his newest ship," he added slyly, watching for her reaction.

"Does it *really?*" Sirena smiled. "Does he think perhaps the Sea Siren will spare his ship if she sees her likeness on the bow?"

Chaezar laughed. "Perhaps. No man knows what *Regan* thinks! But I know he's obsessed with the piratess. I see it in his eyes, as have other men. But . . . I hope, my dear, that I haven't offended you."

"Not in the least," Sirena said, smiling. "Let us both hope it is a good-luck charm for him. I would not want my husband to be disappointed . . . But tell me more, Don Chaezar, about the Sea Siren. Why does she ride the seas?"

"God only knows. All I can say is I wish she was in *my* employ."

"Have you seen her yourself?"

"No," Chaezar replied, tugging at his beard. "But it is said that she is what every man would want in his bed. She is what every woman would secretly like to be—wild and untamed. Speaking from a man's point of view," Chaezar murmured softly, "I wager we would all like to be the one to capture her and tame her. But," he continued carefully, "she is not a wench to be tamed. She is as wild as the sea she rides. The man who could tame her would, indeed, be a man."

Sirena laughed inwardly. "I find this so . . . thrilling—though"—and Sirena lowered her eyes in false modesty—"of course I should not!" she breathed.

"Another glass of wine, dear Sirena?"

"No, thank you. I must be getting back before Regan turns into a bull and tramples the house because of my disobedience. Today I felt the need of a small outing and a little conversation in our mother tongue. The way Regan desecrates our language makes my blood boil."

"It was my pleasure! You must come here, my dear, whenever the pressures of your home become too much for you. My house will always be a sanctuary for you. I—I would defend you with my life if need be," he said gallantly. "Till our next meeting," he finished, bringing her hand to his lips.

On arriving in the van der Rhys courtyard, Sirena instructed Juli: "Hurry now, dear, to the Mynheer. Tell him precisely what we did. Do not worry. If he is angry, it will be at me, not you!" The native girl hesitated on the doorstep, "Hurry in, now. Obey me!"

At the foot of the wide staircase, Sirena turned once more to see Juli knock at the study door. "Oh, and tell the Mynheer not to disturb me for the rest of the day. I have much to pray for this day!" she said, smiling wickedly behind her mantilla.

Pursing her mouth as she climbed to her room, Sirena wondered how long it would take the "bull" to trample his way upstairs. Not long, she surmised, so she had best position herself by the bed, with her rosary, and keep her head bowed. Less than a minute after she had sunk to her knees, Regan burst through the bedroom door, fuming.

"You defied me!" he shouted. "You deliberately defied me!" Sirena said nothing, her fingers moving over the beads, her head bent. "What did you do, alone inside the Spaniard's house? Answer me, damn you!"

"You are a . . . bull, Mynheer. When you address me, you will use a civil tongue. This is not the twelfth century—when a woman was a slave to the man she married. In the future you will *ask* me to do something, you will not *tell* me. Nor will you ever again order me to do as you say. If you do, I shall only be forced to . . . ignore you. Now, please leave me to my prayers."

All this in a calm, almost emotionless voice, soft yet demanding attention.

Uncertainty flickered across Regan's face. Who in the name of God did she think she was speaking to? Some saint, perhaps?

"Did you . . . wish to say something else, Mynheer?" Sirena asked, raising her eyes.

"There is nothing else I need say. You are aware of my deman—wishes in regard to Don Chaezar Alvarez. It would be wise if you obeyed them in the future. Otherwise I *may* have a chance to show what a bull I really can be—by locking you in your room!"

"I would not do that if I were you, Mynheer van der Rhys." The green eyes sparkled and glittered with something Regan could not define. "For, if you do, then you will force me to seek sanctuary in Senor Alvarez's house. I will not be treated like one of the whores who do your bidding in order to win your favor. Leave me to my prayers, as I've asked, and perhaps . . . if I have time . . . I'll pray for your soul."

With a savage gesture Regan reached out and grasped the beads from her hand, snapped the chain in two. He looked at the ruined rosary a moment and tossed it onto the floor.

"You behave, Mynheer, like a schoolboy who doesn't get his way," Sirena shot back vehemently for the first time. She had had enough of this! "Remove yourself from my presence! You offend me!'

Regan stood, the furies of Hell engulfing him as he gazed down into her emerald eyes. Suddenly he wanted to rip the clothes from her body and press her into the softness of the bed on which she rested her arms.

"Your lust sickens me," Sirena said as she read the expression in his eyes. "Go to your whore! Leave me!"

Stunned at her fury—something he had not yet witnessed—Regan could only stalk from the room, his booted feet making harsh sounds on the marble floor.

Chapter Twenty

"Sirena! Sirena!" Caleb shouted as he burst into her room without knocking a few days later. "Listen to me! I just came from the anteroom outside Regan's library. He has cloistered himself there with Señor Alvarez. Regan looked extremely angry when he received the Señor in the entranceway a few minutes ago!"

Sirena gathered up her heavy skirts and followed Caleb downstairs at a near-run. "Station yourself in the corridor and ward off any of the servants who might come this way," she hissed as she leaned against the stout library door.

"Aye, Sirena," Caleb replied, his eyes bright with the excitement of conspiracy.

Her hands clasped tightly to her breast, Sirena pressed her ear to the wood. Smiling wickedly, she pictured both men staring into each other's eyes. Chaezar was speaking, his warm, rich voice carrying through the thick door paneling.

"So . . . now you have come to the point. Mynheer, what could you and I have to discuss other than business, however?"

"Quite simply, the matter of my wife. I know you, Don Chaezar, for the libertine you are. I want you to stay away from her. She is vulnerable at this time in her life, she wishes only to lead a life of prayer. You are making me the laughingstock of Batavia in your pursuit of her." Regan cleared his throat somberly. "She is . . . of course . . . too much of a lady to tell you directly that you offend her. I must do that. So . . . whether you are her countryman or not, I warn you to stay away from her from this day forward!"

Chaezar took a moment to speak. "Sirena . . . has

said this to you—that I 'pursue' her?" he asked suavely. "I think not. And, indeed, on the other hand, she has been most sympathetic to my . . . attentions."

"Are you intimating that you have bedded my wife?" Regan shouted hoarsely.

"Mynheer, I beg of you! We . . . we Spaniards are not a breed like you Dutch. No Hispanic would besmirch a lady's good name—especially a married one's. And no Spaniard would . . . tell of it . . . if he did. However, I can assure you that my attentions have not gone so far with your fair Sirena." Then, quickly: "Though you, Regan, with your whoring ways, what should my feelings toward your wife matter to *you?* You—who have cut a swath from Sumatra to Guinea a mile wide. I'll wager," Chaezar laughed quietly, "you've bedded every female who's able to walk without the aid of a cane! But you'd best be careful, Regan," the Spaniard warned. "These Javanese beauties are well versed in the art of poisoning their lovers when something doesn't go their way!"

"You speak of my 'cutting a swath from Sumatra to Guinea.' By God, Chaezar, you have always been right behind me to pick up where I left off!"

Don Chaezar Alvarez chuckled loud enough for Sirena to hear. "What you say is true—but there's a difference between us: I use discretion; I don't tread like a bull elephant and leave my mark wherever I go. We Spanish would never darken a woman's good name—be she a lady of quality or a whore."

"Bah!" Regan said brusquely.

Sirena heard a chair scrape the floor and judged that her husband had risen. Chaezar would be grinning at the sun-bronzed Dutchman as he paced the richly carpeted room.

"But enough of this talk!" Regan finally resumed. "I reiterate what I asked you here to tell you: Leave my wife to her prayers!"

"And I'm telling you, Regan, the decision must be hers. And besides, the lovely lady cannot sit by her bed during every waking hour! If she chooses to visit me . . . But, I agree—enough of this prattle! You must settle your own marital problems with your wife. What's more, I find it in exceedingly poor taste to discuss a man's spouse with him."

A chair moaned and Sirena knew that Don Chaezar had risen. Dare she stay a moment longer?

"There is, however, one thing I should like to say to you before I leave, Mynheer. Your ship now boasts the lovely carving of the Sea Siren. Do you really think that the lovely pirate lady riding the seas of late, these past months, will not molest you or your ships if she sees her likeness on the bow of your vessel?" The Spaniard laughed quietly. "She has you bewitched, my friend. Ah, I see by the look on your face that it's true!"

"I think no such thing. I merely wanted a figurehead for my ship, and the Sea Siren—beauty that she is—seemed ideal for it. Make no more of it than that, sir! But there is . . . an item of true business that I called you here to speak of. Will you take a seat again?"

"For a moment I thought you were going to forget to detail what you merely mentioned to me in passing, the other day in town. You said then that you wanted to plot a trap that will be so well constructed, so escape-proof that the Siren will raise a white flag and fall to her knees, begging mercy!"

Regan explained his plan, which, Sirena heard quite clearly, was that each of them should take a convoy of three vessels, combined as it were into a fleet, and place a cordon around the western tip of Java, including the Sunda Strait and the coastline west of Batavia, along which the Sea Siren frequently disappeared. The ships' sails should be tinted black, as hers were; and they should maintain their vigil for a week.

"Several of my own ships have just been careened," Don Chaezar responded, "so that I'll have the sails dyed and will be ready to set them to sea within two days. However, in this joint expedition I have one condition: the Sea Siren is not to be killed, or injured in any way—though of course her ship must be dismantled and her crew hanged."

"I've no stomach for killing women, as you seem

to think!" Regan shot back. "Of course I agree to your condition."

"I hesitate to ask you this, Regan, but who gets the prize? The Spanish or the Dutch?"

Sirena held her breath as she waited for her husband's reply.

"Don't hedge, Chaezar. What you're asking is who gets the Siren—you or me!"

"You *are* an uncouth lout, do you know that, Regan? Very well, that's what I want to know."

"It's quite simple," the Dutchman replied. "Whichever of us is man enough to take her. I rather think she shall be mine."

Well, is she now? Sirena smiled to herself. We'll just see about that!

Suavely, the Spaniard prepared to make his exit. "Shall we merely say that 'To the victor go the spoils'?"

With the grace and speed of a cat, Sirena raced out of the anteroom and across the broad main entranceway to the staircase, where she pretended to be in the act of coming downstairs. As the Mynheer conducted his guest to the front door, she did not see the Spaniard reach into his waistcoat pocket and produce a small package.

"By the way, friend Regan," the representative of the Spanish Crown said softly, "several months ago we agreed on a small wager as to which of our ships—the *Rotterdam* or the *Sevilla* reached Capetown first. As you recall, they began their journey at the same hour. Thanks to the indolent lout who captained the *Sevilla,* you have won the wager. I'm sure you'll find this token"—he extended the packet to his host—"a bit more valuable than the amount we agreed upon." And with that he left.

After a pretended survey of the kitchen, Sirena had returned to her room, upstairs, and had briefed Caleb on what she'd heard.

"They'll wait out there in the straits until they grow old—for the Sea Siren won't be ensnared by them! Then they'll each think a spy told her not to go to sea—and each will think the spy is in the other's camp, for they both want the Sea Siren for herself alone! Man are so stupid, so really stupid. Except for you, Caleb," she added hastily.

"Does this mean we won't go out to sea again for more than a week?" the boy asked.

"That's exactly what it means. But," she said quietly, "we'll set sail if—as I believe he will—Regan finally sends the convoy, both his ships and Chaezar's, home and then returns last, alone! We'll catch him with his fleet gone home. I doubt that the expedition—'the fleet,' as they call it—will even last a week. Don Chaezar will not have as much patience as is needed. Furthermore, both men will believe the other let the plans become known, in some way, to the Siren; this will make for dissension among the Spanish and Dutch vessels of the fleet."

"You'll—you'll not harm the Mynheer, will you, Sirena?" Caleb asked anxiously.

She smiled. My, how the boy admired the loutish Dutchman. "Go to your room now, little brother. Back to your studies for a time. We will speak more later."

No, she would not "harm" Regan, Sirena told herself when the youth had left. But she would best the man! That was what she wanted, wasn't it?

Then, sinking down onto the soft coverlet of her bed, she let her thoughts race. What else did she want of Regan? Did she want to gaze into those steely eyes of his and murmur words of love to him? Did she, indeed, want to be taken on the wide deck of the *Rana,* the ship tossing and thundering against giant breakers to the rhythm of lovemaking? Yes . . . she admitted it to herself for perhaps the first time.

But, sitting up straight as a ramrod, she suddenly reproached herself: I *must* kill him. I've lied to poor Caleb! I swore to take vengeance on Isabel's killer. And, though perhaps only indirectly, Regan van der Rhys is that man. He may not have wielded the cutlass, but—

Perspiration broke out on her brow. The thought of taking Regan's life was so abhorrent that she trembled. What was happening to her? She rose and went to stand by the window overlooking the garden. Her hands were folded and her eyes glazed as she stared out at the exotic flowers beyond. And then a knock sounded at her door, jarring her from any further thoughts.

"Come in," she called, and Regan entered, his eyes raking the room.

Sirena willed her face to blankness. She waited, her heart thumping in her chest. What did he want now?

"I've just seen Señor Alvarez to his trap."

Her glittering green eyes looked directly into the mocking angry blue ones of her husband. "And how is Cha—Señor Alvarez?" she asked softly.

"At the moment he is well. However," he said harshly, "he may not remain in that state much longer if he does not put an end to the rumors that are floating about the island."

Sirena's lips closed tightly.

"And you add to those rumors by your visits to him?"

"I have entered his house but twice," Sirena asserted calmly.

"Twice is twice too many times!" Regan fired back. "Everyone in Batavia is calling me a fool. Why only last night, Gretch—" He caught himself, but too late.

Anger shot up Sirena's spine, her eyes smoldered as she gazed at her husband. Her eyes belied her soft tones, as she answered. "A 'fool'? But you were that, long before I arrived—and long before you married me. When one is a fool to begin with, nothing can change the matter, unless," she said coldly, "it is to be made still a bigger fool. And you, Mynheer, are quite adept. You need no help from me! What do you want with me? Why are you here?"

Regan's eyes narrowed to mere slits. Her words were infuriating . . . but why did she have this strange effect on him? He should, by rights, hate her—and whip her—for what she'd said.

Instead, he posed a question: "What is it . . . about Don Chaezar Alvarez that so fascinates you, my dear?" Then, quickly, as she lowered her gaze: "Don't deny it. I see it in your eyes!"

"Don Chaezar is a fellow countryman, as I've told

you before. *He* . . . is a gentleman. He speaks my native tongue as it was meant to be spoken. I find him gallant. Do you know the meaning of that word, Mynheer?" she taunted him quietly.

And stirred him to his depths by that taunting.

He knew he must control his passions. "I shall leave you to your prayers. In fact, that was my main reason for coming here." He reached deep into his pocket and withdrew a long circlet of pearls. "I broke your rosary, as you may recall. I thought you might like to say your prayers on these perfect, cultured pearls—which may give your laments more meaning than the mere stained glass beads you used before. But say some prayers for me—we 'heathens,'" he said mockingly, "need all the help we can get!"

Regan tossed the pearls on the bed. Curious, and with an expression of remembrance, Sirena walked to the bed and gathered them into her hands. "Where—where did you get these?" she stammered, turning pale.

Noting her shock, her husband said softly, "I won them in a wager." He didn't tell her who lost the wager to him. He did not want her to know she held in her hands something of Don Chaezar's. Then he turned swiftly on his heel and strode from the room.

Outside his wife's room, Regan stopped short and looked back at the closed door.

Sirena had not admitted to a relationship with Alvarez. Of course not, how could she have dared? The more he thought about the possibility of Sirena's loving Don Chaezar, the more Regan's mind whirled. Despite her mourning, despite her attitude of calm, might she not have . . . ? He raged inside. Had the cur Chaezar bedded her? Regan drew in his breath; a million small, wriggling worms seemed to be gnawing his belly.

He slammed one fist into the other. "I'll kill the bastard!" he all but shouted. The vision of the two coupling, moaning in ecstasy was suddenly so vivid.

Anger getting the best of him, he stormed back into his wife's room, kicking the door shut behind him.

Sirena now stood near the window, the pearls clasped in her hands, tears streaming down her cheeks.

Heedless of her torment, Regan yelled out: "*Have* you bedded Alvarez? Have you? I want an answer!"

With a swift movement, he tore the pearls from Sirena's hands and pulled her to him. Her eyes gleamed wet, her breathing was ragged.

"Answer me!"

Her lips remained closed. Savagely he pulled her even closer to his heaving body and brought his lips crashing down on hers, hot and blazing as he held her prisoner.

Sirena felt her breasts caressed by urgent hands. Felt, too, her own resistance to him melting—

Then, abruptly, she was thrust away from him. Mocking eyes laughed into hers.

"Alvarez may be a gentleman. But can he stir your blood as I just did?" He glared at her, sure of his conquest. After a moment, he changed his tack, and an acid pleasantry came into his voice: "But, remember, Mevrouw . . . ours is to be a marriage in name only . . . Until your period of mourning is over. And that will be some months yet, will it not?" he chuckled evilly.

Sirena stood stunned, her head reeling, her eyes deep pools of murky water. She knew that to retaliate in her present state would give her feelings for Regan away. Sick and wounded, she turned her back to him, her head bent.

Watching her heaving back, Regan wished to grasp her, cradle that dark head to his chest and stroke that soft hair. He wanted to murmur soft, not harsh words to this lovely creature who had come to him, been contracted to him, from so far away . . .

Instead, he marched angrily from the room, muttering obscenities that she might hear. But, once outside, he took a deep and painful breath and gnashed his teeth. What is coming over me? he wondered. First I wanted Sirena . . . then the Sea Siren . . . and now Sirena once more. How she makes me forget even Gretchen! How this black-clad virgin controls me—I never thought it could happen to *me!* To me,

Regan van der Rhys—my own master and slave to no woman!

The new role did not please him at all. With a steady hand he lit a cigar, shut his eyes briefly to avoid the blue-gray spiral of smoke.

Regan spent the next two days in a turmoil. He would issue an order and five minutes later countermand it. The crews of his private ships were beginning to look upon him as a madman.

Today he smoked cigars continuously as he paced the office rooms like a caged lion. Thoughts of Chaezar Alvarez and his wife lying naked in an opulent bed with lacy hangings set his teeth to rattling. Did she moan and breathe hard for that rutting pig? Did Alvarez make love to her like a gentleman, or like a savage? Regan wanted to strike out, to bludgeon, to kill, to rape, to ravage as never before. After the Sea Siren was captured—by dint of their joint fleet—he would kill the Spaniard. He would show him no mercy. He would slit his throat as if he were a stray piece of wild game. Would Sirena cry over the villain's mutilated body? The picture of her standing over Chaezar's still form, crying unashamedly for all to see, set him in such a frenzy that he kicked out at the leg of a table that stood in his way—and the pain in his foot was so excruciating he had to clench his teeth to keep from crying out.

Regan cursed himself for a fool a thousand times over. He had always prided himself on being a man of his word; he never reneged. Why in the name of Satan had he promised Sirena that the marriage was to be in name only, until her mourning was done? I'll never be able to bed her now unless she comes to me, he thought, thanks to my promise, and to Don Chaezar Alvarez! And thanks to the cursed Spaniard she may not come to me even after she doffs her black gowns!

Am I then to go through life staring at her across the table, he asked himself, remembering the feel of her fast-beating heart, the half-moans she made. Is this—is this the punishment I've earned for the life of sin I've led? he reproached himself suddenly. For my whoring ways, as someone has put it?

Sirena was now in his blood just as was the Sea Siren, and he was doubly frustrated. And last night, when he'd tried to bed the Javanese woman he had been after for months, it had been a fiasco. The woman had spat at him! Today the island was doubtless buzzing with the tale!

Chapter Twenty-one

A week had passed, the joint fleet had departed Batavia harbor, and the town—deprived of its commissioners for the Spanish and Dutch crowns—seemed lifeless except for the mounting fear that the Spaniard and the Netherlander and their ships had met with some terrible end.

Sirena had no such fears.

She paced the elegantly hung bedroom, her fists clenched at her sides, in one of them the knotted rosary of cultured pearls. A hundred times since his leaving her room that night, nine days ago, she had asked herself how Regan himself had had the gall, the cruelty beyond measure to give them to her. To give to her her sister Isabel's precious prayer beads! It was beyond belief! And now . . . now she had no choice: she must bring him down. Yes, little brother, she muttered to herself, I must kill him after all. God help me, I must kill him! His giving me the rosary wipes out all doubt now that he might not have had anything to do with my sister's death!

At a timid knock on the door that connected her chamber to Caleb's, she called out bitterly, "Come in!"

The boy knew what was in Sirena's mind, and had become deeply saddened over the past few days. He looked up at her with tears in his eyes.

Heedless of his feelings, as she knew she *must* be, she queried: "Caleb, is the *Sea Siren* ready to sail?"

The boy looked puzzled. Three times that day he had told her the crew were at the ship, all preparations made. "It's time to leave, Sirena—if we must make the tide. Aren't you ready?"

She sighed. "Yes, I am ready, Caleb. But this time I have little heart for our journey—though I know what I must do. You have seen the pearls, little brother, and I have told you whose they were."

"But the Mynheer told you that he won them in a wager."

"My husband, though an experienced liar, was not trying to deceive me. He was, indeed, challenging me. And . . . my young friend . . . this may mean that he knows I am not his intended!"

Sirena watched the stars with mixed emotions as she stood by the ship's rail. The stars were so far away and so bright. Isabel had been like them in a way: bright, shining, and a faraway object too—remote and ascetic. But Isabel's star had been snuffed out.

Jan, her first mate, touched her lightly on the shoulder. "Capitana?"

Snapping her thoughts back to the reality of her mission, she turned to the blue-eyed Dutchman.

"Willem has just come back from the end of the cove," Jan told her. "He says the fifth ship has passed by the mouth of the river. Thank the Lord for our good moon tonight—else he'd not have been able to see. He believes that the flagship, the Mynheer's own, will not be long in following."

"Then we must up anchor, leave our old hiding place here, and sail downriver to meet him—just beyond the shallows and rocks. It's a dark night, withal, and neither the five ships that have already gone by, nor those at anchor in Batavia, will spy us. If Regan is too close to shore, what's more, we'll lure him farther out into the open sea so that he and I may play out our battle unobserved and unhindered!"

Nevertheless, minutes later, as the *Sea Siren* eased out of the quiet waters of the cove into the swiftly moving river, Sirena's hands were clammy on the ship's wheel. Could she go through with it? Could she kill Regan van der Rhys? Then a vision of her sister Isabel floated before her, and her hands clasped the wheel fiercely as she straightened her back and squared her shoulders. She knew what she had to do, and she would do it!

The ship neared the mouth of the river and Sirena's eyes watched the threatening rocks as she guided the frigate through the narrow channel and eased it into the open sea once more.

At the cry that went up from the men—ever amazed at her ability to free the *Siren* from her hiding place—she sent down word with Jan that they should speak softly. Their words might carry over the water, and though their dark sails gave little hint of the ship's whereabouts, she wanted to surprise Regan's vessel.

And, suddenly, there it was—black-rigged like her own ship, alone on the inky-watered Java Sea.

"Take the wheel now, Jan," she called.

"Aye, Capitana." As he gripped the circle of wood, he continued: "She's in no hurry, Capitana. See, she travels at a mere six knots or less—and with half-furled sail. A sad ship she'll be, too, returning after seven long days and nights with no sight of her prize! Her men will be anxious to see their wives."

"If they see their wives," Sirena said ruefully, and her first mate's smile vanished. He, as well as Caleb, knew her intent this time. "She's far enough offshore so that our encounter will not be seen," Sirena went on, "but we must be quick about it. We've the advantage: the breeze urges us toward her! Caleb," she barked to the boy who sat dejectedly near the stern rail of the *Siren,* "go below, so you'll neither be seen nor hurt. Off with you now!"

"Aye, Sirena," Caleb said as he extended his hand manfully to her. "Good luck . . . Sirena." With difficulty he had held back his tears.

"Caleb," she said softly, pulling him close to her breast, "if it is any consolation to you, at this moment I don't know if what I'm about to do is right, in the sight of God and man, or not. All I know is that . . . I have to do it." She pressed the boy close for a moment. Then: "Get below now. Hurry!"

She turned to Jan. "Pass the order to tighten sail."

In little more than a minute her command had been obeyed. They were a good crew, these Dutchmen she employed. Not one of them would defy her, even though their hearts might not be united on what she planned to do this night.

Jan was at her arm again. "We travel at eight knots, we'll overtake her in minutes. See, there she is—dead on our bow." Suddenly, the confident first mate showed alarm. "Look! She's sighted us, and— But, by the gods, she's sailing off—she's afraid of us!"

"Yes, Jan. Together with her fleet she had no fear of the Sea Siren. Alone, she's a coward!"

In the *Sea Siren*'s chase after the Dutch brigantine, her smaller and lighter hull gave her the advantage. Surely and swiftly the frigate gained on the Dutchman.

Then, with a resounding crash, the ram of the *Siren* pierced the stern of the brig. Shouts and curses rang out aboard the larger ship as Sirena's crew shouting joyously and ran to the side of the *Sea Siren.*

"Do not board the brigantine," Sirena shouted to her men. "Not yet. I want to speak with her captain."

Regan, stripped to the waist, stood near the brig's sterncastle, his eyes glaring, his breeches clinging tightly to the hard muscles of his thighs. Nimbly, Sirena swung herself up into the rigging of the *Siren* and stared down at him.

Suddenly, she heard one of Regan's crew shout, breathlessly from the bridge: "But, Captain, she flew her black sails—and the moon was behind the clouds until a moment ago!" Then, silence, as a shot rang out and the crewman fell wounded to his knees.

"Ho, there, Willem! Enough! Await my orders!" Then she spoke to Regan: "Come aboard, Captain, if you like. I will set no foot on that rotten wood you command. She sinks in an hour's time with one good broadside shot from my crew. You are growing fat and lazy like all Dutchmen. A little alertness on your part and you may have outrun me. You see now that you have nowhere to go but the water. Can you swim, Captain?" she shouted.

Regan stood on the stern, his eyes murderous. So she was on the Spaniard's side after all! Why else did she lay in wait and attack him? And to use black sails! Damn! Why didn't the moon come out so he could get a good look at her? Suddenly he laughed, white teeth gleaming in the yellowish light.

"What do you want from me? You have almost single-handedly ruined me, what else do you want?" he shouted as he watched the long-legged creature nick the air with the point of her cutlass.

"Your life, Captain. Also the life of the one that carries a hook for a hand. Turn him over to me and perhaps I'll spare your life."

Regan laughed again, his arms raised, his feet sure on the rolling deck. "What do you want with the man who uses a hook for a hand? I carry no such man aboard this ship. Tell me why you seek this man," he demanded, his eyes taking in her scanty attire.

"The day I run him through I shall post a notice; until that time, it is my affair! Into the jolly-boats or you die. It's your choice, Dutchman!"

"You can't win. My men will kill the lot of you. Surrender to me and I'll see that it goes easy with you at your trial."

Sirena's laughter rippled across the water. "You seem to have made a mistake, Dutchman; it is I who captured you. I could run you through before you could blink an eye. I should surrender to you? Fool!" she shouted.

"Wrong, lovely lady, look to your stern, it is I who have you captured. The galleon on your stern is mine. She weighed anchor in the mangrove swamp not far from here. Your mistake," he said bowing low.

Sirena swiveled and saw the cannons jutting from the gunwales. The Dutchman was right, she was outnumbered. She would have to fight. Firing cannons at this close range would imperil the frigate.

"All hands to the deck!" Sirena shouted. "It's kill or be killed! I would have let you go, Dutchman, now you leave me no choice," she said, leaping from the rigging to land, feet firmly planted on Regan's deck. She stood a moment, her breathing ragged as she brought up the cutlass in a jaunty salute. She felt a jolt of pain in her shoulder as steel met steel. The air rang with shouts and screams as metal clanged against metal. Shots seemed to come from nowhere and men toppled to the deck like flies. Out of the corner of her eye she saw her mate, Jan, drop his cutlass just as a cutthroat was about to run him through. With the speed of a cat, Sirena turned, leaped over a pile of rigging, and slicked her cutlass with a high wide arch; the man's arm as well as the cutlass rolled to the deck. Jan looked up at the woman in front of him and grinned. "Aye, Capitana, a fierce blow it was. I'll be in your debt."

Her men fought valiantly, as did Regan's crew. The battle raged, with the crew from the *Sea Siren* having the advantage. Great clouds of black, pungent smoke lay heavy in the air from the burning brig. Rubbing her eyes, Sirena turned to attack a crewman bent on cutting her down. Just as she drove him backwards over the rail a thundering shout ripped through the air. Breathing heavily, she strained to see through the thick smoke. It was Jan's shout that made her turn and see the man bent on slashing her in the back.

"Blackheart!" she shouted. "So," she screamed, bringing up the cutlass to hold him at bay. "Willem, Jan, Jacobus," she shouted, 'I have a score to settle with this beast. Clear the decks!"

"No need, Capitana, the Dutch have shouted for quarter."

Never taking her eyes from the man in front of her, she called her order. "See to our wounded, theirs as well as our own. Lower the Dutchmen into the jolly-boats after their wounds have been seen to. Sink the galleon and gut the brig! Let no man interfere with what I'm about to do. Willem, stand guard over Captain van der Rhys."

All eyes watched the woman with the cutlass as she advanced to a point and then stopped before the burly Englishman. "So, you would have run me through from behind! Coward!" she spat. "I told you there would be a time and a place! This is it!" she said, her voice deadly in its calm.

"I'll give you a fighting chance which is more than

you gave me. En garde!" she shouted as she flexed her knees and brought up the cutlass and slashed at the man's weapon. His arm flew backwards and he was stunned with the force of the blow. He recovered quickly and jabbed straight for Sirena's midsection. Nimbly she sidestepped as her weapon again struck out, this time glancing down the side of his arm. Blood spurted as she laughed at the look of terror on Blackheart's face. "How does it feel, Blackheart, to see your arm in tatters? Guard it well, for I shall strike till I lay the bone open." She feinted to the right, the cutlass finding its mark across the man's shoulder. The crack of the shattering bone brought cheers from the *Sea Siren*'s crew. Regan stood, mouth agape, awed by the woman's expertise. How in the name of God did she find the strength to heft and wield the heavy cutlass like a man? Before Blackheart could recover himself she slashed downward, ripping his leg from thigh to ankle. Crimson blood leaked onto the deck and he slipped, trying to regain his position.

"Let me hear you beg, Blackheart!" Sirena spat. "Shout for quarter and I'll throw you into the sea."

"Never!" the man hissed.

Sirena held the cutlass loosely in her hand as she watched Blackheart's agonized face. "You have one leg left, surrender to me, otherwise you give me no choice."

"Never!" the man spat, using his injured arm to strike out with the cutlass. His eyes never saw the blade as it ripped his other leg from thigh to toe. Sirena stepped backward. "You have just seconds to surrender." Glazed, hate-filled eyes stared into hers, the cutlass dropped from his hand.

"Stand like a man and fight! Damn your eyes! Fight, I tell you!" Sirena screeched. With one quick movement she had the fallen cutlass in her hand. She tossed the weapon to the man, and spoke softly: "I want that weapon in your hand when I kill you. I'll have no man say I ran you through unarmed!" Blackheart staggered, the cutlass hanging loosely in his wounded hand, the other hanging loosely at his side.

"This is the last time I'll give you the chance to

ask quarter. What is it to be?" she menaced, the cutlass straight in front of her. For answer, Blackheart spat in her face. His weapon, thrust forward, aiming for the soft flesh of her midsection, took Sirena off guard.

In the instant reflex of protecting herself, Sirena sidestepped Blackheart's attack, her cutlass parried and found its mark in the flesh of his belly, and he crumpled to the deck, lifeless.

Trembling with the overpowering emotion of a long-sought revenge accomplished, Sirena's eyes were pinpoints of flame. "I gave him the opportunity to ask for quarter. He had his choice. I could have done no less than I did. Right or wrong, I'll live with my choice."

As a man, Regan understood this. Her grievance against Blackheart must have been all-consuming. No, he thought, she could have done no less.

Sirena's arrogance returned and she faced Regan with confidence. "Be truthful, Dutchman, have you ever known a woman like me? Admit you'd like me for your own. I see I've scored. Lust leaps from your eyes like frogs from a pond!"

Unable to control himself, Regan pulled free of his captors and planted his feet firmly on the deck within inches of Sirena. "You would challenge me, is that it? Has it become a matter of honor?"

"Yes," Regan menaced. The Siren had lost all claim to womanhood in Regan's furious opinion. She cursed like a man and fought better than most men. He wanted to meet with her in the excitement of a duel. Then, when he had subdued her, cowed her, he wanted to meet her in the excitement of passion.

Sirena read his thoughts accurately and excitement coursed through her veins. "Willem, toss Captain van der Rhys his weapon!" Turning once again to Regan she said harshly, breathlessly, through clenched teeth, "There's no need for this duel." Suddenly she didn't want this duel to happen. Her mind sought frantically for another way to bring vengeance upon him. The idea of piercing his flesh, drawing his blood, was repulsive to her, but, if she must to save herself, she would.

The cutlass came up with lightning speed and slicked across Regan's chest, perforating his shirt and drawing blood. Regan did not take his eyes from the wild untamed she-demon before him. He brought up his weapon with slow deliberation and back-stepped, swinging the blade with a wicked flourish, nicking the buttons on Sirena's blouse. Her creamy, jutting breasts spilled from their confinement.

"You whoring bastard!" Sirena screeched as she fought to keep her blouse together. Being displayed before the crewmen's gawking eyes was too much like that other time aboard the *Rana*. Reckless fury overtook her, blocking out all reason. Beyond all feeling, she dully realized that in her aimless swings with the cutlass Regan's blade was slicing at her fingers and hands, the sticky wetness of her own blood making it impossible to hold her blouse together. Tears of rage blinded her as she brought up the cutlass and thrust it frenziedly at Regan's arm. "I said I'd kill you and I will!" she shrieked. "I hate you!" Again the blade flashed, and she lunged, driving the point of the cutlass through the sinewy muscle of his forearm.

His slate-blue eyes darkened as Regan sucked in his breath. Damn the witch! She said she would kill him and she meant it. There was no doubt in his mind that she was tiring, and were those tears falling down her cheeks?

"Kill me," he said softly. "I'll fight no more. Look to the stern, your men have been seized. We tricked you! You can't win, lovely Sea Siren. You may have me pinned to the halward but you still have to kill me, can you do it?" His eyes darkened and glints of admiration shone as he gazed at the woman breathing in ragged gasps, her jutting breasts rising and falling with each breath.

"You have wounded me as no man has ever wounded me," Regan breathed. "I'll fight to the death, is that what you want? For one of us to die, to spill more blood on these decks."

Sirena backed off. "If I loose you, what then?" Sirena gasped.

"My men will secure your men in the hold and return to Port Batavia."

"That is your bargain?"

"Yes, no more bloodshed."

"You lie," Sirena spat. "I don't believe you."

"I may be many things, but never a liar. You have my word. Even if you kill me now, this minute my men will draw and quarter every man in your crew. Make up your mind," he said harshly, "so I can see to my wounds."

Indecision overwhelmed Sirena. The men watched and listened carefully for her reply.

Slowly and deliberately, Sirena advanced one step, then another. She looked deeply into the man's eyes. She leaned still closer and at the moment she withdrew the cutlass she smiled. "I bested you, Dutchman, admit it. Admit it to your men. Now! For if you don't then I shall pierce you again, this time where it will do the most good."

Regan threw back his head and roared with laughter, his injured arm hanging limply at his side. "All hands," he shouted, "the Sea Siren bested me in a fair duel. Toss her men in the hold, board ship, and a pint of grog for every seaman."

"First," Sirena said, bringing up the point of the blade against Regan's back, "first, you will see to my wounded. When their wounds have been dressed, you will give every member of my crew ale. Understood, Captain," Sirena said softly, the point of the blade nicking the broad back in front of her.

"*Ja,* you heard the . . . lady. Heave to, lad. Who is to dress my wounds?"

"Don't look in my direction, Captain. For if you do, I fear it may be salt I pour in your wounds." Regan laughed as if it were a joke.

"I believe you, Siren. You never give quarter, do you?"

"Never," Sirena cried passionately. "This battle was not necessary. I told you I was finished with you. The wounds you carry are of your own doing. I feel no remorse. Die for all I care! You'll get no help from me!"

"So it's an impasse, is it?"

Sirena laughed, her eyes dancing as she answered: "An impasse? Hardly, Captain. You are almost bankrupt, your cargos are at the bottom of the sea along with ten of your ships. You stand before me with wounds I inflicted and you call it an impasse?" She laughed again. "Hardly!" Regan clenched his teeth at the musical tinkle of her laugh. Damn her eyes, she wasn't human. Or was she . . .

Caleb, hiding in the shadows behind the frigate's rigging, watched in alarm as Regan dueled with the Sea Siren. A thick dense fog was rolling in, adding to the apprehension fluttering in his chest. If either Sirena or Regan should be killed, how would he feel about the survivor? So engrossed in his own thoughts was Caleb that he failed to notice the turnabout of events which saw the crew of Regan's brig become the captors of the *Sea Siren*'s men.

Each minute seemed an eternity. Nervously, he pulled his cap lower on his head, his tumble of hair tucked beneath it. What a fool he'd been, why had he been so mesmerized by the duel he had failed to notice the Dutchman's crew take the advantage over his fellow crew members! Hardly daring to breathe, Caleb heard Regan order his seamen to take Jan, Willem, and the others to the ship's hold. His quick ear also picked up Sirena's demand that her men be given their pint of ale. The message was clear! Silently, on cat-feet, Caleb darted in and out of the shadows to the *Sea Siren*'s galley. Somewhere in the kitchen's stores Martin had placed the dull, green bottle of laudanum.

Hiding behind the forecastle rail, he wondered how he could board the brigantine without Regan's notice. The thick lines that lashed the *Sea Siren* to the Dutch brig tightened and slackened, squeaking with protest as the heaving sea closed and separated the gap between the two ships.

Sirena must have been reading his thoughts, when next she spoke to Regan: "Surely you'll allow me to change my blouse, Captain van der Rhys. I hope you are gentleman enough not to expose me to the crew this way."

Caleb couldn't hear Regan's reply but he must have agreed, for Sirena leaped to the rail of the sterncastle, waited for the gap between the ships to close, and deftly leaped aboard her frigate, Regan in her wake. As they stepped across the deck toward the captain's cabin, the boy heard Sirena tell Regan she had an ointment for their cuts. First she said she wouldn't help him with his wounds, now she was offering ointment. He smiled to himself; this must fall under the heading of 'wily woman.'

As soon as the cabin door closed, Caleb put the laudanum bottle between his teeth and boarded the brigantine, confident Sirena would occupy Regan long enough to give him time to dose the ale.

As Sirena leaped aboard her frigate, she spied Caleb's slight, crouching form hiding in the shadow of the forecastle rail. She had every confidence in the boy and was positive he had picked up his cue and would soon be aboard the Dutchman's brig mingling among the seamen and offering to help serve the apportioned pint of ale. It would be up to Sirena to detain Regan long enough to allow Caleb free movement. A thick, almost tangible bank of fog was drifting in from the horizon, its web of gray already obscuring the moon.

Regan was close behind her, she could almost feel his breath on the back of her neck. She hastened her step and pulled open the cabin door, her mind racing backward to remember the condition of her quarters when she had seen them hours ago. She desperately tried to recall if she had left anything about which would reveal her identity. It had occurred to her before this how foolish men were. Change a woman's hairstyle, her clothes and manner, place her in a location or situation where she wasn't expected to be, and a man wouldn't recognize his own mother! The only thing a man recognized was whether he found a woman desirable or not.

Stepping into the dark cabin, groping for the table on which rested a lamp, Sirena grasped the glass and sent it crashing to the floor in what seemed like an accident. Murmuring a vague oath which cursed her clumsiness, she picked up the flint box and after much fumbling managed to light the small lamp on the wall at the far end of the cabin, noting with satisfaction the low level of oil and the weakly flickering flame. Turning to keep her face in the shadows, she moved over to her bunk and withdrew a coffer of medicines from beneath it.

"If you'll come over here, Captain, I'll bind your arm."

Regan seemed doubtful, even suspicious. Using his foot, he knocked a three-legged stool against the door to keep it open. His frosty blue eyes raked the room looking for hidden weapons. Seeing nothing to cause alarm, he stepped toward Sirena, who was sitting on the bunk unrolling a length of dressing. As he moved, glass from the broken lamp crunched beneath his foot, the only sound in the heavy, moist air.

It was then Sirena noticed the absence of another sound, that of the frigate's bow bumping against the sterncastle of the Dutch brig. Good work, little brother, Sirena thought with delight, realizing that Caleb must have cut the lines connecting the two ships. The frigate was now drifting free, each wave widening the distance from the brig.

She had meant to change her blouse to cover her near-naked bosom, but on second thought negated the idea. Perhaps the expectation of seeing rosy-tipped breasts spilling from her tattered blouse would divert Regan enough so that he wouldn't notice that each wave separated him further from his men.

Regan sat beside her on the bunk, as she silently smoothed an ointment on his wound and bound it with slow and deliberate movements. Sirena felt his eyes upon her and was becoming more and more aware of his nearness.

He broke the silence. "This is unheard of in naval history, I'd stake my life on it," he growled. "Two adversaries doing battle then binding each other's wounds. Perhaps we're both more civilized than we imagined. It's a wicked scar you carry on your arm, Siren, and fairly recent from the looks of it."

"Aye," Sirena grumbled, a harsh note deepening her voice, "a memento from the scurve Blackheart."

"You've taken your revenge on him now, does it make you happy to know he's dead?" Regan asked, his tone mocking.

Sirena stood up and, with her back to Regan, clenched the back of the chair near the table. "Happy? It delights me!" Her voice held a hatred so intense it raised the hackles on Regan's neck. "His death is food for my soul, nourishment for my spirit. I only regret I cannot kill him twenty times over and twenty times more! I'd dreamed of the moment, yearned for it as a thirsty man longs for water. But the scum even denied me this! He chose to die a coward and rob me of my victory. I find no victory in killing a coward."

As she spoke her supple spine stiffened, the muscles in the backs of her incredibly long legs tautened, accentuating the delicious curve of her buttocks. A deep curl of heat arose in Regan's middle and he was conscious of his prophecy that one day he would bed the Sea Siren. It was then Regan noticed a dark stain on the back of her blouse. "You could do with a bit of that ointment. Come here!" he commanded.

Sirena bristled at his tone, was ready to turn on him and loose her wrath. But she was tired, every nerve within her clamored for relief. Also, she reminded herself, she had to give Caleb every chance. Wearily, she joined Regan on the narrow bunk, allowing him to bathe the backs of her hands with the water from the ewer and apply the ointment.

His attitude as he went about seeing to her cuts was so serious, so intensely solicitous, he made her laugh. Regan was embarrassed by what he imagined was an unmanly picture of himself tending to her wounds like an old nursemaid. Gruffly, he ordered her to turn around.

Sirena stifled her laughter when she heard his forbidding tone and obediently turned her back to him. Roughly, he pushed her down on the bunk and, before she could protest ripped the bloody, tattered blouse from her back.

Siren's petulant mouth opened in a silent scream of protest, her body flexed and arched attempting to break free of his grasp. Her eyes squeezed shut, her sob was muffled against the coverlet. No, she pleaded silently, not again! Dear God, she prayed. Please don't let me be raped again!

"Hold still, Sea Witch! I don't mean to hurt you. Blood from the cut on your back dried to your blouse. There was no gentle way to remove it!" Pressing her down against the mattress, Regan bathed away the blood, gently cleansing and tending the cut.

Slowly, Sirena felt the tenseness and the fight drain out of her. The feel of his fingers on her flesh was soothing, delivering her into a state of mind where she felt warm and peaceful. Through half-closed eyes she saw the lamplight flicker and become more diffused. No doubt due to the fog creeping in through the open cabin door. The flickering, dimming lamplight was hypnotic, lulling her into a dream-like state. She felt him apply the soothing ointment, tenderly dabbing it on with his fingertips.

Regan cursed the dimming lamplight, and hurried at his task before the lamp gave out altogether. Wiping the greasy salve from his fingers on her torn blouse, he stood at his full height and gazed down at the Sea Siren.

Her wealth of heavy dark hair covered the side of her face, obscuring all but the tip of her chin and a glimpse of her brow. Her body had relaxed, the taut readiness abated; her arms extended over her head, with her hands open and still.

Beneath her upstretched arms the soft spill of her full, round breasts was visible. The long, low slope of the small of her back, rising again to the firm, spherical hillocks of her bottom, ending in the firm-fleshed lines of her slightly parted thighs, aroused him, beckoned to him as sweetly as the song of the legendary sirens for which he had named her. Quietly, gently, he leaned over her and pressed his lips to the hollow of her spine.

Sirena felt him touch her again, gentle teasing touches, warm, warmer than the night air. Forcing her heavy-lidded eyes open, she saw the lamp had finally flicked its last light, the cabin was in a gray-black darkness, swathed in a haunting, isolating fog.

She sighed, reveling beneath his light touches, feeling him lean against her, aware of the comforting weight of him. He lifted her salt-scented hair off the back of her neck and shoulders and suddenly she realized the touches she felt were kisses, trailing warm and moist across her shoulders, the nape of her neck. Feeling his breath on her skin, she heard a barely audible groan escape his lips.

With an indrawn breath, Sirena turned onto her back, encircling him in her arms, offering her mouth for his kisses. His powerful hands were in her hair, his lips burning hers. Her arms cradled his head to her breasts, her body arched beneath him. She wanted him, needed him as she was sure no woman had ever wanted a man.

His mouth was on her throat, her breasts, eliciting moans of ecstasy from somewhere deep in her soul.

When he pulled away from her she clung to him, enticing him back with her passion-bruised lips, gentling away his remaining reserve and her own with daring, intuitive caresses of her tongue.

Forcefully, he pulled out of her embrace. He removed his boots and appreciatively grazed his hands over her firmly fleshed legs. Slowly, he worked the buckle of her belt, sensuously he tugged her cut-off trousers over her curving hips, delighting at her grace and strength of limb when she lifted her haunches to aid him. Finally, he pulled the clothes from his own body, tearing and ripping them, having no patience for their restrictions.

Sirena's senses whirled and soared, making her dizzy with passion, bringing her to the borders of lust. There was no escape for her now, she had lost her resolve just as she had secretly known she would have lost it on her wedding night had he come to her then. But all that was behind her now. His lovemaking was driving her to the brink of wantonness.

She answered his caress with sensuous embraces, responded to his kisses with a sizzling animal passion she never dreamed she possessed.

Unabashedly, she invited him to awaken her sexuality. His lips covered her breasts, her stomach, her thighs . . . She moaned with exquisite joy as she turned her welcoming body this way and that, pliant to his demands, relishing the newfound sensuality he awakened in her.

Regan delighted in his bewitching Sea Siren, withholding the moment of completion to further savor her charms. He rejoiced to find his passion matched by her own.

He could barely see her in the dim light of the cabin. The fog had enveloped the moon, quenching its light in a bath of gray mist. Her lissome, supple beauty was perceived through his fingers. The delicious fragrance of her, the silken texture of her skin heightened his desire as he fondled and explored her secret charms. Her lips tasted of the sea, and her pleasure in him was unaffected, her responses genuine and unpracticed.

Almost innocently she would seek and find the most sensual caress, exalting in the pleasure and inspiration she gave him. Against his lips she moaned, begging, imploring, "Have me! Have me now!"

Afterwards they slept, entwined in each other's arms.

Sirena awakened at the first light of dawn. The hazy mist still lingered in the cabin, but she knew that in a few hours the sun would burn it away. Regan still slept beside her, his body emanating a feverish heat. His face was flushed with fever, his lips appeared parched and dry.

Her eyes flew to the bandage she'd wrapped around his arm the night before; a yellowish, bloody stain seeped through the linen. Tears welled in her eyes. "Querido," she whispered against his feverish temple, "I did this to you!" With horror she realized that the blade she had cut Regan with was the same with which she had killed Blackheart. Coming from that hulk of evil and into Regan's arm, no wonder the wound was unclean.

Disentangling herself from his embrace, she climbed out of the bunk and dressed quickly. On deck she scanned the horizon for signs of the Dutchman's brig, praying that Caleb had been successful. There, coming toward her from the north coast, was the brig's silhouette. Now she would suffer the ordeal of waiting to see who manned the brig, her men or Regan's.

Sirena went back to Regan and placed a cool cloth on his feverish brow. She contemplated changing the bandage on his arm but her ignorance of whether she would be doing more harm than good stopped her. As she changed the cloth on his forehead she attempted to sort out her feelings for this man, her husband. In the end her emotions were still unresolved.

She only knew that he was her enemy, one she had started out to kill. When had she changed her mind? Was it when Caleb wished her luck. How could she kill him . . . she loved him! Her beloved enemy!

A shout reached her ears. "Ahoy *Sea Siren!*" She recognized Jan's hoarse shout. Caleb had succeeded! In that instant she determined she would return Regan to the care of his own men, aboard his own ship.

Sirena and Caleb stayed below in the galley as Regan was lifted aboard his brig. Should he awaken she had no wish to see him, she felt too vulnerable to face him in the light of day.

As she instructed, she heard Jan warn the Dutchman's first mate to head directly for Batavia if he wished to see his captain live. Later, when the Dutch brig was safely out of sight, Sirena went on deck and changed course for the mouth of the River of Death between the "Sisters of Fire."

Leaving the wheel to Caleb, Sirena then went to her cabin and threw herself down on her bunk. While she lay there, exhausted by emotion, fraught with anxiety, she slept . . . and dreamed of the passion and ecstasy she had shared with Regan the night before.

Caleb gently shook Sirena's shoulder. "We're home. If we ride swiftly we can arrive just as dusk settles."

Sirena rubbed at her sleep-filled eyes. "I must have slept a long time," she said, puzzled.

"I told the men to allow you to sleep. We managed well. The decks have been scrubbed and the wounded are taken care of. I'm sorry, Sirena, I guess I am still a boy. I was so frightened I could not make my mind think. If I had been quicker, perhaps none of this would have happened," he chastised himself. "Will Regan die?"

"He won't die, Caleb. He carries a vengeance in him that won't allow him to die just as I do. Have no fear, little brother, when we arrive home under the cover of dusk, he will already be under the mothering influence of Frau Holtz." As Sirena spoke those reassuring words, she prayed to the God she had renounced that the man she loved would live to hold her again.

Chapter Twenty-two

"Gretchen!" Chaezar exclaimed his surprise. Not so much because of her explosive entrance into his private office but because of the early hour. A small, knowing smile tugged at the corners of Chaezar's mouth. Obviously Gretchen had spent a restless night alone in her bed, a rarity which always left her in ill humor; otherwise, she would have lain abed till noon recovering from the strenuous activities of the previous evening. Still smiling, he soothed, "May I say you are exquisite this morning?" Chaezar's black, heavy-browed eyes slid over her body familiarly. It had been too long since he had shared her bed, a situation he would hasten to remedy.

Seeing the light of appreciation in his gaze, Gretchen preened and was slightly mollified as she could be by the flattering glance of a handsome man. "You may," she said finally.

She had chosen a lightweight, handwoven fabric from India, artistically dyed in great splurges of green and blue on a background of palest yellow. A wide-brimmed straw hat festooned with yellow tea roses protected her flawless, clotted-cream complexion.

"To what do I owe this visit?" Chaesar asked.

"Isn't it early in the day for you to be abroad? Is something wrong?"

"Everything's wrong!" Gretchen pouted as she paced Chaezar's office nervously. Turning on him suddenly, she threw her gloves on his desktop. "You said you'd hear something about that boy! That was weeks ago!" She stamped a pretty, silk-shod foot on the red Oriental carpet.

"And I have, just before you arrived," Chaezar said smoothly, impervious by now to Gretchen's display of temper. "I would have paid you a visit a little later in the day, when I could be certain you were alone." Any other woman on Java would have either been insulted or at least blushed at his obvious slur on her morals. But not Gretchen. She never minded comment on her sexual activities, in fact she welcomed them. "You won't like hearing what I found out, Gretchen. The boy is gone."

"What?" she shrilled. "How?"

Chaezar repeated what he had learned in a voice devoid of emotion. "As we already know, the child was merely a baby, not more than four when we arranged to relieve Regan of his wife. 'The Hook,' as our mutual friend is popularly referred to these days, made the agreed-upon arrangements to see the child was cared for. This he did by *selling* the child to a rich Shintu chief. This chief purchased the boy for one of his wives, who was barren and desired a child. The boy was well cared for, doted on actually until he was somewhere around the age of six. At this time it is purported there was a war between feuding tribes and the child was taken as a slave. After this point all trace of him is lost. The boy's former owner is convinced the child was press-ganged, as all trace of him stops at the Banda quay in the Banda Islands.

"Oh my God," Gretchen wailed. "Now what do we do?"

"Do? There's nothing for either of us to do. We wait."

"Wait? Wait for what? For Regan to find out and have him kill us? You're insane, Chaezar! You've played me false from the beginning. From the moment the *Tita* set sail you had no intention of letting

Regan go free. I thought then that you gave in to me too easily. You wanted Regan out of your way in that damn Spanish prison. True, you managed to kill his wife for me, but that was just so I would be indebted to you. All along it was Regan you wanted out of the way. You weren't helping me at all, you greedy swine! It was convenient for you to kill Tita, so you did. But never for me! For yourself! And now that it has come time for us to pay for our . . . sins, you'd let me hang for yours as well. You won't get away with it, Chaezar! If it comes to Regan finding out, I'll tell him your part in it. If I have to die, so will you. Why in the name of God didn't you place the boy with a missionary?"

"If you'll remember correctly, we had little time to do more than we did. I don't much care for the tone of your threats, Gretchen," he said softly, stroking his luxuriant beard.

"You'd sell your mother for a piece of gold, don't deny it," Gretchen sneered. "And 'The Hook,' what did you find out about him? If Regan finds him, the charade is over!"

"Pray God the Sea Siren finds him before Regan does." Chaezar's voice betrayed a hint of his inner agitation. "The man must have been warned and has taken to land again. Otherwise, he would have been sighted long ago."

"Do you think an inner-island search would help?" Gretchen asked hopefully.

"It's worth the effort."

"When will you send someone to the islands to start inquiries?"

"Would today suit you?" Chaezar smiled wickedly, drawing her close to him. "Perhaps in the meantime we could . . ." His words were muffled against her lips.

So overpowering was the wave of revulsion that washed over Gretchen, she had the feeling she was drowning. Once again she must barter her flesh as a means to her ends. Her mind hated the Spaniard's soft, caressing touch, but her traitorous body welcomed it. If only Regan knew how she sold her body time and time again with only one thought in mind: to make him hers.

Chaezar's lips were soft and demanding as they sought the warm, moist recesses of her mouth. Shuddering inwardly at the close physical contact, she forced herself to respond, at first unwillingly then willingly as desire coursed through her body. It was a simple matter to pretend these were Regan's arms that were holding her. Soft moans escaped her as the pressure on her mouth became more insistent.

Chaezar released her suddenly. "Not here," he said thickly, "the servants." Half dragging and half carrying her, he led her to his chambers and immediately ripped the gown from her body.

Gretchen, her passion momentarily abated, narrowed her eyes and forced back the screams of protest at the damage done to her newest gown. If it had been Regan who tore her gown to shreds she would have helped him. She would do anything for Regan. She would give up all the gowns in her massive wardrobe. Her sultry eyes narrowed again—well, perhaps not all the gowns, but half of them. If only Regan would say just once, I need you, I want you, she would do anything . . . anything!

Desire once more coursed though her as Chaezar's nakedness met her flesh. His dark hands grasped her long golden hair. He twined it about his fingers, as he suckled her breasts with their rapidly hardening cherry nipples. Slowly, insidiously, he manipulated every part of her silken softness till she cried out with frenzied desire.

Fire danced and rippled through her, threatening to engulf her, and still he caressed her at this maddening slow pace, exploring every inch of her warm, wet flesh with his nibbling lips, darting tongue, and plying fingers.

Lost in her moment of desire, Gretchen imagined herself once again under the stars with Regan, making wild, passionate love. A small cry escaped her as she felt the familiar pressure within her. The world exploded as Regan's name escaped her parted lips.

Shocked, she found herself in a heap on the floor, staring up into the wild, rage-filled eyes of Chaezar

Alvarez. "So, I come out second best with Regan's whore," he spat with controlled fury. His tone softened abruptly, frightening Gretchen still more. She could handle his fury but never this soft, dangerous mood. Slowly, she got to her knees and backed away from his outstretched foot. She had no desire to have her face disfigured.

Chaezar bent down and pulled her to her feet. He would kill her, she was sure of it. With the instinct of a trapped animal, she lashed out, gouging and kicking, raking her nails down the Spaniard's chest, drawing blood. "Bastard! You'll not kill me!" she hissed, her breasts heaving with the exertion.

She lashed out with her foot, only to have it become caught between his legs and they both went down in a tumble on the floor. Gretchen grabbed handfuls of the black, curly hair on Chaezar's chest and yanked. A womanly, high-pitched shriek tore from the Spaniard's throat.

Rolling across his nakedness to make her escape, she was stunned to feel his hardness beneath her. Her fear was replaced with disgust. Instinctively she knew what she had to do. Once Chaezar was lulled by his satisfied passions she could escape.

Her strong, slender hands gripped his shoulders and forced him back onto the floor. She gazed deeply into his passion-filled eyes as she pinched his nipples. Slowly she raised herself and mounted him.

Chaezar closed his eyes as she took him in, a saturnine grimace distorting his features as Gretchen rocked back and forth, first taunting him with slow movements, then faster and faster as she was engulfed in the delight of her own pleasure. Spasm after wild spasm gripped Chaezar's body and soon he was breathing deeply with satisfaction. He was lost to a world where he indulged his aberrations.

Seeing her chance, Gretchen scrambled to her feet and donned her torn and ravaged clothing. Without a backward glance she quietly left the room, knowing she would never return.

Chapter Twenty-three

Frau Holtz stood next to Regan's bed in the darkened room where the sun-bronzed giant thrashed about in delirium. Her expression was more dour than usual, reflecting the pain and pity churning within her. Lifting her eyes, she gazed at the doctor and read worry and indecision in his face.

Clearing his throat, the short, outmodishly dressed physician turned to avoid the housekeeper's accusing glare. "The wound is to the bone, but it will be a miracle if he doesn't perish of the fever. Regan will become a madman if he loses his arm. Someone must stay with him every moment. Where is Mevrouw van der Rhys? She must be told."

"The Mevrouw will come shortly. She's been in retreat, and shortly before the Mynheer was brought home she called for her bath water. It won't be long now." Frau Holtz's disapproval of her mistress was evident in the tone of her voice.

"I can't wait about for her, Frau Holtz. Night has already fallen and Mevrouw Sankku, the clerk's wife, is ready to birth her first child. Follow the instructions I gave you and I'll be back in the morning. If his fever hasn't broken, I may have to take his arm." The doctor's voice said this was more than a possibility, it was inevitable. "Hurry the Mevrouw along. Make her understand the situation. Tomorrow's sunset may see her a widow!" Picking up his heavy, black bag, he followed Frau Holtz to the door.

The housekeeper muttered to herself as she retraced her footsteps to Regan's door. She looked in and satisfied herself that he had not changed position. The drug the physician had administered was taking effect.

Sirena hurried down the hall toward Regan's room. Frau Holtz seemed to be guarding the door, a worried, forbidding expression lining her plain peasant's face. "The doctor has just left. He'll return in the morning. He's worried he may have to take the Mynheer's arm . . . if he lives!

Sirena gasped, "I'll go to him at once!"

Frau Holtz moved to block the doorway. "The doctor said I was to stay with him and nurse him." The housekeeper's tone was guarded, her expression suspicious.

"I will see to my husband, Frau Holtz, I won't be interfered with! You will repeat the doctor's instructions of what must be done and I will do it. Quickly now!"

The housekeeper's eyes were cold and unreadable as she stepped aside to allow Sirena passage into Regan's room. In a bone-chilling tone she repeated the physician's instructions.

"Mevrouw, how will you manage if Mynheer needs to be restrained?"

"My brother Caleb will help me, Frau Holtz."

Stepping closer to the bed, Sirena stared down at Regan's fever-flushed face. She clenched her fists to still their trembling and forced her face into lines that would not betray her inner emotions. She had done this! Unable to restrain herself any longer, Sirena dropped to her knees and gently touched Regan's feverish brow. He lay so still, so quietly, as quietly as death must lay. Her fingers felt scorched by their fleeting contact with his brow. Her eyes traveled downward to his bandaged arm which lay atop the coverlet. Blood and pus were already soaking through the bandages. Tears glistened in her eyes, illuminating them like stained-glass windows in a chapel. She had done this! She must help him!

Sirena lifted her eyes and held the housekeeper in a steady stare. In a voice that was stronger than she felt, she ordered, "On your way back to the kitchen send my brother to me." In that one simple sentence she had challenged Frau Holtz's right to be with Regan. Sirena imagined she could almost hear Frau Holtz's nerves crackle with rage but she kept her gaze steady, with an imperious lift to her chin. Whatever Frau Holtz was about to say in retaliation, she apparently thought better of it and accepted Sirena's dismissal. Head held high, her coronet of salt-and-pepper braids adding to her regal bearing, Frau Holtz left the room.

Regan began thrashing about on the bed again and Sirena attempted to soothe him with cool compresses and gently reassuring murmurs. Caleb quietly entered the room; he took in the scene, and winced when he saw the tears shining in Sirena's eyes.

"How . . . how bad is he, Sirena?

"Very. Look at his arm. Frau Holtz told me the doctor's instructions and gave me these powders he left. But I don't trust them. Go to my room and bring me those powders in my medicine chest. They're the same kind you used to save my arm; pray God they'll help Regan."

"But . . ." Caleb began, indecision flashing in his eyes. "Perhaps the doctor *did* know best."

"No buts, Caleb. We have to take the chance. The doctor has so little faith in the prescription he left that he fully expects to amputate in the morning."

Regan again stirred fretfully, and tried to speak. Sirena grasped his hand in a firm grip and spoke soothingly. Her soft words seemed to calm him and he quieted. Placing a cool cloth on his forehead, she gently wiped his face and neck. "I've done this to you, Regan, but I won't let them take your arm. I won't let you die like that, you have my word on it," she said quietly.

Regan's blue eyes opened, and were cloudy and pain-filled. He looked up and tried to focus on her face. But the face was a blur as were her words. Nevertheless, he felt comforted by her presence and by her gentle touch. His heavy fringe of eyelashes fluttered and closed.

Moments later, Caleb reentered the room, Sirena's medicine chest under his arm. "Sirena," he said, "the smell in here is worse than bilge! What is it?"

"It's his arm, Caleb. I think what you smell is the onset of putrefaction. That's probably why the doctor feels the arm must come off. We'll have to reopen the wound to clean it and when we do he'll scream to the high heavens. You'll have to hold him down and he'll fight like a tiger. First secure his good arm to the bedpost, then the injured arm. You'll have to straddle his chest to keep him down on the bed. Do you think you can do it?"

"I'll do it," Caleb said, his young mouth set in a grim line.

Within minutes Regan was securely bound to the bedposts. Caleb was in position across Regan's chest, pressing the hard, muscular shoulders down into the mattress. Sirena quickly unwound the bloody bandage over the wound, drawing in her breath at the sight of the gash. "Caleb, was my arm this bad? Look quickly!"

Caleb gulped when he saw the festered opening oozing blood and infected pus. "It might have been, but we didn't let it get this far. What kind of scurves does Regan employ on his ships that not one among them knew how to treat the wound until they could get to port?" Sirena sympathized and understood the anger she saw in Caleb's face. The boy admired Regan and it was inconceivable to him that Regan's men could have neglected their captain this way.

Steeling herself for what was to come, Sirena withdrew a sharp knife from her medicine chest. She lit a candle and drew the blade through the tip of the wavering flame. Without hesitation, she slit the wound along the original cut with a fluid motion. Blood and pus spurted and drained from her lancing. Caleb forced Regan down on the bed, exerting all the strength within his sturdy twelve-year-old body. Regan growled and cursed and damned the monster eating his arm. In his delirium he imagined he was the object of a shark attack. This, Caleb understood from Regan's ramblings and the boy was once again in awe of the bronzed sun god who would curse and swear and fight like the devil and never give in to the most feared fate of any seaman, death by those greedy demons of the sea—sharks!

"I have to drain the pus. Hold him Caleb, he'll rave like a madman." Drawing in a great breath, Sirena pressed the edges of the wound together.

Regan's cries and thrashings jolted her backwards. When she regained her position, she swabbed away the fresh blood which was now free of the yellow-green pus. Her movements were hurried as she lavishly sprinkled a dull-yellow powder over the wound and covered it with a thick strip of bandage.

Caleb and Sirena were totally engrossed in Regan, so much so that neither of them heard Frau Holtz enter the room. Suddenly Sirena was jerked back away from Regan and soundly slapped across the face. "Witch!" the housekeeper spat vehemently, "what do you think you're doing to the Mynheer?" Wildly, Frau Holtz yanked Caleb off Regan's chest.

Sirena retailiated angrily, grasping Frau Holtz's arm and flinging the woman against the far wall. Panting from the exertion, Sirena gasped, "Are you mad? The Mynheer is fighting for his life. Why are you behaving this way?"

"I saw what you were doing, you're a witch! What have you and your brother done to him? He's as still as death! The doctor will hear of what you've done!"

"If left to that stupid doctor's devices, I would be a widow by morning! Now get out of here and don't come back!"

The stately housekeeper rubbed her shoulder. "You'll regret this, Mevrouw," she hissed viciously.

"Perhaps I will," Sirena retorted, "but the order still stands. Get out and don't come back!"

The sharp slam of the closing door made Caleb sigh with relief. "We must have looked like a coven of witches sacrificing Regan in a ritual. I can understand what she must have thought when she saw me sitting on his chest and you leaning over his arm, your hands smeared with his blood!"

A slow smile broke out on Sirena's face as the ridiculousness of the situation hit her. "I can see your point, Caleb. Nevertheless, that one takes too much upon herself!" Sirena's cheek was beginning to smart and she knew there was a brand from Frau Holtz's fingers on her face.

Caleb and Sirena decided to alternate their watch over Regan. Taking the first watch as Caleb slept atop a quilt in the corner of the room, Sirena sat next to the bed, her slim white hand covering Regan's.

From time to time Regan moaned and thrashed on the bed. Sirena would speak in a low, soothing tone and he would quiet. At one point, his sun-darkened hand sought hers and he tried to grasp it, only to have his strength ebb. Moans of pain darkened his features. Sirena's eyes were tortured as she watched Regan fight the fever. Again she changed the dressing on his injured arm. Something was wrong, the signs of putrefaction were more evident than before. Frightened, she bent to look closer with the aid of the lamp. Merciful God!

On trembling legs she raced to the corner to wake Caleb. "Quickly! Come see his arm." Shaking with fear, Caleb looked at Sirena.

"Lock the doors and come back here!" Sirena rapidly told Caleb what had to be done. "It will take strength you don't have, Caleb. You will have to find a way to be strong. He can't move the arm. I'll do it," she said through clenched teeth. "If he's not to lose his arm, it's the only chance he has." Before she could think twice or change her mind, she held the long, flat blade of a knife to the candle flame. Regan struggled and writhed beneath Caleb as he fought for escape from the pain. Caleb sat atop Regan's chest with his hands pressed into his hard, sinewy shoulders.

"It's done, Caleb. Put cool cloths on his forehead, while I see to the dressing. I think you can untie his arms now."

"No!" Caleb said fearfully, "leave him tied till the fever abates." Sirena agreed while she sprinkled the yellow powder over Regan's seared flesh and laid a clean dressing on the arm.

"Will it work?"

"God only knows. There isn't anything else to do. Now all we can do is wait. Go back to sleep."

Regan lay quiet, breathing in uneven gasps. Sirena held his hand and dozed from time to time. Toward dawn, she fell into a quiet sleep.

Regan opened his eyes and focused on the woman on the chair next to him. Wearily he closed his eyes, his arm wracked with pain. What in the name of God was wrong with him? Where was he? His vision blurred as he tried to look around the room. He needed help. His glazed vision settled on the sleeping woman on the chair with her hair hanging loosely from its pins. The Sea Siren! Would she help him? He opened his mouth to cry out when she woke and leaned over him. Soft soothing words were being said but he was unable to distinguish what they were. Somehow they were like a balm to his ear. Gentle hands wiped his face, cool lips touched his forehead, his cheeks, and his mouth. Opening his eyes he stared into the depths of green-water pools. Why would the Sea Siren cry for him? He had to speak, to ask what was happening. Gasping, he opened his mouth only to have those same cool lips cover his. His head swam dizzily as remembered sensations flooded his body.

"I'm sorry, I'm so sorry," Sirena said softly. "I didn't mean it to come to this. It would have been better if I killed you." The tears she had long held in check were now streaming down her cheeks.

"You bested me, Siren," Regan said, his voice rough and hoarse, his head whirling.

"Shh," Sirena said, laying a finger to his lips. "You must rest now to regain your strength." Regan slept, his mind whirling backwards in time to the decks of the black ship and the embrace of the Sea Siren.

"It is time to change the dressings. I'm almost afraid to look, little brother. The doctor will be here soon and we may have some problems."

Her first thought was to pull the dressing away with one motion. Some inner voice warned her to ease it off. "Look, Caleb," she whispered excitedly, "a scab is forming."

Caleb breathed a sigh of relief as he looked at the thin crust which was forming over the wound. Sirena herself closed her eyes in relief.

"What of his fever?" Caleb asked anxiously.

"We can do nothing but let it run its course. We'll continue with the cool cloths and the medicine."

"I'll watch him if you want to bathe and change your clothing," Caleb volunteered.

"Don't take your eyes from him, Caleb. Continue with the cool cloths and I'll return as soon as possible."

Sirena was in the process of buttoning the sleeves of her gown when Caleb burst into the room. "The doctor says he'll have to amputate his arm and Regan is half awake! Hurry, Sirena!"

"What! The fool! Did he look at the arm?"

"Aye. But he says the poisons are in Regan's body from the arm and that is why the fever still rages. Don't, please don't let them cut off his arm!" Caleb pleaded as they raced down the corridor.

Sirena flung open the door, her eyes wild, her hair streaming down her shoulders. "What is this my brother tells me that you will take the arm? What foolish talk is this?"

"Look to your husband, Meurouw. Do you see how the fever engulfs him? The poisons from the arm are all through his body!"

"The arm is on the mend! Open your eyes, old man, open them wide! The dressing is clean and the wound has crusted!"

"I have been Mynheer van der Rhys's physician for many years. My judgment has never been questioned before!"

Regan lay, his eyes half open, listening to the exchange between the doctor and the Siren. They wanted to cut off his arm. No, that wasn't right. The doctor wanted to cut off his arm and the Sea Siren was opposing him.

"You will not take his arm," Sirena said coldly.

"It's necessary. Do you think I like the idea of taking off a man's arm? Especially a man like Regan? I tell you, it's necessary!"

"And I tell you it's not necessary. The fever will run its course. The arm mends. My husband is half lucid, why don't you ask him before you make any more decisions?" Sirena said quietly, her eyes chips of frozen seawater.

"The man is in a delirium, he can't know what is going on. I am the physician!"

"And I, Mynheer Doctor, am his wife. I say the arm stays."

What were they babbling? Regan thought. Why was the Siren saying she was his wife? And that fool of a doctor, why did he want to cut off his arm? Why was the Siren saying the arm was to stay? Hadn't she been the one who laid it open? Did she want him to suffer still more? What good would he be with only one arm?

Regan tried to motion for silence. His mouth felt dry and full of lint. He had to make them understand the arm was to stay. He would rather be dead than lose it!

Sirena, seeing Regan's desperate condition, bent low and whispered soothingly, "Have no fear, I'll not allow him to take your arm." Her calm, soft tone reassured Regan and he closed his eyes and slept.

"The matter is ended. I will care for my husband myself. When my husband recovers, you may discuss this matter with him. Till then, your services are not required. Good day, Mynheer Doctor. Caleb, show him to the door."

Left alone with Regan, who seemed to be resting quietly in spite of the ferocious fever, Sirena sank down into a chair. Quaking with anger, fraught with anxiety, she couldn't suppress the one thought which kept surfacing: What if I'm wrong! Have I saved his arm from that bloodthirsty physician just so Regan can take it into his early grave?

Tears came unbidden to her emerald eyes as her mind rebelled from the thought that she might never again know his caresses, perhaps someday, his love . . .

Chapter Twenty-four

Sirena and Caleb occupied themselves in Regan's room. Quietly dusting tabletops that needed no dusting, opening or closing the shutters on the long windows, bringing fresh water, adjusting the bed-cover, changing wilted flowers for fresh, doing all sorts of busywork in an effort to keep themselves from thinking about Regan. His fever had broken the night before and after one or two lucid moments he had fallen back into an exhausted but natural sleep. Now Caleb and Sirena hovered about him, anxiously awaiting signs of Regan's awakening.

The faint rustling of the covers brought Caleb scampering to the bedside. "How are you, Regan?" Caleb asked, trying to restrain his exuberance.

Regan frowned and tried to bring his vision into focus. "You've been very sick, Regan, but you're on the mend now! Your arm gets better every day and you've been without the fever since yesterday."

Regan's eyes roved the room frantically and came to rest on Sirena, who was calmly seated in a chair, rosary in her hands. Wearily, he closed his eyes again. Why had he expected to see the Sea Siren? How ill had he been? "How long have I been home?" he asked, his voice hoarse and low.

"Six days, Regan," Caleb replied. "Sirena's been taking care of you all that time." Vaguely, Regan was aware Caleb had dropped the title "Mynheer" and was using his Christian name. A certain satisfaction permeated his weakened body. Once again his blue eyes closed and he heaved a deep sigh.

Satisfied Regan was lucid, Sirena stood next to the bed and looked down at him.

"We Dutch are hardy stock," Regan said hoarsely.

"Hardy stock is it?" Sirena laughed with a hint of mockery in her voice. "And I thought perhaps it was my prayers on the cultured pearl beads you gave me. You did say that perhaps if I prayed on real pearls my prayers would carry more weight." She lowered her head a trifle and said, "I am happy you're better, Regan. Come Caleb, he still needs much more rest."

Regan regained his strength quickly, and Sirena found he required her ministrations less and less. She soon began devoting herself to his affairs outside the house: delivering messages to the clerks in his office, dealing with the most urgent business matters. She had learned from Caleb that Regan asked every day if there were any word of the Sea Siren. It gave her a certain vicarious pleasure to know Regan was obviously hopelessly enamored of the ruthless female pirate. When she realized to what extent Regan dwelled on his fascinating "mistress of the sea," Sirena took extra pains with her appearance to obscure the most obvious similarities. She kept her hair brushed sleekly back into the heavy knot at the back of her neck; a black lace mantilla covered her head and cast dark, lacey shadows on her whitely powdered face. Cumbersome, black gowns cut to obscure her figure were as integral to her wardrobe as her softly modulated voice and prayerful manner were to her demeanor.

Every now and then Regan would look at her speculatively, almost searchingly. At these times Sirena would practice a little trick she had been employing for the months since she had arrived in Regan's house. Just a humble little dip of her head and the sides of her mantillla would fall against her face, obscuring her features behind a web of mystery. Before her mirror she had experimented with more elaborate hairstyles, but in the end had decided the sleek style brushed severely back from her high forehead suited her purposes best.

As the Sea Siren, her fine-boned face was largely concealed by a brightly colored bandana tied around her head just a few inches above her delicately arched eyebrows. Still, when Regan's eyes swept over her face searchingly, she experienced a chilling fear of discovery.

One month to the day of being laid low by the Sea Siren's blade, Regan, who had been ambulatory for several days, sent word to Sirena that Chaezar was giving an impromptu dinner that evening.

Sirena smiled to herself, looking forward to the dinner party. She had been more or less housebound since Regan's illness. It would be good to get out again. Leave it to Chaezar to give a party to take his guests' minds off the ominous rumbling which had been emanating from the Sisters of Fire for several weeks. The whole of Java was uneasy about a possible eruption. In fact many families had left the island, pleading the need for a change of scene. No one was fooled, an inner panic lay beneath the public actions of most Batavians.

At the appointed hour Sirena descended the stairs to join Regan, who waited for her in the drawing room. His eyes flicked over her approvingly as he offered his arm to escort her to the carriage. As always, Sirena wished she could dispense with the drab figure-concealing black gowns. She would have loved to wear something more colorful and revealing to dazzle him.

Seated next to Regan in the carriage, Sirena asked lightly, "What's the purpose of this dinner? I assume there's a purpose, isn't there?"

"So, at last you've discovered there are few things Chaezar Alvarez does without an ulterior motive."

Not caring to engage in an argument concerning Chaezar, Sirena bandied, "Does this dinner concern the Sea Siren?"

"Yes, it does. She must be captured and brought here to Batavia." Even while speaking of the Sea Siren's capture, Regan's face revealed his desire for the infamous piratess.

"How do you plan to capture her? She's slipped through your fingers time and again."

"I'm not sure how yet. Tonight some scheme will be arrived at. I don't understand her motives. She could have killed all my men and me along with them.

Instead she allowed my brig to sail to port because I was wounded and needed a doctor. If I only knew why she hunts this man called The Hook perhaps I would almost accept this havoc she enjoys creating. I saw a look in her eye I can't name. She's possessed by a devilish drive to find The Hook!"

"Is she as beautiful as they say?" Sirena asked cautiously, watching his face covertly under cover of the dark night.

Regan spoke slowly and carefully, as if he were carefully choosing each word. "I've seen many beautiful women but the Sea Siren is something more. She's as wild as the seas she rides, as sultry as the equatorial air, dangerous as the seasonal monsoons, as hauntingly beautiful as a rare gem. There's liquid fire in her veins and a promise of a kiss plays on her lips. There's no other like her if one searched the world over."

Sirena's pulses quickened. She knew Regan was thinking of the night aboard the frigate, alone in each other's arms, separated from the world by a blanket of isolating fog. His voice was warm and husky, his frosty blue eyes looked far off into the distance.

"You seem to be enamored of her, Regan, are you?" Sirena asked softly, thrilling to his low, intimate tones, wanting him to continue speaking of the Sea Siren, forgetting for the moment that he thought he was speaking of a totally different woman.

Instead, Regan turned to her in amazement. "You have a bold tongue! Strange question for a wife to ask her husband!"

"Not really. What I find strange is that you haven't answered me!"

Regan was saved from a reply by their carriage arriving at Chaezar's palatial home.

After the elaborate dinner at Chaezar's table, Regan and Sirena, along with Chaezar, and Gretchen and several captains and their wives whom Sirena vaguely remembered meeting before at her wedding and Chaezar's elaborate ball, retired to the drawing room.

In this room Chaezar's distinctive tastes were successfully mirrored. Cool blues and pale yellows dominated the color scheme, enhanced by the delicate teak and ebony tables clustered close to the white damask upholstery on the spindly-legged gilt chairs.

Gretchen was resplendent in a low-cut gown of silver net atop a shimmering blue petticoat. As in the dining room, she contrived to place herself at Regan's elbow, ready at the smallest provocation to smile up at him, dimpling her chin and displaying her splendid startlingly white teeth. It wasn't Gretchen's shameless flirting that rankled Sirena, because she knew Regan was obsessed with the Sea Siren, it was the pitying glances Gretchen tossed at her that made Sirena's nails itch to rake that pink face.

Chaezar moved to the center of the room and held up his hand for silence. "Mevrouw Lindenreich has kindly agreed to sing for us this evening. Any business can be discussed later. Gretchen, if you please."

Pretending a coyness which didn't become her, Gretchen allowed Chaezar to lead her to a position next to the spinet. Seating himself at the instrument, Chaezar ran his fingers lightly over the keys. The tune was unfamiliar yet hauntingly lovely. At her cue, Gretchen began to sing, in French, a love ballad about the undying love of a pretty street urchin for a grand duke.

If she were to be honest with herself, Sirena had to give Gretchen her due. Her voice was a high, clear soprano, colorful and rich. The room was hushed, every eye on the beautiful Gretchen who only had eyes for Regan.

Sirena, whose back was to Regan, imagined he was preening in Gretchen's bold flattery. Slowly, Sirena turned to steal a glance at the effect Gretchen was having on him.

Regan, with his usual easy grace, sat on the delicate gilt chair holding a snifter of Chaezar's rare brandy, long legs stretched out before him. His agate gaze was centered on Gretchen, the lines about his square lean jaw relaxed and softened, a smile played about the corner of his mouth. The looks traveling between Regan and his silver-blond mistress excluded everyone else in the room. How many times had Gretchen sung for him when they were alone and free to indulge themselves in the promised sensuality of her songs?

Several gentlemen shifted uneasily in their chairs. Regan's connection with Gretchen was well known and before Regan's marriage to Sirena these same gentlemen were happy enough to jab elbows into one another and smile knowingly. But now! The glances traveling between Gretchen and Regan were making them most uncomfortable, especially before their wives who, pitying Sirena, would take great care not to suffer her embarrassment themselves. The reins would be tightened in many Batavian households.

Sirena's body temperature rose several degrees. How could Regan denigrate her this way? she thought hotly. I wonder if Gretchen would find him so attractive if he'd lost his arm? Somehow Sirena knew Gretchen would want Regan if he were armless and legless and a mindless idiot. Beneath that blond, voluptuous almost vulgar beauty was a passionate woman who, despite her amoral behavior, truly loved Regan van der Rhys. Realizing this, Sirena felt almost sorry for Gretchen. Regan had used Gretchen, had toyed with her and would continue to do so, never for a moment taking her seriously.

Gretchen concluded the last of her songs and basked in the applause and compliments paid her. At last she turned her triumphant hazel eyes to Sirena. "Your voice is lovely, Gretchen," Sirena said truthfully.

"Thank you," Gretchen said simply, a shard of ice in her polite pleasantry. Gretchen's eyes sought Regan, who was still sitting easily on his chair contemplating the burnished liquid in his glass.

Chaezar stepped over to Sirena, and said in a clear voice, "And now, Sirena, perhaps you would honor us likewise."

"Oh no, I couldn't," Sirena protested meekly over a chorus of gentle pleadings from the party guests. She was about to plead a headache when she looked into Gretchen's eyes. Hate spilled from them and had the look been a tangible thing, Sirena would have been struck from her chair.

"I'd love to play for you," Sirena said, smiling up at Chaezar. He drew her to her feet and led her over to the far end of the room. Seated near the spinet, the glow of the lamplight illuminating her complexion to perfection, Sirena softly strummed Chaezar's ornate Spanish guitar, testing the chords, reverberating the deep tones, playing staccato on the high notes. Her audience complimented her with rapt attention.

She played a succession of short, lilting, melodious folk songs which induced her audience to tap their feet and clap their hands in rhythm, caused their faces to be wreathed in lighthearted smiles. The tunes ended, Chaezar and his guests applauded with delight, and yet Sirena sat, her head bowed in concentration, her fingers poised on the strings. The room became hushed, everyone was alert with expectation. Suddenly, Sirena's fingers flew over the strings, and the music was alive and vibrant. Chaezar moved close to Sirena and dropped down on one knee, his dark, brilliant eyes intent upon her face. He knew from the opening strains she was about to play for him the flamenco, food for the passionate Spanish soul.

It was then he heard it, so perfect in tone at first he thought it was the guitar. Then the sound blossomed and poured forth, spilling into the hushed corners of the room with perfection and clarity of pitch—Sirena's voice.

She sang the flamenco with inspiration, and her audience was caught up in the music's sensuousness, especially Chaezar, who understood its sweetness and poignancy, and could follow Sirena through each movement knowingly, savoring its promise.

As Sirena sang, she looked at Chaezar. He seemed to be transported, her music moving him across the thousands of miles back to Spain.

Regan watched his wife and Chaezar through flashing cold eyes, his mouth set in a tight, grim line. What did Chaezar think he was doing poised on one knee inches away from Sirena and gazing up adoringly into her face? And Sirena! His cool, aloof Sirena. Was her poise, composure, and cool reserve only for him, Regan? Was there a fiery nature and passionate soul, as passionate as her music, beneath that mask of constraint? Was it only for Chaezar the mask was allowed to slip, revealing beneath it a temptress, bold and exciting?

Regan quickly swallowed the remainder of his brandy and frowned. The heat from his hand had warmed the liquor beyond what he considered a pleasing temperature. Bah! he thought, treacherous friends, a flirtatious wife, warm liquor!

When her song ended, Sirena lifted her head and looked across the room to Regan. His face was flushed with anger, his sheaf of white-blond hair spilled across his sun-darkened brow, emphasizing the burning rage in his eyes.

Chaezar and his guests gathered about Sirena, applauding her enthusiastically and declaring their praise—everyone save Regan.

Later in the evening, Sirena found herself bored by all the talk and speculation about the Sea Siren. She found herself squirming and fidgeting on the gilt chair. Her back ached with strain, her stomach was queasy and she was feeling light-headed. She'd experienced this feeling quite often during the past weeks and, having no patience for illness, attributed it to being confined to the house nursing Regan and missing the fresh, free-spirited air of the open sea. Perhaps if she refreshed herself she'd be better able to tolerate the balance of the evening.

Excusing herself, Sirena made her way to the ladies' chambers to splash cologne on her wrists and neck. Sirena was smoothing her hair when she looked up to see Gretchen enter the room.

"You did it purposely, didn't you?" Gretchen hissed.

"Did what?" Sirena asked, puzzled.

"Made a fool of me by strumming on that box! You did it on purpose! You won't win, you know; Regan is mine! He's been mine for years!"

"Now I see what you're talking about. The songs

you sang were an excuse to bait me. I hesitate to remind you that I am married to Regan. If he had wanted to marry you, the choice was his." Sirena knew her calm, unruffled attitude was infuriating Gretchen.

"There wasn't any choice and you know it! The contracts were arranged long ago!"

"Contracts have been broken over less trivial things. If he wanted you he would have sought you out. I find this discussion in poor taste. If you'll excuse me," Sirena said, gathering her skirts in her hand to pass the angry-eyed German.

"I'm not finished!" Gretchen spat, as she jerked Sirena's arm to push her backwards.

"That was a foolish move, Gretchen. What if one of the other ladies were to enter the room?"

"I don't care. I have more to say!"

"I have nothing to say to you. Now let me pass."

"You're so cool, so confident. Why is that? If I had a husband who bedded every whore from here to Cape Town regardless of her color I wouldn't be so smug."

"Why are you concerned? Regan isn't your husband."

"He would have been if it weren't for you," Gretchen spat.

"I find that hard to believe."

"Bitch!" Gretchen hissed angrily as she reached out and grabbed Sirena's arm, throwing her off balance. Sirena collided with the wall and brought up her arm to shield her face from Gretchen's clawing attack. Sirena's hand bore deep, bleeding gouges. The German poised for still another attack and Sirena found her hand instinctively reaching for the hilt of her cutlass. With a lithe movement she brought up the inside of her arm and jarred Gretchen's hands away from her face and rendered the blonde a stinging blow. Sirena, having the advantage now, gave Gretchen a push and yanked at her heavy blond hair. Sirena wasn't surprised to see a handful remain in her hand. She was gazing at the curls in her hand when the door opened and Chaezar and Regan entered.

"Two spitting cats," Chaezar grinned. "Who was the victor? Ah, Gretchen, it would appear it wasn't you. Tidy yourself and come join the party."

"She doesn't even fight like a woman," Gretchen spat. "Look at her. Not a hair out of place!"

Regan's blue eyes traveled to his wife and was puzzled. How could Sirena have fought a cat match and been the victor? Gretchen was right, there wasn't a hair out of place.

Regan found his glance traveling to Sirena for the remainder of the evening. There was something about her that made his blood rush through his veins. He knew he had imbibed too freely of Chaezar's excellent brandy. Perhaps he wasn't fully recovered from his illness. Was it the alcohol that made him imagine the Sea Siren's beautiful laughing face superimposed over his wife's aloof, reserved features.

Apprehension knotted in the pit of Sirena's stomach each time she felt Regan's eyes on her. He was looking at her almost as if he knew of her secret identity.

The party ended close to midnight. Regan and Sirena were the last to leave. Courteously, Regan apologized for his wife's behavior.

Angrily, Sirena interrupted, "I need no one to make apologies on my behalf. I merely defended myself. You men defend yourselves against the Sea Siren, don't you? Should I have allowed Gretchen to scratch my eyes out and rip my gown down the front as was her intent?"

"Indeed not!" Chaezar said, bowing low over her hand. "You never need to apologize for anything in my house. I must be allowed to reinstate my hospitality, Sirena. Say you'll be my guest for lunch this week. That is if you are permitted," Chaezar said, looking at Regan defiantly.

"You seem bent on ignoring my wishes, Chaezar," Regan said coldly, his words slightly slurred because of the brandy he had consumed. "I have no desire to insult you in your own home, but I've warned you once and I won't repeat myself. The Mevrouw has many duties to occupy her time."

"What duties?" Sirena challenged. "I'm bored to

tears. Chaezar," she addressed the Spaniard airily, "next you know Regan will have a chain about my neck to lead me to and fro." Her laughter tinkled out into the dark night.

Regan drew in his breath.

The ride home was made in silence. Regan seethed inwardly because of her open defiance and ridicule. If he ever knew for certain she had taken the Spaniard as a lover, he would kill her!

Sirena rode next to Regan and tried to keep from being jostled against him. She hoped she was wrong about what she was reading in her husband's eyes. She inched further away from him, sensing she could smell his open lust.

In her room with the door locked, she shed her gown and was in the process of loosening the pins from her hair when a knock sounded at the door. Clutching the gown to her, she approached the door fearfully, hoping against hope that her maid Juli had stayed awake and was coming to brush her hair.

Sirena called softly through the door, "Yes?"

"Open the door, I want to speak to you."

"I'm preparing for bed, Regan, and I've many prayers to say before retiring," she explained in a calm voice that belied her inner turmoil.

"You'll find this door at your feet if you don't open it! You've got till the count of five!"

Sirena gasped. She had been right! God, where was Caleb—Juli—anyone! Quickly, she pulled the gown over her head and fumbled clumsily with the long buttons. On the count of four, with a yard of buttons still to go, she swung open the door and stared up into her husband's face.

Regan measured her disarray and the panic in her eyes. Why in the name of God should she fear her husband and not that bastard Chaezar? Incensed by fury and too much brandy, he sauntered over the threshold and locked his arms across his massive chest. "It's occurred to me, Sirena, the last time I was in your room I asked a question and didn't receive your answer. I want it answered now!"

Sirena pleaded ignorance, though she knew full well what he was asking.

"Your memory seems to be as convenient as Chaezar's. He also pleads ignorance when I discuss the matter with him," Regan said bitterly.

"Regan, I don't know what you're talking about," Sirena protested.

"Have you taken the Spaniard for your lover? This evening you made a fool of me again with your coquettish looks at the Spaniard. Everyone noticed and Chaezar himself was the cat in the cream crock. I won't have it!" he raged, unlocking his arms and stalking her.

Sirena frantically clutched the gown over her heaving breasts as she tried to figure a way to elude him.

"Answer me, damn you! Is Chaezar your lover?"

"I refuse to answer you, you're drunk and don't know what you're saying. You'll be ashamed of yourself tomorrow."

Regan's face showed his uncertainty. What was it about this woman that could cow him as if he were a child? Roughly he reached out and pulled her against him.

"I want you," he murmured huskily, his lips seeking hers.

Sirena fought his embrace, but her struggles were useless against his powerful arms. Ignoring her protests, he picked her up in his arms and cradled her head to his chest, all the while whispering soft, indistinct phrases.

Almost tenderly, he laid her on the bed and began to remove her gown. Head reeling, Sirena gasped, "Please, Regan, you mustn't. Please don't do this to either of us! We won't be able to face each other tomorrow!"

His lips found hers again, his hands worked at her gown. Lost in the moment, Sirena could only surrender to the feelings engulfing her. All was forgotten and she was again in the cabin of her frigate, the *Sea Siren,* surrounded by the isolating fog. Then she remembered the wicked scar on her arm—if he saw it the game would be played and she the loser.

"Regan! Stop!" she cried hoarsely, pushing him from

her as she rolled across the bed to escape him. He said nothing, his eyes said it all. She was his wife and he meant to have her.

Drunkenly, he stumbled toward her. She knew if he got his hands on her she would be powerless against him. She backed away, groping behind her for a weapon to stave him off. Her hand closed over a silver-backed hairbrush. "Don't come any closer, Regan," she threatened, hefting the brush.

Still he advanced on her, tearing his shirt open and removing his belt.

Hysterically, she cleared off her dressing table, throwing each object directly at his head.

Fists clenched so tightly his knuckles stood out starkly white, he fended off her attack. When her supply of weapons on the dressing table was exhausted, he watched to see her next move. Menace glowed in his eyes, there was a smirk about his mouth, he looped the end of his belt through the heavy brass buckle, making a noose.

"The devil take your soul, you filthy scurve!" she shrieked.

Still he advanced, portending lust making his eyes as indigo as the night.

"You're not man enough to make me come to you, to make me want you, so you think you'll rape me! Never! You pig of a whoreson!"

Still he advanced.

Her only escape was the door. Regan seemed to realize this. Hampered by her dragging skirts, she stumbled, her arm reaching, clawing for the knob.

In a flash of motion, Regan looped the belt around her wrist and yanked her to him, the threatening smile playing about his cruelly twisted mouth. Half dragging, half carrying her to the bed, he flung her upon it, looped the long end of the belt around the bedpost, and ran it back through the buckle, fastening her securely.

Panting with exertion, Sirena lay there wild-eyed, anticipating his next move. Still glaring at her, he knocked the glass chimney from her bedside lamp and extinguished the smoky flame with the palm of his hand.

After a moment he came to her, locking her kicking legs between his knees. He fell on her, naked now, ripping and tearing the clothes from her body. She could feel the hard network of muscles beneath his sun-ravished back.

Despite her struggles, his hand grazed her body, his fingers tangled in her hair, his lips sought hers, parting them and seeking out the warm recesses of her mouth. Wearing little else but her silk stockings, her body was covered by his, which pressed her into the soft bedding.

His kisses covered her lips, her cheeks, her eyes, her throat. In spite of herself, Sirena was aware of a building response. This was Regan, the Regan who had taught her about lovemaking aboard the gently rocking frigate. She closed her eyes, she imagined she could smell the thick, pungent, salt tang that rolls in with a sequestering fog.

Like the sea, Sirena felt her resistance ebb to be replaced by a surging tide of passion. Her lips answered his, her body arched against him. Just as she felt herself succumb, drowning in a sea of desire, she heard him whisper against her ear, "Not man enough to make you want me, am I?"

Her answer was to pull his head down and press her warm, passion-bruised lips to his.

Chapter Twenty-five

Sirena felt rather than saw the man at her side stir and move from the bed. His movements were quiet as he dressed. Completely awake and aware of the happenings of the past several hours, she could only wonder if the man who stood so quietly looking down at her was aware of her dual identity.

Locked in the throes of passion, some inner warning had penetrated her mind, warning her to keep the wounded arm out of sight. Drunk on brandy and passion, Regan could well have missed the telltale scar. Pray God he did.

Her heart ached as she watched him walk to the door. In the dim moonlight she saw him stop, turn and gaze toward the bed where she lay. She wanted to scream, to call him back, to have him come to her bed and lay next to her where she could cradle his head to her breasts and kiss his mouth in forgiveness.

She forced her breathing to be steady and moved slightly, as if asleep. The sound of the closing door forced her head into the pillows to choke the tears and sobs that racked her body.

Regan stood outside the door, uncertain of the sound coming from the room. Quietly, he opened the door and flinched when he heard her heartbreaking sobs in the darkness. He forced himself back into the dimly lit corridor. His shoulders slumped dejectedly as he made his way to his room. Inside he poured himself a generous glass of rum and stood staring out the wide windows. He was angry, puzzled, and indignant. Another glass of rum and his blue eyes darkened, taking on a murderous look as he gazed out into the dark shrubbery.

Caleb woke, his hair tousled and damp. Trembling with fear, he crawled from the high bed and walked to the wide windows. Why did he have such murderous dreams? The last, which woke him, had sent fear coursing through his veins. They had been sailing the *Sea Siren* home when Sirena called him to show him her arm. Only it wasn't her arm, it was Regan's growing from her shoulder and it was laid open to the bone. Sirena was asking his help in winding the cultured-pearl prayer beads around the wound to close it. He had gasped in fear because the shimmering pearls were covered with the thick oozing slime that ran from the wound. One of the seamen was shouting from the shrouds that the Dutchman was returning for his arm. Then Caleb had wakened.

Though it was barely dawn, he knew he would

never be able to return to sleep. He would go to the kitchen and take some cheese and walk to the wharf. Perhaps some cheese and fruit, he thought as his stomach grumbled hungrily.

Dressing quickly, he descended the steps quietly and felt his way down the dark corridor. He stopped in midstride as he saw a faint light shine from Regan's office door. Was Regan working or did he also find it impossible to sleep? Perhaps they could talk. He'd offer to get cheese and fruit for Regan. Caleb tiptoed into the room and stopped short. Regan was sprawled in his big chair behind his desk, a rum bottle clutched in his hands.

"What are you doing up at this hour, Caleb?" he asked, his speech slurred as he brought the rum bottle to his lips.

"I couldn't sleep. It's too hot and I had a bad dream. I thought I'd get some cheese and fruit, then go for a walk to the wharf. Can I get you something to eat?" he asked, eyeing the rum bottle.

"It's not food I need, boy. Sit down and talk to me."

"Is something the matter?" Caleb asked hesitantly. "Is something wrong at your offices? I see you've many papers on the desk before you."

"Many papers," Regan answered solemnly, taking another pull from the rum bottle. "Do you see this paper?" He fumbled among the sheaf on his desk.

"Yes, I see it. What is it?"

"It's my copy of the marriage contract with your sister. It's the first time I've looked at it. I never wanted to see it before. I never wanted this marriage." Suddenly Regan laughed as he waved the paper and the rum bottle in the air. "Do you see this? I haven't read it, I can't read it! This damnable curly Spanish writing. You read it to me, boy."

Regan waited for Caleb to begin. He wanted to hear the words that would absolve his guilt for forcing his way into Sirena's room and demanding his rights as her husband.

Worms of fear crawled over Caleb's belly as he heard the demand. He knew the words on the contract as well as his own name.

"Read it to me," Regan said, tossing the paper

across the desk, spilling the rum at the same time. Again he laughed. Nervously, Caleb reached out to pick up the marriage contract and, with a slight hand motion, maneuvered the paper onto the sticky puddle of rum.

"I'm sorry," he muttered, as he picked up the contract and smeared the rum over the written words. "It's difficult to read," he murmured, "with rum soaking the paper."

"You'll manage," Regan said, watching Caleb suspiciously, "read me the words!"

"It . . . says that . . . Sirena Elena Esthera Ramos y Córdez," Caleb whispered, substituting Sirena's name for Isabel's, "oldest daughter of Don Antonio Córdez Savars, is promised this day to Regan Pieter van der Rhys. It says . . . that both elders are in agreement, that joining these two old, revered families is an honor for them both. Then it goes on to define the financial agreements."

"Is that what it says?" Regan laughed drunkenly.

"Yes," Caleb whispered. "Shall I put it away?"

"Don't put it away, throw it away! I'll replace it one day with a divorce paper!"

"Why would you do that?" the boy quivered.

"Why? Because I would, that's why." Rum dribbled down his chin and he wiped it away with an angry gesture. Hearing that Sirena was legally his wife had in no way assuaged the guilt he felt because of the way he had forced himself on her.

"You see before you a broken man. My business has been ruined by that damn devil Siren. I've lost face with my men. I've been bested by a woman, wounded nearly fatally. And . . ." the rum bottle found its way to his mouth again, "and I'm no longer a man of my word. Today was the first time I ever went back on something I gave my word on."

"One little mistake, Regan. Perhaps the problem can be mended. Right now you're not thinking straight. Tomorrow you may feel differently."

"When a man loses his honor, there's nothing left," he hiccuped drunkenly.

The man looked so lost, so humble, Caleb was off the chair and behind the desk in a second's time. He knelt at Regan's knee, his brunette head raised to look into Regan's blurred eyes. "What is it you did, Regan, that you feel cannot be mended?" He wanted to comfort this strange man with the sad eyes. What could he do? What could he say?

"To speak of the matter only makes me . . . fetch me a bottle of rum. I don't wish to speak of my dishonor."

Caleb uncorked the bottle and handed it to Regan. Regan tilted the bottle and drank greedily.

"Perhaps if you speak of the matter it won't be so bad," the boy said softly.

The Dutchman looked down at the boy at his knee and frowned. A large bronzed hand reached out clumsily to touch the dark head. He drew the boy closer to his knee and spoke simply, all signs of drunkenness gone. "Perhaps you would understand, you're almost a man. I gave my word to your sister that our marriage was to be in name only. Tonight I violated her like a madman. I used her. I was an animal. I'm torn two ways. At first, I had thoughts of only the Sea Siren. She was in my blood, she still is and will remain so forever. She will always be a part of me. And then there is your sister, my wife. As each day goes by, I see in her things that please me. She crawled into my blood when I least suspected it. One woman pulls me one way and the other pulls another."

"But the Sea Siren tried to kill you! How can you love her?" Caleb tried to distract him from his comparison.

"She could have killed me, but she didn't. I think now I understand what drives her. She carries a vengeance in her as I did. I know now I can never bring my wife back from the dead. The ship which was named after her lies at the bottom of the seas. And my son . . . I don't know if he's alive or dead.

"If he's alive, I can only hope someone cares for him and gives him a good life. I no longer carry vengeance in my heart. It is over and done. The Sea Siren taught me this. I see what vengeance has done to her, what it did to me. One day she'll find her quarry and then she'll be at peace. Till then, she'll never give up. I respect this in her."

"If you could capture her, what would you do?" Caleb asked hesitantly.

"I don't know. Perhaps I'd kill her so I could rest without her on my mind every second of the day. She can never be mine. She's as free as the wind and the seas. I doubt there's a man alive who could tame her and call her his own."

"I think you're such a man, Regan. I think you could capture her and make her love you."

"One cannot make someone love them. On the other side of the coin is your sister. She crept into my blood and she is possessing me like the Sea Siren does." The bronze hand idly stroked Caleb's dark head as he spoke. Caleb was still, the sensation so pleasing he never wanted to move. It was almost like having a father. "What will you do now?"

"Now I'm going to sleep. And you, my boy, get some food in your stomach and go for that walk to the wharf. But before you go, I have a present for you. Open the drawer of the desk. It's yours."

Caleb reached into the drawer and withdrew the small model of the *Tita.*

"Regan, you mean to give me this?" the boy asked, his eyes lighting with happiness. "But I can't accept it. It's all you have left of the *Tita,* your wife and son."

"That's why I'm giving it to you. There's no need for me to stare at it every day and torture myself. Didn't you hear me when I said the Sea Siren taught me something? There's no room in this world for vengeance. It's over. The *Tita* is yours. What do you think of the carving on her bow?"

Carefully, the boy turned the ship around in his hands. His eyes widened at the carving. "She's beautiful. Was this your wife? Did the same man who carved the *Java Queen* do this?'

"The same man. Tita was the most beautiful girl on the island when I married her. It's an exact likeness."

"She . . . she looks like someone . . ." Caleb shook his head, unable to place the likeness in his mind. "I'll treasure it. Thank you, Regan."

"There's no need for thanks. I wanted you to have it. Perhaps it will give you pleasure. It gave me only pain and vengeance. Go now and see to your stomach. I can hear it howling from here."

Regan leaned back in his deep chair and rubbed his temples. His brain felt as if it were on fire. He needed sleep. With one sweep, he gathered all the papers, including the marriage contract with its wide stain of rum on it, and slipped them haphazardly into the box. Why look at them again? The boy had read the words. Why continue to torture himself?

Chapter Twenty-six

Chaezar leaned back and crossed one elegantly clad leg over the other, his cigar held loosely between long, slender, graceful fingers. His dark eyes were warm and soft as he gazed at the woman seated across from him.

"Your beauty leaves me almost gasping for breath," he said suavely as he stroked his pointed beard. Sirena watched, fascinated at the soft sure strokes he gave to his luxuriant beard, much the way a man would caress a woman. Sirena leaned back languidly and said, "I'm pleased, Chaezar that you find me beautiful. But then we Spanish have always had an eye for beauty." Why was she so relaxed? Was it the wine? She felt so . . . so delicious. Chaezar smiled sensuously, his dark eyes lighting.

Sirena basked in the warm tones of her native tongue. An attractive man, a glass of excellent wine, and . . . She was jarred from her wicked thoughts as Chaezar spoke:

"I've desired you from the first moment I saw you. You're the most beautiful woman I've ever seen. Let's not fence, beautiful lady. I want you for myself. Divorce Regan! I'll whisk you away to a place where we'll live a life of luxury and ease. I'll treasure you as one does a rare work of art."

Sirena was shaken. What was she to say? She wouldn't fence. "Chaezar," she said lightly, "you covet another's wife." She smiled and sipped at the wine she held in her hand. It was an effort to keep her eyes open. Shaking her head to clear it, she said softly, "I find you most . . . gallant. When we speak our native tongue, I warm to you. I appreciate the way you have befriended me. However, I don't think that Regan will be too quick to give me a divorce." She held up a hand to ward off Chaezar's outburst. "He takes his pleasures where he finds them. I know this. But, he will never agree to a divorce. Yes," she said teasingly, "I am not above a little dalliance on the side. When I am ready," she added hastily as she noticed his eyes grow hot and wanton.

"I wouldn't want to rush you into any decision you were unable to carry out." His voice was soft and sensuous as he rose to his feet and looked down at Sirena. Her heart whipped in her chest for a moment as she gazed into his smoldering, dark eyes. She blinked again as Chaezar helped her to her feet. She swayed, held his arm for support. What was wrong with her? Why did she feel so . . . so delicious and abandoned? She smiled to herself. Why was Regan looking at her like that? No . . . not Regan, it was Chaezar who was looking at her with passion in his eyes. Why was she so confused? She licked dry lips as she tried to focus her eyes. Her vision seemed blurred and a strange feeling was engulfing her. Suddenly she wanted to rip the clothes from her body and stand naked before Regan. Would he like her body? Regan didn't have dark eyes and olive skin. She shook her head to clear it. Regan had blond hair and blue eyes. What was Regan saying? Whatever it was, he was speaking Spanish fluently. He must have learned Spanish secretly to please her. Regan would never do anything to please her, what was wrong with her? She felt herself being half led, half carried down a dim corridor. Soft murmurings as she felt a warm breath on her neck. She had to get these clothes off. The compulsion was so strong she tried to quicken her step. She felt herself picked up bodily and carried through a doorway. She tried to focus her eyes but she could only see vague shadows in the semi-darkened room. How was Regan to see her body if the curtains were drawn? She smiled. What did it matter as long as he could feel?

She felt her clothing being removed. Her own hands fumbled with the small hooks as she tried to remove her gown. Within moments she was standing naked and erect, her arms outstretched to welcome the man opposite her. Gently, he lowered her to the bed and immediately was atop her. She cried out as soft hands caressed her body slowly at first and then more urgently. The urgent caresses were unleashing some wild, clamorous passion so far held in abeyance. Her glistening, demanding body writhed on the bed . . .

Sirena woke to bright light streaming through the wide windows. She stretched luxuriously as she let her eyes rove the room. Where was she? Startled, she sat up in bed, the thin cover falling from her. She looked down at her nudity and again let her eyes circle the room. Memory flooded her as she pulled the cover to her chin. "Mother of God!" she cried out in anguish. Hiding her face in the mound of pillows, she let her thoughts race. Did she . . . ? Weakly, she brought her hand to her mouth. Yes, she remembered everything now. Regan—no, not Regan, the Spaniard . . . How could he . . . ? How could she have . . . ? The wine . . . after she drank the wine she started to feel . . . there must have been something in the wine . . .

Tears formed in her green eyes as she recalled how she had fumbled with her gown. Merciful God, how could you let this happen to me? she cried silently. Slowly, she threw off the thin covering and looked at the nakedness that betrayed her. Gradually, the green eyes darkened till they resembled chips of jet. Lust! She spat the word. Men were the animals of the earth, not the four-legged beasts which roamed at will. Chilling anger at her circumstances washed over her as she rose and dressed. What would the servants think? What would Frau Holtz say when she returned? How long had she been here? Where was that bastard Spaniard? How would he look upon her now? Did he leave to save her the humiliation when she woke?

Sirena shuddered as she remembered the feel of his hands on her body. She had to leave this house! She had to get home! Home! Where and what was home?

In her daze, rushing to leave the house, Sirena took a wrong turn and found herself in a large, sunlit room lined with shelves and decorative display cases. The sunlight streamed through the iron-meshed windows, glancing off the various objects carefully arranged atop the shelves. Chaezar's treasures. The display was so ostentatious that despite her hurry, Sirena stopped a moment. Knowing Chaezar's liking for the accouterments of wealth, she wasn't really surprised to see rows of precious crystal goblets, intricately carved figures of jade from China, wrought-gold serviceware from India, tiles set with semi-precious stones from Northern Africa. In the back of her mind she thought that Chaezar would be very upset when he discovered he left the heavy ebony door unlocked.

Just as she was about to leave, the light dazzled off an object on a lower shelf, catching her eye. Stunned, gasping with shock, she walked slowly toward it, her mind denying it was what she thought. Slowly, almost hypnotized, Sirena stepped across the room. It couldn't be! Disbelievingly, she took it in her hands and turned it upside down. It was! Isabel's confirmation crucifix. There were her initials engraved under the base—I.T.C., for Isabel Theresa Córdez.

Sirena's mind raced in circles. When she reached the obvious conclusion, she was staggered. Nevertheless, she knew her assumption to be correct. Regan *had* received the cultured pearl prayer beads in a wager. A wager with Chaezar! Chaezar, not Regan was Isabel's murderer!

Regan was innocent and she had come so close to destroying him! Killing him! All the while it was Chaezar's cutthroats acting under Chaezar's orders.

That's why Regan was so puzzled when she ran Dick Blackheart through! Regan had absolutely no knowledge of Blackheart captaining the ship that assaulted the *Rana*.

Thank God she had been spared killing Regan. Now she would never have to put herself to the test. Could she have actually done it? Could she have pierced that beloved flesh and watched his life ebb before her eyes? No! her mind screamed out in agony, she knew now she never could have done it. Regan's death would have been her own. The realization was stunning and yet she knew it was a fact. She loved him! Hopelessly, desperately! She loved him.

It all fit. Chaezar would naturally have dismissed Blackheart for losing the *Rana*. A little paint and new sails and Chaezar would have had another ship to add to his fleet. Perhaps that was what happened to Regan's *Tita*. Chaezar was behind that, too! Refurbishing the *Tita* and renaming her *Wanderer*, Chaezar was richer by another valuable ship. Only he hadn't known about Regan's son's initials carved on the quarterdeck. If Regan suspected as she did, it was small wonder he hated Chaezar so.

Sirena glanced once more at the heavy gold and mother-of-pearl crucifix. She would have liked to take it with her. It disgusted her to think of it resting on Chaezar's shelves like a trophy. But she replaced it on the shelf. Under no circumstances could she take the chance of arousing Chaezar's suspicions. First she must decide how to gain revenge against the despicable Spaniard.

Boldly, she opened the door of the house and came face to face with Frau Holtz. The old housekeeper did not fail to notice her glittering green eyes or the triumphant set of her firm chin. She almost looked like a satisfied . . . The Mevrouw had been gone over four hours. Luncheons rarely lasted more than a socially respectable two.

Sirena noticed the suspicious look immediately and spoke coolly: "It was such a lovely day I decided to take a drive to the wharf and see the Mynheer's new ship. Was there something you wished to say, Frau

Holtz? No, then I suggest you continue with your duties."

A glib story. She would wager her last gulden that the Mevrouw had been nowhere near the wharf today or any other day for that matter. What kind of religion did she embrace that she would pray with the beads, then go to the Spaniard's house unchaperoned and stay for four hours? Next she would say she was going to have a retreat in her room. What did she pray for? Surely not divine guidance. What would the Mynheer say when he was informed of this affair? A smile played around the corners of her dour face as she envisioned the master's anger.

Angrily, Sirena ripped off her gown and flung it in the corner. She would have to find a way to dispose of the offensive-looking garment. A feeling akin to hatred raced through her blood as she recalled the look on the housekeeper's face. She had looked as if she could read her mind and see into her soul. How could she have let the Spaniard do what he did? That she wasn't a willing partner—indeed, a drugged partner—didn't enter into it. Would he hold the events of the afternoon over her head in some way to get to Regan? Now she knew what Chaezar wanted, to ruin Regan! What a fool she had been! The green eyes were cold with hatred and vengeance as she looked out the large windows into the lush tropical garden. Chaezar would pay, countryman or not! She realized the enormity of her plan. How would she learn of the Spaniard's activities? She would send Caleb to the wharves to watch and listen. There would be a way, she would see to it!

What was happening to her? First Regan comes to her room and then Chaezar drugs and rapes her. Then she discovers Chaezar was responsible for Tio Juan's and Isabel's deaths! God in Heaven, was this what I was put on earth for, to be a receptacle for men's lust?

The desire to kill the Spaniard was so great she had to force her hands to remain still. She could picture her hands around his neck, choking the life from his body. When he gasped and turned blue, she would ease up the pressure, let him gulp for air, then exert more pressure. She would continue this until his lungs burst from the effort. Tears burned her eyes at the injustice of it all. Flinging herself on the bed, she cried great heartbreaking sobs.

"Where has Regan been all this time?" she asked a worried-looking Caleb.

"He's gone to the inner islands for some business matters. He'll be gone ten days."

"Ten days! And you didn't tell me! Why?"

"He just left this morning. Please don't, Sirena, please! Leave him. You've ruined him. No more."

Sirena stood quietly and looked at the boy. "I understand how you feel. I also feel the time has come when you don't tell me everything Regan says to you. It's all right, I told you I understand. This time it's the Spaniard's turn. With Regan on land we shall take on the Spanish fleet. Chaezar set sail two days ago with an escort of three. This time, since I have no definite plan of return, we'll say we are going to visit a friend of my father's on one of the islands. There is no one to dispute either of us. Take the message to Frau Holtz and if she questions our return, simply tell her we will return when we have become bored, no more no less. We'll leave the carriage at the wharf for safe keeping and from there we'll ride to the *Sea Siren*. We'll leave under cover of darkness. I promise you, I shall not attack any Dutch ships."

One day was much the same as the next. The *Sea Siren* would lay in wait in a cove or inlet and, at the passing of a ship, would sail out of her hiding place. If the ship were Spanish, in the blink of an eye it would be attacked and her crew scattered on the seas. The *Sea Siren* would then retire to her haven and await the next passing ship.

On the evening of the eighteenth day, Sirena gave the order to tighten sail and head for the straits. They were going home.

"Sixteen of the Spanish fleet at the bottom of the sea. Not bad, little brother, we averaged almost one a day."

"But you still haven't found the man with the hook."

"I will. It's just a matter of time."

"Ten knots and we arrive at the mouth of the river," Jan called.

"Sail ho!"

Sirena swiveled and saw the sail, a bright speck in the noonday sun. "Sight her flag!"

"Dutch," came the reply.

"Rest easy, little brother, I gave my word that I'd leave Regan be. It's the Spaniard who's responsible for the events aboard the *Rana* and Isabel's death. Straight ahead, tighten sail," she called her orders.

"What if she fires into us?" Caleb asked anxiously.

"A promise is a promise, yet what would you have me do?"

"Run!" he answered.

"I run from no ship. I said I wouldn't attack the Dutch ships and I'll keep my word. You haven't answered me. If she fires into us, what will you have me do? Think carefully, little brother, it's our lives you answer for."

Caleb nodded. "We fight but only if she attacks us."

"She had us in her sights, Capitana," Jan shouted. "I see her cannon on the port." The air split with the sound of cannon. One, two, then three in quick succession tore the decks of the frigate.

"Fire!" Sirena gave the order.

It was of no use, the frigate had lost her maneuverability and limped along in a frantic effort to elude the Dutch brig. But it was not to be. The brig sailed true and berthed alongside the frigate, evidence of the *Sea Siren*'s attack smoking her decks.

"So, we meet again," the blue eyes were no longer mocking, but sad.

Sirena looked into his eyes and wished she could brush away the pain she saw there. She felt helpless in the face of his pain. Her love for him had disarmed her to a greater degree than if she had been stripped of her weapons, the ship, and her crew. Her love held her prisoner. Not by word, gesture, or glance could she reveal her feelings. She must play out this farce, her role as the Sea Siren, one last time.

More wounding than a scabbard's edge would be Regan's mocking laugh if he should suspect her tumultuous emotions.

"You seem to have lost your appetite for fighting, Captain van der Rhys. I, too, have had enough of this bloodshed. I was homeward bound. I wouldn't have attacked your ship. You're wounded as am I. Your ship is in no better shape than mine. Both will sink within hours if they're not shored up. What's it to be? I can sail on with my men or I can fight till one of us dies. The decision is yours."

"There's nothing to fight for, Sea Siren, I went in search of the man with the hook. I found him on one of the inner islands. He's aboard my brig. I'm taking him to Batavia to be judged and sentenced."

"You have the man?" Sirena asked, shock making her green eyes murky as the water beneath her, all thoughts of Regan and love erased by her desire for revenge.

"He's my prisoner."

"He belongs to me, hand him over! This time I won't play the weak-kneed woman."

"Neither of us is fit to judge this man. Let others do it."

"I'm his judge and I'll sentence him! Don't let all this have been for nothing. I can't give up now. Hand him over to me. I promise you if you do that, this is the last you'll see of me."

Regan frowned. "Tell me why you want this man and then I'll decide."

"I'll tell you nothing. We hold the advantage," she said brazenly, knowing she lied. "It's a personal matter of mine and mine alone. Turn him over to me and I'll allow you and your crew to go unharmed. If you don't," she shouted clearly, "I'll run you through. Make fast work of your answer, for I have no patience this day."

Regan stood on his collapsing stern mere feet from Sirena on her bow. Perhaps if he gave her what she wanted he could get her to let her guard down and then attack her and bring both the Sea Siren and The Hook to Batavia.

"Well!" Sirena shouted.

Regan nodded. He called an order and the man with the hook was standing next to him.

"Give him a cutlass and swing him aboard," Sirena shouted, her eyes glittering in anticipation of securing her quarry.

"No, Captain; no, Captain. Quarter! Quarter!" The Hook shouted.

Sirena laughed. "Why is the coward yelling for mercy? I have not made my objective known." She laughed, the tinkling musical sound carrying over the water and bouncing back with an eerie shriek. She leaned nonchalantly into the rigging, her cutlass held loosely in her hand. Fearfully, the man with the hook tried to edge away from Regan, only to find himself with a hold on the rigging and swinging toward the bow of the *Sea Siren.*

"Don't move!" Sirena ordered sharply, her cutlass pointed at his midriff. "Captain van der Rhys, I think it would be best if you lowered your jolly and had your men descend the ladder before I forget my generous offer. You're to follow them directly. If you don't," she shouted, "I'll keep my promise and run you through. You could salvage your ship if she was shored within the hour; if not, she sinks. I prefer that she sinks. Look lively now. Till we meet again!" Sirena raised her cutlass in a salute and gave him a mocking bow. Regan stood as if carved from stone. She was as tricky as a fox and wily as a minx. Briskly, he gave the order to leave the ship.

Sirena turned and jumped from the tackle box with the stealth and speed of a panther. Her eyes glittered as she swung the cutlass in wide swaths in the air. The breeze ruffled the greasy lanks of hair on the man's head. His eyes held fear as he brought his own cutlass up to ward off a blow.

Sirena lashed to the right and to the left, giving no quarter. The man fought valiantly but he was no match for the hate-filled woman who swung her blade with an expertise Regan had yet to see matched anywhere. Sirena darted to the left and slashed downwards with the cutlass, ripping the man's boot to the toe. She brought up her hand and the cutlass sliced at the man's ear. When it dropped to the deck, Sirena lowered her cutlass and pierced the flesh and taunted the man.

"You bleed like a pig!" she shouted. "Already your head is covered with blood. The sight sickens me. Let us get this over with. I'm tired of this play!" With a lightning movement she jabbed to the right and the sound of steel against steel rang in the bright sun. Quickly, she withdrew and brought her arm up with all the might she could muster, knocking the cutlass from the man's hand. Sirena drove the point of the cutlass through the man's shirt sleeve and pinned him to the wall.

The man's eyes were filled with fear as he gazed into the glittering eyes of the woman before him. He looked from one man to the next. He would get no help from them.

"Why do you want to kill me?" he whined. "What did I do? I do my job and take my pay."

"And a few other things along the way," Sirena said softly. "I want to hear you say the name of the man who employed you when you sailed with that pig Blackheart and attacked the Spanish frigate *Rana*, killing her crew and raping the women. Finally you murdered one of the women with your hook. You slit her from her throat to her gullet. Remember? Now! The name of the man!"

"Chaezar, Señor Chaezar Alvarez!"

"I already knew. I wanted to hear it from you!"

"What do you want from me?" The Hook whined.

"I want you to pray."

"Wha—what?"

"Pray! I want to see you pray!"

"I—don't—know how—"

"Then you had better learn quickly. I won't tell you again. Now pray!" Sirena flicked the cutlass, making small knicks on the man's arm as he attempted to do her bidding.

"Holy God—"

"Go on!"

"Holy God—"

"You said that before, now pray!" She jabbed the cutlass, drawing blood from the man's arm.

"Holy God, help me—"

"Your God doesn't seem to hear you. Louder, much louder."

"Merciful God, help me—"

"Louder! He still doesn't hear you! You appear to have a problem. Where is this God you pray to? One would think he would answer so heartfelt a plea. Try again, this time on your knees! Loudly and clearly. I want every man aboard this ship to hear your prayers!" Again she knicked the man's arm and, to his horror, more blood spurted. "I want them to hear your prayers just as they heard my sister's when you raped and killed her!" Fear at her words was like a live thing in the man's eyes.

"You're not praying. Loud and clear!"

"Merciful God," the man whined, "help me, don't let this crazy woman kill me! Help me!"

"For some strange reason this God of yours isn't paying any attention," Sirena said softly. "Why is that, do you think?"

"Don't kill me!" the man whined.

"I'll be your God!" Sirena shouted. "Pray to me!" She reached into the pocket of her blouse and withdrew the pearl rosary. With one movement she had it looped around the man's neck.

"I'm waiting!"

"God help me," the man pleaded.

"Yes," Sirena said conversationally, "I'll help you, just the way you helped my sister. I'm going to listen the way you listened to her."

Sirena gave the cutlass a vicious swing and brought the end of it down on the man's shoulder. The loud crack of the splintered bone was fierce on the quiet deck. "Pray!" she demanded coldly.

"Mother of God . . ." *Crack!* and the cutlass sliced the air.

The man's face convulsed in pain as Sirena brought up the cutlass a third time. "Kill me!" the man groaned. "I can't stand the pain." Sirena stood and looked at the man.

"Throw him overboard. Let his compatriots see to him."

The man's screams would ring in Sirena's ears for a long time as her men grasped him under the armpits to heave him over the side. Suddenly there was bedlam and—Regan and his men on the deck of her ship.

"You made one mistake too many, my lovely Sea Siren," Regan said mockingly. "You were so set on your vengeance you thought we would do your bidding, and accept your generous offer of our freedom after you sacked our ship. The tables are turned now!"

Coldly, in a ringing voice, he issued orders and the frigate's men were secured in the hold. She was defenseless.

"Swing aboard ship, shore her, and secure her tight as a drum. You have less than an hour—heave to, lads. Now," Regan said briskly, "we'll go to your quarters and see what this is all about."

"Take your hands off me or I'll kill you!" Sirena spat, her green eyes shooting sparks of flame.

"With what? I have your cutlass," he laughed, swinging it in the air.

Sirena followed Regan to her quarters. She defiantly stared into his eyes. "Are we to play your game of lust again? Will you make love to me here in this room or will you do it on the decks, like the animal you are, for all to see? You'll have to rape me, for you'll never take me of my own free will. I'm finished. There's no feeling left in me. I found that which I sought. I completed my mission and the end is here. Monies will be paid to your bank account for all the damages you suffered at my hands. Get on with whatever it is you have to do."

Casually, Regan tossed her a rapier. Instinctively, she reached up to grasp the hilt. She eyed the long, slender weapon and laid it down next to her. "I told you I was finished. I'll fight no more."

"The tables are turned now. I have the upper hand and now you have lost the desire to duel." Regan laughed, the sound harsh and guttural in the still cabin.

"Think what you will, I'm finished. At this moment I don't care if you rape me or kill me."

Regan frowned. She meant it. The mocking green

eyes he remembered were now dull and flat and . . . lifeless.

"What if I take you back to Batavia?"

"Then do it, don't just stand there making idle threats. I told you that I was finished, how many times do I have to repeat myself? You Dutch are a stupid lot!" Sirena leaned back on the hard bunk, her long tawny legs extending in front of her. Nonchalantly, she toyed with the handle of the rapier at her side. Regan stood mesmerized at the sight of her long, creamy legs. His eyes traveled to her thighs and stopped, the rapier almost dangling from his hand. When he raised his eyes to look into hers, her hand grasped the hilt of the rapier and, with one fluid motion, she knocked his weapon from his hand. The tip of the silver blade rested directly below his navel. "It would be advisable if you didn't so much as breathe, Captain van der Rhys, for if you do this weapon will travel downwards at an alarming rate of speed. I'll castrate you without a second thought. Now back off slowly if you desire to have your manhood remain intact. Breathe softly, Dutchman, for I have no patience left. To the ladder now and shout your orders to board your ship. If you hurry you may save her."

"All hands board the brig," he shouted loudly. Silence greeted his order and a burly head appeared at the top of the ladder.

"Aye, Captain," he said as he jumped with the aid of the rigging to board the brig. The other seamen followed him and then Regan departed.

Sirena stood on the bow, her green eyes laughing merrily. "Good-bye Dutchman! Remember what I said about the monies finding their way to your bank account. A notice will be posted at Batavia announcing my retirement! My apologies," she said, bowing low.

"Tell me something before you leave. Would you have . . . ?"

"Castrated you? You'll never know, will you?" she replied, laughter bubbling over in the sea-green eyes. "You're free, Dutchman, as free as I am. Perhaps now we can pick up and try to live what passes for a normal life." Each gave the other a mocking salute with the tip of their rapiers as the two ships sailed away. Tears formed in the emerald eyes for the things that might have been.

The Sea Siren was dead.

Chapter Twenty-seven

Regan sat in his office, his face a veritable thunder cloud as he looked at the empty space where the model of the *Tita* had rested. Would he ever be the same again? The Sea Siren had found that which she sought and she had conquered it. Was it a mistake to hand over The Hook to the woman? He thought not. If nothing else, he gave her peace. He would never forget that glorious, long-legged creature. Never as long as he lived.

He had other matters to occupy his mind now. His son. He now knew that his son lived somewhere. His journey to the inner islands had been fruitful. If he had to, he would move heaven and earth to find him. When he had been bearing down on The Hook, the scurve had babbled like an old woman, and revealed the fate of his son on that horrible day aboard the *Tita* so many years before. He should have known, if not at least suspected the wily Gretchen and that bastard Chaezar. He would kill them both with his bare hands!

He knew he had to think carefully before he made a move. He would attack the Spaniard on his home ground and kill him! And Gretchen, that bitch! He'd draw and quarter her and hang her on the wharf to rot in the sun! His thoughts were interrupted by a sharp rap on the door and the entrance of a tall, blond man.

"Captain Dykstra, how go the repairs on the *Whispering Wind?*"

"The galleon will be ready next week. What's this scuttlebutt I hear?" the man asked.

"What was it you heard?" Regan asked.

"Scuttlebutt has it you found The Hook and turned him over to the Sea Siren."

"What you heard is true. She gave her word she retires from the sea."

"And you believed her?" Dykstra asked, amazement lifting his voice.

"Yes, I believe her."

"They say her treatment of The Hook was brutal!"

"Yes, it was. But she didn't kill him, she threw him overboard and my crew picked him up. He'll do no more harm, so battered is he. You must remember something, Dykstra, men have been fighting wars and destroying their enemies since the beginning of time. And men have, through the ages, arrived at a formal code, a set of ethics and honorable conduct. Not so women. War is new to her, power to destroy her enemies untried. When a woman meets her enemy she has no code of ethics. She's unhampered by a sense of honor. She has a much keener sense of kill-or-be-killed than we men. A woman faces her enemy and destroys him.

Seeing Regan's serious, reflective mood, Captain Dykstra changed the subject. "Chaezar Alvarez left the island. There's a great deal of speculation as to where he's gone, but nothing definite. The only thing certain is that he'll be gone at least two months."

Regan glared at Captain Dykstra and the man groped for another subject. "Frau Lindenreich," Dykstra said more confidently, "has accompanied her latest lover on a buying trip to India. The man's a merchant and has promised to supply her with the richest silks in the East to refurbish that endless wardrobe of hers."

Regan's scowl deepened, his mood became blacker. "Chaezar will be gone for two months, you say? Why, do you think?"

"Personally, I believe Señor Alvarez is to meet

his superiors in Cape Town to give an accounting of his losses. He'll have a lot of explaining to do."

Regan, Dykstra in his wake, strode through beaded curtains and into the anteroom of the most exclusive brothel in Batavia. "Clarice!" he shouted drunkenly, "where the hell are you? As madam of this whorehouse, get your ass in here! I've brought you a new customer and don't send me any of your disease-ridden hags. Nothing but the best for my friend," he said, reeling into the beads. Frustrated, he grabbed a handful of the colorful beads and ripped them from their hangings. Hundreds of beads scattered and rolled across the floor. He laughed at his destruction and, wobbling on unsteady legs, he muttered to Dykstra, "I always hated those damn things. They remind me of prayer beads."

Clarice ran into the room. Regan van der Rhys had taken the place apart more than once. "Stop calling my brothel a whorehouse! What you do here is your own business, but I thought you gentleman enough to keep it to yourself. This is an establishment. Your money alone has made me fat and rich." She kicked angrily at the beads with her plump, slippered foot. "In the future, treat my furnishings as if they were your own. I'm tired of redecorating after your visits."

Regan laughed uproariously at her little joke. "Dykstra, old friend," he said, clapping the nervous captain on the back in an expansive mood, "I've kept this 'establishment' operating. I'm their most valued customer. Don't believe anything Clarice tells you. All she does is bank what I spend here. She's probably worth more than the two of us together."

A smirk on her plump, jaded features, Clarice was busy pouring rum into ruby crystal goblets. Regan could burn the place down, for all she cared. He'd always make good and then some, in retribution. "Luanna isn't here right now." Clarice smiled slyly. "I have two new girls, both of them are virgins, perhaps they could profit from your vast experience." She hoped she had sparked Regan's interest. It was time Luanna, Regan's favorite whore, was set back a few steps. She was getting caught up in her own importance lately. Regan's preferring someone else could shake some sense into her.

"Two virgins," Regan hiccuped drunkenly, "I'll take them both!" Seeing a flame of interest in Dykstra's eyes, Regan said magnanimously, "On second thought, Clarice, give them to Dykstra. I'll pay!" he said, downing the glass of rum. "What have you got left?"

"Nothing," Clarice answered flatly, "the other girls are otherwise engaged."

"Well, disengage them," Regan boasted, "all of them!"

Worried for her trade, Clarice soothed the impetuous Regan. "Regan, why destroy your image? In your condition you wouldn't be much use to one girl, much less seven. Let me get you a room for a few hours. Sleep and then I'll send in everybody and anybody you want."

Regan looked at her with drunken suspicion. "I'll wait for Luanna."

Clarice led the two "virgins" into the room. They were beauties, there was no doubt about it. They were small, and delicately boned, almost childlike. Slim narrow hips extended into lean, lightly muscled thighs. Nubile, budding, coral-tipped breasts peaked out from gauzy shifts. They were a smooth skinned ochre-color. Their eyes had an Oriental slant. Clarice introduced them to Captain Dykstra, ignoring Regan. Eagerly, they began to paw and pet the perspiring Dykstra.

The girls led him up the stairs to the second floor. Regan, standing at the bottom of the steps, appraised their gracefully swinging hips and saw one of the girls reach back to caress Dykstra's haunches. "Virgins, my ass!" he mumbled accusingly to Clarice.

The madam shrugged and gave Regan a conspiratorial wink. "He'll never know the difference."

Regan wiped the smile off Clarice's face by issuing an edict: "I'm only paying for one! Now get me that room, I'll sleep off this drunk and then I'll take care of your girls, all of them!"

Luanna was tiny, a porcelain doll. Jet hair flowed to her waist. Her small, naked breasts were firm and high. Her body was hairless in the Javanese tradition.

"Regan," she cooed softly, "Madame Clarice told me you were here." She smiled beguilingly, her small, white, sharp-pointed teeth nibbling at her full, lower lip. "Have you been waiting long?" Regan grunted, neither an admission or a denial. Because of the rum he had consumed he didn't know how long he had been there. Only his aching head told him it had not been long enough.

Luanna slid into the bed next to him, wiggling her hips seductively as she slid into his embrace. She put her mouth against his and nibbled his lips, searching his mouth with her tongue. Regan lay still, accepting her caresses, willing himself to concentrate on her charms.

What was wrong with him? Luanna had always excited him, heated his blood to boiling, he could never get enough of her. Now her charms were ineffectual, her body was too thin, too small, her breasts too hard and lacking voluptuousness. Her musk scent was unpleasant to him. His mind kept searching for fuller, softer breasts, lean, long haunches, the scent of spindrift. The Siren! That's who he longed for, the damnable Sea Siren who was his nemesis.

Luanna's hands caressed him searchingly, sliding over his body in a hot embrace. Realizing her failure to arouse him, her lips became hungrier and she pressed her body still closer.

Suddenly, abruptly, she sat up in bed, her eyes accusing and murderous. "So, you didn't wait for your Luanna after all," she hissed. "How dare you come to me spent and exhausted from the embrace of another?" She was enraged, seething with jealousy. She eyed him calculatingly, her lips curled back over her pointed little teeth, which now seemed carnivorous and deadly. She would rather have him dead than have him solicit another whore. To be rejected by Regan for another one of Clarice's girls would mean the toppling of her position in the ranks. A position she guiltily knew she had abused. As Regan's favorite she had enjoyed being pampered by Clarice and looked at with envy by the other girls. Rather than pay homage to her successor, she would kill him first!

A slight snore filled the small, otherwise silent room. In a frenzy, Luanna was off the bed and reaching for the stiletto she kept hidden in a dresser drawer. She pounced on the bed, the knife poised. Her movements jarred Regan awake. He leaned over and grasped her arm, knocking the stiletto to the floor.

Chaezar's words rang in his ears: "You have to be careful, Regan, these Javanese whores are well versed in the art of murder." Regan shuddered at how close he had come to fulfilling Chaezar's prophecy. Luanna was up and reaching for him with sharp, talon-like fingers. He threw her against the wall, grabbed his clothes from the chair near the door and made a hasty exit.

As he raced down the stairs, naked, his clothes in his arms, he bellowed, "Dykstra, you son of a bitch! It's time to get out of here! No virgin's worth your life!"

His near-white thatch of hair practically standing on end, his face flushed, he was completely sober now. He passed in front of Clarice, who was laughing uproariously.

"I see you're in a hurry, Regan," she shouted as he leaped through the door. "We'll settle up the bill another time!"

Sirena passed her days in distracted idleness. Chaezar's sudden departure had left her feeling frustrated and empty. Time dragged and would continue to drag until he returned and she could plot her revenge.

Occasionally she dined with Regan, but neither of them had much to say. That night in her room stood between them and made communication impossible.

One afternoon Caleb came to her room. "What is it, Sirena? What's wrong?" he asked. In the six weeks that had passed since she had found The Hook she had become irritable and demanding. Restlessness created a hollow look about her eyes.

"I think I'm going mad," she answered. "Are you happy, Caleb?"

"Happy enough," Caleb confessed. "Regan keeps me busy. He's taking me on a cruise to the inner islands. He says he wants someone to meet me. Why is that, do you suppose?"

"When did he first mention this to you?"

"It was just after you dealt with The Hook. Remember, Regan was returning with him from the inner islands? He called me into his office and told me. His eyes were so sad, I know he grieves for his son. When I was there he told me he knows his son is alive and he's determined to find him. Regan's eyes are haunted and he drinks more than what's good for him. You must have noticed the change in him, Sirena."

"I rarely see him, how could I notice a change in him?" she replied bitterly.

"Regan asked me if I remembered who the carving on the *Tita* reminded me of."

"And did you?" Sirena asked vaguely.

"No, and it bothers me. It seeems so familiar. Let me get it and show it to you. Perhaps you will notice something."

Caleb was back in minutes, the small model held securely in his sun-browned hands.

"It's beautiful," Sirena said, taking the model from his hands. "Whoever did the carving is a master craftsman."

"Regan said it's an exact likeness of his wife Tita. Look at the carving around the eyes. You can see separations between her eyelashes. Isn't she beautiful?"

Sirena ran her hands over the small carving and looked into Caleb's eyes. Her own were narrowed as she gazed at the boy. It couldn't be. Yet . . . "Tita was a native princess, I imagine her eyes were inky-black."

"Brown," Caleb corrected. "Regan said they were soft as a dove's, and her hair was like silk, her skin was like spun honey."

"She must have been very beautiful," Sirena said sadly.

"What is it, Sirena? I see such sadness in your eyes."

"It's nothing. I guess I'm just bored."

"Does the carving remind you of someone, as it does me."

"Yes, it does look familiar. I think it's the eyes. What do you think?"

"I agree. That's what I told Regan was familiar to me. He just looked at me and smiled."

"I'll think about it and if I decide who it is I'll let you know," she said, handing back the model to the boy.

Caleb scampered off happily, his model clutched in both hands.

Sirena sat frowning. It was impossible yet everything would almost point in the direction of . . . Had Regan noticed the resemblance? If he had, her game was up. Suddenly she gripped her stomach as a violent attack of nausea overcame her. God in Heaven, not again. What ailed her? Suddenly her eyes widened and she gasped. Her mind raced as she gripped her stomach and fought back the retches. Wearily, she lay down on the bed, tears streaming down her cheeks. Please, God, no, don't let it happen. Not now, not after all I've been through.

Sobs shook her body as she buried her face into the smoothness of the pillow beneath her head. How would she explain it? Regan would never believe her. Would he kill her? Did she care? Yes, she whispered, I care, for I love him. I love him too much to let him know. I'll have to leave. Soon she wouldn't be able to hide the obvious. Already she had noticed Frau Holtz looking at her with more than her usual suspicion. I have to do something. And Caleb. What of Caleb? What would be best for the boy? Her head whirled and the only consolation she could offer herself was the certainty that this child was Regan's. The signs had appeared long before that afternoon with Chaezar but long after the event's aboard the *Rana*.

"Sirena, I'm going to the inner islands with Regan today. I don't know how long we'll be gone. Will you be all right alone?"

"Of course, why do you ask?"

"You don't look well to me. The circles under your eyes get darker each day. Is there anything I can do?"

"I don't think anyone on Java has been getting much rest! Not with these nightly tirades from the volcano." The Sisters of Fire had been reminding the islanders of their presence more frequently with their ominous tremors and belches of hot cinders. Many natives had escaped from the Dutch plantations, slipping away by night in their dugout proas. Still, the stubborn Europeans refused to acknowledge the threats. They doggedly remained on Java, fearful of losing the fruitful properties they had amassed.

"When do you leave, Caleb?" Sirena asked, anxious to divert his attention away from herself.

"Sometime this afternoon. Regan says he must be here when Señor Alvarez returns. He has a score to settle with him. He blames Chaezar and Frau Lindenreich for his son's disappearance."

"Caleb, if for some reason I'm not here when you return, I want you to stay here with Regan. This is to be your home from now on. Someday you'll understand. I promised you the *Sea Siren* and she'll be yours, when you're of age. I'll see to it that she's sent here for you."

"Where are you going?" the boy asked, fear leaping into his eyes as he clutched her arm.

"I'm not sure. You must trust me and tell no one what I just said to you. I can't stay here any longer. For Regan's sake I must leave. Please believe me when I tell you that I don't want to hurt him anymore."

"Will you take the *Sea Siren?*"

"Yes, I shall take her. Alone."

"Alone!" Caleb gasped.

"Your promise, little brother."

The boy gulped but promised, his body shaking with fear.

"There's something I must tell you. I'm almost positive that what I am about to tell you is true. I couldn't leave and not let you know. I think Regan suspects but isn't sure. Until that time, you have a right to know but you must not let Regan know and you must guard this secret until such time as Regan acknowledges it."

"What secret?"

"Remember the carving on the bow of the *Tita?*" The boy nodded. "You thought it reminded you of someone and so did I." Sirena grasped the boy's shoulders and looked lovingly into his eyes. "Tita was your mother and Regan is your father. I've suspected for a long time but wasn't sure. You say Regan is taking you to the inner islands today. He'll want someone to look upon you and give him details. You must not let on that you know. If you do, he will think it is some sort of trick. He has to acknowledge you himself. Once he realizes that you are not my brother, he will know that I am not what I pretend to be. Now do you see why I must leave? Don't cry, little one, you'll soon gain a doting, loving father. Already I see the love creep from his eyes when he looks upon you. You'll have a full, rich life."

"And you, what will happen to you?" Caleb looked worriedly at the woman who had been his Capitana and his sister.

"I will be fine. You mustn't worry about me. Will you keep the secret?"

Caleb nodded dejectedly. "I'm too big to cry," he blubbered.

"You're never too big to cry," she said, holding him close to her chest. "You have to hurry now, it's almost the noon hour. Don't look back, little brother, go out that door and join your father." You'll always be my little brother, she whispered to herself as the door closed on her gathering tears.

Sirena looked around the small cluttered room and forced herself to walk through the door. She would go downstairs and leave by the front door. Who was there to question her, certainly not Frau Holtz? And if she did, what could she do about it?

Walking around the courtyard, she saddled her horse and mounted it. She sat for a moment, looking at the house. Who was there to miss her? Perhaps the boy, but in time he, too, would forget her. She spurred the horse and narrowly missed colliding with a dark shadow emerging from the driveway.

"Chaezar! What brings you here?" she demanded coldly.

"And what brings you out at night, atop such a fiery steed?"

"I'm bored," she lied. "Regan isn't here. He took the boy to one of the inner islands this afternoon."

"To the inner islands?" Was she wrong or did she detect fear in the man's voice?

"Yes," she answered him simply.

"Is it true he turned the man with the hook over to the Sea Siren?"

"Yes, it's true. Have you just returned, Chaezar?"

"Several hours ago. I came as soon as I heard. Now you say that Regan has gone to the inner islands. That's strange, he rarely goes there."

She knew Chaezar was baiting her for more information. "But you're wrong, Chaezar. He's been going there every week for the past month." Sirena sensed the man's fear at her words and enjoyed it. Nevertheless, this wasn't the time to deal with Chaezar. To take her leave of him, she said, "If you'll excuse me, I'll continue my ride. I'll leave a message for Regan saying you called."

"That won't be necessary. Perhaps you'll allow me to join you on your ride. The evening is much too lovely to be alone."

"Your pretense is admirable; however, I prefer to ride alone. I have many things I wish to think about. I haven't forgotten our last meeting, Chaezar, nor will I forget it in the future."

"Ah, my little dove, what can I say?" He threw his hands up in a helpless gesture. "I'm a man, you're a beautiful woman. I was lost in the moment, and may I say it was a memorable moment?'

Sirena flushed. "You tricked me! The wine was drugged and you were the one who drugged it. You knew I'd never crawl into your bed otherwise!"

"Dear Sirena, you sound like an angry virgin. If I recall correctly, you were quite enamored of me that afternoon and surprisingly experienced, despite the rumors of Regan never having bedded you."

"Pig!" Sirena spat. "You want only to ruin Regan and you thought by seducing me you could break him and achieve your ends. I could understand an honest seduction, but not this contrived affair. I think Regan has something to settle with you."

"What sort of threat is that?"

"It's not a threat. I don't know what he's been doing, but my brother tells me that these trips to the islands have something to do with you. And that's all I know," she said, jerking the reins from his fingers.

Chaezar gripped her wrist, twisted it, and nearly dragged her from atop her horse. Sirena kicked out, struggling to free herself from his surprisingly strong grasp. Pulling backward, Chaezar's grip ripped her sleeve, baring her arm to the moonlight.

Viciously, Sirena lashed out, aiming for his eyes. Shocked, Chaezar stepped back, giving Sirena her chance to escape. Spurring the animal, Sirena's heart hammered in her chest. Even though it was dark, the moon shone quite brightly and his face had been hate-filled. Had he seen the scar? Would he have recognized it as the wound a slicing cutlass leaves? There was no doubt in her mind that if he wanted to he would overtake her and . . . What would he do?

Unknown to either of them, a tall stately figure had watched them from the window. She had been so near she might have reached out and touched them. Frau Holtz's face was set in dour lines. She had suspected for some time the Mevrouw was hiding some terrible secret. She had noted that every time the Mevrouw went into retreat the Sea Siren wreaked her havoc.

Juli said the ailment the Mevrouw claimed to suffer left a film, white and salty like spindrift, on her skin and hair. Then finally, spying from the garden, she had seen the Mevrouw and Caleb climb into the house through the window.

Frau Holtz had secretly championed the Sea Siren and had admired the piratess's triumph. Frau Holtz, along with all the female sex, knew what it was like to be impotent in the face of men's strength.

The main reason Frau Holtz disapproved of the Mevrouw wasn't because of her deeds at sea, but because she believed Regan was being cuckolded. Now, seeing the wild hatred in Sirena's face, the viciousness of her escape from Chaezar, Frau Holtz admitted her mistake. Swiftly, she calculated the days till Regan's return. She must tell him. Frau Holtz knew another secret—Sirena was pregnant with Regan's child.

Chapter Twenty-eight

The cool night air cloaked Sirena as she spurred the beast beneath her. Twice she reined in the gelding when she thought she heard hoofbeats behind her. Satisfied, she continued her journey to the *Sea Siren*.

She dismounted and stood quietly listening for any sound other than the usual night cries of the birds. The frigate lay in her berth like a dark, ghostly phantom. She gave the gelding a hard slap to its rump and prayed he would find his way back home.

Quietly, she crept aboard the dark ship and headed for her cabin. The night lay before her like an oblong grave. She would have to ready the ship under cover of darkness. Her nausea was returning and she felt decidedly weak as she bent to hoist the sail. Her feet were sure on the gently pitching deck and she gave a startled cry as her toe touched something soft and yielding.

"Who goes there?" came a hoarse sleep-filled shout.

"Jacobus! What are you doing here? You startled me."

"I didn't think you would mind if I slept on the deck. It seems the older I get the fancier my notions. I can't sleep on land. I didn't think you'd mind and at the same time I keep my eye on the ship for you."

"No, I don't mind," Sirena said, trying to fight down the nausea that threatened to erupt. "I'm taking the ship back to Spain. If possible I'd like to set sail before midnight."

"You'd sail without a crew? But Capitana, that is not wise! Do you know what the bounty on your head is? It was posted two days ago. You won't stand a chance on the seas alone. It will take but an hour to get the crew together."

"How much is the bounty?"

"An outrageous sum," Jacobus said, grinning.

Sirena raced to the rail and retched till she had to hold her ribs for support.

"And you think you can sail this ship in your condition? Wait here, Capitana. I'll be back in an hour." Sirena nodded weakly. She sat in a pile of rigging, her head between her knees to stop the whirling dizziness. Jacobus was right. What in the name of God had possessed her to think she could make the trip to Spain alone? It would take months and she had given no thought to provisions. Fool, she chided herself.

Tears welled in her emerald eyes as she let her thoughts wander to Regan. Soon he would know everything. What would he do? What could he do? Perhaps he would be satisfied to find his son and forget about her. Would he be able to forget the Sea Siren or his wife? Was she in his blood as he was in hers? It didn't matter now, nothing mattered except getting back to Spain. Back to her homeland where she could lick her wounds in private and give birth to Regan's child. She would go into seclusion on her country estate to give birth, and there she would remain. She thanked God for the financial security which would enable her to provide for their child. Their child, hers and Regan's.

The tears continued to roll down her cheeks as she let her mind dwell on Regan and the child she carried within her. Was this then to be the punishment doled out to her by the God she had renounced so long ago? She would live out her life in solitude with every luxury money could buy, but her life would have no love, no meaning, save that of the child, Regan's child. A lonely succession of days floated before her eyes, each one longer than the next. Would she be able to survive without the love she carried in her heart for the tall, blond Dutchman?

Swaying dizzily, she grasped the rigging for support as Jacobus quietly came aboard.

"Food, Jacobus, I didn't think of food. It's to be a long journey and I forgot."

"Aye, Capitana, we brought the provisions. Go below and we'll get the ship underway. Jan can take the wheel. Do you need help?"

"I'm afraid I do, Jacobus," she said, extending her hand. How strange, she mused to herself as the old man led her to her quarters, never before did I ask for or accept help. "Raise the Spanish flag, Jacobus. I'm going home!"

"Aye, Capitana, the Spanish flag it is."

"It would be well if you secure this ship before we set sail. There'll be a storm before the new day is out."

"And fierce it will be. I noticed the other day that the waters are warmer than usual."

"I fear what it means, old man."

"There is no need to be afraid, Capitana, I've ridden these seas all my life and those volcanos haven't spit out yet."

"There's always the first time, Jacobus. Never before have you noticed the water so warm either, am I right? And the mist, even in my sickened condition, I can tell that thick yellow fog is unnatural.

"Jacobus," she said, clutching his thin, sinewy wrist, "first we sail into Batavia. I made a promise to post notice that when I've caught The Hook I'm retiring from the sea. I wasn't serious at the time I made it, but I am now. To Batavia first, Jacobus. Speaking of posting, who posted the bounty on my head?"

"Captain van der Rhys. It is said that he borrowed heavily from all of the merchants and cleaned out his bank account. He said he would have you one way or the other."

"What's to happen to me if I'm caught?"

"He said you would belong to him and he would decide then what was to be done with you."

A vision of herself slit from throat to navel floated before her eyes as she drifted into an uneasy slumber.

Chaezar rode home in a fury. How did Regan find out? The Hook, of course, but would he have been fool enough to tell everything? Yes, the man was a coward. How fortunate that Gretchen had left the island for a visit. If he were to blame the whole of it on the German woman, would Regan believe it? Not likely, he was no fool.

There was only one means of escape, and although it was premature, he'd have to take it. The African Gold Coast, to the beginnings of his latest enterprise. A nutmeg plantation that would undercut the East Indian trade, built from the fertile nuts he had been smuggling out for the past four years. His first crop would be in soon and, although small, it would rock the trade foundations of the Dutch East India Company. The house he had built was there waiting for him, and if he ever hoped to live in it he must get away from Regan, now.

Her face grim and purposeful, Frau Holtz stood on the edge of the wharf shielding her eyes from the smoky cinders falling about her. She squinted through half-closed lids and willed a sail, Regan's sail, to appear on the horizon. Where was he? It was time she opened his eyes, told him that his wife was actually the infamous *Sea Siren,* and was carrying his child. The tall, imposing woman blanched when she thought of the expression on his face when she told him that his remarkable wife had also left him. A look of utter hopelessness crossed her face as the vague rumblings beneath her feet increased in tempo. She always feared the Sisters of Fire erupting—the whole island would burn to a crisp and her with it.

Frantically, she paced the wharf, her arms crossed over her heavy breasts. She couldn't just stand waiting here forever. She had to do something. The falling cinders were already clouding the air, making visibility almost nil. Clenching her strong wide teeth in an agony of indecision, she marched purposefully toward the offices of the Dutch East India Company.

Panic had taken hold. Evacuation of the island was all that mattered. As fast as a ship left the harbor another was filled to capacity, making way to the open sea with its cargo of terror-stricken humanity. Men, women, and children, their belongings in sacks, raced to the wharf to board the waiting ships. Others looked skyward, their faces filled with a mixture of fear and disbelief. Would the Sisters erupt? Brushing impatiently at a stray cinder that singed her bare arm, Frau Holtz opened the door of the offices and stepped inside. Chaos reigned. Captains and merchants were busily stuffing papers and ledgers into satchels and gathering their personal belongings. She listened to the babble of high-pitched hysteria with alarm.

"I tell you, it's only a matter of hours," Captain Dykstra said harshly. "There's no way we can escape this time. The entire island has to be evacuated. The question is, can we do it in time?"

"Women and children first," Captain Kloss said quietly. "Has anyone heard from Regan?"

"I wish to know if Mynheer van der Rhys has made port," Frau Holtz interrupted anxiously. "I'm Frau Holtz, his housekeeper, and have messages of grave importance to deliver to him personally."

"No one's seen or heard from Regan. Not since yesterday, when he took the boy to the inner islands. I happen to know he expected to make his trip a short one. He should be returning some time today. God, I wish he were here now with his gift for organization. It would be best for you, dear woman, if you went to the wharf and got aboard a ship. When I see Regan I'll tell him that you wish to see him. Go now, while there's still time!"

"*Ja,* I go," Frau Holtz said wearily. So, these men also knew what she knew in her heart. The Sisters would erupt and place everyone on Java in danger. She had tried, what more could she do?

Sirena gave the order to weigh anchor. Jacobus looked at her questioningly. "Are you sure, Capitana, that you know what you're about to do? The *Sea Siren* won't find a welcome in Batavia."

"I know that, Jacobus; however, a promise is a

promise. I said I'd post a notice in the offices of the Dutch East India Company when I settled matters with The Hook. I must keep my word. That will end the matter once and for all."

"The cinders and the ashes are falling more heavily. You'd best make quick work of your mission. We must be safely out to sea when the Sisters spew their hot rocks and lava. Pray God there isn't a tidal wave, for then we're all dead!"

Sirena, her mind elsewhere, barely heard the warning Jacobus issued. Nimbly, she jumped from the ship and almost collided with Frau Holtz. The housekeeper was standing on the wharf, shielding her eyes with her strong hands. What in the name of God was the woman doing here in Port Batavia? Sidestepping her, Sirena raced to the offices of the Dutch East India Company and rushed inside. Bedlam greeted her. Her eyes raked the wall for some sort of board to hang her notice on, when she spied a slab of cork with a reward notice posted for her. She blanched slightly at the grim words of Regan's: Dead or Alive. Quickly, she posted her own notice. Swiveling around the noisy room, she noticed two sea captains staring at her, their hands full of papers. Quickly, she placed her hand on the hilt of the cutlass that hung at her side and spoke quietly: "I came here to post my notice. I see that the time is not quite appropriate; however, it was a promise I made and one I felt honor-bound to keep. The *Sea Siren* is now part of the past." Both captains looked at her with strange expressions on their ruddy, weather-beaten faces. Was it safe to turn her back on them? Undecided, she backed up, her hand sure on her cutlass. No man made a move to follow her, or comment on her statement. So be it.

Outside, she saw women dragging small children by the hand as they wailed piteously and brushed at the hot ash dripping from the skies. Absently, she brushed ash from her bare arms. As quickly as she brushed it away, it covered her again, sometimes leaving small scorches on her soft flesh. Jacobus was right, they had to get to sea! She must think of the child, Regan's child! She had to protect the unborn babe!

She raced to the wharf unmindful of the people who stopped to stare at her near-nakedness, the cutlass swinging at her side. As she neared the wharf she noticed Frau Holtz turn in her direction. Should she leave the woman here? If she did, what would become of her?

"Frau Holtz, you must come with me. The island is no longer safe. Are you leaving on another ship? Are you waiting for someone?"

"I . . . I must find Mynheer van der Rhys. I must tell . . ."

"There's no time for that now. Come with me! Regan is at sea. Come, there isn't much time." Forcefully, she tried to grasp the housekeeper's arm, only to have her jerk it away.

"Jan," Sirena called, "come here! Bring some of the men, hurry, there's no time to lose." Soon her men stood on the dock next to her.

"What is it, Capitana, what can we do?"

"Get this woman aboard ship, even if you have to carry her. She won't be safe here. Use force if necessary."

"Aye, Capitana," Jan muttered as he grasped one arm and Willem the other. The two seamen struggled with the tall, heavy woman, eventually getting her to the plank leading to the ship. Sharp curses rang in the air as they grappled with the housekeeper. To her dismay, Frau Holtz found that she was no match for the burly seamen and, in the end, acquiesced.

"Capitana, perhaps we should offer the services of the *Sea Siren* to help evacuate the island. What do you think?"

"What do I think, Jacobus? I think the smell of blood is still too strong on our decks for these good people to want to set foot on our ship," she said mournfully. "I'll go aboard. You can ask if anyone wishes to sail with us. We'll take as many as wish to go. Try!"

"Aye, Capitana."

Nimbly, Sirena leaped aboard the frigate and looked around her. Already there was a dull-gray carpet of ash aboard the decks of the frigate. Small mounds smoldered and smelled of sulphur.

Shielding her eyes from the cinders, she watched for Jacobus's return. She was not surprised to see him climb the plank alone.

"They say this is a ship of death and they don't wish to be saved by a devil woman. In all honesty it was the men who said it, Capitana. The women and children were willing to climb aboard, but the men said there were two galleons waiting for them."

"It's just as well," Sirena said glumly as she kicked at a mound of smoldering ash. "Hoist the anchor and let's leave this godforsaken island before she burns to a cinder."

"Capitana," Jacobus asked hesitantly, "is the bounty notice still hanging in the offices?"

Sirena laughed mirthfully. "It lays in shreds on the floor amidst the smoldering ash."

Chapter Twenty-nine

Gretchen Lindenreich looked around her empty rooms and swore viciously. They had all deserted her, every last stinking one of them. Slaves! Ingrates! Give them a home, food and honest work, and they turned on you for their thanks! Fear cloaked her perspiring body as she peered at the falling ash through her wide window. What did it mean? Never in her wildest dreams had she imagined that this time would come to pass. Now, the damn volcano was finally going to spew forth all the venom it carried in its bowels.

She had to pack and get out of here without any help. Damn Sudi, damn the houseboys, damn everyone to Hell! Trunks! Where were the trunks? Damn Sudi.

Close to hysteria, she raked her fingers through her thick golden hair as she tried to recall where the trunks were stored. Behind the kitchen wall. Running to the kitchen, she slipped and fell. Cursing Sudi and the houseboys, she picked herself up and dragged the massive trunks into the middle of the floor. She bent down to open one and was revolted by a layer of mildew spotting the trunk's lining. Frantically, she searched for a rag to wipe at the hateful black stains. Damn Sudi, she should have cleaned the trunks—all those beatings and still she didn't learn. Damn her soul to Hell! She couldn't put her expensive clothes into those moldy trunks. She rubbed at the offensive stains only to find that she could not remove the black spots.

She found a large towel and laid it on the bottom of the largest trunk. It would have to do. When she arrived at her destination, wherever that might be, she'd remove the clothing and air out the trunk. That would be her first order of the day, to have her trunks cleaned and aired and some sweet-smelling cologne placed inside. It was a wonder vermin weren't crawling inside. Damn that Sudi!

Where was Regan? Would he come for her, knowing she was alone? And Chaezar, where was he? Busy saving his own neck without a thought of her. Damn his soul to Hell, too! If it weren't for his slipshod maneuvering she'd now be married to Regan and he would be saving her precious gowns. And there wouldn't be mildew in her trunks. She would never forgive him for the mildew. "Damn Chaezar! Damn Sudi!" she muttered as she pulled at her hair and tried to think what she should do next.

Should she go to Regan's house? If she arrived there with her trunks he couldn't send her away, he would have to help her. Regan's broad back would get her trunks to the wharf where he would load them on one of his ships. Yes, she would go to Regan's. Stopping in midstride she negated the idea. What if he knew? Instead of carrying her precious trunks he'd kill her and stuff her into one of them. Oh, Regan, damn you! Why didn't you marry me?

She started pulling first one gown then another from

the depths of her spacious wardrobe. What to take? Everything! She'd leave nothing behind. That damn Sudi would come back and steal everything in sight. Self-pity welled in Gretchen's eyes as she sought each dress and carefully looked it over for the odious mildew. She wondered if the fungus in the trunk would creep up on the garment.

Tears spilled down her cheeks as she fumbled with each item of her elaborate wardrobe. Frantically, she rubbed at each and every hemline and then carefully folded the gowns and laid them tenderly in the trunk at her feet. She needed help. She was tired and her head ached. Her eyes felt puffy and she must look a sight.

Where in hell were all the men who had professed to love her when she lay in their arms? Where were they now when she needed help with this damnable mildew? Home with wives and families, that's where they were. No one cared about her. Not one person on this whole godforsaken island cared about her. She was alone and she would have to manage all by herself. She'd show them all! Tears formed anew at this silent declaration and she brushed angrily at the salty streaks.

She stretched her long neck trying to brush her heavy hair back off her face. The heat was suffocating. She didn't ever remember it being this hot. God in Heaven, did it mean the Sisters were due to erupt? The smell of the smoldering shrubbery was creeping into the house, making it difficult to breathe. She had to hurry.

Quickly, she raced to the kitchen and returned dragging the second largest trunk, then another trip for the third and last. This time she didn't bother to try to wipe the mildew from the trunk's lining, she just ripped the sheets from her bed and threw them into the trunks, hoping they would protect her gowns. Sweltering in the unbearable heat, her silk stockings curling and twisting about her slim legs like snakes, she cursed the abysmal heat and everything and anything that came to her mind as she continued her packing.

The trunks were filled to overflowing and there were still gowns in the closet. What to do? Raging with the injustice of her plight, she draped a gown around her neck and tied another around her waist after carefully rubbing at a dark black spot. She would have to take extra care that the gown didn't come loose and trail on the ground. Angrily, she stamped her feet and wiped at her brow.

Jewels! She hadn't packed her jewels! Stomping over to the small coffer, she grabbed brilliant stones and placed them in a drawstring reticule and carefully pulled the ties. She looped it around her neck, heedless of her appearance. The ribbons and pretties with which she loved to adorn herself—what of those? They weren't packed either. Another drawstring purse was filled and then it too was looped around her neck. Wailing, she dragged the heaviest of the trunks outside to the cobblestone courtyard, where her fleeing staff had left a broken-down, flat-back wagon used for hauling food and sundries from town. Someone had hitched a broken-down old nag to the wagon, then abandoned it, preferring Gretchen's spirited team of greys and her comfortable carriage which had a roof to act as protection against the falling cinders. Pushing and shoving the massive trunk, she cried to all the gods in the heavens to help her. Receiving no reply, she again pushed the trunk, only to have it lurch against a large boulder next to the wagon. How was she to get it to the wagon? Even a man would be hard pressed to lift it down.

There was only one thing to do. Quickly, she opened the trunk and ripped out her gowns and then heaved the heavy trunk aboard the wagon. Helter-skelter, she piled the gowns back in only to find that the lid wouldn't close. She banged with her fist, breaking one long tapered nail and then another. Blood gushed from one rosy-tipped finger and she stared at it, mesmerized. Tiny red drops fell onto the yellow gown she had tied around her waist. Choking with the acrid smell in the air, she ripped the yellow gown from her side and tossed it onto the smoldering shrubbery. Angrily, she stomped back into the house and repeated her actions with the two remaining trunks.

The trunks secure, Gretchen climbed into the driver's seat and stared at the nag that was to haul the wagon. The old roan looked as if she could barely stand. The muscles in her flanks twitched involuntarily from the stinging hot ash singeing her worn, fraying coat. The animal's eyes widened in alarm when she pulled on the leads. The old roan was practically beyond feeling. The noxious sulphur fumes and the asphyxiating heat were fast becoming beyond her endurance.

Gretchen fleetingly wondered if the animal would be able to make it to town, hauling the heavy wagon and cargo of precious gowns. Her trunks would get to town if she had to beat the dying nag every step of the way. An image of Chaezar flashed through her mind—an old nag begging to be beaten! If he were here, she'd oblige him gladly—damn him!

As she flicked the leads, the beast moved at a slow, dragging pace. Impatiently, Gretchen wiped at her soot-streaked face and squirmed in her seat. She was soaking wet, perspiration dripping down her back and under her breasts. Irritated, she moved her neck, heavy with the dress and the drawstring pouches. She would never give any of them up! Never! She would suffer!

Gretchen was thrown off balance and at first was at a loss to explain what happened. Convulsing with hysteria, teetering on the brink of madness, she gritted her teeth and strained to tighten her hold on the slippery thread that connected her with sanity. The earth lurched and shook and Gretchen with it. A scream was birthed in her soul and welled up through her breast, pushing against her tightly clenched teeth, wrenching her jaws apart, finding its release in a high-pitched, almost inhuman yowl.

Cruelly, Gretchen snapped the leads over the stumbling horse. How was it those damn servants had left it behind? Because, she answered herself, it was half dead. Just as the wagon reached the town the horse stopped dead in his tracks and lay down in the middle of the road. Gretchen climbed down from the wagon. "Get up, you stinking piece of horse-flesh, get up, do you hear me?" Savagely she kicked at the animal. The beast lay perfectly still. Again she kicked, screaming at the top of her lungs. "We just have a little way to go, get up, get up this minute before I take the whip to you!

Crawling on her hands and knees, she inspected the beast and willed a sign of life to stir the animal. "Get up, you useless old nag!" she screamed, pulling the carcass's ears. Her sweating palms lost their grip and Gretchen went sailing backwards, tumbling head over heels to land sprawled out and staring dumbly at the dead beast of burden.

Furious, she realized she would have to go the rest of the way on foot. Climbing aboard the wagon she pushed and tugged at the heaviest and largest of the trunks pushing it over the side. To her dismay, it landed in a pile of sooty ashes. She then pushed over the other two trunks, their contents spilling into the dark, curling ash. Rage gripped her as she climbed down from the wagon and she gave her shin a vicious scrape from ankle to knee, tearing and chewing the last of her silk stockings. She remembered she had forgotten to pack the others.

For the first time she realized that she was just past the outskirts of town. She had passed through the gates in the thick walls that surrounded Batavia. Coming into town by a little-used road, she had not seen anyone.

A heavy blanket of cinders fell from the sky and settled on her skin. She looked around at the buzzing town. Women held children by the hand, dragging them toward the wharf and carrying parasols to ward off the the falling cinders. She watched in horror as a particularly large cinder fell on a brilliantly colored parasol, setting it aflame. Servants—loyal servants who didn't desert their employers—helped with baggage and carried small babies as their parents carried the most necessary belongings. Gretchen wondered vaguely how many times you had to beat servants before they became loyal. On the verge of hysteria, Gretchen managed to drag one of her trunks a good eight yards before she collapsed at the side of the road. She would never make the wharf this way. She looked down at the soot-singed gown she wore and recalled its cost before she ripped it into thick slices.

She tied a flimsy knot and looped it through the handle of the trunk. She then tried to drag the baggage by placing the rag over her shoulder. She hadn't gone two feet when the rag came free of its knot and she was right back where she started.

Mad with fury, she shook her head to free it of the odious cinders. She could feel the singed, brittle ends of her lush blond hair. Her skin not only smelled scorched, it actually was in many different places. She would go to the wharf and ask for help. There would be men there, strong men, who would be able to carry her trunks. She would ask, she would beg, she would barter her body, something she had always done successfully.

The first man she saw was a tall, dark-skinned native holding a child. "Help me!" she screeched. "I need someone strong and big like you to carry my trunks. See, there they are back there in the middle of the road." Getting no response to her plea, she cursed the man, telling him to put the child down and demanding that he help her. The tall man glared at her with hatred, gathered his child closer to him, and walked silently away, leaving her standing alone cursing. Gretchen raced to the farthest edge of the wharf where men were helping women and children into the jolly-boats for their brief sail to the galleons.

"You must help me," she cried passionately. "Someone has to help me. What am I to do?" The faces that looked at her were cold and hard. Finally she came to a bent old man helping two small children aboard the jolly-boat. "Help me," she begged. "It won't take long."

"I'll help you as soon as I get the children safely aboard."

"Never mind the children, their mothers can see to them! My trunks are all I have left! You must help me!"

"There's no reason for baggage. We take only children on this trip. You'll have to leave all your baggage behind. Save yourself. Help me with these children, they're orphans and have no parents to look after them."

"Help you with those sniveling brats after you tell

me you won't take my trunks? You must be insane, old man!"

Why wouldn't anyone help her, she muttered to herself as she trudged back up the road, all the while brushing the hot cinders from her scorched flesh. She stumbled, breaking a heel on one of her slippers. Limping in a lopsided manner, she reached her trunks and heaved a sigh of relief that they were still intact. What if someone had stolen them while she pleaded with that old man? Why wouldn't anyone help her?

Suddenly she laughed, a harsh cackle that grated on her own ears. Of course! Why hadn't she realized before? She could have saved herself untold agony. She didn't look beautiful! She was dirty and messy, that's why everyone was looking at her so strangely. She would change her gown and go back to the wharf and then all the men would fall all over themselves with offers of help. That was all she had to do, change her gown and dress her hair.

With her last ounce of strength she dragged the largest of the trunks into a secluded spot along the road. Almost reverently she raised the trunk's lid. Which one to choose? They were all so beautiful and each did something special for her. Preening, she cocked her head this way and that, finally deciding on a pale lavender with gold threads.

Angrily, she flicked at a hot ash. She was in the process of extracting the lavender gown when a large, smoldering cinder fell on the gauze-like material, catching it in a winking, pinpoint of flame. Hastily, she tried to beat it out with her hands only to spread the flame further along the fabric. The faster she pummeled the gown the faster the flames seemed to spread, till a spark flew upward to land in her hair. In her frenzy she tried beating at the gown with one hand and raking the other through her wild, burning hair.

"Not my gowns, I can't lose my gowns!" The hungry flame devoured her gown, nipped at her soft white body. Where was Regan, the man who loved her, adored her? All reason gone, her fingers scorched to the bone, she beat at the flames. Two men noticed her dismay and raced to help her.

She was a walking incendiary, it was impossible to recognize her. The men tried vainly to smother the flames, but Gretchen, raving in her lunacy, fought them off. "My gowns, my gowns, save my gowns!" she cried before she collapsed on the ground, a mass of charred flesh more dead than alive. They heard her say calmly, pathetically, "I'll never be beautiful again."

Regan settled himself behind the desk in his captain's quarters aboard the swiftly homeward-bound brigantine. His feet propped on a desk corner, a cigar held loosely in one hand, he was a picture of complete relaxation, but his eyes were dark and angry.

"Wha—what do you wish to discuss?" Caleb quivered.

"We both know that the missionary said you were the child the man with the hook left in his care. He also said that a blond German woman and a dark Spanish man were asking questions about the same child. You. We both know you're my son. I think I knew in my heart you were of my blood the moment I set eyes on you. I was temporarily blinded by other things and took my wife's story at face value. Now I am fully awake and aware of what goes on around me. Now you will tell me the meaning of this charade. We will get down to father-and-son business later. For now the truth and nothing but the truth."

Caleb gulped and brushed at his eyes. His fists clenched, he started his story. "Two years ago I was on an errand near the wharf. I was hit on the head and when I woke, I was aboard ship and out to sea. And there I remained till about a year ago when one day we had made port and I was being flogged for not doing my duties fast enough. A very kind gentleman, Señor Juan Córdez, rescued me and offered me passage home if I would serve aboard his ship. I said yes and we set sail. He nursed me and took care of my back. I felt I owed him my life for the way he intervened in my behalf. We were within one week of Batavia when our ship was attacked by pirates. The marauding ship carried a Dutch flag so everyone aboard thought she was one of your ships."

"My men have no orders to attack ships at sea," Regan said angrily.

"She flew the flag of the Dutch East India Company," Caleb said stubbornly. "We all believed she belonged to you. The men attacked and killed Señor Córdez, my benefactor, and they raped and killed one of the women aboard. It was the man with the hook. He raped her and even after she was . . ." the boy shook his head. "I don't want to talk about it."

"You must talk about it! Now tell me the rest," Regan said.

"He cut open the woman from her throat to her navel with his hook and threw her overboard. Her name was Isabel. She was promised to you in marriage. Her sister told me as did her uncle that she was a holy woman and wanted nothing more than to lead a life of prayer. She accepted the marriage she was to have with you but she would have preferred to go to a nunnery. Her sister . . . Sirena, fought like a wild woman but she was overcome and severely wounded, much as you were wounded. You both carry like scars down the arm. They . . . they took turns raping her, one after the other, day after day. She was sick and burning with fever and wanted to die, but God wouldn't allow her to have such an easy death. I managed to steal some medicine from the captain's quarters and I did the best I could for her. Twice she almost died and twice God spared her. When she was delirious, she spoke of strange things. She said she would take Isabel's place and marry you and . . ."

"Finish it, boy."

"She said she would ruin you as you had ruined her sister and herself. She said she would never be able to hold her head up again. She said no man would want her if they knew what had happened to her. We agreed to pretend she was my sister—and you know the rest. Sirena is the Sea Siren."

"Yes, I know."

"You know?" Caleb's eyes boggled at the calm statement.

"I've suspected for some time, but I knew my suspicions were correct only a few days ago."

"You won't kill her, will you?" Caleb pleaded. "Please. Time after time she spared your life when she could have killed you. Please, Father."

"And the Spaniard. What of him?"

"She hates him. She only went to his lunches to glean information about his ships. She said he's a traitor to Spain. If she could have, she would have killed him. It is you she loves."

"Has she said this to you, boy?"

"No. She didn't have to say anything to me. I could read it in her eyes. She told me you were my father before she left. She said I was to let you tell me yourself."

"Left!" Regan shouted. "Where did she go?"

"Back to Spain. She left the day we sailed to the inner islands. She took her frigate and plans to sail alone."

"Alone! It's impossible!"

"Sirena can do anything she sets her mind to," the boy said confidently.

"She can, can she?" the Dutchman barked. "You know everything about this woman who is my wife."

"Aye, I know her well. Better, perhaps, than you, and you're her husband. Did you know that she carried your child, Father?"

"What?"

"Sirena's going to have a child. I heard Frau Holtz ask Juli all kinds of personal questions about Sirena. I haven't exactly been sheltered, Father, I know what she was asking. And," he added ominously, "she wasn't feeling well the last time I saw her. Again, she didn't tell me this. I've watched her and I've seen the sickness overcome her and the way she tried to hide it from me. It was in her eyes. There was so much sadness there I wanted to run and tell you, but she forbade me. I swore my allegiance to her aboard the *Rana*. I owed it to her and her uncle. I could do no less."

"Blind! I've been so blind!" Regan's voice was tormented.

"You must go after her and make her come back! She'll never be able to sail to Spain in her condition."

"I thought you said she could do anything!"

"Well, almost anything, when she is feeling well. When she's sick, like on board the *Rana,* she needs help. Please, Father, go after her."

Regan drew the boy to him. "We should be discussing how happy we are that we found one another and here we stand, you pleading for the Sea Siren and me feeling like the blind fool I am. Do you know I posted a bounty on her head that . . . God," he groaned, "what if some wild marauder finds her and kills her? Fool, fool." he cursed himself. "Come, we'll go after her."

The boy looked at his father, his jaw just as stubbornly set. "Why?"

"Why what?"

"Why are you going after her?"

"Because you said she is ill and needs help. You pleaded with me!"

"Then I won't go if that's your only reason," the boy said angrily.

"But you . . . what is it you want from me? One minute you asked me to go after her and then when I agree you refuse to go."

"I'll go only if you tell me the real reason why you seek her out."

"I thought you were only twelve years old. You think like a man," Regan said, clapping the boy on the back. "You want to hear me say I love her, is that it? I do, son, I love the Sea Siren and I love Sirena, my wife. It is well that I didn't have to make a choice between the two of them."

"You love the Sea Siren after what she did to you?"

Regan nodded. "I too saw strange things in those green eyes. The things I saw in my wife's eyes. That was the one thing she couldn't change."

Chapter Thirty

As Caleb stood at the wheel, Regan watched him, a lump in his throat. A feeling of pride filled him as his gaze lingered on the raven-haired boy. He shuddered at how close he had come to never finding him—and without Sirena, he probably never would have. His heart ached for the sight of her. Was the boy right? Had she left the island? Would he ever see her again?

Was it possible Caleb was mistaken about Sirena being pregnant? No, he discounted the notion, Caleb wasn't mistaken. But how? When?

His memory soared to a night of darkness and shadow, the sound of breezes in the rigging; the warm, moist blanket of sequestering fog; the rocking of the quiet ship on the silently rolling waves. She had been magnificent that night! The excitement of their duel, the sparks flying from her eyes, her sense of drama, her exultant victory over that coward Blackheart. Regan could understand, now, why she had to kill the man. He, himself, could not have done less.

She was a paradox, an enigma. A fighting, snarling cat one moment, then a ministering angel the next as she tended his wounds.

Regan's memory of that night was acute and distinct. So acute that it seemed as if he could conjure her out of the spindrift. His concentration was so great he seemed to feel her presence and he found himself listening for the sound of her laughter. His eyes ached for the sight of her as she had appeared that night, his hand burned for the feel of her satiny, cool skin. He remembered, the sweet, salt-fresh perfume of her billowing dark hair, the sensuous, lissome length of her body, the voluptuous spill of her full breasts, the soft, gripping strength of her thighs . . . All this and more called to him, arousing the familiar deep curl of heat in his middle.

Her passion had equaled his own, he knew she wanted him as much as he desired her. Their union had been complete and total in its perfection, and because of it she had conceived his child. Their child, Sirena's and his.

The vision of the Sea Siren dropped away and in her place was Sirena, his wife, reserved and aloof. Sirena, his wife, who spent more than one afternoon engaged in lengthy lunches with Chaezar Alvarez. Every fiber of his being rebelled at the thought that the child she carried could be Chaezar's.

Forcing his attention away from the murderous thoughts he was entertaining, his eyes searched the sky hoping for some sign that he was wrong about the threatened events. Never during the period since the white man's arrival in Java, had the Sisters of Fire erupted. The most they had done was growl their ominous warnings and then subside like great sleeping cats. But the smell of sulphur was heavy in the air and it was becoming more difficult to breathe. Was it wise to go back to Port Batavia and hope against hope that Sirena would still be there? Would she know enough to go to the wharf and get aboard ship? He *had* to know. There was no other choice but to return to his home and see for himself.

Besides, he needed provisions if he was to sail for Spain. He had explained to Caleb that you couldn't sail blindly without preparation. The long journey would not be an easy one. Perhaps he would be able to overtake her and save some precious time, bur first he had to see if she had really left the island. Surely if she stayed, Frau Holtz would have seen to her and, along with the rest of the household help, aided her evacuation. Frau Holtz could be depended on. He was sure of it. But would Sirena listen to her?

"We've lost sail, there's no breeze . . . Father," Caleb complained. "We're losing time and . . ."

"And you feel that I am not doing anything, is that it?"

"I think we should be searching for Sirena. You promised," the boy said accusingly.

"Listen to me, son. You can't just take to sea blindly. Look to the skies, the Sisters could erupt momentarily. What if you're wrong and Sirena didn't follow her plan and go to sea, what if she's still at the house waiting?"

"Sirena does what she says she will do," the boy replied stubbornly. "She's sailing the frigate alone. She needs help, your help."

No sooner had the boy spoken than Regan shouted, "Look at the sky!" Flames were on the horizon and a loud thunderous boom split the air.

"Pray God that everyone left the island," Caleb said piteously. "What happens, Father, if Sirena is at sea and there's a tidal wave? She told me she sails alone!"

Regan's eyes took in his son. "I thought you told me she was a better sailor than any man, those were your words to me, weren't they?"

"Yes, but . . ."

"No buts, Caleb. Is she or isn't she a better sailor than me or any man?"

"Yes," Caleb answered defiantly. "Sirena can do anything!" he said loyally.

"Then there's no problem, is there?"

"But this time she sails alone. What if the tidal wave comes and she's washed overboard. She could capsize."

"I doubt there will be a tidal wave. You're going to have to trust me, son. I'm doing what I think is right. We're going to Port Batavia to see if she did indeed leave. We're only six hours from port. There may be others who will need our help. When we see what the situation is, then we'll go after Sirena."

"You promised, Father, you promised me," Caleb shrilled. "Sirena never broke a promise, she said honor is all-important. How can you, my father, and Sirena's husband, break your word? If you do I'll never forgive you till the day I die. I'll find her myself!"

"You must love her very much," Regan said quietly, as he looked compassionately into Caleb's eyes.

"Sirena is the reason I'm alive today. She's the reason I'm standing next to you on this deck calling you "father" and you're calling me "son." Sirena is the reason for everything. I could never live in your house without Sirena even if you are my father. I have to find her! I have to see her!"

Fear crawled into Regan's eyes. The boy's tone frightened him. He'd find her one way or another. He would leave and search for her—of that there was no doubt. He must keep his promise to his son. He must search for Sirena and bring her home with him. Even if the child she carried was Chaezar's . . .

"Well," Caleb said stubbornly, "what's your decision, Fath—" The word stuck in his throat as a picture of Sirena floated before his eyes.

"I'll keep my word. As soon as we're sure she isn't at Batavia we'll sail for Spain. Agreed?"

"Agreed!" Caleb said firmly.

Helga Kloss, holding her parasol at a jaunty angle to protect her head from the hot, falling ash, marched down the road to the wharf. Behind her followed a laughing, singing parade of young, brown-skinned children.

Mevrouw Kloss led them in song, her short, round body stepping with a light rhythm. Though her lips formed the lyrics and her voice lifted in tune, her innards were twisted with fear. Dear God, she prayed fervently, though her face was wreathed in smiles, please God, help me get the children to the ships!

The children, ranging in age from infancy to six years, were all members of the Christian Mission of Batavia, where Helga spent a great deal of her time as a volunteer.

As they marched along singing, grief clutched at Helga's heart. The mission was gone, destroyed by fire, taking with it countless young lives and that of Father Miguel, who had come to Batavia to care for the orphans and bring them to God.

When word was brought to the mission that the ships were in the harbor ready for evacuation, Helga had been readying the little ones to leave with the help of a few of the older girls. The thatched roofs on the mission compound were already smoldering when Helga had lined up her young charges in the courtyard.

"Start the children on their way to the wharf, Mevrouw Kloss, they're so small they won't be able to walk very fast. The others and myself will catch up with you in no time," Father Miguel had said. "We still have preparations to make for our journey. We'll need our mattresses and fresh linen for the little ones." The tall, dignified missionary kept his voice light, almost jovial. It was important that the children not be frightened. Hysterical children would be impossible to handle.

So Helga, taking her cue from the dour-faced Father Miguel had burst into one of the children's favorite songs and led them singing along the forest path to the wharf. Half an hour later, while cutting across the hilltop, Helga peered through the falling ash in the direction of the mission. There, below her, she witnessed a holocaust of flames. The thatched roof of the main building had fallen in, taking part of the walls with it.

Quickly, almost without thinking, she turned the parade of children to the far side of the hill, "*Kinder!*" she called, "This way! Quickly!" Clapping her hands and singing louder, though she thought her heart would break, Helga led her children out of sight of the burning disaster below them.

She longed to go back, to help somehow, but when she looked upon the eager, trusting faces of her young charges, she knew she couldn't leave them. She must get them to the wharf. And so, she led them onward, her voice lifted in song, her heart swollen with grief.

At the back of the parade were the older girls and boys carrying the infants too young to walk. Glancing back, Helga saw their cheeks damp with tears, their lips trembling with suppressed sobs, but still they followed her example and sang on as they trudged down the hillside along the dusty road to the city. The air was rank with sulphur. Some of the children cried aloud, protesting against the scorching cinders that singed their tender, young flesh. Tremor after tremor shook the earth, but faster and faster they walked, louder and louder they sang. The wall surrounding Batavia was in sight. Hopefully Helga prayed that her husband, Anton, would be on his ship waiting for them.

A particularly violent tremor knocked a little girl off her feet. Snatching her up, Helga directed the children, "Lay down, *Kinder!* See! Do like me, *Kinder.*" To demonstrate, she lay down flat, shielding the little girl from the ash with her body.

The sky was dark and ominous, the air almost unfit to breathe. Distant thunder-like rumblings crashed through the sulphur-thick atmosphere. Her determination bordered on panic. The gates of the city were only yards away. "Hurry! *Kinder!* Hurry! To the ships!"

Herding the children along the streets, she saw one little boy fall to his knees, stunned. The back of his head was bleeding, at his feet rested a dark, gray rock. "Dear God!" she heard herself cry, "has it come to this? Please, Lord, they're only children!"

Picking the child up in her arms, she and the older children hurried the babes along to the wharf, to Anton. Helga ran till she thought her heart would burst. The burden of the child in her arms dragged her down, yet somehow she found the strength to go on.

The wharf was within sight. Soon, soon now, the children would be safe. People were running out to them, running to save the children. European and native alike, all with fright-distorted faces, were running to help her little orphans. "God bless them," Helga cried, tears burning her vision as she ran, "God bless them!"

Each child was swooped up into the protective arms of an adult. Sharp, rapping sounds vibrated the plank dock. The Sisters were spewing a pelting of rocks, hot and dangerous. They felled several people instantaneously, and children screamed in pain and outrage.

Helga caught several blows on her back, but she hardly noticed them in her determination to see the children safe. Working quickly, the children were handed into jolly-boats to be rowed out to the ships in the harbor. Thick, heavy tarpaulins were used to shield them from the hurling missiles. Happiness beat in Helga's heart when the last child was handed over.

People swarmed into the jollys after the children. Just as Helga was about to join them a wail of terror reached her ears. Turning about, she looked in the direction from which the sound came. From behind some crates stacked on the dock she saw a little girl, not more than five years old. Barefoot, her little mission dress hanging in tatters under which could be seen burns and blisters, the child's condition wrenched Helga's heart.

Running toward her, Helga surmised that the adult who had taken charge of the little one had been felled by falling rocks. Sweeping up the pathetic, wailing child, Helga ran for the jolly.

An explosive roar split the air. Instantaneously, the vicious pelting of rocks became heavier, knocking the breath from her, crashing against her body and head. Helga went down, the child beneath her shielded from the flying missiles by her bulk.

Several sailors, seeing what had happened, hoisted themselves out of the jolly and scrambled to Helga's aid. Cursing the wounding rocks, protecting their heads with their arms, they reached Helga's fallen body.

One seaman suffered a blow just above the eye. Bloodied and blinded, he fell to his knees. A second seaman went to his aid, a third reached for the whimpering child.

The little girl, fright widening her black, almond-shaped eyes, clung to Helga's body. Her arms reached for Helga's neck and held on tightly, refusing to leave her patron for the rescuing arms of the seaman.

"Hush, baby," the seaman said soothingly, despite the brutal beating he was receiving from the falling stones, "there's nothing to be done for her now. She's gone to be with the angels."

The little child seemed to understand. She was about to place herself in the sailor's arms when she turned back to Helga and placed a loving, grateful kiss on Helga's death-pale cheek.

Captain Anton Kloss watched the destruction of Batavia from aboard his ship where he waited for his wife Helga to join him. From beneath the protection of the overhung quarter deck, he witnessed buildings crumbling from the ravages of fires ignited by the red, glowing rocks showering from the sky. Trees were aflame, their trailing, dancing fires consuming everything in their hungry path. Burning portions of the deck hissed steamily as they toppled into the heated waters of the harbor. "Helga, Helga," his heart cried out.

Before his eyes he saw the land vibrating, the tremors causing high, frothy waves to rock his ship. The heat from the fires, even though a safe distance away, scorched his face and seared his lungs.

An ominous rumbling which grew into a roar, caught his attention. Off the horizon to the west it was possible to see the crest of the steaming, fire-spitting Sisters. As he watched, the horizon grew red, orange, yellow, then white with heat and smoke. The sound of the volcanos' roar was building to a crescendo.

The last thing Captain Anton Kloss was ever to see was the tops of the twin Sisters exploding. The last thing he would ever feel was the enormous shockwave that knocked him unconscious into the unnaturally warm waters of Batavia Harbor.

The yellowish, greenish water was churning beneath Regan's brig. A hot, humid breeze rifled the sails and the ship clipped along, each swell bringing them closer and closer to Port Batavia. Twilight's last pink streaks fought the yellowish air for supremacy as the day ended. Regan stood on the bow of the brig, the spyglass to his eye. The island looked devastated, not a soul stirred. He had a sinking feeling in the pit of his stomach. What if she were dead? Would he want to die too? If she lived would he fetch her back and could he live with another man's child in his house? He was pulled from his thoughts with the boy's anxious cry, "Land ho!"

The brig glided smoothly into what was left of the harbor. "Lower the jolly-boat," Regan ordered.

"There's nothing left," Caleb cried, his eyes scanning the charred docks and piers strewn with rubble of buildings that had toppled from the earth tremors and fire.

"There's a bit of the offices left—look, son." With a brisk order for his men to search the town for survivors, Regan joined Caleb in racing for what was left of the Dutch East India offices.

"Look, Father, here's your cigar box," Caleb said, handing a scorched brown humidor to Regan.

Regan looked around, his eyes settling on a large chunk of cork atop his battered desk. Relieved, he knew his captains had been here and taken everything with them. Caleb swung around to hand his father the cigar box and knocked the cork to the floor. "Look, Father," he cried, "look at this!"

Regan speared the rough paper pinned to the chunk of cork with the tip of the knife.

Caleb stood next to his father and quietly read the words aloud from the paper:

" 'I, the Sea Siren have retired from the seas. My mission is completed. I found that which I sought and now leave the Spanish and the Dutch to their business of trading.' " It was signed with a large sprawling *S*.

"You see, Father, I was right. This was the last thing she had to do before she left. This notice wasn't here when we left for the inner islands. I told you, Sirena never broke a promise."

Regan's eyes narrowed into slits as he looked at the boy. "You were right. I'll order the men to search out the root cellars and store all provisions on board. We'll set sail immediately." His eyes lowered to the scattered strips of charred paper at his feet: his personal bounty on the Sea Siren.

"Thank you, Father," Caleb said humbly.

Regan stood on deck, his thoughts whirling. Why was he doing this? For the boy or for himself? He admitted his love for the woman and it was a hard lump to swallow. How had she gotten into his blood like this? How had he allowed it to happen? Sighing he got to his feet, his eyes cold and hard. Somehow he blamed himself for all that had happened.

Even for Sirena's present condition. If he had had his wits about him he could have stopped that bastard Chaezar. He realized now that Sirena was like no woman he had ever known. If he had listened to her and . . . perhaps this never would have happened. How could she have fallen prey to that oily Spaniard? He must have taken advantage of her and she was afraid to tell him for fear of his wrath. "God help me, God help all of us," he breathed softly.

"Everything is aboard, Father," Caleb called.

"Then give the order to hoist anchor," Regan ordered grimly.

Chapter Thirty-one

Sirena lay on her hard, narrow bunk, her mind a beehive. Visions of Frau Holtz being dragged forcibly by Willem and Jan swam before her eyes. That it was for the housekeeper's own good sounded weak even to her own ears. The austere housekeeper had fought like some caged wild animal at which men were poking sticks. Eventually, with the aid of a few drops of laudanum, she had finally succumbed and was now sound asleep. What would happen when she woke? Sirena thought she wouldn't be surprised if the woman jumped overboard and attempted to swim back to Port Batavia. She grimaced as she pictured the aging Frau Holtz floundering in the water with sharks circling her. She would no doubt wag her finger and say, "*Ja,* I swim home, leave me be!"

Breathing heavily as if some ponderous weight lay on her chest, Sirena moved about on the narrow bunk trying to get comfortable. In the midst of her squirming, an ear-splitting boom shook the air. Panic gripped her as she slid from the bunk and raced up the narrow ladder to the deck. "God in Heaven, what was it?" she demanded of Jan, who stood at the wheel coughing and sputtering.

"The Sisters," he said curtly. "They had growled their warning once too often, now they've taken their revenge and are spewing everything in their guts on the villages and the wharves. God help any of those who remained behind. I've heard of such things many times but never thought I would live to see it happen."

"What . . . How . . ."

"Capitana, the rocks she spills out will be glowing red with fire and set flames to anything they touch. When the rocks have finished falling then the lava will run and suck everything under it. The lava will cool before it reaches the town, but the plantation groves are finished," he said glumly.

"The children, the old people . . . what of them?" Sirena cried in alarm. Caleb and Regan! Were they safe? God in Heaven, she should have stayed and waited.

"Look about you, Capitana, as far as the eye can see are ships of every description. You saw for yourself the men were helping to evacuate the island."

"But there was so little time," Sirena protested.

"What you say is true. It's over now. When the lava cools the men will return to the island and try to rebuild and start over."

"But that will take years," she said in a muffled voice.

"Aye, years. Many years and then there will be years after that while they wait for the trees to grow again. If they grow at all," he said ominously. "It will depend on how much damage the lava did and how heavy it lays."

Sirena shook her head in wonderment at this bizarre happening. Thank God she had dragged the housekeeper aboard or she would no doubt be lying under the burning wharf.

"Jan, how long will this odious choking air be with us?"

"Till the wind shifts, and then it may be days. Go below, Capitana, where it is not so thick. I can manage the wheel."

"All right," Sirena acquiesced, "I want to look in on the housekeeper to see how she fares."

Quietly, Sirena opened the door of the cabin which had once housed Caleb and where now the aging housekeeper slept. For some strange reason, tears burned at her eyes when she gazed down at the sleeping woman. Wisps of iron-gray hair lay on her high, wide forehead and her skin was soot-smudged, giving her an old, haggard appearance. Without thinking, she brushed gently at the stray locks of hair and gently wiped the dirt from the housekeeper's cheekbones. Frau Holtz stirred fretfully, muttering under her breath. One long arm brushed the air and then lay still at her side. Sirena turned to leave when the faded blue eyes opened.

"Frau Holtz, it is I, Sirena. I just came to see how you were. Try to sleep, you look worn out."

"Ja," the woman said harshly. "I am tired and find it difficult to breathe, why is that?"

"The Sisters erupted a while ago. The air on deck is horrendous. It is best to stay below and rest. I'm going to do the same. Have no fear," she said gently, "I'll put you ashore as soon as Willem says it's safe."

"Ja, I have no liking for ships and water. I want my feet on ground with trees and houses around me."

"I understand, Frau Holtz. I'm sorry that the men had to force you aboard. You see, I couldn't leave you behind to . . . die. I knew you must be on the wharf waiting for something, and everything was in such chaos I had to do something."

The housekeeper shook her head. "I was waiting for the Mynheer."

"Then he wasn't on the island?" Sirena said in a relieved tone.

"No, Mevrouw. He never returned with the boy." Boldly, her faded eyes took in Sirena's scanty attire and she pursed her mouth into a tight, grim line.

Sirena smiled slightly at her disapproving look. "I find that my . . . costume is . . . different and gives me much freedom. Perhaps if you wished I could fashion a similar one for you," she teased.

The watery eyes twinkled suddenly. "*Ja,* Mevrouw,

and a sight I would be. If I was younger, perhaps, and with the body you have I might agree. As it is, I will have to keep these rags on my back," she said, looking at her scorched and tattered gown of gray silk.

Sirena laughed happily. "Tell me, Frau Holtz, how long have you known of my . . . dual identity?"

The housekeeper smiled. "From the moment I noticed the spindrift in your hair. Ailment indeed! You may have been able to fool your husband, but you couldn't fool me!"

"You knew and didn't tell Regan?" Sirena's voice held an incredulous note.

"*Ja* . . . I'm not the only one who knew your secret. Didn't you ever question the sturdiness of the trellis at your window or the stoutness of the vine which you climbed up and down? On the nights when you were gone, Juli and I lashed it to the trellis on more than one occasion. Caleb isn't quite as nimble-footed as you. Many times I stood in the courtyard and waited for your return. There was one time when I posted Juli at the top of the rise to be your lookout. I was worried," she said simply, "you'd been gone for weeks!"

"And yet you kept my secret from Regan? I can't fathom it, Frau Holtz."

"*Ja* . . . I was proud of your daring feats. I cheered you behind closed doors as did most of the women in the Indies."

"I don't understand, I thought the women most of all wanted to see me drawn and quartered. Now you say you were proud of me. Why?"

"The van der Rhys family always treated me well, but before I came to them I've had my share of suffering at men's hands." Her eyes became stormy as they seemed to be looking into the distant past.

Pulling herself back to the present, Frau Holtz continued, "Every woman has, at one time or another, wanted to strike out at men for the injustices imposed on us. But Mevrouw, some day that will all change!" Frau Holtz said earnestly. "The Sea Siren was a forerunner of the woman of the future. Now do you understand why I'm proud of you?"

"I . . . I think so." Suddenly Sirena laughed and bent down to embrace the older woman. "You knew all the time," she marveled.

"*Ja,*" Frau Holtz smiled happily.

"Then that makes us compatriots of a sort, doesn't it?"

The housekeeper nodded, then asked: "Where do you go, Mevrouw, when you leave me off at one of the islands?"

"Back to Spain. There's nothing left for me here."

"And the child you carry?"

"You know that, too?"

"I've lived a long time, Mevrouw. There's little that I don't know. Besides," she smiled, "there's that look in your eyes. You're in your fourth month. Have you felt the babe quicken?"

"Yes. But I'll arrive in Spain before my time is due. I'm sorry that you won't be with me," Sirena said sincerely.

Frau Holtz stirred from the bunk and tried to smooth her dirt-smeared, singed gown. Placing a gentle hand on Sirena's shoulder, she said softly, "Your husband should be with you at this time."

Tears gathered in Sirena's eyes. "It cannot be." The housekeeper nodded dejectedly and muttered obscenities about stupid men.

"I think I'll rest a while. Please don't go on deck till Willem calls and says we've sailed clear of the noxious air."

"Very well, Mevrouw, I'll see if there isn't something I can do about tidying myself. Rest well."

Weary to the bone, Jan slumped over the wheel, his eyes burning with the thick sulphurous vapor. His chest was paining him unbearably and by the minute he was finding it more difficult to take a deep breath. When was Willem going to relieve him? Soon, he prayed, otherwise they would be tossing his lifeless body over the rail. He forced his eyes open and tried to stand erect, but the effort was too great and he found himself slipping . . . slipping into merciful oblivion. The wheel swung a full half circle and remained still as his heavy body slumped over, pinning it firmly to its base.

Below decks, Sirena slept while Frau Holtz, her tidying completed, lay back down to rest. Willem and the rest of the small crew stirred with the sudden lurching of the ship, thought little of it, and continued with what they were doing.

The frigate drifted for hours, miles off her course, leaving the cluster of evacuating ships behind. To the west of her stern a sleek galleon with an escort of two rode the churning, boiling waters. The frigate and her crew slept peacefully as the still thick yellow vapor began to dissipate.

Chaezar Alvarez held the glass to his eye, a satanic look on his face. He had known if he waited long enough he would find the frigate. At times it paid to be patient. From the looks of things there was no one aboard the small frigate, no one at her wheel, which was why she was drifting so aimlessly. With luck he could come up behind her and throw a grappling hook aboard and lash his bow to her stern.

Now that his personal victory was almost within his grasp, he could allow himself the luxury of relaxing. Regan was ruined! Port Batavia burned to ashes. Only the thick wall surrounding the city remained. The nutmeg trees were destroyed with no promise of more in the near future. He, and he alone, would command the entire nutmeg trade. He felt as if he, and he alone, had commanded The Sisters to erupt to further his plan. With an evil smile, he cast his eye at the frigate's stern to see if anything moved on the decks. Soon, within minutes, the Sea Siren would be his. His and his alone! He'd take her to the kingdom he prepared in Africa. He'd reign as supreme ruler with the beautiful Sea Siren as his queen.

He had known for months the true identity of the Sea Siren. Dick Blackheart, who had captained the attack upon the Córdez family, had come to him with the sorry tale of how the spirited Spanish girl had outwitted him and sent him and his men adrift in a jolly. It all fit in with the unlikely story Sirena and that brat she called her brother told of a storm at sea and her miraculous rescue by fishermen. At that point he had accepted her story just as everyone else on Java had. To do otherwise would have dangerously implicated him in the crime of piracy and murder aboard the Córdez's frigate.

Even after the Sea Siren launched her initial attack, he had no reason to suspect Sirena's duplicity. It could have been coincidental. But when he had Regan's figurehead of the Sea Siren stolen from the artisan who carved it, in order to smite Regan, he had naturally had a look at the carving: the likeness was unmistakable. That fool van der Rhys, who had aptly named the piratess Sea Siren, so close in sound and spelling to her actual name Sirena, appeared not to notice the resemblance between the figurehead and his wife. But Chaezar, with his sharp, appreciative eye for beauty, was certain of Sirena's dual identity.

Seeing Sirena raging against Gretchen, her eyes filled with fire, had held further proof. So many times he had been tempted to reveal his knowledge to her. How often he had thought her to be on the brink of telling him herself. The Sea Siren had made his position as head of the Spanish shipping trade most precarious. She had brought ruin on the Spanish fleet, had cost him a small fortune in personal business losses. Yet he had done nothing. He had played along with Regan and the others in their plans to capture her, knowing that they wouldn't.

Chaezar's sense of drama had been tittilated. He intended to play the game out to the end. His fortunes did not rest with the Spanish trading fleet, they rested elsewhere with casks of fertile nutmegs and a kingdom on the African coast.

Chaezar's eyes narrowed to a menacing glare when he thought of his fertile nutmegs. By the time he had discovered the twenty-four casks were missing he had other matters on his mind. Regan had been closing in on Gretchen and himself, discovering bit by bit that they were ultimately responsible for the death of his wife, the loss of his son, and the long, hard years he had spent in a Spanish prison. Chaezar had been unable to pursue the loss of his nutmegs when he had been so concerned about keeping one step ahead of Regan to save his life.

The night he had met Sirena in the garden he had come to take her away with him, to offer her the life of a queen, to save her from Regan! But the foolish woman hadn't even given him the chance to speak—sharp points of hatred had shot from her eyes. She had still been angry about the afternoon he had drugged her and taken her to his bed to sample her passionate charms. Then she had become defensive of Regan, telling Chaezar that her husband had sailed to the inner islands. Chaezar had expected to hear that Regan had gone again in pursuit of his son, but not quite so soon.

Chaezar had been frightened, he had grabbed for her. His intent was to force her to go with him. In her struggle, Sirena's sleeve had ripped, baring her arm to the moonlight. There before him had been the ultimate proof that his deductions concerning her dual identity were correct. He had seen the wound on her arm, the one Blackheart had told him about!

Sirena Córdez van der Rhys was the indomitable Sea Siren! Chaezar licked his lips, he was aware of a stirring in his loins. He wondered what it would be like to be dominated by the infamous piratess. He would have her wear the scanty costume she wore aboard her ship, she would be a magnifcent fantasy come to life as she wielded the whip!

The first grappling hook was thrown aboard the spectral, black frigate, and moments later it was lashed to the galleon and Chaezar's men were boarding her decks. When the last of his men climbed aboard, Chaezar followed. It was pointless to take unnecessary risks, he reasoned, one could never be too careful around the Sea Siren. Right this very minute, she could be watching for her chance to kill him. She could be hiding in some dark cranny of the ship waiting for him to show himself. When he was satisfied that his men had the situation in hand, he ordered the woman brought on deck.

Sirena looked blearily at the coarse man who grabbed her arm, yanking her from a sound sleep in her hard bunk. "My captain wants you on deck, now!" For a brief moment Sirena panicked, thinking herself back in time with Blackheart's scurvy crew.

"Take your filthy hands off me. Who are you? How did you get aboard this ship? Loose me, I say!" she cried shrilly. Her answer was to be dragged, half stumbling and half falling, up the ladder to stand on deck. "Chaezar! What are you doing here? What is this?"

"Would you like an embroidered lie or the plain, simple truth?" he asked gallantly as he made a low, swooping bow in her direction.

"Plain truth will serve for now," Sirena said bluntly.

"I plan to kill your crew and take you with me to my kingdom."

"And if I choose not to go, what then?"

"There is no choice. You will come with me, it's as simple as that."

"Never!" Sirena cried passionately. "I wouldn't cross the deck with you, let alone stand next to you."

"Then I shall force you to watch as your men are drawn and quartered, one after the other. When your decks are rivers of blood, you'll reconsider," he said cruelly.

Sirena blanched at the Spaniard's words. From the look in his eye he clearly meant what he said. Merciful God, help me, she prayed.

"Why must you kill my crew? What have they done to you?"

"It's not a question of them doing anything. I want no tales carried back to the islands. You might say I'm making my escape. Men with tongues will talk. I can't afford that in my position."

"You would kill as cold-bloodedly as that? What kind of evil man are you?"

"Am I so different from you, Sea Siren? You killed and reaped rewards for what you did. I'm merely doing the same."

"I never killed for the sake of killing," Sirena spat viciously. "Your thinking is warped, Chaezar. It is you who deserve to die, not these old harmless men. I'll strike a bargain with you. Let them go and I will go willingly with you. My word as the Sea Siren."

Chaezar groped for words. It would be better to

have her come with him willingly than to have to use force. "Your word that there will be no tricks?"

"My word."

"Very well, climb aboard my galleon. Bring nothing but yourself. Understood?" Sirena nodded, and was gracefully swinging herself aboard the galleon as Frau Holtz emerged from the stairs with a blunderbuss in her shaking hands and a frightened look on her face. In the blink of an eye the weapon was dashed against the tackle box and the woman stood, tears streaming down her ruddy cheeks, the point of the cutlass at her throat.

"Hold!" Sirena shouted. "She's my companion, leave her to come with me. I'm not asking you, Chaezar, I'm telling you."

"Very well . . . I've no stomach for killing old women. You may have your companion. Just remember that is one more favor for which you have me to thank. Order your men to remain silent of these doings or you will find this rapier coming out your back! *Comprende?*"

"Willem, you heard Señor Alvarez. You will do nothing to jeopardize his sailing. He has guaranteed me safe sailing, as well as Frau Holtz. You will do me one small favor perhaps." Willem nodded carefully, his eyes peering deeply into those of the woman across from him on the other ship. "See to it that the *Sea Siren* is repaired and her proper name restored to the bow. Be sure that my little brother receives her in good condition. Will you do that for me?"

"Aye, Capitana, I'll see that the boy gets the frigate." He raised his hand to his forehead and gave her a jaunty salute as he watched the heavy ropes being cut, separating the galleon from the *Sea Siren*.

Sirena turned to Frau Holtz, tears in her eyes. She clenched her teeth so as not to show any emotion before Chaezar.

Unable to contain herself, Frau Holtz screeched, "Heathen swine, dirty cutthroat pigs! Bastard at birth and bastard till the day of your death. The Lord should have you choke on your heathen tongue and swallow it."

"If you don't close your mouth, dear lady, it shall be you who chokes on your tongue."

Frau Holtz, her face as crimson as a passion fruit, closed her mouth into tight, grim lines. "May the devil carve your heart from your skinny body and hang it on his fork!" she muttered beneath her breath.

"Take the ladies below to their quarters and lock them in," Chaezar ordered brusquely. "It's time to change course and head for my new kingdom!"

Chapter Thirty-two

Regan's heart ached when he looked at the morose boy at his side. A hard, bitter look crossed his face and he smarted at the idea that a child so young should be experiencing such feelings. Words were of little comfort, he had discovered. Caleb had one thought and one thought only, and that was to find Sirena and bring her home.

"She goes too slow, Father. At this rate of speed we'll never find Sirena! There must be something you can do. Don't you know any shortcuts to save time? Sirena always said if one looked hard enough one could solve any problem. And we have a problem. What if we never find her?" he cried brokenly.

"I have no control over the winds, son," Regan replied patiently. "You must trust me."

"If Sirena doesn't want to be found then she won't. Not you, not the Spaniard, not even I will be able to find her," Caleb said dejectedly.

"I told you I'll sail these waterways till I find her, what more can I do?"

"Sirena is like a wounded animal now, she hurts inside, not just for herself but for the baby," Caleb said in a suddenly adult voice. "What if she's taken to land? She doesn't care anymore, that's why I'm so worried about her. She's given up, nothing matters to her. I saw the look in her eyes and I tell you, Father, she's not alive anymore, just a shell."

Caleb's words cut Regan. It was almost impossible for him to imagine the forceful Sea Siren and the compassionate, lovely woman he called his wife stripped of her vitality and determination. A shudder coursed through him as he turned his eyes to Caleb. No matter how brave his father's words, Caleb read fear in his cold, hard eyes.

A week passed, then two, and then three. Caleb was openly discouraged and antagonistic toward Regan. Regan, his nerves as tightly strung as the guitar Sirena had strummed, could only look with pity into the eyes of his son.

"Sail ho!" came the cry from the rigging. Caleb leaped to the rigging and climbed to the topmost sail, his eyes hopeful and alive for the first time in weeks.

Regan lowered the spyglass from his eyes, a thoughtful look on his face. It was the *Sea Siren* and she carried a Spanish flag atop her mast. To the naked eye she sailed as if she were heavy with cargo. Caleb's jubilant cry made him raise the glass again.

"It's the *Sea Siren,*" Caleb shrilled as he slid down the rigging. "It's Sirena, Father, it's Sirena!"

There was something wrong, Regan could feel it in his bones. He put a gentle hand on the boy's shoulder and tried to quiet him. His touch held no comfort. Caleb was off and running to the stern, his hands shielding his eyes.

"I see Jacobus and Willem. Sirena isn't on deck, she must be in her cabin," he cried excitedly.

Even at this distance Regan could see the grim lines on the faces of the two men on deck. He was right, there was something wrong!

"Ho! *Sea Siren,*" he called loudly. "Call your captain to the decks."

"This ship carries no captain," Willem called harshly. "What is it you want? We carry no cargo."

"What happened to your captain? I speak of the Sea Siren, if you lie to me I'll carve your tongue from your mouth."

"Willem, Jacobus, it is I, Caleb. Where is Sirena? Answer my father, he means her no harm."

"Ay, boy, if I could make our capitana stand before you I would. She is no longer aboard. The bastard Spanish devil, Alvarez, attacked our ship shortly after the Sisters erupted. He took her prisoner, along with a woman we rescued from the wharf at Port Batavia. Her name was Frau Holtz. Our capitana made a last request as she left the ship. She entrusted the crew to bring the ship to port and to have her repainted and hoist a white sail. She was to be turned over to her little brother. We gave our promise. We could do no less as she saved our lives. The Spaniard was bent on killing every man aboard. She said she would go with him if he let us go free to bring the ship to port. There was no way we could fight. We were outmaneuvered and outmanned. The Spaniard's ships were heavily armed and he had an escort of two."

"Where did he take her, Willem?" Caleb called shrilly.

"If I knew I would have sailed after the stinking bastard," Willem said viciously as he spat in the water. "My guess would be Spain, but I'm not sure. I heard one of his crew mutter something about there being no welcome for him there, so it's possible he heads in another direction. I wish there were more I could tell you, young Caleb. Unfortunately, we weren't within earshot for long, the Spaniard took her aboard and immediately set sail. I didn't think he would keep his promise to let us sail free, at any moment I expected a good broadside to this frigate."

"How . . . how was . . . Sirena, Willem?"

"She was . . . ill. The woman will look after her. There's nothing more I can tell you. With your permission, Captain, we'll continue with our journey to the cove where the *Sea Siren* is to be careened and repainted. When you next see her, lad, she'll carry her true name. She's yours now, with the wishes of the Sea Siren." With a low, flourishing bow, Willem made his way to the wheel to relieve Jacobus and to continue his mission.

Tears of frustration pricked the boy's eyes as he gazed upon his father. "Even at the last she thought of me. Now do you see why I must find her? Tell me,

Father, what captain do you know who would do as Sirena did to protect her men? Not one, I'll wager," he cried hoarsely, his young voice rising and falling shrilly. "Not one. Each would only want to save his own skin at the expense of the others. I told you, Sirena is like no other. She made a promise and she kept it."

Something strange and sad fluttered in Regan's chest as he stood at the rail. The boy was right. There wasn't one man in his employ who would have given of himself to let another go free. The sun-bronzed hands gripped the rail he leaned on, a new determination coursed through him. "And I," he said quietly and with deadly calm, "will find your . . . sister. I may be many things in your eyes, young Caleb, but this I implore you to believe. I'll find her, for you and for myself."

Caleb looked at the tortured face opposite him. Gently, he lay a darkened hand on his father's arm. "We'll find her . . . together."

"You must stir yourself, Mevrouw, it's been weeks since you last walked on deck. You must have fresh air and move your muscles. Laying abed won't do you or the baby any good. I beg you, Mevrouw, come on deck with me. The winds are brisk and the spindrift is lovely."

"I can't bear to look upon that devil Alvarez. I'll want to kill him with my bare hands. If there were only some way that I could . . ."

"There is no way. You must also get that notion from your head. Day and night there are two guards outside this door. The Spaniard knows you couldn't fight in your condition."

"In my condition! I'd fight the Devil himself in my condition if I thought it would do me any good. You're right, Frau Holtz, it's useless to even dream I could overpower the bastard. However," she said viciously, "I won't always be in this condition."

"Mevrouw, at that time you will have an extra burden, one you do not have now, the babe."

"Ah yes, the babe. You'll care for the babe while I

carve the manhood from the Spaniard's body," Sirena said conversationally.

Frau Holtz's eyes protruded at her calm words. There was no doubt in her mind that Sirena would do exactly what she said she would.

"I think you're right, Frau Holtz, a brisk walk on the deck would do me wonders. Shall we go?" she asked, getting up from the hard bunk.

The two women strolled along the wide decks, the brisk trade winds ruffling Sirena's hair, bringing a glow to her pale cheeks. "It's been too long." Sirena sighed as she stopped to peer over the rail. The clear, azure waters brought a lump to her throat. A small school of fish swam beneath the surface—how effortlessly they moved beneath the sparkling water. Heaving a sigh, she stirred herself and moved from the rail to rejoin Frau Holtz.

"So, you decided to join the living," Chaezar said urbanely as he leaped to their side agilely. "Perhaps I'll join you, it's a beautiful day."

"If you so much as take one more step," Sirena said, stopping in midstride, "then I shall go below. I don't want your company now, or at any time. If you must walk, then walk alone. I warn you, Chaezar, stay out of my sight."

"Very well, Sirena, I've no wish to force myself upon you."

"It's well you've learned your lesson. The last time was a freak circumstance." Angrily, she turned on the Spaniard. "You drugged me, in my heart it was Regan no matter what you want to believe."

"I'm a patient man. I map every detail before I make a move. Bear that in mind. When next you sleep with me the only drug in your veins will be passion and desire." With a slight nod of his head he backed off a step, and Sirena, seething inwardly, continued her stroll along the deck.

Sirena looked at Frau Holtz, despair in her eyes. "It was all I could do to keep my hands still. I wanted to choke the life from his body and watch his face turn blue."

Her quiet voice sent a chill through the housekeeper as she laid an arm around the girl's trembling shoulders. She spoke soothingly of the warm weather and the sultry breeze, hoping to take Sirena's mind off the brief encounter with the Spaniard.

Chaezar impatiently paced the close confinement of his cabin. The child she carried within her was his! He knew it in his heart. Why did she persist in saying it was Regan's? He knew the marriage was never consummated. Even Regan would never go back on his word. How could he have reneged on her period of mourning? No, the child was his. Still, if it made her happy to think of it as Regan's, if fooling herself kept her oontent, let her. She would be due for a rude awakening when the baby arrived. The child would be olive-skinned with dark, glossy hair. What more proof could a man want? There was no way she could deliver a golden-haired, blue-eyed baby, of that he was certain.

It was two months since Regan sighted the frigate, *Sea Siren*. Since that time, he had questioned every ship he encountered. There wasn't one that had seen the Spaniard. Despair would have engulfed him time and time again were it not for Caleb. Each time he let his shoulders slump or his eyes grow weary, the boy was there to bolster him, A strength which knew no bounds surged in Caleb's slim, youthful body.

"I think I'll weigh anchor at the next port and add fresh provisions. Perhaps we can learn news from some of the merchants."

"I'm sure we'll find something we want to hear. I feel good today," Caleb said jauntily.

A pall of gloom settled over Regan as he made his way back to his cabin, a dejected Caleb trailing in his wake. It was almost as if the ocean had opened up and swallowed Sirena.

One weary day followed another as the ship continued her journey to Spain. Caleb became fretful and openly defiant and constantly apologized for his behavior. Regan was fast becoming a man obsessed with the thought that the Sea Siren was dead. There was no other explanation. Two more days, he told himself wearily, and he would dock at Alvarez's home port.

"The Spaniard told me this morning that we are near land. By sundown," Frau Holtz said grimly.

"It's just as well, Frau Holtz. My time is almost here. I want a fresh bed and a soft pillow for my head. Where is this place we are landing, do you know?"

"I know as much as you, Mevrouw, the northwest coast of Africa."

Suddenly Sirena grasped the old housekeeper's hand. "Have I told you how grateful I am that you're here with me, Frau Holtz? I don't know what I would have done without you. I'll never be able to repay you."

"I want no payment." The women clasped hands and the housekeeper was the first to disentangle herself. "I must gather together the few belongings we have and be ready when Señor Alvarez gives the order to disembark."

"I think I'll lie down for a while, my head pounds with the thought that I'll be forced to live in the same house with that bastard Alvarez and that my child will be born under his roof."

Frau Holtz clenched her teeth. If there were only something she could do, but what? She was an old woman and old women were useless. Would the Spaniard guard her as he had done these past months aboard his ship? Nodding morosely, she thought he would take no chances that the woman called Sea Siren might escape him. Where was Mynheer van der Rhys now? Would he search for his wife or would he think she had died when the Sisters erupted?

Her small tasks completed, Frau Holtz sat down on a hard chair to await the Spaniard's orders to disembark. From time to time, she dozed off only to be jerked awake by some loud noise on deck or some slight stirring Sirena made in her cramped bunk.

A hard rapping on the door startled her. Still, she heaved a sigh of relief. It would be good to see trees and houses and have solid ground beneath her feet again.

Gently, Frau Holtz helped Sirena to her feet. She moved clumsily, her added weight a burden as she climbed the ladder with Frau Holtz's help.

The two women stood on deck as the galleon glided effortlessly into her slip at the wharf.

So, Sirena thought, this is to be my temporary home. There was no doubt in her mind that the word temporary meant just that.

Caleb and Regan disembarked onto the busy dock in Barcelona, Spain. Leaving orders with his crew to lay in stores, Regan immediately asked directions to the harbor master's offices.

Caleb watched his father's jaw tighten and his eyes narrow expectantly. He knew Regan believed he was close to his goal of finding Sirena and the scoundrel Chaezar. Not many nights ago, at the ship's wheel, Regan had confided to his son: "Sometimes Caleb, I feel as if that bastard is so close I can smell his greasy hair oil and garlic breath!" It was merely wishful thinking, Caleb realized. Somehow the boy felt that Sirena was no closer to him than she had been when they left Java.

The dignified harbor master extended every hospitality to Regan and Caleb. It was an honor to receive the Dutchman who, if rumor was correct, had a very good chance of being named governor of Java —a post the Burghers of Holland had deemed necessary. During the leisurely midday meal which they were invited to share, Regan adhered to Spanish protocol and refrained from discussing business. It was over steaming cups of coffee that Regan broached the subject of Don Chaezar Alvarez.

Disbelief darkened Regan's features at his host's response. "You're sure of your facts, Señor? It isn't that I don't believe you, it's just that Alvarez painted such a glowing picture of his superiors' opinion of him here in Spain that I doubted he could ever fall out of favor. Now you tell me there's a price on his head and that for years he's been smuggling unlimed nutmegs to some far-off place where he's going to retire and reign like a king."

"It is sad but true, Mynheer van der Rhys. We've only discovered this recently, and allowed him to stay on in the Indies till another of our men was properly trained. If he hadn't taken matters into his own hands he would have been relieved of his duties one month from today."

"Your new man will have his work cut out for him," Regan sympathized. Briefly, he told the aging Spaniard of the devastation the Sisters had brought to port Batavia.

"Via con Dios, Mynheer. The most encouragement I can offer you at this time is purely speculation. The African coast is the only place Alvarez could hope to plant his unlimed nutmegs. If you have no success, then it would be wise to forget the matter for the time being. Alvarez will eventually poke his head out, much the way a turtle does. And when he does, you'll be standing by with a stick."

"Thank you for all your help, Señor, but I can't give up now!"

Back aboard ship, Regan cursed himself a fool a thousand times. Why hadn't he thought of the African coast? Even if he had to search the entire length of Africa he would find Sirena.

"What do you think, Father?" Caleb asked excitedly.

"I think the old harbor master was right. Alvarez has gone to Africa. If only I had thought of it, we could have saved ourselves months at sea. Soon, I'll feel that skinny bastard's neck beneath my fingers," he said, flexing his sun-darkened hands.

"Soon, Father, soon we'll have Sirena back with us."

"Yes," Regan answered, his thoughts spinning to Sirena. Could it have been almost nine months since that night aboard the spectral, black frigate when he had fulfilled both his obsessions: the possession of the Sea Siren and the consummation of his marriage.

Chapter Thirty-three

Frau Holtz lay in her bed listening to the soft moans that came from the bed adjoining hers. She decided she would pretend to be sleeping until her Mevrouw called for her. Sirena would prefer to be alone with her pain for as long as possible. Instinctively, the German housekeeper knew this and would defer to Sirena's wishes.

Frau Holtz was, for the first time in many years, frustrated by her helplessness. Not having had a child of her own or even attended at a birth, she was uncertain and unsure of her ability to help Sirena. Preparing for this moment, the housekeeper had inquired of Chaezar's staff and had located a midwife. The woman on which Sirena must depend to see her through the birth was far from the fastidious housekeeper's liking. Ebony-black, old and cronelike with a shocking gray mane of wiry hair, the woman appeared stupid and slow and exceedingly dirty. Even her name was unpronounceable; it sounded to her Germanic ears like Tsuna Muub. Whatever, the Mevrouw needed her and hers was the only knowledgeable assistance available.

The only fact Frau Holtz was certain of was that the baby would be healthy and strong. Hadn't she seen to it herself that Sirena ate properly, hadn't she insisted Sirena take daily walks to keep fit? Since coming to this godforsaken hole in the universe, she had made Sirena sit outdoors in the shade of the trees. The fresh air had been a boon to the pale-faced Sirena, and despite her constant objections, she had thrived under Frau Holtz's relentless care.

The moans were increasing and Frau Holtz sensed a struggle in the next bed. Quietly, she got up and slipped downstairs to the vast kitchen. She roused the shiny, black cook and through sign language was able to convey that the midwife Tsuna Muub was needed. The ebony-faced cook smiled her understanding and roused her sleeping husband to fetch the skinny, crone-like midwife. Without being told, the cook set to work heating water in her heavy kettles, humming a strange, toneless melody in her deep, throaty voice. Believing her message understood, Frau Holtz returned to Sirena, stopping only to take a fresh pile of clean bedding from the chest in the linen room.

"Frau Holtz, I'm so glad you're awake. I didn't want to disturb you, but I think my time has come," Sirena gasped, her hands grasping her swollen middle. Perspiring from the heat and exertion, she wiped her forehead with the back of her hand as the pain subsided, a trembling yet brave smile on her face.

"I've sent for that witch, Tsuna Muub, God help us."

Sirena laughed. Poor Frau Holtz, how she hated to admit she needed anyone's assistance, least of all a black-as-night, emaciated African's. And the way she pronounced the old woman's name!

A few moments later, the door swung open and Tsuna Muub stepped across the threshold authoritatively, her yellow-rimmed black eyes darting around the room evaluating the situation. Frau Holtz stood near Sirena, as if to protect her from the old woman, whose appearance did nothing to instill confidence. Her skinny, almost skeletal form was draped with evil-looking trinkets and what appeared to be human teeth and bird feathers. Tsuna Muub padded to the bed on bare feet and faced Frau Holtz defiantly, daring the German to keep her from her patient.

With a grim face and low, disapproving grunt, Frau Holtz stepped aside. Another contraction squeezed a grunt of pain from between Sirena's clenched teeth. Alarmed and feeling useless, Frau Holtz stepped aside.

Tsuna Muub threw back the light sheet covering Sirena and expertly placed her hands over her protruding belly, pressing and feeling. Speaking in what Frau Holtz called gibberish and through signs, the old midwife told Sirena it would be a long while before the child was born. Then Tsuna Muub, with surprising strength, pulled Sirena into a sitting position and mumbling insisted Sirena get to her feet.

Frau Holtz, her maternal protectiveness overwhelming her, began to protest in emphatic German. Tsuna Muub, proud of her craft, argued back in her own dialect. Sirena practically had to prevent the two women from strangling each other.

"Frau Holtz, Tsuna Muub! Stop this at once!" Still they persisted in their argument. Only with the onset of another contraction during which Sirena clutched the bedpost did the women direct their attention to her.

Tsuna Muub rushed to Sirena's side and, taking her arm, led her at a quick, shuffling pace back and forth across the room. The contraction eased more quickly this time and Sirena smiled her relief. "I think the old witch just may know her business after all; that pain was stronger than the others and yet it was easier to bear. My legs didn't cramp up and it subsided more quickly." Frau Holtz's glance rested on Tsuna Muub, and while it wasn't friendly or even approving, there was a kind of relief behind it and perhaps a glimmer of respect.

Through the long hours before dawn, Sirena walked miles back and forth across the carpeted floor, the last hour leaning heavily on Frau Holtz's arm.

The German woman's hair was escaping the long braid which hung down her back, her nightdress and wrapper were damp with perspiration, and worry and fear crept from her eyes. Tsuna Muub, after raising the foot of the bed on two stacks of books and changing the bedding, had ensconced herself on Frau Holtz's bed and directed the pace Sirena must keep during her labor pains. Between contractions she allowed Sirena to sit on a hard straight-backed chair to renew her strength for the next pain. Every so often she would break into a low chanting, a satisfied expression that bordered on smugness playing about her thin-lipped, toothless mouth.

Even when Sirena protested she couldn't walk another step, Tsuna Muub insisted, her hard, surprisingly strong hands prodding Sirena to her feet.

Once, when her protests overcame the spindly native, Sirena lay down on her bed in exhaustion, with Frau Holtz mopping her brow in tender sympathy. Another labor pain seized her in a grip of unrelenting agony. As soon as she was able, Sirena struggled to her feet breathlessly explaining to Frau Holtz that as much as she hated to admit it, Tsuna Muub was right. Walking did help.

Half an hour later, when the pains were coming hard and fast, Tsuna Muub motioned to Sirena that it was time to take to her bed. The midwife's wizened little monkey face bent close to Sirena and her hands pressed low on Sirena's abdomen. Issuing a knowing grunt, she began to prepare Sirena for the birthing.

Frau Holtz leaned close and whispered to Sirena as if Tsuna Muub could understand her. "Mevrouw, if you want I could ask Señor Alvarez for some laudanum. Just a drop or two if the pain becomes unbearable."

"No!" Sirena exclaimed, grasping the Frau's strong wrist, "I'd die before I asked him for anything! Under no circumstances are you even to consider it. Promise me!"

It was the most difficult promise Frau Holtz ever made. Each pain Sirena suffered the Frau suffered; she shared each long moment of anxiety with the mistress she had come to love. "*Ja,* I promise, Mevrouw."

Tsuna Muub had busied herself by tearing a strip of sheeting and twisting it into a thick rope. Quickly, she slipped it over the top bedpost and tied the ends in a thick, bulky knot. She then demonstrated the use of the rope to Sirena. When a pain began, Sirena was to take a deep breath and pull herself upward to the top of the bed. Then she was to release her breath in quick, light pants.

"Like a dog, Mevrouw," Frau Holtz said incredulously, "the witch wants you to behave like a dog!"

"And they never seem to have as many problems giving birth as we humans. I'll try her method, she was right about walking," Sirena said, perspiration wetting her cheeks. "Frau Holtz, my friend, if you see I'm about to scream will you place your hand over my mouth? Please! So far Chaezar doesn't seem to know what's happening. I don't want him to know. Promise me, a woman's promise to another woman," she gasped as a pain gripped her and she pulled on the rope.

Sirena lay gasping, consciously trying to follow Tsuna Muub's instructions. Her thoughts whirled in her head. What if she should die? What would become of the child? What if the baby died? How could she go on without Regan's child to hold and love, to give her a reason to live?

A small bird-like cry escaped Sirena as her frightened, anguished eyes sought those of Frau Holtz. "Remember your promise to me. That was the worst so far," she said, using both hands to grasp the rope to her. With all her strength she pulled, trying to move her heavy body to the top of the slanted bed. Her teeth were clenched, her hair was wet and shiny with sweat. "God help me," she groaned.

Tsuna Muub began to lift Sirena's nightdress. "You'll not touch her with those filthy hands!" Frau Holtz snapped harshly, slapping the black woman's hands away from her mistress. Not understanding, Tsuna Muub again reached for Sirena, and again the German slapped her hands away. Having little patience remaining and fraught with worry, Frau Holtz pulled the spidery little woman to the washstand and motioned to her to wash her hands.

Tsuna Muub acquiesced, realizing she must placate this nervous, bossy woman if she were to get about her business. Frau Holtz handed her a bar of fragrant soap and Tsuna Muub took such delight in its creamy texture and heady scent it seemed she would never stop and the baby would birth itself. Frustrated, Frau Holtz watched Tsuna Muub stop once more to sniff the fragrant lather. The scrawny native then motioned for Frau Holtz to bring water from the kitchen. Hesitant to leave Sirena alone with the crone, the Frau left, realizing the only way to get the water to the room was to go fetch it herself.

When she returned carrying a heavy cauldron of water, Tsuna Muub was prancing about the room, shaking her amulets and chanting. Sirena was pulling on the rope of sheeting, her eyes rolled back in her head.

Suddenly Tsuna Muub stopped her chanting and rushed to Sirena's side, taking the rope from her and indicating she was to push. Sirena needed no instruction, nature was her teacher. Low in her back a curl of pain began, and her body responded to an ancient, instinctive response. With a low, animal grunt she began to bear down, down, down, her body arching and pushing with a will of its own. She bit her tongue, she tasted blood. God in Heaven, would she ever be able to unclench her hands? Then, blessedly, the pain was gone and she was aware of Frau Holtz's gurgle of laughter as she held aloft a tiny red baby emitting a lusty yowl.

"A boy, Mevrouw. A golden-haired boy!"

A smile on her lips, Sirena watched the Frau bathe her son with gentle, adoring hands. Her last conscious thought was, now Caleb has a brother.

Chapter Thirty-four

Daintily, Chaezar dabbed at his mouth. His narrowed eyes raked his lavishly appointed dining room and a smug look crept into them. It was his and his alone. If Sirena chose to share it with him then it would be theirs. Slowly, he lowered his eyes to the gold-crested plate resting before him. A slight smile tugged at the corners of his mouth. Gold plates were something he had promised himself for many years. When he had the merchants dine with him they would be impressed with his apparent wealth. When they saw how huge his nutmeg plantation was, they would be even more impressed and hasten to make him the supreme ruler of the coast. With Sirena to grace his drawing room and sit at the foot of his table, there was no way these peasants could refute his authority and his dominance. He would be the supreme ruler. Some of his nutmeg trees were four years old. Another few years and he would safely control the entire trade in this commodity.

His actions were slow and deliberate as he folded the napkin in a precise triangle. Carefully, he lined it up with the knife at the side of his plate. He took one last sip from the gold-rimmed goblet at his side and then centered it in the middle of the gold-crested plate. There was no use prolonging the moment. It was time to see the new addition to his household. He had deliberately let days go by so that Sirena could regain a little of her strength. He had refrained from asking for a description of the babe. In his heart he knew the child would have a wealth of dark hair and olive skin. He had feigned indifference till he thought he would choke on his own saliva. Now he would confirm his belief.

Gracefully he slid back the high-backed cane chair from the lace-covered table. He stood a moment to look once more at the perfectly appointed table. Satisfied, he strode from the room, a fragrant cigar in his hand.

The door of Sirena's room was slightly ajar. He stopped short, his hand poised to knock. Frau Holtz, in the process of crossing the room, noticed his form in the doorway and quickly walked over to the slight opening and peered out. "What is it you want, Señor?"

"I wish to look upon the new addition to my household. Be so good as to open the door."

"The Mevrouw is resting now, Señor."

"It is not the Señora I wish to see but the babe. In the future, you will address her as the Señora and not the Mevrouw. I find the term offensive to my ear."

Frau Holtz inclined her head a fraction and opened the door wide for him to enter. "The babe lays near the window," she said harshly.

Chaezar hesitated a moment, then slowly walked to the cradle which held the new babe. All he could see was a mound of bunting. He was about to bend over for a closer look, when Frau Holtz pounced on the cradle and literally scooped the small bundle into her arms. A smile on her face, she peeled back a layer of bunting to expose a small pink face crowned with a mass of golden fuzz. Slyly, she watched as hatred danced in the Spaniard's eyes. The black pools were murderous as he nodded his head for the housekeeper to replace the baby in its cradle.

"A fine specimen, wouldn't you say, Señor? The babe will be robust and healthy. He thrives by the day, giving his mother much happiness. It is a pity the father isn't here to share her joy," Frau Holtz said craftily.

Gathering his wits together, Chaezar merely nodded and hurriedly left the room. Outside in the dim corridor, he let his eyes fall to the mangled cigar he held clenched in his hand. He let it fall to the tile floor and slowly ground it beneath his booted foot till the fragrant tobacco was nothing more than a mass of pulp. It was such a tiny head, one good stomp and all that shimmering golden fuzz would resemble the tobacco at his feet.

So he had been misinformed. Regan *had* bedded his wife. Perhaps the situation was not lost yet. If Regan were to be informed that he held not only his wife but his new son in captivity, he would come here and then he would have his final revenge on the man he had hated all these years. If necessary, he would make him watch as he took his wife right under his eyes and then make him watch along with Sirena as he killed the golden-haired bundle that lay in the cradle. He had to be the victor! Too long he had come out second to Regan. Not this time! Not ever again! He must find a way to send a message back to Port Batavia even if he had to send a fully-manned cargoless ship.

Casting a last hateful look at the tobacco at his feet, he pulled a fresh cigar from his waistcoat and, without a backward glance, left the corridor for his offices.

"Mevrouw, the Señor finally came to look upon the babe while you rested," Frau Holtz said, a smile on her wide mouth.

"And what did the Señor have to say about my robust son?" Sirena asked.

"He said nothing. His eyes held murder, your son's murder, if we don't guard him day and night. Never have I seen such hatred in a living person. He will do something that only God will know. He's a vengeful, hateful person, Mevrouw."

"I've known that for many months. You're right, Frau Holtz, he was expecting to see a dark-haired baby. We must guard the little one with our lives."

"Listen to those lusty bellows, your son wishes to eat again."

Sirena smiled at the baby's cries. His lungs were magnificent, one could almost believe he was heard all over the house.

Day after day, Sirena nursed the baby and then would rest, Frau Holtz always at her side. Wearily, Sirena would move and stir herself at the old housekeeper's prodding. She knew the woman was right, it was just that everything was becoming too much of an effort. Dread seemed to enter through every pore in her body. She had a particular horror of the visits Chaezar made to the small nursery. He would come many times and stand looking down at the small bundle, sometimes with hatred in his eyes and sometimes with no expression at all. Sirena feared the blank unreadable looks the most. She felt he plotted her son's death and her own. If only he would say something, anything was better than those moments when he entered unannounced and sent fear scurrying through her body, not for herself but for the small son she loved.

One brightly sunlit day, Sirena had just finished nursing the baby and was about to place him back in his cradle for a nap. She looked up to notice Chaezar leaning against the door frame, his eyes thoughtful as he watched Sirena remove the baby from her breast and arrange her wrapper before getting up to place the baby in its cradle.

"I have been inquiring for a wet nurse for you," he said urbanely.

"You what?" Sirena's tone held outrage.

"A wet nurse," he repeated. "You are fast resembling a sow and I find the sight offensive to my eyes. As soon as a suitable nurse is found you will turn the child over to her." The emerald eyes glittered dangerously but Sirena said nothing. "The reason I'm having a wet nurse for you is that it's now time for you to take on the duties for which I brought you here."

"And what are these . . . duties?" Sirena asked coldly.

"You will act as my hostess and be a charming wife. Everyone believes you are my wife. It wouldn't pay to dispute my words. It's two months since the birth of the babe, and time to wean him from your breast. You'll have much to occupy you without some squawling brat to worry about. Besides, I don't wish to see all the lovely gowns I purchased for you destroyed by dripping mother's milk."

"And if I refuse your . . . offer of a wet nurse, what then?"

"Then, dear lady, there will simply be no babe for you to worry about at all. It would be wise if you did as I suggested. Lately, I find that I have little . . . patience," he said, smiling cruelly.

"You have the audacity to hold me prisoner, tell your friends that I'm your wife—and that this is your son, no doubt—and you want me to act the loving wife. Your stupidity amazes me, Chaezar. I would kill you in a moment if I could. How do you expect me to carry on this farce?"

"My dear, something brilliant will occur to you, of that I'm sure. After all, we do have the child's best interest at heart, don't we?"

"You are a bastard pig, son of a whore!"

"And, dear lady, what does that make you?" A lecherous smile lit his face as he gazed at her protruding breasts. "The wife of a bastard pig, son of a whore. How would you ever prove differently?"

"As long as I know that I'm not your wife that will suffice for me. There is no way in this whole world you could ever make me your wife."

"As I said, I'm a patient man. With the health of your . . . son at stake, I think we both understand each other. Tonight there will be an intimate dinner for a dozen people. One of the servants will bring you a gown and appropriate jewels. Afterwards, I expect you to behave like a wife should.

"Dinner will be served at sundown. I wish you downstairs a good hour before. We shall toast your son's health with a glass of wine. Until then, my dear," he said, his eyes opaque in the dim afternoon glow.

"Frau Holtz, Frau Holtz, did you hear that? Did you hear what he has ordered me to do? Sow! And he wants to bed me tonight after his dinner. What am I to do?" she wailed. "If I don't do as he says one of his murderous guards will surely kill the little one. And you too, Frau Holtz. There's no choice open to me, is there?" At the compassionate look on the housekeeper's face, Sirena nodded. "I thought so," she murmured, "I swore to myself a long time ago that I'd never again be used by anyone. I meant it then and I mean it now. I won't crawl into his bed like some yearning whore. I won't do it!"

"But the—"

"I'll think of something. I still have several hours left. I'll think of something," Sirena said confidently.

Even from aboard ship Regan and Caleb could see the layout of the harbor town. The slips at the wharf were new and numerous, the raw unweathered wood bespoke the port's recent burgeoning. It was said that all the harbors along Africa's coast were undergoing this surge in trade. Unlike the sophisticated harbors of Europe and the Indies, the African ports were crude and rustic.

The commerce here was not spices and silk and foodstuffs, but a new resource that filled the merchant's pockets. It was called black gold or black ivory, but both terms meant the same thing: the African slave trade. The dirtiest, most sordid and obscene cargo ever carried in a ship's hold. Slaves.

Regan jumped to land, Caleb behind him. As their feet touched the dock, a jumble of small children ran to them laughing happily. Regan squatted and gathered a dark-eyed, black-skinned little boy to him. He spoke slowly and through gestures asked his questions. The child smiled shyly and grasped Regan's hand and took him along the planked walkway that led into one of the buildings. Shyly, he pointed out a white-haired man and then ran laughing from the building, the other children close behind.

Quickly, Regan explained his wants and the old man nodded. "There is one such as you speak of. I myself have not met the man, but he resides at the southern end of town. He has built a magnificent house and they say he is wealthy beyond anyone's dreams. He brought a wife and son with him. I have heard just this morning that this evening is to be his first entertainment. It's said he's sort of king and she is his queen. I fear," the old man said gently, "that I do not understand such talk. To introduce her to our people is one thing, but to proclaim oneself king and queen is beyond my comprehension."

"How do I arrive at the . . . king's house?"

"It would be best if you went by horse. I can allow you the use of two of mine if you return them to me. Ride to the clearing and follow the trail to the very edge of the jungle. There you will see a walkway carved through the dense foliage. Follow that till you again come to a clearing and there you shall see a mansion beyond your wildest dreams. That is the home of the man you seek, the one who calls himself a king."

Regan thanked the elderly gentleman and climbed astride the beast he was shown. Caleb followed suit, his eyes glassy in anticipation.

"Does this mean it is the end of the journey, Father? The man he spoke of is Señor Alvarez, is he not?"

"No one, save Alvarez, would appoint himself a king," Regan said coldly.

"Then he must mean Sirena is his queen," Caleb cried jubilantly.

"A more unwilling queen I could not imagine," Regan replied harshly as he spurred the horse beneath him. Now that he was so close he didn't want to waste even one second. Caleb found it hard to keep his seat on the massive beast beneath him. His head reeled giddily as he held onto the reins.

Within an hour, Regan reined in the horse and sat looking at the three-tiered house in front of him. The old man was right, it was a house fit for a king. Was it best to march to the front door or wait for cover of darkness and then stampede the dinner party? He looked at the shining eyes of the boy opposite him and slid from the horse.

No sooner did his feet touch ground then he was pinned by strong black arms. He looked up to see hard black faces peering down at him. A look to the left was all he needed to know that Caleb was in the same predicament. So, the bastard was afraid he might turn up on his doorstep; otherwise, why the guards? What was he protecting? His newly found queen and son? Then the son would be a prince. Regan forced the laughter back in his throat as he strained to free himself from the powerful arms that held him prisoner. Seeing that it was a useless effort, he relaxed and told the boy to do the same. They were literally dragged by the giant men to the rear of the house, where one of Caleb's captors picked up a heavy hammer and hit a stinging blow to a round metal shield hanging from a tree. Within seconds, Alvarez was framed in the doorway, an evil smile on his face.

"So! You have decided to pay my little kingdom a visit. I must say, Regan, you have the manners of a barbarian. A gentleman never comes uninvited." He clucked his tongue in disapproval.

"Your manners make me want to retch, you fop," Regan said acidly. "I've come for my wife! Or should I say your queen?" Suddenly he laughed. A sound that set Chaezar's teeth on edge. "Did Sirena willingly become your queen or did you . . .?"

"Or did I what, you crude lout? I only had to make her the offer and she all but fell at my feet. Why are we standing here, come inside and let me show you how a gentleman of breeding presides over a kingdom. You do know how to behave indoors, don't you?" Chaezar asked caustically.

"I can hardly spill your blood all over your carpets when I'm hampered as I am. Have no fear, Chaezar,

I won't stink up your . . . kingdom." Again he laughed, a cruel mocking laugh that made Chaezar uneasy.

Chaezar turned aside and spoke quickly and softly to one of the servants waiting in attendance.

Sirena finished dressing, a grim look on her face. With a grim warning to Frau Holtz, she had her hand poised to open the door when two servants entered the room. One of them thrust Sirena aside and immediately rushed to the cradle and deftly picked up the small bundle in one hand. With a wild screech of rage Sirena was on him, digging her nails down his bare back with Frau Holtz attacking him from the front. The second guard rushed to help the first and threw Sirena across the room, where she lay stunned with the force of the impact. Frau Holtz was gouging and kicking the guard who held the baby and screaming at the top of her lungs. Effortlessly, he shoved her aside and she landed in a heap next to Sirena, the breath knocked from her body. Sirena was on her knees, shaking her head trying to clear it when the door closed behind the men.

Rage and fury like nothing she had ever experienced before ripped through her as she stood and tried to calm her trembling, shaking body. She would kill the bastard with her bare hands if she had to. Swaying dizzily, she helped Frau Holtz to her feet and raced from the room and down the long, dim corridor. Where would they have taken the baby? To the first-floor level and Chaezar's study, or to the kitchens. She half fell and half ran down the winding stairway and arrived at the bottom panting for air. The sight that met her eyes was one she never expected to see. Regan and Caleb held prisoner by four black giants. Her eyes raked the room and came to rest on the guard who held her son in one arm.

Breathing raggedly, she shouted, "Return my baby to me, this instant!"

"Go back to your room unless you want to be a witness to the murder of your husband and your son," Chaezar said coldly.

At the cruel words, Sirena backed up a step out of Chaezar's reach and let her eyes go to Regan's. God in

Heaven, what was that look in his eye? Murder, rage, despair, and . . . was it love? Swaying with her new knowledge, she then looked at Caleb. She smiled at the boy and spoke softly, "So, little brother, you could not let me go to my homeland without you. I'm sorry that you find me in such a strange house with such a strange man." Her tone was purposely light and gentle as she moved a step closer to the breakfront behind Chaezar. She flicked her eyes to Regan and noted the slight nod. She sidled up to Chaezar and said in a soothing voice, "I'm his queen, did you know that, Regan? Chaezar appointed me his queen. I was to assume my duties today. Tonight at dinner, as a matter of fact. What does this mean, Chaezar, is the dinner party canceled?"

Chaezar frowned at this strange conversation. Why hadn't the guard returned her to her room? Now he had to make a choice. She was in the way.

"I have to kill Regan and that snotty-nosed brat of his. And then the baby. I find that I won't be able to live in my new kingdom with ghostly reminders of Regan. Guard, remove the blankets from the babe. Let van der Rhys gaze upon the child."

Regan struggled to free himself but found that with each movement the hold on him became tighter.

Sirena watched his agate eyes widen in incredulous shock at the realization that Sirena could never have birthed this fair-skinned baby if the father had been dark and swarthy like Chaezar. What he had hoped for had come true, the child was his.

Too late the truth of the child's paternity dawned on Regan. Sirena had seen his doubt change to certainty as his eyes acknowledged the child's fairness. He had expected to see Chaezar's child, never his own! His expression was branded on her heart. She would never forget the incredulous shock on his face just as she would never forget Isabel's screams.

A film blinded Regan's eyes as he gazed upon the small golden head. But his eyes were glazed with fear when they turned to Chaezar. "You'd kill an innocent child and have no remorse? What kind of devil are you? You must be insane! Let the boy and the infant go free and kill me instead. Send them to the Indies and my people will care for them. In the name of God let them go!"

Sirena was now almost abreast of the crossed rapiers that hung behind Chaezar and over the breakfront. With panther-like speed, she had the rapier free of its hook and had shoved Chaezar out of her way.

Armed now with a weapon, she danced her way over to the dark-skinned guard who held her son. The tip of the rapier nicked the small of the man's back and skirted around to his frontal regions. While the man might not understand her language, he understood which direction the rapier was moving. With a nod to Frau Holtz, the woman ran to the perspiring guard and clasped the baby to her bosom in such a fierce grip he squealed his outrage at such rough handling.

Sirena waved the rapier and shouted for silence. "It is you against me, Chaezar. Tell your guards, in whatever language you prefer, to stay out of this battle. For, if you don't, your tongue will never help you to utter another word."

Chaezar mumbled a few guttural words and the guards quietly left the room.

"Regan, Caleb," Sirena said quietly, "you are not to interfere, is that understood? Even if I am coming out second best, you are not to lift one hand in my direction. If you do, I shall cut you down as I did the others who stood in my way." Regan's tortured eyes nodded agreement and Caleb's held confidence as he fought to keep from clapping his hands. He knew who would be the victor, so he could promise anything.

Sirena backed off, hampered by the length of her gown. With a few deft movements, she had it slit and hanging in kneelength tatters.

"It is a fight to the death, is it?" Chaezar asked.

"To the death. Make your choice, Chaezar, a quick clean death or mutilation?"

"Mutilation! Before you die, I want you to have the supreme pleasure of watching your son's blood run over this tile, then your husband's and then, lastly, when you beg for death, I shall leave you to die a slow and painful death."

There was no need for Sirena to answer in words,

the message was in her eyes. Chaezar blanched a moment and blinked before he brought up the rapier.

"En garde!" Sirena called, and the battle was on. Chaezar feinted to the left, bringing up his rapier to slice thin air as Sirena nimbly sidestepped him and swiveled to bring her rapier down across the length of his back. She pivoted with lynx-like grace and brought up her arm with such force, she drove Chaezar back as she jabbed again and again. The Spaniard was perspiring freely as he tried to meet steel with steel. Each time he raised his blade, she would sidestep and jab at his legs. Both of Chaezar's legs were bleeding profusely as she again raised the rapier in a high wide arc and brought it down across his chest. Breathing heavily, she backed off and gasped, "Do you want it clean and quick or is it still mutilation? Answer me now, for I wish to see how much blood runs in your traitorous veins."

"I told you, mutilation, I want to see you weep over your son's blood!" Hate emanated from his eyes as he jabbed and the tip of his weapon drew blood from Sirena's bare arm.

"Neither of us will live to see my son's blood on this tile. The only blood that will drop on this floor will be yours, and if you aren't careful they will need a jolly-boat to row you out of here," she said viciously as she landed a wide slice to the man's chest. "Already your blood runs in many places. Look about you . . . King, and see what is happening to the marble floor in your castle," she taunted as she knicked the tip of the blade across his cheek. No matter what he did, he couldn't make the rapier touch her flesh, she was always one step away from him and his weapon would flounder in empty air, giving her the advantage time and time again. He was tiring and she knew it as she kept up her rapid-fire movements, a jab here and a jab there and then he would feel the warm stickiness trickle from his wounds. Sirena feinted to the right and slipped in a small puddle of blood, losing her balance. Caleb screamed as Chaezar bore down on her, the rapier posed over her neck. Sirena rolled away and sprang to her feet, her eyes hate-filled. "So, cut my neck off, would you?" she shrilled. She lashed out and pinned him to the wall, her breathing ragged. "Your last chance, Señor, quick and clean or the ultimate end?"

Insanity glistened in his wet, dark eyes. "Someday you'll love me," he murmured, "just as I love you."

Sirena never knew what happened. One moment she had him pinned to the wall and the next he had moved, jerking her backwards, the tip of his rapier at her throat. The baby uttered a high-pitched wail and Caleb shouted as she lost her balance and her rapier sliced downward, keeping the promise she had made.

Chaezar's screams rang in the room, vying with the infant's high-pitched cries of hunger and fear. A wide puddle of blood formed on the tile and trickled near her feet. Sirena imagined she could hear the drops as they fell. Chaezar's eyes remained open and glazed as Sirena stood over him, the rapier hanging loosely at her side. "I told you many times that a woman is not a thing to own and possess. She's a creature of God with a free will of her own. It was you, Chaezar, who made me kill you. You should have realized that this rapier I hold in my hand was a scythe of vengeance. It was your choice, Chaezar."

"You win, Sea Siren, take your . . . son and go . . . home." A bubble of blood rose to his mouth and dribbled down his chin. The glazed eyes closed as Sirena dropped the rapier and fell into Regan's outstretched arms.

Chapter Thirty-five

The baby's high-pitched wail startled Sirena. With a quick movement she sprang from Regan's arms and was across the room near Frau Holtz with her arms extended. "Give me my son," she said, her voice husky and edged with desperation.

"Yes, I would like to see the infant myself at close range," Regan smiled.

"No," Sirena said coldly, clutching the baby to her breast. "This is my child! He's hungry and needs a fresh change of linen. All this excitement isn't good for him." Slowly, she backed away from Regan as he advanced toward her, his intent clear. He meant to see the baby at close range and nothing would stop him.

A vision of Regan's startled look when he noticed the golden head was all that Sirena needed to remind her of which side of the fence the Dutchman sat on. He'd been shocked when he saw the rich golden hair and fair skin, since it was jet hair and olive skin he expected to see. Men, bah! Bastards, the lot of them. Ignorant beyond insult. One would think he'd have the decency to mask his feelings. He was closer now, almost upon her. Lynx-like, she literally tossed the baby to Frau Holtz and spun around the rapier in her hand. "I told you once, Mynheer, that this rapier could move as fast as the bird takes to the wing. I meant it then and I mean it now. One more step and you'll join Alvarez in a similar death. Breathe easy, Dutchman, the choice is yours."

Regan laughed harshly, the sound grating in her ears. "You'd deprive your husband a look at his own flesh and blood? You would kill me for this?" His harsh voice sounded incredulous to Sirena.

"The child is mine, he goes back to Spain with me," Sirena spat.

"Your child! Would you have me believe this was a virgin birth? It's only on the whim of nature that the child is mine. He could very well have been Chaezar's."

"Bastard! Son of a whore! Pig! Animal!" Sirena screeched at the top of her lungs. "Not another step or I'll kill you. Move!" she raged, her eyes glittering angrily.

"Not till I look upon my son," Regan said calmly as he advanced still another step. Her rapier came up with such speed Regan backed up and matched her cold, frozen look. "Enough of this foolishness. Frau

Holtz, bring the baby to me. His mother doesn't wish me to move another step."

"No." The one word was an iron command and Frau Holtz stopped in her tracks. "Remember the talk we had aboard ship, Frau Holtz? That's my child you hold in your arms and I tell you to take him to the nursery. I'll follow you and feed him shortly."

"And I'm telling you to bring the child to me this minute. If you don't then you'll feel my wrath," Regan said briskly.

Frau Holtz looked at the glittering eyes of the woman before her and at the mocking eyes of the man next to her. She lowered her own eyes to the small bundle and squared her shoulders. Who was Mynheer van der Rhys to command her to give the child to him? He wasn't paying her wages. Come to think of it, there had been many months with no wages. If he had only asked instead of demanding. Her head high, her cheeks suffused with rosy color, she opened her mouth and uttered, "No, the baby belongs with his mother."

"So, she has worked her magic on you also, Frau Holtz," Regan said sadly. "Is it too much to ask to let a father see his own child?"

"Yes," Sirena spat, "you ask too much. One moment you're convinced the child was the Spaniard's and the next you're convinced he's yours. What if I were to tell you he belongs to Captain Dykstra? What would you say to that? Speak up, Regan, I can't hear you!"

Regan stared into her angry eyes. He wanted to grab her by the hair and drag her to his lair like a prehistoric caveman. His stomach muscles knotted as she returned his stare, her eyes mocked him as Frau Holtz backed away from them and headed for the nursery. How could he allow her to best him in this issue, that of his son? There was no way she would win this battle. He had lost one son and he wasn't going to lose a second! Before he could help himself the words were out of his mouth: "I haven't forgotten those lengthy luncheons with Chaezar and the sparkle in your eyes when you returned. The whole island was talking of your affair with the Spaniard. Deny it, now this minute, that you never bedded the Spaniard! I want to hear your denial. I can't hear you, Sirena," he almost sing-songed.

Sirena cursed herself for allowing herself to be placed in the position of having to make a denial. She could not, she would not lie. Her cheeks flushed with color and her bottle-green eyes turned murky as she gazed into his. How could she say she had bedded the Spaniard but only because she was drugged? Would Regan believe her? Would he believe it was his name on her lips when Chaezar had his way with her? Not likely.

Regan waited for the answer he dreaded. His agate eyes implored her to refute his accusation. When she remained silent, her eyes glittering and her face still as if carved from stone, a chain of steel closed around his heart. Why did he think she would deny the allegation? Was he hoping against hope that the charge was false when he knew it wasn't? Why did he care? Why was he standing here next to her making demands and why was she holding a rapier over him threatening to slice his manhood from his body? The child was his and he meant to have him. And he would have her too . . . when he was ready. The woman hadn't been born who could resist him.

He shrugged elaborately and backed off still another step. The agate eyes warmed and he smiled slightly to show her he was bowing to her demands. Sirena sighed inwardly and thanked God she could lay down her weapon. One killing was enough. She had wrestled with the question of whether she could harm Regan once before. Then she had decided she could never pierce that beloved flesh. Now she knew she would have carved the heart from his body if he had attempted to take the baby from her.

Regan watched her through narrowed eyes and decided he had been magnanimous enough for one day. "Go, see to our son," he laughed. "Caleb and I will see that a meal is prepared. You'll be called down for dinner. We sail for Batavia the first thing in the morning, the crew will have set in stores by then."

Sirena didn't bother to answer him. She had no intention of going anywhere with him, least of all to Batavia.

His mood jovial, Regan clapped Caleb on the back. Caleb wasn't fooled, not for a minute. Regan was a wounded lion. This was a show of bravado and he would brazen it out to the death. Sirena was right. Men did think with their loins. That it was his father made no difference to him. She had won again. But only for the moment. Regan would have the baby. He had the law on his side. What could Sirena do in the face of the law? She couldn't kill everyone with that deadly rapier of hers. Besides, she was a mother now and mothers didn't do things like that.

A horrible vision of Sirena fighting a duel with a baby clutching at her leg made him gasp. His father cast a disapproving look in his direction. He had to talk to her. There had to be a way to get her to stop and listen to Regan. She loved him and he loved her. Why couldn't life be simple? Why did there always have to be problems? If it wasn't for that oily Spaniard everything would be all right. His eyes fell to the streaks of blood on the marble floor and he winced. So much blood! For a skinny man, the Spaniard had bled a lot. He shrugged. He deserved to die and if Sirena hadn't killed him, then Regan would have.

"I know you want to see your new brother and I'm sure Sirena won't have any objections to your looking at him—go ahead, boy," Regan said kindly. "I'll see to having . . . this removed and the blood cleaned up. We don't want to dine with congealed blood at our feet."

Caleb shuddered at the words and bolted from the room in search of Sirena and his new brother. He skidded to a stop, not knowing which direction to take in the enormous house. Caleb bellowed at the top of his lungs, "Sirena!"

Frau Holtz stuck her head out of the door and beckoned him in as she craned her thick neck first to the right and then to the left. Satisfied that her former employer was nowhere in sight, she held the door wide and Caleb scooted through. He couldn't help but hear the bolt slide across the heavy door after he was inside.

"Little brother, so we meet once more. Come here," Sirena said, holding out her arms to the boy. Shyly, Caleb let her embrace him without flinching. He was too old for this motherly display of affection. Mothers always wanted to do that to children. Now that Sirena was a mother she would be wanting to kiss and hug him all the time. He grinned slightly and decided he could bear with it. He could never deny Sirena anything. "Come and see your brother. I think he has your eyes. What do you think, Frau Holtz, does little Mikel have Caleb's eyes?"

"*Ja,* he has the boy's eyes and the jaw of his father and the hair of his father, and soon his hands and feet will grow to the size of his father's," the old woman said dourly. "At the moment his disposition is his own, but for how long can only be a guess."

Sirena smiled in spite of herself. The housekeeper adored the infant and would die to protect him.

Caleb stood fidgeting on first one foot and then the other as Frau Holtz pulled back the blanket and he gazed at the small pink face crowned with golden fuzz. Caleb frowned—what was all the fuss? It didn't look like much of anything. He shrugged elaborately and said something polite to Sirena.

Sirena laughed, "I know exactly what you're thinking, that he looks like a plump, dried fig, right?"

"I . . . I didn't say that," Caleb stammered.

"You didn't have to, little brother. I fear I taught you too well. But I told you to speak the truth, the infant looks like a dried fig at the moment. Soon he'll be beautiful and grow to be a handsome, sturdy boy like his brother. I hesitate to say this, but you resembled the little one yourself when you were little. All babies look like this when they're first born."

Caleb gulped with emotion, "I'll teach him everything I know."

"I'm sorry, Caleb, that won't be possible. I'm taking the baby back to Spain with me. You'll be leaving with your father to go back to Batavia. Perhaps one day you'll come to Spain and then you can visit with your little brother. It has to be," she said sadly at the look she read in the boy's eyes. "I told you a long time ago that this could never be. Too much has happened for me to go on with Regan. Chaezar and Gretchen would always lay between us." She shook her head sadly. "No, it can never be."

"Sirena you must listen to me. Regan is downstairs pretending to be jovial. He doesn't fool me at all. We've been to Spain and back searching for you. He'll have the baby and that's all there is to it. The law gives him complete control over his son. You of all people know that. What are you thinking of to deny him the sight of his son?"

"The right of . . . never mind. It doesn't matter. The child is mine and I'm taking him to Spain."

"The baby is Regan's too, and he says he's taking him to Batavia. He'll use the law if he has to. I think he'd kill you, Sirena, if you tried to take the little one."

Sirena blinked. The boy's words didn't shock her, it was the certainty in his voice that sent fear coursing through her veins. "He's mine!" she shouted.

"And Regan's," Caleb said quietly. "Think about what I said, Sirena. Regan's not thinking with his loins now. His mind is crystal clear and sharp as an ax. The baby has a father."

Sirena and Frau Holtz watched the slender boy's retreating back as the baby Mikel fell into a quiet sleep. He had a father, true, but one who did not love his mother.

Regan had little trouble in bringing the black-skinned household staff under his command. They were terrified of this tall, golden-haired sun god but they followed his pantomimed commands faithfully. Chaezar had instilled fear in them, but was incapable of commanding their respect.

Within moments the servants removed Chaezar's battered, bloody body, and pails of steaming soapy water were coursing down the marble stairs. Soon there would be no trace of the scarlet blood which stretched across the floor like gay streamers at a pagan festival.

Satisfied that his orders were being carried out, he headed for the kitchen regions and managed to make himself understood. Dinner would be served at eight and a messenger was sent to tell the guests who were to arrive of Chaezar's untimely death. After seeing the messenger dispatched, he gave the order for bath water and sent Caleb to the horses for clean clothes from his saddlebag.

An hour later he rapped smartly at the door of the nursery and waited for admittance. He was not surprised when Sirena herself opened the door and stood aside for him to enter. She pointed to the small wicker cradle and watched as Regan gently pulled aside the coverlet. She heard his indrawn breath and smiled to herself. The bastard *would* take the sole credit for the small miracle of Mikel's birth. Regan bent over the basket and picked up the tiny babe. Sirena watched, her face passive. She saw the love in his eyes, felt the tenderness as he cradled the small bundle to his chest. Their eyes locked in a fleeting moment of understanding.

"His name is Mikel," Sirena said quietly.

"Mikel is a good name. It's a strong name. I approve of your choice," Regan said seriously.

"He has your chin," Sirena said.

"And your feet and hands!" Frau Holtz blustered.

"*Ja,* I see all these things, I'm satisfied," he said, placing the baby tenderly back in its cradle. He straightened the thin covering and placed his sun-darkened hand on the golden head for a moment. "A son is the greatest gift a woman can give a man," he said quietly, almost as if he were talking to himself. At first Sirena thought he meant her to hear the words but changed her mind when he straightened from the cradle and, without looking at her or Frau Holtz, left the room. His eyes were far away, focused on some other time and place, perhaps reliving the moment he first looked at Caleb. A stab of pity forced Sirena to blink and bite into her lips to prevent herself from crying out.

Regan, Caleb at his side, walked through the lush tropical gardens as dusk settled around the massive, ornate house that had been Chaezar's palace. He squinted into the semi-darkness and clenched his teeth at what he saw. Row upon row of nutmeg trees as far as the eye could see. The bastard! How could he have betrayed his own country as he did? The trees must be destroyed.

Caleb, sensing his father's mood, spoke softly in the gathering dusk: "Father, what will you do? If we sail at dawn as you said, there's no way for you to do anything about the trees."

"After dinner I'll either set fire to the groves, or along with the servants from the house, I'll rip every tree from the ground with my bare hands."

"There must be thousands," Caleb said dubiously. "If you set a fire it could easily get out of control."

"Not if it's done properly. I'll think on the matter while we look upon this . . . kingdom. Tell me, young Caleb, have you ever seen anything to equal this?"

Caleb shook his head as he craned his neck to look at the house behind him. "It is fit for a king. Señor Alvarez must have spent fortunes to have this built."

At the mention of the Spaniard's name Caleb felt the stiffening in Regan's arm and wished he hadn't spoken. Thinking to take his mind off the dead man, he spoke of the baby: "And do you think he looks like a dried fig, Father?"

Regan laughed, a happy sound in the quiet evening. "Now that you mention it, he did resemble a dried fig. But then so did you. Before long he'll be a strapping young man much like yourself. His name is Mikel. What do you think of that?" he asked proudly.

Caleb rolled the name around on his tongue and smiled. "Yes, I like the name, my brother Mikel," he laughed.

"You'll have plenty of time to get acquainted with the little one on the voyage home."

Caleb looked at his father, a puzzled look on his face. "You know a lot about babies, Father. I thought men left that to the mothers and nurses."

"That's true in some households. My children are important to me. One day all that I have will go to my sons. Many a night I myself walked the floor with you when you had a fever. Your mother and I took turns sitting by your side and taking care of you. We wouldn't trust you to a nurse." The harsh voice had softened and was almost humble.

"Does Sirena know you feel like this, Father? Perhaps if you explained she wouldn't hold such bitterness toward you. She says the baby is hers and she'll take him back to Spain."

"The child belongs to both of us. She won't take

him back to Spain. She'll sail with us in the morning to Batavia. The baby will need her. She has no choice in the matter. There are laws that govern matters such as these and Sirena knows she must do as I say."

Caleb spoke hesitantly: "A compromise . . ."

"There will be no compromise. She'll sail with us."

"She'll kill you if you try to take her baby," Caleb said nervously. "I saw it in her eyes."

"And I'll kill *her* if she tries to take him from me. An impasse, woudn't you say?"

"A compromise, Father, that's the answer." A feeling of doom settled over the boy's shoulders as Regan swung him around to face him.

"I said there will be no compromise. The child is mine!"

"He belongs to Sirena, too, she gave birth to him."

Regan dismissed the boy's quiet words as if they had no meaning. "The child is mine," he repeated coldly.

Caleb shook his father's hands from his shoulders and backed off a step. "A baby should stay with his mother," he said stubbornly, his eyes angry and unforgiving.

"If it comes to a decision, which ship would you sail, boy, mine or Sirena's?"

Caleb ground his teeth together while he clenched his fists at his side. He met his father's cold blue eyes and clenched his teeth even tighter.

Regan knew he would get no response from the boy. In his heart he knew what the answer would be if the boy chose to reply. His shoulders slumped and Caleb gulped back a sob which threatened to choke him.

Why couldn't they solve their differences and start a new life, Caleb agonized inwardly. He was torn as never before and now he had more cause for worry. Perhaps he should take the new baby and run away and then they would see what fools they were. Dejecttedly, he walked back through the sweet-smelling gardens and into the house.

Regan poured himself a generous glass of wine from Chaezar's bountiful wine cellar and sat down to think. He had to think! His eyes burned and his arms ached, for Sirena, for the Sea Siren. He was a fool! Why had he said the things he did? Why couldn't he get the picture of Alvarez and Sirena out of his mind? She didn't deny his allegation, so therefore that meant she had bedded the bastard. It was true the child could have been Chaezar's. Still there had been no need for him to say the cutting things he had said. For a moment, a tiny brief moment, he had read something in those glittering green eyes. Sadness, remorse? Whatever, it was gone too quickly for him even to be sure he had seen something. Caleb was right, she would kill him if he took the baby from her.

Yet, there was no way on this earth he would let her take the child from him. She would have to come back to Batavia with him. The child would need its mother at this tender age. Perhaps if he promised her something she would come willingly. What could he promise that could ever make her come willingly? Nothing. There was nothing she wanted from him except her son and that was the one thing he could not, could never, give her.

Then he would have to trick her somehow. Caleb said she never lied. He would trick her and then make her promise him she . . . Wearily, he shook his head, his mind whirling. What could he say to this cold-eyed woman who carried his name and was the mother of his son? There had been a time aboard ship when he swore she felt the same about him as he did for her, and then that time in her room when he had behaved like a wild animal. Would she forget that so easily? Now that he knew she had bedded the Spaniard he would never be able to get it out of his mind. Visions would always float before his eyes. Would he be able to make love to her like a husband and not let thoughts of Alvarez come between him and the woman he wanted to love? Why did he even want her, why did he still lust for her? What was there about the green-eyed witch that could set his blood to a boil and make him light-headed with desire? He wanted her as he had never wanted anything in his life. He wanted her at his side with his children. He would love her as no man ever loved a woman before. Why couldn't she see that? Why did she have to hate him and torment him as she did? Was she being torn as he was? No. She felt nothing for him, she had made that clear from the start. The question was, could he live without her? Could he live in the same house with her and not go near her? Never!

Angrily, he kicked a teak chair and cried out with pain. It wasn't the pain in his booted foot that caused him to cry out but the pain of his own inadequacy. What in the name of God was he to do? If he wasn't careful he would be lying in a pool of his own blood while his wife and two sons and that damnable housekeeper sailed off on his brig. She couldn't kill him, not the father of her child—or could she? For the first time in his life he was alone, truly alone, and he didn't like the feeling. This was a time in his life that he wanted to share. That also was strange, he had never had the desire to share anything with anyone, not even Tita. Why did Sirena have this effect on him?

Angrily he drove his clenched fist into the softness of the brocade sofa on which he sat. If he told her he didn't believe the things he said about her and Chaezar, that he just said them to make her angry, would she then . . . ? He drove his other fist into the softness of the shiny sofa and knew the answer. It was too late. There was nothing left in her now but love for her son, and soon he would take that from her too. There was no answer for him anywhere.

He poured himself more wine and drank it in a gulp. He poured another and then still another glass. By the time the servant went to fetch Sirena to the table he was roaring drunk and Sirena watched him through narrowed eyes and felt saddened.

"Are you packed for the trip tomorrow?" he asked, his speech slurred. Sirena didn't bother to answer but picked daintily at the fish on her plate.

"Answer me, damn you! I asked if you were packed," he enunciated clearly, to be sure she understood. Receiving no reply, he stood up and glared at her. Still she didn't answer, only toyed with the food on her plate.

Regan picked up the decanter of wine resting next to his plate and waved it in the air. "Damn you, answer me! I don't talk to hear myself. If you aren't careful," he said, his eyes gleaming, "you may find yourself on the floor and me atop you."

Sirena raised her eyes to meet his and smiled slightly. "They will be ready when you are, Mynheer," she said softly.

Sirena was fully aware of the effect she was having on Regan. She had utilized the hours before dinner in a hot bath, scrubbing the imaginary vestiges of Chaezar's blood from her body. She had dressed her long, dark hair in soft, wide waves with the heavy curling ends caught up in a shell comb at the top of her head; so different from the severe, slick knot at the nape of her neck he was used to seeing.

Chaezar had filled her clothes presses with gowns of indescribable beauty. Light silks, heavy brocades, cloth of silver and cloth of gold. Gossamer gauze creations to adorn a goddess and beaded satins fit for a queen . . .

"You're to wear these," Chaezar had proclaimed while Sirena was still heavy with child. "After the birth, of course, to celebrate the birth of my son," he added confidently.

"Then I shall never wear them," Sirena spat in retort, "for there's nothing to celebrate. This child is Regan's!"

". . . nothing to celebrate," she had told Chaezar. But she had decided to wear one of his lavish offerings this evening to impress Regan who, aside from seeing her near-naked in her Sea Siren costume, had never seen her dressed in anything but the black dresses of mourning and heavy, concealing mantilla.

Seizing a gown of rich, vibrant topaz from the clothes press, she had muttered angrily, "You were right, Chaezar. The gowns are to celebrate . . . your death!"

Now, when Regan looked at her, she knew he was excited by what he saw. The jewel-toned topaz brought yellow cat-like glints out in her green eyes. Her skin paled against the vibrant color to the hue of buffed ivory, set off by her shimmering dark hair. Her breasts, always high and full, blossomed over the top of the trim-fitting bodice with a new voluptuousness.

"They! Who is they? I asked you if you were

packed? You speak in riddles," he said, drunkenly eyeing her cleavage. She didn't fail to see him wet his dry lips as he forced his eyes to look into hers.

"They. Frau Holtz and the baby. I assume Caleb can take care of his own needs."

"Are you packed?" he thundered as he brought the wine bottle crashing against the side of the table.

"There's no reason for me to pack. I'm not going with you. You have the right to claim the child. I, too, know the laws. Frau Holtz is this minute securing a wet nurse for Mikel. Now if you'll excuse me," she said, rising from the table. God in Heaven, if she didn't get away from him she would be blubbering like a baby. Baby. She was giving up her baby to Regan and would never see him again. What kind of God are you, she implored silently, to force me to make still another decision that will haunt me for the rest of my life?

"What do you mean you aren't coming?" Regan shouted, all signs of drunkenness gone.

Sirena was halfway around the table and blinking rapidly to hold her tears in check. A glistening drop lay on her cheek as others formed in the emerald eyes. Regan looked at her in awe, his heart thundering in his chest. He had never seen her cry. The effect was devastating! He felt deeply ashamed and guilty. He weakened in the face of her tears. "The child needs you, Caleb needs you," he said huskily. "Won't you reconsider and come with us?"

Another tear fell to her cheeks and her shimmering eyes pleaded with him, as her heart leaped in her chest. Say it, Regan, say you need me, she silently implored. That's all you have to say and I would follow you to the ends of the earth. But you must say the words! Her lips trembling, she bit back the words. She waited a moment and then, blinded with tears, she raced from the room.

Regan slumped in his chair and cursed loudly and clearly. What did she want from him? If she had told him to crawl to her he would have, didn't she know that? God, what did she want? Those tears! His heart ached with the thought that he had caused them. Why hadn't he told her he loved her? What was wrong with him? Why couldn't he say the words?

Sirena raced to her room, racking sobs making her body shake from head to toe. She flung herself on the bed and howled like a banshee. She knew in her heart that he would never be able to forget that she had been ravished by pirates and, he suspected—correctly—by Chaezar. He wouldn't allow himself to love her. She had always known that her past would come between them. Their loving time on the *Sea Siren* and the time in her room were just accidents—animalistic actions. There was no love involved, just lust. On his part, she sobbed to herself. "I love him!" she cried into the softness beneath her. "I love him!"

Frau Holtz entered the room quietly and heard her Mevrouw's words. Her own words caught in her throat. So, Sirena did love Regan after all. Frau Holtz hadn't been sure for the past several hours. Gently, she brought the crying woman to her chest and cradled her much the way she held the small baby who lay in his cradle.

"Cry, Mevrouw, don't hold it in any longer." Sirena cried and cried as the old housekeeper stroked her dark head. Finally, she could cry no more and raised her face to meet the old woman's. "Tell me," she said shakily, "have you found a wet nurse for Mikel?"

Frau Holtz chose her words carefully lest the woman next to her find out she was lying. "There was no one. I couldn't get my idea across. Anyone capable of nursing Mikel has a family of their own and does not wish to leave Africa. I did the best I could, Mevrouw. I'm afraid that you'll have to go with the baby; otherwise, he'll surely die," she said ominously.

"How can that be, Frau Holtz? Did you offer money? Isn't there one among the natives who would make the trip? Are you sure you did everything you could?"

"Everything, Mevrouw. I did everything, Mevrouw," she said piteously. "You must go back to Batavia."

"I can't go, don't you understand? The longer I stay with the baby the harder it will be for me to leave in the end. Already my heart is in shreds. Every day will make it that much worse."

"You can do it," the housekeeper said sharply. "You have done harder things in this life than this. It is your child we speak of, you must do it. There's no other way!"

Sirena failed to see the old eyes dance with delight as she nodded. She would go with the baby. When he was old enough to be weaned she would leave him in Regan's and Caleb's capable hands. Nothing mattered anymore. Life was over for her.

It was nearing dawn as Sirena sat by the window nursing the baby. She let her eyes go to the window and was not surprised to see a roaring fire rip across the fields of nutmegs. So, Regan would burn Chaezar's magnificent kingdom and it would be no more. If the wind shifted the house would go also. Perhaps it was best. Another hour and she'd have to be ready to leave. Sorrow cloaked her body and tears again welled in her emerald eyes. Dear God, help me! she cried silently. I'm tired, help me, there's nothing more I can do. A glistening tear fell on the small golden head and the baby sighed contentedly. Was she carrying some invisible cross that said she was to go through life in torment? Was she never to find happiness? Wearily, she placed the small bundle in his bed and went about the business of preparing to leave.

Dawn had barely come when Sirena walked through the door of Chaezar's palace without a backward glance. She avoided looking at the scorched fields and the heavy smoke that lay to the west of her. Caleb trotted next to her like a happy puppy. He didn't know what made her change her mind. All that was important was that she was sailing with them to Batavia. He sighed in relief because now he was spared from making a hateful decision. From time to time he had pestered Frau Holtz for "just one more look" and constantly asked to hold his brother. He had known he could never leave Sirena or Mikel.

Regan's face, too, wore a look of sublime relief. He had sent for Frau Holtz and his new son, Mikel, hoping against hope for a last look at Sirena. He prayed that she would at least come downstairs to say goodbye to Caleb. It was almost beyond his belief when Sirena announced she was returning to Java with her son. Regan's eyes lighted and a smile spread across his face. Sirena's face wore a chisled look as she carefully picked her way over the cobblestones. There was no way she would acknowledge Regan's smile.

Sunlit days and star-filled nights aboard Regan's brig were almost a balm to Sirena's spirits.

The three-month voyage was uneventful as far as Sirena was concerned. She spent long sunny days on deck with Mikel in his small cradle. He grew by leaps and bounds in the warm, salt air. In his spare time, Caleb would look at the baby fondly and make inane sounds in an attempt to make him laugh. Mikel would oblige and Caleb would rock on his heels in delight. Regan himself made daily morning pilgrimages to her quarters to play with his son and eye him adoringly. From time to time he would pick the baby up and make faces at him. Mikel would regard him solemnly and at times his face would pucker up and lusty yowls would be forthcoming. When this happened Regan would rapidly hand him over to Sirena, a sheepish look on his face. No words passed between them at these times. It was enough that she was aboard ship and Regan seemed content to leave things as they were.

Only once, when a particularly heavy fog rolled in, did Regan search her out at the rail and help her back to the cabin. The touch of his hard callused hand on her arm sent her to trembling and she was not oblivious to his heavy breathing. He explained away his concern for her by saying he didn't want her to get disoriented and fall overboard thus depriving his son of his nourishment. Sirena grimaced at his words and cursed the Dutchman under her breath.

His grip on her arm became more secure as he led her to the steep ladder below. His touch was fire on her cold, damp flesh. Her foot betrayed her on the flimsy ladder and she fell against Regan, crying out in alarm. Regan himself emitted a small groan as she fell against him. Suddenly his hands were in her hair, his lips crushing hers. He wanted her as never before and she was responding in a like manner. Moans of ecstasy escaped her parted lips as Regan's mouth sought her throat, her breasts. Her senses whirled, her passion bordered on wanton lust. Sirena arched her back and opened her eyes to look at Regan and noted that the fog had shrouded everything in its gray, ghostly pallor. They seemed abstracted from their surroundings. Two lovers lost in a moment of time, isolated in a magical cloud of mist that seeped and swirled around them as their arms entwined around each other. Scorching lips met hers in a desire so fierce Sirena became dizzy. She felt her gown being ripped at the throat and immediately felt the mist wrap itself around her nakedness. Regan ground his lips against hers as his hands caressed the tautness of her breasts. His lips left hers for a moment, and he moaned huskily, "I have decided to overlook your affair with Alvarez. I knew that your passion would never be cooled by any other than me."

Regan's hands cradled her head gently as he again brought his mouth crashing down on hers. From some deep recess in her mind she heard his statement, but she was drowning in a pool of her own passion, her animal lust drawing her further and further: *Decided . . . overlook . . . affair . . . only he could . . .* All he had to do was wait . . .

"Bastard!" she shrieked, dragging herself from his arms and tumbling down the ladder. "Lusting bastard animal!" she shrieked. "Pig fodder and dung are only equal to your rottenness! Whoring bastard!" she continued her tirade. Regan stood with his arms extended and a stunned look on his face. "I'll slice that manly organ from your body when you sleep! I'll kill you yet, you whoring bastard pig, may vermin nest in that white thatch you call hair!"

"What . . . I don't—"

"Animal! You think of nothing save that which rests between your legs, bastard. You'll not use me again to salve your lust. I'll pray that dry rot settles on your organs," she spat.

Regan blinked. What had happened to her? One minute she was a passionate, lusting woman and the next she threatened to slice his manhood from his body. What did he do, what did he say?

Caleb said she never lied and she never broke a promise. He would secure his door at night. Visions of Chaezar laying dead, his manhood severed from his body, set Regan's teeth to a near-rattle.

Chapter Thirty-six

The orange ball of sun was just dipping into the cool waters of the horizon when Regan brought the rig into Port Batavia. He let his eyes scan the new wood at the wharf. His captains must have returned unharmed and started the business of rebuilding. Most of the trees were gone. Those that remained resembled ghostly specters in the deepening twilight. The office buildings were being rebuilt or repaired. Many strong backs would be needed before the harbors and wharves would be ready for the everyday life the islanders were used to.

Vaguely, he wondered how many of his good friends had gotten away safely and how many would never return to feel the warm easterly breezes and watch the graceful breadfruit trees as they dipped and swayed. He was saddened by his thoughts until a lusty yowl broke his mood. He looked toward the stern and saw Sirena holding the baby. He had no time for sadness. He had much to be thankful for. Two sons! Who could ask for more? He would do his share of rebuilding the island and hope that his sons would come to love it as he did.

Sirena walked to the bow, the baby secure in her arms. He bobbed his head trying to see everything. A motherly smile on her face, Sirena cooed gentle words to him. Seeing Regan advance on her, the smile left her face and she clutched the baby tighter. Not a word had passed between them since the fog-shrouded night on the ladder. Regan had avoided her deliberately. And just as deliberately she had sought him out time and time again. She would stand and stare at him with a strange look on her face. She smirked to herself as she watched him betray himself in many small ways. A forgotten word to the crew, a sharp tone with Caleb, a nervous jerk of his usually steady hand, a telltale twitch of his cheek. There were more ways than one to skin a cat, and when she was finished with this cat he would not only be minus his fur but his tail as well.

A rich bubble of laughter wafted across the deck and Regan bristled. She was always either laughing or smiling and there was never anything for her to smile about. Was she trying to drive him out of his mind? If indeed that was her purpose, she was almost succeeding. Not for the world would he admit, even to Caleb, that he slept with a bolt on his door. Many times he had caught her eyes on his lower regions and a strange smile on her lips, and then all through the night, visions of Chaezar would haunt his dreams.

"We're home," Regan said curtly. Sirena ignored him completely as she let her gaze travel over the wharf and the various stages of rebuilding. She wondered how much damage was done to the house and if it was habitable. She would sleep under a tree if necessary. Once inside Regan's house, she would be at his mercy. The rules would be his and she would have to abide by them. Or else, she thought coldly, she would kill him. She looked fondly at the baby in her arms and sighed. A few more months and he would be weaned. A sob caught in her throat as she watched Caleb lower the jolly which would take them to the wharf. A few months would pass in the blink of an eye. She had to decide on a course of action and make the most of it. She would live one day at a time and then she would be ready when Mikel was weaned. She would walk to the wharf, not look back, and cut the island of Batavia and all its inhabitants from her heart.

Standing on the wharf, dry land beneath her, she decided she hadn't missed solid ground at all. The hot dusty streets were busy with men and children. Everywhere there was noise of hammering and construction.

These people were rebuilding not only their town, but their lives. New, raw wood glistened in the still twilight. Torches were being lit so the men could continue to work in the cool of the evening. At this rate they would have the island to its former condition before long.

"Regan! I thought you would never get here," Captain Dykstra shouted to be heard above the hammering. "We've been busy, as you can see. Your house is habitable but needs repairs. We've been doing one house at a time. The offices are intact and ready to be opened for business." He lowered his voice slightly. "There's a message for you from the Grand Pensioner himself. Your personal presence is requested in Holland. Wouldn't be surprised if you don't become the next governor," he said jovially.

Regan nodded. "How many were . . . ?"

"Too many. The Medrics, both of them. Helga Kloss, Gretchen Lindenreich, scores of others. Mevrouw Kloss died helping the children get away. With Gretchen, no one seems to know what happened. And you know the Spaniard left before the holocaust."

"He's dead," Regan said coldly. "Fetch me a wagon, Daan, so I can take my family home."

Sirena's heart leaped at the mention of Gretchen's death. Foolish woman, she chided herself, there would always be another whore to take Gretchen's place.

Within a week of settling in, Regan announced at the evening meal that he would be leaving for Holland the following morning. Caleb was to stay behind and look after his little brother. Regan said he would return as soon as he could, but he expected to be gone for five or six months. Sirena blanched at his cold, impersonal tone and managed to finish her dinner somehow. Caleb seemed oblivious of the undercurrents that passed between them. Frau Holtz hovered near the double doors leading to the kitchen, a sour look on her face. For a bridegroom, her employer left much to be desired: at times the temptation to let him feel the toe of her stout boot was almost more than she could bear. Couldn't he see the haunted look in the Mevrouw's eyes. Was he blind?

"I wish a discussion with you, in private," Regan said coolly as he rose from the table. Sirena nodded and followed him to the cool, dim library he called his home office. He motioned for her to sit down and offered her a glass of wine. She declined both, her eyes roaming around the room and coming to rest insidiously on his lower regions. Regan faltered a moment and gained control of himself. She would no longer make a fool of him.

"I want your promise that you will not leave this island until I return. If you fail to give me your word I shall have a guard posted at the front entrance and one at the back." The green eyes were the color of a grassy meadow, quiet and tranquil. She uttered not a word as she waited for his next demand. She knew there would be others, there were always more demands.

"When I return you will have settled yourself in my chambers. Mikel will be in Frau Holtz's care. I plan to exercise my rights as a husband. I don't wish to hear yea, or nay, at this time. You will do it, understood?" Sirena smiled again and let her eyes travel to the window and the lushness outside. She couldn't care less about his demands. Let him demand till the end of time and then some.

"Caleb tells me you never lie or break a promise. It would be a shame for the boy's idol to have feet of clay. Your promise, Sirena."

Caleb would have to learn sooner or later that she wasn't perfect. How could she have let him build such a perfect image of her in his mind? "I'll make no promises to you, Mynheer. The boy is just that, a boy. He has no right to expect me to be perfect, I'm human. No promises. You have the right to Mikel, I recognize the law. But, you don't own me and I shall do as I please."

"We're married," Regan said harshly.

"Bah, a piece of paper that says we're man and wife. Fool! Look at your paper again. It says Isabel is married to you. The contracts were signed by Isabel and you. The wedding is a farce. I'm a fallen woman, a disgrace. I am like your whore, Gretchen. Don't talk to me of marriage rights and what you expect, for if you do, then you may get more than you bargain for. If I wanted I could take the child and leave here, now this minute. Prove that you are married to me! Prove that Mikel is your child!" The green eyes were murderous as she spoke in a dangerously controlled tone. "I also know that one way or another I would lose. I have no desire to do battle again. Mikel is yours. But not me. Never me. I won't be owned, not now, not ever. And even if I were married to you I wouldn't allow you to own me. I'm not some object that you can boast about. If you have nothing further to say then I'll get back to my child—excuse me, your child, the one I'm caring for. I'm only his mother. I don't count for anything. Good-bye, Regan, and don't do me any favors by hurrying back."

Rage boiled in Regan as he watched her turn her back on him. With a long arm he spun her about. His eyes were vicious as he clasped her arm.

"This has gone on long enough! You come into my house full of lies and deceit and make a fool out of me in front of my friends and business associates. You wreak havoc on my ships and send my cargos to the bottom of the sea. You marry me under the name of your sister and have the gall to continue to live the lie. You carry on a blatant affair with my rival under my nose and go off to Africa with him and when you tire of him you kill him! Is that what you have in store for me? Dead men lie at the bottom of the sea because of you. You bewitched my son till he thinks you are a goddess and then you birth my son. Not my son, you conceived him alone! You can do anything, or so Caleb says. You allowed me to make love to you aboard your ship and then again here in my house. Ah, I see that you are about to protest. Think, lovely lady, you laid willingly in my arms and enjoyed our union as much as I. What do you want from me?" he asked brokenly. "Tell me, do you want me to crawl across this room and hang on your skirt, to grovel for your attention? Tell me, what is it you want from me?" The agony in his tone ripped at Sirena's heart. Even if she told him how much she loved him he would never believe her.

"Love is giving entirely of oneself," Sirena said

quietly. "It's true I allowed you to make love to me and it's also true that I enjoyed it as much as you. I gave of myself entirely. Something I never thought I could do, not after . . . not after . . ." a lump rose in her throat as she tried to find the words.

"What can I do? What can I say? There must be some way to reach you. Just tell me. What do you want from me?"

"My son. Will you give me my son?" Sirena asked, holding her breath as she waited for his answer.

Regan eyed the woman in front of him. "And if I were to give you your son, then you would share my bed, is that it?"

Sirena smiled. "Believe what you will," she said lightly, "I can always kill you when I'm ready. I'll stalk you at night the way a wild animal stalks its prey. I'll tell the child you died, glorious in battle—if he should ask, that is." Her tinkling laughter bounced off the walls and Regan felt a shudder ride up and then course down his spine. He raised his hand, gave her a stinging blow to the side of the head. Sirena saw the blow coming, but stood still, taking the attack fully on the side of her head. She reeled, stunned with the force of the blow. He had actually hit her! She staggered away from him and shook her head. Deliberately, she let her eyes narrow and then lower to a spot six inches below his belt. She forced her eyes to remain open for a full minute and then she knew nothing more.

When she woke she was alone in her room and the baby was wailing his head off. Dazed, Sirena climbed from the bed and picked up the crying baby. Gradually, she relaxed as her mind quieted. This was all she needed, this small warm bundle, her son. She wouldn't think about the past hour and what had transpired downstairs. It didn't matter. Regan would leave in the morning and she would never see him again.

Tears glistened in the sea-green eyes as she laid the baby in its wicker cradle. Time would heal her wounds. Time had a way of taking care of everything. Why should she care? Why should she feel sorrow? Time and time again Regan had flaunted his lust with

Gretchen and every available female on the island. That was the worst humiliation of all. Sex! Was there anything in the world besides sex as far as men were concerned?

Storm clouds gathered in the green eyes as she walked to the small balcony and watched Regan stride around the courtyard, a cigar clenched in his strong, white teeth. He looked murderous. Would he trust her alone on the island now that he was leaving? While Mikel was his son, he had no right to Regan's name. Regan had no legal claim. Mikel was hers. In her heart she knew that there would be some way for the Dutchman to force his will. He would have the guards posted around his house and she would never be allowed to leave. He didn't care, all he wanted was his child. Would Caleb help her? Whether he would or wouldn't, she couldn't ask him. Those days were gone forever. This was a new time and a new place.

Regan stopped his long-legged strides and looked up at her balcony. He stood for a moment and slowly and deliberately brought the cigar to his lips. She watched his eyes narrow as he squinted at her through a haze of blue-gray smoke. Angrily, she walked back into her room and lay down on the bed. She was so tired. She couldn't remember a time when she had been so bone tired. All she wanted was to sleep. Sleep, the great escape. Her eyelids became heavier and heavier as she let thoughts of Regan float away on the warm gentle breeze that wafted through the wide windows. Sleep was an escape, a balm to the soul.

Frau Holtz woke her shortly after sundown and brought the baby to her. As the infant nursed at her breast, Frau Holtz casually mentioned that the Mynheer had left the house a short while ago. "He went to his ship and he'll sail at dawn. He was in a killing mood! He goes to Holland!" Still she received no reaction from Sirena, and she frowned. "He left instructions a mile long," Frau Holtz said sourly. "There are guards positioned around the house and around your frigate, and if you attempt to sail her Mynheer's orders were to gut the ship."

Carefully, Sirena lowered the sleeping baby to the

cradle. Here at last was the reaction Frau Holtz was waiting for. "Are you sure of what you say? You didn't make a mistake?"

"No, Mevrouw, no mistake. In fact, I think the Mynheer wanted me to hear his orders to Captain Dykstra. You're his prisoner!"

Sirena nibbled on her full lower lip, her thoughts racing. One day the guards would grow weary. Sooner or later they would become lax and then she would do as she pleased. She would not be held prisoner, not ever again. Regan should know that.

With Regan gone, the house took on a new emptiness. Caleb was quiet and a wary look had come into his eyes. Mikel seemed more fretful in the late morning, the usual time of Regan's daily visits. Frau Holtz grumbled constantly, trivial things rattled her as never before. She also took on a wary look as she went about her household chores. It seemed to Sirena that all eyes were upon her.

There were men, strong, forceful men, who worked outside, supposedly making needed repairs. She wasn't fooled. As soon as she set foot out the garden doors all work stopped and she could feel their eyes watching her every move.

Several weeks after Regan's departure, Sirena walked to the stable, her intention to ride as far as the eye could see. She wasn't sleeping well and she had to do something to tire herself. She would ride to the *Rana* and let her eyes feast on the sleek lines of the frigate. While she saw no one following her, she could hear distant hoofbeats behind her. Regan's men would follow her to the ends of the earth if they had to.

She reined in her horse and sat quietly drinking in the sight of the freshly painted frigate. She looked to the bow and was pleased to see the name *Rana* painted in bold white letters. It looked ghostly in the gathering dusk. When would the frigate travel the seas again? Would she be taken care of and careened and who would see to it, surely not Regan—or would he? He did appreciate the maneuverability of the frigate, perhaps he would lay claim to the ship and hold it for the boy. Sirena became saddened as she thought of her ship laying dormant in the bright blue waters. At the moment, it looked as dead as she felt. It needed a hand on its wheel and someone to hoist the sail just as she needed the caress of Regan's hand and a kind, loving word to make her whole again.

A group of men came out onto the *Rana*'s decks and stood watching Sirena. So, Regan was as good as his word. He had posted guards everywhere.

Willem stood on the deck, Regan's men behind him as he watched the slim figure astride the tall horse. Somehow he had thought she would return before this. He watched her, a knot in his throat. How could the Dutchman do this to her? He had heard Regan give the orders to his burly men. He had said in clear, cold tones that his wife was not to set foot on the ship while he was away. If she did then they would be dead, even if he had to search the world over for them.

Regan had looked at Willem and old Jacobus and had lowered his tone. "My wife wishes you to see about careening this ship and putting her back into shape. If you obey my orders, you can continue to stay aboard. One false move and your death will be fast and fierce!" The Dutchman had then lowered himself into the jolly-boat and headed back for the wharf.

Willem had whispered to old Jacobus and then laughed. They knew in their hearts when their capitana was ready, those burly men of Regan's were as good as dead. They placed a small wager between themselves and settled back to wait. The day would come soon, they were sure of it.

Sirena shielded her eyes from the low-lying sun and frowned. Was that Willem and Jacobus on deck? The reins in her capable hands, she felt the horse rear backwards, but still she didn't take her eyes from the tiny figures on the quarterdeck. She had to know! She brought her gloved hand to her forehead in a jaunty salute and was rewarded with a greeting of waving hands. A smile touched her lips as she spurred the horse beneath her. They had seen her and that was all that was necessary.

The blood raced in her veins as she rode the horse at a fast gallop. Regan had been wise in not forcing her men from her ship. At last he was beginning to understand. It was her ship and her men. It was well he hadn't tampered with either. Perhaps there was hope for him after all. She knew now that she had to do something. She had to fill her days with something meaningful. She had started to wean the baby gradually and now she had more time to herself. One couldn't just idle days and weeks away foolishly when there was so much to do. Tomorrow would be the first day of a new life, a new life that she would have to fashion for herself.

Sirena greeted the faint pink dawn fully dressed, a pail of soapy water in her hands. To Frau Holtz's horror, she worked till noon and then stopped to feed her squawling baby. She then had some breadfruit and marched out to the gardens where she hoed and weeded. When she finished, she picked baskets of fruit and vegetables and carried them into the massive kitchens. Frau Holtz rushed to her, but when she saw the determined look in her mistress's eyes she continued with what she was doing. She fed the wailing baby his evening meal and then rode out of the clearing, her destination, the quay where she could gaze out on the *Rana*.

Day after weary day passed with Sirena working tirelessly. She knew that her child's destiny could only lie with Regan and she felt she must do her share to help build that destiny before she left for the last time. She worked in the house, getting it back into shape for the Mynheer's return, she worked in the gardens and the fields carrying rubble to the big drainage ditches to spare the men for more important work. Literally falling asleep on her feet, she would feed her baby in a trance-like state and only come alive when it was time to take her daily ride to the quay where she could look down at her *Rana*. She would then ride back to the house and fall into bed and sleep like the dead. Frau Holtz grew more concerned as the days wore on. The Mevrouw was too thin and her milk was fast drying. There were deep hollows in her cheeks and dark smudges under her lusterless eyes.

Sirena was walking through the courtyard to the house when the groom met her and explained that her horse had lost a shoe and advised her against riding it. Sirena agreed and decided to walk through the gardens. The beautiful, sweet-smelling flowers that she had tended annoyed her, the graceful breadfruit trees grated on her nerves. She closed the iron gate of the garden and started out across the fields. Here her footstep quickened and her eyes lit up in speculation. She let her foot scuff the dry gray ash. In a moment she was on her knees and digging with her bare hands—down, down through the ash. Was it possible? Could it be? Again she dug frantically, her mind racing with her discovery. She moved further on and once more dug with her hands. Her eyes were shining as she stood and looked around her. She, and she alone, had the power to secure Mikel's future. Swiftly her mind calculated the time Regan had been gone and the time left before he would return. There would be time she decided, time for her to secure her son's destiny. Could she do it? She had to do it!

Racing back to the house she sought out Frau Holtz and explained her plan. The old housekeeper looked at her in amazement. "But Mevrouw, you are only a woman, how can you do it? You will drop dead in your tracks. Will you, at least, allow me to help you? We can leave Mikel with Caleb and work from sunup to sundown. I'll be at your side. It is time these men on this island looked at us with something besides . . ."

Sirena laughed. "Were you about to use word lust?"

"*Ja,* but it was you I was thinking of, not myself. It has been many years since I saw lust in a man's eyes for me."

Sirena clapped her hands in glee. "Arrange for the flat wagon to be in the courtyard at dawn tomorrow. We'll ride out and be back by late afternoon. On second thought, we'll need two wagons. You, Frau Holtz, must drive one of them." The old housekeeper nodded, a look of battle in her eyes. Sirena wasn't sure who she was going to do battle with, but never had she seen the old woman so animated. Together they would arrange Mikel's and Caleb's future! She thought with irony that Chaezar's treachery would aid her. Perhaps they would think kindly of her in the future when the nutmeg trees were thriving and their harvest was rich.

It was something she had to do. She knew she couldn't let the ground lay fallow, not when she had it in her power to make it rich again. Regan's heart must have been near to breaking when he had to set fire to the groves of nutmeg trees in Africa.

Late that night when she went to bed at last, she fell asleep almost instantly. Visions of Regan, riding through the rows and rows of nutmeg trees that she and Frau Holtz had planted, plagued her dreams. He rode endlessly, calling her name over and over again. She woke in the morning with tears in her eyes and a salty taste in her mouth.

She dressed comfortably, it would be a backbreaking day for her. She hoped fervently that Frau Holtz was up to the hard labor.

Hot, sweat-filled days passed, each more tiring than the one before. They were clumsy at first, these two women filled with one purpose, but gradually they managed to get into the rhythm of their task and worked without wasted motion. They started at sunup and worked till dusk was low over the hills. They trudged home in clouds of gray dust with only one thought in mind: tomorrow was one day closer to finishing the task they had started.

"There's one barrel of nutmegs left," the housekeeper said tiredly. "We should finish by dusk."

"I think, Frau Holtz, that we should be proud of ourselves, we have accomplished a tremendous job. There were days when I thought my back would break, and my arms fall off. And you are more tired than I am, I can see it in your eyes. It was foolish of me to allow you to do such hard labor. If anything happened to you, I would never forgive myself."

"There is no need for worry, Mevrouw, I did what I did for you and the child. If I had to do it again, I would. A few days of rest and I'll be fine. What of you? You're thin, the sparkle of life is gone from your eyes."

"I'll survive, Frau Holtz. I think I'll bathe and go riding."

"You torture yourself!" Frau Holtz said sternly. "Why do you ride to the quay every day and look upon your ship? You plan to leave when the baby is weaned? I read the decision in your eyes many days ago. The days are numbered," she said sadly.

Sirena had to continue her evening rides to the quay regardless of how tired she was. She knew Willem and the others well. Each night they waited to salute her. Each night she returned their greeting. It had become a ritual. One night soon she would not appear on the quay and her men would deduce that they should make ready to sail, for the next time they would see her would be when she had made her escape.

More days passed and Sirena lapsed into a state bordering insanity as the fruits of her labor failed to make a showing. Was the ground ruined forever? Had all the back-breaking plowing been in vain? Day after day, she rode out to the fields to oversee the cultivation. The men Captain Dykstra had been able to secure for her were practiced plantation hands. Had she been insane when she turned over the earth in the hopes the nutmegs would grow once more? They should have sprouted by now.

Another week passed and Frau Holtz came on the run, her thick arms waving wildly. She grabbed Sirena by the hand and dragged her through the house and out to the fields. Triumphantly, she pointed to a miniature sprout peeking from the black soil. "Your son's destiny," she said happily.

Sirena smiled as she let her eyes travel the neat rows of planting. Tiny green shoots sprouted as far as the eye could see.

Chapter 36

The baby Mikel was fully weaned. The nutmeg trees were a foot high and thriving in the warm, humid air and daily rain. Caleb had just returned from the wharf and told her that a ship had just pulled into harbor and they had sighted Regan two days out of port. Sirena's heart leaped at the words and immediately turned into a hard lump that made breathing difficult.

So, tonight there would be no ride for her to the hills. Martin and Willem would be in readiness for her arrival. In cool, brisk tones devoid of any emotion, she ordered Frau Holtz to pack her trunks and have them sent to the wharf where the *Rana* was secured. The old housekeeper went off to do her Mevrouw's bidding, her watery eyes stormy with anger.

Sirena argued with herself. She had made no promises and she was a free woman. Regan had no hold on her. She would leave her son in his hands and . . . Why did she even think of these things? This part of her life was over. Somewhere, someplace, there was a new life waiting for her. In time the wound in her heart would heal—if she managed to live that long. For days now she had felt like the very life within her was draining away. She had seen the concern in the housekeeper's eyes and how she had forcefully held her tongue to avoid a confrontation. She meant well, Sirena knew this and held only respect for the old woman. But Sirena had made her decision and she alone would have to live with it.

Sirena awoke, her ears alert to a strange sound in her room. She opened one eye and saw Regan standing over the baby. She forced her breathing to remain calm and even. She waited patiently for him to leave the room, her heart fluttering madly in her chest. She felt rather than heard him move, and she knew he stood next to her bed. She remained still, and eventually he left as quietly as he had come. When he closed the door behind him, Sirena turned her face into her pillow and sobbed.

The following morning, Frau Holtz entered Sirena's room and helped her dress. "Your trunks have been loaded in the wagons. Caleb still sleeps. Is it wise for you to leave without telling him good-bye?"

"I cannot bear another good-bye. The boy will understand. The little one will never miss me, not with you in charge of him. You will take good care of him, won't you, Frau Holtz? she asked anxiously.

"I shall care for him as if he were my own," the old woman said brokenly.

"Regan is back so I must leave. I'm sure that after he satisfied himself that I was here as well as the baby, he will have gone to sleep. This will be the best time for me to leave. I don't know why I waited so long. I should have gone weeks ago."

I know why, the housekeeper thought sourly, you could not bear to leave without one more look at the Mynheer. No matter what you tell yourself, that is the answer.

"Quietly now, I don't wish anyone to know of my going. What do you think, Frau Holtz, a trip down the vine or through the front door?" she asked impishly, trying to make the old woman smile.

The woman shrugged, no humor in her eyes. The Mevrouw was leaving, what did it matter how she left? One way was as good as any other.

"I'll leave by the front door. There is no reason or cause for anyone to stop me. I'm free as the birds. I belong to no man. Good-bye, Frau Holtz, I shall remember you in my prayers. Take good care of my son."

The old woman couldn't restrain herself. "What prayers? I haven't heard or seen you pray in a month of Sundays. Pray that the little one survives without you."

"He'll survive." She descended the stairs and came to an abrupt halt at the bottom. Regan was towering over her.

"Goodbye, Regan," she said quietly. "Please, allow me to pass." Her eyes were pleading as she spoke. "Your son is upstairs, waiting for your return." She moved to go around him.

Regan fought the bellow that threatened to choke him. She was leaving and there was no way he could stop her. She didn't belong to him! She had never belonged to him! He had been proud to receive the appointment of Governor of Java, and knew Sirena would be a perfect first lady for him—but now he would rule Java alone. Miserable and alone. His eyes implored her to give him some sign that she cared, some faint look, anything. How could he allow her to walk out of his life?

Sirena, her heart thumping so madly in her chest she was sure he could hear it, begged him with her eyes to say the words that would make her stay. Why? Why couldn't he say what she wanted to hear? Was she so repulsive that he couldn't wait to be rid of her? This couldn't go on, she couldn't continue to torment herself. With one last imploring look that Regan met with bewilderment, she walked through the door.

Regan's shoulders slumped as the door closed. The sun was gone from the room, the life from his body. On lagging feet, he walked to his office and sat down, the rum bottle in his large sun-bronzed hand. He would get drunk. He would drown out all feeling in him. No sooner had he downed his first drink when the door burst open and Caleb burst into the room, his eyes pools of fright and anger.

"She's gone! Father, she's gone! Why did you let her go? And," he shrilled hopelessly, "she left Mikel behind. She didn't tell me good-bye! Why did you let her go? After what she did for you, how could you allow this to happen? You lied to me!" he accused vehemently. "You told me you loved her. Why did you lie to me?"

Frau Holtz, not to be undone, pranced into the room

and picked up where Caleb left off. "What am I to do with this child? I am an old lady. I know nothing of small babies. This child needs a mother, already he wails," she said, pinching the soft flesh underneath the blanket. The baby let out a lusty yell and Frau Holtz immediately placed him in Regan's arms, but not before she gave him another gentle pinch. "You are his father, see to the child. Perhaps you can convince *him* he needs no mother!"

"What is this conspiracy you have laid for me?" Regan sputtered, his grip on the howling baby precarious. "Both of you will stay out of my affairs from this moment on!"

"Bah!" the housekeeper snorted. "What affairs? You have none with the Mevrouw gone."

"You lied to me!" Caleb howled, tears forming in his dark eyes. "I'm leaving your house. I'll go and stay with Captain Dykstra if he'll have me. You said you loved her, that's what you said. Those were your exact words, Father, that you loved her!"

Was there no peace for him anywhere? What were they doing to him? Why couldn't they see that Sirena didn't want him. He couldn't force her to stay in his house.

"I didn't lie to you, Caleb, I do love her. But I cannot, I will not, force her to live in my house if she doesn't want to."

"If you love her why didn't she stay?" Caleb asked, puzzled now where a moment ago he had been angry.

Frau Holtz stood erect and spoke imperiously. "Because he chose not to *tell* her he loves her. He takes these important matters for granted. He thinks because he is a man, she will *assume* that he loves her!"

"Then this is what Sirena meant when she said men think with their loins. I wasn't sure exactly how that applied to you, Father. Thank you, Frau Holtz, for explaining the matter to me."

Regan choked back a gasp of rage at these words.

"I think perhaps, Father, Sirena is doing something else that I never fully understood before. She is being a wily woman. You do know what that means, don't you?" Caleb asked anxiously.

Frau Holtz, angry now beyond human feeling,

spoke harshly: "When did you tell the Mevrouw that you loved her? When did you tell her that you couldn't live without her? When did you tell her her eyes were like the stars and her skin like . . . ?"

"Enough!" roared the harsh voice.

"Enough. No, it is not enough. Look through the windows and let me know what your eyes see, Mynheer."

Regan strode to the wide windows and gasped. Nutmeg trees, a foot high!

"The Mevrouw and myself planted those trees. She said it was to secure the destiny of her son and young Caleb. She planted those trees for you. For you, Mynheer! Who but a woman in love could do that for a man? What woman could give up her son to a man she didn't love? You have much thinking to do, Mynheer. When a man needs a woman, he shouldn't be afraid to tell her so. If you hurry you may still catch her!"

Regan eyed the rum bottle stubbornly. What did some cranky old woman and a boy not yet dry behind the ears know of love? He would think on the matter—after he finished the warm rum. "Leave this room!" he shouted. "And take this squawling child with you."

"What am I to do with him? Without his mother he is lost," she said, giving the infant still another pinch. Fresh yowls of outrage split the air in the tension-filled room. Regan, a look of despair on his face, looked to Caleb and told him to go play with his brother.

Caleb flatly refused and strode through the doorway, a smile on his face. The baby's cries continued to waft through the house, and finally he heard the door slam shut and the wails stop.

Regan drank greedily. Were they right? Was that what she wanted, to hear him say he loved her? Were women so foolish that they had to hear those soft words? He had never spoken them and he wasn't about to start! A devil perched itself on his shoulder and whispered dark words into his ear. What did a few words matter? It was true he had never said these things. She should have known that he loved her after they . . . Why did he have to say the words? The rum bottle found its way to his lips and he downed the last of its contents in a fast gulp. Quickly, he uncorked a second bottle and drank greedily. He set the bottle on the desk with slow, precise movements and stood looking at it. He could do two things. He could stay here and continue to drink or he could go after her. If he went after her he would have to tell her all the things that were burning in his heart. He would have to tell her he loved her, that he was dead without her. He would have to say he needed her, that he wanted her at his side when their child grew to manhood. He would tell her he wanted many children to romp and laugh through his house. He would tell her Chäezar Alvarez and Gretchen Lindenreich were things of the past that they would put behind them. Could he say all these things to her? A vision of the rows and rows of nutmeg trees made his eyes blur. And the lusty howls of his son rang in his ear. What kind of woman was she? She was . . . his. He eyed the rum bottle again and then knocked it to the floor.

At best, his seat upon the horse was unsteady. He cursed the rum bottle and then he cursed himself. When he was finished he felt no better, so he cursed once more; this time, Frau Holtz was the recipient of his verbal abuse. Dull-witted old hag, what did she know of love? He cursed the fact that upon his return the night before he had stopped at the wharf and set the guards free to do other chores for him. Now that he was home he thought there would be no need for guards. What a fool he was. Would he never learn to listen to his instincts? Some tiny little thing had needled at him as he told the men to go to his offices and make themselves useful to his captains. He hadn't missed the smile that passed between Jacobus and Willem. At the time he merely thought they were glad to see the last of the big, burly men that had lived on the ship these many months.

He wiped the sweat from his brow as he spurred the horse faster and faster. If Sirena had set sail immediately she would have a two-hour head start on him, and with the brisk breeze she would make excellent time. By the time he stored a few provisions and got underway he would lose another two hours. Where would she go? Spain? Or would she ride the lonely sea until they were one?

A worm of fear crawled around his belly and inched its way up to his throat. The pain was so real he had to gasp and fight for breath. Where had that thought come from? Was it the empty look in her eyes? Did she somehow convey to him that she no longer cared to live? Would giving up her son to him make her want to die? Why, in the name of all that was holy, hadn't Frau Holtz thought to say something about that? It was his gut that told him something was wrong. Sirena was not a woman to give up her son. Not to him, not to any man. And why had she planted those damnable nutmeg trees and where in the hell had she gotten the fertile nutmegs to begin with? His mind whirled with these thoughts as he continued to spur the horse forward.

Sirena climbed aboard the frigate and greeted her small crew warmly. She gave the order to hoist the anchor and went below. There was no point in looking toward the town of Batavia. She never wanted to see it again. All she wanted from now on was to stare at the water till her eyes fell from their sockets. The sea was her only friend. It would never betray her. Her mind wandered to the time when she was a child playing with Isabel under the trees. She had been so happy then. Now there were no more happy days. Only days filled with vengeance, hatred, and sorrow.

Old Jacobus quietly entered Sirena's quarters several hours later to convince himself that his Capitana was still alive and well. There was no doubt that she was different. She was a shell of her former self. He wished there was something he could do for her. Too many times he had seen that same look in the eyes of men went to sea and never returned. Feeling helpless, he withdrew from the doorway.

Hours later, Sirena stirred fretfully and finally woke. For a moment she was disoriented as she looked around her quarters. She rubbed her temples and blinked her eyes. She had a raging headache and it was stifling in the close quarters of the cabin. She longed for a cooling bath and some fresh, tingling cologne. She would settle, instead, for removing her heavy clothing and wearing the abbreviated costume she had worn as the Sea Siren. At least she would be able to breathe, to move, and the spindrift was all she needed in the way of cologne.

It was close to midnight when she relieved Willem at the wheel. The air felt heavy and oppressive, they were on the brink of a storm. She was proved right moments later when a vicious bolt of lightning ripped across the sky and a doom-like roll of thunder split the air. The waves beneath her churned and rolled the frigate. As bolt after bolt of lightning lit the sky Sirena thought she saw a ship on her stern.

It was old Jacobus who heard the grappling hook find its mark. He blinked as he saw Regan van der Rhys climb aboard the frigate, alone. Delight danced in the old man's eyes as Regan made his objective known. Willem joined Jacobus on deck and listened to Regan, smiles on their lips. They nodded slightly as Regan motioned for them to go aboard his brig.

Regan watched the men as they swung aboard his brig. The taut ropes holding the ships were straining in the fierce storm. He pulled his cutlass from his belt and looked at the rope that held the two ships together. He threw the grappling hook to Willem and slashed at the rope, his face grim and purposeful.

Sirena fought the wheel and was about to fall in weariness when she felt a presence behind her. "Willem," she shouted, "take the wheel, I've had enough!"

"Do my ears deceive me?" Regan shouted to be heard over the crashing waves. "You've had enough!" His voice was incredulous.

"Regan!" she gasped. "How . . . what . . . ? Get off my ship," she spat. "Who let you aboard? Where are my men?" She fumbled for her rapier and was stunned to find it missing from her belt.

"It would seem that we must fight with words this time," Regan grinned. "I have things that must be said to you. Things you must listen to!"

"I'm past the stage where whatever you have to say will be of interest. Get off my ship!"

"You'll listen to me if I have to lash you to the

wheel. I haven't come this far to have you make a fool of me."

"Very well, say whatever it is you have to say and leave. This is my ship!"

Regan looked at her and was amused at her tone. He loved to see her when she was spitting and fuming and snarling at injustice. She would demand her rights as a person, as a woman. She was the kind of woman with whom a man could build a future. A woman who would endure. She was his woman! She had been his from the moment he first saw her on the bow of her ship. She was his future!

"Did the cat get your tongue?" Sirena taunted. "Why do you look at me that way?"

"What way?" Regan asked mockingly.

"Like . . . like . . ."

"Like I love you? I do. I love you as I never thought it possible for a man to love a woman, Sirena. I need you to make me whole, I can't live without you at my side. Chaezar and Gretchen are in the past—"

"No, they're not! They're standing here between us as if they were living and breathing." He motioned to interrupt her, to tell her she was wrong, that all their pain and torment and suffering was behind them. He loved her, that's all that mattered.

"No . . . Don't stop me, Regan, you have to know." The words welled up in her throat, almost gagging her. "Chaezar," she began hesitantly, her voice barely audible, "Chaezar seduced me!" It was out. She could see the pain in his eyes. She knew he didn't want to hear this, she was hurting him, but there was no other way. If there could ever be love between them, the truth must be known.

"Listen to me Regan, Chaezar's attempts to bed me were fruitless. All his flattery and pretty phrases were in vain. I think I knew even then that I loved you." Sirena saw a slight lifting of the pain in his face. He raised his gaze and looked long and deeply into her eyes.

"Chaezar even tried the direct approach and invited me to become his mistress. When all else failed he drugged me." Her shimmering green eyes met Regan's in direct confrontation. "He made love to me. In my drugged state I imagined Chaezar was you. I really believed it was your arms about me, your lips on mine. Chaezar was with me but I was making love to you. Loving *you!*"

The pain cleared entirely from his eyes and the gaze that met Sirena's was free of all doubtful shadows.

Sirena had never loved him more than at that moment. He had been ready to accept her, to love her, to share his life with her, without any explanations. It would have been enough for him to know that she loved him. He had let the past bury the dead and had come to her for one reason only. *He loved her*.

"Sirena, nothing is important. Nothing but you. I loved you from the moment I set eyes on you. I loved the Sea Siren and then I came to love Sirena, my wife. Somewhere along the way they merged and became one. It's you I want to carry my name. It's you I want to share my house. It's you I want to be the mother of my children." Why wasn't she saying something? Why was she looking at him with such horror? Had he been a fool to listen to Frau Holtz and Caleb?

Sirena listened to the words and couldn't believe her ears. Was that God she prayed to finally, after all this time, answering her prayers? Would she really be released from the nightmare of her shattered spirit, of her broken heart?

It must be a trick, she thought frantically. Or else she was dreaming. Regan would never tell her these things. How could she believe she wasn't dreaming? Her eyes widened and her hands went slack on the wheel as Regan came closer and closer. She wasn't dreaming, his touch was real, beautifully, ecstatically real.

As suddenly as the *Rana* had entered the squall, just as suddenly they had left it behind. So could the past be left behind. They knew this with a sureness neither of them had ever felt before.

The air was cool and fresh. No fog spun its disguising, isolating web between them. The moon came out from behind dark clouds and shone down on Regan and Sirena. In the clear, silvery light they gazed at one another and saw the longing and love in each other's eyes.

Regan pulled her to him, his lips burned into hers, igniting their flames of passion. Hungrily, she answered his kiss, her body pressed tightly against him. She could feel the life re-enter her soul. He made her alive with his touch, with his kiss. She was warm and loved and happier than she ever dreamed possible.

He pulled the bandana from around her head. The wind lifted the dark, curling tresses and whipped them about her face. "Why did you do that, Regan?" She smiled, her eyes glowing with happiness, her tinkling laugh sailing across the water.

Enfolding her tightly in his arms, he whispered, "I wanted to see the Sea Siren just once more."

Captive Embraces

To Mary

Chapter One

1628

The late afternoon sun dipped low on the western horizon, suffusing the tropical isle of Java in a red glow that crept through the tall, narrow windows and reflected off Luanna's slim naked beauty. Sleekly formed hips, narrow as a boy's, caught the sun as she raised her arms to undo the pins at the back of her head, allowing her jet-black hair to cascade to her slim waist. Her small breasts were firm and high; her body absent of hair as was the Javanese tradition. Luanna was fully aware of the sensual picture she presented to Regan van der Rhys. As the most sought after and notorious prostitute on the island, it was her business to know how to appeal to a man's lusty appetites.

Regan watched Luanna's preparations; mentally comparing her to a sultry feline. She moved toward the bed where he waited, sliding in beside him, pressing her hips suggestively against him. Her oblique, dark eyes smiled into his. Regan pulled her to him, conscious of her slender length against his flesh, feeling his responses rise to a throbbing urgency. Her skin was cool and fragrant, her hair perfumed and silky, falling over his face as she kissed and nibbled artfully at his lips. He returned her embrace, tasted her mouth, enjoyed the suppleness of her body. His hands found her breasts and he heard her make a faint sound almost like the purring of a contented cat. He wanted to taste, to feel, to lose himself in her, to forget.

Passions mounted and he tumbled her beneath him, burying his face in her cloud of hair, experiencing the slow curl of heat in his belly, aware that Luanna was matching his movements with a rhythm of her own.

Luanna's hands kneaded the broad muscles of his back, drawing him closer, excited by his increasing passion. Her thighs closed savagely around him, locking him to her as she felt herself being swept away by the wild emotions this man created within her. "Regan . . ." she moaned against his demanding mouth, tasting the sweetness of the wine he had consumed.

She was aware of the thick golden fleece on his chest brushing against her breasts, stimulating their coral tips to stand erect, the hard flat muscles of his stomach pressing against her, the strength of his arms and hands, the clean masculine scent of him. Each of her senses was heightened and filled by this man who could make her feel as though she'd never known another lover, who could make her believe she was created for his pleasure alone and, in giving that pleasure to him, find her own.

Her fingers traced the lines of his face and, even with her eyes closed, she could perceive his image. The brightness of his hair was like moonbeams captured on the water, thick and crisp and whitened like the grasses on the hillside during the summer. His heavy brows gave such a defiant, determined expression to his cool, agate-blue eyes, eyes that could pierce a woman's soul and make her his slave. The bronze of his skin, warmed by the sun and stung by the sea; his full sensitive lips—his smile, white and strong—the cleft in his chin which gave him a certain boyishness and endowed his handsome, almost craggy features with a vulnerability.

Touching his broad shoulders and rock-ribbed torso, she knew the power of this man, a force and energy that made a woman aware of her own defenselessness. But she also knew his gentleness, his consideration. She was reminded of it and reassured by it with each caress stirring her desires and leading her to the threshold of ecstasy. His hands reached down to grasp her hips and she gasped with anticipation. His mouth closed over hers and she began to moan and he carried her with him. Together they spun over the threshold of sensuality into the universe, whirling on a roll of thunder and blinded by a flashing bolt of rapture. In the quiet of the room she heard his voice, deep and heavy, "Sirena . . ."

Afterward Luanna's fingertips traced the frown that furrowed his brow. Lightly she kissed the slight downward pull at the corner of his mouth. She had seen him this way many times in the past months and she knew he only came to her when his passions demanded release and he needed the arms of a woman to comfort his sorrow. "There was a time, Regan, when I would have cheerfully killed you if you had whispered another woman's name while you lay in my arms," she said softly, watching the traces of bitterness cloud his eyes. "Do you know you call out for her?"

"I don't know what you're talking about!" Regan growled, making a move to leave her side.

"No, stay here with me," she whispered, pressing him back against the bedding. "It's time you told someone of your grief."

Regan turned and looked at Luanna's lovely face beside him on the pillow. "There is nothing to tell." Wresting himself free of her, he rose from the bed and reached for his clothes.

Luanna sat up, her long hair falling over her shoulders, cloaking her nudity from his eyes. "You lie! Each time you come here to be with me it is *her* name you call out. Don't you think I feel it in your touch? It's not *my* body you reach out for, it is *hers!*"

"Leave me alone, Luanna. You don't know what you're talking about." He spoke in a monotone, teeth clenched, frightening in his intensity.

Still, Luanna persisted. "I know. I am not stupid! Ever since you came back to Java with your wife and infant son you do not seek Luanna's arms. You want no other woman, only Sirena. Yet, since your young son died it is to Luanna that you come with such loneliness in your eyes."

"Nonsense!" Regan growled as he fastened the buttons on his shirt and reached for his boots.

"It is not nonsense. Do you think it is only Luanna who sees this change in you? Bah! You men! Always so strong! But a woman knows, Regan."

"It's your female imagination," he bristled, angry

with this turn in the conversation. "I don't come here for advice, Luanna," he smiled with bravado.

"You can't fool your Luanna. It is not for me that you cry out at the moment of release. It is for your wife... Sirena! Go back to her, Regan, go to your Sirena. I can't bear to see your heart breaking this way. Don't you think I know a man starved for love when I see him? Go to her. Bare your heart to her. Make her love you. Force her if you must. Break through her grief, Regan, make her see that she needs you and loves you!"

Regan was taken aback by the sincere tears he saw in Luanna's eyes. In the manner of a woman she saw straight through to the root of his problem. "Is this what I've come to, Luanna? A man who evokes a whore's pity?" he asked softly.

"And the best damn whore in all the Indies!" Luanna defended proudly.

Tentatively, he stretched out a hand to brush away the tears glistening on her smooth round cheeks.

"Get out of here, Regan! Go back to your Sirena!" Picking up the bedside lamp, she held it threateningly. "Go home to your wife!"

Silently Regan left the room, closing the door quietly behind him.

Twilight was descending again upon the long stretch of lawn that came to an abrupt end at the edge of the dense primeval jungle surrounding the van der Rhys mansion. From here, the busy growth of Batavia, Java's primary seaport, was unnoticed. The vibrant foliage insulated the house's inhabitants against any intrusion from the outside world. The splendid dwelling and outlying plantation had become the entire world to Sirena van der Rhys in the six months since the death of her only child, Mikel.

Tonight, as every night, Sirena took her place near the delicate pane-glass doors leading out to the garden, to stand sentry. Her deep green eyes penetrated the falling darkness as her mind trod the path to the edge of the lawn where Mikel's lovingly tended grave rested.

If the once ebullient servants in the van der Rhys home were subdued and watchful in her presence,

Sirena did not notice. If their once spirited steps were now a quiet shuffle, she did not care. If Regan looked to her for a sign of affection or a soft word, she did not think to respond. Sirena's only thought was of Mikel. His world was her existence; his eternity her fate.

Regan watched his wife from beneath lowered eyelids as she stood near the doors. The muscles in his lean, clean-shaven jaw tautened as he observed her shoulders slump and her classic profile turn once more to gaze out over the lawn. It had been an error of judgment to allow Sirena to place Mikel's grave so close to the house. He should have insisted that the child be placed beside his grandfather in the small plot of ground at the far end of the nutmeg grove. This standing guard, playing sentinel to a child six months cold was bringing him to the breaking point. He ran a sun-bronzed hand through his thatch of wheat-colored hair and groaned inwardly.

Why couldn't Sirena turn to him? Where had he failed her? Could she not see that the loss of their son was as painful a cross to bear for him as it was for her? Couldn't she see that sharing the loss would make the burden lighter for both of them? Where was the woman he had once known? Where was his Sea Siren? Had the spirit left her at the same moment the breath had left Mikel's body?

Regan closed his eyes against the mournful sight of Sirena and he saw her once again as he remembered her; tall and slender, an expression of supremacy on her delicate features, the light of challenge burning in her eyes. Once again he reveled in the memory of her long raven tresses swept by the sea's errant winds and the haughty set of her shoulders and the daring lift of her chin. He lived again the moments when he had seen her with a mantle of spindrift clouding her hair and settling in a salty wetness on the smooth, tawny flesh of her long, sensuous limbs.

How long had it been since he had heard her laugh? He imagined he heard it now as he had that day when he first saw her aboard her phantom ship, nearly six years ago. She had been a sea witch as she stood with feet placed firmly apart, the rapier's point dug into the deck and her rippling laugh coursing over the waters to taunt him. Then, he had been aware mostly of her abbreviated costume which revealed much of her swelling breasts and all of her lightly muscled legs.

He had never seen a woman as beautiful as the Sea Siren and he realized that beneath the somber, heavy gowns which had become Sirena's regular attire, the same beauty still lurked. The same loveliness, yet so much more. Her skin was still buffed ivory. Her eyes, once flashing emeralds, now without luster beneath a thick black fringe of lashes, were nevertheless wide and slightly tilted at the corners, giving her an Oriental appearance. And her full, sensuous lips were now drawn into a firm line. But once they had been mobile, smiling over strong, dazzling teeth. Motherhood had ripened her beauty and softened it. Though still as slim as a girl, there was a lushness about her.

His arms ached to hold her, to press her head lovingly against his chest and fill her world with love and tenderness and share with her again that all-encompassing yearning for one another. His desire to love and be loved was only secondary to his wanting to comfort her, to be comforted.

Yet Sirena had denied them both this sweet release from grief. She had spurned his advances and turned him away. And fool that he was, he had allowed it. His desire to see her comforted had controlled his passions. In his respect for her grief he had determinedly quelled his needs for her as his wife.

Currently, as Regan shifted his weight in the deep armchair he knew that the constraints of that respect had reached the breaking point. He wanted her, he needed her now! Mikel was dead and if the situation were allowed to continue there would be no respite from the eternal sorrow.

Night had fallen swiftly and the edge of the lawn was barely discernible. There was no moon to light a silvery path to Mikel's grave. These were the times Sirena dreaded the most—when Mikel was shrouded in darkness.

The sound of Regan shifting in his chair caught Sirena's attention. In the glass panes of the doors she saw his reflection. A deepening grudge burned within her. It was this emotion that was the only part of her still alive. She returned her attention to the darkness outside and recalled her horror the day Regan had come upon her soon after the child's death when she had been placing a lantern upon his grave. "It's for when the nights are black and long," she had explained tearfully. She had expected Regan to understand. Instead he had wrung the light from her hand and sent it crashing against the simple stone marker. There had been a fury in his blue eyes and a tensing of the muscles along his jaw.

"Mikel is dead!" he had exploded in a demonstration of rage. "There is no earthly light which can ease his soul. Where's your Christian belief, Sirena? Were you not taught that all little children find their place beside the Lord?"

"My son," she had returned, "was fearful of the dark!"

"Your son!" Regan had bellowed. "Was he not also mine? Would you deny me my own grief that he should be taken from me so cruelly?"

"You bury what misery you feel in your damnable office. You leave this house with thoughts of business on your mind and give not a second thought to your own flesh and blood placed so heartlessly beneath this ground. Tell me, Regan, was it for you Mikel called in the night when a stray wind would blow out his lamp? Did you hurry from your bed to cradle him and chase away his imaginings of winged creatures?" Sirena's face became alive with anger. "More than once you pulled me back against you with reassurances he would be over his terrors that much quicker if I paid them no mind! When I think of the times I heeded you, when I rested again in your arms and closed my ears to his whimpers to listen instead to your soft murmurings of love, it grates my soul! And now you would deny him this final respite which we alone can give him—a lantern on his grave!"

Regan had appeared as though struck full in the face. His features whitened, his mouth drew downward with sorrow. "You would have me believe Mikel cried out in fear. Think back, Sirena, and know the truth for what it is. When Mikel suffered nightmares, there was no chance for anyone besides you to go to him. I swear there were moments when I felt as though you kept your slippers on your feet perchance he should call to you. And those whimperings. Childhood dreams! The boy never turned in his sleep or sighed over dreams of angels that you didn't rush to his crib to watch over him. If there were indeed nights when I was able to take your thoughts from him and turn them to me, they were rare indeed!"

"Now you would have me know you were jealous of your own son!"

"No, Sirena," Regan had said truthfully, his rage calming and a tenderness creeping into his tone, "both of us know we exaggerate. It wasn't nearly the picture we paint. You were a loving mother and I a loving father. We both know this. Scenes of our son resting against your breast still haunt me. Would that we could have another child to soothe your sorrow and lighten my heart." A gentleness shone in Regan's eyes as Sirena looked up at him. His golden head had been framed by the blue of the sky and the deepness of his eyes paled the heavens. He pulled Sirena close, crushing her against him, reveling in the feel of her breasts firm and full against his chest and the fragility of her waist's small span.

Sirena's senses had been filled with him, this man who could still quench her desires and fill her life and consume her, robbing her of every thought save him. The sun had beat warmly against her back but warmer still had been contact of their flesh; her body against his, his mouth upon hers, drinking in the sweetness of her kiss.

Regan's hands had explored the soft swell of her breasts and he had reached lower to press her hips more firmly against him. Their thighs had strained toward union and their breath came in rasps of long-suppressed passion. Here was life, here was promise in Regan's arms. His fingers found the lacings of her gown and she had felt the bindings loosening and the touch of his hand against her bare flesh. Her arms had tightened about his neck, pulling his head down to her, feeling his breath upon her cheek. She had offered him her mouth, her breasts, her rapture and the sweet remembered sharing between them became alive again.

Regan had been overcome with the return of his ardor and had felt the desire within his wife bloom to full flower. The sensation was heady, drowning his senses in the flood tide of longing for her. He had tasted her salty tears running in rivulets down her cheeks to the place where their lips met.

Sirena had felt herself on the verge of giving herself to him when the sound of Regan's booted foot crunched upon the splintered glass from the lantern. The sound had penetrated her being and imbedded itself in her soul. Fraught with anger she had wrested herself from his embrace. "Would you take me here within sight of Mikel's grave? Where is your decency? Upon the very earth which covers his tiny coffin? You rutting scurve! To think I almost was a party to your perfidy!"

Regan's gaze locked with Sirena's. Slowly and deliberately he had ground another shard beneath his heel. "Where will you lay with me, Sirena?" he asked in controlled fury. "Not anywhere near here, not within the walls of our bedroom, not upon a deserted windswept island . . . where, Sirena? Where will you give yourself to me?"

The brilliant sparks had seemed to fly from Sirena's eyes, the furies unbound her rage as she had turned to face him. Were she a dragon her nostrils would have spewed fire, were she an angel the vengeance of Heaven would have crashed down upon him. Her voice was a low, menacing hiss and the cords of her neck bespoke hatred. "I am not Gretchen Lindenreich. That German bitch, that flagrant whore, who would have no respect for those things sacred. She would have lain with you upon any grave, upon any deserted isle, indeed upon the Avenue of Lions within the heart of Batavia for all of Java to witness!"

Regan had knotted his hands into fists, his rage consuming him, depriving him of all good sense. "How easily you spit Gretchen's name," he had menaced, "now that she's dead and therefore no threat. Leave the dead be, Sirena."

"How quickly you jump to her defense! If that

German bitch were here among the living, we would not be here spitting like two cats. You'd be in her bed!"

"You could do with a bit of the warmth Gretchen yeilded to me!" Regan had heaved in injury.

"To you and any other man upon the island!"

"Gretchen was always there," Regan had said in a lowered tone, his eyes piercing Sirena's with meaning.

Her eyes had murdered him as her reflexes had their way and the palm of her hand stung the flesh of his cheek in a resounding blow.

Without a second's hesitation, Regan had retaliated in kind, sending her a blow which had knocked her off her feet and left her sprawling upon the shallow mound of Mikel's grave.

That had been nearly six months ago and the same measured footsteps by which he had left her there, sobbing upon the soft earth, were now advancing upon her as she stood sentinel at the doors. She looked again at Regan's reflection in the dark glass and saw there an expression about his mouth and a light in his eyes which spoke of his intentions.

Sirena withdrew from the doors and skirted past a small table, her movements wary and her sea-green eyes feral. Her fists, alabaster white in the dim lamplit room, clenched tightly into balls as she turned to face her husband.

Her eyes pleaded with him; her breath caught in shallow sobs. She thrust her chin upward in a silent demand that he understand her feelings. Still he advanced, slowly, purposefully. She was assaulted by a memory of a long-ago occasion when he had confronted her just this way, with the same deliberate glinting in his eyes. Then he had taken her against her will. Regan had had his way. Rising above her desperate agony, Sirena managed to whisper, "I need more time, please, Regan. Don't do this to me. Just a little longer."

Regan stalked her slowly, insidiously, the magnitude of his strength looming between Sirena and the glowing light. His shoulders were massive and appeared even broader in comparison to his tapered hips and lean length of thigh. The white shirt he wore emphasized the bronze of his skin and was open to the waist, revealing the golden fur on his chest. He held his arms at his sides, his strong, capable hands barely touching his tight-cut breeches, calling to Sirena's attention the swell of his manhood beneath the thin, buff-colored fabric.

Regan realized the effect these movements were having upon Sirena. He could see the wild look of apprehension in her eyes and sense her sharp anxiety with each step he took. Within him, he was aware of a desire to quell her misgivings and tell her of his yearning for her, the longing, the agony of this life apart from her, the need to be yet still within the reaches of her gaze and the aura of her presence. He needed her as he needed the air he breathed and the blood which coursed through his veins. He needed his wife, for she alone could ease this void in his heart. Yet these words would not come from his lips. He knew she would find argument with them and he would spend another night alone with his arms hopelessly reaching out in his sleep to cradle her close to him. If Sirena were to become his wife in every way, as she had once been, it would call for stronger methods.

"You have avoided me long enough, Sirena. You asked me for just a bit longer months ago and since that day, we have been separated in more than body. We have separated in spirit. I've respected your wishes, but the time has come for you to respect mine." His voice was low and matched his deliberate motions.

"Please, Regan, a little longer," Sirena breathed, taking a step backward.

"Do my ears deceive me, are you pleading with me? The Sea Siren begging?" His laugh came harsh and tinged with menace in the quiet room.

"The Sea Siren is dead. That was another life, long ago. Before Mikel, before everything." Still Regan advanced and Sirena read the determination in his eyes. She felt his powerful emotions as if they were tangible. Ironically, she remembered the effect his blue eyes had once had upon her. She knew how they could render her immobile, bent on his bidding.

Regan advanced another step as Sirena clutched at the edge of a square table, keeping its width between them. "How long?" he taunted. "A day, a week, a month? How long?"

"I don't know. Just a bit more . . . I . . ."

"My patience is at an end. Six months is more than any man can be expected to bear. You're my wife and I expect you to act like it!"

"I can't . . . not yet . . . just—"

"Mikel is dead. You can't bring him back! Put it behind you and go on from there. If you don't, then we're both doomed. There can be other children; we have years."

"Easy for you to say, your arms aren't empty! I was his mother, he was my flesh and blood! I've had everyone taken from me, everyone I loved. Tio Juan, Isabella—and now Mikel. This godforsaken land has taken everything from me." Sirena's gaze became misty and her lower jaw trembled from suppressed tears.

Regan's heart went out to her. She was so vulnerable, so defeated. "And what of me, love? I haven't been taken from you. Can't you find some small joy in the fact that we still have each other?"

Regan's words caught Sirena's attention and stirred her from the depths of self-pity. The lamplight behind him cast deep shadows over his rugged face but there was an emotion to be read there which made Sirena issue a slight moan. Regan was a virile and vital man, not one to be put aside to spend the remainder of his days in celibacy. She loved him, she knew that, yet her arms seemed weighted and strapped to her sides, her feet frozen to the floor. There was a dull ache deep within her as she recognized his loneliness, yet she was powerless to lift her arms to embrace him. Her feet refused to take that first small step which would take her to him and find her crushed against him, sharing the burden of grief and finding joy in loving.

Regan watched the play of emotion flash across Sirena's face. He saw the thick, black fringe of lashes close over her wide, cat-like eyes. He experienced a weakness, an anticipation of hunger soon to be fed, a longing and yearning near the brink of being fulfilled. Her moist lips parted and he could not take his gaze from them, remembering their warmth and sweetness as they clung to his, easing his passions and replenishing his sense of wonder that this vivacious goddess, who had once been named "Sea Siren", should have chosen him above all other men to gift with her love.

Regan's heart thundered in his chest. Somehow he had to stir Sirena from her apathy and make her come alive. Again he pressed, "Am I to think I count for nothing?"

"That's not what I meant . . ." Sirena stammered. "I speak of what was mine. My flesh and blood."

"You told me once that a person can't own another. You didn't own your uncle and your sister. We were both parents to Mikel."

The dark head lifted, her sea-green eyes turned murky. "Mikel was mine. I gave birth to him and now he's dead. That fool of a doctor killed him and you let it happen!"

Regan's shoulders slumped, but only for a moment. "There were two doctors and they both agreed. Even the natives, who have lived with the fever for as long as memory, agreed. Mikel was beyond saving. Place no blame on my shoulders, Sirena. If it's children you want, then you'll be pregnant nine months out of the year," he grinned mischievously.

Her eyes sparkled dangerously. "So you can run with every whore from Java To Sumatra? No thank you."

"You expect too much," Regan said with forced evenness. "I'm a man and six months is—"

"Too long to be faithful!" Sirena interrupted. "Say it, Regan. You don't care how I feel and what I think. All you know is that you must have your lust satisfied. Then go satisfy it somewhere else," she hissed, her eyes narrowing, the delicate line of her jaw tight and forbidding.

"I will do exactly that," Regan growled, "but not until—"

"Think again, Regan. I'm only yours if I want to be." Sirena said softly, blood surging through her. "I have no intention of playing this cat-and-mouse game. I know what you want. I know what all this is leading to. I gave you my answer once and I will only repeat it one more time. I am not leaving this island!" She came around the table, stepping close to him, challenging him, speaking slowly, giving each word its full weight. "I stay here with Mikel. I will not live with the thought of the damnable jungle creeping over my son's grave, obliterating it! I stay here. When I begged you to leave while Mikel was still alive, you refused. Now the shoe is on the other foot. I'm staying here! Go, go to Spain and see to my holdings. That's what you want. You want to take everything from me. Take it. I no longer care!"

"Your inheritance is mine, but only in the eyes of the law. You speak as though your holdings are my sole interest in you. Still, someone must put them in order," Regan said defensively.

"And you're that someone! I know the laws, you made me painfully aware of them a long time ago. What I own is yours, not mine, not ours, yours. Take everything that belongs to me and I'll still survive to tend my son's grave."

Regan drew his breath in sharply. "The child is dead, you must stop grieving. Life is for the living," he said, reaching out for her.

"Leave me alone," Sirena warned, grasping a decanter of wine, holding it aloft.

"And if I don't? Will you fight me when I simply want to claim what is mine?" Regan asked churlishly.

"Why can't you be more patient? Why do you have to be such a bull? Listen to me, Regan," she said softly. "Much has happened to me. So much, too much to forget. My arms ache to hold Mikel. My eyes burn for the sight of his sweet face. My heart is dead. In time I'll accept my loss, but that time hasn't come. I do love you. I'll always love you, but you can never replace that which I felt for my son. Why won't you understand?"

His agate eyes clouded, spelling their own message of loss. "He was my son, too. We should share our grief. We should comfort each other. I tried to ease your agony but you rejected me just as you rejected Caleb. How do you think the boy feels?"

Sirena's hand, holding the decanter, lowered. A new pain came into her eyes when she thought of young Caleb. She adored him. He was like a brother to her. A much-loved brother. But he wasn't Mikel. Somewhere in her mind it registered that Regan was too close, almost upon her. "You have Caleb. He is your son, your flesh and blood. I have nothing. You lost one son. I lost my *only* son! I have nothing. Nothing!"

Regan grasped her arms, pulling her across the floor, her heavy, black skirts trailing.

"Take your hands off me! No man will ever again subject me to rape and that includes you!" she snarled, her teeth bared. "Sooner or later you'll have to release one of my hands and the moment you do, you'll be blinded. I'll pluck your mocking eyes out of your ignorant head!"

Regan merely laughed, the sound raising the hackles on the back of Sirena's neck.

"Damn your soul to Hell!" Sirena shrilled, her fists beating against his hard chest. Regan's hold on her forearm was viselike, yet she continued to struggle. Her legs thrashed out at him from beneath her cumbersome skirts.

Regan locked both her thin wrists in one large hand, his other drawing her face to within inches of his. He looked deep into her stormy eyes and grinned. This was the Sirena he knew and loved. This woman of determination, of vitality; who would fight and spit and turn the fates to her advantage; who could stir his blood and arouse his passions; who would meet him on equal footing or see them both dead before admitting failure. Sirena, his Siren. This was the temptress who was the creator of her own destiny; who would never compromise with what life sent her way but would rush out and meet life and savor it and change that which was not to her liking.

He forced her face still closer and crushed her mouth with his. "Devil!" he shouted furiously as he drew back, blood oozing from his lip. His grip loosened momentarily and Sirena wrenched free, racing to the long, curved stairway and up to her bedroom and the security of its locked door.

In a rage Regan bounded up the steps, his arms reaching out in an attempt to catch her by the skirt.

Fleet of foot, Sirena eluded him and breathlessly gained the top of the stairs. Regan was close behind her, careening in a zigzag pattern, his heavy shoulders glancing against the wall.

Sirena reached her bedroom and successfully slammed the door, turning the key in the lock. Her eyes wide and staring, she backed across the room, cursing herself for her foolhardiness. A wooden barrier would never stop Regan; she should have run through the garden doors and out into the jungle. There, in the dark, hidden from view, she could have bided her time until Regan's fury cooled.

Regan threw himself against the door. Once. Twice. The third time the teak splintered as a result of his force and Sirena's spine stiffened as she prepared herself for his attack. Regan stepped over the fallen fragments. His head lowered, glaring up at her from beneath hooded lids, his mouth a line of grim resolution.

"Have you no respect for bereavement? Have you no respect for your son's death or his mother? Do you think of nothing save that which rests between your legs? Get out of here! Satisfy your lust somewhere else!"

Still he came, step by step, shoulders hunched, eyes blazing.

"Leave me to my mourning. I'm warning you, Regan . . . ," she said huskily, backing into the room, putting the width of the bed between them. An instant later Regan was across the bed, his arms reaching for her. Sirena jerked her arm free of his grasp and felt the fabric of her sleeve rip as she luched around the foot of the bed.

"Bastard!" she shrieked. "Tear my clothes, will you?" The lamp found its way into her hand and sailed past Regan, missing him by a scant hairbreadth. A crystal scent bottle followed. Regan tried to brush the scent from his clothes. "Now you smell like the brothels you play in," Sirena gasped as a brush and then a heavy jar sailed toward him.

Regan chuckled, "How is it you know how a brothel smells?"

"Whoring bastard!" Sirena shrilled. "You talk in your sleep. I learn everything about you when you sleep. I ask you questions and you, fool that you are, answer me." Suddenly she laughed, a high, silvery tinkle that bounced off the walls and came to rest on Regan's ears. He flinched at the sound but leapt across the bed.

Deftly, she sidestepped him, flinging a small, jeweled coffer at his head.

"If that had found its mark, I would be seriously hurt," Regan growled.

"I know," Sirena answered softly, "you've grown fat, Regan. You're slow and clumsy, like all Dutchmen," she trilled. "Rich food and too much rum has added inches to your girth. I have no desire to bed an obese man," she taunted. "Find your way out of my presence."

"You can't win, Sirena. I mean to have you and I will. Come here to me and we'll make a new son." The instant the words were out of his mouth he wished he could take them back. Never had he seen such unleashed fury.

The room was a living explosion of objects hurtling as though they had a life of their own. Dresser drawers and anything that could be lifted had to be reckoned with. Dodging a high-flying shoe, he covered his head, cursing all Spaniards and women in general. Sirena returned his oaths just as quickly and vehemently. "All you want is for me to be ugly and heavy with your child."

"I'm a man," Regan said through clenched teeth, "and you're a woman!"

"Which means what?"

"Which means I'm the superior. We're not fighting with weapons now. Now it's man versus woman and the man is the stronger."

"I have only your word for that. Chaezar Alvarez made the mistake of thinking the same thing," Sirena said quietly as she gauged the distance between herself and the doorway.

"Chaezar," Regan sneered, "was an animal, not a man! I am a man, Sirena, your husband, and when I say I mean to have you, I will! You are also coming with me when I leave for Spain. I've had enough of this nonsense," he said, racing toward the door as soon as he saw what her objective was.

Roughly he grasped her by both shoulders, his fingers biting cruelly into her flesh. He issued an epithet of disgust as he threw her onto the bed. The breath driven from her body, Sirena could only gasp. Regan stood looking down at her, his face a mixture of emotions. "I mean to have you . . . one way or the other," he said distinctly. "And make no mistake, you'll be aboard my ship in the morning. I have just now decided to hasten my departure and you will be with me!"

Sirena lay quietly, her eyes half closed. She neither acknowledged hearing his words nor that she cared what he stated.

"Stand up!" Regan ordered.

"No."

Regan pulled her to her feet. "Take your clothes off," he ordered. "You always did have a penchant for wearing mourning garb. When you first came here, you hid yourself beneath your black gowns and your prayer beads. All the while you were commanding a ship, playing the part of a lady pirate. Lady! Bah! You were no more a lady than the monkeys in the trees. I'm sick of this drab attire. Take it off!"

"No."

"Then I will do it for you," Regan snarled as he tore her gown from throat to navel. Her breasts, free of their restrictions, were taut and erect beneath the thin chemise she wore.

"Remove the rest," he commanded sharply, his eyes on her quivering bosom.

"No."

Staring steadily at his face, Sirena felt the rest of her gown slip to the floor and lay about her feet. Regan's hands were clenched into fists and it was with effort that he opened them to lower her gently to the soft mattress. She remained limp, her eyes wide and unblinking as his lips crushed hers. Desire mounted in him as he touched and caressed her, knowing which delicate caress awakened her desire and response.

Caught in his passions, he mouthed sweet words of love as his lips feverishly sought her mouth, her throat, her breasts. He willed her to respond, demanded it, needed it.

His kisses were gentle and expert as he worshipped her. Tenderly, his lips clung to hers, softly he tasted the sweetness that was hers alone. Their breath mingled, the pulse of her throat beat a tattoo against his hungry mouth. She was warm and supple beneath him, her breasts flattened against his chest, her hips answering his.

A small cry escaped her as he kissed her with passion-bruised lips. Her senses whirled and soared, making her dizzy with a joy that bordered upon lust. Her arms closed about him, drawing him nearer.

She craved his touch, the taste of his mouth, the smell of his skin. She had been starved for him and she hadn't even realized it. She had been so caught up with thoughts about Mikel that she had lost all touch with her own feelings. She had turned away from Regan because he could make her aware that she was alive and she hadn't wanted to be alive. She had denied Regan and herself. This man she adored with her whole being, wanted her, needed her, and she had needed him in return.

Now he had put her back in contact with life. And she wanted to give herself—her body, her love—to him. Her sensuous embraces were answered with Regan's scorching passion. Moaning with ecstasy, she turned her body in his arms, pliant to his demands, relishing the sensuality that was rising to the surface. A sensuality too long held dormant.

Exulting in his pleasure, Sirena sought for and found the most sensual caress and was enraptured with the pleasure and inspiration she gave him. Against his lips she murmured, "Have me, have me, Regan. For now, for tomorrow, for always . . ."

Afterwards they lay in each other's arms, both of them having found peace. Sirena's eyes closed languidly.

"Darling, have you changed your mind? You will come with me, say it. I need to hear you say it." Regan's voice was warm and his arms tightened about her, urging her answer.

"Shhhh," Sirena whispered, laying a gentle hand on his lips. "We'll speak of it later."

"No." Regan's tone was gentle. "We must discuss

it now. I want you to travel to Spain with me. Caleb is in school in Holland. We'd be closer to him in Spain. Say you'll come." He was just making a formal gesture in asking. There wasn't a doubt in his mind that her answer would be in the affirmative. "Your holdings must be put in order. You've always wanted to return to your homeland and now I'm ready to go with you."

"But Mikel. I can't leave him," Sirena said tearfully.

"Sirena," Regan said kindly, "Mikel is gone. Staying here won't change anything."

"I can't. I can't leave. I hate this island and what it has robbed from me," Sirena cried, "but I can't leave. How can you be so inhuman as to ask me such a thing. Didn't Mikel mean anything to you? How can you want to abandon the one thing our love created? I don't understand you, you're his father."

"*Was* his father. Why don't *you* understand? Day after day you sit there by his grave and pull the weeds so the jungle won't claim that small mound of earth."

"I can't leave," Sirena repeated, burying her head in the pillow. "Don't force me to go with you."

"No, I won't make you do something against your will," Regan said sadly. "But I've decided to leave in the morning. If you change your mind . . ."

He was answered by Sirena's sobs as she buried her face deeper. Regan stretched out beside her, holding her, comforting her. God, how I love him, she thought. Why can't I do as he asks? He meant to go with her or without her. Regan never made half statements. How could she survive without him? How could she desert Mikel?

Sometime during the long night Regan quietly left their bed. He stood looking down at Sirena for a long moment, etching her lovely features upon his memory.

Sirena stirred, feeling his glance as though it were a loving caress. She sat up in bed, hair tumbled into a wreath of cloudy darkness, eyes bright with unshed tears, and cheeks flushed with emotion. "Regan, your ship isn't ready to set sail. You planned this trip for the end of the month, why are you leaving so soon?"

"You know the answer to that, darling. It's become a simple matter of choice. Mikel or me. Last night reminded me how much I love you and need you.

There's no place in my life for half a wife. Come with me now, Sirena. Be my love. Take Mikel with you in your heart."

She dropped her eyes, not being able to bear seeing the pain in his. When she again looked up, Regan's look was cold and bitter. "Then this is good-bye, Sirena. If you should ever tire of your prayers and your vigils, perhaps you will join me in Cádiz. But *I won't wait forever, Sirena.*"

"I understand," she said flatly. "Have a safe voyage," she whispered, her throat constricting with her words.

"Sirena . . . I . . . ," the words were lost as she lay back against her pillow, her face calm, her eyes tearless. Regan smacked one large fist into the palm of the other hand and looked down at her. She appeared as if she were already dead and his heart went out to her. Was there nothing he could say to bring her out of this lethargy? Last night there had been a fire in her. He glanced about the room and saw the shambles they had created with their struggling. Was that the only way he could bring about her response? Did he want to spend the rest of his life raping his own wife, begging her for a physical expression of caring? For the first time he accepted the fact that she would never journey to Europe with him. Never join him on a new adventure. She had made her choice and he would have to acknowledge it, no matter how difficult it might be.

When Regan left, Sirena lay on the tumbled sheets for some time. Emotion flooded through her, threatening to drown her, choking off air. Regan . . . Regan . . . her heart cried. She cried for the love they had shared, the life they had made together . . . the son they had lost.

Why couldn't Regan realize that somehow her loss of Mikel was easier to bear when she was near the little plot of ground where the child rested.

Sirena rose and scouted the room for her dressing gown and slippers. A smile brightened her face as she perused the wreckage of the evening before. He had been magnificent. He had conquered the feelings of emptiness engulfing her. He had demanded her love and had received it. He had been right. She did need his love. She did want it. She was a vital woman—a woman grown used to feeling the arms of her lover around her and the passions he could arouse in her.

The house seemed suddenly empty. More desolate than it had when Caleb had gone off to school in Holland. Then, she still had Mikel to fill the day. And Regan to fill the nights. Now it was the loneliest she had ever known it to be. Even Mikel's death had not made her feel this way. Regan's leaving had made it become no more than a frame, a dwelling. Regan had made it a home.

Down the stairs she ran, out to the garden. The dew glistening on the lawn soaked through her slippers and the chill morning air made her shiver.

Heedless of the wetness, Sirena knelt beside the grave. Images of Mikel's laughing face scampered through her memory. "Mikel . . . Mikel . . . ," she cried, throwing herself face down over the shallow mound as she had done on so many days in the past. Only this time she could not feel her son's presence. This time he seemed so distant. Pathetically her fingers dug into the soft earth, clutching, gasping, refusing to be separated from her child. Heaving sobs shook her body, tears mingled with the dew. Her grief was a lonely monster strangling her, cutting off her life, making her one of the living dead.

To her own amazement the name she cried out was not Mikel's, it was Regan's. Over and over she repeated his name, suffering his loss. Then an image of herself crept into her consciousness. It was of an old woman, alone and unloved, weeping over the grave of a child hundreds of years dead. She was empty . . . There was no comfort to be derived from this little plot. Mikel wasn't really beneath this ground, he was in her heart. He was in Regan's heart. No matter where Regan would go, no matter what he would do, he would carry Mikel with him. And so could she. She could leave Java and take Mikel with her. He would always be with her in a place that was warm and bright.

"Regan! Regan!" she called, stumbling across the

wide lawn, running, running toward her love. "Regan!"

Up the stairs and into her room, searching and seeking for her gown, her shoes. She would go to Batavia and tell him to wait for her. She would go anywhere with him, now, tomorrow, forever! And Regan would wait, she knew he would. They would come home together and see to closing the house. There was packing to be done and Frau Holtz would need time to gather together her own possessions. They would be together. Always together.

"Frau Holtz!" she yelled from the top of the stairs, "Frau Holtz, where are you?"

"Ja, I am here," came the reply from the old housekeeper as she began to climb to the second floor.

"No, don't come up. There's no time. Have a horse brought around to the front of the house for me."

The urgency in Sirena's voice alarmed the aged woman. "Is there anything wrong? Where are you going, Mevrouw?"

"No time to answer questions," Sirena said with exasperation. "Just do as I say!"

"Ja, I do it!" Frau Holtz agreed as she turned on her heel toward the back of the house. Her step was lighter than it had been in months and for some strange reason her bones didn't ache as badly as they had just a moment before. A smile on her wizened old face, the housekeeper went to find the stable boy. This wonderful change in Sirena was a miracle. Only yesterday she had thought that she would never see that spark of life lighting Sirena's eyes again. *"Ja,* I do it," Frau Holtz repeated to herself. "I do anything to see her alive again!"

Galloping down the dusty road to Batavia, Sirena laughed and urged the horse onward. Her long, dark hair billowed out behind her, her eyes flashed vibrantly, her smooth cheeks were flushed with excitement and she carried in her the picture of Regan's face when she told him she would never let him depart without her. They belonged together. They had the strength, the wonder, of their love to draw upon.

Wildly thrashing the horse's flanks, she urged it faster, faster, to Regan.

Down the elite Avenue of Lions she galloped, then through the narrow little streets to the offices of the Dutch East India Company. The wharf was a cacophony of longshoremen and traders. They turned to glance at her in amazement. The horse's hooves beat like drums upon the planks leading out over the water. Regan's office was at the far end of the wharf and she could see his mount tethered outside the door.

Sirena rushed into the offices, breathless and disheveled and looking more beautiful than she had in months. The Company clerks dropped their quills, their mouths gaped open in astonishment. Not stopping to make explanations, Sirena burst into Regan's office, her face wreathed in smiles, her eyes glowing with anticipation.

"Regan, darling, I'm coming—" the words were choked off in her throat. Instead of Regan there was their friend, Captain Dykstra.

"Peter," Sirena asked breathlessly, "where's Regan? I have wonderful news for him—" Captain Dykstra's handsome features were drawn into a scowl and something in his bright blue eyes frightened her.

"Peter, where is he?" Sirena asked again, this time quietly, almost subdued.

"Peter?"

"Sirena, he's gone."

"Gone? Gone?" she stammered, not comprehending what he meant. "But that's impossible? I've come down here to tell him I've made up my mind. I've decided to go with him, go anywhere with him? Where has he gone?"

Peter Dykstra's throat swelled with emotion. He knew Regan and Sirena when they were first married. He had seen their love grow and now the pain in Sirena's eyes was almost more than he could stand. Wordlessly he took Sirena's arm and led her over to the window facing the sea. There, just at the horizon she perceived the top of a sail.

Her flashing, green eyes searched Peter's wildly. "He's left? Without me?" She needed no answer; it was there in Captain Dykstra's face.

"The tides were right, Sirena. He said there was no sense putting off sailing. I tried to stop him, his ship hasn't been properly careened for such a long voyage. I told him it was foolhardy but he wouldn't listen. He never listens!" Peter grumbled.

Staggering to a chair, Sirena dropped heavily into it, covering her face with her hands. Beneath her nails was the thin, black line of dirt that had come from digging her fingers into the earth on Mikel's grave. Gone! Regan was gone! "Peter, you've got to help me. I must go to him! Help me," she implored, reaching out and clutching his sleeve.

Peter Dykstra was helpless. Her agony was clearly apparent and mirrored that of Regan's which he'd witnessed earlier. "I can't help you, Sirena. There isn't a ship in the harbor ready to make sail. Even if there were, they're filled to the brim with cargo. You'd never catch him. The best you can do is wait a month when the next ship sets sail for Europe."

"The *Rana,*" Sirena said hopefully, "I could—"

Peter Dykstra shook his head. "No, you couldn't. She's not seaworthy. She's been in drydock. Be reasonable."

Sirena looked to the window. Even from where she sat, she could see the tip of Regan's sail drop over the horizon. Peter was right. She could never catch him.

"Sirena, let me take you home," Peter said softly, touching her hand in consolation.

"Home? Where is that?"

Chapter Two

Month after dreary month passed with Sirena doing no more than making a daily pilgrimage to the burial site. Afterward she would sit in the garden until the rains came, then return to the house and apathetically work on embroidery. She grew thin and gaunt, the hollows in her cheeks more pronounced with each passing day. The once vibrant green eyes were now as dull and lifeless as her spirit.

Nearly five months had passed since Regan had left, and Frau Holtz was observing Sirena from the doorway. She would never forget that morning when Captain Dykstra had brought Sirena home from the wharf. Regan was gone. Over and over Sirena whispered the words, tears glittering in her eyes.

Regan's leaving alone had taken the life from the Mevrouw. By nightfall Sirena had been put to bed with a raging fever, and it had been several weeks before she regained even a semblance of her former strength. The absence of those she cared for most was almost more than she could bear. Sirena had never again spoken of joining Regan. It was almost as though he, too, were dead and buried. Every so often Frau Holtz would encourage Sirena to talk about him, hoping that in doing so Sirena would be persuaded to leave Java and follow her husband. Always she would receive the same response.

"If Regan had loved me, he would have waited for me. It's obvious he wanted no part of me. He knew I didn't want to leave Mikel and he was counting on it to keep me here. No, I won't chase him. I want nothing to do with a man who doesn't want me."

From her position near the door, Frau Holtz noticed a figure on horseback approaching the long drive leading to the house. She squinted into the bright sunlight and realized it was Peter Dykstra.

Wiping her hands on her apron, the housekeeper hurried out to meet him. It would be good for Sirena to have company.

"The Mevrouw is in the garden, Captain Dykstra. Come, I'll take you to her. She will be happy to see you. Visitors don't come very often."

Captain Dykstra drew his breath in sharply at the appearance Sirena made. What in the name of God has happened to her? Alarmed because of the news he brought, he debated a second and then sat down beside her.

"Peter, how nice to see you," she said, her voice a

thin wail. He looked at her dull expression and flinched. Yet he knew he must tell her why he had made the call.

"How have you been, Peter? You look well."

"Sirena, I've come to tell you something. I have some disturbing news." She appeared so ill—no, that wasn't it exactly; she appeared tired, exhausted; as though life had become too much for her.

Sirena tilted her head out of the sun's direct glare. "Yes, Peter, I'm listening. Is something amiss at the office?"

"No, the Company is still doing well. I have information concerning the *Spanish Lady,* Regan's ship." Sirena waited patiently for him to continue. Her face was unreadable.

"The reports I received were . . . incomplete, to say the least. What I'm trying to say, Sirena, is that the *Lady* was sunk off the coast of Spain. No one is certain if the hands were captured by a marauding ship or lost at sea. There was a violent storm and that's all I know. I myself just arrived back from ports near Cathay and the Far East. One of the men returned to port only this noon hour and gave me the message. I'm sorry, Sirena. If there's anything I can do, feel free to ask."

Peter Dykstra's brow was beaded with perspiration. It was unbelievable, she registered no emotion at all. He glanced at Frau Holtz and then back at Sirena.

"You must feel terrible about this, Peter. I know Regan was your friend." She reached out and patted his hand in consolation. Her touch was ice cold, sending chills racing up his spine.

"Certainly I feel terrible, Sirena, but I must say you're taking it rather well. He was my friend, but he was your husband!"

"You have just learned that Regan is lost to you today. He's been lost to me for months. Ever since he sailed away from Java, leaving me behind. My grief is an old one, yours is fresh. Forgive me if I didn't react the way you anticipated, Peter. But I can't. I feel as though I died a year ago and no one has had the decency to bury me. Thank you for coming here to tell me. Now, if you'll excuse me, I want to be alone."

Dykstra rose from the bench. She was right. Her

sorrow was an old one. She was dead inside. He heard it in her voice and saw it in her eyes. Regan may be dead but he hadn't left behind a widow. His wife was dead long before he was. He placed a tender hand on Sirena's shoulder. "Remember, if there's anything I can do—" He realized she wasn't listening.

Frau Holtz watched Captain Dykstra as he rode toward the road leading back to Batavia. She stood closer to Sirena. The elderly woman was also puzzled by the Mevrouw's lack of emotion.

Suddenly Sirena laughed. "It's a trick! Can't you see through it? This is Regan's way of getting me to come to Spain. He must need my signature on some documents or something of the sort. He has no interest in me, only in my money. I never thought he would do anything so drastic! Imagine. Regan, one of the best seamen in the fleet, allowing his ship to be sunk. Never. The *Spanish Lady* could ride out any storm no matter how violent."

"Mevrouw, I know Captain Dykstra told you on the day Regan left that the ship was not fit to sail. And I, myself, heard them arguing two days before the Mynheer left. Captain Dykstra was telling the Mynheer that the six months that he had been filling himself with rum the vessel was unattended. Captain Dykstra warned the Mynheer and told him to have the *Lady* seen to. There was no time to do it; the Mynheer left before he could—"

"Poor Frau Holtz. I should have realized how Peter's news would upset you. You've taken care of Regan since he was a small boy and you love him like your own." Tenderly, she took the housekeeper into her arms and comforted her while the old woman shed tears for Regan.

Something crept into Sirena's heart. "Frau Holtz, do you really think that something has happened to Regan?"

"I only tell you what I heard with my own ears. I woud not lie to you," the old woman sobbed. "I raised that man from the time he was a boy. He would never trick you into believing he was dead. For what reason? For your name on a slip of paper? No, he would find his way around that. And it is not to pull you away from Java. If he wanted a woman, there is always someone beautiful ready to fall into his bed. No, Mevrouw, you may be his wife, but I know the Mynheer. Something terrible has happened. I can sense it!"

Sirena comforted the other woman and felt a sinking sensation in her own heart. Perhaps Frau Holtz was right. But then that would mean that Regan was dead! No, she couldn't believe that. She would never believe that. Not Regan!

A week passed and then two without Sirena going to the small grave. From her position on the balcony, she watched the jungle creep closer to the shallow mound. At the end of the third week, the vines had already trailed over the little marker, and she was aware that within the next few days there would be no sign that a much-loved little body rested beneath the lush foliage.

Dry-eyed, she called for Frau Holtz and pointed to where Mikel rested. "It's gone. I can leave now. I'm going to take the *Rana* and set out for Spain. Do you want to remain here or will you come with me?"

"Ja," Frau Holtz said sternly, "I've been packed since the day Captain Dykstra came here. Your trunks are mostly ready also. Jacobus and your crew have already taken the ship out of dry dock and she is well stocked with provisions and ready to sail. We only wait for you."

Sirena swallowed hard and looked at the housekeeper. "I still say it's a trick! Yet my heart tells me otherwise. Dismiss the servants and give them ample wages. Close the house and we'll leave."

"Ja," Frau Holtz said happily. *"Ja.* If anyone can discover what has become of the Mynheer, it is you, Mevrouw."

"Ja," Sirena teased, "it is me."

The *Rana*'s crew greeted Sirena joyously, their faces filled with delight. It was old Jacobus who bowed low with a grand flourish and then impulsively gathered her close and swept her across the polished deck. Sirena giggled for the first time in months, her eyes sparkling. "Take me to my homeland, Jacobus. Take me to Spain."

"Aye, Capitana, your homeland it will be. But it will be you who takes us there. There's not one among us fit to captain this ship. If the boy Caleb were here, it would be a different matter. Have you heard any more news of the captain?"

"Why are we standing here?" Frau Holtz demanded. "The longer we stand here mooning around the less time we'll have to search for the Mynheer."

"This is my first mate," Sirena said to the grinning seamen. "You heard the lady, hoist the anchor and raise the sail. Jacobus, take the wheel, and I'll relieve you shortly."

"Aye, Capitana," Jacobus answered, using the name her crew had given her when they had ridden the seas on their vengeful mission to locate and destroy the man known as "the Hook." He had been directly responsible for the death of Sirena's sister, Isabella, and their search for him had led them through an adventure it would fill a book to tell. She had been Sirena Córdez then. Proud and beautiful, as she still was. She had been humiliated and badly used by a band of ruthless pirates. When she and the young boy, Caleb, plotted their escape, they had taken command of an elusive vessel and she had earned for herself the name "Sea Siren," in her thirst for revenge.

It was to Regan van der Rhys that her sister Isabella had been betrothed. Sirena had taken her dead sister's place and married the impassioned, sun-gilded master of the Dutch East Indies whose lusty tastes were stifled by his marriage to the seemingly demure Sirena. The Sea Siren and Regan clashed on land as man and wife and on the seas as enemies, before finding that they loved and desired each other more than either had ever thought possible.

Jacobus smiled. Nothing would give him more pleasure than to sail the seas with her again and discover what new exploits the future held.

Frau Holtz bustled around the cabin, unpacking the trunks and tidying, muttering something about sloppy seamen and the mildew that was fast taking hold between the floor planks.

Sirena chuckled as she tied her blouse in a knot beneath her full breasts. "I'll leave you to your housekeeping duties and take the wheel from Jacobus."

On deck, the wheel in her grip, Sirena felt as though she had taken a grip on life. She was at peace. A feeling which had eluded her for too many months. A feeling she relished and accepted.

Lashing rain beat against the tall, narrow windows of the expansive, gray stone building across the canal from The Hague. For once Caleb van der Rhys took no notice of the harsh weather which cursed Holland. Usually, his mood would blacken with the low, scudding clouds and his thoughts would invariably return to the sun-filled days of the East Indies. He detested this country, the school he attended, and the boredom of his existence. The regimentation of his days was a far cry from the excitement and danger he had experienced at sea when he served as cabin boy to Sirena van der Rhys, his stepmother. In those days she had been known as the Sea Siren and he had fought beside her as she wreaked her revenge on those who had made her life a living hell. He had been a badly misused cabin boy, indentured from ship to ship, when she had found him and had made him her friend.

Because of Sirena he had been reunited with his father, who had thought him dead for many years. Regan was everything a young man could hope for in a father and Sirena, who had met her lusty match in Regan and married him, was more than a young man could wish for in a stepmother.

Caleb stood before the tall looking glass, smoothed his dark hair and straightened his silky, white cravat. He nervously brushed minuscule specks of dust from the sleeve of his jacket and stood on one foot, rubbing the toe of a polished boot against the back of his other leg. Satisfied that the tips of his boots were dazzling and his cravat was properly tied, he brought himself to full height and purposely restrained himself from running headlong down the corridors to the austere front parlor to greet Regan.

Caleb had been wrestling with Latin when the dormitory messenger had interrupted his studies and relayed the information that Mynheer van der Rhys was awaiting him downstairs. In the midst of his excitement, Caleb held a single wish in his heart; that Regan had come to take him out of school and return with him to Java. Mingled with that hope was the certainty that Regan would view him as a full-grown man and accept him as such. Caleb glanced once again in the mirror and straightened his shoulders and lifted his chin. There was no denying that he was no longer the boy Regan had left behind in Holland. Caleb's features had matured. The soft, boyish roundness had disappeared from his jaw and he had been shaving regularly for more than six months now. His coat fit snugly around his broad shoulders and emphasized his muscular build. In a few months he would be eighteen, surely old enough to make his own way in the world and take his place as a man among men.

He bounded down the steps three at a time and only had a second to tighten his lips over an ebullient whoop of joy.

Caleb walked into the sparsely furnished parlor where visitors were admitted. His dark eyes lighted at the sight of his father, then immediately darkened to a scowl. "Sirena isn't with you?" he asked accusingly.

"No," Regan answered, his voice little more than a deep growl. "I told you in my letter not to expect her. Why do you torture yourself with the thought that she would come here? Look at you!" Regan said jovially, trying to distract Caleb from his thoughts, "I left a boy and now I return to find a man!"

Caleb stood next to his father at eye level, a replica of his father except for his dark hair. "I'm pleased you accept me as a man. Then you understand my feelings and have come to take me out of school."

"No, Caleb, that is not my intention," Regan answered with a deep sigh. Why did everything have to come to an opposition of wills? Caleb might be his own son, yet he was more like Sirena than Regan cared to admit. At times it seemed to him that Caleb had never had another mother; that Tita, the Javanese princess who had birthed the boy, had never existed. It was Sirena who had formed the boy's spirit. And like Sirena, Caleb spoke his mind and was willing to fight to win his objective.

"Father, I gave you my word I would stay until the end of the term, but when it is over, I'm leaving. I'm through with this dark land that is Holland. Nor will I stay with you in Spain. I'm going back to Java."

"You're going back for Sirena, is that it? I always knew that if it came to a choice, you would choose her over me, your own father."

"I just said I was going back to Java. I plan to sign on a ship with Captain Dykstra. I'll look in on Sirena and see how she's faring without a man in the house. You shouldn't have left her alone on the island," he said flatly.

"And you refuse to forget it or understand why! You'll always hold it against me, is that what you're saying?" Regan's face deepened into an angry frown and he impatiently tossed back the fringe of white-blond hair which fell across his tanned brow.

"No, Father, that's what you're saying," Caleb parried. "I have no mind for school and being a gentleman. I'm going back to sea where I can be what I want to be. And if my going where I belong means I lose my father . . . " Caleb shrugged his shoulders in a gesture of pretended indifference. He loved Regan and Sirena and he rationalized that what they did with their own lives had little to do with him. But the pain was still there and now it rose in his throat like bitter gall. He hoped that Regan would not test him and refuse to understand his feelings.

"This is not what I came all the way to discuss with you," Regan said quietly, settling himself upon a stiff, hard-backed chair and reaching in his pocket for a cheroot.

"When I saw Sirena wasn't with you, I immediately surmised that," Caleb lowered his voice. He searched the inside of his own jacket for a black cheroot which he lit with a glowing taper from the ever-present fire that had slight effect on the damp room. Offering Regan a light, he tossed the taper into the flames and sat opposite his father.

Regan had never seen Caleb smoke until now and was strangely rankled. Chalking it up to regret that his son was so close to manhood, Regan forced down his misgivings when he noticed how appropriate the thin, dark roll of tobacco seemed in Caleb's large, capable hands.

"Why are you so hostile to me, Caleb? I thought I had explained the entire situation in my letter. If you are truly on the threshold of becoming a man, surely you must make an effort to understand and accept the fact that Sirena and I are a thing of the past."

"Even a man can't ignore cruelty, and that's how you're behaving. By now, word must have reached Sirena that the *Spanish Lady* was sunk off the coast of Spain. What torment Sirena must be going through believing you are dead! I can only hope my letter explaining that you are alive and well reaches her before she suffers overmuch. Even now, I'm puzzled as to why you've come here." Caleb eyed Regan boldly, unnerving his father.

"There's a matter we must discuss. I was hoping for a quiet hour alone with you so I could explain something to you."

Caleb's eyes were dark and cold as he looked at Regan, daring his father to say what he had come to say. Caleb, himself, was silent, his expression hostile. Under his father's scrutiny, he stood and walked the few paces to the fireplace to flick his ashes onto the burning logs.

"Sit down, Caleb. We must talk."

"I prefer to stand, thank you."

Regan's eyes were speculative as he looked at his son. The shock of seeing this tall, muscular youth was still something he could hardly come to terms with. His voice was hesitant and then gradually it quickened, gathering momentum as he watched the angry look in Caleb's eyes turn to incredulity. "When I left the islands, I knew in my gut Sirena would never come with me. Don't ask me how I knew, I just did. I was convinced she would never leave the island nor would she leave Mikel's grave site. You must understand that I sincerely believed this. I still do. Our life together is over. From now on, it is only we two. When I was picked up by the ship that rescued us, I went to Spain and met the Córdez business manager in order to explain the circumstances of Sirena's and my parting."

Regan cleared his throat as though he were reluctant about continuing. "I have taken over the handling of all the Córdez holdings." Suddenly, his voice thickened and his agate-blue eyes took on a faraway look. "I know I must make a new life for myself and that is what I intend to do. In fact, I've already begun. I've divorced Sirena," he said huskily.

Caleb kept his silence but his eyes accused, judged, and found his father guilty. Without another glance in Regan's direction, he turned and walked from the room.

"Caleb, come back here," Regan shouted. "That part of our life is over! Finished! We have to make a new beginning here!" His eyes searched the long corridor, willing Caleb to return. He went back into the front parlor and sat down heavily, his heart hammering in his chest. Head reeling, he smacked one large, bronze fist into the other. Caleb was gone, just as Mikel was gone. Just as Sirena was gone.

Caleb would never forgive him, never come back to him. The same woman who had returned Caleb to him was taking his son away. What he had now was a divorce from a woman he loved dearly, and a young woman of excellent breeding who was demanding marriage in exchange for her wealth and virtue. God! What had he done?

His broad, muscular shoulders slumped as he looked toward the doorway where Caleb had taken his exit. Something churned in the pit of his stomach. Was this what Sirena had felt when he left her? Was this the damnable emptiness she lived with, this total loss?

Chapter Three

The *Rana* berthed in Cádiz, Spain, nine weeks after leaving Batavia. The voyage, usually taking anywhere from twelve weeks to five months, had been speedy owing to excellent weather and a good wind. Since reaching the northern limits of the African continent, Sirena had discontinued wearing her familiar sea garb. Wisely, she realized as they reached the more routinely traveled shipping lanes, her abbreviated costume of slashed short breeches and a blouse tied snugly beneath her full breasts would raise questioning eyes. Worse yet, it was possible her reputation as the Sea Siren might have preceded her arrival into the more civilized reaches of the world and being recognized would make her an easy mark for some adventure-seeking sailors wishing to gain the reputation of having conquered the infamous female pirate.

Spain's ancient seaport was buzzing with activity. Longshoremen were loading and unloading cargo and the horizon was impeded by a forest of ship's masts.

As Sirena leaned over the quarterdeck rail drinking in the familiar sights about her, a deep anxiety in the pit of her innards began to creep insidiously around her spine. Throughout the voyage, she had convinced herself beyond doubt that she had left Batavia because of Regan's manipulations and trickery. He *couldn't* have gone down with his ship! This was just his way of luring her off Java.

Yet, throughout the voyage, she had found it more and more difficult to discount the possibility that she might be wrong. Sirena bit into her lower lip, her green eyes narrowed against the fear which kept bobbing to the surface like the cork on the end of a fisherman's line. Regardless of Regan's expertise, regardless of anything, she knew that the sea was a powerful mistress and oftentimes did win the battle she waged with the sailing vessels that dared to cross her domain!

Sirena had been wrestling with this thought ever since Captain Dykstra had brought her the news, even though she had been careful not to admit it to herself. But when they had sighted the tall cliffs of Gibraltar, she would find herself more and more often whispering silent words of prayer that Regan would be found safe and sound. She loved him, God, how she loved him! Please God, let him be well!

Sirena was broken from her pathetic prayers by a harsh cry from the *atracar obreros,* those longshoremen who made their livelihood by unloading the wealth of the world from ship's holds.

"Hey, Capitán," one burly, sweat-beaded *obrero* called to Jan, assuming he was the Captain of the *Rana,* "what you carry in your hold? Feathers? You ride high on the water."

"No cargo, *amigo,"* Jan answered. "You'll find no work here!"

"Where you coming from, Capitán?"

"Java, the East Indies."

"And no cargo?" The burly dock worker shook his head incredulously. He turned to his small contingent of men and tapped a finger to his temple.

Sirena laughed. Jan turned and looked at her, his face flushed with color. "They think you're *loco,* Jan. Who ever heard of traveling halfway around the world without a cargo to make the journey worthwhile?"

"Perhaps I should have referred him to you, Capitana," Jan teased. "If he learned that a woman captains this ship, he would forgive the stupidity of sailing without cargo and merely think me crazy for sailing under a female."

"A hungry woman!" Sirena laughed. "I wonder if Jacobus has any of those biscuits and hot coffee left. Come, Jan. I'll need you to run interference for me if Jacobus has already cleaned his galley and stowed away the larder."

Over old Jacobus' protests, Sirena and Jan leaned their elbows on the galley table and sipped at their steaming mugs of coffee. "Tell me, Capitana, how long has it been since you were last in Cádiz?"

"Tio Juan, my sister Isabella and I sailed from Cádiz just before we arrived in the Indies. Like all old cities, it hasn't changed from what I could see of it from the quarterdeck."

"Then you are familiar with the city?"

"Certainly," Sirena answered. "A grand place it is, too. I always loved it when I was a child. As a matter of fact, my family still owns a magnificent *casa* not far from the dock area. It sits up on a hill and from there it is possible to see the ships in port. It belonged to Tio Juan, but now it is mine." Sirena's eyes turned murky with sorrow. "How I loved to visit my uncle when I was a child, Jan. Isabella and I would race up and down the cobblestoned courtyard and our dueña, Magdelena, would throw up her hands and screech that we were children of the devil. Then, Isabella and I would go somewhere and hide and giggle till our sides hurt. Tio Juan would listen to our dueña's complaints about our incorrigible behavior and pretend to be angry with us. But all the time he was scolding us for Señora Magdelena's benefit, we could see his eyes twinkling and a barely concealed smile hiding behind his carefully trimmed mustache."

"You loved your Tio Juan very much, Capitana. It is there to be seen in your eyes."

"Yes, Jan. Both Isabella and myself cherished him very much. But it was my father who was my hero. He was tall and dashing and always carefully groomed. I thought he was the most magnificent person ever put on earth. He was greatly respected by all and feared by most. But for my sister and me he was the kindest, most loving man. His arms were always open for us to run to and he would swing us up, high above his head. And he loved us to a fault."

"And it was from him you learned the ways of the sea?"

"Yes. Isabella and I were very different in nature." Sirena's voice became husky with emotion.

"If it pains you to speak of her, Capitana, I will understand."

"No, Jan. It has been so long since I have spoken of Isabella, though she is never very far from my thoughts. When we became of age, Isabella and I were sent to the convent school. She was the model of decorum while I . . . I was . . ."

Jan smiled. "I can imagine. I can see where the good nuns had their hands full with you."

"How right you are," Sirena laughed, and picked up her mug for another swallow of coffee. "In fact, it reached a point where my father was implored to take me out of the school. Isabella remained behind with the nuns and I traveled the world aboard my father's ships. It was from him I learned to sail the seas. Tutors were brought aboard to teach me, and my father insisted that I excel in my studies. While he pampered me in almost every way thinkable, he was, nevertheless, a taskmaster. If I did poorly with my studies, I was forbidden my turn at the wheel or my lesson in fencing. These things I savored, so it wasn't often I gave my tutors any trouble. Summers, Isabella would travel with us. It was she who tried to undo my hellion ways by showing me the manners of a lady. Poor Isabella, how often I would hear her say that I was giving her gray hair at the tender age of twelve! You see, Jan, I was surrounded by gentle, loving people and my early years were very happy."

"Aye, I can see that. Was it on a voyage with your father that you came to the Indies?"

"No." Sirena's eyes became overcast again. "If my father were sailing this ship, the fates wouldn't have turned against us as they did. Tio Juan was a businessman and knew very little about commanding a crew. My father had already died. It was due to a drunken, stupid captain that the *Rana* was attacked by pirates and the lives of Tio Juan and Isabella were lost." Sirena's last words were whispered, charged with sadness. She would never forget what had happened to them on that cursed day. A happenstance that had changed her life forever.

Frau Holtz burst into the galley. "Mevrouw, if you are to go ashore, it would be best if you began to dress. You can't go about the city dressed in the gown you are wearing, it is not befitting someone of your station."

Sirena glanced down at the drab, light woolen gown she had hastily donned over her sea costume before they sailed into port. "Yes, I'm coming, Frau Holtz. I was just reminiscing with Jan." Placing her mug down on the rough-hewn table, Sirena stood up resignedly. "While I am changing, Jan, take a walk on the dock and find out what you can about Regan's ship. I won't leave the *Rana* until you report back."

As Sirena pushed her head through the delicate lace camisole which covered her stays, Frau Holtz went about getting her shoes and gossamer stockings. "Do you think Jan will learn anything about the Mynheer's whereabouts?" the housekeeper asked. Sirena noted that the woman was very careful to omit the very real likelihood that Regan might have gone down with his ship.

"Fairly certain. I told Jan to check in with the harbormaster. Most assuredly, if anyone knows the circumstances surrounding Regan's ship, that official does. I imagine it's only a matter of time now and I'll come face to face with my husband." Sirena tried to make her voice as casual as possible but a glimmer of her anxiety came through.

"Ja, most certainly, the harbor master will know," the Frau agreed. "Am I to believe you no longer think the Mynheer has tricked you, Mevrouw?"

"Yes. After thinking many hard hours on it, Regan would never tempt the fates by pretending to have lost the *Lady* at sea. But I'm certain Regan is safe and sound. He's much too expert a seaman to become a casualty at sea. Besides, how many times he's boasted that he has more lives than a cat."

"Ja," Frau Holtz grumbled. Her heavy brows came together in a look of consternation. Even cats only had nine lives and Regan's colorful and adventurous past would seem to suggest that he already had outdone that number.

Three days later neither Sirena nor her crew had found any information about Regan. It was only known that the *Spanish Lady* had gone down off the coast of Spain as she traveled toward Cádiz.

Each time Sirena had gone in search of details concerning Regan she had started out in high spirits, certain of learning his whereabouts. Each evening she had come back to the *Rana* more defeated than the day past. Her crew searched earnestly for word of Regan van der Rhys, but they too returned to the ship without news.

Sirena's optimism began to flag. She had tried in vain to locate Señor Arroya, Tio Esteban, the Córdez family business manager. She knew without a doubt that if Regan had come into Cádiz, he would have seen Esteban Arroya concerning the takeover of the Córdez fortunes. But Tio Esteban was somewhere in Salamanca and was not expected to return for several months.

At first Sirena considered going to Salamanca in search of Tio Esteban, but the possibility of missing him somewhere along the way was deterring. She had to be doing something, anything! Besides, no one in his offices could give her assurance that he had not traveled on to Italy to visit with his daughter who had married a banker from Milan. The prospect of sitting in Cádiz awaiting her uncle's arrival grated on Sirena and all indications pointed to Regan having gone under with his ship.

Hour by hour Sirena puzzled the problem, becoming more depressed and fearful. Regan! Regan! Her heart cried. She squeezed her eyes shut and prayed. "Please, God," she whispered, tears welling behind her lids and gathering on her thick lashes. "Please, God. Give Regan his life, don't let him be dead. Please, God, please. I was such a fool, I should have listened to him, I should have left Java with him. Forgive me for putting my grief for my dead baby above the love I have for my husband. Above You, God. We've all lost so much, suffered so much. Me, Regan, Caleb. Please, don't let me lose the only love in my life. Please, God, please!"

On into the night Sirena prayed, and it was morning when Frau Holtz found her slumped beside her narrow bunk, tearstained face at last peaceful in sleep, her sister Isabella's rosary clutched tightly in her fist.

Sirena refused to eat her breakfast as well as her lunch. She stayed secluded in her cabin, thoughts of Regan whirling through her head. She remembered how on their last night together, they had battled each trying to impose their will on the other. She shed bitter tears when she recalled how long she had pushed Regan from her. How many nights she had lain in her solitary bed castigating him over and over in her mind, refusing to regard his need for her, refusing to admit that she needed him. And when at last they had found one another again, it had been like a sip of cool water after an interminable dry trek on the desert. They had sipped and then drank deeply, at the well of love and tenderness they were each capable of giving. And after their loving they had lain in each other's arms, at last finding peace.

And now this torment. If only she knew for certain whether Regan lived, or had died at sea. She couldn't go on this way. This not knowing was killing her as surely as an arrow through the heart. And there was no one, nobody to whom she could go! She had rejected not just Regan, but Caleb as well. How unfair she had been, how selfish! Caleb was more than a son to her. He had been her friend, her little brother, and no son of her own flesh could ever take his place in her heart. Yet she had actually hated the fact that it was Caleb who lived and Mikel who had died.

Caleb! As if seeing the light for the first time, Sirena cried aloud, "Caleb! Regan would have made contact with him! Frau Holtz! Jacobus! Jan!" she called excitedly, flinging open the narrow door of her cabin. "Make ready to sail! To Holland!"

Chapter Four

"Mynheer van der Rhys," the housemaster said imperiously, "I believe you were informed a lady awaits you in the visitor's room. You will not ignore me as you did our young dormitory messenger," the elderly scholar warned sternly. "A gentleman never keeps a lady waiting. Be on your way, now, before she thinks you have a sorry lack of manners."

Caleb frowned. "I have no wish to see anybody." Since Regan's visit weeks ago, Caleb had kept himself apart from the young society which he had learned to enjoy. He supposed his female visitor was still another of his friends' sisters come to flirt with him and break the heavy black mood that engulfed him.

"Did I hear you correctly, young man? Ah, I see I did. Of course, I can't force you to see her, but it is especially awkward since the woman says she has traveled all the way from Java to see you."

Caleb's head jerked upright, his dark eyes alight in wonder. "Did you say Java, sir?" Not waiting for an answer, he took off at a dead run for the parlor.

"Sirena!" he shouted boisterously. "Is it really you?" He wrapped her in his strong arms and swept her off the floor. "I was leaving as soon as the term was over to come back to Java. The days drag on and on and at times I thought I'd never see you again. You look beautiful. How did you get here? Never mind, I know. The *Rana!*" Abruptly, his exuberance faded and he put her a little distance from him. "You heard," he said softly, "that's why you've come. You've had word from Father."

"Regan! You know where he is?"

Caleb nodded. Sirena's joy was so full, so ebullient she threw her slender arms about his neck and hugged him fiercely. "Oh, Caleb, I'm so happy to see you. And Regan, where is he? God, I can't wait to see him again. To tell him it was all my fault, the doings of a foolish woman who loves him. Is he well, where is he?" she asked anxiously.

"Father is in England." What was he going to do? How was he going to tell her? He hadn't seen her this happy in ages. He couldn't allow her to go to Britain and find Regan without knowing. He must tell her.

Sirena clung to Caleb, her beautiful face alight and happy. "I'm so happy to see you. Now we can be a family again. I'm sorry it took me so long to get over . . . never mind. That's all behind us now. Just think, Caleb, if I take the *Rana* I can see Regan in a matter of days. Won't he be surprised? I can barely wait to see the expression on his face. I know that he's lost patience with me, but I told him I would be able to leave Java as soon as I had settled things in my own mind. Do you know, Caleb, I was ready to depart with him but his ship had already sailed? I was a fool, but I'll make it up to him. I swear I will. And to you, Caleb," Sirena babbled, not noticing the anguish in Caleb's eyes.

"Tell me, little brother, have you missed me?" Again, she didn't wait for a reply. "You're so grown. You're an adult!" she said, her voice colored with amazement. "I always knew you'd make a fine man, I just didn't realize it would be so soon. Frau Holtz is with me, what do you think of that? It was no small feat, I can assure you," she laughed. For the first time, she noticed Caleb's silence. "I'm sorry. Just listen to me. I haven't given you a chance to say a word. Sit down and we'll talk. It's just that I'm so excited," she said, hugging him again. "Tell me about school and how you're doing. Tell me everything, don't leave a thing out."

"You didn't receive my letter, did you, Sirena?" Caleb said, licking his dry lips, his dark eyes tormented as he looked at Sirena.

"Letter? No, I must have left Java before it arrived. No matter. I'm here and you can tell me in person."

Caleb began hesitantly. "I hate school. I hate these shoes and I hate Holland," he said calmly, gathering steam as he spoke the words. "I hate the interminable rain, I hate books! I hate Latin! I hate everything! *I Hate My Father!*"

Sirena's eyes betrayed her shock. "Caleb! I've never seen you this way! What's come over you? Regan only wants you to have the benefit of an education. He isn't punishing you by sending you to school. He sent you here for your own welfare. I don't want to hear you speak of Regan that way. Now tell me what's troubling you. Perhaps we can work out a solution."

"There is no solution," Caleb said miserably.

Sirena's heart went out to him. For all his size and budding manhood, Caleb was still more of a boy than a man. "Come, little brother, it can't be as serious as all that. Two heads are better than one. Tell me what it is and we'll find a solution."

"You're too late, Sirena. You came too late," he said in a thin voice that threatened to break.

"It's never too late. I know we've lost touch with one another since you've been at school, but we're still every bit the friends we were before."

"You don't understand," Caleb blurted. "Regan divorced you! That's why I hate him!"

Sirena's face drained of all color and the room seemed to whirl about her. Caleb thought she would faint and he cursed himself for his bluntness as he reached out to support her. He fanned her face with his handkerchief. "Sirena, are you all right? Forgive me. I hadn't meant to tell you this way. It was all in my letter. Every blasted word of it." Damn his father, damn his soul to Hell!

"Sirena, I couldn't let you go to Regan not knowing." Sirena's dark lashes fluttered open, her emerald eyes sick and begging for an explanation. Caleb helped her to her feet and again apologized for being inconsiderate.

Sirena rubbed her temples and gazed at him, her eyes blank. "I must be certain I understand what you've told me. Regan divorced me?"

Caleb nodded, his eyes guarded.

"No! It isn't so! I know Regan went to Spain to take over the Córdez holdings . . ." Sirena's voice was heavy, her eyes pleaded with Caleb to deny what he had told her. Yet, somewhere within her, all hope died. She knew Caleb would never be so callous to say such a thing were it not true. Her eyes widened, the delicate lines of her jaw tightened as did her small clenched fists. "Regan divorced!"

Caleb again nodded miserably.

"Why?"

"Father thought you would never leave Java. That your lives together as man and wife were over," Caleb whispered.

"I told him I just needed more time, just a little more time and to please be patient with me. Caleb, did he tell you this himself?" Sirena asked. One small hope which had blossomed died when she saw Caleb avoid her in misery.

"Yes. He came here to the academy and told me himself. I had already given him my word that I'd stay here until the term was over; otherwise, I would have come to you in Java. I heard it from his own lips that he divorced you."

"But how? I don't understand," Sirena breathed as she sank down into the same hard-backed chair that Regan had used.

"Sirena, nothing is impossible for those who have money. Here in Holland divorce is not unusual. A little greasing of the palms to facilitate the necessary paperwork and a handsome stipend to the clergy and a *Royal* marriage can be nullified."

"What else did your father say when you spoke with him?" Sirena's voice was just a shade above a whisper, her hands rested in her lap, palms up, fingers still, in a humble facsimile of supplication.

"I'm ashamed to admit it, Sirena, but I behaved like a child. I ran from the room and refused to speak with him again. Sirena, I don't care what he does any longer. As far as I'm concerned, he has no son. I don't want him for my father.

"Sirena," he asked anxiously. "What are you going to do?" He had noticed her green eyes turn dark and dangerous.

"How many days until the term is over?"

"Ten."

"Do you want me to remain in port and wait for you and then we'll look into this matter together?"

"I'll leave with you right now."

"Perhaps you can. Let us speak to the headmaster and see what he says. If he's agreeable, then we will leave this place of little sunshine."

Caleb noted that each word she spoke was slow and precise, her emotions under control. Only her eyes indicated what was going on inside her and, from the sparks shooting in their depths, her emotions were murderous. Upon confrontation, the headmaster was more than amiable to their plans. Caleb had been a constant source of irritation ever since he had arrived. What could he possibly learn in ten days that would be worth the rascal's impatience and aggravating manners.

"I'll wait outdoors, Caleb. Hurry and pack your belongings."

Away from Caleb's scrutiny, Sirena relaxed, her emerald eyes narrowed in thought. Divorce me! Take my money, will he? Not as long as I live! No, that wasn't right. Not as long as *he* lived. Whoring bastard! Soon as her back was turned, he leaps into bed with another. He was no better than a wild, blood sucking pig! Spend my money on some other woman, will he?

She slammed her fists into her sides. "I knew I should have killed him when I had the chance. Divorce me! Dirty Dutchman!"

He would pay for this, she thought as she let her gaze focus on the canal and the shimmering water. She would brand him with two large S's. One on his buttocks and one on his chest. She'd fix him. "You'll never live to spend money," she cursed. She'd send his branded body back to those damnable nutmeg trees she had nearly broken her back planting for him. And this was the thanks she received. "I'll brand an S on his forehead, too," she said viciously as she kicked out at the iron bench beside her. She winced with pain. Leave me to die on that godforsaken island, will you? Well, I'm here now! And if you're not ready for me, it would behoove you to get ready. I'm ready to fight! For you, Regan, she sobbed inwardly. I'll fight for you, to get you back. I won't let you go, Regan, I can't! I love you.

Chapter Five

The red gold of the setting sun was hidden by the heavy, gray clouds which hung over the wharves. Long shadows were forming into a haze, obscuring the topmost sails of the tall ships which lined the waterfront. Here and there, the yellow gold of a lantern dotted the buildings and illuminated the oily windows of the merchants' shops crowding the docks.

Jacobus and the *Rana*'s crew stood at the rail watching Sirena and Caleb climb from the carriage which had brought them from the academy. Sirena's green eyes were flashing angrily and the delicate line of her jaw was grim and determined. Even from this distance, Jacobus could see something was wrong.

Caleb was taking long strides to match her furious pace. Caleb. The boy was now a man, forged in his father's likeness. The beauty of height was there as was the magnificent breadth of shoulders. There was no doubt he was Regan's son. Except that the boy's hair was dark where Regan's was the color of winter wheat; the seed hadn't fallen far from the tree.

Frau Holtz hurried to the rail for a glimpse of Caleb. She, too, saw immediately that Sirena was behaving strangely. The old woman brought her hand to her mouth and shivered inwardly. Sirena was walking as though she were a puppet and invisible strings were attached to her limbs.

Sirena moved up the gangplank keeping her gaze straight ahead, neither looking right nor left. Jacobus eyed her warily and with a slight motion of his hand warned the others to remain quiet. He knew that burning look, and it struck a chord of warning within him.

"Hoist anchor," Sirena said tersely. "We sail for

Spain." With a nod to Caleb, she moved jerkily toward her quarters and a change of garments.

Caleb, his expression forbidding and unreadable, nodded slightly to the crew and held out his hand to Franco, the second mate.

"You've grown, boy," Franco said quietly. "School must have agreed with you."

"It's good to have you aboard again, Caleb," Jan welcomed him softly.

"The last time these old eyes saw you, you were a mere child. And now you're a strapping young man. We missed you," Jacobus grinned. "It's good to have another pair of reliable hands aboard. Welcome back."

Frau Holtz gathered him to her bosom in a motherly embrace and was momentarily startled that it was her head resting against Caleb's chest and not the other way around. Standing on tiptoe she whispered, "I must talk with you. Now!" she added urgently.

The crew busied themselves readying the *Rana* for departure, having taken on stores as soon as they had made port earlier that day. Soon the frigate's tightly strung sails billowed and thumped as they caught the early-evening breeze.

Frau Holtz led Caleb to her cabin. "What is it? What happened back at the school—and don't lie to me. What's wrong?" Her voice took on the harsh note it always did when she knew something was troubling her Mevrouw.

Caleb debated for a moment before speaking. His gut churned as he tried to find the right words to answer the housekeeper. "Sirena . . . Sirena, for the first time in her life has . . . No, Frau Holtz. It's not my place to discuss it with anyone. Sirena will have to tell you."

The elderly woman looked at Caleb and grimaced. "I see they taught you many things at your fancy academy. I admire your loyalty to the Mevrouw; but, perhaps, if you were to tell me what it is that's troubling her, the crew and I could help."

"Frau Holtz, at this moment there is no one on this earth who can help Sirena. You must believe me when I tell you this. For now, she must work it through in her own mind. Nobody, not even you and least of all me, can help her."

"And you learned all this from books?" the housekeeper asked snidely, indignant to be excluded from Sirena's troubles.

Caleb grinned. "No, Frau Holtz. Not books. You must remember Sirena was my teacher for a long time. I learned many things from her, things that I . . . Never mind. It's not important for you to know what I learned from Sirena or my books."

"You may have been taught many things, but the lesson you have learned best is your father's arrogance! Be careful, young man. that you're wise enough to handle this haughtiness. You may look like a man and you may act like a man, but are you a man in here where it counts?" she challenged, jabbing her finger repeatedly into his chest.

Caleb laughed. "Make no mistake, Frau Holtz. Boyhood is far behind me. And," he said coolly, "I am my own man. I make my own decisions and I lead my own life."

"Brave words," the Frau noted petulantly, taken aback. Caleb's smile was so like Regan's. "I suppose you're going to tell me that you are now a master in the art of self-defense and can handle a weapon as well as the Mevrouw and the Mynheer."

"But of course," Caleb teased. assuming an air of self-importance to irritate her. "I have earned several medals at the academy for fencing. I am considered an expert!" he exclaimed confidently.

Frau Holtz could feel the iron-gray hairs at the back of her neck stand out with her agitation. These van der Rhys men were all alike, loving the sport of needling her to distraction! Although she knew he had purposely exasperated her, she believed his statement about the medals implicitly. Could Sirena's pupil and Regan's son be anything less than an expert with the rapier?

"May we talk later, Frau Holtz? I could never climb the rigging in these foppish garments." He smiled as he looked upward to the crow's nest and the old housekeeper was again struck by his handsomeness. The virile ruggedness of Regan's features was clearly evident, but Caleb had also inherited dark eyes and hair from his Javanese mother. Along with her exotic coloring, he had received a certain gentleness in the soft tilt near the corners of his eyes and a sensuousness in the pout of his lower lip. Regan's handsomeness and Tita's loveliness had spawned in Caleb a refined elegance which, while totally masculine, was still no less than beautiful. Tall and broad-shouldered with the flat stomach and lean haunches of youth; a noble head held proudly by the strong column of his neck and dark hair with warm, golden glints that was thick with a tendency to unruliness. A high, intelligent brow accentuating sensitive eyes. Frau Holtz suffered a twinge of sympathy for the women who would throw themselves at Caleb's feet. And if he followed in Regan's footsteps, which Frau Holtz was certain would be the case, it would take the most remarkable of girls to snare that wild heart. As remarkable and magnificent as the Mevrouw, the Frau smiled to herself, and then beware, young Caleb, for your fate will be sealed by a pair of honeyed lips and smooth limbs.

"Frau Holtz," Caleb's voice broke her thoughts, "I'm so glad you agreed to accompany Sirena." His tone was soft and intimate. On a sudden impulse, he leaned down to kiss her warmly on the cheek before going below to change clothes.

"Young whelp," the Frau muttered to herself, gently touching the spot where Caleb's lips had touched her. He has no right to return looking like he does, she grumbled inwardly in the way of the aged when the young are grown, leaving them without a child to nurture and guide. The world wasn't ready for two van der Rhys men.

At loose ends, Frau Holtz sought out toothless Jacobus and complained bitterly of her inactivity and fears that something was wrong with the Mevrouw.

"Aye. I, too, saw the odd expression in the Capitana's eyes. Agh! It does no good to worry and speculate. All in good time. She's not so proud that she won't ask for help if she needs it. She knows we're here and she has only to ask. Amazing how the boy has grown, eh? He's a fine figure of a man. Resembles his father."

"In more ways than you know," Frau Holtz commented. "I wish I knew why we were going to Spain. I've been accustomed to an orderly life, not this seafaring way I'm being forced to cope with. I feel like a water gypsy without a home. I'm too old for this."

"We're all growing old. I never thought I'd live to see the day when I wanted solid ground beneath my feet, but my bones are beginning to ache and my eyesight's not what it used to be. I've been giving serious thought to becoming a landlubber. If you've a mind to, we could set up housekeeping on some small island," Jacobus said wickedly.

"That will be the day!" Frau Holtz responded haughtily. "What would a fine woman like myself want with a toothless old man?" To add emphasis to her words, she let loose with a high-flying blow in the direction of Jacobus' ear.

"Who knows?" Jacobus smiled, dodging her cuff. "If you change your mind, let me know so I can prepare myself for the wedding."

"Get your addled mind on sailing this ship," the housekeeper said tartly as her face flushed a rosy hue. "I've no mind to end my life in these waters."

"I'm not a sailor, I'm the cook!"

"Then go and see to your galley," she answered over her shoulder as she flounced off in the direction of her cabin. Her first marriage proposal—and it had to come from a toothless old man who admitted his eyesight was failing. She sniffed to herself as she looked at her graying hair in her mirror, smoothing the coronet of braids she wore atop her head. A slow smile crept onto her lips. At least she could go to her grave knowing she had received one proposal.

Alone in her cabin, Sirena refused to allow her mind to dwell on the heart-stopping information she had received this afternoon. She concentrated on the tasks at hand and, for the moment, that consisted of freeing herself from the lengthy row of fabric-covered buttons running down her gown.

Sirena had taken special care with her toilet earlier

that day in her eagerness to appear unchanged to Caleb's eyes when she went to see him at the school. After a much-needed bath to cleanse her skin of the spindrift, she had taken extra pains with her dress. Frau Holtz had spent hours with a heavy flatiron, pressing the folds from a deep-gold afternoon gown with intricate ruching around the neck and sleeves. Petticoat after petticoat met with the Frau's sizzling iron and the steam rose from her table and heated her cheeks into a fiery red. While Sirena had dressed her luxurious, ebony hair into a modish style atop her head, leaving a long hank to curl winsomely over her shoulder, the Frau had fussed with the frothy wisp of veiling which decorated the feminine version of the wide-brimmed Cavalier's hat Sirena had chosen to wear.

Now her rakish chapeau was carelessly thrown on her bunk; its crisp veiling had wilted in the dank, moisture-laden air and its curling feather looked as tired as she felt. When she had changed into her abbreviated costume and tied her blouse tightly beneath her voluptuous bosom, she reached for her high-heeled black kid boots and pulled them on over her slim, well-shaped calves up to her long, supple thighs. She would not think about what Caleb had told her. She would concentrate on her ship and her crew. Once the *Rana*'s wheel was in her hands, her world would be right side up. She clenched and unclenched her hands as she paced the narrow confines of the cabin, her heels beating out a tattoo of emotions.

How much could one person be expected to bear in this lifetime? How in God's name had she allowed this to happen to her? Was it her fault? Was Regan to blame? Don't think about it, she warned herself, as she continued to pace distractedly. Did it matter whose fault it was? All that counted was that Regan no longer loved her and had divorced her.

Her shoulders shuddered convulsively and tears gathered in her eyes. Didn't Regan realize how much she loved him? So many times he had told her of his love for her. How could he cast her aside like a stale cigar and leave her to smolder to ashes.

The quivering shoulders grew still. She relaxed her hands and ceased pacing. Was she or was she not a woman? The taut shoulders relaxed and her hands grew limp. Her emerald eyes sparkled momentarily and then grew misty again. Time. Time was the answer.

Suddenly her shoulders slumped and tears again threatened to well her eyes. Regan would find another to hold in his strong arms. His soft words of love would be whispered in the ear of some other woman.

A sob caught in her throat. How could a love like theirs die? A vision of a faceless female in Regan's embrace swam before her. "No!" she cried in torment. "*No,* no, no!" The pain in her breast was sharper than any knife wound. "No!" she screamed and her cry held the anguish of all the women who had gone before her when they had lost their lovers.

It was Caleb who heard her high-pitched wail first, and it was he who grasped Willem's arm to restrain him from running to the Capitana. "She is in no danger. Leave her. When she comes up on deck you will see she will be in control of herself. She needs this time alone." Willem glanced at Caleb, a look of wonderment in his eyes.

Jan's expression questioned Willem as they watched Caleb stalk across the deck. His bronzed skin glowed in the last light of day and his surefooted stance was all too familiar. Mynheer van der Rhys had stood like that on the deck of his burning ship, stripped to the waist, his breeches tattered at the knees, a grim, purposeful expression on his chiseled features.

Away from the cloud-shrouded coast of Holland, the sea's fresh winds dusted away the low fog and the red glow of the setting sun reflected off the calm, azure sea through the sterncastle's mullioned windows. Sirena glanced about and then headed for the deck. She relieved Jan at the wheel and shouted her orders. "Look to the sky, there's a storm blowing in from the west. Full speed away," she called. "If we're in luck, we might be able to outrun her by changing course. Caleb," she yelled harshly, "why are you standing about? Move! Anyone who sails on my ship must do his share of the work!"

Caleb, who had been coiling a length of rope, straightened and stared at Sirena. She was tightly strung and boiling with determination. Still, she had never taken her vengeance out on him and this new, bitter note in her voice when she addressed him pierced his heart. He clenched his teeth and bent to his task. The line secure, he nestled himself in the shrouds, beyond the reach of Sirena's attention.

From this level, Caleb could observe Sirena as she held her stance at the wheel. She was a magnificent seaman. The sea and the approaching storm would never beat her. There was a time when Caleb would have said that nothing in this world could best Sirena. But that had been before Mikel's death and this treachery of Regan's. Sirena had always said that no man would ever get the better of her. Regan divorcing her had proved how wrong she had been and now she would have to come to terms with it. In his heart, Caleb knew that she would never, could never, accept it. Without Regan, Sirena would be an empty shell.

And what of Regan without Sirena? Was he whole? Would he find life to his liking without her? For one brief moment Caleb pitied Regan. Then, setting his jaw, he decided he would no longer take sides. They couldn't keep playing him like a string on a fiddle. Whatever they would do, they would do it without him!

Watching the nearing storm, Sirena picked up the horn near the wheel and shouted orders. "All hands to the deck to secure ship!"

The wind howled in the rigging as she steered the frigate under closely reefed sails. She kept her bow pointed into the wind as much as possible. Gigantic waves spun by the gale into curly, white combers rolled continuously from the west. Spindrift flew in flakes, stinging Sirena's face as she fought the wheel.

Nature's fury demanded her full attention. Hands gripping the wheel, all other thoughts fleeing her mind, she stood erect and brazened the onslaught. Lightning flashed, illuminating the horizon. Spectral clouds assumed violent shapes and scudded across the sky. Rain had not yet begun to pelt the decks, but it was out there waiting for her. Sirena knew the rain was her enemy, just as the fizzing sea foam whipped by the winds was, just as Regan was now her enemy. Rain could beat the strength out of a man, wearing and draining his vitality bit by bit, sip by sip, like a vampire draining life's blood. It could choke off a man's air by driving in solid sheets, whipping up the nostrils and down the throat. The rain could pound a helmsman from the wheel and the wind could lure a ship onto a certain course of destruction.

Fleetingly, her mind questioned one method of destruction versus another. Regan or the storm? Which was worse? For now, the storm, she answered herself. Fearing the worst, she lashed herself to the wheel with a length of narrow sailcloth.

The rains came and Sirena, blinded by the savage downpour, kept the *Rana* to its heading by instinct. Her body was battered by the elements and her hair came loose and beat against her face, twisting about her neck like insistent, strangling fingers. When physical strength began to fail, an iron will to survive became her mainstay. She must see Regan again. She must hear from his own lips that he no longer loved her. She must see his face, touch him. "Damn your soul to Hell, Regan van der Rhys!" Sirena screamed. "You're mine! Mine!" And her howl was matched by the furies of the storm.

The wind buffeted Caleb against the quarterdeck rail and only by taking a fast hold on the rigging was he able to pull himself across the deck to Sirena. "I came to help," he shouted to be heard above the elements.

"I don't need your aid," Sirena shouted, never taking her eyes from the sea swells.

"You're tiring. Let me take the wheel. This is no time for you to play *Conquistadora*. Now hand the wheel over to me! I'll get behind you and loosen your bindings. Get ready!"

"Get back to your post! An error on your part allowing her to lay broadside and broach will be the end of us! We cannot change positions now. Hear me well, Caleb! I captain this ship. When I have need of your assistance, I'll ask for it!" she shouted above the howling winds. "And," she added ominously, "don't interfere in my affairs again!"

Caleb gave her a long, level look and made his way back to his former position. Tons of water suddenly crashed onto the frigate's decks, threatening to stave in her hatches. The massive onslaught of water crashed upon him just as he grasped the rigging.

Sirena called out, but was too late. She watched the water pick Caleb up and swoop him down the deck. She screamed but knew the sound did not reach the crew. "Please, God, let him be all right," she prayed. "If it weren't for you, Regan, I wouldn't be here battling a storm with your son. If he drowns, it will be on your conscience, not mine!"

It was nearly an hour before Sirena ran the frigate before the wind to the northeast and into calm water. "Caleb . . . Caleb, where are you?"

"Up here, Sirena. Were you worried about me?" came a weak answer from the quarterdeck.

"Of course I was worried. I'm responsible for every man aboard my ship."

"For a moment I hoped you were concerned for me personally," Caleb retorted bitterly. Sirena offered no reply as she loosened the bindings which held her to the wheel.

"Now you can take over," she said to Caleb, "until I get someone up here to take your place." She watched as he made his way forward, his body drenched, his dark hair falling low on his forehead. How like Regan he looked. She stood a moment and watched as he planted his feet firmly. The hard, sinewy muscles in his arms bunched as he straightened his shoulders, grasping the wheel securely. He was as tall as Regan and almost as muscular. Sirena felt a lump rise in her throat as she watched him, his mouth grim, his dark eyes angry and smoldering.

Caleb noticed her walk away, no words spoken between them. Her shoulders slumped slightly and her arms hung limply at her sides. She stumbled once and rejected Willem's arm when he extended it. From his position, Caleb watched her bring the back of her hand to her eyes to wipe at her tears. He couldn't help her. Only Regan could do that and he was far away living a new life.

Frau Holtz clucked and crooned as she assisted Sirena in shedding her sodden clothing. The older woman wrapped a towel around her mistress' wet hair and made her comfortable on the hard, narrow bunk.

As if by magic, Jacobus appeared at the door with two steaming cups of coffee. "I laced them liberally with rum. The Capitana appears to need it. And," he said grinning toothlessly, "this is a gift of love." He handed the Frau the second mug. "The first of many," he quipped as he backed hastily out of the doorway, reading the woman's intention of dashing the scalding brew at him.

Comfortable and dry, the hot mug in her hands, Sirena leaned back on the bunk, her long, tawny legs curled beneath her. "I see many questions in your face, Frau Holtz."

"And I see strange things in your eyes, Mevrouw. If you need someone to talk to, I'll not ask any questions."

Sirena sipped at the coffee and spoke carefully. She exerted great effort to keep her countenance blank and her eyes unreadable. This ache was solely hers and she did not need anyone to share the burden. "Regan went to Spain, secured my holdings, and then he set sail for Holland, where he divorced me. I no longer have my inheritance nor my husband. He plans to pension me off, using my money."

"Mevrouw! What are you talking about?" Frau Holtz asked fearfully.

Suddenly all Sirena's control dissolved. "Didn't you hear me? Regan divorced me."

"Bah! I will never believe that. He loves you like no man has loved a woman. Didn't he chase you halfway around the world to prove it to you?"

"That was a long time ago. This is the present!"

"Then why are we going to Spain? What are you going to do? It would seem to me that if the Mynheer is in Holland that's where we should have stayed."

Sirena took another drink before replying, "At this moment I'm as near destitute as a person can be. I have nothing save this ship and my personal belongings. I must see my family's solicitor and guardian of the family's estates."

"But, Mevrouw, you just told me the Mynheer has confiscated everything."

Poor Frau Holtz. Sirena had never seen her so staggered with shock. Not even on the night when Mikel was born and she had had to relinquish Sirena's welfare to the wizened, black African midwife. "True, Frau. Regan has, by law, the right to my inheritance. But I am hoping that Tio Esteban will have kept my mother's fortunes intact. The law reads that Regan is entitled to the Córdez wealth, I'm hoping the Valdez fortunes from my mother's side of the family do not come under that requirement. Poor Tio Esteban, I can imagine his shock when Regan presented himself to claim my property."

"Forgive me, Mevrouw, but are your holdings from the Valdez family as great as those your husband controls?"

"Dear lady, remember Regan is no longer my husband," Sirena reminded bitterly. "And yes, the Valdez fortune is even greater than that of the Córdez. The reason it has remained intact was my father refused to accept one *peseta* of my mother's inheritance. He said he was a young man and capable of making a living and building his own fortunes."

"What will you do?" the Frau asked, wringing her hands in sympathy. She knew the loss of the estates meant nothing to Sirena. It was the loss of Regan's love which could deal a lethal blow. "Will we stay in Spain? Have you given any thought to the future?"

"What future, old friend? Everything escapes me save for the fact that Regan has divorced me. I can't think beyond that point. When I speak with Tio Esteban, then I'll make my decisions. Have no fear, we won't make our home aboard ship. I know how you yearn for solid ground beneath your feet."

"And Caleb? What of the young man? Where will he go, what will he do?"

Frau Holtz watched Sirena's green eyes cloud. "I'm certain Caleb will see to his own future. He claims to be a man, let him act like one."

"He's a magnificent youth. A replica of his father."

"Yes," Sirena sighed. "He's seen the best and worst of his father and the best and worst of me. Let us hope he has learned wisely from his experiences with both of us."

"He's gone further than that," Frau Holtz said with a touch of awe, remembering her conversation with Caleb when he first boarded the *Rana*. "He's quite knowledgeable in book learning and he claims he is a master of fencing, having won many medals."

"Has he now?" Sirena said with interest. "Perhaps we can have a small exhibition for the crew. I'd like to see for myself how much he has learned."

"I have a feeling, Mevrouw, that you might be surprised at what the young man has learned. He's more confident than his father at the same age. I knew it was a mistake to send him to school. I told the Mynheer that it was a mistake. Did he listen to me? No. He said Caleb needed to be educated and the boy certainly is that."

"Frau Holtz, with growth comes knowledge. We must accept the fact that Caleb is no longer a boy but a man. I know how your arms ache to hold a child," Sirena's voice became softer, almost a whisper as she thought of little Mikel. "But for Caleb's sake, accept the fact that he's now a man," she repeated, her voice again strong and confident.

"Somehow I could accept it more readily if he didn't act and look so like the Mynheer," Frau Holtz said sourly, inadvertently reflecting Sirena's own feelings.

Chapter Six

The journey from Holland to Spain was exquisite torture for Caleb. How long he had yearned for the feel of the deck beneath his feet while he had been at the academy. How he had dreamed of Sirena's beautiful face and coming beneath her loving gaze. And for the sight of his father, too, he grudgingly admitted to himself. Now, everything was in turmoil thanks to Regan's doing.

Day after day Caleb watched Sirena as she stood at the wheel, her hands tightly clutching it. Her green eyes held smoldering fires, her face was a frozen mask of fury. Although she spoke quietly, there was a cold ring of steel in her voice. No one questioned her or gave her cause for anger. Even Frau Holtz kept her distance and remained silent.

What would Regan do when he came face to face with Sirena? Caleb imagined the duel. There was no question in his mind it would come to a duel, that the two of them would pace off and attack. In Caleb's imagination, the sound of the hasps as the hatch was lifted became the sound of rapier against rapier as Regan and Sirena fought once again. God, no, he muttered to himself. He never again wanted to see his father and Sirena square off against one another. Regan would kill her this time. Motherhood and grief would have taken their toll on the long-legged creature who now stood at the helm. She would not be a match for the dynamic Regan van der Rhys.

A land bird flew close to the swiftly moving *Rana*. Soon, thought Caleb, soon they would sight Spain and make the port of Cádiz. Then Sirena's real troubles would begin. She wouldn't be able to tire herself with exhausting hours at the frigate's wheel so when she *did* finally lie down in her bunk, a heavy sleep could be her escape. He, also, would be forced to face much unpleasantness. He could feel it in his bones. What would Regan's reaction be when he discovered that he was with Sirena? Would he feel betrayed and enraged or would he be secretly relieved that Caleb could look after his ex-wife. Ex-wife? Caleb felt the need to spit even as he thought the word. He tossed his dark head and knew he didn't care what Regan thought. Not now, not tomorrow, nor the day after tomorrow.

"Caleb, take over," Sirena called.

Caleb hastened to do her bidding, glad to free his mind of his tormenting thoughts.

"Within the week, barring bad weather, we should sight Spain. Home," she said with a wistful note. "My birthplace, Caleb." Abruptly, Sirena snapped herself from her melancholia. "Three hours at the wheel and then have Franco relieve you. We'll have a fencing lesson after our meal? What do you think?"

Caleb's heart leapt to his throat. Was she going to practice to prepare herself for meeting Regan? Caleb gulped but agreed to the match, hoping he would make a worthy show of himself. Although he had practiced the sport with the best masters Holland could offer, he knew that when Sirena was at her finest she could have easily taken any of his teachers. Still, the fear kept niggling at him that Sirena was not as quick as she had once been and that she would make an easy target for Regan's onslaught if it were ever to come to a confrontation. His thoughts brightened as he remembered Sirena as she had once been. Fleet of foot, quick of reflex, feisty and daring, determined never to allow any man to put her at a disadvantage. She had been filled with torment and the need for vengeance just as she was now. He knew from experience the effect that emotional state had on her; it could give her impetus and heighten her reflexes and accentuate her expertise. He would have to bring into play everything he had ever learned in order to make a worthy opponent and not make a fool of himself.

Below deck Sirena unsheathed her rapier and looked at it for a moment. Slowly, she ran her fingers down the smooth shaft of steel and flexed the slender blade. Suddenly, she dug the point into the floor with a quick, fluid motion. She smiled at the shocked look on Frau Holtz's ruddy face. She held her arms out before her and clenched and unclenched her honey-colored hands. "Still nimble, wouldn't you say, Frau Holtz?" she laughed and withdrew the weapon from the floorboards. Swiftly, she spun about and rested the blade's tip against the portly woman's middle.

"Extremely nimble," the Frau grimaced.

"A few simple exercises and practice sessions with Caleb and my form will return," Sirena observed confidently.

"And then . . . ?" the old housekeeper asked quietly.

Sirena shrugged her graceful shoulders. "Just that. My form will have returned," she answered airily. "I've never killed for the sake of killing, Frau Holtz. You know this is true. It is only that I feel it to my advantage to keep in form," she laughed. "I believe I'll rest until it is time for our meal. Wake me when it's ready, will you, old friend?"

"*Ja.* I wake you. Sleep, Mevrouw." The housekeeper settled herself on a hard, wooden chair and waited for Sirena to doze off. Her faded blue eyes were sad and tender. The Mevrouw had had more than her share of misfortune and, if she could find some escape from the loss in sleep, then the old woman decided no one would rob Sirena of it by awakening her.

As Frau Holtz stared down at Sirena, her heart lay heavy in her ample breast. Sirena had suffered more than any woman should. Everything had been stripped from her. Her wealth, her property, the man she loved and the son she adored. Only Caleb remained, the flesh of another woman. How long, Frau Holtz wondered, would it be before Sirena found Caleb too painful a reminder of Regan? Hadn't she already seen a coldness creep into the Mevrouw's eyes when she looked at the boy? Wasn't there a strident, hostile note to be heard in her voice when she spoke to Caleb? Frau Holtz shook her iron-gray head and attempted to turn her thoughts to happier times.

Jacobus had outdone himself in the preparation of the evening meal and it was with glowing pride that he placed a serving of flaky, baked, freshly caught fish before Frau Holtz. He had conceived a special treat for them by digging into his treasure trove of potatoes and frying them with one of his precious onions. Fresh vegetables were always a luxury aboard ship and from somewhere in his larder he produced a finely shredded cabbage stewed with morsels of salt pork and seasoned with vinegar.

Frau Holtz sniffed haughtily at his small miracle and began to pick delicately at her platter. To Jacobus' delight, one forkful was followed by another and another, until the Frau's plate looked as though it had been licked clean. The crew was more vocal in their appreciation, and the compliments were music to Jacobus' ears.

Only Sirena and Caleb ate sparingly. If anyone noticed their apparent lack of appetite, it went unmentioned. All knew they were measuring each other for the dueling match and both contenders knew an empty belly made a better warrior.

A brisk breeze blew up with the approach of evening and Caleb waited for Sirena to appear on the quarterdeck. The crew had gathered about, propping themselves against the rail or lazily lolling on the hatch doors. Caleb was aware of an exhilaration building within him.

Sirena appeared on deck, dressed as she always was when at sea, in her short, tatter-edged breeches and full-sleeved blouse which she tied tightly beneath her high, proud breasts. She had wrapped a multicolored silk scarf about her head to keep her long, heavy hair from flying into her face. Caleb felt a familiar pride in her as he watched Sirena walk toward him. It was easy to see why she had captivated Regan's passions. Open admiration shone in his dark gaze. Time and motherhood hadn't changed her at all. She was still as sleek as a cat and moved with a feline's easy grace. Her sinfully delightful legs were enhanced by the knee-high, black kid boots which were a part of her uniform, and her hips were still narrow and swung seductively when she walked. God, thought Caleb, how could my father turn away from such a magnificent creature.

There was nothing sexual in the way Caleb appreciated Sirena. He loved her, yes, but as a sister, and he hoped that one day he would find himself a woman as captivating and as exciting as Sirena, although at this moment he was certain that another such as she could never exist.

"Are you ready, Caleb?" Sirena asked, her eyes bright with challenge.

"Aye, Sirena, ready and waiting," he answered, a grin splitting his face.

"Then select your weapon," she instructed, holding forth the hilts of two rapiers. Caleb reached out, chose one and tested the thin blade by bowing it against the deck.

"You'll notice the fencing tips are in place. I wouldn't want you to take revenge for some real or fancied offense," she laughed, a sour note in the tone. "We stepmothers have a reputation for being evil, or so you may have heard. Does the weapon meet with your expert satisfaction?" she teased lightly.

"More than you realize, Stepmother," Caleb answered wickedly, taking fast swipes at the open air, the blade singing in a high-pitched whizz.

"If you're ready then, *en garde!*" she ordered, taking a stance, feet spread for balance, rapier extended.

Caleb moved to stand opposite her, his lean strength adding to his princely grace. He waited for her to take the first thrust and she did, the tip of her blade piercing the space between his arm and his midsection.

Sirena brought up her arm and flexed her knees, slashing again at Caleb's weapon. The blow nearly knocked the rapier from Caleb's grip and he took a firmer hold on the hilt. Sirena's strength surprised him and something in her eyes was unsettling. For a brief instant he wondered if she would have cut him with her first thrust had not the fencing tips been affixed.

Caleb took the initiative, aiming for Sirena's midsection. She parried, recovered and nimbly sidestepped as again her blade struck out. His arm flew backward and he was astounded at her agility.

Caleb parried, feinted to the right and touched the tip of his weapon to her shoulder. *"Touché!"* he shouted exultantly.

"So, Caleb, the lessons you learned under your fencing instructors were not for naught. How nimbly you handle yourself," she breathed heavily. "You are a greater challenge than I imagined." Quickly, her rapier touched the hard flesh of his thigh and he jumped backward away from the pressure. "You still have difficulty with your concentration; someday it may mean the end of you."

Caleb's eyes widened then narrowed. Something in the tone of Sirena's voice and the wicked glare in her clear green eyes chilled his blood. Allowing her opponent no time to regain himself, Sirena plunged onward, driving Caleb back against the rail. Time and again the tip of her weapon sought his flesh, time and again he parried, eluding the dangerous thrusts.

Fine beads of perspiration glistened on Sirena's upper lip and it was evident to all who watched that she was hard pressed to see the contest to its finish. She moved with the grace of a cat, but to Caleb's knowing eye she had become slower, out of practice. Her offensive tactics were contrived to conceal her deficiencies.

For an instant Caleb considered allowing her this win. He felt it would abate some of her torment and perhaps restore her faith in herself. A small voice called to Caleb. Let her win, let her win. It's what she wants, what she needs! Save her this disgrace before her crew.

So totally against his principles were Caleb's thoughts, that he rose to his own defense. His movements were those of a dancer, light and sure-footed. His motions were limited to protecting himself from her onslaught. He knew that at any time he could take her. The muscles in his back were bunched in anticipation. His blood ran fast, but his breathing remained light and unlabored. He had almost decided to give her a further advantage over him when he saw the smile on her face. Macabre! A grimace more than a smile. Deadly! A hatred burning from within. Caleb knew in that instant that Sirena was not seeing him, Caleb, within pointed range of her weapon. Her adversary was Regan.

Sirena's heart pounded within her breast. Her arm was heavy and becoming impossible to lift. The rapier which had once been an extension of her own limb had become awkward and alien to her. Still, she pushed Caleb backward. Her blade came up with lightning speed and slashed across Caleb's chest. She did not take her eyes from him. She watched him feint from one side to the other, always staying out of reach. Only the clash of steel upon steel could be heard above her ragged breathing. She was out of condition and she knew it, and her possible failure drove her onward with a vengeance.

The falling night lengthened the shadows, and in the half-light Caleb seemed to become Regan. Regan whom she hated; Regan whom she loved. Caleb's costume enhanced the resemblance to his father: white shirt open to the waist, baring an expanse of bronze chest.

Reckless fury overtook her, blocking out all reason. Beyond feeling, she took the advantage again, swiping at Caleb's weapon, sending a jarring blow near the hilt where he gripped it, sending the rapier sailing across the deck.

The silence of the onlookers was ominous, bated, waiting for Sirena's next move. Jan stood ready to intervene, knowing Sirena's mood had become lethal, waiting to step in to Caleb's defense if necessary.

"Pick up your weapon," she ordered in a tightly controlled voice. "This contest is not over."

Caleb stepped across the deck, the hackles raising on his neck as he reached for his rapier. He had sensed a change in her since the contest began. This was the old Sirena—as she had been when she met with her enemies. But *he* wasn't her enemy! He was Caleb! Astounded that her feelings toward him had changed so radically, Caleb moved mechanically back to the opposing position.

Horrified, he and the crew watched Sirena pointedly remove the protective tip from her blade. Glaring at him through half-lowered lids, she warned, "You see what I have done. Protect yourself, remove the tip from your weapon!"

The crew was aghast. Frau Holtz held her breath, disbelieving what she had just heard. The old woman's hand groped the air in horror. "No! No!" she heard herself cry out. Had Sirena gone mad?

Caleb watched Sirena as she advanced. Her eyes penetrated his being and held him locked in a stare. Again her blade flashed, and she lunged, aiming for his heart. Tears of rage blinded her as she thrust again, this time with frenzy.

Caleb's gaze darkened as he effectively parried the offensive thrusts. She had backed him across the deck again. Soon he would be off balance if he couldn't distract her long enough to turn around. "Kill me if you must, Sirena. I'll fight no more!" he breathed, dropping his weapon defenselessly to his side.

Something in his words, in his voice disarmed her. She had heard those words before, but where? Who had said them to her in that same deep, gentle voice. Regan! Regan had said those words to her in the heat of a duel. The night had been dark as it was now. She had found the pirate Blackheart aboard his ship and she had met the swarthy Englishman at swords' point. Then she had killed him. How many men had she killed? Oh God, is this the divine retribution You have sent me?

Dick Blackheart, the worst scurve ever to ride the seas! He had murdered Tio Juan, seen Isabella slain, raped Sirena, then offered her to his filthy crew. The night she had killed Blackheart, Regan had said those very words to her. "Kill me," he had said softly. "I'll fight no more . . . You can't win, lovely Sea Siren. You may have pinned me halward but you still have to kill me . . . Can you do it?" His eyes had darkened and glints of admiration shone as he had gazed at Sirena.

But she hadn't killed him, although there were times afterward when she almost wished she had. That night of bloodshed had ended in incomparable passion.

They had slipped aboard the deserted *Rana,* previously named *Sea Siren,* to bind one another's wounds. The cabin was dim, the oil from the lamps gone, the globe shattered. Regan had noticed a telltale stain on the back of her blouse.

"You could do with a bit of ointment. Come here!" he had commanded.

Sirena had bristled at his tone and was ready to turn on him and loose her wrath. But she had been tired, every nerve within her clamored for relief. Wearily, she had joined Regan on the bunk, allowing him to bathe the backs of her hands with water from the ewer and apply the salve.

His attitude had been so intent as he went about the business of dressing her wounds. Gruffly, he had ordered her to turn around and Sirena had surprised herself by obeying. Roughly, he pushed her down on the bedding and, before she could protest, ripped the bloody, tattered shirt from her back.

"Hold still, Sea Witch, I don't mean to hurt you." Pressing her against the mattress, Regan had bathed away the blood, gently cleansing and tending the cut.

Slowly, Sirena had felt the tension of the fight drain out of her. The feel of his fingers on her flesh had been soothing, delivering her into a state of mind where she felt warm and peaceful.

From touch to caress, he had made love to her. He had awakened her sexuality with his lips, covering her breasts, her stomach, her thighs. She had moaned with exquisite joy and had welcomed him, pliant to his need and demands. They had shared love that night in the sequestering fog. Here, aboard this very ship, in her own cabin; her own bunk. Even now, she could almost hear her own voice as she had moaned against his lips, begging, imploring, "Have me! Have me now!"

Sirena saw Caleb give an imperceptible shake of his head to someone behind her. It was distraction enough for Caleb to change direction away from the rail. He began to move to midship, fending off Sirena's slicing weapon with the clash of steel. Still, she advanced on him, taking leaps to bridge the distance he managed to put between them. Her mouth was set in a straight line, her eyes murky with anguish and tears glistened on her flushed cheeks. Caleb understood. And with that sudden comprehension came a sharing of her pain and, at that moment, he would have given his life to rid her of it.

Again and again she attacked, her rapier making singing noises as it dangerously passed his ear. In her madness she had opened herself to attack. She had left herself unguarded. Caleb could have easily brought her down.

The crew waited; Frau Holtz covered her eyes. Jacobus stepped closer to the Frau and comforted her, hushing her mindless wailing.

Back, back, she drove Caleb, back against the mizzenmast, trapped between the great solid shaft of wood and the rage of the Sea Siren.

Wordlessly, she made her intent clear. Her rapier's tip slashed at his shirtfront, leaving tatters of the white cloth. Caleb could hear her deep heaving, saw the tears falling like silent soldiers on her cheeks.

Jabbing, she had him trapped; he could feel the heavy knots of the rigging hard against his back. She was so close he could feel her breath upon his cheek, but still he would not defend himself.

Sirena raised her arm, the rapier's point aiming directly for his neck. With a cry of the forsaken damned she lunged forward, the last shred of her sanity compelling her to deviate from her intended target. The point buried itself in the mizzenmast mere inches from Caleb's convulsing throat.

For a long moment they stared into one another's eyes. The horror of her actions dawned on Sirena and she shuddered with shame. Caleb held his arms out to her in forgiveness.

Holding her close, he whispered, "Sirena, forgive me for looking so much like my father."

Trying to control a torrent of tears, Sirena's body shook. Her proud head hung low in shame and she would receive no comfort for what she had almost done. Not trusting her voice, she silently turned and walked slowly across the deck to her cabin.

Frau Holtz and the crew watched as she stepped inside and quietly closed the door, shutting out the world, preferring to suffer in isolation.

Sirena spent the next three days confined to the cabin, refusing to open the door even for Frau Holtz. Food left outside was left untouched; and when the Frau pressed her ear against the solid oak frame, no sounds could be heard from within. Only the lamp lighted within gave the housekeeper reason to sigh with relief.

Several times Frau Holtz implored Caleb to break down the door. "I'd do anything for you, Frau Holtz," he answered softly, "anything but this. I know Sirena, and she needs this time without interference." As he murmured the words, the housekeeper saw the depths of sympathy. His thoughts were plainly visible. Caleb was of the mind that Sirena had locked herself away because she could not bear the sight of him.

"I know what you're thinking, Caleb," Frau Holtz soothed, "and you're wrong. Sirena loves you."

"No, Frau Holtz," he replied, "that was in the past. Now when she looks at me, she sees my father and she can't bear it. If I thought it would give her any peace, I'd throw myself overboard and be done with it."

The woman clasped him tightly. "Never say that. Sirena would be lost without you; all she needs is time to straighten things in her own mind."

Caleb patted her reassuringgly. "I know. Of course, you're right. There's no doubt in my mind she *will* come to terms with the divorce, sooner or later. Meanwhile, she has to face me and the memories I conjure. She'll come out of this; I have faith in her."

The Frau released Caleb from her embrace and did not refute what he had told her.

On the fourth day, when the housekeeper tried Sirena's door, she was surprised to find it open. Balancing a laden breakfast tray on her hip, she kicked the door wider and entered, her sharp eyes raking the cabin. Sirena sat on the side of her bunk, her hair disheveled and her clothing wrinkled and untidy. The room looked exactly as it had the last time the Frau was in it, just before the contest with Caleb. So, Sirena had spent the past days huddled atop her bunk, sorting out her thoughts and emotions. From the expression of weary resolution on her face, apparently Sirena had come to terms with herself.

The fragrant aroma of coffee captured Sirena's immediate attention. "I'll be needing a bath, Frau Holtz. Will you see to it?"

"*Ja*, I will see to it," the old woman answered, a

cheery note in her voice as she spread honey on one of Jacobus' biscuits and handed it to Sirena.

Sirena ate voraciously and swallowed down the last of the coffee while the Frau went to ask Jacobus to heat water for the high-back, copper hip bath. Jan and Willem returned with the water, deftly handling the heavy pails as though they were weightless. They offered her a jaunty salute and, after several moments' conversation about latitude and longitude, Sirena dismissed them.

The Frau watched her Mevrouw carefully and saw that the hot water and fragrant bath salts were working their own special magic in restoring Sirena's spirits. She watched Sirena's green eyes take on their familiar glitter and her mouth hover somewhere between a smile and a pout.

As Sirena went about dressing in her abbreviated sea costume, Frau Holtz asked innocently, "*Ja,* it is good to see you yourself again, Mevrouw. Am I to take it you have come to terms with what the Mynheer has done?"

"Yes, Frau Holtz, you could say that. I know exactly where I stand! And I can tell you I don't like it one bit!" Sirena's movements became as angry as her emotions as she pulled on her tall kid boots. "Divorce me, will he!" she muttered. "Pension me off, as he no doubt intends to do. Oh, Regan is too much the gentleman to think of me destitute and starving and he certainly wouldn't like to consider me taking to piracy to seek a living! No, he'll see to it that I'm given a generous allotment."

She slipped a brilliant silk print blouse over her smooth shoulders and tied it tightly beneath her jutting breasts. "Cast me aside like an old shoe, steal my inheritance! Bastard!" she cursed, to Frau Holtz's stunned amazement. "He'll rue the day he ever left Java!"

"How do you intend to do this?" Frau Holtz asked fearfully.

"You heard me, I'll get it all back and then some," Sirena shouted, "one way or another. And Regan, too! He'll not get away with stealing from me and then divorcing me!"

"But, Mevrouw," Frau Holtz soothed, "the law reads that a husband has control of his wife's holdings. You relinquished all rights to your inheritance when you married him. That is hardly stealing!"

Sirena turned to the other woman. "Well, I call it thievery! Listen, old friend, when I was Regan's wife, anything and everything was his, with my blessings. When I knew he loved me, I gave myself and all I owned to his safekeeping. I trusted him, with my heart, my life, everything. Well, he's betrayed that trust! Oh, I know all about men who become tired of their wives and look for excitement in another woman's bed. The most those wives can hope for is that their husbands do it discreetly, leaving them the tatters of their dignity to shield themselves from the mockery of the world. Regan has not even left me this. He has stripped everything away from me and left me to live from his charity. Yes, I told you it was quite possible Tio Esteban has my mother's fortune in safekeeping for me, but it is essentially the same. I don't even have a sham of a marriage to hide behind; he has left me a scorned woman!"

"No, I don't believe it," the Frau protested. "There's an error, a misunderstanding. Never have I seen two people so much in love . . . so right together . . . The Mynheer is—"

"The Mynheer is stupid!" Sirena finished her sentence. "He should know better than to do this to me. Does he think I'll sit idly by while he philanders around and spends my money? He thinks I'm still in Java. He considers himself safe and free to do as he wishes . . . with my money! Oh! I can almost see him, so smug and content with himself. Hear me well, Frau Holtz, I'll get it back, every last penny. He's going to live in England. Hah! If he can still call it living, when I'm through with him. I'll take everything that's mine; and, if he's lucky enough to withhold a single pound sterling I'll shove it down his throat! He has his own wealth from liquidating his properties in Batavia. Let him go back there and uproot those awful nutmeg trees I nearly broke my back planting for him. You, too, Frau Holtz. Don't you remember the long hours we spent restoring the plantation after the volcano erupted, leaving nothing behind but ashes? And who reaped the harvest? Regan! And what does he do? He takes everything I worked so hard to give him and runs to Spain where he can take everything my family struggled for. My inheritance, my ships, everything!" Exhausted from her tirade, Sirena threw herself on her bunk and stared up at the ceiling.

Sirena's anger was a relief to the Frau. Too long Sirena had been lethargic, a shell of herself. Anything, even this rage, was better than that stillness.

Later, on deck, Sirena held the wheel, which was nearly as tall as herself, in her capable hands. This was where she belonged. The tang of the salt air, the spindrift spraying her ivory cheeks as she stood with her feet firmly placed on the rolling deck. This was home. Yet, there was something missing. A tight feeling of discontent still lay heavy on her. Home was the deck of the *Rana* but, soon now, she would have to face the world and society. She wondered if somehow it was stamped on her features that she was a woman who had been found lacking by her husband. That she was unwanted, rejected, scorned. An icy-cold glare crept into her eyes and she was aware that a part of her retreated into herself. Was she destined to ride the sea for the remainder of her life, a soul-less being, hiding from the world's condemnation?

Chapter Seven

Sirena sailed the *Rana* by rote. Hour after hour, she stood at the wheel, her eyes on the bright, glistening waters of the Atlantic. As time passed, the strangeness in her eyes became more pronounced. She never allowed anyone to take the wheel from her when the weather became rough. Frau Holtz explained to

Caleb that it was Sirena's way of punishing herself. Caleb nodded and managed to stay out of Sirena's range of vision whenever possible. It seemed that every time she noticed him she would complain about something he had or hadn't done. No matter what he did, it was not to her liking. Her eyes would become bitter and defensive when she spoke to him or when he offered to help her.

Once, when she was nearly asleep at the wheel, Caleb crept up on her and gently led her back to her cabin. She had looked at him in the old, loving way and said softly, tears in her eyes, "You are your father's son. If I seem . . . if it's hard for you . . . what I mean is—"

"Sirena, there's no need for words. I understand. My presence is unbearable for you. It's well that we talk now for when we reach Spain on the morrow, I will leave you there and make my way to England. I'm telling you this so you'll know where to reach me if you should ever need me. All I ask is that you don't hold me accountable for Regan's actions. My days of defending you to each other are over. I'll start to make a life for myself. I'll work hard and, if I'm lucky, I may one day meet a woman like you. I'll demand that she be as beautiful as you, as intelligent; and I'll insist that she loves me more than you do. You see, Sirena, I know you do love me. And I care very much for you, Sirena," he said, so softly that a rush of tears began to form in Sirena's eyes. "Now," he said on a lighter note, "do you think I'll ever find the woman of my dreams?"

"If there is such a woman, you'll find her. I wish you well, little brother."

"Sirena, about Regan. I—"

"Not to worry. I'll manage and I'll survive. I have endured worse than this. I'll make a new life for myself and I might even be happy. I'll miss you. Remember, this ship is yours. I promised you would receive it when you came of age, and I believe the time has come. The necessary title will be made out to you when we reach Spain. I'll take Frau Holtz with me, but the crew is yours. I'm certain they would be honored to sail the *Rana* with you as her master."

"Your men will never leave you, Sirena. Besides, I

feel they resent me. I'm not blind. I've seen how they react to me. They don't understand why your feelings toward me have seemed to change, and I don't feel that I should explain. No, they're loyal men. And Jacobus would be loath to separate company from Frau Holtz. I've heard that he's proposed marriage to her."

"Is that why she's been curling her hair and borrowing my lip rouge?" Sirena giggled.

"I'm glad you still have a sense of humor, Sirena. For a while I was very concerned for you. Sirena, I owe—"

"Shhhh," Sirena said as she held a finger to his lips. "I understand perfectly. Whatever I may have done for you, you have returned twofold. No thanks are needed. I ask only that you care for the *Rana* as you would for this fine, beautiful, intelligent girl you're looking for. Caleb, you must have money! At the moment I have none but that will be remedied as soon as I see Tio Esteban. Take my jewels. Please. Another time and another place, you can repay me. I insist," she stated firmly.

Sirena looked away as she saw a slight, glassy film swim over Caleb's eyes. "I'll talk to you later, for now I must rest. Take everything out of the coffer from beneath the bunk. Be certain you get a good price for the pearls, they're perfectly matched."

"I'll haggle without mercy," Caleb grinned.

"Little brother, can you ever forgive me for my actions when we . . . when I nearly—"

"Sirena, no apologies are necessary," Caleb interjected softly, his brown eyes gentle with loving understanding. "What is past is past. What is important to me now is that I know you love me." He took her in his arms and held her close, warming her with his love, sensing the rigid core within her bend a little as she accepted his embrace.

"Sirena," he whispered huskily, "I know how dead you must be feeling inside, how lost. I know you feel there is nothing inside you to offer, no warmth, no love. So, for the time being, just accept my love. Just take it and keep it as you always have. I make no demands on you, what is a brother for if he can't love his sister?"

Sirena was choked with emotion. How well Caleb understood her. How kind he was. "Caleb, I am more proud of you at this moment than I have ever been. You have become a man in every sense and your consideration is more than I deserve."

"Hush, Sirena. You know you deserve everything, more than I can ever give you. I am who I am because of you. I owe you my life and I need nothing more from you than to hear you call me 'little brother.' "

Sirena was overcome. "You are my little brother, Caleb, in the fullest sense of the word." Fiercely, she clutched him to her, tears stinging her eyes. *"Vaya con Dios,* little brother. We will meet again."

She released him and Caleb brushed his lips across her tear-streaked cheek, too moved for words. Before the divorce, Sirena almost never cried and her futile sobbing was tearing at his heart.

When he returned to the deck, Caleb motioned for Jan to join him at the rail where they stood looking down into the ebony, swirling waters as the *Rana* plowed her way gracefully through the waves. Caleb spoke quietly. "Listen to me, Jan, for I must speak with you. When we reach port tomorrow, I plan to lay in provisions and sail the *Rana* to England with a crew of my own. Sirena has given me permission to take all of you with me, and nothing would please me more. But I told her these sailors would insist on staying with her. She needs all of you. I can't stay here with her," Caleb said sadly. "Every time she looks at me, she's reminded of my father. I can't go on tormenting her day after day. She's going to make a new life for herself and she needs your support."

Jan looked away. The sadness in the young man's eyes had a haunting quality, and Jan felt his emotions rise up to choke him.

"Jan, you and the crew must be curious to know what's happened. My father divorced Sirena. She didn't know until I told her at the academy. I had to tell her. I couldn't let her go to her solicitor in Spain and find out from someone else. Do you understand what I'm saying?"

"Yes, I'm afraid so. Rarely have I seen a love like

theirs. I'm sorry for the Capitana. Of course, we'll stay with her. The strange look in her eyes haunts all of us."

"Have you ever seen that look before, Jan?"

"No. I've tried to put a name to it but it eludes me. Have you ever witnessed it, Caleb?"

"Yes," Caleb answered, without hesitation. "Once, a long time ago, when the *Rana* was assaulted by Dick Blackheart's pirates and they raped Sirena and killed her uncle and sister. The expression you see in her eyes is humiliation and scorn. She's been rejected by the man she loves, by the man with whom she had a son. You must help her. If I thought for one moment I could be of some use to her, I would stay and not a soul could drive me away. Unfortunately, I'm the one person she can't bear to see. For that reason, I must go."

Jan nodded in agreement. He knew how strong the bond between Sirena and Caleb was, and he knew what it was costing Caleb to leave Sirena this way.

"I wonder if you and the others would do me a favor when we reach port? I want the name of the *Rana* changed to read *Sea Siren*. Will you do that for me while I see about laying in provisions and getting a new crew together?"

"Hell, I'll do it myself!" Jan grasped Caleb's shoulder and shook it roughly. "We'll watch over her, have no fear. You'll be in England, you say? If I ever find myself there, I'll be sure to look you up."

"Make that a promise and tell the others the same. I have to relieve Willem at the wheel. Remember, Jan. Watch over her."

"Aye, with our life, Caleb."

The sun was high when the *Rana* docked once again in the port of Cádiz. Sirena stood on deck and looked in frustration at what was once her homeland. She no longer felt a bond with either Spain or Java. It was as though she didn't belong anywhere.

"We can go ashore now," Caleb said quietly. "It's time to say good-bye, big sister. I wish you well and good fortune. You'll find happiness. I know it as surely as I know I must take my next breath. Godspeed,

Sirena," he said gruffly as he gathered her into a strong embrace.

Sirena watched as he leapt ashore, carrying his shirt in his hand, his strong, bronzed back rippling from the impact of hitting solid ground. He shaded his eyes and gave her a jaunty salute before he raced off in search of men and supplies.

"Godspeed, little brother," Sirena whispered hoarsely, her throat working convulsively. Behind her, the crew had gathered, their jackets and sea bags slung over their shoulders. They watched her expectantly, waiting for their Capitana's orders.

Sirena eyed them all with fondness and compassion. They had brought her to Cádiz and because they had declined Caleb's offer to sail with him, they were left stranded without a ship. She couldn't allow them to leave her now. Where would they go? The sea was the only life they knew. "Willem has gone to hire a conveyance to take me to my solicitor's office. I pray that he has returned from his journey by this time. Currently, I can't tell you what my plans are, but you are welcome to make your home with me. The decision is yours. My offer is sincere and I won't harbor ill feeling for any of you who do not wish to join me."

Sirena waited, hardly daring to hope that the loyal sailors would accept her offer. When the unanimous shout of affirmation rose up, she had to fight to keep her tears in check. They were her friends, and loyalty of mind and spirit was all that was necessary to bind them all together, no matter what happened in the future.

Frau Holtz stood on one side of her and Jacobus on the other as they descended the gangplank to the dock. "Don't look back, Capitana," Jacobus suggested. "She's only timber and a bit of sail." Sirena gulped and bit into her lip. She faltered only once before squaring her shoulders and marching up the walkway, with her crew trailing behind, singing lustily of bawdy women and ripe love.

Willem removed his cap and bowed low with a sweeping flourish as he ushered Sirena and the Frau into the carriage he had summoned. With final words of how the crew could be found in the taprooms dockside, Sirena promised to send Jacobus for them as soon as she had made arrangements to occupy the stately Córdez *casa* which overlooked the harbor.

Frau Holtz settled her ample form beside Sirena, carefully pushing aside her Mevrouw's crisp, finely striped gown of pearl gray and black taffeta. Glancing covertly at her mistress, she appreciated the delicate open ruff that was cut to reveal Sirena's slender throat and lush rise of bosom. From beneath the wide-brimmed Cavalier hat, set firmly atop her glossy, dark curls, Sirena's attention was fixed upon the scene outside her carriage window.

This was still the Cádiz of her childhood, and she doubted it would ever change. Here the sun still baked the whitewashed buildings and the shadows still offered a cool respite from the heat. Children ran the streets playing with a stone and stick, calling to each other in spirited voices. The narrow cobbled streets reached in curving roundabout paths to the crests of the small hills overlooking the harbor. Red-tiled roofs overhung terraced courtyards and sported hanging pots filled with exciting blossoms, as though they were badges worn proudly upon a soldier's breast. Every once in a while, it was possible to glance into the alleys between the houses and see clotheslines hung with linens and bedding to catch the sun and the fresh ocean breezes. Sirena could remember sleeping upon pillows that had aired in the sunshine and smelled of the salt tang. She had lain her head upon many pillows since she was a child, but there was something special in the winds which blew into the Cádiz port. Rife with the natural elements, there was also a sense of excitement and life; something which was a part of Cádiz itself.

"Where are we going?" the Frau questioned, breaking into Sirena's thoughts.

"The first order of the day is to inquire after Tio Esteban, Señor Esteban Arroya. When we were last in Cádiz, Tio was not in his offices. He was visiting his daughter and journeying on to Italy. He has always handled the business dealings of the Córdez family; and, since I was a child, Isabella and I referred to him as uncle."

Since Sirena did not continue with any further information, Frau Holtz kept her peace and allowed her mistress to turn her eyes once again to the window and her reverie.

Chapter Eight

The coach turned into a side street and the horses heaved their burden to the top of a steep hill. Sirena craned her neck for familiar landmarks and pointed out the structure which housed Tio Esteban's offices.

Sirena motioned Frau Holtz to follow her and entered the building, blinking in the dimness after the golden brightness outside. It was just as she had remembered it from her school days: chairs with faded green cushions lined one wall and the fiber carpet produced puffs of dust that made her sneeze. Frau Holtz wrinkled her nose and Sirena knew she itched to take a pail of soapy water to the small chambers. A low, carved railing separated the end of the room where a wizened man sat behind a cluttered desk, sleeping peacefully.

Sirena unlatched the railing gate, stepped over to the hunched form and gently shook his thin shoulder. "Tio Esteban, wake up. It is I, Sirena Córdez." She stooped to plant a kiss on his brow. "Tio, it is really me, don't look so surprised."

"Surprised! Child, you're a sight for these old eyes. I knew you would come in spite of what your husband said."

Sirena looked into his alert face and felt a sadness that he should have aged so. Once-plump cheeks were sunken and wrinkled, and the wealth of dark hair had receded and was snow white, standing in tufts around his ears. Never a tall man, he seemed shrunken, and fine blue veins stood out starkly on his thin hands.

Only his eyes were the same, always bright and piercing.

"I heard you had come to Cádiz when I returned from Italy. Since then, I've waited for you every day. I've turned over my accounts to others long ago. Alas," he laughed, "there is no one who wants a doddering old man handling their affairs." His dark eyes fell upon the formidable figure of Frau Höltz.

"Frau Holtz," Sirena introduced, "Señor Esteban Arroya, Tio Esteban." Frau Holtz murmured a greeting and seemed flustered when the lawyer leaned over her hand and respectfully grazed his lips against her fingers.

Señor Arroya went about placing chairs near his desk and he gestured for the ladies to make themselves comfortable. "Sit down, child, there is much to speak of. I know little of what you've made of your life since your husband has been handling your affairs. Last word I had from you was on the birth of your son, Mikel."

Sirena's eyes glittered with moisture and this did not go unnoticed by the elderly gentleman. "No, no, I did not mean to make you cry. Your husband told me your sad news. Mynheer van der Rhys also told me other things. Odd, scandalous things . . . ," his eyes twinkled with devilish lights. Glancing toward Frau Holtz, Señor Arroya's eyes became guarded.

"Speak freely, Tio, there is little the good Frau does not know about me. As a matter of fact, she proclaims to know me better than I do myself," she laughed. "Though I hesitate to admit it, there are times when I am certain she is correct. What things did Regan tell you?"

"Stories of a female pirate! The Sea Siren, men called her," he whispered conspiratorially. "And he told me that this enchantress had retired from the sea to be his wife! *Escandalo!* Blasphemy!" he roared, all the while his eyes twinkled proudly.

"Sí, Tio, a scandal yet most necessary. For the soul, *comprende usted?* It was for what was done to Tio Juan, Isabella and to myself."

Gently, the elderly man patted Sirena's hand. *"Comprendo, niña,* Your husband was kind enough to inform me of the details. *Sí*, much sorrow you have suffered," he sighed deeply. "The news I have to give you will not lighten your burden."

"Tio, don't feel you must spare me. It is important that you tell me everything."

"There was little I could do," he explained. "The law reads that I must turn over your properties to him. *Perdonar, niña*, forgive me."

"Tio, I do not place any blame on you. Please, you must understand. I know that what happened between my husband and myself was as much my fault as it was his. It is over and done with. Now, I must gather up what remains to me and begin over again."

"And still you love him. I see it in your eyes. That, child, is one thing that will give you away. Your eyes, even when you were a child, they were a mirror of your emotions. Tell me, what happened?"

"It is over, there is nothing to tell. Regan no longer loves me and has divorced me."

Rage filtered through the old gentleman's charming demeanor. Sirena expressed his thoughts verbally. "*Sí, bastardo*. No more questions, Tio. Tell me, where do I stand with regard to my mother's inheritance. I would imagine that the circumstances have changed since Isabella's death. And the house on Via Arpa here in Cádiz?"

"*Sí*. It is already in readiness for you. As for your other holdings," he hesitated, "they have been transferred to *Inglaterra*."

"England! Why England?"

Tio Esteban's expression fell into mysterious lines. "Because, Sirena, I felt that is what you would ultimately do, so I saved you the bother. I know you, child, I know you so well I was not even surprised to learn that you had taken to the seas as an avenging angel for the deaths of Juan and Isabella. You always had the fire and fight any man would admire in his son but would mourn to find in his daughter. And then there was a certain look about Mynheer van der Rhys when he spoke of you."

"But, Tio—"

"No, Sirena, allow me to finish," he brushed off her protests with an extended hand. "I said I knew you and I am glad to see I was not wrong in doing what I did. I knew you would never consent to wed a man you did not love and I knew that love would last a lifetime. You would never toss off something as important to you as your marriage with a shrug and a witty comment that you had made a misalliance. Never you, Sirena. And, apparently, not your Regan. There was a somber tone in his voice. And when I tried to persuade him to breach the differences between you, he became enraged. The anger of a man who thinks himself rejected by the woman he loves."

"I don't wish to hear you continue with this, Tio," Sirena implored, pain evident in her misty green eyes. "Frau Holtz," she turned to the formidable woman beside her, "make him stop. Make him stop telling me these things."

"Nein, nein, Lieblich," the Frau soothed. "Señor Arroya is merely telling you what I've believed all along. Listen to him. Let him give you his reasons."

Sirena brought herself under control. *"Perdonar,* Tio. I'm sorry. You don't know all the circumstances. Continue, tell me why you've transferred my meager investments to England."

"It is really quite simple, Sirena," Tio Esteban smiled cherubically. "It is simply because that is where your husband—"

"Ex-husband."

"Ex-husband," the Señor amended, "is going to reside. I believed you would someday make the decision to follow him there and correct this mistake you have both made."

"And you are saving me wasted time by forming that decision for me. Is that it?"

"Sí, and because I am an old man and I knew you would forgive me my whims."

Sirena smiled. "And I suppose there is nothing here in Spain for me?"

"Nothing, Sirena," Tio Esteban said softly. "That which you seek is waiting for you in England."

Turning to Frau Holtz, Sirena sighed, "Then I suppose it's to England we will go."

"Ja, to England," the Frau confirmed dourly. The prospect of still another sea voyage was not to her lik-

ing. Her stomach still grumbled from the last one and her legs could not yet seem to hold her up properly on dry land.

"And as to your fortunes being meager, Sirena, I'm certain you will be pleasantly surprised. You mustn't forget that Isabella's holdings reverted to you and are not a part of the original marriage agreement. Furthermore, they did not come into your title until after your husband obtained his divorce."

"You sly fox," Sirena laughed.

"A mere technicality but one which would hold up in a court of law, I assure you," Señor Arroya smiled craftily.

Sirena hugged him enthusiastically. "Now I know why my father and Tio Juan referred to you as a treasure. When can I book passage to England?"

"We will come to that. First I wish to discuss your affairs." Sirena watched as the man shuffled papers on his desk and finally extracted a thick, yellow packet tied with string and sealed with red wax. "Everything is here inside. Read it over carefully and understand what you read. In brief, you are an extremely wealthy woman. I doubt if in your lifetime you will touch the capital. I have sent everything necessary to a distant cousin of your mother's in England. He has since communicated with me and said that everything is in order. His son, Tyler, is more directly involved with the business as his father grows older. Be assured that both father and son are trustworthy, else I would not have involved them in your affairs. I understand that the son, Tyler, is a bit of a rogue—very dashing, a ladies' man. You know the sort. However, he is sharp of wit. You could have none better to advise you. There is a letter from him and I included it in the packet I've given you. He has offered several plans of investment. I replied that I trusted his judgment and told him to make whatever plans are necessary. I've been told he is quite handsome, this Tyler Sinclair, and you may find him to your liking," the Spaniard said cunningly.

"No matchmaking, Tio. Regan—what did he say his plans were?"

"He seemed interested in importing and exporting. A trade he is very well equipped to handle seeing how his background is firmly entrenched in the success of the Dutch East India Company. You will no doubt cross paths sooner or later. He has the bulk of the Córdez fortune at his disposal and, by the time you reach London, he will have established himself. You are entitled to a share of his dividends. I haggled for twenty-five percent but he drove me down to twenty. Monies are to be paid quarterly to Tyler Payne Sinclair. If Señor van der Rhys defaults, the entire business reverts to you."

"Tio, how did you manage this?" Sirena asked incredulously.

"Ah, so you appreciate that your husband is no fool. He is a shrewd businessman. But I remained stubborn and threatened to withhold my cooperation in transferring the Córdez titles. Knowing it would mean a lengthy delay and one in which these corrupt Spanish courts would find a way to line their pockets, he agreed."

"Threats have never worked with Regan," Sirena observed, puzzled.

"Would it help you to understand that I threatened to shoot him dead with this," Tio Esteban withdrew a rusty blunderbuss from the depths of his desk drawer. "He knew I meant it. The twenty percent will hamper him in the beginning but, when he starts to show a profit, he will manage very well. I believe he would rather starve than default on his payment. At first, he wanted to pay you three percent," the old man cackled gleefully.

"Tio, you are marvelous," Sirena laughed, throwing her arms around his skinny neck. "So, we will all be in England."

"Yes, I am certain that you will be pleasantly met by the arrangements that have been made for your arrival."

"My arrival? Tio, how could you have been so sure I would go to England?"

"As I told you, I felt I know you well enough to predict your actions. I already instructed Señor Sinclair to purchase a home for you. Something befitting a woman of your station and wealth. It was to be furnished and made ready for you whenever you decided to use it. Go to see Señor Sinclair when you make port in London. A new life awaits you. Leave all the unpleasantness behind. Regan was one man, there are others who would fall at your feet in worship of you."

"*Gracias,* Tio, for everything. I'll do the best I can, more than that I cannot promise."

Señor Esteban stood up from his desk and reached for his walking stick and hat. "Oh, yes, I mustn't forget to tell you, there are stories circulating here in Spain and also in England of a sea witch known also as the Sea Siren. Sailors do have their way of spreading rumors. It seems that Señor Sinclair has heard of this enchantress. If one reads between the lines, he could easily become enamored of such a sultry woman."

"Tio, you didn't tell—"

"Of course not. My allegiance is to you, Sirena. I would not propagate such gossip," he said sternly. Then, turning to her again, "Your wicked past is done with. It *is* over, isn't it?" he asked fearfully.

"Certainly, Tio," Sirena's laugh tinkled across the room and seemed to brighten the shadows. "Now, let us see about passage to England."

"I take it by your sour expression that you don't care to sail under another captain, Sirena."

"This is so, Tio. The last time I sailed with someone else at the wheel besides Regan, the fool had us captured and Tio Juan and Isabella lost their lives."

Frau Holtz shuddered visibly.

"Calm yourself, good woman," Señor Arroya soothed. "Perhaps, we will find the situation will remedy itself." Dark eyes dancing, Señor Arroya led the ladies out into the bright sunshine and the waiting carriage. When the coach at last reached the harbor, he directed the driver to the dry docks.

"Follow me, child. There is something I wish you to see—the last ship your grandfather commissioned. She is almost complete but I want you to see the lady before she receives her final coat of paint."

Sirena accompanied the ageing family friend to the fitting berth. She walked along the planks, which were covered with sawdust, and relished the heavy scent of varnish, paint and hewn wood. Familiar sounds of hammering and sawing assaulted her ears and she thrilled to them. She had been brought here many times when still a child and watched amazed as the skillful hands of the artisans created a thing of beauty and purpose.

Esteban Arroya pointed to the farthest berth and watched for Sirena's expression as she drew in her breath, amazed. "Tio!" she exclaimed. "He did it! He really did it! Abuelo Córdez made his dream come true!"

Sirena's eyes skimmed over the graceful ship, her sharp gaze committing every detail to memory. The sleek vessel seemed to come alive beneath the hands of the artisans. On the bow, men spread shimmering coats of varnish on her deck stanchions and rails while others, with smaller, more delicate brushes, dabbed at the figurehead of a lusty, buxom woman. Awestruck, she watched as men began taking in a main mast, shortening the purchase as it upended. Not daring to speak, Sirena knew that if all wore well, the great spar would drop to keelson. She waited, praying. The masts were the spines of the ship. They were as essential as life and death.

"Tio, I still can't believe it! Grandfather said he would do it someday and he has. My hands itch for the wheel. Tell me, what was the reaction of the others in Cádiz when they heard he finally built his dream ship? And see the copper bottom? Just like a petticoat peeking from beneath a lady's skirt. How did he manage to design her to be so graceful? Look at the way the bowsprit and the jib boom point toward destiny. It's almost as if she had the confidence instead of her captain. I never thought I would live to see this," she cried excitedly. "Look, Tio, at the dolphin striker, the blade of her cutwater, the swooping sweep of her cathead."

"I see, I see," the elderly man laughed indulgently. "I wish your grandfather had lived to see this ship." Then the old eyes clouded over. "No, I'm glad he wasn't here to listen to the ridicule and the jibes the other builders would have heaped on him. Today, they still claim she'll never make open water. Your grandfather drew the plans and had her nearly finished when he died. Your own father and Tio Juan were too busy with the business to care much for his dream. So here she stayed in dry dock, nearly completed. I saw to it that monies came out of the business to keep her sheltered and in prime. If your father and uncle ever knew, they never said anything to me and I never pressed them. I had extreme confidence in your grandfather, Sirena, and I knew that his dream only waited for the right captain. I believe that captain is you, and I wish you well with her."

"Gracias, Tio, thank you for everything. And you will be there to see this sea spirit skim the waters like the nymph she is. She is years ahead of her time and may the heavens bless my grandfather for having had the courage to build her. He designed my frigate, Tio, and there is no finer ship in water than the *Rana."*

Señor Arroya smiled at the young woman who radiated with delight. Sirena Córdez had loved the shipbuilding industry ever since she was a child and she still retained that joyful ebullience like a child at Christmas. She had come into his offices that afternoon, somber and constrained. The break in her marriage and the loss of her son had taken their toll and there had been a bitterness in the thrust of her lower lip and in the fine lines between her brows. He had been right in ordering the completion of this ship. He had given her back some small happiness, an indefinable part of her beginnings, a glad eye to the future. The elderly gentleman narrowed his eyes and scanned the day and the weather. Aside from the busy carpenters' pounding, the day was quiet. The gentle lap of the water against the wharf was calming. A flock of gulls screeched and swooped down from the sky and flew off again, leaving behind a stillness. As he looked again at Sirena, he imagined he could hear her heart thumping and her pulses racing as she committed every line and detail of the ship to memory. "She's a beauty and she'll sail you true to your course, Sirena. Whatever it may be."

"Oh, Tio, I can't wait to get her into open water," Sirena laughed, her green eyes flashing. "And yes, Tio, I believe you are right. The *Sea Spirit* will carry me on whatever course I chart. For now, my bearings lead me to England, to Regan."

Her voice became soft, almost a whisper as she murmured Regan's name and the lawyer muttered a silent prayer that this beautiful woman would find that which she sought.

Reluctantly, Sirena followed Frau Holtz and Señor Arroya back to the carriage that would take them to the Villa Valdez on Via Arpa. As they settled themselves in the jostling coach, Señor Arroya broached a problem. "Your aptly named *Sea Spirit* is considered a disaster. I doubt you will find a reliable crew."

"No problem, Tio, my own has decided to remain with me. Sons of the sea, they're as reliable as the rising sun."

"Your ship is a work of art. Two thousand tons, carved from the finest oak and hard pine, and fitted with wooden nails. She carries miles of canvas on her yards. She's every captain's ideal."

"No, Tio, the Sea Spirit is *this* captain's ideal. She's mine and only mine. A small wager, Tio. How long do you think it will take me to reach England?"

"Three weeks, plus a few days," the gentleman offered, giving Sirena a conservative length of time.

"Two weeks to the day," Sirena smiled. "I can see my departure now. When we release her mooring lines and ease away from the wharf, her sails will gleam as the crowds watch. I can see her heel in the wind, just enough to show the unusual. Her hull will pick up reflections of the water, like first morning dew on the petals of a flower. She's born to the sea. I can feel her pulsate and throb with life. She's magnificent!"

The old Spaniard grinned. "Two weeks, eh?"

Sirena answered, her face wreathed in smiles, "Not a day more."

"Then a wager it is," he laughed again, a sound like the rustling of dry papers. Usually much more conservative in his bets, Señor Arroya glanced at the long-legged creature sitting opposite him. He was a fool to wager with her. If Sirena Córdez said she would dock in London in two weeks, then two weeks it would be.

The ride to the Villa Valdez was short. "What do you think of Cádiz, Frau Holtz?" Sirena questioned. "You've been so silent since leaving Tio Esteban's office. Perhaps you don't look forward to another trip, is that it?"

"Ach! My poor feet are not even accustomed to the feel of land and already you talk of more weeks on water. Also, I am not so impressed with your new ship as you are, Mevrouw."

"What troubles you, Frau? Don't you think the *Sea Spirit* gorgeous?" Sirena smiled indulgently at the elderly housekeeper, knowing that the woman would never find beauty in a ship. Now a house, that was different!

"Who ever heard of a ship with a copper bottom. Ships should be made completely of wood. Wood at least floats!" the Frau blurted, her brows pulled down in a scowl.

"If Grandfather designed her, she will float," Sirena soothed, patting Frau Holtz's gloved hand. "If you like, you can remain behind in Cádiz. Tio Esteban will watch over you for me."

"Watch over me, will he?" the Frau sniffed haughtily. "And who will watch over you? *Nein,* I go with you but I do not like it." Not for all the tea in China would she allow Sirena to go off to England without her and, if it meant she must sail aboard a doomed ship to stay with her mistress, she would do it.

The carriage wheels clattered over the worn cobblestones up the winding streets toward the Valdez Villa. Before reaching the top of the incline, Señor Arroya begged to be let off a short distance from his home. When Sirena protested that they could drive him to his doorstep, he insisted that the short walk would help to increase his failing appetite. After warm *adios* and a promise to come for lunch the next day, Sirena and Frau Holtz continued on to their destination.

"You still haven't told me what you think of my birthplace, Frau Holtz."

"All the buildings look alike," the German woman complained. "Why are all the houses so white? And the streets, they are all so narrow and winding. I wouldn't care to walk them after dark. *Nein,* I do not think I like it."

"All the streets lead to the sea and they twist about so the incline is not so steep. Cádiz is an ancient and wealthy city. Ah, good friend, you lack the soul of a romantic. We'll have to do something about that. However, we will only remain here long enough for the *Sea Spirit* to be completed. At the rate the carpenters are working, it will only be long enough for me to walk again the halls of my mother's home and to taste the fruits of my homeland."

"Ja," Frau Holtz murmured, not at all convinced.

"When you see the Valdez estate, you will fall under its spell," Sirena chattered on to relieve the housekeeper's apprehension of strange places. She had lived so long on Java it was understandably difficult for her to acclimate herself to new surroundings. "At one time many gardeners were employed to keep the gardens and orchard in prime. The Valdez home was the most beautiful in Cadiz. Tio Esteban said the house had been kept in good repair but I'm certain it will require your firm hand." With that statement the Frau seemed to glow. "And the gardens, wait till you see them. Oranges and grapes in the arbor. And home-pressed wines! We'll have a bottle of Valdez wine with our dinner tonight. Oh, Frau Holtz, you have no idea how much I've missed Spain. Even I had forgotten how much a part of my homeland I really am. Java seems like a lifetime ago." A frown settled over her lovely features. "It doesn't matter now," she whispered as the Frau reached for her hand. "Look! There's the villa!"

Frau Holtz leaned toward the window and looked to the top of the hill. There, in sprawling splendor, was Sirena's home. The tiled roof was constructed to overhang the walls on all four sides and myriad pots and ceramic jars were hung, filled to overflowing with bright blossoms and fragrant herbs. As the carriage approached, outbuildings could be seen in the distance and the Frau surmised these were the servants' quarters. The walkways were pebbled with white stones and glittered in the sunlight and directed the eye to the deep shadows where light, airy furniture, suited to the outdoors, blended in with the foliage. The two-story building sported grilled windows and a balcony embraced the top floor.

The next hour was spent doing all the things that

women naturally do when taking occupancy of a new dwelling. The first action Frau Holtz performed was to survey the spacious kitchen area and the linens. Sirena reacquainted herself with several of the servants and was introduced to the others. She toured the home of her childhood and complimented the staff for their care and vigilance. She took Frau Holtz by the arm and led her through the rooms, pointing out this article or that and relating a story connected with each. Finally, with last instructions to a houseman on where he could find Jacobus and the message that the crew was to join her for dinner that evening, Sirena closed the door to her room and settled herself discontendedly on the bed where she had spent her girlhood dreams.

It's true then, she thought to herself, there is no going back. Only ahead. I don't belong here. This isn't my home. I should be feeling something, she thought sadly, I should be happy to be here. How many times in the past I've thought about it. But without Father, Isabella and Tio Juan here to share this with me, it's all so empty. My home was anywhere Regan was. Regan and Mikel. But Mikel was taken from me and I drove Regan away. No, she cried silently, closing her eyes against the cool greens and soft beiges of her room, this is no longer home. The Villa Valdez, it is only bricks and beams and long-ago memories. This part of my life is over. Perhaps one day Caleb would want to live here with his bride. If not, the house could rot and decay and become part of the earth on which it stood.

Without warning, a round ball of black fur jumped onto the bed beside her. "Ah," Sirena said, "don't tell me you too are homeless with no one to love you. There is nothing in this life more terrible. I love him so much," she crooned as she stroked the cat's sleek head. "I gave all I had to give and it still wasn't enough. I stopped giving and I destroyed the only love I'll ever want. I have nothing more to offer to any man. I gave it all to Regan." Sirena nuzzled the kitten and whispered, "I'll make him love me again. He has to. I'll seek him out, tell him how much he means to me, that I love him. I'll beg, I'll plead, I'll do anything, say anything if only he'll love me again!" she cried brokenly, oblivious to the stranglehold she had on the animal. In defense of itself, it struggled from her arms and lashed out at her cheek, leaving behind a long scratch. As the kitten leaped from the bed, Sirena ran her slender fingertips over the wound and studied her bloodied finger. Her emerald eyes narrowed as she once again traced the length of the injury. "And if there is nothing I can say or do to make him mine, I'll kill him. He belongs to me and I to him. He loved me once and he'll love me again!"

As she stopped weeping, an anger rose in her for the life she had led. She held her bloodstained finger before her and recalled what life had had to offer her since she had last seen Cádiz. Raped at sea by pirates, drugged and raped by Chaezar Alvarez. A life of deceit and lies to gain vengeance on Regan because she blamed him for the deaths of Tio Juan and Isabella and the crimes against her. Marrying Regan, loving Regan, giving him a son born of that love.

A niggling voice whispered something about her destiny and nutmeg trees. Trees she had labored to plant to insure her son's future. Now her son was dead and the trees still stood. Regan deserting her. Refusing to wait until she had adjusted to Mikel's death. Assuming control of the inheritance left her by her family. Then insult of insults, offering to pay her three percent and poor Tio Esteban fighting for her interests. "Beware, Regan van der Rhys!" she intoned doomfully. "I'll track you down and in one way or another we'll come to terms . . . my terms!"

Frau Holtz stood concealed near the door which she had quietly opened. For the first time in her long life, murder was in her heart. If possible, she would wield the weapon herself. The Mynheer must have taken lessons from the Devil himself.

The housekeeper gathered the anguished Sirena in her thick arms, soothing her with gentle pats and tender cluckings. All the while she muttered oaths and obscenities in German to which Sirena nodded her agreement, but punctuated with swelling sobs of: "I love him! I love him!"

Chapter Nine

"The only word which describes the *Spirit* is sleek," Jan boasted proudly. "Even her name seems to fit her, Capitana."

Sirena nodded, "It does have a nice sound, doesn't it?"

"Aye!" Jan agreed exuberantly. "The *Sea Spirit* rolls off the tongue and doesn't get caught in my teeth. She's long and smooth, the way I like my women," he laughed as he ushered her aboard.

"She has the *Rana*'s lines." She ran her hand along the quarterdeck rail and then nodded to her crew. The ship was completely acceptible to their Capitana. "A master of designs built this ship and we must do him proud." Sirena assumed a regal stance as she issued her first order aboard the *Sea Spirit*. "Hoist the anchor to set sail. Willem, take the wheel, and Jan, see to the halyards. Jacobus, ready a meal fit for royalty. We dine at dusk."

"Aye, Capitana," they chorused. It was Jan who observed the Capitana closely. She wasn't fooling him for a moment. She still carried the same look as when she had boarded in Holland. Perhaps when they reached England, the haunted expression would cease.

The sailing was uneventful as far as Frau Holtz was concerned. All this fuss over a length of sail and planks of wood were beyond her ken. She didn't marvel at how easily this copper-bottom tub cut the water. She wasn't at all impressed with the well-hung rigging or the cut of the jib. True, the cabins were more spacious than aboard the *Rana,* and the fresh varnish and shining settings were easier on the eye of a scrupulous housekeeper. But she couldn't share Jacobus' enthusiasm for the superbly equipped galley because it wasn't *her* domain. Yet she did listen tolerantly to Jan's prideful boasts about the ship's responsiveness. It was Sirena who occupied the Frau's thoughts. The Mevrouw spent long hours alone in her cabin and Jan and Willem took their watches at the wheel. Jacobus spent long hours in the galley concocting what he hoped was tempting fare for the Capitana who, in turn, merely picked at the proffered food. All in all, it was not a happy voyage. The crew became subdued when Sirena strummed on her guitar on the moonlit deck and sang haunting love songs with a strained voice. At such times Frau Holtz wanted to wring Regan van der Rhys' bullish neck.

Two days out of the port of Cádiz, Sirena again had her sea legs. Looking toward the sky, she knew she was in for heavy weather. Her heartbeat quickened at the thought of a storm. This would be her chance to see what the *Sea Spirit* would do in a heavy gale. Already she could feel the approaching fog. Soon it would snake its way across the water and come to rest on the decks, wrapping itself around her legs and body like tentacles.

Sirena looked toward the sky again, willing the thoughts of Regan to flee her mind. She had to keep her mind on the *Sea Spirit* and her crew. Since she hit open water she had been plagued by a strong westerly wind. Her eyes were blank, almost unseeing as she watched the fog creep up on the *Sea Spirit*. She flinched when she saw that it was creeping around her boots and crawling up her thighs. A shudder ripped through her, demanding she pay attention to her position at the wheel.

"Sail ho!" came a shout from the rigging.

"What flag does she fly, Jan?"

"None that I can see, but she's tightened sail."

"All hands to the deck! Four men to mount the shrouds, four men to the yardarms—they'll slice the rigging if she's bent on attacking us."

"She's a clumsy ship, Capitana," Jan called. "From the looks of her she won't heave to in a gale under a reefed main topsail and that's what we're going to have shortly. If she's bent on attacking us we have the advantage. Marauders, wild marauders," he spat angrily.

A deafening crash sounded as a cannonball made contact with the *Sea Spirit*, splitting a hole in the deck. The crew ran to check the rolling cannon. The crackling and rending of broken wood was deafening. "Bastard!" Sirena shouted hoarsely. "You'll pay for this."

"Fire!" Sirena ordered. "I'll steer the *Spirit* directly astern at full speed and our ram will puncture the other ship's stern. Look lively now and tighten sail. We'll survive the damage to the deck, at best it was a lucky shot and one she won't repeat. Steady as she goes, the gale is whipping up. She can't tack. Fire!" Sirena commanded again.

As the cannonballs found their mark a large cloud of thick black smoke whipped upward, followed by a deafening screech of splitting timbers and decks as another missile found its mark. Sirena could see, even in the fog, that men toppled over the side as other seamen ran to check the sails.

Sirena shouted the order to take over the other vessel. "Quickly, she'll sink within minutes."

"Lower the flag," Jan yelled as one of the men swung out with his cutlass at an approaching seaman.

Sirena stood on the bow of the *Spirit* and watched as her men fought tooth and nail with the seamen who stayed on the marauding ship.

"Secure her," she screamed to be heard above the sound of clanking metal and the snapping and crackling of the burning wood. With an agile move, she grasped the rope from one of the crew and leaped aboard the fast-sinking brig, her cutlass rattling on the deck as she landed.

"Who captains this ship?" she demanded arrogantly. "Answer me quickly and honestly or you'll see your tongue flop at your feet like a fish out of water."

A tall and heavy man stood apart from the others. From his dress and cocked hat, Sirena knew he was the captain. They locked stares. Sirena's lip curled in distaste as she watched him sweat while his chest heaved, his thick lips trembling in fear.

"A small error on my part," the captain said hoarsely. "Who are you?" he demanded as his beady eyes took in her scanty attire.

"The Virgin Mary," Sirena said coolly. "What do you carry in your hold? No lies."

"Crystal and silk. It's mine, I stole it fair and square," he blustered.

"I can well believe you did. Now it belongs to me. Where you're going you'll have no need for the cargo. I, on the other hand, fancy I could use such articles. Quickly, Jan. It will bring a good price if we can manage to sell it someplace."

"What about these scurves?" Willem called out.

"Toss them overboard and if you feel charitable, lower the jolly boats. If not, let them drown," she said callously.

"All cargo aboard!"

"All hands back to our ship!" She jumped the widening gap between the two vessels with agility. "That's it, Jan, heave way from this scurvy brig! She'll not last long. Steer before the wind, quickly now!"

The *Spirit* now on a westward course, Sirena stood at the bow, one hand on the cutlass, measuring the sea. The churned-up waves beat furiously against the ship. It would still be a fight to best the wind and she might have to veer off the south or north until the gale changed somewhat.

What seemed like hours later, Sirena shouted happily, "The worst is over, calm waters ahead." Jan looked at Willem with a smirk on his face. "The Capitana hasn't lost her touch; her expertise is as great as ever."

"Aye," Willem agreed. "For now we must see to repairing and shoring up the *Spirit*. The booty will bring a grand price in London. Not that we have need of money, but it is nice to know that it rests in one's sock should the occasion ever arise for a quick buy."

"Well done, men," Sirena called. "You haven't lost your touch in the heat of battle."

Jan studied her carefully. She might be wearing a smile but it never reached her eyes like in the old days. He shifted uncomfortably, first on one foot and then the other. Time. Time was the answer to all things. There would be a day when the sparkle returned and the glow would be back. For now they would wait and watch and help when they could.

The *Sea Spirit* glided into harbor on a depressing, rainy day in early February. Ice floes were choking the Thames and churned beneath the vessel's bow. A dense fog was settling over the wharf as Sirena and Frau Holtz retired to the captain's quarters to prepare for their excursion into the heart of London. The first order of the day was to go to the offices of Tyler Payne Sinclair, Esquire, and the second was to make inquiries concerning Regan. After that, Sirena would locate Caleb to see how he was faring, if he was still in port.

The moment Sirena was docking in London, Caleb van der Rhys was striding through the doors of the Owl and Boar taproom to meet with his father.

The air of the cavernous room was hazy with tobacco smoke. The sound of sizzling grease could be heard coming from the open hearth where a haunch of pork was slowly turning on a spit. The stale odor of ale and the damp sawdust strewn about the floor assailed his nostrils, as he peered into the gloom searching for Regan. Caleb sighted him some moments later in the shadow recesses of the room. He was having a conversation with an elegantly clad gentleman who was obviously of the aristocracy. Both were guzzling ale and wore serious frowns.

Caleb strode the length of the floor, his lithe figure weaving between the milling patrons being catered to by lusty serving wenches. He was so intent upon reaching his father he failed to see the admiring glances of the bawds and the open speculation of the men who sipped their ale.

Caleb swung a lean, muscular leg over the rough plank bench and seated himself. He offered no greeting but signaled to the serving maid for a drink. His eyes were darkly hostile. The aristocrat interpreted the look and excused himself from their company. It was Regan who spoke first. "How did you find me?" he asked bruskly.

"It wasn't difficult," his son replied coolly. "I've been in England for several days. I noticed your offices near the docks and assumed you frequented one of the taprooms nearby. I thought it better you learn about my presence here in England from me rather than from someone else. I plan to stay, at least for a while. Ultimately, I intended to take advantage of the new shipping outlets in the colonies. For now, I'll feel my oats and see if I'm capable of making a living on my own."

Regan's face was forbidding. Caleb's casual manner irritated him, and he still remembered their last meeting at the academy in Holland. "I'm afraid you've come at a bad time," he said harshly. "My money is tied up and there's not much left for further investments. After our last meeting I didn't expect to see you again, least of all in London," he added bitterly.

Caleb's mouth was compressed into a thin, tight line. "I didn't come here for money or for your help. I came looking for you as a son to his father. I ask for nothing; I want nothing from you."

Regan's expression remained unchanged as he measured his son—filled with a hostility as consuming as his own. How was he to reach him? What could he say? Should he offer to take him into his small, fledgling business? Would Caleb reject his offer? In a tight, constrained voice Regan asked, "What ship did you sail from Holland?"

"In a manner of speaking, you might say I worked my way to Spain and from there I sailed my own frigate to England." Regan's smoldering blue eyes questioned the statement but he said nothing. "Sirena came to the academy to see what I knew of your whereabouts. She was frantic that you had gone under with the *Spanish Lady* off the coast of Spain. When she learned that you were hale and hearty, her relief was heartbreaking, considering what further information I had to offer. You see, Sirena knew nothing of the divorce until I was forced to tell her." Caleb's eyes met Regan's, the air between them charged with smoldering rage. "Because of the effect my news had on her, I was released two weeks early from my studies and sailed with her to Spain. In Cádiz she turned the *Rana* over to me as she had promised long ago. Having nothing else to give me, she gave me the Córdez jewels. Before I turned them into gold I wanted to hear from your own lips that you . . ." Caleb hesitated, hoping Regan would give some sign that his feelings for Sirena had altered. That he didn't want to honor the divorce, that he still cared for her and what happened to her.

"Spit it out, say it, don't talk around it," Regan ordered, his voice level and impersonal.

"You've taken everything else she had, why not the gems?" He hadn't meant to say it that way. He hadn't meant to be so cruel. But Regan's manner incited him to cruelty. He wanted to see Regan as helpless and as crushed as Sirena was.

"If Sirena gave them to you, then they are yours," Regan growled through clenched teeth. Just her name, just hearing Caleb say she was as near as Spain sent shock waves through his body, almost choking the breath from him. Had she come for him after all this time? He controlled his face so that it became impassive, and waited for Caleb's next words.

Regan had finished his ale and was well into another and still his son had said nothing. Unable to keep himself under control, Regan started to rise from the table when Caleb motioned for him to sit down. "Very well, Father. I see that you're not going to ask, so I'll tell you about her anyway. I owe you that much and I'm certain Sirena wouldn't mind. First, however, I want it understood that I'll not be a go-between. As to facts, she seems to be handling matters. She is aware that you have seized her fortune. I would have stayed with her, worked my fingers to the bone if necessary, but she wouldn't have it. The truth of the matter is, Father," Caleb used the address cynically, "Sirena can't stand the sight of me. I remind her too much of you. In time this will change; I must believe this; but for now, I can't bear to watch her suffer. I love Sirena, and you have taken her away from me."

Regan swallowed another gulp of ale and sharply slammed the mug on the table. He turned away from Caleb, not wanting to look directly into the bitter face of his own son.

"You've taken something that can never be replaced. You told her you loved her and then you divorced her, stripping away everything that was hers. I can never forgive you for leaving her the way you did."

"Dammit, boy," Regan roared, uncaring of inquisitive glances. "What do you mean, 'never.' You well know Sirena will be fine. Why continue with this?"

An intense rage erupted in Caleb, blinding him to the fact that Regan was his parent. His hand clamped over the arm Regan rested on the table. Caleb could feel the tension and anger between them. Through clenched teeth he hissed, "I saw Sirena suffer at the hands of pirates. I watched her when they mutilated and murdered her sister. I witnessed her grief when her uncle died. I was there when they strapped her to the mizzenmast and whipped her. It was I who brought her a tattered, filthy shirt to cover her nakedness. And even after these bodily abuses she was never as debased as by you!"

Regan shrank back, his conscience stung by the hurled statements. There was no way he could explain what had happened between Sirena and himself. How could he tell Caleb of the endless hours he had watched his beautiful wife wish herself into the grave alongside Mikel? How could he hope to make Caleb understand that the last night he spent on Java he had held Sirena in his arms and had felt the wonderful revival of soaring passions? How could he describe his joy—and the final rejection? Even though she had gone in search of him, it was too late! Life had too much to offer and Regan was determined to live it to the fullest.

"Whatever happens to Sirena, Father, whatever road she chooses to follow, she'll do so alone. It will be interesting to see who makes the most of the situation." Caleb swilled his ale and drained the mug.

"And which side of the fence do you sit on, Caleb?" Regan asked harshly.

"Neither. But, there is something you should know. I heard a bit of scuttlebutt as I was preparing the *Rana* to leave port. I learned that Sirena's enterprising crew has managed to put a price on your head. There's not a one of them who would blink an eye at seeing your heart cut out for what you've done to their Capitana. And from what I understand, contracts in the underworld are more binding than impressive legal documents. Even thieves and cutthroats have their code of honor, Father.

"However, that is not what I meant to tell you. I was happily tossing down the brew in a taproom in Cádiz when I discovered that by some technicality of the law, Sirena is entitled to not only her mother's, but her sister's and Tio Juan's holdings. The Valdez estate is a hundred times greater than that of the Córdez. So, you see, Sirena is far from destitute. I'll give you one small bit of advice—as a son to his father," Caleb said quietly. "Once before you underestimated Sirena. This time, it wouldn't be wise."

"You tell me all this then claim that you don't take sides. Do you take me for a fool?"

Caleb threw back his head and roared with laughter. Regan was jarred and his eyes widened at the outburst. It was like looking at a ghost of himself. "I recall Sirena giving you the answer to that question several years ago. Do you want me to refresh your memory?"

"Let's talk cold, hard facts, Caleb. The monies I've taken from Sirena are an investment. On the first of each month I am to pay her twenty percent of the profits and a healthy sum of interest on the principal."

"That's very generous of you, Father. As Sirena says, you're pensioning her off with her money," Caleb smirked.

"Hear me well, you young bull. If I hadn't taken over Sirena's wealth, the Spanish Crown would have. That country is forever in the throes of upheaval. This way, she'll be paid a comfortable sum on a steady basis. If the Spanish government had seized her property, she would have nothing. It is I who will be working twenty hours a day to make this business endeavor survive. It is I who will build the firm. My father made the Dutch East India Company what it was and then it was through my labors that the trade increased and grew to what it is today. Tell me, what better man than myself to take charge of her affairs? Transferring those holdings into my own name was for the sake of expediency."

"What you say would be true," Caleb countered. "If you were still married to her," he added bitingly. Standing up, nearly knocking the plank bench over, Caleb said, "Father, that is the one thing I hold against you. In my eyes you stole from her." With a last stony look into Regan's icy blue eyes, Caleb threw down several coins and turned on his heel, leaving his father hunched over his tankard of ale.

Regan sat, reviewing his meeting with Caleb over and over in his mind. Sirena in Spain. She had finally abandoned the little gravesite. All the angels in Heaven would never have convinced him she would ever leave Batavia. He had acted too hastily. Why hadn't he waited as she asked? Sirena, with the flashing emerald eyes and satiny skin. Sirena, with hair the color of a raven's wing. A tight band seemed to close around his chest as these thoughts whirled through his mind.

His sun-darkened hand reached beneath his vest and withdrew a paper, crackling as it was unfolded. Regan studied it with narrowed eyes. It was legal and binding. Aside from the twenty percent dividend Arroya had forced out of him, the paper stipulated Sirena was to receive half of all the profits on a quarterly basis. Before any and all expenditures, her money was to be set aside in a separate account. It had been Regan's own idea—one the Spaniard had no knowledge of. When his business flourished, as Regan knew it would, Sirena would share equally in everything. Why hadn't he shown the document to Caleb? Because, he answered himself, Caleb wouldn't have believed it. He would have thought it a trick.

Regardless of what was said, Sirena would always come first with Caleb. She was, and would always be, all things to the boy. Regan knew instinctively that Caleb would die for her if he had to. A vision of himself and Sirena floundering in shark-infested waters with Caleb flinging out a lifeline was so clear Regan almost choked on his drink. There was no question as to who would be saved. Caleb's emotions were as easily read as Sirena's.

Regan's eyes raked the dim room and he was startled to see that Caleb had seated himself with several seamen. Caleb ordered rum and drank it down with a gulp. He ordered another, then a third. The sailors joined in with a fresh bottle, while a giggling wench plopped herself on Caleb's lap and nuzzled his ear. Regan watched his son whisper something and the girl giggled again. Regan's gut churned as he observed Caleb's finely tapered hand slip inside her low-cut bodice.

Caleb drained his tankard and reached beneath the wench's skirts. She nuzzled closer and pointed to the far end of the room where a stairway led to the second floor. Caleb threw back his head and roared with laughter. Regan wanted to drag his son back by the scruff of his neck as he watched Caleb make his way up the stairs with the voluptuous redhead slung over his shoulder.

Angrily, Regan settled his bill and stomped from the taproom, wondering if every father saw his own youth through his son. The thought struck him that he wasn't certain if seeing Caleb with the lusty wench rankled him because he regretted the loss of his own carefree youth, or because he wanted to save Caleb from the same mistakes he had made. Whatever the cause, he had relinquished all rights for any voice in how Caleb behaved.

When Sirena emerged from her cabin, with Frau Holtz in tow, the men of the *Sea Spirit* whistled their admiration. Following the style of the day, Sirena wore a long-waisted, closely cut gown of topaz silk trimmed with wide bands of delicate lace running down the front of the skirt and also accenting the cuffs of the full-blown sleeves and wide, revealing neckline. The matching silk hose felt smooth and luxurious against her skin and the frilly garters that held the filmy gauze taut over her thighs made Sirena feel decidedly womanly and almost decadent. After weeks at sea wearing kid boots, the lightly constructed high-heeled pumps—a deeper shade than the gown—made her feel like dancing and she loved the way they peeked shyly from beneath her rustling petticoats. These French-influenced garments were so refreshing after wearing the bulky, awkward styles that were the accepted attire in Dutch-governed Java.

When Frau Holtz had seen the dresses that Sirena had ordered in Cádiz before sailing on to England, she had sniffed her disapproval and firmly stated that she intended to keep on wearing her stiff, concealing

Dutch-style clothes. "These," she had scowled, "are too like the raiments of a certain blonde German woman." She was referring to Gretchen Lindenreich, whose vanity and lack of morals had been well known.

"They are not quite what that slut wore, Frau Holtz. Although the way she turned Regan's head, she may have been wiser than I gave her credit for being. I have it on the word of the dressmaker that this is what fashionable women in England are wearing and I mean to take advantage of every means at my disposal. And if a show of smooth skin and feminine form can be of benefit, so be it."

Sirena had chosen to ignore Frau Holtz's negative thoughts when she skimmed back her ebony hair into a thick coil at the nape of her neck and allowed a wispy fringe of stray curls to fall flirtatiously over her forehead. Angling a wide-brimmed hat of satiny bronze atop her head and adjusting the frou-frou of feathers before stabbing it securely with a long hatpin, she picked up a pair of gloves and turned to measure her effect on the housekeeper. "Do I remind you so much of Gretchen?"

"*Nein*. There's none of the whore about you, Mevrouw. But . . ." she hesitated.

"But what?" Sirena prompted, trying to hide her annoyance with the Frau.

"But nothing, Mevrouw. Come, we must be on our way. Too long you've amused yourself before the mirror." Quickly, the Frau had averted her eyes, not wishing Sirena to press her further. What she had been about to say was that, although the Mevrouw was obviously a lady, unlike Gretchen Lindenreich, there was something about the look in her eye which reminded Frau of Regan's former lover—a hungry look.

Frau Holtz grumbled and complained about the close confines of the coach. Truth be known, she would have much preferred remaining aboard ship arguing with Jacobus and complaining about his accomplishments in the galley.

"How can that driver see where he's taking us in all this murk," the housekeeper complained. "We will meet our death at his hands, mark my words," she groaned, clutching her iron-gray hair as the wheels rumbled over a rut in the road. "Is this what London is like? Where's the sunshine? Everything is so cold and damp. Already my bones ache!"

Sirena's own temper was short and she replied in cool, biting tones. "As I remember it, the warmth and sunshine of Cádiz were not to your liking either. Perhaps I should send you back to Java. If you insist, I'll have the driver stop and you can walk back to the ship!"

Frau Holtz looked toward the grimy window and reviewed her situation. The streets were muddy and in sore need of repair, and unsavory-looking beggars lingered about. Even as she peered out, several ragamuffins came running beside the slowly moving coach, hurling clods of filth at the vehicle.

"Shall I have the driver stop?" Sirena asked, a smile breaking on her lips, taking a small, perverse delight in the formidable housekeeper's reluctance to leave the safety of the carriage.

"Nein," Frau Holtz grumbled. "The Mevrouw mustn't go about this vile city unaccompanied." She then sat back and clasped her thick arms before her, sniffing audibly and rocking herself back and forth to ward off the chill.

It was midafternoon when their carriage turned onto Thames Street, which ran parallel to the river. London was a polyglot of the ages, old and battered and hinting of evil, but also brimming with color and a certain decadent beauty. The streets and by-ways were narrow, most of them unpaved, and down either side, or sometimes in the center, ran the sewage troughs. Houses leaned heavily upon each other, creating an obstacle to light and air. Thames Street was lined at intervals with scarred and beaten posts which served to separate the traffic from the narrow, pedestrian walkway.

The streets were crowded with porters struggling to carry their staggering loads of merchandise and they issued vile epithets at any who impeded their hasty progress. Vendors and merchants pushed their carts through the alleys and housewives swarmed to purchase their wares. Merchants loitered in their doorways, cajoling, beckoning, even physically urging customers into their shops.

The skyline was punctuated with church steeples stabbing the gray air, and their clanging, musical chimes added to the cacophony. The center of life was the innumerable taprooms and inns which were denoted by the swinging signs painted brightly with ogle-eyed owls, blue bulls, golden lions' shields and swords, and burly seamen swigging tankards of ale.

The air was thick with malodorous smoke from the chimneys and soap stewers. Impervious to the stench, beggars, cripples and minstrels vied for the carelessly tossed coins from silk-stockinged dandies and elaborately coiffed ladies. Sedan chairs burdened smartly liveried footmen and, peeking from behind the closed draperies, an occasional member of the "quality" could be seen. Often it was quicker to traverse the streets of London on foot, even though it was dangerous. Traffic was frequently stalled several minutes at a time due to an overturned cart or a religious procession to one of the churches that seemed to be found at every turn in the walled city.

As their coach made its progress down Thames Street, Sirena absorbed the tempo of the city by drinking in the sights through the grimy coach window. Suddenly, her attention was caught by a sign hung above the door of a corner establishment. **Imports-Exports, R. van der Rhys.** "Driver, Driver," she called, excitement rising in her voice, "what street is that we just passed?"

"That be Saint Dunstan Hill, milady."

Frau Holtz, quick to perceive a situation, glanced backward through the muddied glass and noticed the sign. "Sit down, Mevrouw," she urged, "before we overturn on this murderous road."

Sirena stood up, leaning precariously out the hastily opened window for another glimpse of the sign. Regan! Regan! She felt herself being forced back into her seat by Frau Holtz and, when she lifted her eyes again, they were glistening with unshed tears. *"Kind, Kind,"* the Frau soothed, "child, child, the time will come soon enough." She sought Sirena's shaking hand and clasped it tightly, the heated words of moments ago forgotten in the compassion for her Mevrouw.

Sirena committed the location of Regan's establishment to memory and settled back in her seat, the sights and sounds of London no longer diversionary.

When, at last, the rocking coach stopped at the corner of New Queen Street and Cloaks Lane, Sirena and Frau Holtz disembarked with the aid of their driver, issuing him instructions that he should wait for them. Here the neighborhood improved markedly.

Head held proudly, Sirena approached the wide brick steps leading to the offices of Tyler Payne Sinclair, Esquire. Her hand poised to knock on the multipaned glass door, a chill washed over her as she debated her next move. A sidelong glance at the grim countenance of the elderly woman beside her made her square her shoulders as she swung open the door.

The inner vestibule was well lit, a welcome sight after the dinginess without. Unlike Tio Esteban's office, this was opulently furnished. Sitting at the far end of the room was a secretary perched on a high stool, leaning over ledgers. Coughing lightly to attract his attention, Sirena waited to introduce herself.

"Sir Sinclair has been expecting you," the cranelike young man stated in a cultured voice. "I'll tell him you have arrived. Won't you make yourself comfortable?" he asked, gesturing toward masculine leather couches.

"No, thank you," Sirena replied. "If you will just tell Sir Sinclair I'm here."

The secretary smiled appreciatively at her, taking in every detail of her appearance. Then his glance settled on Frau Holtz's stern expression and he hurried to do Sirena's bidding.

From out of the inner office stepped a tall, dark-eyed man attired in the current elegant fashions without assuming some of the more ridiculous feminine exaggerations. His doublet was of blue brocade and revealed a wide expanse of snowy white linen shirting which was laced at the neck and wrist. Following the trend, in place of the stiff, unbecoming ruff, his waistcoat fell into a casual, wide collar of deepest indigo velvet. His boot tops were loose and ornamented with spurs as was the style since the start of the conflict between Catholic and Protestant. For the most part the animosity between the two factions was still contained in Germany but outcroppings of it were slowly creeping across the continent and threatened to engulf most of Europe.

Turning his gaze on Sirena, he exclaimed, "Mevrouw van der Rhys," clearly enunciating the Dutch form of address. "Welcome to England, welcome. Had I known your ship had docked I would have sent a private coach for you."

"Thank you, but it wasn't necessary. Frau Holtz, from all appearances, this is Sir Sinclair." Sirena flashed a winning smile at him. "Congratulations on your knighthood. Señor Arroya told me it was quite recent."

Tyler Payne Sinclair was unnerved at having such a lack of manners in not introducing himself formally. Usually at ease with any situation, he was babbling like a schoolboy instead of a man in his twenties in front of this raven-haired, green-eyed goddess. Taking a breath to recover himself, he leaned over Frau Holtz's hand and bowed, murmuring his pardons. At a loss again for greeting the housekeeper before he paid his compliments to Sirena, Tyler decided to forego the amenities and simply took Sirena's offered hand and pressed his lips to her fingers.

Sirena didn't miss Frau Holtz's disapproving indrawn breath, nor did she fail to notice Tyler Sinclair's open admiration mingled with a devilish glint as he observed her over her slim, white hand.

"Please, be seated. Allow me to offer you a glass of wine. You must both be weary from your drive from the wharf." Sirena inclined her head in acceptance while the Frau flatly refused the offer.

"This is excellent Maderia," he said softly. "Perhaps you'll recognize the bouquet."

Sirena studied Sinclair over the rim of her crystal goblet and was amused by the expression she read in his eyes. She liked what she saw and her emerald eyes lightened. He was handsome and well built. He'd look magnificent stripped to the waist on board ship with the wind ruffling his black curls. His gaze was direct, and his eyes the color of ripe chestnuts beneath thick, straight brows. His features were masculine and regular, but there was a sensuality in the mouth, and when he smiled, a cleft developed in his chin. Sirena noticed he had caught her in her open inspection of him and reddened slightly. "Excellent wine, thank you."

Tyler Sinclair drew a chair opposite Sirena and seated himself, his long legs stretched out in front of him in a relaxed pose. "Allow me to apologize for the beastly weather," he laughed. "I imagine Englishmen have been apologizing for it for centuries. Tell me, when did you arrive in London and on what ship did you book passage? I'll send someone to see after your baggage. Was your voyage comfortable?"

Sirena placed her goblet carefully on the small table nearby and spoke softly. "We sailed on the *Rotterdam* and we had a most enjoyable trip," she lied. There was no need for the man to know she captained her own ship and commanded her own crew. It didn't pay to tell everything. In fact, as of late, she believed it was best to reveal as little as possible. She would be wary of how much she divulged to this handsome rake with the devilish glint in his eyes. Very careful, indeed. Even though Tio Esteban had assured her of Sinclair's honesty, she would still rather keep her own counsel and maintain a silence about her personal life.

"You are aware that I've been in communication with Esteban Arroya, are you not? I see by the packet in your hand that you did indeed visit the gentleman. I'm certain he explained how he came to my father and myself and turned your affairs over to our care. If it will be more agreeable, I will come to call on you the day after tomorrow and we will discuss your affairs in greater detail. You must have had a wearying day and I don't wish to burden you now. Let it suffice to say that all is being handled according to Señor Arroya's specifications; meeting your approval."

"That will be most appreciated, Sir Sinclair. It has been a hectic day and I'm certain Frau Holtz is in need of her rest. As to my baggage, there is no need for you to send for it. There are final arrangements I must make at the ship and Frau Holtz will see to it. I understand that you have been commissioned to purchase a house for me."

"Yes," Tyler Sinclair stated, with a degree of enthusiasm. "It is a grand house in a very fashionable section of the city. It is on King Street, just across from Saint James Park. Westminster Abbey is down the road a piece and you're not far from Whitehall itself. It has been furnished for you, exquisitely so, according to my mother, the Baroness, who has a certain eye and flair for such matters. I trust it will be satisfactory."

"I'm certain of it, Sir Sinclair. I hope the matter didn't inconvenience you too greatly."

"On the contrary. I rather enjoyed making the purchase and haggling over the price. Once you are settled, the Baroness intends to set you on a social whirl. Prepare yourself," he cajoled. His grin lighted his eyes and encouraged the rakish cleft to appear on his chin.

"Servants?"

"Everything has been seen to, so my mother assures me."

"Perhaps you will stay to dinner the day after tomorrow?" Sirena flashed a smile and was amused at its effect.

"I would enjoy that greatly, Mevrouw van der Rhys." Damn the woman, Tyler thought, that smile near takes my breath away and leaves me sputtering like an idiot. "There are a few matters which must be seen to as soon as possible. Among them is your . . . one of them is Mynheer van der Rhys."

Sirena felt her heart begin to pound at the mention of Regan's name. God in Heaven, would it always be like this? Struggling for control over her emotions, Sirena asked, "How is Regan?"

"Hale and hearty. He's established his import-export business and I imagine he'll do very well with it. He has some very sound ideas and, of course, his endeavors with the Dutch East India Company are to his credit. As a matter of fact, we discussed his plans at some great length. I can see by your expression that this puzzles you. Your . . . ex-husband must keep me informed of his business dealings and open his ledgers to me at the first of the month. I wish I could tell you he was amenable to it, but he's not. He objected quite strongly. Thanks to Señor Arroya's shrewdness, the Dutchman has little choice but to do so."

"Did you mention to Regan that I was expected in England?" Sirena inquired quietly, averting her eyes from Sir Sinclair's in an effort to conceal her emotions.

"I saw no need to discuss your plans with him." Tyler could see this turn in the conversation was causing Sirena a good deal of pain and he admired the way she kept herself in control. God, what could the Dutchman be thinking of to leave a woman like this? The man must be a fool! Yet, in his dealings with Regan, Tyler realized van der Rhys was anything but a fool. The Dutchman was a sharp businessman of keen intelligence. In fact, had they not been working at opposite sides of the court, so to speak, Tyler would have taken a sincere liking to him.

"Then Regan has no idea that I'm here, or for that matter, that I've left Java."

Tyler's brown eyes narrowed slightly and he observed the grim lines around Sirena's mouth. Was it possible she still loved the Dutchman? Esteban Arroya had given no indication that this was the case. There must have been something irreconcilable to have driven two such vitally attractive people apart. Without a doubt, she was one of the most beautiful women he'd ever seen. He sensed she held banked fires in check. Regan van der Rhys' eyes betrayed the same haunted look as Sirena's. If she did love him still, what would she say once she learned of rumors linking the Dutchman with the lovely, fair-skinned Camilla?

"Ladies, the hour grows late and the fog seems to have rolled in thicker than before, if that is possible. You must allow me to escort you to your new home. The streets aren't safe. On your drive here you must have noticed the presence of an inordinate number of street riffraff. Not since the founding of Bridewell have we had such a convergence of scoundrels on the city. The matter would have been seen to quicker except for this damnable fog which has settled itself on us for the past week. The special committee of beadles has been attempting to round them off to Bridewell but they keep escaping and moving deeper into the city.

Today, at the noon hour, I heard that Graie Friars—a hospital for beggar children—is filled to overflowing. These vagabonds bring their entire families and when they get rousted, they leave the offspring behind. I shudder to think what condition Saint Bartholomew's is in."

"St. Bartholomew's?" Frau Holtz questioned, disliking London more by the minute.

"A hostelry for the poor," Tyler explained. "These beggars bring disease with them and there have been noises of a cholera epidemic. These institutions may sound cruel, but the people are fed, clothed and given medical attention there. As for now, the streets aren't safe."

Frau Holtz recalled the milling throngs of urchins and their hostility when their carriage drove by. "We would be most grateful for your company!" Frau Holtz exclaimed. *"Ja,* Mevrouw?"

"Yes, thank you, Sir Sinclair. Also I want to thank you for all you've done in my behalf." She rose to her feet and looked into his chestnut eyes and for the first time since leaving Batavia she was fully aware of being a woman. A woman who was being admired by a tall, dark-haired, dark-eyed, attractive man.

"Must we be so formal? Please, call me Tyler; I'm still not comfortable with my new title. There's time enough for that when my father passes on and I'll be the Baron Sinclair."

Sirena laughed, the first genuine expression of amusement Frau Holtz had heard from her in more months than she cared to remember. "Then you must call me Sirena. My legal and formal name is too staggering for the human tongue."

"As I well know, having written it several hundred times in preparing a legal brief. See here," he said, reaching across his desk for a slip of cream-colored parchment. "You are, as it says, Sirena Magdelena Consuela Ramosy Córdez. You no longer carry the van der Rhys name. You are a free woman."

His words were a shock. All the color drained from her face and she felt weak-kneed. Tyler raced to put his arms protectively around her. Through the shock of hearing that years of her life had been erased, that she was no longer a van der Rhys, Sirena was aware of Tyler's steady support. She heard his quick intake of breath as he gazed down at her. She watched as he moistened his lips with the tip of his tongue.

Sirena smiled in spite of herself. She liked this strong, lusty man. What was it Frau Holtz was always saying? Ah, yes, "A bird in the hand is worth two in the bush." This bird would be well worth taking in hand. His tail feathers were definitely plumed. And then, too, if Regan found another man attracted to her, he might . . . Deliberately, Sirena leaned more heavily into the closeness of Tyler's embrace and lowered her thick lashes. She allowed her mouth to quiver slightly before carefully extracting herself from his arms. She held his gaze with her own, her eyes grass-green and shimmeringly moist.

Frau Holtz was scandalized and tapped her foot on the shiny floor to get the Mevrouw's attention. When Sirena still paid no notice, she coughed as though she were strangling on a fish bone.

A smile tugged at the corner of Tyler's mouth and Sirena found it infectious and laughed aloud. Tyler gave her a heavy-lidded wink before he led her to the door, Frau Holtz blowing her nose with gusto in their wake. What would the Mynheer think? It dawned on the old German housekeeper that the Mynheer would not be in a position to think anything. The Mevrouw no longer carried his name and she was free to do as she pleased. Vaguely, she wondered if Sirena would insist on being referred to as Señorita now that she carried the Córdez name again.

Harrumph! she snorted as she again dabbed at her watery eyes. This Tyler Payne Sinclair was a handsome man, she would give him that. And from where she sat she could tell he had breeding and manners. The Mevrouw could do worse!

Chapter Ten

When the hired coach pulled into the circular drive in front of the massive, white stone building, Sirena was disappointed that the heavy mist obscured her first glimpse of her new home. As she climbed down from the coach, it was impossible to see more than a few feet ahead. Tyler Sinclair took her hand in his and offered Frau Holtz his arm, escorting them up the cobbled walk to the wide double doors which sported gleaming brass fittings and a bulky knocker. Sirena strained to peer through the gloom, but relented as the wide doors were opened by a young girl. The servant ushered them inside and Sirena suppressed a smile when Tyler pinched the maids cheek, making her flush and stammer a greeting.

"Peggy, see to the ladies' comfort. This is Señorita Córdez and her housekeeper, Frau Holtz."

Peggy curtsied, uncomfortable under the scrutinizing gaze of Frau Holtz. "Would you like a cup of nice, hot tea, Mrs. Holtz?" Peggy asked quaveringly.

"It's *Frau* Holtz, not Mrs.," the housekeeper answered sternly, ready to pull the house staff under her indisputable control. "And we would all like tea to be served."

"Not for me, if you please, Frau Holtz," Tyler broke in, then turned to Sirena with his explanation. "I'm sure you're exhausted, and there are matters which I must attend to. Before I leave, I'd like to show you the house."

Tyler led Sirena into the parlor, which was to the right of the spacious foyer. "Well, Sirena, what do you think? Was my choice suitable or not?"

"It's lovely," Sirena said sincerely. "It's so spacious and opulent. Even in Cádiz, I've never seen a home like this. And the furnishings! Magnificent. Velvet, brocade, completely to my liking," she said, running her hands over a rich, sky-blue settee. Everything in the expansive parlor was done in shades of blue. The velvet hangings at the windows were a rich hyacinth color and the tiles in the floor picked up the indigo tones in the matching chairs, strategically placed around the room. The glowing luster of the oak-paneled walls shimmered in the bright, lamplit room. A monster of a fireplace with an intricately carved mantle adorned the far wall. Huge tubs of evergreens stood near the burning hearth, giving a cozy appearance to a corner where a many-tiered bookshelf stood. Colorful paintings hung about, giving added light and beauty. "It's exquisite," Sirena said as she touched a high-backed chair. "It's very peaceful."

Tyler smiled happily. My mother will be delighted to hear you approve of her choices. For weeks she's been in a dither. However, if there is anything not to your liking, you are simply to say so and not worry that you will offend her."

"If the rest of the house is like this, the Baroness has worried needlessly. Tell your mother that I am very pleased and could not have done better myself. Please tell her that I will call on her at the first opportunity to express my thanks in person."

"You will make her very happy," Tyler said, hesitating to interrupt her .He was intoxicated by her light, Spanish accent and her flashing green eyes.

When Tyler had made his departure, with the promise to come to dinner the day after next, Sirena turned to Frau Holtz with instructions. "Before we complete our tour, please make arrangements with the footman to bring our luggage from the *Sea Spirit* and inform the crew where they can find us. I have no desire to ride through the city again if things are as unsettled as Tyler told us."

"Ja, I was hoping you would not go back near the wharves. Just the thought of those beggars sets my teeth to chattering," the Frau intoned, her obvious disenchantment with the City of London evident.

Sirena left the Frau to her errand and climbed the stairs in search of her room. After inspecting several opulently furnished bedrooms, Sirena came upon a door to the left side of the second floor which opened on a large, combination bed and sitting room which was obviously meant for her. It was restful and feminine, decorated with care. The satin bed coverings and window hangings were apricot with heavy russet fringe. The low settee and the deep chairs were covered with heavy brocade of the same colors. Cherrywood tables were placed around the room, some accented by silver bowls of cut flowers while others held small, porcelain figurines. A massive painting hanging above the cold hearth cried for attention. Sirena judged it to be a scene of an English countryside in autumn. The rich golds and oranges blended with the apricot furnishings and the rich browns of the thick carpet underfoot.

Alone at last with her thoughts, Sirena's shoulders slumped as she lowered herself onto the settee. How was she to stay by herself in this magnificent house? How was she to carry on a life as Señorita Córdez as though her marriage with Regan had never been? What was she doing here? Why had she come? She had come because of Regan. He was the beginning and end of everything. He was the reason behind her every thought.

Tomorrow, as soon as she awakened and dressed, she would go to St. Dunstan Hill and seek him out in his offices. Street ruffians be damned. She would make him tell her face to face that he no longer wanted her, no longer loved her. She had to hear it from Regan himself. Then and only then would she believe it. Until that time she could dream and she could hope that it was all some macabre misunderstanding.

Sirena was weary, yet she could not close her eyes and rest. Her mind whirled and her stomach churned at the prospect of seeing Regan shortly. As soon as she had seen where his offices were, she knew she would go to him. She had known it when she was still in Cádiz. She had felt the need to see him as long ago as when she had seen the tip of his tops'l skim over the horizon in Port Batavia.

Sirena leaned her head back against the settee, her thoughts swimming with Regan. And when sleep did come, it was to dream of a tall, muscular man with hair the color of ripe wheat.

Within a matter of hours Frau Holtz had her domain under control. She issued orders in a firm voice and waved her arms imperiously for all to know that she meant business. Within moments she had the cook in tears, the footman stammering, and the downstairs maid in a state of utter confusion. She swept through the downstairs like a Dowager Queen. She informed the staff she wouldn't tolerate sloppiness, wastefulness, laziness, or slapdash cleaning methods. She also declared she was in the habit of making a daily inspection to see that her orders were carried out and woe be to those who fell short of their mark.

Her tirade over, she demanded a light tray for Sirena and carried it upstairs to her quarters. When she saw her mistress napping, she tiptoed from the room and sat down at the top of the stairs. Listlessly she ate the food, then carried the tray back to the kitchen. She decided she didn't like this place or the people in it. Where in blazes was Jacobus? When the baggage had arrived from the *Sea Spirit,* she was surprised to see that Jacobus was in tow. When she questioned him as to how he had pried himself away from his precious galley, he had answered perfunctorily that he didn't trust the Capitana's luggage to anyone and that he had come along to be certain it was delivered in one piece.

Although the Frau grumbled and complained that she didn't need Jacobus hanging about the house and getting underfoot, she was nevertheless glad to see a friend. Now, she was in search of him. Where could he be? Perhaps she could devil him into a game of checkers. But Jacobus was wise to the way she cheated and he wouldn't make any bones about telling her subordinates about it. She shook her iron-gray head and decided she would make it cards.

She found him in the greenhouse, which was an extension of the kitchens. He was puttering around with a small trowel, a look of confusion on his wizened features. "Madame Holtz," he said sternly, "there is nothing I don't know about my ship's galley and the sea. However, I don't know anything about flowers except that I like the way they look and smell. Here," he said extending a delicate bloom for her inspection, "I thought of you when I cut it. I believe it's an English rose."

Frau Holtz let out a small yelp as she fingered the thorny stem. "You old sea salt," she sputtered.

"I warned you that the bloom reminded me of you. It's as sharp and thorny as your tongue," he grinned toothlessly, "yet it is as beautiful as you are."

Frau Holtz flushed a bright crimson. "Oh scat! You old fool," she exclaimed as she fluttered her apron as though shooing away a pesky fly. "There's nothing you can do out here; can't your old blind eyes see it's getting dark? I thought we might have a game of cards. Or perhaps just keep each other company. I'm afraid I don't like it here," she said forlornly.

Jacobus felt drawn to the dour-faced woman. "You've got me to talk with anytime you feel the need for it. While we're out here, tell me what I'm supposed to do in this glass cage."

Frau Holtz glanced around with a practiced eye and placed her hands on her hips, a look of concentration pulling the corners of her mouth. "Jacobus, I don't care what you do with the flowers. The Mevrouw won't care what you do with them and neither will anyone else. My advice is do whatever you want. No one will know the difference. Why should you care?"

Jacobus shrugged. "I only meant to make myself useful and I really like flowers. I'd like to try my hand at them."

"Suit yourself," said the Frau. "Come inside for that game of cards and perhaps another piece of pie?"

Jacobus eagerly followed at the mention of the pie. It was the best he'd ever had and that cook in the kitchen was no fool. It would take some doing to get her to show him how she had made it.

As soon as Sirena got up in the morning, she had the entire household in an uproar. She demanded pails and pails of steamy water for her bath. She had Peggy tending her as a personal maid and the poor girl was all a dither when Sirena insisted she press one gown and then another only to change her mind a third time. Finally, settled in the tub, she asked Peggy to bring her scents from the still unpacked baggage. Peggy handed her new mistress a slim bottle of amber liquid and thoughtlessly Sirena tipped it into her bath water. Recognizing the scent, Sirena slapped angrily at water sending out small showers in every direction.

"Have I done something wrong, Mistress?" Peggy inquired fearfully.

"No, how could you know? Go now, leave me to my bath, I'll call you when I need you." Sirena's voice was stern and Peggy wasted no time in escaping her mistress' wrath.

Sirena slipped down in the tub, the hot water draining her tension. She was ashamed at having treated Peggy so harshly. The girl couldn't have possibly known that Sirena disliked the scent she had unwittingly poured into the bath. Civet musk, heady and sensual, wafted to her nostrils. She hadn't worn this particular fragrance since her wedding night. Wedding night! Sirena scorned, reliving her own personal embarrassment. The day had been endless and exhausting. She had married Regan under duress, it had been part of her plan to avenge Isabella's death. At the time she had still held Regan responsible for the treachery committed upon her and her family.

Throughout her wedding day Regan had remained attentively at Sirena's side. Considerate of her needs, introducing her to the guests she had not met before, he was the picture of a delighted groom.

Sirena's nerves had been strung as tautly as the violin strings on which the musicians played. She had passed through the celebration as if in a dream. Nothing had seemed real or to have substance. The food was tasteless, the wine flat, the conversation meaningless.

Later, alone in her room, Sirena had prepared for bed. The windows overlooking the gardens were open, allowing the night breezes to carry the sweet aromatic scents of the flowers and spices inside. She had slipped away from the last of the lingering wedding guests to seek the peace of solitude. As she had climbed the stairs, she had looked back and her eyes had been drawn to Regan. As if her glance were a physical touch, he had turned from his conversation and looked at her and their eyes had locked. After a long moment, she had turned her head and proceeded up the stairs.

By the time she had reached her room, her heart was beating wildly, her pulse throbbing savagely. His one, brief glance had desired her, coveted her, and she had seen that he regretted his promise to free her from sharing his bed. She had recalled the smile that had played about his lips when he made that promise. Could it be he had no intention of honoring it?

In spite of herself, Sirena had taken elaborate pains with her toilette. For a final touch, she had placed a few precious drops of civet musk on her pulse spots; it had enveloped her in a cloud of heady sensuality.

She had arranged a soft, loose knot atop her head with wispy ringlets feathering her brow and the nape of her neck. Satisfied that she created an alluring picture, she had waited . . .

Over and over she had rehearsed the scene in her mind. Regan would tap on the door seeking admittance. Hesitantly, shyly, she would admit him. His eyes would cover her hotly, their searing passion and need burnishing her soft flesh. She would stand with her back to the dim lamplight, allowing him to discern the voluptuous outline of her body through her thin lavender nightdress.

He would stand close to her, the musk intoxicating him with desire. His hand would reach out and touch the soft ringlets falling against her cheek and then caress the silky skin of her neck. Roughly, desperately, he would pull her against his muscular body, his breath would come in a light, wine-scented panting. His mouth would seek hers in a long, enveloping kiss. Drawing away, his eyes would burn into hers, pleading, begging her to release him from his promise.

Tormented, Sirena broke from her reverie. That had been her wedding night! Ashamed, she covered her face with her hands. Regan had never come to her room, had never pleaded for her caresses. He had left the house; she had heard his footsteps, had heard his horse's hooves. He had gone to Gretchen Lindenreich's. He had given the Teutonic bitch the satisfaction of knowing that Regan had left his nuptial bed to fly to his Valkyrie's arms and die a little in the throes of passion as she transported him to Valhalla.

Sirena pummeled the water with her fists. She had planned on humiliating Regan by her sweet rejection of him. Instead, he had never come to her. The sharp talons of scorn raked her as though she were again reliving the night Regan had left her for the German whore, denying Sirena even the right of refusal.

Frau Holtz entered Sirena's room and waited on the settee for Sirena to complete her bath. All of this for that bull-headed Regan van der Rhys. And if she was any judge of men, he wouldn't even notice. All these lavish preparations would be for naught and the Mevrouw would be devastated.

"Have you decided which gown you wish to wear?"

"The emerald silk."

Frau Holtz was laying the dress on the bed when Sirena changed her mind. "No, Frau Holtz, the scarlet I think." The Frau pursed her mouth and replaced the green with the scarlet. "On second thought, it is such a depressing day, I think I'll wear the yellow. Regan likes yellow."

Three hours, nine gowns, and four pairs of slippers later, Sirena was finally clothed. Frau Holtz heaved a sigh of relief as she watched the Mevrouw flick her cheeks with red Spanish paper and pat her hair. When she turned for inspection, the old housekeeper blanched slightly when she saw how low the neckline was cut.

"What do you think?" Sirena questioned.

"I knew you'd go back to the emerald silk. How else do you think you look? Beautiful, *ja*, beautiful. The Mynheer will be entranced."

Sirena clenched and unclenched her fists while Frau Holtz went to call the footman. What if Regan turned her away? What if he refused to even speak with her, saying the marriage was ended and there was nothing to discuss? What if! What if! There was no use speculating on it. She had to see him, it was as simple as that. She had to see for herself what his reaction was when he saw she was here in England.

Frau Holtz watched Sirena climb into the carriage;

Jacobus sat beside the driver. The Frau's throat felt constricted and she found swallowing difficult. What would become of Sirena if Regan rejected her? Would she become withdrawn and hollow-eyed the way she was in Batavia or would she revert to her former ways and fill herself with vengeance and hate? Whatever, Frau Holtz knew her life would be miserable and difficult if Regan turned Sirena away.

Through the streets of London, Sirena rode. Several times throughout the trip she heard Jacobus and the footmen cursing and beating off the riff-raff and beggars who impeded their progress to Saint Dunstan's Hill. The drive, which normally took less than an hour, was dragging into nearly two, and Sirena became fretful that Regan would leave the office for the day or that business would call him away. Why oh why had it taken her so long to decide on her gown? Regan never cared for women's trappings. If he still loved her and was happy to see her, he wouldn't care if she were dressed in sack cloth and ashes.

The carriage stopped on the corner of Saint Dunstan's Hill and Thames Street. Her head high, her back ramrod straight, Sirena raised her hand to knock on the door of Regan's offices. All she had to do was turn the handle, the door would open, and she would see Regan. They would look at each other and . . . and what? What would she say? How should she behave? She had to do the talking and the explaining before Regan could protest, or should she wait for Regan to explain why he had divorced her?

Quickly, before she could change her mind, Sirena entered. Regan was standing beside a large wall map, his arm raised to place a marker on what looked like a navigation route.

Just the sight of his broad back sent shivers up Sirena's spine. She saw him tilt his head as though he pondered a different route from the one he originally intended. He moved slightly and then rocked back on his heels. He hadn't changed. He still carried himself well, his hair was still tousled and pale. Her arms longed for him, her lips burned for his kiss. She felt herself being restored; just seeing him again did that for her. All this time, since they had been apart, she had only been half a person. Now, with Regan so close, she could be whole again. If only she could hear him say it had all been a mistake, that he still loved her.

"Regan," she said softly, from somewhere within her soul. His name was out and spoken before she even realized she'd uttered it. His name was a plea, a cry from the depths of her heart. She saw his muscular back tense. Slowly, as though caught in a void of time, Regan turned to face her. His eyes held an expression of incredulity. If he recognized the emotions behind the sound of his name, he gave no sign.

Sirena let herself drink in the sight of him. All her wants and needs were there to be read in her emerald eyes. She had to say something, make a move. She felt rooted to the floor, her tongue thick and swollen. "You . . . you look well, Regan," she finally managed. He hadn't changed at all. His square, chiseled features were the same. The sheaf of light golden hair was rakish and falling low over his brow. His agate eyes were aloof, just as she remembered them.

The muscles in his arms bunched as Regan clenched his fists at his side. His tone was cool and almost mocking as he looked at her. "And you look well, Sirena. I see you've managed to put your grieving behind you. And do my eyes deceive me, you've lost your rosary!"

"Regan . . . I—"

"You just thought you would come to England and pay me a visit. Is that what you're about to say? You're too late, Sirena. Whatever you came for is not here." His voice was harsh as he stared at her through narrowed eyes. "Look around you. What you see is what I am. A small, dingy office with room for only one person. I am a one-man company, but someday I'll make the van der Rhys import-export a rival to the Dutch East India. I agreed to the terms your old Spaniard demanded. Your solicitor receives your payment on the first day of each quarter as I agreed."

"That's not why I'm here, Regan. I wanted to see you and talk to you. I want to know; I want to hear from your own lips the reason you divorced me. I want to hear you say you no longer love me. Say the words and I'll leave and never bother you again. Tell me why," she cried brokenly, daring him to tell her, refusing to believe he would. "I loved you, Regan! I love you now! I gave you everything I had; my heart, my soul, my body. I gave you a son. I loved your son, Caleb, as though he were my own. I would have lain down my life for you. Why? Simply tell me why? I have nothing . . . you've taken everything. Even Caleb has turned away from me." Great tears welled in the bottle-green eyes, but remained in check. "Why?" It was a cry birthed in her soul and erupting from her throat in an explosion of torment.

Regan stiffened as he noticed her outstretched hand. "How prettily you beg, Sirena. I remember another time such as this when you pleaded. You said you needed more time to come to grips with losing Mikel. I didn't believe you then and I don't believe you now. You've led a life of lies and deceit. Trickery was your mainstay. You've spilled blood and laid with Chaezar, then told me it was because you were drugged. I forgave all these things when you gave birth to our son and I loved you as much as you now profess to love me. When Mikel died, there was no sorrow greater than mine save your own. You wouldn't let me help you come to terms with this terrible happening in our life. I begged you then for days, for weeks, for months, and you scorned me. Again I asked you to come with me to this new land where we could make a fresh start for ourselves and you refused. You said you would never leave Mikel's grave. Because I forgave you everything and because I loved you, I believed you. You left me no other choice. If we must place blame, Sirena, let us be certain to place it where it belongs."

"Yes, Regan, place the blame on me. I want it, I deserve it. I accept it." The tears spilled over onto her smooth, ivory cheeks, running in rivulets, but her voice held firm and she controlled the quaking sobs she felt rising in her breast. "I accept the fact that I demanded more patience than you had to give. I was wrong when your body cried for mine and I turned away. I did deny you the comfort I should have given. I accept the truth that I would not be comforted. My shoulders are not as broad as yours, but lay the blame on them. I'm truly sorry for the way things worked out. I'm here now to make amends and I beg you to come back and begin again. Forgive me, Regan, it was my love and my anguish for our son that blinded me. Our son, Regan, not just mine or just yours. Can't you forgive me?" Regan said nothing, his expression unreadable.

An inner voice niggled at Sirena. Get down on your hands and knees and crawl to him if that's what he wants. You already know how much it hurts to be without him. Beg! Isn't that what you said you'd do? She waited, watched. The corners of Regan's mouth pulled down and the familiar mocking look was there again. She squared her shoulders slightly. She must have been mad! Women didn't have to grovel to men, at least not this woman to this man, she thought bitterly. "I see that you will not allow yourself to utter the words I want to hear. Why is that?" she asked in a dangerously low voice.

"There is no need for further discussion," Regan replied coldly. "We are divorced. It is just as well you came here today, there's something I want to tell you. I've met someone. I plan to marry her if she'll have me. So you see, Sirena, it really is over between us."

Please, dear God, help me, Sirena prayed silently. Don't let me falter now. With every ounce of strength within her, Sirena steadied herself. Her emerald-green eyes flashed a warning as she met his gaze. Her words, when they came, surprised her, for they were as completely controlled as Regan's.

"I want to be certain I understand." She enunciated each word slowly and carefully. "We are divorced. By your decision. You plan to marry another. Everything you've taken from me by what you claim is your right, I will reclaim. You may have it now, but," she said so faintly that Regan had to strain to hear, "I will get it back. You won't spend one cent of my money on another woman. What's mine is mine. Not yours, no longer ours, but mine! Believe what you will, do as you wish, but consider this the only warning I'll give you. Oh, and one other matter," she added casually. "I looked over the agreement you made with Señor Arroya. I've made a slight change as the gentleman said was my prerogative. I no longer want a profit statement. I want more shares of this company. See to it that the matter is handled. In three days it will be the first of the month."

"You want what?" Regan bellowed in outrage.

"I want my payment to buy extra shares in your company. I have great faith in you, Regan. I know that if you work twenty hours a day as I did in the nutmeg fields you will make me a rich woman. You should have learned to read Spanish. It is the bottom line on the contract you signed. Your bold, brave signature rests directly beneath it. Shares, Regan, and don't stint yourself."

"The law—"

"I've had enough of you and your damnable laws. I'm sick and tired of you telling me what I can and cannot do. You have no choice in the matter. Think of it this way; it will increase your capital to improve the business. Play me fair, Regan, else I'll kill you. I can't make it plainer than that. And don't think I'll shed tears of remorse. There is no judge in this land who would convict me when they learn what you did to me. In case you're not aware of the fact, the Valdez fortune has come into my hands. If one has enough money, judges and lawmakers can be bought. Just as husbands can be."

"If there is one thing which sickens me, Sirena, it's a jealous, spiteful woman," Regan sneered.

Sirena's laugh tinkled off the walls. "A *rich,* jealous, spiteful woman!" Again, her green eyes flashed dangerously. "It would be advisable for you to work your fingers to the bone . . . for me. And if I am in a generous mood, then I will allow you to continue . . . ," she laughed again, ". . . to continue to make a living for me. *Adios,* Regan."

Regan watched her leave, her loose-limbed stride regal and confident. Damn woman! He sat down slowly on the hard chair and put his head in his hands. She had come to England, for him. Why had he been so bull-headed and so cold to her? Just the sight of her had almost driven the breath from his body. She hadn't changed since he had last seen her, damn her. If anything, she was even more beautiful. His heart thundered in his chest. It had been all he could do to keep from crushing her to him.

What had he done? God in his Heaven couldn't have convinced him she would ever have overcome her despair and come to him. He had believed her implicitly when she cried that she would never leave Mikel's grave. And here she was, threatening to ruin him as she had almost done once before. A wild, frightening feeling churned in his guts as he recalled the dangerous glint in her eyes. He had seen that look before and had seen the results of the emotions behind that look—when she had mowed down the scurrilous pirate, Dick Blackheart!

When she had enjoyed her escapades as the Sea Siren, Sirena had waited for the day when she could repay Blackheart for what he had done to her and her sister. That day had come, just as she had known it would. And now she was threatening to ruin something that he, Regan, was building. Not this time, Sirena, Regan thought as he gritted his teeth. He groped for some way to protect himself from her. Some way to get his hands on a healthy income that had nothing to do with the money he'd vested for Sirena. Something apart from the business.

Over and over he mulled things in his mind and his logic kept bringing him back to the same point. Camilla Langdon. Daughter of Sir Stephan Langdon, a wealthy landowner and financier.

Actually he had been seeing quite a bit of Camilla since coming to England. Not that he sought her out; she just seemed to be at every party or dinner he attended and had more or less attached herself to him. Recently, whenever asked to a social function, it was assumed he would bring Camilla with him.

A forced smile tightened on Regan's lips. He could do worse than a lovely, young, fair-skinned heiress, couldn't he? And he'd already told Sirena that he intended to marry. Well, perhaps it was a bit before the fact. He knew instinctively that Sir Stephan would welcome the alliance. As for Camilla, he would swear she was hot for him. Besides, what better way to protect himself from Sirena's allure than to be a happily married man?

Sirena collapsed in the coach, heart-racking sobs engulfing her body. Jacobus cradled her in his thin, sinewy arms and let her cry. He cursed the Dutchman silently and wished him a slow, painful death. Poor Capitana. There was no need for her to suffer so. If this was what dry land was going to do to the crew and captain of the *Sea Spirit,* then it would be best to return to sea. He knew in his heart that the Capitana would never depart as long as the Dutchman was here in this hellhole known as London. He made a mental note to speak to Jan and the other crew members and see if they could think of something that would ease the Capitana's anguish. Love was for fools, he reasoned. The sea and ship were his only loves. They didn't break your heart. If he ever went over the side he would go straight to the bottom and not fight the inevitable. He would rest in his watery grave, in the arms of his only true love, the restless sea.

Pale sunshine was streaking the sky when the carriage finally stopped at Sirena's new home. Inside her room, with the door closed, Sirena looked about like a trapped animal. Why had she said what she did to Regan? Where had all her good intentions gone? What had possessed her to threaten him the way she did? Because he hurt me, she cried silently. He rejected me. He plans to marry again. I had to do what I did. I couldn't let him see how he hurt me, I just couldn't let him see.

Anger abruptly shot up her spine and flushed her cheeks. Regan had ruined everything. Now, as before, it was up to her to do something. She raised her eyes to the heavens. Oh, God, I love him. I want him back. I want him to love me. The niggling voice returned. He loves another.

"In a pig's eye!" The ornate, feminine dressing table suddenly found itself leaning haphazardly against the wall, the decanters of cologne and perfume spilling over the thick carpet. A sliver of mirror and a hairbrush smashed against the door and landed in a heap side by side. Down came the draperies as her fist shot through a pane of glass. She looked in wide-eyed wonder at the slim scratch which ran the length of her thumb. She lashed out at the bed and ripped the coverlet and threw it across the room. Her hand found the andiron by the fireplace and she set about whacking whatever fell into her path. "Get rid of me like one of your foul cigars, will you? Marry somebody else, will you? I've ruined you before and I'll do it again. I'll make you pay for what you've done to me!" she screeched. "You married me. You're mine!" she screamed as Frau Holtz rushed into the room, Jacobus behind her.

They looked about at the devastation and quietly closed the door. There was nothing they could do. The Mevrouw had to work things out for herself. She wouldn't thank them for interfering in her rampage. "No," the housekeeper said to Jacobus, "there is nothing for us to do. The Mevrouw will make a decision and she will live with it."

Chapter Eleven

On the Pall Mall, near Charing Cross, the townhouse of the Baron and Baroness Sinclair presided over the affluent neighborhood. The heavy fog which had descended upon London had all but obscured the impeccably tended garden which made passersby pause to enjoy its symmetry and formal landscaping. It seemed to those who had occasion to walk by frequently that the Sinclair garden boasted continually blooming flora regardless of the season. This was mostly due to the efforts and foresight of the Baroness Helen Sinclair herself, who was now tapping her foot impatiently on the library floor and piercing her husband, Baron Charles, with a steely look.

"One would think Tyler would be here to welcome us back to London after our holiday in the country."

"Perhaps the boy had pressing business at the office and he hasn't realized the lateness of the hour. Besides, this weather brought traffic almost to a standstill," Baron Charles said quietly.

The Baroness looked down her long, aristocratic nose and frowned. "When are you going to stop defending Tyler? He's no longer a boy, but an eligible man. You've been too indulgent for too long," she criticized. "How many times have I warned you that he requires a strong hand."

"My dear," the Baron sighed, "on the one hand you tell me he's no longer a boy and on the other you advise me to take a strong hand with him. Every young man must sow his wild oats before he settles down and it will serve to make him a better husband. I was allowed a few oats in my day and haven't I made you a good husband?" The Baron winked at her roguishly, hoping to erase the frown from her face.

"Yes, you've been wonderful," the Baroness answered honestly. "But, Charles, a few oats are one thing. The rascal is sowing an entire field! It has to stop; his reputation is beginning to suffer and then where will he be? We must step in and take a firm hand just the way we did when he was smitten with Camilla Langdon. You must admit, Charles, that if we hadn't stepped in at that time he would have married that snippet."

"Now, now, Helen, I don't think Tyler's reputation will be damaged. You must admit he's more enterprising than those ridiculous fops who walk the halls of Whitehall hoping to be invited to the King's Court. Tyler is a respectable businessman, just as I was."

"True," the Baroness reluctantly conceded, "he does have that. But you must admit it was only because we insisted upon him doing something with his life that he read for the Law. Just as your father insisted you do. It was a wise move on our part and I thank God for it. But it doesn't excuse Tyler from his social behavior. You can't have forgotten how frantic we were when he insisted he wanted to marry that scheming little Camilla!"

"He was immature then. Surely, you can understand his attraction to the young lady. She was and still is a beautiful woman."

"A poor woman. A poor relation!" the Baroness

spit. "And to think I brought her into our home along with that ne'er-do-well father of hers, Stephan Langdon."

"My dear wife, Camilla's impoverished state is something she cannot help," the Baron pointed out kindly.

"I expected you to say that," Helen sniffed. "Camilla and her father are *your* relatives. And don't tell me you haven't been paying their bills! Why couldn't you send them away somewhere where they wouldn't be a constant threat of embarrassment?"

"In truth now, my dear, where could I send them? Camilla would just pine away for London's society and Stephan would literally die if he were away from his clubs and gaming houses. I can't take the responsibility for their lives. If all it takes is an occasional loan and I have it to give, where's the harm? I consider the matter closed." Charles' tone indicated this was an old argument which had been worked over time and again between himself and the Baroness, and both stood firmly and intractably in their feelings toward the Langdons.

"Very well," the Baroness agreed. "But one last thing, Charles. Is it true what I hear about Camilla and that Dutchman keeping serious company with each other? Van der Rhys is his name, I believe. I certainly hope it is. Then I can rest easy knowing that Tyler will have to put her out of his mind once and for all."

"I heard it said at the club that Stephan himself was boasting of the wealthy Dutchman's interest in his daughter. Another source close to Camilla said she is already selecting her trousseau."

The Baroness' face brightened and her blue eyes sparkled at her husband's words. She patted her carefully coiffed hair and smiled. "That means Tyler is safe until some other designing female gets her hooks into him. I believe I'll have a small sip of wine, dear, my throat feels dry. Perhaps it will ease my annoyance over Tyler. We will wait exactly fifteen minutes and if he hasn't arrived, we'll dine without him."

"The hour isn't that late, dear. Tell me, have you heard anything more about this van der Rhys. I know the ladies are forever gossiping behind their hands when an acceptable man comes to town. Every mother within miles will be trying to rid herself of her marriageable daughters."

"We have spoken on the subject," the Baroness remarked coyly. "Actually, there is not much to discuss. He's a handsome brute and seems to be making success in his importing-exporting enterprise. I'm given to believe he's quite wealthy and is considered very, very eligible. Lady Constance told me, when she came to call, that he was received socially and has been invited to every social function that was held while we were away on holiday. She said the men hold him in respect and the women fawn over him."

The Baroness turned her attention to her round-faced husband. It was true what he had said. He did make a good husband and he was an excellent father, even if somewhat indulgent. Of late, however, he was becoming forgetful, and he could ramble on for hours of things that had happened in the past. She reached over and patted his hand affectionately.

"I think I hear Tyler now," the Baron said smiling. He rose from his chair to greet his exuberant son and clasped him firmly on the shoulder.

"Welcome home, Mother," Tyler said, leaning to kiss her powdered cheek. "I had some pressing details at the office, else I would have been home earlier. "Señorita Córdez arrived yesterday. I'll be dining with her tomorrow to go over business affairs. Now tell me, how was your holiday?"

"We missed you," the Baroness sniffed elaborately. "One would think you could have driven out to see us at least once."

Tyler winked at his father. "Mother, I toiled in my offices from sunup to sundown and came home to fall exhausted into bed only to start over again the next day. The Córdez affairs have taken so much of my time I've done little else. And, Father, there is something I'd like to discuss with you after dinner."

"Does it concern the Señorita Córdez?"

"Yes, her affairs are in fine shape and there's an abundance of capital which must be invested. That is what I'd like to discuss."

"Tyler, did the Señorita approve of the house and the furnishings?" the Baroness asked inquisitively.

"She was effusive in her praise, Mother. She asked me to tell you she would call as soon as possible to thank you herself. She's quite a remarkable woman."

"In what way," Baroness Helen asked.

"Well, for one thing, she's beautiful. She is every inch a lady and, as you already know, extremely wealthy. She is intelligent, forthright and I think, Mother, you will grow fond of Sirena."

"Oh, Sirena, is it?" the Baron chuckled.

Tyler correctly interpreted his mother's look and immediately reassured her. "Mother, have no fear. I have no plans of marriage for the present or in the near future. In fact, I'll go one step further and assure you that I'll never marry."

"That is a rash statement, Tyler," his father said, frowning.

"You can't mean it," the Baroness gasped.

Tyler laughed, a low, husky sound which pleased his mother. "I have no desire to marry. And why should I? I have quite a choice among London's most desirable young women. It would be a pleasure to give each and every lady the benefit of knowing me and appreciating my charms. Rest easy, Mother," Tyler amended, "I'll be careful not to tarnish my reputation beyond redemption."

"If what you said is true, Tyler, then I have no hope of grandchildren to daddle on my knee and fuss over."

"Somehow you do not strike me as the grandmotherly type. However, I can always change my mind."

The Baroness sent her son a slanted look and told him not to be too hasty in his decisions. "Perhaps one day the right girl will come along and you'll know what to do."

Tyler laughed and linked his arm through her's as he led the way into the dining room, winking again at the Baron.

At that moment the Baron would have given up his entire fortune to be Tyler's age again, with London's society at his feet.

After dinner, Tyler followed his father into the leather-furnished library and settled himself with a glass of port. His eyes scanned the massive shelves as he slouched into the deepness of the chair. The Baron held out a fragrant cigar and, after both men lit up, Tyler spoke. "Father, what do you think of my investing some of Sirena's capital in Ireland? I'm told there is a great demand for linens and laces. I was thinking of taking a trip there to investigate the business. Perhaps Sirena would like to go and observe first hand what her money would be vested in. I plan to broach the matter with her tomorrow. If my calculations are correct, she could double her investment in a year's time. Providing we can import according to schedule."

"It sounds like a wise selection to me. I've looked into it myself, as a matter of fact. Perhaps you could make a few investments for me while you are there. At any rate, you seem to have worked it out, although possibly the woman may not want to make the voyage to Ireland."

"It's only a matter of a week's sailing, winds prevailing. What concerns me is her husband, pardon, ex-husband. The animosity between those two is so thick you could slice it with a knife. My guts tell me he's not a man to be pushed or coerced and that's exactly what this arrangement he made with Señor Arroya is doing."

"And the other investments? How are they faring?" the Baron asked, blowing a fragrant, blue-gray cloud of smoke into the center of the room.

"Much better than I expected. However, there is a problem. Her affairs take every moment of my time. I'll have to find an associate. I've already asked about for referrals. All I can do for the time being is wait and see."

"You still haven't told me your opinion of this Spanish señorita," Charles noted shrewdly.

"She's a woman held in tight control, but her emotions are not far under the surface. I sensed this almost at once. Sirena is a most gracious lady, and I'm certain I'll enjoy getting to know her better. I believe she is still in love with her former husband, but I'm just as certain she would deny it vehemently."

"Your mother told me that Lady Constance informed her that Camilla Langdon is on the verge of betrothal with van der Rhys. Have you heard this, Tyler?"

Tyler's dark eyes held no answer for his father. "Yes," he said quietly. "I knew they were seeing a great deal of one another. Don't concern yourself, Father. To Camilla, wealth is all important, and van der Rhys is far from being impoverished."

"You've had dealings with the man. If his former wife is still enamored of him as you suspect, what are his feelings for her?"

"I've no idea, actually. If he does become betrothed to Camilla, I can only assume that he does not share Sirena's feelings. I really don't know why they divorced. Sirena is one of the most beautiful women I've ever seen. Whatever the reason, it must have been quite serious, van der Rhys is a bitter man."

"And, you, Tyler, what's to become of you? You're a constant cause for your mother's concern. When are you going to settle down and raise a family. You've a brilliant mind, don't waste it. Curtail this wild, reckless life you seem determined to live and give the ladies in London a rest. I'll wager there are few you haven't bedded. And, mark my words, someday one of their husbands will thirst for your blood."

Tyler chucked. "Father, I've slept with my share. When I take a bride, I certainly hope she isn't a virgin. I find them tiresome. There's nothing I like less than dealing with false modesty and the chore of teaching a foolish, giddy young girl the ways of the bedroom is too time-consuming. By the time she's learned her lessons, you've gotten bored with her and she is free to give some other man the benefits of her education. Don't you agree?"

Baron Charles tried to look urbane and sophisticated. It was difficult when he had only bedded one woman in his entire lifetime. And at times the Baroness left much to be desired. All the stories of his wild and willful youth were simply that, stories. "Yes, yes, quite right, son, virgins are tiresome indeed."

"And if one of my wild oats should suddenly take sprout, then I'll deliberate the consequences. For now, I'm content with things as they are."

Baron Sinclair looked at his son and thought he saw a sadness in the depths of his brown eyes. Yes, it was definitely there. Charles sighed inaudibly. So, it still pained Tyler to think of what might have been with Camilla.

Sirena had dressed and was ready for Tyler Payne Sinclair's arrival for dinner. The topaz gown she wore complemented her ivory skin and deepened the color of her eyes. She had arranged her hair in a thick coil at each side of her head and a pearl shell comb took on a special lustre against the gleaming black locks. She knew she looked attractive and knew that Tyler would appreciate her toilette this evening. A man is a man, she thought smugly. A pretty face, a show of flesh and they fall at a woman's feet.

She smiled as she recalled her interview with the noted dressmaker, Mrs. Wittcomb, earlier that day. The small birdlike woman had arrived at Sirena's invitation and proceeded to measure lengths of pattern muslin. Mrs. Wittcomb, her mouth full of pins, had stood back to survey a hem and thought she had never seen a better model for her expertise with the needle. The Spanish woman was slim and lithe yet well fleshed in important areas. The smooth ivory tones of her skin could complement almost every color of the spectrum and her dark hair was a relief against her cool, incredibly green, dark-fringed eyes.

"I'll take this and this and this," Sirena said quietly. "And you mentioned a particular bolt of fabric. May I see it now?"

Mrs. Wittcomb reverently unwrapped a length of cloth from its protective layer of rice paper and held up a shimmering length of serpentine green silk that seemed to light up the room. Sirena drew in her breath and handled a corner of the fabric. "Perfect, Mrs. Wittcomb. Now, this is the way I would like you to fashion the gown."

The tiny woman's mouth dropped open as she listened. "Can you do it?" Sirena asked, a smile tugging at the corners of her mouth.

The seamstress nodded, her eyes perplexed. "Madame, I feel I should tell you that such fashions have not been worn in London."

Sirena shrugged. "That is no concern of mine. Stitch this gown first, exactly as I described it to you. How soon do you think I can have it?"

"A fortnight?" Mrs. Wittcomb answered hesitantly. This would be an important account for her and she was grateful to have been chosen on the suggestion of Mrs. Wilks, Sirena's cook. Once the merchants and vendors learned there was a rich woman new to England, the Spanish lady would be besieged and she, Mrs. Wittcomb, would have little chance for her trade. "Madame, you're certain . . ."

Sirena's bottle-green eyes flashed but her voice was quiet and controlled. "Very sure."

Mrs. Wittcomb lowered her head and pursed her mouth. Such a lovely woman, yet with this particular gown she would be an overnight scandal. Well, she was paid to sew and not to speculate on the morals or choices of wealthy ladies.

Sirena smiled again as she remembered how Mrs. Wittcomb had bustled out of the house, burdened with her bolts of fabric and a scandalized expression pinching her features.

A calculating gleam shone in Sirena's eyes. The gown would be a sensation and she could almost predict Tyler's reaction to it. There was no denying he was an attractive man. If she were careful and shrewd, she could pit him against Regan and see if jealousy was the answer. It was a shame to use Tyler this way, yet desperation called for desperate measures. The difference between men and women was not so great. If she could feel jealousy because Regan planned to marry again, Regan could easily find himself eaten with jealousy over her relationship with Tyler. Sirena frowned, her delicate, arched brows puckering low over her blazing eyes. If Regan ever should marry, she knew she would be like a wild jungle animal. But Regan wasn't married . . . yet.

Shaking off thoughts of impending doom, Sirena

straightened her shoulders and glanced about the opulently handsome drawing room. Everything boasted the sheen of newness and was obviously designed for comfort. The crimson settee and the matching armchairs were placed intimately near the open hearth. Rich, vibrant oil paintings adorned the paneled walls, adding warmth and color. Heavy draperies shot through with thread the color of recently minted gold hung at the windows and long paned doors leading to the side yards. In the center of the Italian marble mantle a large, trailing fern rested in a silver bowl. The fronds were tapered, long and graceful, and glistened like uncut emeralds. It was a pleasing room and Sirena was comfortable in it. The subdued lamplight glanced off a nearby cherrywood table bearing a silver tray with a decanter of ruby red wine. For a brief moment she felt guilty using Tyler the way she intended. Pushing away the uneasiness, she decided she would make it all up to him when she and Regan were together again.

While she waited for Tyler, she allowed thoughts of Caleb to creep into her mind. She wondered how he was faring and realized again how she had hurt him with her rejection. Even when he said he understood her feelings, she wondered if he really did or if he had said it to allow her to save face.

Sirena was jarred from her thoughts as Frau Holtz ushered Tyler Sinclair into the room. The old housekeeper watched as the gallant knight brought Sirena's hand to his lips, then gazed deeply into her eyes. Harrumph! she snorted as she backed from the room, closing the carved mahogany doors with a loud bang.

Tyler looked at Sirena and smiled approvingly. "Allow me to say how lovely you are this evening."

"You may," Sirena laughed and the formality was shattered. "Please, sit down and let us get this bothersome business done with so we can enjoy dinner."

After an hour, Tyler gathered his papers together and placed them carefully in a smart leather case. "As you can see, you're a very wealthy woman, Sirena. Are you satisfied with the way I'm handling your investments?"

"Quite satisfied. You mentioned prospects in Ireland. Are you certain my investment will be recouped by the end of the year?"

"Oh yes, but I would like you to make an inspection and see for yourself. My thoughts were to leave as soon as possible, but I looked into the sailing schedules and the only ships leaving port for Waterford are those of Regan van der Rhys. We'll have to wait till the first of the month to see what opens."

"I'll have to think about it, Tyler. I'll let you know," Sirena said quietly, her mind racing. Why did she have to book passage on another ship when her own sat in the harbor? If she were careful, she might be able to manage something. She smiled slightly. Everything was working out just as she planned, in fact better. "There is one other matter I'd like to discuss with you before dinner is announced. I went to see my . . . I saw Regan yesterday and I'm sorry to say we didn't part on the happiest of terms. I told him I was taking advantage of my prerogative for shares in his company in lieu of cash exchange."

Tyler laughed, "Very clever, Sirena. Would you care to join me in my practice? I can use a helping hand."

"No, I have no head for business," Sirena smiled. "Tell me about your practice, Tyler. Do you enjoy it?"

"Yes and no. If I were as rich as you are, I think I'd be a scoundrel living off my income. My father, the Baron, turned over the business to me several years ago. It's a sort of tradition in my family. It is thought to be the cure for keeping first-born sons from becoming outright reprobates," he laughed.

Sirena liked the sound of his low, lusty laughter. "In time you'll require a son of your own to take over the tradition. Tell me, is there a lady somewhere in your affections?"

Tyler sobered at her words. "One day perhaps. For now, I enjoy my position as a bachelor. I must admit," he grinned, "at times it gets to be a bit of a bore dodging matrimony-minded females. As I said, I'd like to be a scoundrel, a dashing rake without conscience, who loves a woman and leaves her without a backward glance."

"But, Tyler, Tio Esteban warned me that you already enjoy that reputation," she giggled.

"Ah! balm for my soul! What I actually meant was I'd like to be a highwayman, something wicked and unlawful, a rogue. I think everyone dreams of an exciting life. When I was a boy I wanted to be a notorious pirate with a patch over my eye. Unfortunately, I learned that to legitimately wear one I should have to lose my eye. As I grew older, I had a desire to rob from rich and beautiful women while I kissed them scandalously, leaving them breathless with only warm affection in their hearts for me. However, when I approached maturity I had no desire to hang by my neck, so I relegated my dreams to oblivion and began to practice law."

"I can understand how dry it must be after your exciting dreams," Sirena cooed. "Ah, there is Frau Holtz; come, dinner is ready."

Sirena enjoyed the elaborate dinner of roast duckling as Tyler regaled her with tales of his many near trips to the altar. Frau Holtz was beside herself as Sirena laughed and complimented the dashing Tyler Sinclair. She became alarmed as Sirena's eyes took on a sparkle and her wit became pronounced.

When the dinner was over, the housekeeper was in a state bordering shock when Sirena offered to play her guitar for the Englishman. Quietly, she withdrew from sight and listened as Sirena softly strummed the strings, testing the chords. Her audience of one sat in rapt attention as she began the opening strains. Frau Holtz knew immediately that Sirena was going to play a flamenco. "Poor man," the Frau muttered to herself, shaking her head, "he hasn't a chance."

When Tyler first heard the tone, he thought it was the guitar. The sound blossomed and poured forth, spilling into the hushed corners of the room with perfection and clarity of pitch. Sirena's voice.

She sang the flamenco with inspiration and her audience of one was caught up in the music's passion. It was Frau Holtz, standing outside the door, who understood the sweetness and the poignancy behind the notes. Sirena might be looking at the Englishman, but she was singing for the Mynheer, wherever he was.

The song over, Sirena lifted her eyes and felt a sharp jab of disappointment that it was not Regan who was sitting across from her. It should have been Regan with his sheaf of white-blond hair falling low on his forehead, his agate eyes loving her, devouring her. Instead, she looked into dark eyes filled with admiration and interest. Sirena was flattered; Tyler was a most attractive man. Handsome actually, and if she weren't still in love with Regan, she would have found it very easy to be attracted to him.

She smiled coyly, refusing to play again. Tyler's praise was genuine and enthusiastic. Sirena rose, indicating the evening was over. Graciously, she extended her hand and, as always, Tyler touched his lips to it.

"Thank you for a most enjoyable evening, Sirena. We must repeat it someday soon. I'll be in touch with you in a day or so. Good night, Sirena." His lips touched her hand again and lingered there a moment longer than necessary. Sirena felt the current of emotions run between them. How easy it would be to fall into his arms, offer her mouth for his kisses. She was lonely, so lonely, and she knew somehow that Tyler was also looking for a relief from the same thing. There was a bit too much bravado in his voice when he said he had no plans for marriage. Sirena suspected that Tyler was in love with someone who did not return his affections. How easy it would be to console one another, to reach out for the warmth of another, the tenderness, the affection. But where would it lead to? She had nothing to give him. Her heart was Regan's. And if her instincts were correct, Tyler was floundering in the same lonely sea.

Their eyes met. "Good night, Tyler. Sleep well," she said softly.

Dockside, at the Owl and Boar, Caleb was talking to an aristocratic gentleman by the name of Lord Farrington. The interminable fog was still hampering trade, so Caleb had taken to whiling away the hours at the inn, enjoying the brew and the company of a particular serving wench the boisterous patrons called Sally.

Over the period of days since Caleb had met at the inn with Regan, Lord Farrington had conscientiously engineered a continuing acquaintance with him. The stylish, older gentlemen had watched with interest whenever Caleb carelessly tossed a generous handful of uncounted coins on the stained table to pay for his meal and ale. To the nobleman's eye it seemed that several fierce-looking thugs, who were regular patrons of the Owl and Boar, also had more than a cursory interest in Caleb's overflowing pockets.

"Have you been waiting long, love?" asked Sally as she ambled seductively over to Caleb, swinging her ample hips and greeting him with a slow smile.

Caleb, who was well into his cups, reached for her and swung her down onto his lap, burying his face in the soft skin of her throat.

"Tush now, sir!" Sally pretended indignance. "How you men do handle a poor girl. By a Jew's eye, I'd swear it'd been years since you had a tumble instead of last night. Here, here," Sally laughed, disentangling herself from Caleb's arms, "let me show you the new ribbons I bought at the Change with the coin ya gave me." Sally brought her fingers to her bosom and leaned over to show Caleb the bright, pink ribbon she had woven into the laces of her soiled and dingy chemise. "Now, don't that do somethin' to ya, love?" she asked, noting the way Caleb's attention was focused upon the swell of her breasts. He was a handsome devil, and any wench on the wharf would be glad to have him put his shoes under her bed.

"It does something, all right," Caleb groaned, holding Sally tighter and reaching inside her bodice, making her squeal.

Lord Farrington's attention was again brought to the two thugs who now were lingering near the stairs. Sally seemed to notice them too and a silent look passed between them. Turning to Lord Farrington, Sally giggled, "Surely you won't be missing myself and the young lord here for a few minutes, will you? Heave to, sailor," she said to Caleb, rising from his lap and pulling him to his feet. "You and me go upstairs and Sally will take you to the moon. Heave to, now."

Dizzy-headed, Caleb stood and lurched after Sally

as she tossed her red curls and called out greetings to a familiar face.

Caleb was in a stupor, there was no doubt about it. How could any man who drank a bottle of rum expect to do a woman justice when the prospect of sleep was more attractive? Farrington realized he should have warned young Caleb about flashing around the coins he carried and the small pouch of gemstones which hung from his belt. It was clear that Caleb had hardly any knowledge of the evils of the city. It was not unheard of for a doxie and thieves to conspire together and to roll a man while he was engaged in romantic pursuit. And now, for the past hour, Lord Farrington had noticed the two ruffians eyeing Caleb and watching his every move. And when Sally had given her silent signal before leading Caleb up the stairs to the bedroom, Farrington knew without doubt what the end results would be.

Aubrey Farrington drained his tankard, pushed his chair back from the rough table and stood up as he reached for his walking stick. I think I'd best get a bead on this situation, he thought to himself. Fluffing the frou-frou of ruffles at his neck and brushing an imaginary speck from his impeccable shirtfront, he drew himself up to his full height and made as if to leave the establishment. When he was about to step out into the thick fog, he turned to see the move he was anticipating. The burly thugs were making their way to the second floor.

It was no gallant gesture of the samaritan which propelled Lord Farrington back across the crowded room to the bottom of the stairway. It was more a protection of his own interests. Caleb had been very generous with his company and his pocket, buying food and drinks for him. The stylish aristocrat was loath to see this come to an end, as it certainly would if the young man put up a fight and the two crooks spilled his brains out.

His walking stick securely in hand, he made his way to the upper level. Carefully, in the dimness of the corridor, he extracted the concealed rapier from its sheath. He paused in a small alcove and smiled to himself as he listened to the lusty sounds coming through the door. Ah, to be young again and know what I know now, he sighed.

Suddenly, he was aware of soft footfalls approaching. The same moment he heard the door being thrust open he followed the thugs into the room and shouted to Caleb, "Move, boy, they want your money and your life!"

Caleb's brain was fogged with rum and his eyes had difficulty focusing on the quick events. Sally's mouth was open in horror and she visibly shrank beneath Caleb's weight.

"Move, boy!" Farrington shouted again. "Do you mean to tell me a roll with a bawd is more important than your life?" he demanded, as he flourished his rapier in a wicked slash at one of the scoundrels.

"I'll be damned, who is he?" shouted the other thug as he attempted to pull Caleb from atop Sally, meanwhile brandishing a cudgel. "You said you'd take care of things," he yelled accusingly at the horrified serving wench.

"Out! Out!" Aubrey Farrington yelled. "Or I'll have the watch on you." With a last flourish of his weapon he drove the defenseless men through the door and down the stairs. A few minutes later Sally followed them, hastily pulling on her chemise and dragging her stained skirts behind her. The throng of patrons in the taproom howled their approval as the thugs grabbed hold of Sally and tore from the inn, swearing oaths at her and each other.

Lord Farrington climbed the stairs again and entered the room where Caleb lay stretched on the bed, deep snores of oblivion coming from his mouth. Looking at Caleb's lean, muscular body, Aubrey Farrington again longed for his youth. There was something aside from Caleb's generosity which appealed to him. He was about to toss a dirty quilt over the man's prone form when Aubrey thought differently. With a mighty shove, he rolled Caleb's inebriated body over the side of the bed onto the floor. Then he gently took the quilt and covered Caleb's lower regions. Carefully removing his own doublet and waistcoat, Lord Farrington smoothed the covers on the bedstead and lay down, placing his walking stick, which held the concealed rapier, at his side.

As the impoverished lord had nowhere else to sleep this night, due to an unkind landlady who had given him boot for nonpayment of his rent, this was as good a place as any. When the young man woke, he would tell him how he had single-handedly saved his life and fortune. A born gambler, Lord Farrington was certain of the outcome. He made himself comfortable and dozed as he waited for Caleb to waken.

It was dawn when Caleb muttered in his sleep and rolled over. At his first sound, Lord Farrington was awake and smiled expectantly to himself.

Caleb sat up and scratched his head. His tongue licked at his dry lips. He seemed surprised to see he had spent the night on the hard floor. Before Caleb even noticed his presence, Lord Farrington spoke. "Dear boy, how good to see you are awake and well."

Caleb's eyes focused questioningly on the gentleman. Rubbing his eyes and stretching to relieve the aches from a long night on the hard boards, Caleb stood up reaching for his clothes. "What, may I ask, are you doing here? And how did I leave my bed for the floor?"

Lord Farrington informed Caleb of the night's happenings, eyeing him suspiciously. Only the dried spots of blood from the wound the aristocrat's rapier had dealt to the thief's arm convinced him that the lord spoke the truth.

"And so you see," Aubrey Farrington explained, "when I came back in here to stay guard over you through the night, I found you there on the floor. I'm afraid, dear boy, your weight was too much for me, so I made you as comfortable as possible; and, since the bed was not being used, I did not think you'd mind if I availed myself of it."

Caleb touched the pouch of gems at his belt and dug in his pocket till his fingers came in contact with his coins. All seemed to be as it should.

"I hope she was worth it," Lord Farrington said smugly.

"She was," Caleb grinned, vaguely remembering an expanse of smooth, white skin and full, ripe breasts.

"Why don't we order a bit of breakfast and talk. I have several things I'd like to discuss with you."

"Anything to get this taste out of my mouth," Caleb muttered, as he glanced down to his jerkin and the stains that marred its front.

"Only a ruffian drinks rum from the bottle," Aubrey said distastefully. "That is one of the things I must discuss with you. However, I find I am temporarily indisposed. I left my purse at home and I must impose upon you for my meal."

Caleb nodded; he would agree to anything just to get out of this stinking room and get a drink of something in his mouth.

Settled downstairs in the taproom of the Owl and Boar, Caleb waited for the lord to broach whatever was on his mind. The moment Aubrey finished with his breakfast, he daintily pulled his immaculate handkerchief from his sleeve and dabbed at his mouth.

"Young man, I see you are in need of a small amount of guidance. I recall last eve you told me of a ship, a frigate, I believe you referred to her. As I told you then, but you have no doubt forgotten, I have been thinking of how you could put this ship of yours to good use and make a fortune."

Caleb turned to signal the barkeep to pay his bill, obviously not interested in any schemes this elderly, but dubious, gentleman had to offer.

"If you are amenable, that is," Lord Farrington pressed. "Hear me out. Not long ago I heard of a ship that was berthed in Marseilles, France." Aubrey Farrington lowered his voice to a bare whisper. "It was a gambling ship. The French call it a 'folly' and it is frequented by the richest and most fashionable of society. The ship's owner made a killing," the lord said winking at Caleb. "Now my proposition is this. At the moment I find myself with very little capital. I may as well tell you the truth. My landlady, and a dastardly woman she is, had literally tossed me out on the street with nothing save what is on my back and my reliable walking stick. I have lived my life by my wits and the generosity of . . . er, friends. If we could manage, somehow to get enough together to buy gaming equipment and refurbish your ship with trimmings to give it atmosphere, we too could prosper. I have my title, which is by the way, legitimate. And I do know anyone who is anybody. I can offer you my expertise and inherent good taste which would insure the success of the endeavor. Well, what do you think?"

When Caleb didn't answer immediately, Aubrey threw in another morsel. "It's known that women of breeding frequent these 'follies.' Not only do they spend their money freely, they give of their favors just as generously. For a healthy young man like yourself, what better business to go into? That clap-ridden wench you bedded last night is good enough for a common man, but not for two such as ourselves."

Caleb pretended thought. It might be a good idea and he would be available to keep his eye on his father and Sirena, who was bound to show up in England sooner or later. No matter what, Sirena couldn't stay away from Regan when she learned where he was.

"And how would the profits be divided?" Caleb asked craftily.

Lord Farrington took the plunge and hoped for the best. "Half, what else?"

"The ship is mine. The money is mine. I will be giving you a home. No, fifty percent is not satisfactory."

Aubrey Farrington gulped again. He had underestimated this cocky, young provincial. Seeming to give in with good grace, he said, "Very well. A quarter to me, seventy-five to you."

Caleb shook his head. "You will be receiving the food I provide and will no doubt play against the house. You are a gambler, are you not? I think ten percent as your share is more than fair. Take it or leave it."

Lord Farrington's face split into a wide grin. "I'll take it!" The young rascal should only know I would have settled gladly for two, Farrington thought. They shook hands and the bargain was sealed. Caleb van der Rhys and Lord Aubrey Farrington would open a gambling ship to entertain the bored rich of London.

Chapter Twelve

On the second floor of a modest-looking gray stoned dwelling on Lime Street, Regan van der Rhys prepared himself for the evening ahead. His movements were fluid and unhurried. Not so his thoughts. They raced like a wild bird caught in a snare. Just that afternoon Sir Stephan Langdon had visited his office and told him the reason for Baroness Sinclair's reception that evening was to introduce a certain Spanish lady, newly arrived from her homeland.

Regan rubbed his chest with a strong, bronzed hand. Why was it every time he thought of Sirena, he experienced this damnable pain in his chest, like a giant vise squeezing the breath from him? He shook his proud, leonine head and buttoned his fine lawn shirt. He glanced at his image in the long looking glass and tried to calm his angry eyes. Brushing at his sheaf of blond hair impatiently, he bent to pull on his boots.

Regan van der Rhys stomped about his room, his agate-blue eyes cold and hard. His stubbornness was evident in his lean, square jaw and the way he kept smashing one capable hand into the palm of the other. Something was happening to him, something he didn't like, something over which he had no control.

Until the day Sirena had stepped into his office unannounced, weeks ago, he had been trying to put the pieces of his life together, to sort them in a semblance of order. Now his life was upside down again.

Shortly after his meeting with Sirena, he asked Camilla Langdon for her hand in marriage and was accepted. Now that he was betrothed to Camilla she was the woman who should occupy his thoughts, not Sirena.

Regan forced his thoughts to conjure up a vision of

the pink-and-white Camilla. He had to blink several times before he could focus and, when he did, it was emerald eyes and dark hair that looked back at him. It was ivory skin with a tawny glow and a wide, sensuous mouth with pearl-white teeth that smiled at him. His arms began to ache as did his nether regions. "Bitch!" he shouted hoarsely to the empty room. Even here in England she sought him out, threatened him, lied to him and taunted him. Was he never to know peace? Would she haunt him for the rest of his days? And merciful God, what would she do to the poor, unsuspecting Camilla, who had led such an unspoiled, sheltered life?

Sirena would make short shrift of her with a few well-chosen words. The petal-cheeked Camilla would be little more than pulp if Sirena took matters into her own hands. Camilla certainly was no match for the wily, cutlass-wielding Sirena. Come to think of it, he wasn't so positive he was a match for her either.

Had she truly come to see him, as she said, or did she have an ulterior motive? "Now she wants shares in my business," he blustered to his reflection in the mirror. "She'll watch me work seven days a week so she can have her share, and she'll fritter it away on costly gowns and fine furnishings." Regan felt his shoulders bunch at the thought. There had to be an answer.

Bitterly, he accepted the fact that Sirena had *all* the solutions! With the way his luck ran when it came to dealing with Sirena, she would own the damn company in a year's time. He would break his back carving out his business and she would sit back and live lavishly on his efforts. "My ass!" he thundered to the room.

A more pleasant thought crossed his mind. Sirena wouldn't be able to touch Camilla's fortune. He would have to be very careful to see that a strict accounting was kept and that not a cent of Langdon money was invested in the import-export business he was building. If he made an error, Sirena would get her hands on that, too! Time was the answer. He needed it to work out some plan to outwit Sirena. Hadn't he already taken the first step in asking Camilla to marry him?

Regan surveyed himself again and wondered at the sour expression on his face as he thought of being wed to the delicate Camilla.

Regan lifted the heavy knocker on the Langdon front door on fashionable Drury Lane and waited for the family retainer to admit him. He was impatient this night and in no mood for cooling his heels waiting for Camilla. He hoped that for once she was ready to leave.

Just as he was about to light a cheroot, he looked up and saw her standing at the top of the wide, circular staircase. She was becomingly dressed in a demure silk gown of daffodil yellow which enhanced her petite, dainty figure. Fragile was the word that came to Regan's mind when he thought of her—defenseless and in need of a protector. And he was that champion.

Before descending, Camilla hesitated a moment for Regan to gain the full effect of her appearance. Her pale blond hair had been laboriously curled into an elaborate coiffure and tumbled about her head in a studied disarray to frame her piquant features and highlight her creamy white skin and soft violet eyes. Her small, pink mouth trembled slightly at the sight of the tall man waiting for her at the bottom of the stairs.

Camilla was picture-pretty with small pearl drops nestled on the lobes of her tiny, shell-like ears and a wide ribbon sash tied about her incredibly tiny waist. She held out her hand for Regan as she neared the last step and looked up at him with a smile that brought out the two adorable dimples in her velvety cheeks.

"You're so handsome, Regan. Every woman at the Sinclairs' will want to scratch my eyes from their sockets."

Regan gulped as an image of Sirena, looming over the delicate flower who was Camilla, swam before his eyes.

"I'm really looking forward to this evening's entertainment. My father tells me that a visitor to our fair

London is being introduced this evening. A Spanish lady, I heard. I understand she is quite beautiful and, therefore, I'll not allow you out of my sight," she cooed playfully.

"You have no fear of me leaving your side, sweetheart," Regan muttered beneath his breath. He would never allow Camilla and the wild, untamed Sirena to get within inches of each other. Not while he was alive, at any rate. His hand shook slightly. Sirena could always remedy that situation if she took it into that unreasonable Latin head of hers.

The hired carriage came to a creeping stop and Regan helped his fiancée disembark to the cobbled drive. Music spilled into the grounds from the Sinclair mansion and every window was aglow with light.

Inside, the vast ballroom was decorated with fresh-cut flowers and massive tubs of ferns. Small, gilt, velvet-seated chairs lined the perimeters of the room. Everywhere servants carried trays bearing cups of punch and sweetmeats of marzipan. A toast was being made as Regan and Camilla entered the room. The guests tipped fragile, long-stemmed glasses to their lips in celebration of the night's festivities.

As the musicians resumed their playing, Regan and Camilla were announced. The couple worked their way down the receiving line to the Baron and Baroness. A portly gentleman behind Regan was heard to mention that everyone seemed present save the guest of honor. He also mentioned it was Sir Sinclair who was the lady's escort for the evening.

Regan's gut churned at the softly spoken words. Where was she? If his guess was correct, she was deliberately going to make a grand entrance on the arm of the dashing rake, Tyler Sinclair.

Tyler apologized for his tardiness for the tenth time. "It was this blasted shirt, you see," he explained again. "Two of the servants are ill and my personal valet among them. So, instead of obeying my instructions concerning my evening clothes, my mother interfered . . . Oh damn! You see," he joked, "if I were a highwayman, this would never have happened. Mother will be having an attack of the vapors about now, seeing how late we are."

Sirena smiled. "So long as it is you who are the reason behind her vapors and not myself, you can save your apologies, Tyler. I really don't mind since it took longer than I expected to complete my toilette."

"And the results are quite fetching, to say the least, Sirena." Tyler glanced at her approvingly. "Green does incredible things to your eyes. You'll dazzle every man at the ball. I intend to keep a sharp eye on you, so be warned. I want to keep you all to myself."

"I won't mind, Tyler, if it's a plan you intend to keep," Sirena laughed softly, edging closer to him on the luxurious seat in the Sinclair coach.

"Sirena," Tyler said seriously, "Regan van der Rhys and Camilla Langdon will be there. I feel it only fair to warn you that you're bound to meet them in the course of the evening. I'm certain you'll be able to carry it off and no one need know you were formerly married to him. Mother and Father both think it's in your best interests not to make mention of the fact. Divorce is still a social blight in England, regardless of the Crown's policies. I'm also certain that Regan has kept the fact under wraps. I doubt if even Camilla knows, otherwise it would be a matter for gossip. It's not a piece of information she could keep to herself."

"Tyler, do you mean to say Camilla is a gossipmonger?"

"When it doesn't affect her own reputation, yes," he answered, the touch of bitterness in his voice raising Sirena's curiosity.

"Surely the girl's mother would have taught her better."

"She lost her mother when she was very young and her father, Sir Stephan Langdon, has never remarried. It's true, Camilla could have done with a firm female hand in her upbringing." Sirena thought Tyler was about to say more on the subject of Camilla, when he glanced out the window and saw they had arrived. "Here we are. The Baroness will be in a carefully controlled rage, if I know my mother. We'll both have to put our best foot forward."

As Sirena and Tyler moved through the spacious

hallway of the Sinclair home, Tyler led her directly over to the receiving line. All heads turned to see the elegant couple and Sirena noticed out of the corner of her eye that the women were whispering and the men were smiling with interest. Where was Regan? All she had to do was turn her head and look for the tallest of men with a thatch of gold hair. It was too late. Tyler was introducing her to the Baron and Baroness. Sirena was at her most gracious as she spoke softly, a lilt in her voice, her eyes demurely downcast. Baron Sinclair was obviously entranced and the Baroness liked her immediately.

"My dear Señorita," the Baroness said delightedly, "you are quite the most exquisite creature in the room this night. Tomorrow you'll be the talk of all London. Come, stand beside me and receive my guests, they're near dying to meet you."

A thousand greetings and polite exchanges later, the Baroness took Sirena upstairs to a tiring room where she could refresh herself before the dancing began. Baron Charles took his son by the arm and led him to the punch bowl where several elegant young ladies eyed Tyler seductively. Tyler accepted his drink and complimented the ladies with his attention in his own gallant way before joining his father at the far side of the room.

"The Dutchman must be blind," the Baron blustered. "She's lovely, simply lovely, eh Tyler?" he jostled his son's arm enthusiastically, nearly spilling his punch.

"Without a doubt," Tyler answered as he stretched his neck to see Sirena descending the stairs beside his mother. Why he felt this concern for her he could not imagine. With the formidable Baroness at her side, nothing could go amiss. "Father, look, Camilla is dragging van der Rhys to be introduced to Sirena."

"Not to worry, my boy, she has the situation well in hand. Even my faded eyes can see that she's every inch a lady and won't give herself away."

It was Regan who wore the wary look. When he met Sirena's amused emerald eyes, his chest constricted. He felt his muscles tense when he saw how graciously she inclined her head to acknowledge the introduction. His throat closed entirely when she purred softly, "From Batavia, Mynheer van der Rhys! Someday you must tell me of the nutmeg trees which grow there. Why," she trilled, "I've heard tales of women working their hands raw in the fields for their husbands. And then the ungrateful wretches leave them somewhere by the wayside when they are of no further use. Have you ever heard of anything more inhumane?" she asked of the pink-cheeked Camilla.

"Never! What a terrible thing to do. The men must be beasts!" Camilla said, properly horrified.

"Tell me, Mynheer, have you heard this tale?" Sirena asked. "I'd always heard the Dutch brought civilization to Java. Obviously, such is not the case. Don't you agree? Excuse me, I seem to have forgotten your name."

The Baroness hastened to refresh her guest's memory while Camilla looked properly aghast. "I couldn't agree with you more."

"And you, sir?" Sirena pressed of Regan, a sly smirk at the corner of her mouth.

Regan chose his words carefully, his eyes on the creamy shoulders and voluptuous bosom revealed by the cut of Sirena's gown. He felt light-headed and his palms were perspiring. "I believe it is said the tale you speak of involved only one woman and she was a notorious pirate in the Indies waters. A woman who was a skilled liar, a master of deceit, a murderer, and when she reformed her ways, she contented herself with her rosary." Regan cocked his head and stared intently at Sirena. "It was said this lady professed to love the man she planted the fields for; but, when he was forced to leave Java, she refused to go with him. So you see, Señorita Córdez, he did not cast her by the wayside, she preferred not to stay with him."

"How sad. Isn't that a sad tale, Baroness? But it seems to me the tale goes even further. Wasn't there something about the man stealing this woman's fortune and then offering to pension her off with her own money?"

The cords in Regan's neck threatened to burst. Before he could utter a reply, Sirena pressed her advantage. "Miss Langdon, have you ever heard of a more despicable act?"

"Never!" Camilla said forcefully.

"Nor I!" the Baroness interjected. "The rascal should be hanged by the neck!" She was happily enjoying every moment of this playacting.

"Exactly my thoughts on the matter," Sirena said softly. "The end of the story is this . . . lady sought out this . . . gentleman and . . . good heavens, I don't wish to spoil the gentleman's evening. I'm certain he has heard the tale so there is no point in repeating it again. Poor man, poor, poor man," Sirena said sadly, a wicked light in her eyes, as she followed the Baroness to her next guest.

"Darling, she is a striking woman, isn't she?" Camilla asked innocently.

Regan looked down into Camilla's beautiful, piquant face and said harshly, "Sweetheart, she's as striking as a viper!" His mood shattered, Regan felt his gaze trail Sirena every time she was within sight. Never once did she look his way, as far as he could tell.

All through the evening Regan stayed at Camilla's side. Ever on his guard for Sirena to steal a moment alone with his betrothed, Regan even refused a respite in the gardens for a much wanted cheroot. If he could help it, Sirena would not get the opportunity to regale Camilla with further tales of Java and perhaps even go so far as to reveal to his sweet and very young intended that she was once Regan's wife. Consequently, each time Sirena glanced his way, Regan was paying court to the demure flower who was to replace her.

Through the course of the evening, Sirena felt her spirits sink lower and lower. Regan appeared to absolutely dote on the girl. Sirena was reminded of how he used to dance attendance on her. He had been so loving, so tender, so attentive. When he had wanted to be, she reminded herself. Nevertheless, Regan wasn't a man who became preoccupied with a woman unless his interest in her was sincere. And tonight Regan's behavior was almost—her mind grappled for the word —vigilant! Down, down, her spirits sank and her heart was near to breaking. He loves her! He loves her! her heart cried. It's true, Regan loves Camilla!

Toward the end of the evening, Regan settled himself on one of the gilt chairs placed near a huge assortment of evergreens. Camilla had obviously retired to refresh herself. As he waited for Camilla's return, a voluptuous redhead passed him as she was led by her escort to the garden. Regan eyed the woman appreciatively as she swayed seductively and gave him a saucy smile which he returned.

Sirena, who was standing near the evergreens, watched Regan and knew in that split second that he did not love Camilla Langdon. If he had a thousand willing, beautiful women falling at his feet, Regan would have looked right through them as if they'd been carved from glass. When he loved a woman, Regan was the kind of man to whom no others existed. When they were married, after they discovered their love for one another, Regan had never had eyes for another woman. He had been completely faithful and devoted to her.

Sirena's heart lifted, her spirits soared. There was still hope, still that chance to win him back. To make him declare his love for her. To hear him say the divorce had been a mistake. He still wanted her, still loved her!

Suddenly, Regan stood and found Sirena directly in his line of vision. "Don't tell me you sought me out to finish your bitter little tale."

"No," Sirena laughed, her heart lighter than it had been in what seemed like centuries. "The tale is not yet finished. There is still a question as to how it will end." Her voice was quiet, holding Regan in the unexpected tenderness of her tone. The moment between them seemed an eternity, as though time stood still, and they were caught forever in this instant of infinity.

Breaking through the spell she seemed to weave about him, Regan demanded, "Then why have you sought me out?"

"I came to bid you goodnight and to tell you how lovely your child bride-to-be is." Sirena laughed lightly, knowing full well the message she read in his eyes.

Regan stood his ground when Sirena laughed. The sound seemed to settle around him like a mantle, enveloping him in emotions he had been struggling to overcome. He wanted to lash out. Those exciting cat-green eyes were laughing at him, mocking him, tormenting him. God, how he wanted her. Wanted her in his arms, his lips crushing hers.

Sirena smiled, joyously interpreting his thoughts. "Anything more than a formal handclasp would be tantamount to rape, Regan," she laughed. "You divorced me, remember?" she taunted. "Perhaps I'll marry again, myself. No, no, not Tyler. Perhaps someone more impressive, like that gentleman speaking with the Baroness." She pointed discreetly.

At Regan's shocked expression she laughed again. "Would my marriage to Lord Langdon upset you? Ah, Regan, darling, this decadent society we find ourselves in is too much for you." A devil danced in her eyes and her mouth broke into a grin as she continued. "If I were to marry Sir Langdon, who is by the way quite enamored of me; if his pursuit of me all evening is an indication, I would then be your stepmother-in-law. It's utterly fascinating," she laughed once more, the rich peals making Regan quake with rage.

"Bitch!" Regan hissed between clenched teeth, as Sirena left his side in search of Tyler Sinclair.

Inside Sirena was trembling. Had she pushed Regan too far? She teased him unmercifully. It was a dangerous game she was playing and she was fully aware of the consequences should she lose. Yet she was impelled to play on. She had to make Regan aware of her. Make him feel something toward her, and if anger and rage were the first steps to opening his eyes to her then she would have to take her chances and play the game out to the last turn.

She found herself beside Tyler, pleading weariness and asking to be taken home. If he noticed a strange light dancing in the depths of Sirena's eyes, he said nothing. But he looked at her questioningly, for only minutes before he had seen her talking with Regan and she had been animated. Now there was a flush on her ivory cheeks belying the exhaustion she claimed.

"You can't be leaving us so soon," Sir Langdon interrupted them as she bade her farewell to the Baron and Baroness. "The night is still young and you've only given me the pleasure of dancing with you once. Please, won't you stay a while longer?" Though his words were pleasant enough, there was a silent demand behind his request.

Out of the corner of her eye, Sirena noticed Regan leading Camilla out onto the dance floor for the quadrille. Suddenly, her mind made up, Sirena smiled brightly and took Sir Langdon by his arm. "Perhaps one last dance," she said sweetly, looking up into his handsomely craggy face.

Stephan Langdon was a tall man of fifty-five who appeared ten years younger. His slender physique bespoke the grace of an athlete and his manner was gracious and winning. A ladies' man, Sirena thought. She studied him as they danced. His sense of fashion was indisputable, and he wore his frothy white linen and severely cut silver-gray doublet with a flair. His legs were long and well shaped and he seemed not to care for the current fashion of adorning himself with an abundance of jewelry, save for the ruby stickpin in his cravat and a simple, masculine onyx ring on his finger.

His gray eyes were warm with golden lights as they appraised her, and his mouth was full; yet there was nothing weak or feminine about it. Rather, it was well defined and curvaceously shaped beneath a well-trimmed, steel-gray mustache which was just a shade darker than his full head of hair. His arms were strong and his hands square and able. As he talked, Sirena found herself enjoying his company. Sir Stephen Langdon was well versed in the social graces and immediately put her at ease.

"Will you allow me to show you our fair city of London?" he inquired, his arm fast about her waist, his voice warm and sincere. "Nothing would give me more pleasure than to take you to Whitehall and flaunt you before the court or take you for an excursion through Saint James' Park."

"I would like that very much, Sir Langdon," Sirena replied, smiling up into his face.

"Please, as a relative of the Baron and Baroness

shouldn't we find ourselves on more familiar terms? My given name is Stephan."

"Then Stephan it will be. And please do call me Sirena."

"Sirena—how fitting a name for you. Yet, do I detect hidden excitement behind those incredible eyes of yours?" he asked flirtatiously.

Sirena dropped her glance to the floor, not wanting to reveal just how excited she was by the plan she was forming in her mind.

"I did not mean to embarrass you, Sirena. Still, a man can find himself lost in those green depths. Certainly, I'm not the first to tell you this."

"No, not the first," Sirena said coyly, "yet a lady likes to hear it all the same." The music came to an end and Sirena was amused at the petulant look on Sir Langdon's face.

"I had hoped the music would have continued forever," he murmured in a husky voice that, in spite of herself, Sirena found thrilling. His hand on her arm as he led her back to Tyler was gentle, yet there was a certain possessiveness that remained even after he removed it.

"I trust you will allow me to call upon you," he said, lifting her hand and touching his lips to her fingers.

"Please do, Sir Langdon—Stephan," she amended. "I will look forward to seeing you. But you must forgive me this night for I am very tired and must beg Tyler to see me home. Baron, Baroness," she said to Tyler's parents, "there is no way to thank you for the wonderful welcome you've so graciously extended me. Especially, you, Baroness Sinclair, for all the help you've been in readying a home for me. You must allow me to reciprocate your hospitality as soon as possible."

Baroness Sinclair smiled warmly. She sincerely liked this lovely, young Spaniard and was delighted in Tyler's obvious interest in her. "Yes, my dear," she said in a motherly tone, "I can imagine how trying things have been for you tonight. However, there was little to be done about it, you know." By the Baroness' tone and expression Sirena knew she was apologizing for Regan and Camilla's presence. "However," the Baroness continued, "I am glad you count the Baron and me among your friends. London is a strange city." Her expression grew guarded and warning. "Please not to take everyone at face value. There are those who are acceptable in society's drawing rooms, dear, who are quite unacceptable under other circumstances."

Chapter Thirteen

As soon as Tyler departed, Sirena danced her way out the back door of her house to the stables. Pulling her cloak tightly about herself to ward off the chilly, damp night, she rapped on Jacobus' door to awaken the old man. Bleary-eyed, he answered the summons and immediately was put on his guard when he saw her.

"Aye, Capitana, what be the trouble?"

"Nothing, Jacobus. There's something I want you to do for me. Something I can't ask the coachman."

"Anything, Capitana, what is it?"

"I want you to hitch up the carriage and drive me somewhere. And bring a blanket with you. I can promise you it will be a long night."

"Aye, Capitana," Jacobus agreed unquestioningly. "Now, if you'll just allow me to pull on me breeches—"

"Just hurry," Sirena laughed, "and be as quiet about it as you can. I don't want all of London to know what I'm about."

"Aye, Capitana," Jacobus smiled, closing the door for privacy. The toothless seaman was amenable to anything the Capitana might suggest. Had it just been the moonlight or was the old sparkle there in her eyes again?

Through the city Jacobus drove the carriage, following the instructions his Capitana gave him. Due to a piece of luck and a bit of wrangling, she was able to discover from Tyler the address and location of Regan's house on Lime Street. Though the fog was still dense, it had lifted some in the cool night air and the flaring links which were burning at crossroads made it possible to read street signs. Following the now familiar Thames Street, they found Regan's office on St. Dunstan's Hill, turned left to Eastcheapside and then over six blocks to Lime Street.

Finding the address was more difficult, but Jacobus snatched a lantern from the side of the coach and searched the housefronts until he found it.

"It's just as you said, Capitana, but from the looks of it, there's no one home."

"Good! Then we're not too late. I'll leave breaking past the lock up to you, Jacobus. Do you think you can do it?"

"Oh, aye, Capitana. And when I'm finished there won't be a sign to tell it's been picked. But before I have a go at it, do you want to tell me whose home I'm breaking into?"

"Only if you'll keep the secret. It's Regan's. Now, get on with it, will you. We don't want the watch to catch us in the act and I want to be in there before Regan returns."

Without another word Jacobus reached under the driver's seat and removed several tools. "One of these should do nicely," he breathed, looking up and down Lime Street for a patrolling constable. Within a few moments he was finished. "It's done, Capitana. Just go in and close the door fast behind you. No one will be able to tell the lock's been tampered with. Do you want me to go with you?" he asked, fearful for Sirena's well-being.

"No, Jacobus, I told you it would be a long night. Just pull the coach up the street a ways and wait for me there. If things go according to plan, you won't see me till morning."

Even in the dark Sirena thought she saw the old man blush. "Well, it will be a long night at that. Don't think I'll close my eyes till you're safe in your own home," he promised. "Besides, there'll be no sleeping in the likes of this city. I'd wager if a man closes his eyes they'd steal the bed right out from under him, let alone something as valuable as a coach and pair."

Into the dark house Sirena crept, her hands trembling, her heart in her throat. Her eyes already accustomed to the dark from her long ride through the city, she easily found the stairs and quietly mounted them. It had not crossed her mind until she was actually inside that Regan might have a live-in housekeeper in his employ. What a sticky mess that would be if she found herself clobbered over the head to awaken with a member of the constabulary looking down at her. Chills danced up Sirena's spine and, breathlessly, she mounted the flight of steps.

Following the landing she came upon the master bedroom. She knew it to be Regan's room by the aroma of bay rum and the faint but pungent smell of his cheroots. Hastily, before she could change her mind, she straightened the bedcovers and removed her clothes. Naked and trembling with anticipation, she slid beneath the covers and waited for Regan.

The minutes passed at infuriating snail's pace. Time and again Sirena was tempted to rise and throw on her clothes and run into the street to her carriage. Then she would quiet her pounding heart and convince herself she was doing the right thing. I saw the hunger in his eyes for me, she reminded herself. He wants me just as I want him. If the mountain won't go to Mohammed, then Mohammed must go to the mountain. If he can feel my arms about him, know how much I love him, see to what lengths I'd go to have him love me again. He can't refuse me!

She sensed rather than heard Regan's arrival. He slammed the door shut behind him and climbed the stairs. Silently Sirena thanked Jacobus' expertise in picking locks. Obviously, Regan did not suspect anything was amiss. Suddenly, she was seized by panic. Suppose he had not returned home alone. Suppose he had brought Camilla with him. She didn't think for one moment that Regan would patiently await the blessing of his marriage vows before bedding the pretty girl. Regan's need for a woman in his bed was too great to wait for a legal decree.

Tensing beneath the blankets, Sirena squeezed her eyes shut, praying that Regan had not brought her. Almost without warning, Regan was in the room. Gratefully, she realized he was alone. Steeling herself for the moment of discovery, Sirena held her breath.

Not bothering to light the lamp, Regan shed his clothing. Sirena could hear the rustle of his garments as they fell to the floor or chair or whatever was handy. When his boots dropped, Sirena's heart raced. What would he do when he slid into bed and felt her next to him? God in Heaven, what had made her do this? Whatever it was, it was too late to change her mind. Regan was sitting on the edge of the high bed and she could feel the warmth of him and smell the faint aroma of his last cheroot.

As Regan's leg touched bare flesh, he let out a shout and jumped to his knees, imprisoning the interloper between his legs, his hands holding her shoulders firm against the bedding. "Who the blast are you?" he asked, shaking her shoulders in an iron grip.

"I always said you were a bull," Sirena said quietly, her voice as smooth as silk, belying the quaking she was experiencing.

"What are you doing here?" he blustered, recognizing her voice; his eyes penetrating the darkness for the sight of her.

"Foolish man," Sirena breathed, wrangling her arms free from his loosening grip to wrap them about his neck and surround him with her warmth.

Regan perceived her form against the white bedclothes. All of his pent-up yearnings, all of his desires rose to the surface as he slid beside her and encircled her in his embrace. Just the feel of her satiny skin, the nearness of her, caused him to close his eyes with remembered ecstasy. She belonged to him, and only to him. How could he have thought otherwise? A sound escaped him, a sound of pain as he drew her closer. As his lips sought hers, he heard her murmur, "I love you so. Never let me go. Love me, Regan, love me."

His lips crushed hers and her head whirled as her body came to life beneath his caresses. He was gentle and unhurried, his mouth moving against hers. Her senses reeled as she strained against him, trying to make them one.

With infinite tenderness, Regan loved her, putting a guarded check on the growing feverishness he was experiencing. Sirena once again became his pagan goddess. His mind formed a picture of her as he perceived through his fingertips. The ivory luster of her full breasts; her slim waist; her firm velvet haunches. He placed a long, sensual kiss on the silky triangle her nudity offered, and Sirena gave herself in panting surrender.

A hundred times his lips touched her body, satisfying himself in his passion for her beauty. Many details, details hardly noticed before, intoxicated him with their perfection; the flatness of her stomach, the distinct curve of her thighs, the dimples in her haunches, the elegant length of her legs. But he lingered in the warm shadows of her breasts while their coral tips beckoned him in a silent and provocative appeal.

Sirena's body voiced a will of its own. She writhed as though maddened with the desire to offer herself wholly to the searchings of his fingers and lips. And Regan, sensing this in her, resumed his advances, thirsting still more for her boundless beauty and to plant his kisses on the voluptuous moistness of her silky fleece which held such attraction for him.

Regan rejoiced that his passion was met equally and totally.

He felt Sirena brush his hair back from his forehead as she kissed him lightly on the lips. Straining toward him, her body rose and fell rhythmically in obedience to her desire to culminate their love.

Her hands firm against his shoulders, Sirena pressed Regan back against the bed. His breath came in short, rapid gasps; and, when she leaned over him, pressing the fullness of her breasts against his chest, she heard him emit a barely audible groan. Beneath her touch his skin glistened with a gleaming wetness, the fine furring on his chest teased the tips of her breasts and the long, hard length of him brought comfort to her yearning need for him. She tasted every detail of his physique, touched the rippling, muscular smoothness of him. She placed her lips at the hollow of his throat and licked the sweet saltiness she found there.

His hands were on her back, drawing her closer; her legs tangled with his as she held herself above him, her body touching the full length of him, rubbing against him lightly, bringing him to the apex of his erotic desires. She crushed his face against the ripe plentitude of her breasts and reveled in the teasing touches of his mouth. He came alive beneath her fingers and she felt his expectancy throb between them. The contact of her flesh on his was as smooth as silk and her whole being concentrated on giving to him, enjoying the emotions she evoked in him, bringing him pleasure and pleasuring herself.

His well-delineated chest became an altar on which she offered herself; his firm legs were the pillars on which her house of passion was built; his arms were the cushions which protected her from falling into a dark abyss where life had no meaning and loneliness was torture to her heart.

She felt his eyes upon her, delving the darkness, sensing her love. And Sirena loved. Joyously, without reservation. And when she mounted him, they cried in unison for the time they had been lost to one another. And when she felt the river of life warm her from within, she whispered hoarsely, "You love me, Regan, I knew I could make you love me!"

Sirena lay back against Regan, her head cradled on his shoulder, peace and contentment readable on her features. Regan was silent, his breathing steady and even.

When Sirena reached out a hand to touch his chest, she felt him stiffen beneath her fingers and was aware of his retreat from her. "Regan, darling, what's wrong? Aren't you happy we've found each other before it was too late?"

"It is too late, Sirena!" Regan growled, heaving himself from the bed and going in search of his robe.

Hurt and perplexed, Sirena sat up in bed, imploring him with her eyes to look at her, to tell her what she had done wrong. When no answer was forthcoming, she pressed. "Talk to me, Regan! Tell me what I've done to displease you!"

Regan was silent, the only sound she heard was the striking of the flint box and his struggles with the lamp. Abruptly, the room was flooded with the warm, yellow light and her gaze lifted to look into the cold, agate depths of Regan's eyes. His mouth was a thin, grim line and his jaw held stubborn determination.

"Tell me what I've done, Regan!" Sirena demanded, hurt beyond words, her pride forbidding her to share her pain.

"It's nothing you've done, Sirena," Regan said at last, his words clipped and controlled. "You're still the best piece to ever warm my bed."

"Then what is it?" she demanded, tired of parading her emotions before him.

"You're too damned confident of yourself, Sirena. Tell me why I found you here in my bed tonight? Tell me! Wasn't it a damned plot to prove I can still be made a fool over you? Didn't you come here and throw yourself at me so you could reduce me to the idiot you already think I am?"

"No, Regan, no! I came because I love you. Because I knew you still loved me!"

"The words you used, Sirena, at the height of our passion were, 'I *knew* I could make you love me!' I'm a challenge to you, you can't face the fact that I could divorce you as I did! So you came here tonight to tempt me with your kisses and drive me wild with your beauty."

"No, Regan, no!"

In two strides he was beside the bed, his fingers biting into the flesh of her arms. "I won't be used, Sirena, and that's what you've got planned for me in that pretty head of yours, isn't it? You thought you'd come here and remind me of what we had together. *Had and lost, Sirena!* I never did care for a woman who was overconfident of her charms. And if you think I'd allow you to get close enough to me to gain your revenge for what you think I've done to you, think again!" he bellowed.

"Please believe me, Regan!" she implored, crawling

out from under the covers, kneeling, her arms outstretched in a gesture of supplication.

"Believe you! I, who know what lengths you're capable of going to? Remember, it was I who married you thinking you were your own sister! It was my house you lived in while you were wreaking havoc on the business my father and I had spent a lifetime building! You bore my name and slept with another man! You are the epitome of deceit, Sirena, and God help me, but I loved you! I can still love you, damn my soul, but I won't let myself. I'm wiser now and I won't fall into your traps again!" In a gesture as old as time itself, Regan reached for several coins and placed them on a table within her sight. "Little enough payment for a good roll in the sack. Take it, like the good little whore you are, and get out of here!"

Before Sirena could find the words or strength to answer him, he turned on his heel and left the room, slamming the door behind him.

Too stricken to cry, too pained to move, Sirena heard him stamp down the stairs and, from below, there was the sound of shattering glass. Slowly, in choked, laggard movements, she dressed herself. Glancing once about the room where she had found meaning to her life only a short while ago, she closed the door behind her. Soundlessly, she descended the stairs and stepped out into the night, the foggy dark a cover for her shattered, humiliated heart.

Throughout the next weeks Sirena found herself much in demand to attend social functions given in her honor. Though she wore a mask of gaiety for the world to see, only Frau Holtz and Jacobus knew her true feelings.

But there was nobody more aware of what she was suffering than Sirena herself. She knew she was beyond controlling the circumstances of her life. She felt powerless to salvage what was left. The only reason she stayed in London was to be near Regan. Somewhere within her was the small hope that the damage between them could be repaired.

In the dark, lonely hours before dawn, while she lay in her solitary bed, scenes from their last time together flashed before her, warming her in a half-dream where she could feel Regan's arms about her and his lips adoring her. And from this she could draw strength. Regan loved her. Hadn't his arms told her, and his lips? And when he had turned her in his arms, hadn't he reveled in her offerings? Regan loves me, I know he does! And God help me, I love him so much! He doesn't want to admit it because of his pride, but he cares!

Then, just as the early sun was lighting the horizon, her spirits would fall into that desolate abyss. And before she at last closed her eyes in sleep, she would cry with the firm belief that she was only fooling herself. That if Regan loved her, he wouldn't have been so quick to misunderstand what she had meant when she had cried out. Yet loving Regan was the only thing she had left and no matter what pain it brought her, she could not give it up.

One afternoon, Sirena lounged after lunch deliberating on what costume she would wear that coming evening. Frau Holtz knocked perfunctorily and entered, bearing a small, silver tray on which was stacked invitations. Sirena smiled and picked up the first and then another. Near the bottom of the stack she picked up a formal, cream-colored square and laughed delightedly. "This," she said, waving the invitation in the air, "is from Sir Stephan Langdon." She had already explained that Stephan was Camilla's father. "He requests the honor of my company at dinner tomorrow. He would be delighted to be my escort at the Fallows' dinner party."

Frau Holtz watched as Sirena quickly penned off her reply and handed it to the housekeeper for a footman to deliver. The aged woman trembled slightly at the sight of her mistress dancing about the room. What was the Mevrouw up to? Whatever it was, it had to do with the Mynheer.

"Listen to me, Frau Holtz. There's another message to be delivered. I think Jacobus is the man for it. Tyler Sinclair has asked me to accompany him to Waterford so I can examine a factory he wishes to buy. As there aren't any ships sailing on a regular basis there save Regan's and, of course, the small schooners that are not allowed to take passengers, ask Jacobus to go to the wharf and have Jan or Willem go to Tyler's office and say their ship is taking a few passengers. Whoever goes is to act as captain and his reason for going to Tyler should be to inquire as to the levies on Irish laces. When we sail to Ireland, you will accompany me as well as Jacobus."

Frau Holtz frowned at the prospect of a sea voyage, no matter how short; then she found her spirits lifting a little. She had never been so bored and lacking something to do since she had come to this house in England. When the Mevrouw and Mynheer lived together, there was always something going on, sparks were always flying and one never knew if it were safe to leave one's bed from day to day. As always, when the Frau was upset, her thoughts went to Batavia and her life on the islands. How she missed it.

"Jacobus," she called out into the greenhouse from the kitchen window. "The Mevrouw has an errand for you." Quickly she explained and did not fail to see the man's eyes light at the prospect of going to sea again. While Jacobus might say he yearned for dry land, he longed to be once again on a rolling, pitching deck. But, he would never leave Sirena. He had promised to look after the Capitana and Frau Holtz and he would never go back on his word, no matter how miserable he was.

Several days later, baggage in tow, Sirena and Frau Holtz stepped aboard the *Sea Spirit*. Sirena winked roguishly at Jan, who welcomed his passengers aboard.

To all intents and purposes, Sirena and her crew behaved as though they were complete strangers to each other. Willem showed her to her cabin while the others were made comfortable in quarters which had been arranged for them. Sirena whispered to Willem that Sir Sinclair had a tendency toward billiousness in open water. Pray for calm seas.

Willem promised to do his best and, while she carried her baggage into the cabin, he asked how she found London.

"I hate it!" Sirena responded vehemently, her eyes stormy. "For some reason I find myself bound there." She looked into Willem's face, scrutinizing what she read there. She smiled sadly, "I have this feeling, Willem, that something is going to happen to me. I keep telling myself it's my own sense of insecurity, but somehow I feel it's something more. Perhaps it's because I have no home, no roots. Oh, I have a house and I'm told I'm wealthy, but . . . everything is gone," she said softly. "Can you understand that?"

"Aye, Capitana. More than you realize."

"I'm sorry, Willem. Of course you as a sailor understand what it is to be homeless. Forget what I said and sail this ship to Ireland, and I'll let the sea convince me these feelings are just attacks of a woman's fancy."

The *Sea Spirit* was three days out to sea, headed for Waterford, Ireland. Sirena was strolling the deck, Tyler on one side of her, Frau Holtz meandering on the other, her eye to an approaching storm. Sirena, too, watched the encroaching gale warily. Another two hours and they would find themselves in the thick of it. Her flesh tingled and her hands itched to take the wheel, but she forced down her feelings.

Later, leaning over the rail, Sirena watched as the *Spirit* lifted and dipped and sliced through the diamond-shaped waves with all the grace and certainty of a water sprite. She showed she was made of more than just the wood and nails that man had hammered into her. Satisfaction was the *Spirit*'s reward and the roar in her rigging was her ovation. On she raced through billows and groaning squalls. She met the wind and licked up the sea, dipping more than heeling, as if she knew she was the most magnificent ship beneath the sky.

"Sail ho!" came the cry from the rigging.

"Where away?" Willem called as Sirena narrowed her eyes to peer into the gloom.

"Due north and there's another sail on her bow!"

Sirena climbed onto a tackle box and watched as the brig held to her course. Wet down, her canvas straining, the ship held her speed for nearly an hour. With the wind coming aft, Sirena watched as her booms swung out under the reaches of her sails. The water boiled and churned aft until her wake was long and white. Even from this distance, Sirena could see the other ship gaining on the floundering brig.

Her own *Sea Spirit* secure, Sirena watched as the British flag whipped in the wind. She knew in a second what the pursuing ship's objective was, a brig carrying English cargo. Her eyes questioned Jan and he nodded. It was a pirate ship and bent on destroying the unsuspecting vessel. Sirena shook her head slightly. They would not interfere.

Tyler was watching with a keen eye as the brigantine tried to outrun the pirates.

Sirena fought to keep her agitation from showing as she watched the lightning play in brilliant sheets, frolicking over the line of earth and sky. The lady of the sea was unhappy. She was betrothed to the wind, a prodigal and unpredictable suitor.

"Look!" Tyler called excitedly, "it's really a pirate ship!" He could barely contain his excitement as a roar split the air and thick, black smoke eddied upward above the smoking brigantine.

"How does it feel to witness this, Tyler?" Sirena asked. "Do you still entertain thoughts of being a lawless seaman?"

"I'd give anything to be one of those pirates!" he exclaimed, his eyes shining brightly. "I've never seen anything like it. My father used to read me stories when I was a child and it was just like this, the storm and all," he said, waving his hand at the flashes of lightning and the thundering sky. "That's van der Rhys' ship!" he suddenly exclaimed, recognizing the English brig for the first time. "I can tell by the flag she flies. I only saw it being loaded at the wharf just last month. He'll have a bloody fit!" Suddenly he caught himself, "Sorry, Sirena, I suppose those are a share of your profits, too."

Sirena's eyes flashed suddenly. "Are you certain?" she shouted as a roar of thunder split the air.

"Positive!" Tyler announced, his eyes glued to the attacking pirate brigantine. "If I had that booty from the van der Rhys ship, I'd never have to go to those damnable offices again. I could be free to live as I like! I wouldn't have to live by rules and convention. I'd be free!"

"Do you want it?" Sirena asked quietly. In the roar of the storm Tyler wasn't certain he'd heard her or if he'd read her lips. He tore his glance away from hers and riveted his eyes on the pirate ship again.

"I'd give anything in this world for it," he said huskily.

"Then you will have it!"

Tyler didn't notice her leave, so intent was he on his objective. When Sirena appeared, she was in her sea costume; the full-sleeved blouse tied snugly beneath her breasts; her tall, wide-topped boots which rose above her knees and accentuated the long length of thigh exposed by her cropped-off trousers. "All hands to the deck," Sirena shouted, her legs firmly planted on the rolling planks. "We're going to run. The wind has changed to the south!"

Tyler's eyes nearly popped from his head as Sirena ordered, "Haul the yards about for the port tack. Move lively, men, there's not much time!" She looked over her shoulder and grinned at Tyler's obvious shock. "You wanted it. Station yourself securely or you might go overboard and you'll not live to enjoy your booty."

Every crew member knew what lay in store for himself. Each manned his station. The *Spirit* would maneuver a short round to, and in so doing would pivot on her stern under headsails, piling up great lee waves on her starboard side. Sirena had to heist forward and reply to the ship's head with helm at the exact moment. She had to push aft at just the right time, when the helm was moved to shift her forward. She would be forced to lay oil from her bows and, most important, before the order to fill headsails, wait for a smooth. If not, she was in deadly peril.

One false move, no matter how minute, and the *Spirit* would be at the mercy of wind and sea. Sirena took the wheel and it was touch and go. The seamen's cries rained on the wind. The helm shifted and the jib sails and forestaysail rose, cracked in the wind, ballooned and, with the forward seamen playing tug-of-war on the sheets, the mighty foresail reefed, catching a fill of wind and buoying up the fore. The *Spirit* began to swing. The arrogant lady dug her nose into the rolling seas and pushed up more starboard. The lady came about in a boil of water and foam, her port side exposed to the full force of the ferocious wind.

She shuddered, heeled dangerously in the vise of windward and lee seas, rocking, unsure of herself. Then the helm shifted. To cries aft and forward, the headsails spilled their wind as the aft gave bright sail to bear. Foresail was set on the fore and main, yards readied on the port tack sprouted sail. The helm met the press of canvas. The graceful lady groaned, trembled, heeled and shot forward.

"Smartly done," Jan yelled from the stern.

"Willem, the wheel," Sirena called.

"Magnificent," Willem complimented.

"We must make our guest happy," Sirena smiled, satisfied with a job well done.

For better than two hours the *Sea Spirit* pursued the pirate ship. And when they at last had her within reach, Sirena shouted, "Hear this! We take the marauding pirate brig! When we have her, gut her. A pirate on open seas is fair game to any and all. The prize goes to our guest," she said emphatically.

"Aye, Capitana," the crew shouted as they readied a grappling hook to board the brig bearing the Jolly Roger. "The fight's gone out of her and it's all she can do to stay afloat after that storm. A few of the English trader's shots were well aimed from the look of her crew. If we don't take her booty now, it'll go to the bottom," Franco yelled.

Sirena searched out Tyler, who was hanging on to the mizzenmast for dear life, his face pale and white. "Poor Tyler, you're ill."

Sinclair, his hold on the ropes slipping, eyed the long-legged creature before him with awe. He tried to speak, but words would not come.

Sirena brandished her cutlass in the air and laughed aloud. "I'd take the brig for you but she's rotten with toredo worms and practically worthless. The cargo is yours and, within the hour, will be secure in the hold of the *Sea Spirit*. It's all yours, Tyler, but remember, you said you would do anything for the booty. One day I'll lay claim to that promise."

"You must be . . . you can't be! I thought it was a story, a fabrication made for amusement! But you are real!" he exclaimed with excitement. "You are the Sea Siren!"

"Yes, I'm real, not a myth."

"Sirena, that cargo the pirates took belongs to Regan van der Rhys."

"Not any longer. Now it belongs to you," Sirena laughed. "It was fair game. We didn't take it from Regan's vessel, the pirates did. There is a difference. I didn't attack Regan's ship," she said firmly.

"He'll bloody well kill the pair of us," Tyler laughed nervously.

"Do you plan on advertising the fact that you're in possession of his cargo?"

"No . . . but—"

"Then he will never know who sunk the pirate ship or who has his cargo. Unfortunately for the scurves, they repelled the attack and paid with their lives."

Some of Tyler's color was returning. "What should I do with the cargo?"

Sirena shrugged, "You have several alternatives. You can sell it on the black market in Ireland or, if worse comes to worse, you could sell it back to Regan. I should think he'd pay handsomely for its return. Don't forget I get my finder's fee if that's what you do."

"We could bloody well end up in Newgate or strung from the end of a yardarm for this little stunt," he said, scowling.

"Only if your mouth begins to flap," Sirena said coolly. "And before that happens, I'd shut it for you, Tyler. For good, if necessary. Think about it. Right now, you're as guilty as the rest of us."

As Sirena strolled back to her cabin, she bubbled over with laughter. Regan's cargo. What a stroke of luck! Poor Tyler, he'd never be the same!

Regan was in the taproom of the White Dove when word reached him that his ship had limped back into port after being plundered at sea. He stood still, his eyes shocked, as he listened to the sailor's report. He tried to clear his rum-filled head. His tongue was thick and his muscular body moved sluggishly as he tried to grasp the seaman by the arm to demand more information. "What pirate? Was it a woman?" he shouted hoarsely, a murderous glint in his eye. The sailor, frightened for his life, jerked his arm free and backed away from the wild Dutchman.

"I only came here to give you the news as I was instructed. What's this you ask me about a woman pirate? How am I to know if there was a woman," the sailor shouted belligerently. "Go to the wharf yourself and see with your own eyes. All I know is your cargo is aboard another ship and yours limped into port. Your captain told me to inform you the reason word hasn't reached you before this is because he took time off the Cornish coast to shore up your ship well enough to sail back to London."

Regan looked about wildly at the interested, amused faces that surrounded him. It was clear they thought him insane. How could he explain about the notorious Sea Siren to these grog-soaked individuals. If he wasn't careful, they'd lock him away in Bedlam. Goddammit, it had been his biggest cargo so far in his fledgling business, and one that would have paid handsomely. Suddenly, his brain cleared and he tore from the room as if the hounds of Hell were on his heels.

He flagged down the first hackney he spotted and told the driver he'd pay double for a quick ride to King Street. "I'll wring her neck, damn her!" he shouted viciously into the clear night air.

The ride through the city of London did little to cool Regan's temper. Stopping before Sirena's house, he raced to the wide double doors and kicked at them like a petulant child. Frau Holtz, her hair standing on end, opened the door and immediately backed off when she saw the wild look in Regan's face.

"Where is she?" he demanded.

The woman blanched and brought her clenched fist to her mouth. Incensed, Regan tore her hand away and demanded an answer. "Answer me or I'll break your arm and old bones don't mend quickly. Where is she?"

"In her room. The second door from the top of the landing," Frau Holtz whispered fearfully.

Sirena had been in the process of reading a note when she looked up and saw Regan framed in the doorway, filling the opening, murder in his eyes. Sirena held a letter opener loosely, wary and angry at this intrusion. "Don't come any closer," she said vehemently, brandishing the slim blade.

Regan's face contorted with rage. He leaped over a low footstool and slapped her, the palm of his hand drawing blood from her lip. Sirena tried to sidestep the blow and lost her balance just as Regan reached for her flowing hair. He grabbed a handful of the ebony tresses and pulled her to him, ignoring her scream.

"Attack my ship and steal my cargo. Oh, no, not again! Never again!" he shouted. "When I'm finished with you you're going to cry for mercy, beg my forgiveness. In the end you'll beg me to kill you. I warned you, and this time I mean what I say. I've had enough!" he shouted, each word distinct, his voice venomous and full of hate. "You've gone too far!" Intent on his own fury, his hold loosened. With one quick motion, Sirena cut up and lashed through her long mane of hair and found herself free.

She backed off and held the knife in front of her. "This," she said, waving the impromptu weapon, "makes things a little more even between us," she said coldly. "Why are you here? What's your problem? Whatever it is, we could have discussed it like civilized human beings. You don't belong here. I have a paper signed by you that says you are no longer my husband; so get out and take your rage and your stale, sweaty body out of my room. You make me sick!"

"I'll leave when I'm damn good and ready. First you will tell me where my cargo is and when you plan to pay for damages done to my ship."

Sirena stepped her way around the room, Regan stalking her like an animal. "Hear this, Regan. I didn't attack your ship. Pirates hauled your cargo to their brig. Not me, understand? I didn't plunder your property."

"You lie!" Regan hissed. "You'd lie to me with a prayer book in one hand and a rosary in the other. Your entire life is one lie after another. Deceit, trickery, killing are the rules you live by." He pounced on her and she brought up the letter opener in defense. He had her slender wrist in his strong grip as she frantically tried to free herself. He had her trapped. She brought up her knee and thrust it in the direction of his groin. His yell of pain forced him backward as she reached out with the blade and brought it down and around his cheek. She saw the blood spurt from the wound, and Regan doubled over.

"I hope I crippled you," Sirena spit viciously. "Go back to your delicious peach and let her nurse your injuries. I hope you die," she cried. "I told you I didn't attack your ship, and I didn't. You believe whatever is convenient at the time. Just as you wanted to believe Mikel was Chaezar's child. Be glad I didn't kill you because from this moment on you're fair game. You couldn't even give me the decency of hearing me out. No, you come to my house and threaten me and expect me to stand meekly by and take your punishment."

Kicking her way past him, Sirena turned and looked down at him, disgust and loathing written on her features. "You're smelling up my bedroom," she sneered. "Now get out of here. If you can't make it on your own two legs, I'll have the servants toss you out the window."

Regan straightened painfully and looked at Sirena. He blinked as he watched her face break into a smile that stretched from ear to ear. Deftly she reached behind her and grasped a small, silver-backed mirror and tossed it to him. "A small memento of this night. A mistake, but then who will ever know."

Regan's face drained of all color as he brought up his arm to wipe his cheek with his sleeve. His agate-blue eyes became slits as he looked into the mirror and then at Sirena. "You'll pay for this," he shouted hoarsely. "If it's war you want, then it's war you'll get."

"It would seem I've won the first battle. I hope you like the way I've carved my initial on your cheek. Think how nice it will feel when your little darling runs her fingers over it so lovingly. Tell her the S stands for seduction . . . hers!" Sirena laughed, the familiar tinkle that grated on Regan's ears and made his teeth rattle.

"I'll see you dead," he breathed harshly.

"First, you'll have to catch me," Sirena taunted. "And from now on, you'll be so busy seeing to your cargoes, you'll have little time for me. *Adios,* Regan, don't trip over your own feet on your way out."

The ache in his groin was intense but he'd never let her know how she hurt him. He'd walk from the room on his own two legs if it killed him. And it probably would, he thought as an ocean began to roar in his ears. His teeth were clenched so hard he thought his jaw would crack as he turned to make his way down the endless staircase. The white line around his grim mouth caused Frau Holtz to catch her breath. She wanted to help him but his forbidding look prevented her from doing so.

Regan had three steps to go before he reached the bottom. Sirena stood at the top of the landing and called his name. She still held the letter opener by its point. The moment Regan turned she threw and the sleek weapon soared through the air and, by some strange fluke, penetrated the toe of his boot. "I did not attack your ship. *I* sunk the pirate ship that stole your cargo. The rules of salvage make the booty mine." Sirena leaned over the railing and laughed. "Frau Holtz, help him. The poor man seems to be hurt."

Regan brought himself under control and stalked from the house, the stiletto bobbing from the thick leather of his boot.

"Insufferable bastard. If you ever allow him into this house again, I'll send you to sea, Frau Holtz, and you'll never touch dry land again! Do you hear me?"

Frau Holtz gulped, knowing it was useless to argue. "*Ja,* I hear, Mevrouw."

Tears streaming down her cheeks, Sirena made her way to her suite and threw herself on the bed, sobbing.

Regan staggered into his room, his eyes burning with rage as he fell across his bed. He slumped down, his hands grasping his midsection. His mouth was a grim, ashen line as he drew deep breaths into his lungs. She was a bitch! He should have grasped her by the neck and squeezed till her eyes bulged from her head and her tongue turned black. He should have taken her and smashed her against the wall till she was a bleeding, pulpy mass.

He remembered the wound on his cheek and slammed his fist into the hard wood of the headboard. A yowl of outrage escaped him and then he nursed his bruised hand. His blood boiled as he tried to get to his feet, only to fall back on the softness of the bed. He closed his eyes as wave after wave of pain washed over him. There was no doubt in his mind that he could have killed her, stopped her in some way. Why did he always stop short of doing her harm? Why did he allow her to taunt and torment him time and again? Was it because she was in his blood? Because he loved her? How much longer was he going to let her have her way? When was he going to put a stop to it once and for all?

He rolled over on the bed as another wave of pain coursed through him. He had to do something. Make up his mind and stick to a course of action. If only she were more typical, more predictable, then he would feel . . . safer.

He ground his teeth together at the thought. He was a man and she was only a woman. A stabbing sensation surged through his groin with such force, he drove his fist into the bed, tearing the sheet. "Bitch! Goddamn murdering bitch!" he groaned.

Hours and half a bottle of rum later, the pain subsided and Regan slept. His dreams were those of a hunted man with a cutlass-wielding Sirena hot on his trail.

When he woke it was with grim determination to do something. She said she loved him, that her life was incomplete without him. Once and for all he would put her in her place and she would never shake loose from it. "I've had enough!" he roared. "Two can play this damnable game!"

War, she called it. Men fought wars, men won wars. Women *caused* wars! This time it would be no different. He would fight her with the one weapon she couldn't resist, he thought smugly, himself. He would lull her into a false sense of security and then he would strike. Then he would pick up his life and lead it without her interference. He had to do it; she was leaving him no choice. There comes a time in every man's life, he told himself, when he has to do the impossible. And this was going to be it, he thought morbidly. It was time Sirena learned the hard way who the superior force was.

Chapter Fourteen

Caleb sat with his knees drawn to his chin on the sparkling decks of the *Rana* as his gaze followed Lord Farrington and the workmen who were busily following the dapper gentleman's orders. He watched as gaming equipment and box after box of decorations, befitting an exclusive gambling parlor, were brought aboard. There was a wary look in his dark, luminous eyes as he imagined the expression on Sirena's face should she ever see the way her ship was outfitted. And Caleb was certain that sooner or later she would see it. Lord Farrington had told him, only this morning, that handbills were being printed to be distributed through London.

The argument between himself and the aristocratic lord still rankled Caleb, but he was glad to have won. Lord Farrington had presented the idea of having the hull of the *Rana* opened and a dockside room attached, forever condemning the frigate to be moored to land. Caleb had immediately negated the idea, refusing to alter the ship in any way which would impede her seaworthiness.

The soft lap of water against the hull of the ship had an hypnotic effect as Caleb leaned against the quarterdeck rail. He let his eyes travel to the top of the mizzenmast and wished fervently he was out to sea. The back-breaking hours of being a longshoreman had taken their toll. He knew that particular life wasn't for him, but he didn't give up until yesterday when Aubrey Farrington said the gaming equipment was due to arrive. Until that moment, Caleb didn't believe he had agreed to the lord's proposition. Now, it was a reality.

He watched a gull as it swooped toward the shoreline, then take wing and soar overhead. He wished he had someone to talk to, someone other than Farrington, who only cared to discuss business and profits. When he tired of that subject, he would invariably switch to women. Caleb wished Willem or Jan were aboard so he could exchange sea tales. The two old salts would have plenty to say and would entertain him as they had on many nights in Java. It had been a long time, too long. Thoughts of Sirena and Regan seeped into his mind and he quickly pushed them away.

Lord Aubrey Farrington tapped Caleb's shoulder with the tip of his walking stick. "Cal, the men have been telling me of a pirate operating in these waters. I think it best if we take a few precautionary measures to assure the safety of our profits, and our patrons, of course."

An old, familiar feeling churned in Caleb's gut as he stared in disbelief. "What did you say?"

"I said there is word of a pirate operating in the waters off the southern coast. A ship belonging to van der Rhys was sacked and came limping into port with the news. I said we should take a few measures to protect ourselves, sitting out here on the wharf this way."

Caleb's mind raced. Regan's ship! Sirena wouldn't! Not again! He schooled his face to hide his emotions and asked, "What manner of pirate vessel was it?"

"By the stars, Cal, how should I know? A pirate ship, an ordinary pirate ship, whatever that may be!"

Caleb hadn't realized he was holding his breath until the dapper lord uttered his last words absolving Sirena. She certainly wasn't an "ordinary" pirate and, if indeed it was she who sacked Regan's ship, she would have been certain he would know it.

"Well, boy, do you agree we should hire guards?" Aubrey tapped Caleb impatiently with his walking stick again.

"Get that damn thing away from me before I break it over your back! I've told you before I don't like it!"

Caleb threatened and Lord Farrington cautiously lifted the stick out of his grasp. "As far as protection from the pirates, that's ridiculous. But I do agree to taking on a few men to safeguard our cash box from the scoundrels loitering about the docks."

"Yes, I agree," Lord Farrington said smoothly, "whatever you think best," he walked away from Caleb, his stick tapping the deck.

An uneasy feeling settled between Caleb's shoulder blades as he got to his feet. His brown eyes narrowed as he stared across the water at the horizon, to another time and another place, remembering . . . remembering . . .

At the top of the wide, curving staircase in the Sinclair townhouse on the Pall Mall, Baroness Helen Sinclair marched haughtily in front of her husband, her thin form bespeaking her indignation. She was angry, angry enough to spit, and she minced no words in proclaiming this.

"Make no excuses to me, Charles. You had very poor judgment in inviting Stephan Langdon to *my* dinner party!"

"Helen, dear," Baron Sinclair pleaded, "what would you have had me do? When Stephan approached me, he already knew the invitations for your little soirée were out. He simply stated that perhaps his fool of a housekeeper had misplaced it. I knew what he was aiming at; I couldn't profess ignorance."

"Oh, couldn't you?" the Baroness looked down her long nose at her husband. "I should never know why! Charles, when will you learn that Stephan Langdon is ignorant beyond insult?"

Floundering for an excuse as to why he went over his wife's head to invite Sir Langdon to the dinner, Baron Sinclair said innocently, "Stephan seems genuinely interested in our lovely Sirena and she also seems quite taken with him. Perhaps a match is in the making."

"Over my dead body," the Baroness muttered as she lifted the hem of her gown to step down the stairs. No sooner had she settled herself on a settee covered in rich ruby brocade when the first-floor maid announced Sirena and Sir Langdon and showed them into the drawing room where the Sinclairs were enjoying the brightly burning hearth.

As always, the Baroness drew in her breath at Sirena's loveliness, who today was wearing a copper-colored silk which enhanced her fragile ivory skin and shining dark hair. Now, why can't Tyler find himself in love with her, the Baroness thought sourly, disapproving of her son's taste in women. She sighed inwardly, realizing that a man like Tyler could never be a match for the fiery Spaniard. Sirena needed a man like Regan van der Rhys to compliment her beauty and spirit. A man who could take control and offer a constant challenge to her. Tyler was yet a boy compared to Regan. How sad that the marriage between the Dutchman and this beautiful creature had gone awry.

"How lovely you are today," the Baroness said sincerely, extending her hand in greeting.

"Thank you," Sirena smiled. "Your drawing room is lovely, Baroness."

"I ordered the materials from your homeland, Sirena, and brought a draper from Spain to see to the decorating. I'm pleased you like it."

Sirena smiled again and accepted a glass of sherry from the Baron. "Tell me, Sirena," he asked, "how did you enjoy your trip to Ireland?"

Sirena sipped the cordial and looked at the Baron over the rim of the crystal glass. "It was . . . interesting," she said softly.

"I'd like to see some of the laces you brought back from Waterford," the Baroness stated.

"Laces and crystal, Baroness. As a matter of fact, you will receive a small gift of the most exquisite glasses I've ever seen. It should arrive in a day or two. As for the laces, I'd love to show them to you. Perhaps later in the week. They are so delicate and novel in design. I must commend Tyler on his choice of investment. A woman never has enough ribbons and laces."

Baron Sinclair, having little interest in the topic under discussion other than the potential profit to be gained, spoke to Stephan Langdon. "Have you heard that van der Rhys lost a cargo to pirates?"

"Everyone had heard of it," Stephan said harshly. "And to think they sail in English waters! It's not to be tolerated."

"I heard the Dutchman was in a murderous mood when the news was brought to him. The story making the rounds is that he seemed a bit tetched, peculiar. He demanded to know if the pirates were led by a woman. Did you ever hear of anything so outrageous?"

Sirena placed her glass on a small table and raised her eyes to Baron Sinclair. The heavy, black fringe of lashes hid the sparkle in her emerald eyes. "Several years ago there was a tale of a woman pirate that originated in the East Indies. They say there was no seaman her equal. She fought and cursed like a man, and was said to be the most beautiful woman ever to sail those waters. Men named her the Sea Siren, but I understand the Dutch East India Company and its stockholders had other names for her." Sirena smiled, a cool, enigmatic expression that caught Stephan Langdon's eye and interest. "Some say she was a myth, others say she was real and that she still roams the waters searching for prey. I myself inquired of Mynheer van der Rhys if there was any validity to the story since he recently came from the Indies. He told me there was no such person, and, if there was, she's dead now. Knowing this, I don't understand why he should ask about a woman pirate. Perhaps there is something to the rumor that he's a bit unstable."

All eyes turned to Sirena, listening attentively as she continued. "I've no doubt it was pirates who plundered the van der Rhys cargo. Why, just today, I stopped by Tyler's office and he told me a rather wicked rumor. It seems the pirate offered to sell van der Rhys back his own cargo for double what he paid. Ingenious, wouldn't you say?"

"Quite," Langdon said, sipping his wine. "Perhaps that explains Regan's foul mood when he came to call on Camilla. That and the confrontation he had with several ruffians who attacked him and left him with a rather nasty cut on his right cheek."

"You sound so bitter, Stephan," the Baroness said snidely. "One would believe Regan's fortunes, or misfortunes if you will, were your own." Baroness Helen shot Stephan a speculating glance. Lifting her tone, she asked, "Speaking of Camilla, how is the dear child?"

"Very content with the betrothal. And, as you know, Helen, Camilla's happiness is foremost in my heart." Now it was Stephan's turn to throw the Baroness a smirking look. "By the end of the evening she will have him smiling out of his black mood. He's quite enamored of my daughter, you know. One has only to see the way he stares at her. He absolutely dotes on the child."

"Doesn't it annoy you, Stephan, that the Dutchman is nearly old enough to be Camilla's father? You English, I'm finding, have a tendency to be indulgent with your children," Sirena laughed, amusement bubbling in her green eyes.

"Camilla needs a strong hand," Stephan said firmly, defending the situation between Camilla and Regan.

"A strong hand should be her father's responsibility. A girl doesn't need two fathers, Stephan. A husband should be a lover," Sirena purred.

"She's right," the Baroness noted sharply. "Whatever were you thinking of to allow Camilla to become involved with the Dutchman?"

Stephan sighed. "The girl has a mind of her own and once she set her sights on him there was little I could do. Besides, he's quite wealthy and a poor, motherless child could do worse, and my little Camilla *does* love him."

Regan or his money? Sirena thought nastily. She lowered her gaze and offered the Baroness a conspiratorial wink which the regal lady returned.

The dinner party was a success. Sirena and Sir Langdon were joined by eight other couples and all enjoyed the Sinclairs' lavish hospitality.

Because of the Baroness' maternal interest in Sirena, a broad spectrum of society accepted this visitor from Spain with open arms. She was beautiful, intelligent and rich! If any other qualities were necessary to become society's little darling, nobody found them lacking in Sirena. Her entrance into the closed ranks of London's *ton* was successfully accomplished.

Much later, when the evening was nearly at an end, the other guests gone, and only Sirena and Stephan remained, the Baroness and Sirena withdrew to a far corner of the drawing room while the Baron and Stephan enjoyed a private smoke in the library.

The ladies, left to themselves, discussed a variety of topics—the weather, lace, and the balls which were being held. Finally, the Baroness could stand it no longer. Fully aware of the wary look in Sirena's eyes, she attacked forcefully, intent on learning the truth. "You still love him, don't you, dear?"

"Yes," Sirena answered softly, turning her face away from the glowing lamplight, her features cast in mysterious shadows.

"And you'll do whatever necessary to get him back?"

"Yes."

"Even if he loves another?"

"No, not if he truly loved another. He doesn't love Camilla Langdon. He loved me once. He can't have forgotten," she whispered, the passion of her statement charging the air.

"Just suppose, now I said suppose, that what you say is untrue. Suppose he no longer loves you, can never love you again? What would you do?" the Baroness asked, concern lining her otherwise smooth brow.

"What will I do? I think I should simply die. There's no life in me without Regan. He's mine by right of marriage; my religion forbids divorce. In my eyes we are still married and will remain so until death parts us. Not whimsical secular laws. I won't spend my life being half alive. I want it all or nothing!" The eyes Sirena turned to the Baroness were so filled with grief, so tortured with rejection, the older woman was caught in their glimmering sadness.

"But, dear, what can you do? You can't *make* someone love you!"

"Please, Baroness, no more questions. All I know is I must do what I must do. The circumstances between Regan and myself were my doing and I must try to rectify that mistake in the only way I know how."

The Baroness gazed at Sirena with genuine fondness. If only Tyler were man enough for this woman, what sons they would have! "I understand, Sirena, I really do. If there is anything I can do, you have only to ask."

"You are very kind, but this is something I must do alone. But I beg you to remember that I love him."

The Baroness wondered vaguely if she would have gone to any lengths for Charles. She thought not. It sounded like a great deal of trouble for one man. Still, Charles wasn't Regan van der Rhys. She shrugged as the men entered the room, Tyler behind them, returned from a dinner engagement. His chestnut eyes lit up at the sight of Sirena; and, after greeting his mother, he bowed low over her hand and brought her fingers to his lips.

"Tyler, how elegant you are," Sirena laughed. "And who was the lucky lady this evening?"

"Some little drab," he answered, his mouth turned downward. "I was literally forced into this evening by the girl's mother. Since the family is a client of mine, I could not refuse."

"Tell us what we missed, son," his mother smiled indulgently.

"The usual," Tyler said sourly. "Rich food, flat wine and dancing. The musicians left much to be desired. The conversation at dinner was lively, however," he grinned. "Regan van der Rhys regaled the party with the tale of his pirated ship. It seems the scurves offered to sell him his cargo back at double the price."

"Don't keep us in suspense, Tyler, what did the Dutchman do?" the Baroness asked, her gaze going between her handsome son and the lovely Spaniard. Was she wrong or was there a private understanding between the two?

Tyler suppressed his excitement. "He said he has no other choice. He must regain those goods to honor the contracts with his clients, else his reputation will suffer. For a fledgling business, it is to be avoided at all costs."

"How terrible for the poor man," Sirena pretended sympathy. "How often can his business survive such attacks?" she asked, her voice low and throaty, her eyes keen and sharp.

Tyler shrugged, his own glance anxious and wary. "Who can say? It depends on how much he has invested."

Sir Stephan Langdon's aloof gray eyes were disturbed and his tone bordered on panic. "Are you telling me the Dutchman is near ruin?"

"No, that's not what I'm saying. I said it depends on how much of his capital he had invested. He could well lose it all and still be far from ruination. Only a fool puts all his eggs in one basket and that van der Rhys is far from being."

Langdon's face showed relief and Sirena wanted to slap his face till his teeth rattled. If Regan were penniless, Stephan would snatch the lovely Camilla away so quickly he'd leave her breathless. It always came down to the size of the bank account, she thought sadly. Poor Regan, he should only know.

"If you'll excuse me, I've had a long day," Tyler said, getting to his feet. He favored Sirena with a heavy-lidded wink before quitting the room.

"The Dutchman should never have acceded to the pirate's demands," Charles Sinclair said in a miffed tone. "In doing so, he jeopardizes all British trade. Still, it's been quite a while since London has seen this kind of excitement, eh?" He directed his question to Stephan.

"A pity we won't see it through to the end," Baroness Helen interjected. "We will be leaving for Scotland shortly. Affairs of family holding," she said to Sirena. "We may never learn how Mr. van der Rhys settles his affairs."

"Before you leave, Stephan, there's something I'd like to ask you," Baron Sinclair interrupted his wife. He was loath to hear again how she detested the barbarous Scots and their hostile country. "While at my club this afternoon, a group of us were decrying the fact that our young sons of England are deprived of proper training in the art of fencing. A group of us would like to institute such instruction and, naturally, your name was mentioned. We feel it would be a profitable endeavor and would attract scions from all of London. A short-term project actually. We would like you to come in on it with us, Langdon, if you would consider seeing to it that the boys were correctly taught. Since you are an expert of renown, your name would have quite a draw in recruiting students. The tuition would be rather stiff and, if you would agree, you wouldn't be asked to take part in the financing of the school. Your efforts with the students would be your contribution and we all seem to think the profits would be handsome."

"Stephan, there seems to be so much I don't know about you," Sirena murmured. "I had no idea you were a fencing master."

"The best!" Baron Charles bragged as he slapped Stephan soundly on his back. "The very best. He's never lost a match to my knowledge."

"I hope it doesn't upset you, Sirena," Stephan said anxiously. "Some women frown on such accomplishments."

"On the contrary. I find it a very masculine sport," she answered quietly, her face composed. "Perhaps one day you will teach me something about it. I understand the women in France find it an amusing sport."

"I should be honored," Stephan responded in his courtly manner. "I will leave it to you to name the time and place."

In the carriage on the short ride back to Sirena's house, a change seemed to have taken place in Stephan. He was almost withdrawn. Sirena thought he would be full of ideas concerning the fencing academy. But he remained quiet, answering only when spoken to. Taking sidelong glances at Stephan, Sirena scrutinized this man who had become her almost constant escort. He was rakishly handsome and the moonlight, spilling through the coach window, reflected off his silvery hair. His complexion was a bit swarthy and his teeth perfect. She had noted his athletic build earlier, and now she knew how he came by it. Fencing was a demanding sport and one which required top physical condition. She decided he must have enjoyed a reputation as a lothario in his younger days. There was still a certain sensuality about him. At times, when she caught him unawares, she saw him watching her and there would be a certain excitement behind his aloof stare. A titillating excitement she found somewhat pleasing coming from a man of his ilk.

It was gratifying to know that an attractive man found her desirable after Regan's rejection. As though reading her thoughts, Stephan placed his arm about her shoulders and pulled her close. Gently, he placed a finger beneath her chin and lifted her face to look down into her eyes. "Do you know how beautiful you are, Sirena?" he breathed, his voice husky. Slowly, seductively, he covered her mouth with his own in a long, searching kiss. His arms tightened about her and she felt the strength in them and succumbed to it. Stephan was a most attractive man, yet Sirena was surprised by the response she experienced. And when his hand cupped her breast, she allowed it to remain there and enjoyed a small, womanly thrill to be found exciting by a virile, worldly man.

When the coach pulled into the drive to her house, Sirena extracted herself from his arms. She wanted no mistaken impressions that she would allow him to stay the night.

Stephan did not protest her action. Once again, he fell into the same silence and somehow Sirena suspected he was thinking about Regan's money, or the lack of it, whichever the case may be. He walked with her to the entrance and waited till Frau Holtz appeared. Bowing over her hand, he took his leave and Sirena watched him with a frown at the corners of her mouth.

Regan sat in his unheated office poring over his ledgers and papers. The hour was late and his head throbbed. The figures in the columns swam before his tired eyes. If he had more time, just a little more time, he could build a thriving enterprise. If he had it, he could liquidate some of Sirena's holdings to cash, thereby giving him more capital to work with. He had been a fool to start on such a large scale with so little cash and hope that sheer effort would insure success.

Now, he had Tyler Sinclair breathing down his neck demanding shares for Sirena in lieu of pounds sterling. With no other alternative, he had reluctantly agreed.

He couldn't see to affairs here on land and be at sea with his ships to protect the cargoes as well. Life had been so simple in Batavia. What in the name of God ever possessed him to come to England? He longed for the warm, easterly trade winds and the ripe, golden sun. If he had dug in his heels on Java, things may have worked themselves through for him and Sirena. Now, since she had come to England, things had gone from bad to worse.

He rubbed at his aching eyes as a vision of Camilla rose before him. He could always arrange to have the wedding moved up to a closer date and then he could take control of Camilla's dowry. Only temporarily, until he settled his debts. He would make it clear to her in the beginning. He resolved he would return every penny. He had learned his lesson. Never again would he be accused of stealing a woman's money.

There was no point in working the figures over again. Staring at them and wishing wasn't going to change them. Why was he lying to himself? Why didn't he admit he didn't want to go home? He had no home, not really. He remembered his fine house in Batavia and then he compared it to the luxurious mansion which Sirena occupied. Just Sirena living there made her house a home. Frau Holtz's scrupulous care kept it spotless, not like the hap-hazard cleaning methods of his lazy housekeeper.

In a split second his life flashed before him and he knew in that instant he had made the biggest mistake of his entire adult years. One he couldn't alter or repair. Or could he? In order to amend the situation, he would have to go to Sirena and admit his wrong actions. Also, he would have to explain to Camilla that the marriage was off. He would have to face Caleb and the boy would know that Sirena had won again. He would have to close his offices and face the fact that his business had been a fiasco.

Regan pounded his fist on the desk. "No! Never!" he shouted into the echoing darkness. He wouldn't give up! He'd not make that error again. This time he would dig in his heels and make the best of it. If he could simply find some way to get his next shipment to Scotland, he might salvage the enterprise. Caleb would help him. Caleb could sail the cargo for him and wait for payment. The first thing in the morning he would find his son and put forth the offer. And at the same time he would see about liquidating more of the holdings.

Locking the door behind him, Regan stepped out into the gray before dawn. His shoulders slumped as he made his way through the crooked alleys to Lime Street. The closer he got to his house, the heavier his feet lagged. The damp mist circled around him and wrapped him in its arms. His tired eyes were bitter and his mouth was tight. The thin, S-shaped line on his cheek was raw and stiff. He touched his fingers to it lightly and felt a stab of humiliation. Sirena had branded him with her initial. His reason told him it was merely a coincidence, but something deeper, more basic, recoiled at the knowledge that, given a chance, Sirena would have sat upon his chest and carved her name into his forehead. He felt the stubble of growth on his chin and estimated how long it would take for the beard he had started to cover his disgrace.

Chapter Fifteen

London was awake from its night's sleep. The peddlers were hawking their wares. Outside the Langdon residence two overblown fishwives were slapping it out with oily flounders to determine which of them would secure the Langdon trade that day.

Regan had just dozed off into a fitful sleep when his bride-to-be was stirring for the beginning of another day.

It irritated Camilla that she had to dress herself and arrange her own hair. Her pretty face settled into a heavy frown as she looked into the mirror trying for a seductive effect with her long, yellow curls. Disgusted that nothing she could do would ever disguise her girlishness, she threw down the brush and stamped from the room. Why did she have to be all pink and white? she wondered with a pout. Why couldn't she look like that Spanish woman her father seemed so enamored of lately? Her own coloring and features required a softly feminine style of dressing while Sirena Córdez's ivory skin and luxurious jet hair commanded more sophisticating grooming. Camilla hadn't missed the way Regan's interested gaze had followed the sultry Sirena at the Sinclairs' ball. The thought of losing Regan set Camilla into a panic. The Dutchman was the best catch of the season aside from Prince Charles himself, and Camilla wasn't taking any chances on losing him to a dark-haired, green-eyed beauty who was at least five years older than herself!

When Camilla joined Stephan at the breakfast table, her mood hadn't improved. She looked with distaste at the thin slice of bread and at the nearly empty marmalade pot. She knew she would have to distract her father somehow if she wanted to have the jam on *her* bread. There wasn't enough for two. "You seem in fine fettle this morning, Father," she trilled as she snatched the pot from beneath his nose. Quickly, she smeared her bread with the thick, golden spread and then licked the spoon. Correctly interpreting his look, she spoke bitterly, "Yes, it's come to this. I hope you have good news today. You did win at whist last evening, didn't you?"

"Yes," Stephan sighed, "but a paltry amount."

"I hope it was enough to pay the cook. She's threatening to leave, you know. She said she'd finish out the week and, if she wasn't paid her wages, she wasn't coming back," Camilla sneered, her rosy mouth curled in distaste. "I'd love to know just how that hag manages to keep so plump and fat while I'm wasting away to nothing! I'd wager she steals more than she cooks for us! She constantly complains the allowance you give her isn't enough to cover the price of food, but she looks healthy enough."

Langdon looked up from the billet sheet he was reading and smiled perversely. "A certain gauntness adds mystery to your charms, darling."

"Gauntness! Starvation is more the like! It was all I could do to keep from bolting my food at the Waversons' dinner last evening. It's different for you. A man eats a hearty meal and his hostess approves. But women must pick daintily and leave half on their plate. I tell you, I'm starving!"

"Child, self-denial is an attribute to be cultivated," Stephan said piously.

"I don't see you denying yourself anything!" Camilla retorted, her rosy mouth puckered into a bow. "Every night you manage to dine out while I must listen to my innards rumble with hunger. Did you at least win enough to buy some eggs and cheese?"

"Something can be managed, perhaps a few staples. Remember, I have to keep enough for the next game. My credit is doubtful, to say the least."

"Then cheat!" Camilla cried heartlessly. "I'm your child and I'm starving!"

"It's only a temporary state of affairs," Stephan said airily.

"You've been saying that for over two years! I'm warning you, Father, if I don't get a substantial meal in me, I'll be too weak to make it to the altar with Regan. And then all your bubbles will burst!"

Suddenly remembering something, Camilla ran into the parlor and came back with the reticule she carried the night before. From out of the small purse she withdrew a linen napkin. Carefully, she unwrapped the cloth and revealed a leg of pheasant. Ignoring Stephan's disapproval, she began to tear into the tender meat as though it were the last food she would ever see. Stephan Langdon had to clench his fists to avoid snatching it from her hands. He watched as her small, sharp, white teeth tore into the succulent meat, savoring each bite.

"That was a dangerous thing to do, Camilla. What if someone saw you?"

"What if someone did? I don't care any longer. I'm hungry and I could eat a dozen more just like this," she said, licking her fingers and then sucking on the bone.

"Which of us will answer the door today to ward off the bill collectors?" Stephen asked.

"I'm tired of pretending to be the maid," Camilla complained. "You do it. You do make a rather impressive butler, Father."

Stephan eyed her with disgust and turned back to his billet sheet, studying the advertisements.

"Father, I hate to bring this up, but my seamstress is demanding payment and is threatening to spread the word of my poor credit. We really must do something. Your own tailor is making noises about taking the same action. I cannot think of another lie to save my soul. You must do something. Ask Baron Charles for another small loan. He is your cousin; surely he can't refuse you when you tell him how impoverished we are!"

"As for asking Baron Sinclair for a loan, I refuse. It mustn't get about how we're fixed for money. It would immediately get back to van der Rhys. And our fortunes are looking brighter. Only last evening the Baron asked me for my expertise in schooling young scions in the art of fencing. I won't have to invest anything, I'll just reap the profits."

"But that could take months! If only you'd allow me to convince Regan to hasten the wedding. At least in his house there would be food on the table."

"My dear," Stephan placated, "I've been toying with an idea. I think you should go to Tyler and ask for a small advance. He wouldn't dare tell his parents for fear of their disapproval."

"I knew you were out of your mind," Camilla screamed, her fair complexion blotched with rage. "That is the worst suggestion I've ever heard."

"I'm afraid we've no alternative. It's either ask Tyler or starve," he said craftily, watching her carefully.

Camilla looked at the cleanly picked bone and then at the empty jam jar. "Very well."

"Today, Camilla," Stephan urged. "I looked in your engagement book and you have no dinner invitation for this evening. Nor do I. You'll have to do it today or we'll both go to bed without eating. Of course, we could always stop at the Radcliffs' near the dinner hour on some premise or another."

"We did that last week, or have you forgotten?" Camilla snapped.

"We haven't visited the Beckmans or the Palmers lately."

"That's because when we do their butler tells us they're not at home. Father, soon all of London will be wise to us. Must you keep coming up with such weak solutions? Either you're going to have to become more adept at cards or you'll have to take up stealing."

"There will be no need for such drastic measures. Not if you go to Tyler. His money will tide us over for a while."

"How much do you think he'll give me? Enough for a few days and then we'll be right back where we are now. Starving!" she cried bitterly. "And another thing. Why must I do all the worrying about our credit. You're the man of the house and you're my father. You're supposed to take care of me!"

"True, true, my dear. But then I have my reputation to think of," Stephan commented affably.

"What reputation?" Camilla snorted. "If anyone's reputation is hanging for inspection, it's mine. I still cannot believe I'm doing what you ask. Do you realize, Father," she asked, leaning over the table, "if Tyler takes it in his mind to stop my marriage to Regan, where does that leave us? In Newgate! That's where! Bigamy is a serious charge. And if Regan discovers that I'm still married to Tyler Sinclair, he'll kill both of us!"

"Camilla, if this little act of yours is to get me to agree to extend our credit against the Dutchman's name, give over now, child. I've told you. Regan is a serious, sensitive man. And I don't believe his love for you would stand in the way of his better sense. And if you are worried that Tyler will reveal your little . . . er . . . secret, I've told you often enough, I can remedy that situation. I've merely to make a widow of you."

All the color drained from Camilla's face. "You wouldn't! You always said Tyler was our ace in the hole! Father, you must use your brain! The trouble here is Regan, not Tyler!"

"Sweetheart, have you ever thought of becoming a rich widow, or do you feel black is not your color?

And while we're discussing your position in life, have you given any thought as to how to pay for this wedding?"

"How else, I'll be married on credit!" Camilla sniped. "That is, if there is anyone who will still extend us any. A promise to pay up the day after the wedding should suffice."

"As always, you're very astute. I was more or less thinking the same thought. I do hope you will have the foresight to have the larder well stocked before hand."

"You can count on it."

"Tell me, my dear, how did you get Tyler to agree to remain silent about all this?"

"You know as well as I. He knows bloody well if he marries, he gets cut off without a farthing."

"I don't think you have that quite right, Camilla. You mean that happens if he marries *you*," Stephen said smugly. "I told you it was a mistake not to endear yourself to the Baroness."

"It wasn't me the Baroness objected to, Father. It was you! She has no closeness of kinship to give rise to her conscience. Besides, Tyler isn't a fool. He knows our circumstances as well as his own. He agreed to say nothing and that is it in a shell. He also realizes it was a mistake for us to have eloped. And he knows full well the Baroness' unforgiving nature where we Langdons are concerned."

"Thank God for small favors and for Tyler still being in love with you," Stephan said sincerely.

"And what of you? How is your romance going with that witch, Sirena Córdez?"

"I think the lady is quite impressed with me. It's too soon to close in for the kill. I want to woo her a while longer. I've looked into her affairs and, if anything, she's wealthier than your van der Rhys. I feel it safe to say I have the inside peg with her."

Camilla looked at her father and wanted to tell him the chances of making a match with the sultry Spaniard were almost nil. "There must be something to eat in this house," she said, rising from the table. "I'll just bet that miserable cook has a larder stashed away somewhere and she'll tell me where it is if I have to tie her to the spit and roast *her* for our dinner!"

Stephan watched his daughter with an amused look and thought she was the most endearing little cannibal in all London.

The weather was fair; and when Sirena rose she was aware of a vague boredom which she knew would increase before the day was through. She scowled to herself. She wasn't used to this indolent life. Even as a child, she had been physically active. On Java there had been horseback rides into the jungles and along the inland river. On board ship she used her muscles to hoist rigging and stand watch at the wheel. Here, a lady was tightly restricted as to what activities were offered her. Sirena didn't care to adopt the fashion of entertaining vendors and merchants in her suite while she attended to her toilette. In fact, there was nothing she considered more a waste of time than to sit before a mirror half the day while some simpleton dressed her hair and she puzzled over one length of cloth after another.

She longed to walk through Saint James' Park, but that was unheard of among the upper classes. Either a lady went attended in a coach or not at all. The weather still prohibited a picnic in the country where she could stretch her limbs and enjoy clear, fresh air. The prospect of spending another day indoors fell on her like a blight. Suddenly, her eyes fell on a billet sheet which had been brought in with her breakfast tray. It announced the opening of several new shops in the Royal Exchange. The idea interested her and she determined that she would go there in the company of Frau Holtz later that morning.

Frau Holtz busied herself about Sirena's room, happily looking forward to the shopping expedition. Like all other women, the prospect of perusing the many shops and bargain tables at the "Change," as it was popularly called, excited her. Mentally, she made a list of the things she wished to buy. Money was really no object for the Frau as she had been well paid throughout her years as the van der Rhys housekeeper and her needs were few. Besides, on Java, what did a woman of her status need in the way of luxuries save a few new gowns every year and a pair of sensible shoes. But the city of London fired the Frau's tastes. Her few excursions into the park and the marketplace alerted her to the fact the servants of the rich reflected their employers' tastes and pockets. She had become dissatisfied with her plain, black bombazine gowns and yearned for a frill or two at the neckline and sleeve.

Sirena turned to the looking glass for the full effect of her costume. She was wearing a new aquamarine outfit. The color of the Mediterranean, she thought when she selected the velvet fabric. The gown sported a snug-fitting jacket, deeply embossed with golden scrolls at the lapels and full sleeves. Her hair gleamed darkly against the pale color and her eyes were enhanced, looking brighter and greener from under her black lashes. Although severely tailored, the delicate hue lent a femininity to the costume. On her head she set a narrow, peaked hat with wispy veiling falling over her face and an array of exotic feathers decorating the crown. Pulling on white kid gloves, Sirena was ready to depart.

"Is the carriage ready for us, Frau Holtz?" she asked, smiling as the older woman hastened to clamp her plain hat firmly on her gray head and don her heavy, woolen cloak.

"Ja, and Jacobus is waiting for us. He thinks it all fun and games to play footman to you, Mevrouw. Sometimes I wish he'd go back to the ship," she complained. "All he does is spruce himself up in that fine livery you bought him and hang about the house all day plying cakes and pies out of Cook."

Sirena's smile broadened. "Frau Holtz, do I detect a spur of jealousy?"

"*Nein!* And why should I be jealous of the likes of him? I can't shake loose from the man! He's taken it upon himself to watch over the two of us and he does a fine job of that. Whenever I turn about, he's there. He's always underfoot! And God forbid you should return from a party or dinner later than he thinks you should, Mevrouw! Ach! The man's a fool!" she exclaimed, but Sirena noted there was a softening in her eyes when she spoke of the old man.

At the intersection of Corn Hill and Threadneedle Street stood the Royal Exchange. The immense building was in the shape of a quadrangle and encircled a courtyard and galleries that were divided into tiny shops which were attended by comely girls to draw the trade of the gallants and fops who frequented the pubs and eateries. The traffic surrounding the famous marketplace was thick and disorderly.

After a lengthy ride through town along cobblestoned streets and the various disputes with hackneys over the right of way and interminable processions of chicken carts and tallow carts and vehicles bearing every variety of goods, Jacobus' patience was at an end. "Just give a man the freedom of open water," he complained to Sirena. But she knew Jacobus would be heartbroken if she ever sent him back to the *Sea Spirit* with the rest of the crew. Jacobus would be lost without the Frau and herself to look after. He had appointed himself their guardian and he meant to see the job through, whatever the costs to his temperament.

As Sirena and Frau Holtz went into the Exchange, they were assaulted by myriad aromas coming from cookfires and heard the hawkers displaying their goods. Ascending the stairs to the top gallery with Frau Holtz close behind, Sirena pretended not to hear the compliments extended in her direction by fastidiously dressed gallants who hung about flirting with the shopgirls and unescorted ladies. Frau Holtz sniffed and sent them scourging looks as she huffed up the steps after her Mevrouw. Daunted, they left the women to their shopping and bedeviled other likely prospects.

Through the shops the women wandered, stopping now and again to examine a pair of gloves or a length of ribbon. Sirena was caught up in the enthusiasm of the Change. She bought seven pairs of gloves, each in a different color. Frau Holtz, too, was enticed by the bargains. She also bought gloves, two pairs, both black.

Stockings, feathers, fans, laces, buttons, needles, spices, exotic essences, all found their way into their packages. On the lower gallery, Sirena and Frau Holtz happily neared the end of their adventure. The Frau's feet hurt and Sirena's head ached and her nerves were taut from being jostled by the crowd. In the center of the courtyard, merchants dickered over the prices of stocks and mortgages and their prospective cargoes which were coming by ship.

Just as they were about to leave, they rounded a goldsmith's shop and Frau Holtz stopped to admire a pair of earbobs. On impulse, Sirena stepped into the stall and bought them for her friend. The jeweler looked at Sirena with a speculative eye, noting her rich dress and obvious wealth, and he said in a low voice, "If Madame would be interested in a most unusual piece of jewelry, she has come to the right shop."

Sirena glanced at him and was reminded of the wealthy old Jews who used to come to her father's house in Cádiz. She instinctively knew the goldsmith was to be trusted in the quality of his merchandise. Jewelers' reputations were more precious to their trade than diamonds. "If you would care to show me," she said, "I would be most interested."

The man's expression brightened as he glanced warily around his stall. It wouldn't be wise to advertise to the scoundrels who hung about the Change that he had something valuable in his possession. Swiftly, he bent over to bring out a box from beneath the table, and Sirena caught a glance of the spotlessly clean yarmulke covering the crown of his head. The tiny satin cap was in such contradiction to his otherwise seedy appearance that Sirena knew him to be a wealthy man under the guise of a poor merchant. She realized the goldsmith knew it was unwise to sport his comfortable circumstances.

His hands shook slightly as he raised the lid for her. "This came to me by way of the Orient, madame, and when I saw your eyes, I knew it had been crafted for you." Sirena's eyes were fixed on the jewels which lay on a bed of black velvet. There was the most spectacular piece of jade jewelry she had ever seen. It was in the shape of a mandarin dragon with two glowing rubies for eyes. The craftmanship of the pendant and gold chain were exquisite.

Thinking of the gown she had commissioned Mrs. Wittcomb to create for her out of the serpentine silk,

Sirena knew she must have the piece. "You are truthful, sir. It is by far the most beautiful necklace I've ever seen." Her voice was excited and, try as she might, she could not disguise the thrill the object caused in her. She knew it was bad bargaining to allow the merchant to see this, yet she would gladly pay thrice what the pendant was worth to wear it with the gown.

Breathlessly, she told the merchant where she lived and invited him to come by. He introduced himself as Solomon Levy and gave her one of his cards. When Sirena reluctantly placed the royal dragon back in its case and walked away with Frau Holtz, Solomon Levy smiled with satisfaction. He certainly could pick a likely prospect, he congratulated himself. The jade was beautiful, rare and worth every cent Sirena would pay for it.

Goldsmith Levy was an honest businessman with insight as to character and means. When Sirena hadn't inquired about the price, he knew she could afford whatever he asked.

Tucking the box safely beneath the table again, he thought to himself that it had been a profitable day. He experienced a small regret at having sold the pendant. Sometimes at night, when he was all alone and safe from prying eyes, he would take out the velvet box and look at the Chinese jade in the flickering light of a candle. His consolation in losing this enjoyment was that Sirena was as lovely as the pendant itself.

Frau Holtz and Sirena bustled out of the Change, laden with packages. "You wait here, Mevrouw," the Frau said. "Look at the filth on the streets. You'll ruin your shoes. I'll go and fetch Jacobus and the carriage. *I* wear sensible shoes!"

Sirena succumbed to the Frau's mothering. "All right, but leave the parcels with me so you won't have to carry them around." Looking up at the sky, she muttered, "It looks like rain. We'd better get home as soon as we can. I've heard of carriages turning over on the slick cobbles."

"*Ja,* I hurry!"

Standing alone, Sirena ignored the inquisitive glances and bawdy appeals directed at her, a lady without escort or companion. Across Threadneedle Street carriages were lined up waiting for their charges. Sirena strained to see if her coach was among them. A chill washed over her which she attributed to the sun going behind clouds and the change in the air. From out of the corner of her eye, she saw a hired hackney pull out of line on Threadneedle Street and block the traffic behind it. The drivers swore epithets at the impeding vehicle, which seemed to be having some sort of difficulty. Just then, Jacobus came up behind her.

"I'll take those packages off your hands, Capitana," he said softly, relieving Sirena of her burden. "We'll have to cross the road. Corn Hill's impassable; there's been an accident."

Jacobus stepped into the street, Sirena behind him, her thoughts on the royal dragon. When she was nearly across, the hired hack drew into the road, the team of horses broke into a gallop, their driver whipping them into a frenzy. They were almost upon her before she saw them and then it was too late.

Whinnying, snorting, the steeds came. She looked up and saw the dark driver with whip raised, standing with his cloak billowing about him. In that instant, Sirena saw death!

Jacobus saw it, too. He threw the packages away from himself and rushed back to Sirena, tumbling her to the ground and knocking her out of harm's way. The coach plunged forward, the thundering of the horses' hooves loud on the cobblestones.

It was a full minute before Sirena and Jacobus collected themselves to get to their feet. Numerous passersby looked on, but none offered aid. Sirena's velvet suit was ruined; the filth of the gutter staining it beyond repair. Her hands were scraped right through her gloves and she had twisted her ankle painfully.

Jacobus inquired if she had been injured. "I'll be fine, good friend, but what of yourself?"

"I'm only glad I'm not too old to take swift action. You were very nearly killed, Capitana! I swear that vehicle bore down on you with intent!"

"Nonsense, you're imagining things!" she scowled,

remembering something vaguely familiar about the driver of the onrushing hackney.

"Don't tell me nonsense, Capitana. I saw it myself!"

Embarrassed by the commotion she had caused, Sirena was grateful to see her carriage round the corner and drive up to where she and Jacobus were standing.

"Liebchen!" Frau Holtz cried, "what happened? You old fool!" she scolded Jacobus, "what did you do to her!"

"He saved my life, is what he did," Sirena stammered, still shaken. "Move over Frau Holtz, Jacobus has had as much a shock as I did. I want him inside with us."

"Ja, ja," the Frau uttered, a new respect for Jacobus in her eyes.

When they had settled in the coach and were on their way home, Sirena thought of her near miss with death. She must keep her wits about her in this city, she scolded herself. London is a busy place and can be cruel to those who don't keep their mind on the affairs at hand.

Sirena rested her head against the plush interior. The vision of the hackney and its wild, heavily cloaked driver pierced her thoughts. There was something about him she found familiar. Was it the size of him, or the set of his shoulders or the tilt of his head? She sighed and admonished herself for being fanciful. Perhaps it was because of her interest in the arts of self-defense. Fencing required her to develop a certain perception of the way a man moved, his height, his agility. Somehow the driver of the hack reminded her of someone but, for the life of her, she couldn't think who it was!

The ride from Drury Lane to Tyler's offices on New Queen Street should not have taken over half an hour, as Camilla knew quite well. But just before she left the house, dark clouds had descended over London and the populace prepared for the oncoming storm. Hackneys and coaches jammed the streets as people rushed toward home before the downpour obliterated the kennels in the streets and sewage and filth floated about, foul-smelling obstacles to foot and vehicle. Checking the tiny timepiece pinned to her dress, she realized she had been riding for forty-five minutes and was still quite some distance from Tyler's office.

In the gloom of midday Camilla tried to relax. As a native of London, she knew it was useless to prod the driver to hurry or to curse the weather. She lifted the paper shade covering the mud-spattered window and looked out. If anything, the sky grew blacker, the impending rain making the air thick and still. Suddenly, the hackney came to a stop and she leaned forward to see what the trouble was. There, coming out of St. Bride's Lane, was a cart rigged with wooden slats that made it a cage. Inside was a woman, her hair matted with filth and her body emaciated. Camilla shuddered, knowing the cart was taking the poor soul across London to the Bethlehem Royal Hospital, popularly known as Bedlam.

Camilla watched, mesmerized by the woman's suffering. Her rags hung in tatters, revealing her scrawny form and the raw, bleeding sores across her upper chest and bony arms. A sign on the cart stated that it belonged to Bridewell, a combination prison and hospital for women and children. Desperation and panic clutched at Camilla's heart. The vacant apathy and confusion in the eyes of the incarcerated woman brought back fearsome memories Camilla had thought were long forgotten.

How many years ago had it been when she had seen that same vacant terror in her own mother's eyes? She had been only a child, no more than ten. "Mother is very ill, dear," she could still hear her father's voice. "Papa is going to put her in a hospital where they can help her."

"No, no! Please, Papa, don't take Mummy away! Please, Papa, I'll watch over her, don't take Mummy away!" But he had. Stephan had explained to his young daughter in the gentlest of terms that Lady Langdon needed more than the loving care of her family. She needed expert help. Help she would receive from the doctors at the Bethlehem Royal Hospital.

Camilla squeezed her eyes shut against the vivid memory of that last afternoon when she had run into her mother's room and threw herself into her arms in spite of the nurse's protests. But there had been no answering embrace, no loving kiss.

And when, at the last, Stephan had led Lady Langdon down the stairs and into the carriage, Camilla had hated him. Hated him for the times he had spoken bitterly to his wife. Hated him for the cries in the night that had awakened the little girl from her sleep. Hated him for always being a kind, loving father, yet a bitter, cruel husband to the gentle Lady Langdon.

When Camilla looked into the street again, her coach had begun to move and the cart from Bridewell had passed on. Surprised to find her cheeks stained with tears, Camilla searched in her reticule for a handkerchief. The pain was still there, the loneliness of a child missing her mother was still able to come up from the bottom of her soul and engulf her in a black web of helplessness.

Camilla loved her father, Stephan Langdon, in the emotional, all-encompassing way an only child loves her sole surviving parent. She blinded herself to his shortcomings, turned a deaf ear to his outrages and attributed to him all the endearing qualities of a storybook prince. Even their constant financial difficulties she did not really blame on his penchant for gambling and his inbred lack of responsibility. Rather, she believed him when he decried his bad luck. Even being hungry did not daunt her affection for him. If there was no food, they starved together. If they were besieged by creditors; they banded together; if they were homeless, they were homeless together. The only thing she had ever come to count upon in life was his true affection for her, and she rewarded this with her loyalty.

And yet, whenever confronted with a reminder that there was such a place as Bedlam, Camilla experienced a deep-seated hatred for Stephan. It had become the fashion among the gallants and popinjays to pay a penny and tour the asylum to gawk at the miserable inmates. Camilla always constricted with fear and dread as she listened to these tales with a macabre interest. To this day, she did not believe Stephan was *forced* to commit her once lovely mother to that institution. She harbored the niggling belief it was because Stephan wanted his wife out of the way.

As Camilla squeezed her eyes shut again against the boiling brew of mixed emotions which welled up inside her, she had the familiar recurring memory of Lady Langdon laying in her husband's arms without protest as he carried her to the waiting coach, her eyes vacant and staring. Camilla remembered thinking how easily her father had lifted her mother. How delicate and thin she had been, a mere shadow of the lovely, bright-eyed girl whose portrait hung over the mantle in the parlor. And, at the last, when Stephan had closed the carriage door and turned back to the house, Lady Langdon had turned to look at her daughter who was standing in the open doorway, tears running down her face. For the first time in months, Camilla saw her mother make a voluntary movement. Slowly, ever so slowly, the thin, skeletal hand reached up to wave good-bye.

Stephan must have seen a change in Camilla's expression, for he immediately asked, "What is it? What did you see?" and quickly turned to look back at the carriage. For a reason she'd never been able to explain, not even to herself, Camilla looked at Stephan and said, "Nothing, Father. I saw nothing!"

But her little girl's eyes had followed the vehicle down the drive and into the street, waiting for her mother to turn back and look after her. She never did.

By the time Camilla's hackney turned onto New Queen Street, she had made the necessary repairs to her appearance. All traces of tears were gone and she had smoothed and straightened her deep-brown velvet gown. Tyler loved her in dark, rich colors; she had worn the gown expressly for him.

Tyler happened to be looking out his window down onto New Queen Street when Camilla arrived. He was surprised to see her out on such a rainy afternoon. He knew Camilla abhorred thunder and, from the looks of the sky, thunder seemed more than likely. Sourly, he thought to himself, the only thing that could drag Camilla out on a day like this was the need for cash. Tyler mentally calculated how much he could spare her and took a quick glance into his billfold. Since turning that quick bit of profit by selling van der Rhys back his own cargo, it was a good deal more than she would ever expect. Aware of her suspicious nature, he decided he would only give her ten or twelve pounds. It wouldn't do to have Camilla or her sly father poking about in his affairs. All it would take was the smell of money and they would delve into his activities like gophers in a turnip patch.

It was only a minute before he heard her enter the outer office. He smiled to himself as he opened the door and saw his clerk, Whipple, stammering and gawking at Camilla, trying to speak intelligently. Whenever Camilla came to the office, Whipple acted like an ass.

"Hello, darling," she breathed when she noticed Tyler. "Have I come at a bad time for you? Now, you haven't been overworking sweet Mr. Whipple, have you? The poor dear seems overwrought." She smiled in Whipple's direction and the young man's pimples glowed fiercely beneath his blushes. Camilla knew full well the effect she had on the skinny clerk and she reveled in it.

"Not at all, sweetheart," Tyler said, motioning her into his office. As he closed the door behind him, he laughed, "Tell me, Camilla, do you come in here to practice your charms on unwitting Whipple? It's a blasted sin what you do to his nerves. The youth's complexion will never clear if you keep at it."

Camilla laughed, the sound light and girlish and tinkling with gaiety. "Don't be silly, darling, how could little me have such a devastating effect?" she pouted, her eyes sparkling.

"You little pagan, you know you love it when I accuse you of being a *femme fatale,*" Tyler smiled affectionately.

Sighing, Camilla kissed Tyler lightly on the cheek. "You know me so well, dearest, it's a wonder you still like me."

Roughly, Tyler pulled her into his arms, kissing her sweet mouth with savage earnestness. Then, holding her away from him, he teased, "Now that you've gotten what you came for, get away with you and let me be on with my accounts."

Undaunted, Camilla patted her hair back into place and adjusted the brim of her flowered hat. "Tyler, you know why I'm here. Don't make a muddle of it. Father's been having a turn of ill luck at the tables and I'm near to starving! Can you spare me enough to buy a good meal!"

Tyler laughed aloud. "Really, Camilla, from the bloom on your cheeks I wouldn't say you were starving!"

"That's only because I've not taken to eating my red Spanish paper. The bloom you see, dear, is artificial, applied with a deft hand. Believe me, Tyler, I'm starving!"

"Don't burden me with your affairs; go tell your Dutchman. He's more able to fatten you up than I am."

"Darling," Camilla pleaded, "you're not going to be tiresome and have me beg, are you?"

"No, sweetheart, I'm not. Will ten pounds see you over? It's all I can spare right now. It's near the end of the month and Whipple tells me he's taken up the nasty habit of eating right along with the rest of us. It would be a shame to stint the chap of his earnings."

"Ten pounds?" Camilla asked, obviously not caring whether Whipple received his salary or not. "Can't you do better than that? I'm telling you, Tyler, the larder is empty!"

"Twelve pounds, then."

"Fifteen, not a penny less!"

As Tyler pulled the extra five-pound note out of his pocket, he said seriously, "Camilla, sweet, do you always get what you want?"

"Whenever I set my mind to it," she replied, snatching the fiver out of his fingers and looking with interest at his half-opened billfold.

"I think that's what I admire most about you. You set your sights on something and you go after it."

"Father's training," Camilla murmured as she poked the notes into her reticule. "You're certain you can't spare any more, Tyler. My seamstress is badgering me for payment."

"I'll feed you, Camilla, but I won't clothe you. In

a matter of weeks van der Rhys will see to both," he scowled.

"Darling, you're jealous!"

"Bloody well right I'm jealous! If your dear father hadn't such an influence over you, things might be different between us. Mother never objected to the fact that you were penniless, Camilla, only to the fact that you're a little schemer and you'd do anything for your father. Even to the point of selling every one of us Sinclairs down on pauper's row."

"Not *all* the Sinclairs, darling, even a white slaver wouldn't have the Baroness and I doubt the wisest Jew could profit a penny from your doddering old father. Only you, sweet, would bring a handsome profit. I can see you being set loose in the streets of Verona and making your fortune as a gigolo to an Italian Countess." She tossed her yellow curls and giggled, "Remember, I can speak for your talents, darling." She stepped closer to him and trailed her hand down his chest, feeling his heart beating wildly beneath her touch. His hand came up and imprisoned hers and they looked into each other's eyes with a world of longing between them.

Suddenly, a low rumble sounded outside the window and a flash of lightning streaked the sky. Camilla stiffened and buried her face in Tyler's chest, clinging tightly. His arms went around her, feeling the trembling slimness of her, the childlike framework beneath her budding womanhood. At last, she raised her head, tears glistening in her eyes and Tyler was drowning in the droplets skimming down her cheeks. They kissed, tongues touching, breaths mingling, urgent needs blending. And they were lost in one another as they had been when they were little more than children.

Masterfully, Tyler led Camilla to the wide, leather couch in a dim corner of the room. He had not lit the lamps before the start of the storm and the gray halo of light penetrating the windows gave a feeling of intimacy and solitude to the spacious office.

Somewhere between hungry kisses, Tyler had removed his vest along with Camilla's light jacket. And she, impatient with her cumbersome skirts, had slipped them to the floor, leaving on only her chemise and petticoat.

Claiming his lips with her own, she pushed him down on the couch and settled herself in his lap. Under the warm pressure of her thighs, desire was renewed in Tyler. Her tongue slowly followed the outline of his mouth, moistening it, penetrating it. A tremor passed through her to Tyler and she seized his hand, which was resting on her knees, and brought it against her breast.

He could feel the perfect symmetry beneath his fingers. His left arm made a support for her back and Camilla arched herself toward him. The purity of her breasts when he pulled her chemise to her waist astonished him. It had been so long since they were together like this. Not since immediately before Regan came to London. Her skin was a glowing white that seemed almost luminous in the dimness of the room. Slowly, very slowly, despite his lusty impatience, which he was having difficulty restraining, his fingers grazed her satin skin. Her petticoats rucked up and Tyler was excited by a glimpse of a creamy thigh above her stocking.

Fiercely, Tyler cupped her face and kissed her with breathtaking swiftness. Beneath her legs Camilla was aware of his passion for her and of the building need within herself for Tyler. He felt the change in her, felt her rosy crest stiffen beneath his palm, felt the heat from her loins and knew a sense of power over her. He could never get enough of her. The freshness of her skin, the delicate paleness of her hair, the sweet spareness of her breasts and torso; all of her was created to entice him, fever his desires, quell his want for any other woman. And when she was beneath him and her legs clung fiercely to his hips, he knew a sense of coming home. Of a familiar welcome, of a path much traveled and greatly loved. His brown eyes burned with exaltation when he entered her and she trembled beneath him, opening herself to him. Camilla moaned softly, relishing the weight of him. Loving it when he talked to her, whispered to her, told her how he enjoyed her, loved her body, the feel of her. And Tyler knew her almost better than she did herself.

Others could be confounded by her unpredictability, but her moods were like phrases in an often read book to Tyler. He loved her in spite of herself.

He crushed her mouth beneath his, savoring the fullness of her lips, tasting the nectar of her passions. And when he leaned near her ear, he whispered in throaty tones intimate things, bawdy phrases, sultry words.

He withdrew from her, and entered again so forcefully, she cried out and raked his back with her nails, knowing what his next move would be. Tyler rolled over onto his back, bringing her with him, both still firmly joined.

Camilla's heart pounded violently, her tumultuous breathing heaving her breast. "Oh, Tyler, we are made for each other; we are like hand in glove." She looked down at him, at the adoration there in his face. She was aware of his hands, possessing her, driving her to the brink of ecstasy. She felt his muscular torso between her knees and the heat where their flesh joined. And when they both approached the apex of desire, Tyler gently laid her under him once again. He covered her mouth with his as she began to cry out for fulfillment and together they soared and spun out beyond the stars, seeing the moon with rapture in their eyes.

The rain was pelting against the windows as Camilla fussed with her hair and completed the buttons on her jacket. Another sudden clap of thunder unnerved her. If the sky had opened up and lightning had rained down upon London when she and Tyler were locked in each other's arms, she had not been aware of it. She didn't care for the thought of traveling across town in a hired hack while the elements still crashed, but there was no help for it. If she was to get home in time to pay Cook and lay in ample provisions, she would have to leave immediately. Her innards were already growling in protest over the scanty breakfast she had had.

"Are you certain you want to leave right away, Camilla?" Tyler asked. "I know how much you detest storms."

"Yes, but I detest starvation even more. Really, I

must depart. Before I do, though, have I thanked you for your little loan?"

"More than adequately, sweetheart," Tyler kept his voice light and even. Yet Camilla perceived a hint of contempt edging his words and looked at him inquisitively.

"You're quite a girl, Camilla. One can always say you never take without giving. You always pay somehow or other for what you get, don't you?"

Fury fired Camilla's eyes. "I'd like to think this afternoon was worth more than fifteen pounds to you, Tyler," she said caustically.

"I could have gotten the same and more down on Rotten Row for a shilling," he lied, wanting to hurt her.

"Then it's to there you should go, Tyler. And a pox be on you!" her temper flared. "How would you like it if I dropped it in the Baroness' ear that her son frequents the whorehouses in the slums?"

Tyler laughed. "I wouldn't do that, Camilla. My mother is apt to ask you where on Rotten Row your father has opened a house for you."

"You pig!" Camilla screamed, slapping Tyler soundly across the face. "Perhaps I should let all be damned and confess to your beloved parents that we've been married for nearly three years now and you're simply waiting for them to pass on to their reward to claim me as your bride!"

"What, and have me disinherited? Camilla, you shock me," Tyler remarked scornfully. "When I wanted to tell my parents, you and your father talked me out of it. 'Don't do it,' he said, and like a fool I listened to him! I tought it was *my* skin he was saving, but we both know that's not true. I would be ostracized, disinherited and, along with me, your father would find himself resting in the dung heap! It was his own skin he was watching out for. He knew my parents would banish him from their society and the only reason he is acceptable at all among his peers is that he has my father's endorsement. Without that he'd be cast out of those fashionable drawing rooms like a leper!

"Besides, I'm interested to see to what lengths you'd

go to please your Papa. I'll reach my majority of twenty-five in two years' time and that is when I intend to lay my claim to you. Whether you're married to van der Rhys or not! I'll come forward and demand you, Camilla. I have warned you before and you don't seem to believe me."

"You wouldn't dare! You agreed to pretend our marriage never happened. My father paid thousands to have the records obliterated! You couldn't prove a thing!"

"Ah, sweetheart, but I could. You forget the marriage paper both you and I signed, and I'm happy to say your father's signature giving his consent is also present. I have that document, Camilla, and I'll use it. You know how little I care for society. I much prefer my parents' country estate. And a little scandal never harmed a man's acceptability. It's you and your father who will suffer. I've begged you not to go through with this farce, but you insist. You refuse to stand up to Stephan Langdon. Then pay, Camilla, pay by never knowing when I will strike."

"You'll never have the chance! My father would kill you first!" Her eyes blazed, her skin flushed, yet her voice was smoothly controlled. "Only this morning father told me he'd make a widow of me. Beware, Tyler, you know as well as I what he is capable of doing when crossed." Swiftly turning on her heel, she stamped from his office, slamming the door behind her.

Tyler smiled, chuckled, then broke into a raucous laugh. The Langdons both thought Regan was far wealthier than he was in reality. Everything he had been able to secure from Sirena's holdings he had poured into his business. It also occurred to Tyler that Regan thought the Langdons well endowed with property and stocks. He laughed again, the sound bounding hollowly off the walls. They deserved each other, he thought, and he intended to be somewhere about when they learned the truth concerning each other's state of affairs.

Tyler stepped over to the window and looked out. Camilla was just stepping into the hackney carriage. He experienced a knot of jealousy deep in his gut. There was no sense to it, but he knew he loved her.

He probably always would. Why couldn't he pull himself up by his bootstraps and go to his parents and tell them the truth? What difference if they did disinherit him?

Sadly, he knew the truth. The difference lay in the fact that if he were penniless Camilla wouldn't have him. The only small satisfaction he could reap from the whole stinking situation was that Camilla was marrying Regan for the money, not for the man.

Chapter Sixteen

The trees in Saint James' Park burst into bud and then into bloom. King Street, which passed in front of Sirena's house, became a well-traveled thoroughfare as spring spun greenly toward summer. The ladies of London dug through their wardrobes for lighter gowns of pastel colors. Seamstresses experienced the usual rush for their handiwork. Coaches were polished to gleaming, their matched equine beasts curried to perfection. London was wearing the mantle of sunlight and flora like a new bonnet, and a sense of celebration freshened the air.

Sirena was becoming well known in aristocratic circles. When Stephan Langdon wasn't on her arm, it was Tyler Sinclair. Many other prospective suitors sought her company and she often obliged; but when they would promise her their undying love, she would gently and thoroughly put them aside. She had no wish to enter a relationship with any of them. Tyler was a friend and she enjoyed his company; it was strictly a platonic relationship and Tyler never pressed it further. For this, she was grateful. Stephan, on the other hand, was a perfect gallant, but he never insisted on her kisses or to strengthen their companionship. He sometimes seemed intimidated by her, almost cautious, as though a false move on his part would find him cast from her society.

Stephan enjoyed being Sirena's almost constant escort. His status in the social whirl climbed, and he did not fool himself for a moment that it was his charming self who was welcome at the balls and intimate soirées. It was Sirena and her endorsement by the Baron and Baroness and, of course, her money.

Sirena found herself in demand as every hostess requested her presence whenever they entertained. In return, Sirena repaid their hospitality with lavish balls and elegant dinners that were the envy of the entire city. She spared no expense on food and music. Her gowns were the most stylish and beautiful, and her entertainments gracious without ever being gauche.

Tyler watched her budding romance with Langdon with a cautious eye. He wanted to tell her what he knew about Stephan, but decided against it. Sirena was capable of taking care of herself, and would probably resent his interference.

"Nine more days till Camilla's wedding," Tyler moaned through clenched teeth. How was he to attend that bogus affair and behave as though there were never anything between himself and Camilla. For a moment he felt pity for van der Rhys. The poor man was getting it from all ends. Then he experienced a bitter bite of hatred for Regan because he was taking Camilla for his own; would share her bed and know her intimately; would learn to know how satiny those girlishly round arms would feel around his neck; would be offered those smooth, white charms and alluring lips. Tyler still loved her; there was no point in denying it. He was helpless. If his parents ever discovered his youthful marriage, they would disinherit him without a second thought. They loved him; they indulged him in all but this. He knew, without doubt, they meant what they said. Until he reached his majority, there was nothing he could do.

How often he had dreamed of proclaiming to the world that Camilla was his wife and inheritance be damned. Yet, while it would free him from this paralyzing agony of loving her and being unable to claim her, it would also be his total undoing.

The lights on the Thames reflected in the inky water like thousands of fireflies. It was the middle of May and the Royal Flotilla was a highlight of the season. Each year, according to tradition, the King, his Court and invited guests, would gather at the Whitehall Privy Stairs, where hundreds of barges and small craft took on their passengers for a leisurely cruise on the river accompanied to minstrels' rhymes and music. All along the route torches blazed, guiding the way. On the banks the citizenry gathered en masse for a glimpse of their sovereign and his party. Finally, when the flotilla passed beneath London Bridge, the passengers would disembark for food and drink on the bridge itself and dance to the minstrels' jaunty tunes.

Because Tyler's parents, the Baron and Baroness, were abroad in Scotland, he took Sirena to the annual event with their invitations. The night had been warm, yet the air was fresh with the salt breeze from the Channel. King Charles had been most charming to his guests and roamed among them freely, wishing them welcome.

The cruise had been a gay affair and Sirena was still laughing at some ridiculous remark of Tyler's when they walked along Thames Street to find Tyler's carriage. The vehicles were lined up and down the thoroughfare, even extending up Bridge Street and onto Fish. It reminded Sirena, suddenly, of the commotion outside the Change where she had very nearly been run down by the mysterious hackney. Even as she thought of it, her blood ran cold and chills coursed up her spine. She had no reason to suspect it had been deliberate, but the occurrence had come back time and again to haunt her dreams.

"Come back here, ye filthy little sniper!" A man's angry voice rang over the distant celebration coming from London Bridge. Tyler immediately pulled Sirena closer to him, protecting her against an unseen threat. This particular section of London was notorious for beggars and thieves. "Come back here!" the loud masculine voice sounded again.

Without warning, from around the corner of St. Martin's Lane came a barely distinguishable form, careening at breakneck speed directly toward them. Beneath the light of flaring links, it was only possible to perceive it was a child, tattered and ragged, wild-eyed with terror, running away from a pursuer. Behind the child raced a footman, the gold braid on his livery gleaming, the light glancing off the heavy cudgel he waved in the air. "I'll get ye, stinking little hellion!"

Unexpectedly, the hurling figure of the child ran directly into Sirena, becoming tangled in her skirt. In that one, brief instant, Sirena looked into the face of a little girl, not more than ten. Frantically, the child tried to disengage herself. Sirena gathered her close, protectively, smelling the rank odor of unwashed hair and filthy rags. The girl looked behind her, shrieking in terror as her pursuer gained ground.

"Please, Mum, let me go! He'll kill me for sure!"

Looking down, Sirena saw a tangle of curly, brown hair and a thin petite face whose dark, shoe-button eyes were too large for it. Not only was there terror in those eyes, but a stricken expression of mistrust and loneliness, the look of the hunted animal. Twisting in Sirena's arms, the child was gone as suddenly as she had come, running down the street on tiny feet which were bare to the elements. The liveried footman came abreast of Tyler, the expression on his face vicious.

"Tyler! Stop him!" Sirena shouted. The thought of what this burly, rough-hewn man could do to that fragile child was abhorrent to her.

Instantly, Tyler imprisoned the footman, wrestling him down to the ground. They struggled for a while before the servant realized he was resisting a member of the gentry. The footman offered no further resistance and quickly lay still beneath Tyler's grasp. "I'm sorry, sir," he uttered. "You can let me up now."

When Tyler stood, the footman jumped up and began brushing at his clothes, murmuring over and over again how sorry he was to inconvenience the gentleman.

"That's not important now," Sirena said angrily. "I want to know why you were chasing that child?"

The footman stopped what he was doing and said, "I'm sorry to have troubled ye, milady. But the filthy little urchin was hiding in my master's carriage and cutting the brass buttons off the seat cushions, she was.

When I caught her at it, she spit right in me eye! Little trashmonger!" he said scornfully.

"Watch the way you speak to the lady," Tyler warned.

Immediately, the footman lowered his head. It would never do to go against the gentry, that was a lesson he had learned early in life. A rough boy from the slums of Whitefriars didn't become footman to a nobleman by bucking the classes.

"And where were you, that the girl was able to slip into the coach?" Tyler asked. "I'd be willing to wager you were visiting a nearby taproom, eh?" From the way the man shifted, Sirena knew Tyler had hit the mark.

"I was feeling a terrible thirst, milord," the footman excused. "I merely chased the beggar to retrieve the ornaments. I've a wife and four young'uns to support. Them buttons are worth a half-year's wages! My master won't be pleased, sir, not pleased at all," he whined, glancing off in the direction the child had taken.

"Give him five pounds, Tyler, that should more than cover the cost. I won't have him chasing after the poor little thing when we turn our backs."

Tyler reached into his pocket and withdrew a gold sovereign. "The lady's being much too generous with you," he scowled. "I, for one, would have your master discover what a sluggard you are. Here," he said, pressing the coin into the footman's palm. "Now, be on your way and leave the mite be. After you've seen to new buttons, there's more than enough left for your trouble."

"Yes, sir. Thank ye, milady," he stammered obsequiously, as he bowed and turned off in the direction of his coach on St. Martin's Lane.

In the Sinclair coach Tyler watched Sirena. Evidently, the scene with the little girl and the footman had upset her. He had seen a bit of the tiger in her as she protected the waif from the footman.

Sirena knew Tyler was concerned by this sudden silence of hers. Yet, she could not help herself. Somehow the dark, bright eyes of the small child became confused with her memories of Mikel. Mikel, her baby. Beyond the fact they were both children, there was no similarity between the gaunt, dirty beggar with her springy mop of dark curls and the plump, precocious, fair-haired Mikel. Yet, the waif had struck a long, silent chord of motherhood in Sirena and brought with it all the pain of her loss and the need to feel a child near her once more.

She squeezed her eyes shut and barely controlled the shudders of sorrow reborn as she remembered the touch of her son's arms about her neck, the brightness of his smile, the warm, fragrant scent of his hair and the smoothness of his plump cheek beneath her lips. Her heart cried out, her body rebelled at this hollowness, her breasts craved the feel of a child's head resting against it in sleep.

Thankfully, the carriage pulled into the drive; and, before Tyler could disembark and help her down onto the cobbled drive, Sirena tore out of the vehicle and ran past him into the house. The tears had welled up within her and threatened to bellow forth in a scream of anguish. Up the stairs she raced, nearly tripping on her skirts, twisting an ankle, nearly toppling over on her head, till she reached the solitude of her room where she could cry out her rage and enmity to the fates who had taken Mikel.

Jacobus settled himself comfortably beneath the sycamore tree in the garden and watched through rum-soaked eyes the progress the workmen were making. He wondered vaguely if he should offer to help. One look at the bottle clutched in his hand and his decision was made. Why work when he could drink? Completely satisfied with his decision, he brought the jug to his lips and guzzled greedily.

The sound of furious cursing woke the seaman from his half-drunken sleep. His hand still clutched around the handle of the jug, he opened a bleary eye, and grimaced. Hell's bells, now what? He forced his other eye to open and looked around. Was it too much to ask to get a little sleep? An unsavory lot if he ever saw one, he thought virtuously. Paid to work and they spent their time arguing. He vowed to bring the matter to the Capitana's attention as soon as he could get his land legs to working.

He was drunk, he decided, and this was no time to go to the Capitana with anything. For now all he could do was sit and hold his hands to his head to ease the pounding between his ears. Dastardly lot of men. A motion in the thick yew bushes to his left drew his attention and he squinted to see if it was Frau Holtz on his trail with another of her make-believe errands. Ever since she told him what her first name was he knew she meant business. She was not the type of person ever to reveal that fact unless she planned to marry him.

He blinked his watery eyes again. It couldn't be, he must be seeing things, he mumbled to himself as he rubbed at his eyes to clear his vision. Dick Blackheart! Next thing he would be seeing was flying angels with harps. The Frau had warned him that when he started seeing things it meant his mind was being eaten by the liquor. What did a crazy old woman know about visions and rum?

Struggling to his knees, his hands still clutching the bottle, he tried to creep nearer to the hedges. It was Dick Blackheart and he would wager his drink against anything anyone wanted to put up against it that he was right. "Damn and blast," he grumbled. "You there!" he yelled. "What's your business here?"

The figure looked up, then quietly withdrew into the thicket of greenery. When Jacobus opened his eyes again the man had disappeared. He glared at the rum bottle and then tossed it into the hedge. If seeing Blackheart was what rum was going to do to him he would give it up. From now on it was the love of a good woman and strong black coffee. He grinned to himself as he cradled his head in the crook of his arm and was asleep instantly.

In the meantime, Sirena walked beside Frau Holtz, nodding approvingly at the preparations behind her mansion for the party she was holding that evening. The previous owners of the dwelling had seen to it that the grounds were a tribute to horticulture, and

Sirena had hired several proficient gardeners to follow suit.

The weather had held and the lush grasses underfoot were dry. Early spring blooms had burst into color in neat borders surrounding carefully pruned shrubbery. Michaelmas daisies had been brought in, it being too early in the season for their delicate simplicity, and were bowing gracefully in the gentle breezes. The fruit trees and ornamentals sported new green foliage; but most spectacular of all was a strange blossomed tree which one of the gardeners had told her was a raintree. Its leaves were like feathers of spun gold and it held and reflected the sunlight like the armor of a warrior god. The bottom branches dipped in the attitude of a swan, and it was beneath this spectacular sentinel Sirena had ordered the construction of a dais for the musicians.

Long tables covered with exquisite lace cloths were placed in a row alongside the house. Later they would be laden with pheasant, turkey, breast of lamb, racks of veal and succulent hams. "I did as you asked and told the cooks to flavor the sweets with nutmeg, Mevrouw," Frau Holtz smiled. "The Mynheer will think he is back on Java. Even the decorations you have chosen will bring him back to the East Indies. Chinese paper lanterns, the flowers, even the musicians you've hired."

"And you'll never know how difficult it was, Frau Holtz, to find them. Jacobus was the one who suggested trying the wharf for ships coming in from the Indies. He says most sailors are fair musicians. Luckily, a ship arrived carrying several Javanese sailors and two from Bali. I should think their performance will offer a touch of the exotic to the affair."

"Not to mention making the Mynheer homesick," Frau Holtz snorted, plainly indicating she did not think Regan worth the trouble. "All this foolishness! If the people in England would put their mind to work instead of play there wouldn't be so many beggars roaming the streets. All I ever hear is parties, balls, dinners! And now this!"

Sirena laughed. "I take it you don't approve of masquerade balls?"

"Bah! As if these people need the excuse to pretend to be something they're not! And what will the Mynheer appear as? A sheep? And that child he intends to marry, will she dress as a shepherdess? Bah!" Suddenly Frau Holtz was sorry she had mentioned Regan. Sirena's eyes took on a pained expression and the anticipation of being in Regan's company showed in the strained lines surrounding her mouth.

The smile left Sirena's face. "Regan will marry in just six days," she said softly. "I thought for a time he wouldn't go through with it, but he is. I've heard of the lavish preparations being made for their wedding. It's said no expense is being spared. Tell me, Frau Holtz, how can I attend this ceremony and behave as though it meant nothing to me? I've lost him completely," she whispered, "forever."

The old housekeeper's face was bitter. "You will do what you must do. Just as you have always done."

Tears glistened in Sirena's bottle-green eyes. "It was different in the past. I had a hate and vengeance in me then. It was what kept me alive. And when Mikel was born, I had my babe to clasp to my breast and give me comfort. Now it's all gone and I have nothing."

"You will always have me, Mevrouw," the elderly woman said haltingly, trying to keep the tears from her voice. "There are still comforts I can bring you."

"You are my friend, and whatever would I do without you and Jacobus and the others," Sirena said softly. "Frau Holtz, I've been thinking. After Regan's wedding would you like to return to Batavia? Once the marriage takes place I will know there is nothing left for me here."

"Mevrouw, I am an old woman, but I know that it is not possible to run away from life. You're only tormenting yourself. What will you do in Batavia? There's nothing there for you now."

"I could help rebuild the island. There is still much to be done since havoc struck when the volcanoes erupted. But, you're correct, there's nothing there anymore. Or anywhere else, for that matter. I'm a wanderer without roots, no ties. What good is all the wealth in the world if there is no one to share it with?

What use beauty and jewels if there is only emptiness? Even Caleb has deserted me. He has not even come to see me once since I last saw him in Spain. I know he's here in England. Jacobus told me the *Rana* is berthed at the wharf."

"Perhaps he feels he would only upset you by visiting here. Don't doubt that Caleb loves you, Mevrouw," the housekeeper soothed.

"Yes," Sirena sighed dejectedly. "After the miserable way I treated him aboard the *Rana,* I can't really blame him for staying away." Suddenly, Sirena gripped Frau Holtz's wrist, a world of emotion brimming from her eyes. "All I ever wanted was for Regan to love me! When he needed me, after Mikel died, did I really turn from him?"

Frau Holtz gathered Sirena close to her, patting her gently, clucking soothing noises. "Hush, Mevrouw, if you did fail him, the same could be said for the Mynheer."

"How can I face Regan again? Each time I see him, my heart breaks all over again!" The scene in Regan's room when she had waited for him, bubbled up within her. She knew if she gave in to her desolation, it would destroy her, resign her forever to a place where life had no meaning and the needs of the heart were buried beneath a legion of regrets.

Frau Holtz felt Sirena's spine stiffen beneath her ministering hands. And when she looked into her Mevrouw's face, her generous, mobile mouth was pinched with determination and the emerald eyes were flashing with resolution. "*Ja,* this is better. Tonight you must be in his company and your paths will often cross. You will not wear your heart on your sleeve; you will keep up this charade as long as you must!" The housekeeper's voice became gruff as she led her mistress back to the house. "A little nap, you will take, to make your eyes sparkle."

Through the house and up to her room, Sirena walked on leaden feet. She lay staring at the ceiling, waiting for sleep, and her thoughts strayed far away to another time and another place. Regan's face flashed before her, and she threw up her arm to cover her eyes as though warding off a blow.

Fitfully, she thrashed about on the bed. Her slender arm lashed out and knocked the lamp from the nearby nightstand and the tinkle of the shattering glass reminded her of that night, long ago, when Regan had stormed into her bedroom.

It had been after a party at the Spaniard's, Chaezar Alvarez. He had come to her door, demanding to be admitted, demanding an answer to his question. "Is Chaezar Alvarez your lover?"

"I refuse to answer you, Regan, you're drunk!"

Regan's face had shown his uncertainty. Then he reached out and pulled her against him. "I want you," he had murmured huskily, his lips seeking hers.

Sirena had fought his embrace, but her struggles were useless against his powerful arms. Ignoring her protests, he had picked her up in his arms and cradled her head to his chest, all the while whispering soft, indistinct phrases.

Almost tenderly, he had laid her on the bed and began to remove her gown. Head reeling, Sirena gasped. "Please, Regan, don't do this. Don't do this to either of us. We won't be able to face each other in the morning."

His lips had found hers again; his hands worked at her gown. Lost in the moment, Sirena could only surrender to the emotions engulfing her. All the anger and bitterness was forgotten and she had felt herself in the cabin of her ship, the *Rana,* surrounded by the isolating fog. "Regan, stop!" she had cried hoarsely, pushing him away from her as she rolled across the bed to escape him. He said nothing, his eyes said it all. She was his wife and he meant to have her.

Drunkenly, he had stumbled toward her. She knew if he got his hands on her she would be powerless against him. She had backed away, groping behind her for a weapon to stave him off. Her hand had closed over a silver-backed hairbrush. "Don't come any closer, Regan," she threatened.

In the end Sirena had found herself once again on the bed. She had lain there wild-eyed, anticipating his next move. And Regan, still glaring at her, had knocked the glass chimney from the bedside lamp and extinguished the flame with the palm of his hand.

He had come to her, locking her kicking legs between his knees. He had torn the clothes from her body, leaving her naked. Sirena remembered the feel of the hard network of muscles beneath his sun-ravished back.

Despite her struggles, his hand had grazed her body, his fingers had woven in her hair, and his lips had sought hers, parting them and seeking out the warm recesses of her mouth.

His kisses had covered her lips, her cheeks, her eyes, her throat. In spite of herself, Sirena had been aware of a building response. This was Regan, her mind had cried. Regan who had taught her about lovemaking aboard the gently rocking frigate. She had closed her eyes and imagined she could smell the thick, pungent salt tang that rolls in with a sequestering fog.

Like the sea, Sirena had felt her resistance ebb to be replaced by a surging tide of passion. Her lips had answered his, her body had arched against him. She had pulled his head down and pressed her warm, passion-bruised lips to his.

Even now, years later, Sirena could taste his mouth against hers, feel his hands on her body, relive the response he evoked in her. And when she reached out her arms to bring her lover closer, the pain of loneliness clutched her heart like sharp talons.

Frau Holtz looked in on Sirena and found her preparing her hair. The Mevrouw's eyes were wounded and hurt. The sparkle she had hoped to see was missing. "Are you ready for your gown, Mevrouw? Do you need help with the fasteners?" The woman hoped her voice was light and cheerful.

"Yes," Sirena nodded dully. Her reminiscing had left her drained of spirit and life.

Frau Holtz removed several wide petticoats from Sirena's wardrobe. "Will you need three or four, Mevrouw?"

"None," Sirena stated simply, steeling herself for the Frau's disapproval.

"Your gown has its own petticoats attached," the housekeeper declared confidently.

"No, as a matter of fact, it doesn't," Sirena said, "and I don't want to hear any of your objections. Just help me dress and not a word out of you! Now, if you'll come over here and help me with the pins for my hair."

Frau Holtz snapped her mouth shut. It was rarely the Mevrouw worked herself into a black mood like this, but at those times it could be outright dangerous to displease her. If the old woman didn't want to find herself back aboard the *Sea Spirit*, cooking and cleaning for the crew, she knew she'd better do as she was told. It was also possible to make an excuse that she was needed elsewhere in the house, but her inborn curiosity prevented her from doing so. If the Mevrouw was up to something outrageous, it would be best to know it from the first.

Sirena sat at her vanity table, hairbrush in hand, sweeping the bristles through her long, thick tresses. When Frau Holtz picked up the curling iron to heat it in the lamp's flame, Sirena said tersely, "We won't be needing that." She brushed her hair severely away from her face, catching it at the back of her crown and tying it with the Frau's help. Dipping her fingers in the pomade jar, she rubbed it vigorously between her palms and smoothed it over her hair, the light oil bringing out glistening blue-black highlights. The remaining tail of hair was twisted into a full coil at the back of her head and secured with pins. Into it she pierced long, decorative sticks with jeweled tips.

"Mevrouw," the Frau whispered, "you've done your hair like a Chinee!"

"Chinese," Sirena corrected. "If I've done the gardens to remind Regan of the exotic Indies, why should it end there? He always had a taste for Oriental women and I intend to whet his appetite. Now hold your tongue, Frau Holtz, and help me."

From the jars and pots on the dressing table, Sirena produced a vial of Indian kohl and a tiny, pointed brush. With it, she lined her eyes with delicate, thin strokes, sweeping the ends out toward her temples. When she had finished, the effect was startling. The natural tilt of her eyes was enhanced and produced the oblique slant of the Asian eye. A blending of powders, a touch of Spanish paper to her high cheekbones and a gloss over her lips created the effect she sought. The delicacy and piquancy of her features lent themselves perfectly to her artistry.

Frau Holtz was stunned at the reflection in the mirror. "Mevrouw, you look like . . . like—"

"Stop stammering. I know what I look like. It's just as I intended. I look like the Eurasian girls in Clarice's brothel on Java. Since Regan was such a loyal patron of that establishment, I thought he would appreciate this small touch of home." Sirena stood and walked away from the vanity table, unable to meet Frau Holtz's gaze. From the interior of the clothespress she withdrew the gown Mrs. Wittcomb had created for her. The serpentine silk overlayed a heavier, dazzling green satin. When the old housekeeper saw the gown Sirena had commissioned, she gasped.

"Mevrouw! What can you be thinking of? You'll be a scandal!"

"I'll live with it!" Sirena said sarcastically.

"You'll live to regret it, you mean!" the Frau shot back.

"Whatever. Now bring me the new slippers I ordered from the cobbler. Remember, I told you to hold your tongue, I meant it. Hurry." Even as she spoke, she cast off her dressing gown, revealing she wore nothing beneath it save long silk stockings held up by diamond-studded garters. Frau Holtz nearly swooned and was about to ask where Sirena's chemise and underwear were but cautioned herself not to comment.

The shoes the housekeeper found, still in their wrapper, matched the gown and sported ridiculously high heels. "You'll break your neck for certain in these," she muttered.

"That's my worry, not yours," Sirena answered as she slid the shoes on her feet.

"Harrmph! You'll see over every man's head! You—" A wicked look from Sirena snapped the Frau's mouth shut.

Sirena held her arms up so the Frau could slip the gown on. The bodice fit snugly, the wide, open neckline dipping to a point between her breasts, revealing their lush fullness. The sleeves were long and tight, showing the smooth, round curve of her shoulders and the elegant length of her limbs. The long, narrow, sheathlike skirt hugged her body and looked wet, pouring over her hips and down her legs like the tail of a mermaid. The hem in front was slashed and cut away so, when she walked, the length of her silk-clad leg was exposed halfway up her thigh. Frau Holtz gulped. "Mevrouw! The flesh above your stocking shows when you move!"

"It does, doesn't it," Sirena said casually, wondering where she would get the courage to appear like this in public. Refusing to dwell on it, she reached for the jewel box on her dressing table and opened it to reveal the royal dragon pendant. When she slipped it over her neck, the jade rested high on her breasts, drawing the eye to her seductive cleavage. In her ears she hung dangling jade earrings which accentuated her long neck and heightened the ebony of her hair. When she turned to Frau Holtz for a comment, she thought for a moment the woman was going to throw herself against the door to prevent her from leaving. Instead, the Frau pursed her lips and looked down her nose, scowling.

"After tonight, we'll be leaving this damnable country sooner than I imagined! You won't be able to show your face after you make your appearance in . . . in that!"

Chapter Seventeen

Practically all the guests had arrived at Sirena's informal affair, and they strolled through the gardens or danced to the music while others surrounded the long tables where the array of food was amassed. Sirena had yet to make her appearance and Stephan was becoming very impatient. As he looked through the doors out into the milling throng, he mentally counted eight shepherdesses, eleven cavalrymen, nine soldiers of the Crown, three tavern wenches, two medieval knights in full armor, four astrologists, and eight gypsy dancers.

"Father, must you wait in here for our hostess?" Stephan turned and saw Camilla standing beside the Dutchman. His eyes flicked over his daughter, and he thought how tiresome her costume was. Another shepherdess, bringing the total up to nine.

"I thought it only proper, my dear," he answered kindly. "How lovely you look."

"Not very original," Camilla observed, tossing her bright, yellow curls. "However, it was the best I could manage, considering how frantic I am with the arrangements for the wedding. Isn't that correct, Regan?" she cooed.

The Dutchman looked decidedly bored with the whole conversation, and Stephan could imagine Camilla had wearied him with the tedious details of the nuptial preparations. Regan was dressed as a common sailor, his short-sleeved, striped shirt revealing the power in his arms and chest. His visored cap was worn at a jaunty angle over his eyes and his snug-fitting breeches were stuffed into knee-high boots. "You wear the costume well, Regan," Stephan complimented. "You look for all the world like an able-bodied seaman. And allow me to say that scar on your cheek only adds to the effect."

Regan's hand flew up to touch the red line. His agate-blue eyes became stormy as he recalled the circumstances under which he been marked. He swore under his breath. The last place in the world Regan wanted to be this night was here at Sirena's party. But Camilla had insisted, saying how she "simply adored" costume parties and they simply had to make an appearance. As usual, Regan had given in to her whims, but he regretted it the moment he stepped into the garden and saw the decorations. Chinese paper lanterns glowed softly, casting their alluring light amid the shrubbery. He saw the cages holding the tropical birds and heard the Javanese musicians strum their instruments and pound their drums. Even the tantalizing aroma coming from the banquet tables was calculated to remind him of Batavia and the lushness of Java. Grudgingly, Regan had to admit to himself that Sirena's preparations had succeeded in bringing back a vague feeling of nostalgia. Sirena knew his weaknesses and was capitalizing on them. Bitch! he thought as he vowed he would not fall into her traps like the fly into the spider's web.

"Doesn't Father look dashing, Regan? Regan?" Camilla asked again, her blue eyes seeking his. Gaining his attention, she persisted, "Regan, I asked you if Father doesn't look dashing? Have your thoughts flown to business again, darling?" she pouted.

Regan smiled indulgently. "Sorry, sweetheart, what? Oh, yes, very inventive, Stephan," he said, noticing Sir Langdon's costume for the first time. "You make a convincing devil."

"I suppose I should take that as a compliment," Stephan said smugly, brushing away imaginary specks from his black vest and adjusting the long, red satin cloak over his shoulders.

"Where are your horns, Father?" Camilla asked innocently, her sarcasm meant only for Stephan's ears. "And your tail! Surely you haven't forgotten that?"

"Yes, where are your horns, Stephan?" asked a voice behind them. They turned and gasped with astonishment. There stood Sirena, dressed as a Chinese courtesan, the shimmering green of her costume matching exactly the blaze of her eyes.

For a full moment, Stephan was speechless. His eyes took in her womanly curves from the deep wide V of her neckline to the high slash in her hem which revealed her spectacular legs.

Camilla was visibly astonished. She had expected Sirena to dress as a chaste, Spanish lady, complete with high ruff and full farthingale. Not this slender, full-hipped woman who appeared as though she had been poured into her gown. Camilla's feminine speculation took in every detail, from the high crown of dark hair sleeked back from her beautiful face to the outrageously high heels on her slippers. Even the diamond garters winking out from the slash in the front of her skirt did not escape Camilla's scrutiny. Suddenly, she flushed as she realized how ridiculously juvenile she looked beside this full-blown image of seductiveness.

Regan stared frankly at Sirena. His cool eyes were lit from within and a mocking smile played about his lips. She was gorgeous! If he didn't know better, he would think he was in Clarice's brothel, which boasted beautiful Oriental temptresses to suit any man's taste. But Clarice had never imported anyone like Sirena. If she had, she would have increased her business a thousandfold.

Regan's forthright admiration was evident and Sirena considered scandalizing herself small payment for Regan's renewed interest. "You haven't answered me, darling," she directed to Stephan. "Where are your horns?" Her voice was low and as seductive as her dress.

Stephan blanched uneasily. "I . . . er . . . I've got them here," he said, pulling out a cap with bright red satanic horns fastened to it. "I felt rather ridiculous wearing them. Sirena, I've told you how I detest these masquerades."

"Yes, you did, Stephan. However, I like them. They give one the opportunity to see what people secretly consider themselves."

"Heavens, Sirena! I should hope not!" Camilla said sweetly, her voice dripping with honey while her gaze flicked over Sirena's costume.

"And you, little Camilla, how lovely you look. A shepherdess, is it? And where are your sheep?" she laughed. "There aren't many women who can wear that paricular shade of lavender. In Spain, when a child dies, he is laid out in lavender. It compliments the waxy pallor of death." Camilla blanched slightly, but managed a smile.

"Mynheer," Sirena smiled, offering her hand to Regan, "how nice of you to bring Camilla to my little party."

"Little party?" Regan questioned, raising his eyebrows. He could have operated his business for three months on what she had spent on this gathering.

"When we're married, we must have a ball exactly

like it, Regan! I think masquerades are going to become the rage," Camilla cooed.

"But of course, dear, when money is no object, you can have whatever your heart desires. Isn't that so Mynheer?" asked Sirena.

"Only what can be bought with money. There are things, as well as people, that can never be bought," Regan replied curtly.

"Everyone has his price," Sirena said smoothly. "If not money, then something else."

Camilla's hand trembled slightly on Regan's arm. What manner of conversation were they having. The Spaniard sounded as though she were baiting Regan and he was livid. She could feel it in the tenseness of his arm. When Regan became like this, her whole evening was ruined, and tonight she was in no mood to cajole and flatter him into being agreeable. All she wanted to do was eat and eat till she became sick and they had to carry her home. The aromas from the banquet tables were wafting in through the open doors and Camilla's knees felt weak with hunger. She looked to her father to end this conversation between Sirena and Regan; but what she saw there nearly made her mouth gape.

Stephan, having gotten over the shock of seeing Sirena's costume, now had his attention focused on the valuable necklace. The rubies twinkled in the precious jade. For one horrible second, Camilla thought her father's hand would reach up and caress the jewel as it lay between Sirena's breasts. Careful not to catch either Sirena's or Regan's attention, Camilla jabbed the end of her shepherd's crook into the soft leather top of Stephan's shoe and smiled with satisfaction when he cried out in pain. "Oh dear, Father, are you ill?"

Stephan managed to compose himself. "No, no. I'm quite well, thank you." Adroitly, he turned his attention back to the conversation at hand.

"How is your fledgling business, Mynheer? Has it taken wing yet? Or are those vicious rumors true, that because of the pirate attack your wings were clipped, so to speak? I only ask," she said casually, "because I was considering having you export back a hold of nutmegs. I know of a place where they can be gotten at a very good price."

"I'm sorry I can't help you," Regan said coolly. "I have all the business I can handle. I'm afraid it would be impossible to take on any new clients."

"Too many clients! How wonderful!" The emerald eyes flashed warningly. "That can be so easily changed. One trip to sea and poof!" she snapped her fingers, "no more clients."

Her message was not lost on Regan. His own expression became murky and dangerous. "If I should ever find myself without clients, I would be forced to take . . . other measures."

Sirena laughed, the sound causing the fine hairs on the back of his neck to prickle. "It always comes back to money, doesn't it? Money can buy anything."

There was a new tone in Regan's voice when he replied. One Sirena had never heard before. "Take me, for instance," he said. "Money cannot buy my services. There is a word for what I'm referring to, it's called ethics."

"Where I come from, we call it stealing. Whatever it's called here, it's punishable by death. Think about it, Mynheer. Enjoy yourselves," she said, turning to Camilla, "I must see to my other guests. Are you coming, Stephan?"

Regan watched her for a moment, his eyes the color of deep indigo and brimming with cold hatred. Hatred for what he knew she could do to him and hatred for himself because he would not be able to stop her.

Later in the evening, Sirena stood alone in a dim corner of the garden. The stir caused by her daring costume had died down although the women still gazed at her covertly and the men still ogled her everywhere she went. Watching the merriment all around her, her eyes fell on Stephan Langdon as he talked with a buxom lady and offered her a glass of punch. When she saw the woman glance up at Stephan with a flirtatious gleam in her eyes, Sirena made a decision. She would marry Stephan and, in this way, she could destroy Regan's plans to inherit the Langdon fortunes through Camilla. Regan would be left holding an empty bag. Frau Holtz said there were more ways than one to skin a cat and this was the time to do it. It was only a few more days until Regan took Camilla for his wife. If there had been any hope left that Regan would come back to her, it was gone. Dead like the leaves of autumn. All her calculations had gone awry. This party, this costume, everything, had been wasted. Regan was stronger than she thought. Sirena sighed miserably. But she would never let him win. Let him marry Camilla if he must; she would never believe he loved her. Never! A shudder ran through her as she remembered the last time she had lain in his arms and felt him bring her with him to the heights of ecstasy. It was all becoming clear to her. Regan felt he had to fortify himself against her. And the only defense he could rely upon was gold sovereigns. The Langdon money. "And he claims to have no price!" she snorted. "He's determined I won't get the better of him this time. Regardless of how many times I try to tell him I love him, he believes it to be a trick. His conscience pricks him so savagely and he's strangling in his own guilt. He could never believe I would forgive him." Foolish man, she thought, but if it's games he's willing to play, he'll soon find who's the winner.

Sirena strolled toward Stephan, masculine eyes following her every step. As she approached him, he turned and quickly looked about to see if someone else was the recipient of her outrageous flirting. Seeing no one else save a group of chattering women, he preened like a peacock and stepped forward to take her hand in his.

"Darling Stephan, where have you been hiding all evening? I've been waiting for you to ask me to dance. Come now," she said rubbing her hand up and down his arms in a caress.

Stephan's eyes widened and then took advantage of the situation. "Sweetheart, I thought you were too busy with your guests to bother about me. I've waited this whole night for this moment," he said, whirling her onto the dance floor.

Breathless from the quadrille, Sirena laughed up into Stephan's face. He really is quite handsome, she thought. Older men have a certain style, a gaily charming, debonair quality. Seeing her opportunity, she gazed into the gray depths of his eyes. Then, dropping her lids demurely, she said in a wan voice, "How fortunate these ladies are. They're going home with their husbands to spend the night together . . ." She risked a sidelong glance to see the effect of her words.

Stephan swallowed hard and said nervously, "Marriage has a lot to be said for it, Sirena." Stephan couldn't believe his good fortune. The answer to all his prayers. He would have to tread lightly so he wouldn't scare her off. A Jew's toenails! How much was Sirena worth? From the most modest estimations, millions! He almost groaned aloud as he forced his mind back to the matters at hand. "Darling, Sirena, if I thought you would say the word, I'd ask you to share my life with me. However, I realize I could never hope for a young, vital woman like yourself to wed an older man like myself."

"Stephan, do my ears deceive me or have you asked me to marry you?" She let her eyes widen into incredulous wonder.

"If I were to be bold enough to ask you, Sirena, would you . . . could you—?"

"Ask me!" Sirena demanded, annoyed he was taking so long to get to the point.

"Sirena, sweetheart, darling, will you . . . do you . . . I want you to . . ." The words were choking off his air. Damn it, Stephan cursed silently. How often he had planned this, and now at the moment he couldn't for the life of him get the words out.

Her patience at an end, Sirena said, "Yes, yes. I'll marry you! When?"

"Camilla will be married in a week or so. Anytime after—"

"Darling, that will never do! Now that I've found you, I won't let you get away. We will be married immediately before Camilla. We'll share her wedding reception. Until then, it will be a secret. We'll elope! How romantic! I'll count the hours!"

Sirena couldn't believe she had just done what she did! "Darling!" She was actually making herself sick! How would she ever go through with this farce when her heart cried out for Regan? She thought about her impending wedding to Stephan, then recalled the same event with Regan. But she still loved Regan and could never feel the same way about Stephan Langdon!

Regan was talking with several people not far from where Sirena stood with Stephan. Something about that relationship annoyed him. Somehow, whenever he saw Sirena in Stephan's company, he felt the urge to rush over and snatch her away from the silver-haired gentleman who was soon to be his father-in-law. It wasn't jealousy, exactly. He didn't feel this way when Sirena was with Tyler Sinclair, only when she was escorted by Langdon. It was more a protectiveness, he decided. Suddenly, he burst into laughter, drawing curious looks from those around him. Sirena needed about as much protection as a barracuda in open water!

As he watched, one of the musicians brought Sirena her guitar. Excusing herself from Stephan, Sirena made her way to the dais and was seating herself on a chair which had been placed there for her. In spite of himself, Regan found he was moving toward the dais, his eyes locked on Sirena. The overhead lantern cast shimmering light on the sleek and sensuous gown she wore and threw blue-black highlights into her hair. Hungrily his eyes devoured her and he realized his heart was pounding in his chest. Damn her! Would he never get this green-eyed siren out of his blood?

The stage was set and Sirena strummed lightly on her instrument, catching the attention of the guests. The milling throng advanced toward the dais, pushing their way in front of Regan, who contented himself with standing in the shadows.

Sirena's manner was completely composed. She lowered her head, her long, graceful hands plucking the strings. Her back was straight, only the curve of her arms and the bend of her leg breaking the study of perfect linearity. Sirena played, capturing her audience with the lilting music. The light from the overhead lantern swung gracefully on its wire, sending arcs of brilliancy onto her face and illuminating her features with radiance.

Throughout the melody, Regan became increasingly drawn under the spell she wove. Her voice called to him, coming to him like a whisperous feather on the wind, thawing the glacial restraints he had erected between them. He was oblivious to all as her song wove a silken web about him. Forward he moved, skirting the edges of the crowd. He was unaware of time or space, knowing only that he had to be near her, breathe in the special fragrance of her, knowing it would be as fresh as the salt tang and spindrift. His arms ached to hold her, caress her, feel her supple beauty crushed against him. He was hungry for her, hungrier than he ever remembered being, dying for a taste of her lips and to feel the throb of the wild pulse in her throat beat against his mouth.

Sirena felt his smoldering eyes upon her and, when she looked up, he was there, an arm's length away. As she continued with the ballad, she sang for Regan. She saw in his eyes the reflection of her own desire, her own needs. Unaware of the speculative glances about them, Sirena sang of her love, caressing each syllable before she offered it to him, her senses reeling, her heart catapulting across the distance between them and coming to find its home with him. She basked in his attention, preened in his fascination and luxuriated in his adoration as she sang her serenade to him, for him.

The lantern lights reflected on his hair, casting a nimbus of spun gold about his head. She drank in the sight of him, the fires of her passions unquenchable.

She glanced down at her guitar as her fingers sought a change of chord. When she looked up at him again, his attention was directed somewhere above her head, a look of consternation bordering on horror was on his chiseled features.

Regan was distracted by the peculiar swinging of the oil lantern. The light was beginning to make wide, awkward motions, unaccountable in the soft breezes. A rustling in the shadows of the trees caught his ear; and, when he again looked back to Sirena, it was too late! The lantern was falling, the wire which had held it fastened in the tree boughs hanging free.

"Sirena!" Regan shouted, his urgency causing her to leap to her feet. Abruptly, the world about her was ablaze. The lantern crashed to the dais, breaking and splashing the flammable liquid against her skirt and legs, causing them to be ignited by dancing flames.

In an instant Regan had vaulted onto the low platform to push Sirena away from further harm, but not before the planks beneath her feet were a miniature inferno. The party guests shrieked in terror, backing away from the fire. Helplessly, Regan looked about for something to smother the flames. He called to Stephan, who was also retreating, shock and terror written on his face. "Your cloak, man!" Regan shouted. "Your cloak!" Stephan was beyond comprehension.

In a blur of action, Regan leaped for Stephan and tore the satanic cloak from his back and threw it around Sirena's legs, carrying her off the platform.

Several others seemed to come to their senses and break into action. A footman came rushing forth with two planters full of flowers and dumped the moist soil on the burning wood.

Frau Holtz came on a run, fright creasing her features. She had seen the lantern slip and had been pushing her way through the huddled guests. Seeing she could rely on Regan to have things in hand, her concern for Sirena quieted. "Mynheer! Take her into the house! We must see what damage has been done!" Although her voice was strong and confident, Regan saw the white ring of horror about her pursed mouth.

Sirena's hands covered her face and she was very still as Regan lifted her, the Frau taking off her snowy white apron and covering the Mevrouw's legs. She tried not to think about the black charring she saw when she had removed the scarlet cloak.

As she followed Regan inside, the old woman prayed silently, Please, God, don't let her be burned! Don't let her be crippled! Not that, God, never that! she beseeched as she thought of Sirena's vitality and agile grace.

Regan carried Sirena up to her room, the Frau bustled in after him, turning back the bed covers before he tenderly laid Sirena down. Helplessly, he stood by as the housekeeper carefully lifted the apron to bare Sirena's legs. The movement must have caused some pain because Sirena stirred fitfully before falling against the pillows with her eyes shut.

The front of her shimmering, green gown was singed and her silk stockings were burned into an uneven pattern of dark circled holes. *"Ja,"* Frau Holtz said confidently after surveying the damage. "She is burned, but not badly," she assured Regan as he bent solicitously over Sirena's still form.

"When I think of what might have happened to her," he muttered, his voice thick with emotion. "The first time I saw her this evening, I cursed her for her revealing costume. Now I can only thank God she didn't wear those billowing petticoats. They would have gone up in flame like dry kindling." He sank to his knees and picked up Sirena's hand. "Frau Holtz, why is she so still?" he demanded. "You said she wasn't seriously injured!"

"The shock, Mynheer. You seem as though you're in a state yourself; now be useful or get out of my way!" The old authority was in her voice and Regan snapped to attention, waiting for her orders. "While I go down for ointments, you take her gown and stockings off. Cut them off if you have to, but be careful! I won't have you peeling away half her skin with your clumsy hands!"

Regan bent to his task, gently turning Sirena over so he could reach the long row of tiny buttons at the back of her gown. It wasn't long before he realized she was completely naked underneath, and he quickly covered her nudity with a light blanket before the Frau could accuse him of being a ravisher of unconscious women. He undid the diamond garters and began rolling the stockings off her legs. Those magnificent, smooth-muscled legs! They had been what he had dreamed of after he saw her for the first time as the Sea Siren with the *Tita* sinking in the background.

A wistful half-smile played about his mouth as he recalled the first time he had ever made love to her. He had known her as the Sea Siren then and they were alone in her cabin aboard her frigate. He had nursed her then too, a cut received in the heat of battle. The lamp in the cabin was running dry of oil and he remembered cursing the flickering light. She had tended his wound and he had returned the favor. As he wiped the greasy salve from his fingers, he had gazed down upon the most remarkable woman he had ever known. She was lying on her stomach across the narrow bunk. Her wealth of dark hair obscured all but the tip of her chin and a glimpse of her brow. Her body had relaxed from his ministrations and her arms were extended over her head.

Beneath her upstretched arms the soft spill of her full, round breasts was visible. The long, low slope of the small of her back rising again to the firm spherical hillocks of her bottom, ending in her slightly parted, firm-fleshed thighs aroused him, beckoned to him as sweetly as the song of the legendary sirens for which he had named her. Gently, he had leaned over and pressed his lips to the hollow of her spine. In the dark of the cabin, with the sequestering fog creeping in, her lissome, supple beauty was perceived through his fingers. The delicious fragrance of her, the silken texture of her skin, had heightened his desire as he had fondled and explored her secret charms. Her lips tasted of the sea and her pleasure in him had been unaffected, her responses genuine and unpracticed.

And almost innocently she had sought and found the most sensual caress, exalting in the pleasure and inspiration she had given him. And when she had murmured against his lips, "Have me! Have me now!" he had known that this woman would always be a part of his life. She was life!

Frau Holtz bustled in again with an ewer of water and a crock of ointment. "Here, help me!" she commanded, tossing Regan a cloth dipped in water. "We have to get the threads of silk stocking away from the burns."

"She's so still," he whispered.

"Better for us," Frau Holtz said curtly. "There's no pain while we clean."

"How badly is she hurt?" Regan pressed, as he rinsed out another cloth for the housekeeper.

"Ach! It is almost nothing, thank heavens. No worse than a laundress gets from the flatiron."

Regan seemed reassured, and Frau Holtz watched him lean over Sirena and press his lips to her cheek. The tender moment brought tears to the Frau's eyes, and she knew that if Sirena ever dreamed that a frightening incident could bring Regan back to her, she would have doused her head with lamp oil and set fire to her hair!

"Frau Holtz, has anyone been lurking about the house?" Regan asked cryptically.

"Someone lurking? *Nein,* Mynheer," the Frau answered, puzzled at such a question. Suddenly, she was frightened. "Why? Do you suspect—"

"No, no, calm yourself. Still, if I hadn't seen that lantern swinging and hadn't called out to Sirena, I shudder to think what might have been the consequences."

Frau Holtz gasped. "And you think this is the doing of some mischief-maker? *Nein!* It was an accident!" Strangely, a vision of Sirena and Jacobus nearly being run down by a runaway hackney flashed through her mind. She was about to say something to Regan when Sirena began to stir. From a drawer in the nightstand, the Frau withdrew a small bottle of laudanum. "This will help. Let her sleep through the worst of it," the old woman muttered, forcing a spoon of the clear liquid against Sirena's lips.

Silent as they worked, Frau Holtz and Regan wrapped Sirena's legs lightly in strips of soft sheeting. The pins were removed from her thick dark hair and, while Regan sent a servant for fresh water, the Frau removed all traces of makeup from Sirena's face. Once more, looking like herself rather than a Chinese courtesan, Sirena lay peacefully against the pillows.

"Will she be all right?" Regan asked, concern deepening his voice.

"*Ja.* Knowing the Mevrouw, she'll be walking about tomorrow," she replied, watching his actions out of the corner of her eye.

Regan went to kneel beside the bed, gazing down at Sirena's face, praying the Frau's prognosis was correct. He realized he would rather give his life than see her maimed, see her less than she was. A shudder coursed through him, prickling the hairs at the back of his neck and tightening his jaw muscle. Sirena's face was pale, her lips bloodless. That lantern could have crashed down on her head. Killing her. The disfiguring flames eating greedily at her hair, her face. The flaming oil spilling down her back, her breasts . . . Too horrible to think about, Regan's mind reverted to the sound coming from among the trees. Without rhyme or reason, somehow Regan knew this act against Sirena had been deliberately contrived to destroy her!

The slim body on the high bed became restless. Sirena's eyelids fluttered and she sighed deeply. Gradually, her eyes opened, their green lights dimmed by the drug. Barely audible, she whispered, "Stephan."

Regan's head snapped around to where Sirena's gaze was directed. There, framed in the doorway, was Langdon, a nervous expression lining his features, worry and concern darkening his eyes. Before his jealous rage could take hold and he smashed everything in sight, Regan sprinted to his feet and rushed out of the room, roughly pushing Stephan aside.

Frau Holtz's mouth opened to stop him. She, too, had heard Sirena's word and immediately understood that in her drugged state she hadn't realized Regan was beside her and had merely said the name of the first person she recognized. Unreasonably, the elderly woman knew the urge to hit Stephan Langdon, hit him until his teeth rattled. Instead, she moved quickly to the door and slammed it shut in his face.

Chapter Eighteen

"I won't wear these, I won't!" Sirena rebelled at the thin woven stocking Frau Holtz had brought to her.

"Suit yourself, Mevrouw, but when the silk stockings make your legs feel as though they are smothering and they keep your body heat, you'll be sorry!" the housekeeper snapped. "Who can see these beneath your gown? Who will know?"

Sirena made a face as she looked at the unattractive

hose. Reluctantly, she snatched them out of Frau Holtz's hands and fell heavily on the side of the bed to put them on. She had still not gotten over the incident at her party two nights earlier. From all aspects it was a horrifying experience. Not only that, but she was piqued with herself for passing out in a faint. The last thing she remembered was Regan rushing to her aid and sweeping her up in his arms. After that, all was a total blank until the next morning. And to make her mood blacker, each time she questioned Frau Holtz about what happened afterward, all the woman would say was that she had given her mistress laudanum for the pain and dressed her wounds.

Frau Holtz sighed as she watched Sirena fasten the thin woven stockings to her garters. She knew the reason for Sirena's temper. It was because she refused to tell her anything about Regan. How could she tell Sirena how gentle Regan had been with her? How he had helped tend her burns and had worried over her, hovering near her bedside. And then, due to the worst possible luck, that Sirena had looked up to see Stephan standing in the doorway and had murmured his name. No, she determined she would never tell her. It would break her heart and wouldn't come to any good. The Frau knew that Regan would never understand. Hadn't she herself seen the rage in his face?

"I believe I'll wear my bronze day dress, Frau Holtz. Would you get it from the clothes press?"

"Mevrouw, I wish you wouldn't go out today. You only left your bed yesterday afternoon, it's too soon yet! You stay home, *ja?*"

"I stay home, no. There's business to take care of and I've already sent word to Tyler that I would come to his office."

"He can come here. For dinner, *ja?*"

"No. I can't stay about the house." Then her tone softened. "Good friend, I know you worry for my welfare, but I'm fine. Really. Now, please help me. I promise I won't be long. What is the difference if I sit at home or in the coach? I won't be on my feet much; I promise."

Realizing it was useless to argue, Frau Holtz sighed loudly and went about helping Sirena dress.

After a pleasant ride through the city, Sirena's coach pulled up in front of Tyler Sinclair's offices. Jacobus climbed down from his perch beside the driver and helped her to the ground, taking care not to hurry her. If Sirena so much as winced with discomfort, the Frau would have his head.

Sirena mounted the steps to Tyler's office with care. She hated to admit it, but the burns were bothering her, and she was more than grateful that Frau Holtz had had her way about the stockings.

When she opened the door, Tyler was having a discussion with Whipple. When he saw her there, delight shone in his eyes. "How wonderful to see you up and about, Sirena. Did your housekeeper tell you I called as soon as I heard of your mishap?"

"She did, and thank you for the lovely flowers. As for myself, I'm perfectly fine."

Tyler strode over to her and grasped her hands. "I'm glad to hear it, Sirena, very glad. Could I offer you coffee, tea?"

"No, thank you. This isn't a social call, Tyler, but a professional one."

"Sounds serious. Come into my office where we can talk freely."

After she had seated herself near his desk, Sirena blurted, "Stephan Langdon has asked me to marry him and I've accepted his proposal. We'll be married immediately before Camilla and Regan. Just a small, intimate ceremony. As a matter of fact, we plan on eloping. You'll be our witness."

Tyler's eyes nearly popped from his head. How in the world had this come about? He had to tell her, warn her of Stephan! Yet, how could he convince her without revealing his circumstances with Camilla?

"Tyler, you don't seem very happy about my news." Sirena studied him for his reaction.

Tyler smiled, his heart pounding. He had to warn her somehow and let her think it was her own evaluation. Once that jack a napes relative got his hands on her money, it would be the end of Sirena. The stories of Stephan's unfortunate, dead wife were still vivid in Tyler's mind even though he was a mere boy when he'd heard them. He could still hear the Baroness' angry voice when she accused him of gambling away Flora's money. And when she accused Stephan of squandering his wife's inheritance and committing the poor woman to Bedlam, the young Tyler had run and hidden beneath his bed. Stephan was a terrifyingly vicious man and he regretted that he hadn't warned Sirena right from the beginning.

"Sirena, this is rather sudden, isn't it? You haven't known Stephan that long to want to make a permanent tie. Whatever possessed you to consider marriage?"

"That really isn't important, Tyler. I came here to have some business contracts drawn before the wedding. First of all, I want three-fourths of my holdings divided between Frau Holtz and Caleb van der Rhys. All holdings and monies are to be in their name. Of course, it's only to be in trust, they wouldn't inherit until my death. The balance of my wealth is to be placed in Regan's name. Should anything unforetold happen to any of these people, the estate would revert to the survivors. Of course, this is to be in a trust whereby I can draw on the principal if need be."

Tyler relaxed visibly. So, Sirena was not a fool after all. "Do you realize what you're doing? You'll be going into marriage with very little free capital. This could cause a problem," he said, furrowing his brow.

"I'm not entirely ignorant of the law, Tyler. If I dispose of my property before my marriage, it's nobody's concern save my own. For all I know, Stephan could be contemplating the very same thing himself. Regan was able to take the Córdez inheritance away from me and not anyone will find the Valdez inheritance available to them."

"Sirena, I must warn you this is not entirely wise. Have you thought of what Stephan would say? Afterward, when he learns you have only enough to get by on?"

"If and when the time ever comes I need more than what I have available, then you will liquidate some of the capital. It's really quite simple, why are you making such ado about it?"

"Sirena, English law states you are subject to your

husband's rule. You must listen to what I'm trying to tell you."

"No. You must listen to me! I'm paying you a handsome sum to handle my affairs. Not to interfere in my personal life. If you interfere again, I'll be forced to engage another solicitor."

"Very well, Sirena, but don't say I didn't try to warn you. Please," he said, holding up his hand for her to stop talking. "I speak as a friend. You can't possibly love Stephan Langdon; he's old enough to be your father. Have you thought of the more romantic side of marriage?"

Sirena gulped. This was a thought she had been pushing away all yesterday, ever since she had embarked on this scheme to marry Stephan.

"I can see by your face you haven't considered it. Don't rush into this, it's a big step and deserves further consideration."

"Tyler, can't I have a contract drawn up . . ." her words faded off, she knew she was trapped. If she married Stephan, she would have to share his bed. For an instant she almost retracted; then she thought of how undemanding Stephan had been in their relationship. More than a kiss on the cheek or a soft pressing on the lips, he had not demanded. He would probably be just as yielding about his marital rights.

"If you were about to suggest a premarital contract giving you sole rights to your own bed, I must hasten to tell you again English law does not recognize anything of the sort. These things are usually decided upon by the parties involved. Stephan will never submit to any such request. What man would, being married to you? Sirena, when you wed, you lose your voice. Your husband is your lord and you must yield to him in all things. Financial and intimate."

Sirena was thoughtful for a moment. "In other words, what he has is his and what I have becomes his also. That leaves me nothing for myself and we don't share jointly; in fact, we don't share at all. He will provide for me and, beyond that, his obligations end."

"Exactly. At last you understand. Now, perhaps, you will reconsider."

"No. But don't worry, Tyler. Simply arrange things the way I've asked. I will manage Stephan, have no fear."

But Tyler did worry.

It was late in the afternoon when Frau Holtz charged into Sirena's suite, a handbill clutched in her fist. "Mevrouw, Mevrouw, look at this! May the saints preserve us," she cried dramatically. "It's Caleb and look what he's done!"

Sirena snatched the advertisement from the housekeeper, a puzzled look on her face. "Caleb has outfitted the *Rana* as a gambling folly?"

"Not the *Rana*, Mevrouw, he calls the ship *Sea Siren!*" the woman exclaimed harshly.

"I can't believe he would do this! I wonder if Regan is behind all this. Why would Caleb do such a thing? Is this why he hasn't paid me a visit, because he can't face me? Because he's so guilty over what he was planning to do with the *Rana?*" She looked at the paper again. "He plans his opening tomorrow night. Gaming till dawn, food fit for kings . . . It's Regan! I know it is. He thinks he can get back at me through Caleb." Sirena stormed about her room. "He won't get away with this! He probably shares the profits!"

"What does it matter now, what can you do?" Frau Holtz asked worriedly. "You gave the boy the ship to do with it as he pleased."

"Yes, but to go into the shipping business. Not this . . . this . . ." words failed her, ". . . this den of iniquity! And," she shrilled, "you see how he's named this folly the *Sea Siren?* Frau Holtz, somehow I must stop him! I'll go to see Regan. No, I can't. He's a part of this. I have to think. I must decide." She lowered herself onto the settee, her hands at her temples. "Leave me. I must concentrate without any distractions."

"If there is anything—"

"I'll call you if I need you, friend."

The housekeeper closed the door quietly as Sirena leaned back, her eyes closed. "How could you do this, Caleb? My *Rana!* A gaming ship!"

Caleb was so inexperienced. He'd grown up among good, hard-working people. He'd be no match for wicked gamblers and scheming women who would frequent his gaming palace. "Damn you, Regan, you're responsible for this!"

Sirena opened the door to call for Frau Holtz. "Tell Jacobus to ready the carriage. I'll be down as soon as I change my gown."

An hour later, dressed in a watered silk of vibrant rose, matching her temper, Sirena thrust open the door to Regan's house and marched in. Her eyes flashed angrily, the handbill clutched in her fist. "I'll destroy that ship before I let you get away with this! I'll sink it there in its berth! I'll gut it, and when there's nothing left, I'll put a torch to it! And if you stand in my way, you'll go to the bottom with it! The same goes for Caleb. How could you allow him to do this?" she shouted vehemently at the startled Regan. "I should have known—Frau Holtz warned me—but I wouldn't listen. You couldn't get to me any other way so you're using Caleb and the *Rana!*" she shouted viciously. "How could you allow your son to get involved with something like this?"

Regan's jaw tightened as he watched Sirena advance on him, a paper clutched in her hand. "What are you doing here and what are you screaming about? Has something happened to Caleb?" he asked anxiously.

"That's right. Play the innocent! Pretend you don't know what's going on. Your business is floundering and this was a way for you to make money. On *my* ship with *your* son! You'll stop at nothing to get what you want. I'll not permit you to do this to Caleb."

Regan reached for the paper and his eyes raked the bold lettering. "I know nothing of this. This is the first I've heard Caleb was involved with the gaming folly. The only name I've heard connected with it was an old reprobate by the name of Farrington."

"Liar! Trickery! I don't believe a word you say."

Regan grew amused. "Listen to who speaks of lies and tricks. Oh no, Sirena. It's the person who stands in your shoes who is those things. I'm telling you, I know nothing of the matter. I haven't seen Caleb since he first arrived in England."

"If you aren't a party to this, then you put Caleb up to it. Caleb isn't the type to come up with an idea like this. He's just a boy."

"My dear Sirena, you'd better take another look at him. He's an adult with a mind of his own. As usual," Regan drawled, "you only see what you want to. If it's any consolation, I don't approve of this either, but he is his own man. He'll have to learn the hard way if he's to survive in this world."

"The *Rana* wasn't intended to be a den of iniquity!"

"The *Rana* is a ship. Not a shrine!"

At that moment Sirena detested Regan more than she had ever dreamed possible. He had come too close to the mark and she knew it. The *Rana* was a temple of sorts and her immediate wrath was because she felt the frigate which had seen her through some of the worst trials of her life was being defamed.

"Damn you, Regan. I know what I'm talking about! Stop Caleb, stop him before it's too late! Gambling is not a trade which prolongs one's life! Scurrilous gamblers have been known to claim they're being cheated and someone's death usually results. In this instance, it could be Caleb."

"Perhaps you're right," Regan said conversationally. "I have been remiss in my parental duties. Caleb needs a fatherly hand. I'll seek him out and take him to the finest brothel in all of England. I'll see to it that his manly education is complete. And there's no need for you to worry about some gambler killing him. Caleb has mastered the art of self-defense, thanks to a certain female pirate who took him under her wing."

"You'd do that, wouldn't you? You would take your own son to a whorehouse and stand by while he learns the van der Rhys methods in carnality. I swear if you do, Regan, I *will* kill you!"

"So you've told me," he answered harshly. "Do it and get it over with, it has become a source of boredom. But before you do, let me tell you that I think your mothering concern for Caleb is a little late. Motherhood doesn't become you, Sirena."

Sirena blinked as though she had been slapped.

Scalding tears escaped her eyes as she tried to bring Regan into her line of vision. "Motherhood doesn't become you!" Did she hear him say those words? Even he couldn't have said that to her. He couldn't be so malicious. Crystal tears glistened on her sooty lashes. "Caleb is your son. I was wrong to come here; I see that now. I gave him the *Rana* and what he does with it is his affair. I will pray with each breath I take that as a parent you will do the wise thing." Sirena faltered a moment as she wiped at her watery eyes. "I apologize for coming here. Forgive me, Regan," she said, turning to leave.

Regan tensed. She was up to something. Sirena never apologized to anyone for anything. Two long strides and he had her arm in a viselike grip. She was really crying! he thought, stunned. A ploy. She was as wily as a lean, hungry fox. In one heartrending second he saw in her eyes what he thought he would never see again. Defeat!

At his touch, Sirena felt herself stiffen. What was that look in his eyes? Dear God, no, she cried silently as she tried to disengage her arm. Never, never again! Regan would never do that to her! "Take your hands off me!" she cried, her voice tinged with fear. "Leave me be!" she insisted, wrestling loose.

No sooner had she gained her freedom than she turned to run from the room. Suddenly, Regan's fierce hold imprisoned her again. "What is this I see here?" he asked mockingly. "Are you afraid of me? The brave and cunning Sea Siren afraid of a mere man?" he smiled churlishly.

"Let me go, Regan. I don't like you this way," she said defiantly.

"And how is it you like me, Sirena? Do you ever like me? A few moments ago you said you would kill me. You couldn't have liked me then." His voice was as smooth as satin and the gleam in his eyes was as glassy as chips of shaved ice.

"You're right. I didn't like you then and I hate you now!" she snarled, baring her teeth like a trapped animal. "God help me, but I wonder what I ever liked about you!"

"Do you wonder?" Regan smiled, both hands grasping her shoulders, drawing her against him. "Shall I tell you? Don't you already know?"

"Regan! Release me!"

"No, Sirena. You came here to my home. You sought me out. Was it really to tell me about Caleb or did you have another reason?"

"What other motive could I possibly have?" she spit, her beautiful face contorted into something feral.

"Perhaps to seduce me again. You have been known to do that, love." His grip on her became stronger, pressing her against him till she thought it impossible to take another breath. His voice was smooth, yet his tone harbored a seething dislike.

"Regan, don't do this."

"Do what, love? Take you in my arms? You love the things I do to you, my hands, my mouth. Won't you sing for me passion's song? You sang it for me so prettily the last time you were here."

"You're a pig!"

"Ah, love, those are not the words. Don't you remember them? Shall I help your memory? Shall I press my lips to that most secret place where your passions are stirred and your melodies evoked?" Not waiting for an answer, Regan wrapped his arms about her, forcing her head to be still, covering her mouth with his.

Sirena clamped her lips shut, feeling his teeth biting against her mouth, his tongue seeking entrance.

"Tell me what you like about me, Sirena," he taunted, forcing her to her knees on the thick carpet, his menacing face only inches away. He pinned her arms to her sides, knocking her backward, falling heavily atop her. "Tell me, love, let me hear you say the words. Do you like it when I touch your breasts and make them swell?" His hand groped inside the wide neckline of her gown, seeking the firm flesh, questing for the stiffening rosy crests. "What do you like, Sirena? Tell me," he urged, using a silky, deprecating tone.

Sirena remained silent, refusing to speak.

"Do you like it when I cover your skin with my mouth? Do you like the emotions I release in you, Sirena?" His head dropped and his lips were where his hands had been, his tongue teasing her sensitive skin.

This was not Regan, her heart cried. This was not the man who could bring her to the heights of rapture with his tenderness. These were not the hands that had caressed her flesh, worshiping her, adoring her. These were the hands of a beast, the mouth of a devil. When his hands groped beneath her skirts, Sirena stiffened, abhorring his touch. He was using her—worse, mocking her. There was no pleasure in this for him. He wanted to hurt her, wound her, ultimately destroy her. The hostility was there to be heard in his voice as well. What he was doing was worse than a beating, worse than killing her, and he knew it! That knowledge ate at her soul, chipping away at her heart. This was his revenge, his reprisal, to defame her and denigrate her. His pleasure was not in the act, but a brutal attempt to revile her.

She had stripped him of all weapons. She had attacked him and threatened to destroy him and forced him to come to this. The ultimate injury a man could inflict upon a woman. Rape.

She loved Regan too much to allow him to do this. It would destroy both of them. He wouldn't be able to live with himself. He would hate himself and her. He would never be able to look her in the face again. Tears stung her eyes and coursed down her cheeks. "Please, Regan," she cried hoarsely, "don't do this to me. Don't do this to yourself. Please."

Something in her voice stilled Regan's movements. The moment seemed like an eternity and she waited with bated breath. Suddenly, Regan seemed to slump. She heard his breath come in ragged gasps as he lifted his weight from her body.

"Get out of here, Sirena. Get out before you wish I would kill you, or you me. Get out, Sirena, for God's sake go!"

Sirena reached out to comfort him wanting to touch his shock of golden hair, she checked her hand in midair. His pride would be inconsolable if she offered to forgive him. He would never allow it.

Slowly, she dragged herself to her feet, taking a brief moment to arrange her skirts and bodice before departing for the waiting carriage. When she looked around again, Regan was on his feet, his back to her.

"Get out of here, Sirena, and don't ever return."

Imperceptibly, Sirena straightened her shoulders as she exited the house and blinked the burning tears away. She had to get home, where she could give into her humiliation, where no one save herself would see or care.

Sensing a commotion, she looked around to hear a frightened wail. Mikel had cried like that once. Sirena watched in horror as a small, thin child struggled with a man who was bent on dragging her down the cobbled street. "I swear, I didn't take it," the girl pleaded. "I gave you all the money. I didn't keep any." She continued to whimper during her feeble struggles.

Sirena's head jerked up as she raced after the pair. "Unhand that child this minute," she shouted hoarsely, her clenched fists lashing out at the burly, bearded man. Stunned, the man loosened his hold and the child was free, running toward the carriage. "I demand to know what you were doing," Sirena shouted, her green eyes full of venom, her lips curled back into a snarl.

"She cheated me," the man blustered. "She's been keeping some of the coins for herself, that's what she's been doing, and it's none of your affair, my fancy lady. Now she's gotten away and for that you can thank yourself. She'll get a whipping the likes of which she'll never forget."

Sirena brought up her booted foot and aimed a well-placed kick in the direction of the man's groin. "If there's any whipping to be done, it will be you who gets it, not the child. If I ever," she said acidly, "see you near that girl again, I'll have you thrown in Newgate and that's where you'll rot. Get out of my sight," she spat as she turned on her heel and raced to the waiting vehicle and gathered the youngster in her arms.

How wasted she was. She's not much more than a baby and forced to work on the streets for the likes of that slovenly bastard. Gently, Sirena touched the gaunt face and looked searchingly into round, terrified eyes. "I remember you," she said softly. "You had a fistful of gold buttons in your hand the last time I saw you."

The child stared at her, saying nothing.

"There's no need for you to fear me. I'm going to take you home with me and keep you safe. You have my word that nothing will ever harm you again. Do you understand what I'm saying to you?"

The child nodded.

"I promise you that you will be safe with me," she said, hugging the frail figure. "Get into the carriage and wait for me.

"You," Sirena screeched at the driver, "climb down from your seat and tell me why you sat there, letting a grown man beat upon a child and not go to her aid." The man was thunderstruck at her tone and the menacing look on her face, but he descended and stood before her, a sullen look on his face.

"It was no affair of mine," he said defensively. "I would only have gotten the ruffian's boot for interfering."

"Now you'll feel my boot," Sirena said, kicking him in the middle of the shin. At his cry of pain, she kicked again, this time at his other leg. "There's one place left," she said coldly. "If I were you, I would get back up there on your perch and drive this coach home. While you're doing it, remember that a defenseless child could have died for your neglect. Tomorrow I will decide if you are to remain in my employ."

"Oh Missy-ma'am, what you did for me was so wonderful. I will never be able to thank you," the girl said, throwing her dirty arms around Sirena's shoulders. "You helped me. Nobody ever did before. It was always, Wren do this, Wren do that, Wren where is the money and Wren you must get a whipping because you didn't make enough money today. Thank you, Missy-ma'am," she said, smacking Sirena on the cheek with a wet kiss. "I'll do whatever you want. I'll be so good you won't be sorry you helped me. I just love you, Missy-ma'am!" she exclaimed, hugging Sirena again.

Sirena cradled the small dark head to her and smiled. You were wrong, Regan, this child knows and feels that I am a mother. Was a mother, she corrected the thought. She stroked the child's hair the way she had stroked Mikel's. Her heart lightened as she saw the small eyes close in weariness.

Chapter Nineteen

"Sirena, darling, we really must go to the opening," Stephan said firmly. "Everyone will be there. Our absence will be conspicuous. We don't want that now, do we? I like to try my hand at a new gaming table, and your reluctance to accompany me is quite puzzling."

"There is nothing strange in my reluctance to attend this 'gala' as you call it, Stephan. I simply don't wish to come." Sirena's temper threatened to flare. Stephan was speaking to her as though she were a spoiled child. "If it means so much to you, go by yourself."

"I wouldn't enjoy it without you, darling. If you'd rather a quiet evening here at your home, then I will oblige. As a matter of fact, it has been some time since we've had privacy."

When it became obvious that Stephan had every intention of spending the evening with her, Sirena had second thoughts. The idea of whiling away an entire evening listening to him recite the inane gossip he acquired in drawing rooms and taprooms was hardly appealing. Nor did she care to listen politely as he told her of his luck at the faro table or his plans for the fencing academy. Stephan had told her also that Regan was taking Camilla to Caleb's new enterprise and the last person she wanted to face was Regan. It had been only yesterday that she went to his house. It would take some time to get over what had nearly happened. Still, if Regan had recovered himself to spend a night out with Camilla, what was she to do? Hide away in the house and refuse to show her face? "Very well, Stephan, but let us make it an early evening."

"Wonderful," Langdon smiled. "I will do all I can to make the evening a success for you."

Sirena's stomach churned at the thought of going aboard the beloved Rana and seeing Caleb again and all the gaming equipment. She wasn't entirely certain she would be able to contain her irritation over what he had made of the frigate.

Reluctantly, Sirena ascended the stairway to get ready. She took special care with her toilette in order to compensate for what had transpired between herself and Regan. A gown of rich gold with a low, yet modest, bodice was her final choice. She fastened a large, triangular-shaped emerald at the V of her gown and attached matching gems to her earlobes. Her dark hair shone like the sleek feathers of a raven as it took wing. A light touch of Spanish paper brought color to her cheeks and lips.

As Stephan waited for Frau Holtz to bring Sirena's light wrap, he said appreciatively, "Sirena, have I neglected to tell you how breathtaking you are tonight." His gaze centered upon the brooch and his finger itched to snatch it from her bosom. He contented himself with knowing that, sooner or later, his hands would close around it. "By the by, darling," Stephan said sweetly, "it seems as though I've forgotten to bring my purse. Could you extend me some pounds to amuse myself at the tables? A few hundred would do nicely."

"A few hundred what?" Sirena asked sarcastically. "You say it as though you were talking about fish!"

"Darling, I wouldn't ask you save for the fact that until I've established an account at the Sea Siren's tables, I'm at a disadvantage. Of course, we could always stop by my house to retrieve my purse." Tiny beads of perspiration broke out on Stephan's forehead. If she didn't lend him the money, he would have to contrive another lie to keep her from discovering he hadn't a farthing to his name.

"Very well, Stephan, darling," she added the endearment with a curled lip. "I wouldn't want to spoil your evening, would I?"

Suddenly Stephan turned around, sensing an unexpected presence in the room. There stood Wren, her dark eyes shining as she looked admiringly at Sirena.

"Wren! Shouldn't Frau Holtz have put you to bed? It's very late, little one." Stephan raised an eyebrow at Sirena's soft tone and brought his attention back to the child. "Stephan, this is Wren. Curtsy to Lord Langdon, sweetheart," she directed affectionately.

Wren made a quick, embarrassed curtsy and shyly glanced up into Stephan's face. The soft lighting in the room heightened the pink glow on the girl's smooth cheeks and her brown hair bounced in springy curls with her action. Stephan reached out his hand and smoothed the errant locks back from her brow and lifted her chin to study her features. "Wren, now, is it? A niece of yours, Sirena?" he questioned. "Where did you ever find such a lovely child?"

"No, not a niece. Wren was in sorry straits when we found each other. Isn't that right, sweetheart?" Again her tone gentled and Stephan noticed. "I've taken her in as my ward and the situation pleases both of us." Her smile was maternal and loving.

"Sirena, you can't mean to say you've taken a waif off the streets and brought her into your home?"

Sirena bristled at Stephan's tone and tenderly ordered Wren to run off to bed. After the girl left Sirena turned hostile, glittering eyes on her intended. "Don't ever talk in that deprecating manner around Wren. I won't have it!"

Stephan sensed the danger of his actions. Immediately, he amended: "Darling, it is only for your own sake I ask these questions. You're such a child yourself when it comes to the horrors of London. You have no way of knowing whether or not that urchin is part of a gang of thugs and intends to make it possible for them to rob you blind! Haven't you thought of that possibility?"

"Much to my own merit, Stephan, no I haven't. Wren is a loving, beautiful and grateful child. As a matter of fact, I intend to adopt her sometime soon.

As such, she deserves your respect, if not your affection."

Stephan sensed he was journeying on shaky ground. The light in Sirena's eyes had heightened to the glow of molten metal. "Of course, darling, how generous of you. I should never have spoken as I did, regardless of my apprehensions. Forgive me."

Sirena remained silent. Tugging her wrap closer about her shoulders, she moved to the door, waiting for Stephan to open it for her. As she stepped out into the cool air, Stephan turned and saw Wren staring down at him from the second-floor balustrade. Her dark eyes bore into him and held a wise and knowing look that made the hackles on the back of his neck rise to attention. Long after he had closed the door behind him, Stephan could feel the child's eyes boring into his back.

As they rode toward Rosemary Lane, where Caleb's ship was anchored near Barking Church, Sirena listened with half an ear as Stephan droned on and on about gambling halls and fortunes men had won and lost. She seethed and her body trembled. What was wrong with her? Here she was, in a civilized society, and she was behaving like an ignorant schoolgirl. Was it possible that she could only come to life at sea, free to roam the decks of her own ship dressed as the notorious Sea Siren? I've made a shambles of my life, she thought sadly as she felt Stephan inch closer to her in the coach. And, she thought unexpectedly, Stephan nauseates me. And here I am, sitting beside him and I'll marry him in a few days' time. Regan is right. I must be insane!

The carriage lurched and came to a grinding halt. Sirena fell sideways and Stephan caught her in his arms. She swallowed hard to fight back the tears as she righted herself. Strings of festively colorful lanterns lit the wharf surrounding her beloved frigate. The newly painted name on the bow was stark and eye-catching. Elegantly clad women strolled the decks, their arms demurely tucked into those of their escorts as they laughed and chattered excitedly of the evening ahead.

On deck, the newly varnished rails were sleek and

smooth to the touch. For a second Sirena was frightened to walk beneath the swaying lamps, remembering the near catastrophe at the masquerade party. Her attention was directed away from her fears to the bright ribbons and lanterns festooning the wheelhouse. Stifling her annoyance, she allowed Stephan to escort her into the main room, which had once been the crew's quarters and quarterdeck.

The center area was devoted to the gaming tables while the perimeters were furnished with intimate dining tables. A small stage had been erected in the far corner and was lengthened with a narrow runway, making it visible at every angle.

The room was so crowded it was almost impossible to move. Men argued in brisk, friendly tones as they waited their turn at dice or faro. Sirena noticed a distinguished, aristocratic gentleman weaving in and out of the throng, assuring the guests they would all be seen to and each would have their chance. Over and over he repeated that the Sea Siren would be open every night for dining, entertainment and for a toss with Lady Luck.

After Stephan seated Sirena at a dining table, he positioned himself across from her, his eyes continually roving to the dice game in progress. "Go on and enjoy yourself, Stephan, I'll be perfectly happy to sit here and watch."

"You're certain you wouldn't mind?" he asked perfunctorily, already rising from his chair, an excited, hungry look marking his handsome features.

"I'm certain. Go, have a try for me." She saw Stephan's hand go unconsciously to the breast pocket where he had put the money she had loaned him. Gallantly, he leaned over her hand and pressed his lips to it, murmuring a promise he wouldn't be long.

It was some time before Sirena noticed Caleb in the crowded, airless room. Her eyes met his the instant he looked up. She was stunned once again by the close resemblance to Regan. Why did she keep thinking of him as a young boy? It was apparent to everyone that he was a very handsome and, judging from the number of patrons on the ship, promisingly rich young man. Sadly, Regan had been correct in saying Caleb had put his immaturity behind. His shoulders were broad and muscular as he lithely snaked his way among the gay guests. His dark eyes flashed happily and a wide grin split his face as he finally succeeded in arriving at Sirena's table.

When he perceived her cold attitude, his smile faded and his eyes took on a wary, brooding expression, so like Regan's. "I'm glad you came tonight, Sirena. My father is somewhere with his young lady. He wished me success and I was hoping you would do the same."

Even his voice seemed to have changed—low, husky and almost seductive. His evening wear fitted him perfectly, as though the tailor cut it to his precise form. She noted his eye follow a slim, young woman bent on winning at dice. "Hello, Caleb," she said softly. "I can do no less than Regan. Of course, I wish you well. If tonight is any indication of your success, you'll turn a handsome profit. What will you do with your wealth?"

"First, I plan to repay what is owed to you. Then I want to go to the American colonies. How soon this will be depends upon my success here. And what of yourself, Sirena, how do you fare?"

"If you cared how I was, you would have called and not let me discover what you've done with the *Rana* by means of a carelessly thrown handbill. You've inherited a good deal of your father's traits," Sirena said cooly.

Caleb sat down opposite her and said seriously, "I am not Regan, Sirena. Remember that. I made a promise to myself not to interfere in your lives and I expect the same from both of you. I could well be making a terrible mistake with this enterprise, but I will have only myself to blame. Haven't you noticed I'm no longer that young boy?"

"I've noticed," Sirena answered quietly, a part of her mourning for that tousle-headed youth who climbed like a monkey up the masts and through the rigging. "Tell me, Caleb, what do you think of Regan's betrothed?"

Something flashed in Caleb's eyes as he squirmed beneath Sirena's scrutiny. Even in the dim light she could detect the beginning of a flush. "They look well together," he hedged. "My father has had little to say to me since he came aboard this evening. Sirena, what are you going to do—do you plan to stay in England?"

"Did he instruct you to discover my intentions?"

"Of course not. I ask because I'm interested."

"When I decide, I'll let you know. Now, if you'll excuse me, I think I'll try my hand against the house." With a nod to Caleb, she rose and walked off, aware of him staring at her receding back.

This wasn't the old Sirena, Caleb thought dejectedly. Never had he seen her so hostile. Between Regan and himself, they had succeeded in stealing the spirit right out of her. His dark gaze searched the room for Regan and Camilla. His eyes became speculative as he walked in their direction, his attention centering on the beautiful blonde who was soon to be his stepmother.

Regan settled his fianceé beside a portly woman, with whom she seemed familiar, and made his way to the crowded faro table. Just as he turned his back on the ladies, Caleb sauntered up to Camilla and offered to point out the attractions of the *Sea Siren*. Camilla flushed and prettily agreed.

Out on deck, beneath the festive lanterns, Camilla looked up at Caleb. "Regan never told me he had a son. I can't imagine why, since you are a very attractive man."

Caleb smiled, barely keeping himself from grimacing. Regan kept many secrets to himself, he was thinking. Then, looking down into Camilla's fragile face, he realized how reluctant Regan would be to admit he had a son nearly as old as his future wife. "Perhaps Father was frightened I would steal you off."

Camilla looked up at Caleb, the resemblance to Regan amazing. Despite the fact that Caleb's hair and eyes were dark brown while Regan resembled a Norse god, their gestures and stride were the same, as well as the breadth of shoulders and slender hips. But in Caleb, Regan's good looks were almost exotic, owing to the slight tilt of his eyes. "Would you, Caleb? Steal me off, that is?" Her frank appreciation for him was evident in the languorous look she bestowed on him.

"Yes, I suppose I would have," he answered truthfully. She was the most exquisite creature he had ever seen and merely being near her did odd things to his pulse. "Would you have come with me?" he asked huskily.

For an answer, Camilla gazed into his eyes, allowing him to see there a torrent of emotion. Abruptly, she looked away, a faint blush on her smooth cheeks, and retreated slightly as though putting herself out of temptation's way. Several paces distant, she stopped and leaned over the rail, studying the star-filled night.

Caleb felt as though his heart would rise up in his throat and choke him. He had to be near her, even the few feet separating them made him feel as though he'd stepped into shadow after the bright warming sun. She was so lovely, and in her pale blue gown she looked like a spring flower basking in the moonlight.

Sirena's eyes had narrowed as she watched Caleb and Camilla leave the main room. She had thrown the dice and left her winnings on the board, to the astonishment of the company. Quietly, she had followed Caleb and Camilla across the familiar deck. She knew each creaking plank, each worm hole in the salt-scrubbed deck. It was several minutes before she found the young duo at the rail of the stern looking out over the water. Their manner was so intimate she became embarrassed and was about to leave when she saw Caleb bring up his hand and gently stroke Camilla's cheek. The girl leaned her face into the palm of his hand, searching his face as he gazed into her eyes.

Camilla seemed to shiver involuntarily and Caleb swiftly removed his frock coat and gently placed it around her shoulders, bringing it close around her neck. Sirena knew that Camilla had aroused Caleb's protective instincts. She was the first woman he had ever seemed truly interested in, and in the manner of all young men, he imagined himself Camilla's knight on white charger. She flattered his masculinity, catered to his virility and swept him into her carefully spun web.

Sirena watched, all her female instincts knowing Camilla's ploy. Oh, Caleb, she sighed silently. I thought I taught you about wily women! Unbidden to Sirena's mind came the memory of Caleb as a child and his protectiveness toward *her*. She recalled how, as a lad, he had sought to save her from the lecherous crewman, Wooster. He had put his life on the line for her that day, taking up sword against the seaman and risking death, to protect her.

An anger rose up in Sirena, directed toward Regan. Camilla was too young for him. The anger subsided and worry took its place. Caleb was playing with fire when he entertained thoughts of Camilla. If Regan should ever find out, Caleb would be placing himself in as great a danger as he did when he confronted that scurve, Wooster.

Sirena drew in her breath as Caleb's voice carried across to her and she heard him murmur to Camilla that her eyes were unequaled by the stars and her hair was liquid silver in the moonlight. They leaned closer to one another as though pulled by an invisible force. Caleb gathered Camilla near him and brought her lips to his in a long, lingering kiss. Camilla's smooth, white arms tightened about his broad back as she strained closer.

Sirena felt her heart pound as she heard faint words from Caleb and watched them make their way to the captain's cabin where Regan had made love to her so long ago. When they were out of sight, Sirena saw the irony of the situation and threw back her head and laughed, the sound carrying out over the water and coming back to rest at her feet. "You're too late, Regan. Your son has no need of a brothel. Like father, like son."

Back in the main room, Sirena managed to wiggle her way between Stephan and Regan. Regan was making losing tosses of the dice time and again. Stephan, however, had won a modest sum, to Sirena's amusement. From Regan's expression, not only was he losing, he was also on the verge of inebriation.

"Mynheer van der Rhys, I believe Camilla is looking for you," Sirena said, a wicked smile on her face. "She was strolling the deck a minute ago and the poor child seemed lost. I assume she lacks your attention."

Regan turned, glanced at her and left. Stephan took her arm and escorted her back to their table.

"What do you think, Sirena? God, how I wish I'd thought of doing something like this myself. The lucky fellow who owns this enterprise will make a fortune in a fortnight. Lord Aubrey Farrington is part owner, I understand."

"Then you don't realize that your step-grandson is his partner."

Stephan looked at her quizzically.

"Didn't you realize Regan has a full-grown son, Caleb. This is his ship. How nice for you, two entrepreneurs in the family!"

Stephan Langdon seemed shocked to learn Regan already had a son, but he didn't seem altogether displeased. "I had no idea; Camilla never mentioned—"

"It's possible she didn't know."

Mentally, Stephan calculated what effect Regan having a son would have on Camilla's prospects to inherit his fortune. Deciding that the loss would be negligible, he brightened. The younger van der Rhys would certainly extend credit to his prospective step-grandfather. "Whatever. I am proud to have such an inventive young man join my family. Our family," he quickly amended. "Perhaps I can give him a few pointers. For one point, exclusivity is the key to a thriving establishment. Perhaps I should avail this Caleb van der Rhys of my knowledge of such matters. Of course, Lord Farrington has a certain acquaintanceship with these things, but I fear he lacks the important degree of finesse. Is something wrong, Sirena," he interrupted himself, "you suddenly seem very quiet."

"A raging headache, Stephan. I wonder if you would mind calling it a night? We can return some other time."

"Darling, we haven't seen the gypsy dancers yet!" Stephan declared, unwilling to accommodate the request.

"I have seen all manner of gypsy dancers in Spain and I told you I have a headache. If you refuse to escort me, I will avail myself of your coach and go alone," Sirena said hotly.

Stephan recovered himself and spoke warmly. "Forgive me, darling. I allowed myself to be carried away with the gala atmosphere. I couldn't bear to have you suffer. Can you forgive my thoughtlessness?" He became solicitous and led her out onto the deck.

"Look, Stephan, there's the Dutchman and he doesn't seem to have had much luck in locating your daughter."

"Regan, where is Camilla?" Stephan called.

Regan weaved his way to the railing and looked at Sirena first and then at his future father-in-law. "I don't know where the hell she is," he slurred. "An explanation will be in order when I do find her."

"Perhaps I can be of some help," Sirena offered. "I saw her walking the deck with a handsome young man. She called him Caleb, if my memory serves me."

Regan noticed her inflection when she said 'young man.' "And that pleases you, doesn't it? It's made your evening complete," he said savagely, gripping her arm.

"See here, Regan. Remove your hand from the lady; your drunkenness in unbecoming. If a man cannot hold his liquor, he should not drink." Stephan raised his voice.

"If a man cannot control his daughter, then he should not take her out in public," Regan countered menacingly.

"I hesitate to remind you it was you who brought Camilla here. And it was you who left her to her own devices for amusement while you gambled!"

"I knew this was a wicked ship, a wicked, wicked ship," Sirena said coyly. "That is the reason Stephan is taking me home. I really don't think this is a fitting place for a lady and dear, dear Camilla—why, anything could have happened to her. That man certainly was strong. Why, one little flick of his hand and she would be . . . pulp!"

Stephan had no intention of telling the lovely Sirena that the demure Camilla would have the gentleman over the railing in a split second if she wanted. He would have to find her before van der Rhys had second thoughts about marrying her. Stupid girl, what was she up to?

"Stephan, Mynheer van der Rhys is absolutely correct. Camilla needs a controlling hand; and, until their marriage, the chore is yours. The poor child needs supervision. Poor baby, something absolutely awful must have happened to her."

"Shut up, Sirena," Regan said harshly.

Stephan stiffened. He was in a most untenable situation. He hesitated to encourage Regan's wrath and perhaps ruin Camilla's chances, yet he was honorbound to protect Sirena from the Dutchman's insults. "Regan, I must caution you not to speak to Sirena that way. The only reason I won't call you out is you're betrothed to my daughter and you're drunk." Fine perspiration broke out on Stephan's brow.

"Disgusting," Sirena said pertly. "I will overlook his rudeness, Stephan, because I am so worried about Camilla. Do you think we should organize a search party? I, for one, would be glad to help."

Stephan's tone was suspicious. "I believe you said you had a headache and wanted to go home."

"Do you think for one minute I would be able to sleep with that infant lost? What kind of woman do you take me for?" she demanded virtuously. "Come, Mynheer, I will help you find her," she said, taking Regan's arm.

Stephan uttered a cry of relief. "There's no need, darling, here is Camilla now. Young woman, where have you been?" he asked firmly.

"It was such a lovely evening I thought I would explore the deck while Regan had his turn at the table," Camilla said happily.

Regan was glaring at Camilla, and Sirena wondered if he noticed her lips were slightly swollen. Leaning near Regan, Sirena whispered, "You really must tell me where she's been the next time we meet. If for some reason her excuses don't satisfy you, seek me out and I'll be happy to tell you." She gathered her skirts in her hand and deboarded with Stephan, leaving Regan staring after her with rage engulfing his features.

Sirena was very quiet on the ride home and Stephan soon tired of trying to engage her in conversation. Her thoughts swung back to Regan and what he would do if he discovered Caleb was romantically involved with Camilla. Belatedly, she realized she shouldn't have baited Regan. The last thing in this world she wanted was for him to learn where Camilla had been . . . and with whom.

Relations were strained between Regan and his son as it was. This was a breech that would never heal! Caleb's disloyalty and Camilla's infidelity would never be forgiven. She thought of the relationship once enjoyed between Regan and Caleb and a lump swelled in her throat. Theirs was a loving bond and it had always included her and Mikel. They were so alike, the man she loved and his son, and they never forgot for a minute that it was because of her they were together again.

Regan and Caleb had once shared something beautiful and they still could. This breach would not last their lifetimes. Pushing back the tears of regret that something she had almost said would have destroyed the two people she loved most in the world, she resolved she would never tell Regan anything.

Regan helped Camilla into the carriage, all signs of drunkenness gone as he thrust her against the side of the seat. "Now, tell me where you were and what you were doing! You made me the fool in front of your father and that Spanish witch."

Camilla allowed a tear to spill down her cheek. She had no intention of telling him where she had been. Her body still ached for Caleb. The soul-shattering ecstasy in his arms was something she would want again and again. "Dearest Regan, I was so piqued when you left me for a pair of dice, I just knew I had to go outdoors for a breath of air to compose myself. A gentleman was smoking one of those filthy cigars and giving me a headache. When your son offered to point out several attractions of his ship, I agreed. Soon after, he was called away on a matter of business. What harm was done?" she asked softly, nestling closer to him. "Regan, are you jealous? How gallant of you!" she giggled. "I quite adore you when you're like this. And darling, please, you mustn't concern yourself about being made a fool. No one could ever do that. You're so strong, so manly," she breathed. "As for Sirena, she would never consider my behavior unladylike. She's so earthy. Why, she has been in my father's bed many times," Camilla lied. "I'm not a child, Regan. I know what is going on around me, and you must believe me when I tell you my evening was innocent."

A chill washed over Regan. He withdrew his arm from her, his muscles tensed. Camilla continued to speak. "I have a feeling, mind you, it is only a hunch, but I think something will develop between them. I've seen the way she looks at him, and I suspect she would like to become Lady Langdon," Camilla babbled on. "Of course, my father is not a fool. I'm certain he will do the honorable thing and marry her sooner or later."

On and on Camilla babbled, till Regan thought he would lose all patience.

Why did he feel this way? What Sirena did with her life was her own business, just as what he did was his own. Something deep inside him knew that Camilla was lying to him about her evening stroll and about Sirena. Camilla had been with Caleb and . . .

The carriage had come to a halt and Camilla waited for Regan to escort her to her door. "Darling Regan, I am so sorry I neglected you," she pouted. "When we're married, I'll be at your side constantly. I'll be the most devoted wife in all England." She held up her face for his kiss and immediately went into the house.

Regan walked back to the carriage with the thought racing through his head that he should return to the *Sea Siren* and beat the truth out of Caleb. His broad shoulders slumped and he brought his hands to his temples when he relaxed against the seat. Camilla wasn't worth it. He knew he didn't love her; she was only a means to an end. Suddenly, he felt like retching. Sirena was right; even *he* had a price. Nothing was working out the way he planned it.

Camilla danced up to her room and flounced down on the bed. Her thoughts were on Caleb and her hour with him. Tonight, there were no thoughts about her empty stomach and the food she had cached away in her reticule. She lay back, a dreamy expression on her face.

The last patron gone, the bolt secure, Lord Farrington began to count the night's profits. From time to time he smiled happily as he divided the money into separate piles. Caleb watched him, a strange look lighting his eyes. In one night he had become a successful businessman, seduced his father's betrothed and antagonized Sirena. In the last few hours he had left the last vestiges of boyhood behind. He had found love.

When Camilla had crept from the bunk to return to the gaming hall, he had felt no remorse, only complete satisfaction. All the other times and all the other women meant nothing. This time it had been different. Camilla was special.

He sighed happily as he watched Lord Farrington fill two pouches with the profits and separate what they would need to pay expenses.

When Camilla had bent over his naked body and whispered in his ear that she would return, he had thought he had died and gone to Heaven. Clutching her to him, he had kissed her ardently till she was breathless. Gently, he had pushed her away. "Another time," he had whispered in her ear.

"No," Camilla had panted. "Again! Again, Caleb," she had said, slipping her gown off her shoulder so he could see one creamy, coral-tipped breast.

Caleb had licked dry lips and straightened her gown. "Another time," he had stated firmly. Some instinct had cautioned him that this was not the time to satisfy their wants. Another long, passionate kiss and Camilla, her breathing harsh and ragged in the quiet cabin, gathered up her reticule and left, but only after bestowing on Caleb a long and promising look.

"I will count the hours and the minutes," she had whispered.

Caleb grinned and forced his attention back to the present. "Well, how did we do tonight?" he asked.

"With what we took in tonight, we could both live comfortably for a long time. But that's not the end of it, eh Caleb, my boy? A toast, Caleb, to our success," Aubrey Farrington said, pouring wine into two goblets. "To our continued success," he said, regarding Caleb over the rim of the glass. His rheumy eyes narrowed slightly when he noticed the expression on Caleb's face. He had seen that look before, worn it himself as a matter of fact. "And which of the ladies offered you her favors? Don't deny it, lad, it's there on your face."

Caleb shrugged and drained his goblet, not offering any explanations.

"You'll soon discover you have your pick of women, and most will want to crawl between the sheets with you. Do yourself a favor, lad. Taste them all and don't tie yourself to one. There's a long life ahead, long and profitable, and if you play your cards right, it will be very enjoyable."

Farrington laughed at his little witticism and Caleb joined him, leaning back and stretching his long, muscular legs in front of him. He was completely relaxed. When he moved, Lord Farrington was reminded of a large, jungle cat who had felled his prey. Caleb enjoyed his women and made the best of his lusty appetites. Whatever, if he were to indulge his manly prowess, he wouldn't pay too much attention to the profits.

Stephan Langdon burst into his darkened house calling for Camilla at the top of his voice. He had never been so furious with her in her whole life! It had taken all his control not to thrash her there on the gambling folly in the presence of Regan and Sirena. She had very nearly ruined their plans and he would see it never happened again. That romantic dalliance with Regan's son had very nearly cost them the marriage to the wealthy van der Rhys.

Bounding up the stairs toward Camilla's room, the rage welled up in him, reddening his finely drawn features. He knew if he didn't get himself under control Camilla would be the worse for it. "Camilla! Camilla, you little fool! I mean to see you, so open this door!"

Camilla had been lying against her pillows dreaming of Caleb's strong embrace and ardent lovemaking when she heard the front door bang shut announcing her father's return. She knew he would be angry with her and she sincerely hoped he would leave her to herself until morning. She wanted nothing to interrupt her languid thoughts of the tall, dark-eyed young man whom she had only this night discovered was Regan's son. Caleb was vital, daring and enthusiastic. Regan was a strong, fascinating man, but he was so staid, so mature. He lacked imagination. That was the difference, Camilla decided. Regan had never attempted to take her to bed. He treated her as though she were a mere child whose head was empty of everything save a new gown or pretty hats. Regan had never even thought to scratch her surface to find the sensuous woman who lurked beneath. But Caleb, yes, Caleb was quite a man. His youth was appealing, exciting, with a wild, urgent quality no woman could resist.

"Camilla! I mean to see you! Open this door!" For a fleeting moment Camilla was frightened. She had never heard this rage in Stephan's voice directed at her. This was the tone he used with lazy servants or insolent shopkeepers who plagued him for payment. With a shock she remembered this was the voice he had used with her mother, leaving her sobbing and tearful.

"The door is open, Father. Please come in," she said sweetly, ignoring his frame of mind. She would have to keep her wits about her.

Stephan entered. "What in the world were you trying to prove this evening, daughter? Don't you know you very nearly destroyed the betrothal between yourself and the Dutchman?" He advanced on her and she resolved he would not obtain the advantage and reduce her to a cloying, crying weakling. As he had done with Mother, a little voice echoed through her head.

Standing erect, tiny chin jutting in defiance, Camilla faced her father. "Calm yourself. Regan was quite satisfied with my explanations. Besides, Caleb is his son, or didn't you know? He would never suspect his son of being interested in his fiancée. Regan has very definite scruples and, naturally, attributes the same to his son." She had kept her voice steady, had even ended her little speech with a stifled yawn.

Stephan grasped her arm in a hurting hold. "So say you! But you didn't see him when he couldn't find you. There was murder in his eyes, and I don't think he would have stopped to consider who the young man was! As for you, he would have snapped you in two!"

Camilla wrestled free, tears stinging the backs of her eyelids, but she managed to say, "Perhaps. But he was very different with me. And he didn't murmur a word about calling off the wedding."

Stephan was not satisfied with his daughter's assurances. "You can't be smug where the Dutchman is concerned," he growled. "Regan can't be made the fool, like Tyler Sinclair, or even be trifled with, like his son. Now get your wits about you, you little ninny!" He shook her violently to punctuate his words.

"Get your hands off me, Father," Camilla sneered, her voice low and seething. "I tell you nothing has happened between Regan and myself. But perhaps it should! Caleb is much more to my liking! And rich, too! As for Tyler, don't underestimate him, Father. He's not quite the fool you think him!" Roughly, she pushed him away from her. "Ooh! If I had any sense at all, I would quit this whole business and run to Tyler and beg him to tell his parents about us! The Baron and Baroness would accept me if I promised never to have another thing to do with you! It's *you* they object to, Father, not me!"

With lightning speed Stephan brought up his hand and cracked her soundly on her face. Camilla staggered backward, tears springing from her astounded eyes.

"So this is what I get for being a devoted father! Treachery! Bah! You are like all women, faithless, traitorous! Like your mother!" He loomed over her, his face contorted with hate. "I should have done away with you when I did away with her. I should have known you would leave childhood behind and grow to womanhood!" He spit the word "womanhood" as though it were the name of a leprous disease. "As for our plans, they will be executed on schedule. You will marry van der Rhys. After we have secured his fortunes, if you wish, I will make you a lovely young widow. Until then, see you behave accordingly!" He stalked from the room, leaving Camilla nursing her wounded face.

She stared after him, horror mingled with astonishment dulling her pansy eyes. Until this moment she had never been frightened of her father. She had always thought his remarks concerning widowhood were in jest. He had often threatened to do away with Tyler if he became a nuisance, but he had actually seemed serious when he said he *would* rid her of Regan. A chill crept up her spine when at last she was able to face the statement he had made concerning her mother. ". . . I did away with her!" A nightmare memory of her mother's face as the coach drove out the drive flashed before her. Her eyes so empty and hopeless, that simple gesture of lifting her hand to wave good-bye.

"Oh, God! No, God, no!" Camilla gasped, sinking to her knees on the thick carpet. "She knew! Mother knew what he was doing to her!"

Chapter Twenty

Frau Holtz stamped around Sirena's suite going through the motions of helping her mistress dress. The hour was very early, the sun was just breaking over the horizon. The woman's pinched face clearly stated she thought this marriage to Stephan Langdon the most foolish idea the Mevrouw had ever dreamed up. More than foolish, outright stupid! Frau Holtz disliked Sir Stephan Langdon intensely. Whenever she was in his presence, it was all she could do to keep from sweeping him out of the house like a spider.

"You can stop overdramatizing the situation, Frau Holtz. I've explained my reasons to you and enough has been said," Sirena spoke commandingly. "I've decided to marry Stephan and the matter is closed. Now will you help me get ready or should I call Wren?"

"Nein. You'll do no such thing. The poor little child needs her sleep, and she doesn't have to remember

the day you make a fool of yourself," the Frau answered tartly.

"Then hurry and get my shoes out of the clothes press. Stephan will be here any moment." Sirena turned to look in the mirror, patting her hair into place. It promised to be a long day. Her own wedding this morning and Regan's this afternoon. How she would manage to get through it, God only knew. She wrung her hands anxiously, trying to bring some warmth to them. Her whole body was like ice and there was a pounding in her temples. Covertly, she risked a glance at Frau Holtz, some part of her praying the old woman would tie her to the bed and refuse to allow her to leave the house with Stephan. Taking a deep breath, she knew her fate had been sealed. She herself had arrived at this decision and would follow through with it, regardless of the black cloud looming over her. Sirena cast her thoughts and apprehensions away and made a supreme effort to brighten her spirits. She told herself that Stephan was past fifty years of age and his demands on her would be few and far between. And if he should become overzealous in his duties as a husband, she would make short work of that! She meant to keep the upper hand in this marriage and Stephan had better make no mistake about it.

"I wish you would allow me to come with you, Mevrouw. You will need a woman to be with you." The Frau's voice had softened and she was sympathetic, as though Sirena were going to a funeral and would need the support of a friend.

Reaching out her hand and touching the Frau's sleeve, Sirena answered in a like tone. "This is something I must do alone, good friend. Thank you for your offer."

"Where is the . . . the ceremony to take place. Why couldn't you have arranged to have it here?"

"Stephan has a friend who has kindly offered us his home in the outskirts of the city. We will be met there by the clergy. Immediately after, we will return to London, in time for Camilla's wedding to Regan." In spite of herself, Sirena nearly choked on the words. "As you know, Stephan will be living here with us.

He's already moved a number of his belongings here. He is leaving his house on Drury Lane for Camilla and . . . her husband." The last phrase was uttered in a whisper and nearly broke the Frau's heart.

"Mevrouw, I would rather see you face pirates than see you with this man Langdon. There's something about him that frightens me. Don't ask me to explain it, I can't."

To offset the impact of hearing her own suspicions spoken by Frau Holtz, Sirena laughed uneasily. "You've seen me deal with pirates, and they are men, just as Stephan is a man. Why do you doubt my ability to deal with him?"

"Because a pirate is a pirate. It is there for all the world to see. This Lord Langdon wears many faces, and my instincts tell me he's not the person he would have the world think he is." Again, Frau Holtz's face crumpled into worried lines.

"Don't worry about me. If it ever comes to dealing with Stephan, rest assured, I'll know how to go about it!" Even to herself, her voice sounded less assured than her bravado.

Before the footman could announce him, Sirena heard Stephan's carriage wheels on the drive. Picking up her beaded reticule from the bed, and with a cursory glance in the mirror, Sirena swept from the room with a last instruction, "Kiss Wren for me, Frau Holtz, and tell her I'll be getting home rather late. I'll see her in the morning!"

Stephan waited for her at the bottom of the stairs. When he saw her, his eyes lit in appreciation. There was no denying it, Sirena was a beautiful woman, and she was bringing more into this marriage than social status and money. He knew he would not have been half as smug if he were marrying a rich, old woman who would lend him social acceptance as well as an indefatigable supply of funds. As important as it had always been to him, Stephan was discovering, once having gotten it, there were some things more important than money.

Sirena swept down the stairs toward him, her apricot silk gown bringing a fresh, healthy tint to her cheeks and throwing her shining ebony hair into contrast. As she pulled on her matching gloves, she looked up and smiled at him. "Are you ready, Stephan?"

"More than you'll ever know, darling," he reached for her gloved hand and pressed his mouth to her fingers. "You'll need a wrap, Sirena. The morning is still chilly."

"I have it here," she remarked, pointing to a dark brown capelet trimmed with sable. Stephan took it and placed it about her shoulders. His touch against her flesh held a distinct possessiveness and Sirena shuddered slightly. An impulse compelled her to run from this man, run as far away as she possibly could, yet she stood her ground and pulled the capelet around herself as though warding off a blast of cold air. Stephan did not seem to notice, and led her out the door to the waiting coach.

It was so early in the day little activity took place on the streets of the city. Few merchants were up and about at this hour and the citizens, who loitered about the pubs and alleys, were usually worse the wear from the tippling the night before. In the quiet, the bells of St. Paul's rung out, welcoming the new day, to be joined by the melodious chiming from St. Peter's, St. Olave's, St. Botolph's, St. Dunstan's, St. Sepulchre's and, finally, Barking Church near Hounditch Road, denoting the city limit.

They had made exceedingly good time through London, owing to the desolation. Within the hour they were embarking upon White Chapel Street past Goodman's Field to the home of Anthony Webster, where the exchanging of vows would take place.

Stephan became increasingly unsettled by Sirena's silence and watched her as she smoothed the folds of her gown between nervous fingers. "Sirena, tell me you're not angry because I declined to have Tyler Sinclair be our witness. Please try to understand, darling, Anthony Webster is the only witness we need. It seemed unreasonable to drag Sinclair all the way out into the country with us."

Sirena lifted her head. "I don't understand your objections, Stephan. It is only natural I would like to have a friend present at this important event. However, I acceded to your wishes; let's make no more of it." Her tone was cool and reserved, but her fingers still plucked anxiously at her dress.

"You really are a winsome child, darling," Stephan whispered as he put his arm around her and drew her close for a kiss.

Sirena's blood froze and she strangled on her panic. She pushed him politely away, murmuring something about crushing her gown and wanting to look as lovely as possible on this most special day.

Stephan's gray eyes became like shards of ice at her rejection and his already thin mouth pinched tightly, thrusting his stubborn chin outward. Sirena looked at him and wondered that she had never before seen the lines of cruelty in his face. Finding himself beneath her scrutiny, Stephan smiled in what he hoped was a display of affection and released her from his embrace.

"Poor child, every woman has the right to be nervous on her wedding day," he soothed, patting her hand affectionately.

For an answer, Sirena turned her head and gazed out the window at the passing scenery, wondering why in heaven she was here with a man she did not love, could never love, traveling down the road to marry him.

As the coach swung up a wide, curving drive canopied with oak, Stephan reached into his smartly tailored vest and noted that his timepiece had just struck the hour of eight. The watery sunshine had now blossomed to a full golden splendor and promised a beautiful day. "Happy is the bride the sun shines on, darling," Stephan recited, watching for Sirena's reaction. It peeved him greatly that she was pensive and distracted rather than graciously, or even coyly, exuberant over their coming marriage. Regardless of how attractive Sirena's fortune was to Stephan, his ego demanded his bride be flatteringly excited over sharing his name and his bed.

The Webster home came into view, and Sirena saw it was constructed of fieldstone and heavy hewn timbers, giving it a rustic charm. Once inside, however, the rustic gave way to gracious furniture and bright, airy rooms. Anthony Webster, a man close to Stephan's age, greeted her warmly, his bovine, brown eyes smiling into hers.

Weakly, she returned his smile and thanked him for offering his hospitality. "Think nothing of it. Stephan is one of my oldest friends. I was more than happy to oblige."

"Then you will be driving to London with us to attend Camilla's wedding," Sirena said with certainty, relieved she would not have to share the carriage all the way back to the city alone with Stephan.

Anthony Webster seemed at a loss for words. "Why, no, er . . . that is . . . " His eyes flew to Stephan.

Smoothly, Stephan interjected, "Sirena, darling, you have our own wedding to think of, why must you dwell on Camilla's? In fact, Anthony finds it impossible to attend the fair. He has other plans for today concerning his political ambitions. Don't you, Anthony?"

"Yes, yes, as a matter of fact, I do. I was so sorry to refuse, but there was little help for it. Now, let us not stand here wasting time. Justice Tallman is waiting in the drawing room." Squire Webster took hold of Sirena's arm and escorted her through the hall to the flower-bedecked drawing room. "I hope you approve of the decorations." Once again his eyes went to Stephan, who had followed them into the room.

Near the mantel stood a short, rotund gentleman of the cloth, who smiled in greeting. Seeing him standing there brought Sirena's panic so close to the surface, she nearly turned and ran. In fact, she would have if Squire Webster hadn't had such a firm grip on her arm.

The next few minutes swept past Sirena's consciousness in a blur. She realized vaguely that she had signed the marriage contract. She heard Justice Tallman recite the vows and she heard her responses. Her finger, where Stephan had placed an impressive, square-cut, emerald ring, felt heavy and strangely cold. At last, when the ceremony was completed, Stephan embraced her. Her lips were bloodless, her vision foggy, her hands atremble. What had she done? Why had she married Stephan Langdon?

When they were alone once again in the coach returning to London, Stephan kept his arm about her and insisted upon kissing her. When she felt his tongue probe her lips, she was hard pressed not to display her disgust. His tongue was soft and felt thick against her mouth and too smooth, too wet, like a thing alive, like something she could find living a dark existence beneath a rock in the garden.

"Stephan, please," she protested. "Control yourself! We've still Camilla's wedding to attend; would you have me appearing mussed and wrinkled?"

"To hell with Camilla's wedding," Stephan said against her mouth, his hands groping beneath her skirts. "I've waited too long to claim you, Sirena."

"Stephan! Please!" she shoved him away with what she hoped was a smile. "You can't miss your own daughter's marriage! What would Camilla think of me if I kept her father from the most important day of her life?"

Reluctantly, Stephan pulled away, straightening his waistcoat and adjusting his trousers. "You will have your way for now, Sirena. But I warn you; I find you the most desirable woman I've ever met, and I'll be waiting for tonight. Darling," he added as though the endearment were an afterthought.

Sirena looked into her husband's eyes and saw there a terrifying lust. Stephan meant every word he said. Why had she never noticed how glitteringly hard his gray eyes could be? Why had she supposed that Stephan's interest in sex would be merely perfunctory? He had never made advances or pressed her for her favors until this moment. She had been mistaken in assuming that age had dulled his appetite for the nuptial bed. Now, glancing at his slim, athletic body, she realized what a fool she had been.

"I've brought along a trifling surprise to celebrate our union," Stephan announced, reaching beneath the seat to withdraw a wicker basket. Opening it, he revealed two crystal glasses and a bottle of white wine. With an expert economy of motion, he poured the wine into the goblets and handed her one. "To us, darling." He clicked the glasses together and drank heartily.

The wine was cool to her throat and Sirena drank

greedily, holding out her goblet for more. "It's delicious, Stephan."

"I'm delighted you like it, darling. I've saved another bottle for tonight."

Hearing his words, Sirena gulped the wine down, feeling it warm her innards. God, she thought, she would need a whole bottle to herself if she were to get through the hours ahead with Stephan. She had been so purposeful about throwing stumbling blocks in Regan's path she thought nothing of what marriage to Stephan would mean. Regan, she thought, taking another long drink. Camilla would be going home to spend her wedding night in Regan's bed while she would be left to Stephan! She drank again.

Stephan sipped at his wine, savoring the fruity flavor, his eyes darting to his new wife. "I'm glad you like it so well, Sirena. I'll arrange to import it for our wine cellar."

Sirena barely heard him, she was so intent on her thoughts. She had been a fool. Again! The wine had already gone to her head owing to her empty stomach. She tried to review the reasons she had married Stephan. Somehow they all became confused and muddled in her mind.

Sirena shook her head and drained her goblet. She couldn't think. Relaxing against the plush interior of the coach, she allowed Stephan to refill her glass.

Camilla Langdon sat before the mirror applying the finishing touches to her buttercup-yellow hair. The timepiece on her nightstand told her it was nearly ten o'clock. Her father would have married Sirena by this time, and they would be headed back toward London if they had not already arrived. The Langdons had at last secured their futures, Camilla thought sourly. Or at least Father had, she amended. Her own future was still uncertain. She was entering into a bigamous marriage. A vision of Tyler stepping forward to protest her marriage to Regan flashed before her.

Camilla wasn't certain what had gotten into Tyler lately. He seemed more self-assured, self-confident, as though he harbored a wonderful secret. At times she wondered if his financial condition had improved, but then she would think of the paltry amounts he gave her on loan and discounted the idea entirely.

Along with these reflections came the memory of her first wedding day. She had been young, so young and in love. The way only a sixteen-year-old girl could be. They had spent the summer at the Sinclair's country estate, and Tyler and she had been immediately attracted to one another. More than attracted, wildly in love! Stephan had kept a wary eye on the young couple, giving them excuses to be alone together, covering their trysts, condoning their relationship, and, at last, helping them elope and giving his blessing. At first, she thought herself lucky to have such an understanding parent, but then she learned the truth. Stephan had his goal set for the Sinclair money, and what better way to get his hands on it than to have his daughter marry the heir to the title.

Her wedding day to Regan was so different from that day nearly four years past when she and Tyler had run off together. Then she had been breathlessly in love; today she was going through the motions.

Though she considered Regan one of the most fascinating men she had ever met, she was frightened of him. Regan was no schoolboy who could be toyed with. He was a worldly, intelligent man who knew what he wanted from life and went after it. While his treatment of her was always courtly and gentle, she knew his ire could be aroused. She still shuddered to think of the night they had gone aboard Caleb's *Sea Siren* and Regan could not find her. Regan was a challenge and would never knowingly allow himself to be manipulated. Camilla gulped when she thought of Tyler's threat to expose her to the Dutchman. She could almost feel Regan's strong, capable hands closing around her throat. Perhaps that was why she found herself so enamored of Caleb. He was a younger version of his handsome father without that terrifying aura of power which Regan exuded.

Suddenly, a heartrending sob tore from Camilla's throat. "Damn you, Tyler! Why couldn't it have worked for us?" she cried, lowering her head to her folded arms on the dressing table. "We're both too greedy for our own good."

That was how the maid found her when she brought the freshly ironed wedding gown to Camilla's room.

Stephan ushered Sirena through the front doors of his house on Drury Lane. Guests were thronging through the rooms, looking for the best vantage point to witness the wedding of Camilla Langdon to Regan van der Rhys. Gratefully, he realized the shabby furnishings and worn carpets were not noticeable because of the gay decorations and crowds of people. As he led Sirena through to the drawing room, several gentlemen clapped him on the back and congratulated him as father of the bride. He answered their good wishes with a smile, but was concentrating on Sirena, who had had more than enough wine. He felt a slight tug at his arm as she stumbled once and decided the safest thing was to seat her near the doors to the garden where the vows would be said.

As he glanced around the room, he felt an uncontrollable desire to announce that Sirena and he had been married that very morning. The sooner word spread that he had become the husband of an heiress, the quicker his credit would improve.

Sirena allowed Stephan to seat her and she tried to focus on the milling guests. She had definitely drunk too much wine and she knew it, but somehow it seemed the only way to get through the day. An ominous pall hung about her as she saw Stephan smile and speak first to one guest, then another. She hoped he thought she was the blushing bride and that was why she was so remote. She would hate to have him know she was holding onto her chair for dear life as the room spun around her.

Through blurry eyes, Sirena looked toward the rear of the room and saw a manservant open the door to admit yet another guest. Fuzzy though her mind was, she wondered snidely if Stephan had invited the whole of London to witness Regan make a fool of himself. Her eyes adjusted and her attention strained to see the person was Caleb. He entered and fumbled uncomfortably with his cravat and his fashionable narrowly cut waistcoat seemed to strain against his broad shoulders. Her first impulse was to rise and rush to greet him, so relieved was she to see a familiar face from the past. But her feet were anchors and her knees wobbly from the wine, and she sat back down on her chair, hoping Caleb would notice her and cover the distance between them himself.

Caleb scanned the crowd and almost immediately observed Sirena. He turned away, hoping she hadn't seen him. He didn't want to speak with her, to open himself to her possible sarcasm, to expose his vulnerabilities to her. He strongly suspected Sirena knew what had transpired with Camilla.

Before coming to the Langdon house on Drury Lane, Caleb had contrived several excuses which would prevent him from attending the wedding. He knew none of them would be acceptable to Regan, who had made it clear he wanted his son present.

Gnashing his teeth, Caleb reached for a glass of wine from the tray of a passing servant. Two swallows and the glass was empty. He reached for another. He was a cauldron of boiling emotion.

Caleb had never desired a woman the way he did Camilla, and in a few moments she would be his stepmother, married to his father. He had never felt so ashamed as he did for his betrayal of Regan. Even worse was the knowledge that he was allowing Regan to march innocently into a marriage with a woman whose disloyalty would ultimately destroy him. And yet, selfishly, Caleb could say nothing. If he implicated himself in Camilla's infidelity, whatever bond existed between Regan and himself would be severed beyond healing. He hated Camilla for what she was doing, and yet, just thinking about her made him want her. Her pale yellow hair in the silver of moonlight creeping through the porthole of the *Sea Siren;* her skin, alabaster white against his own darker body. Her scent . . . her feel . . .

Unexpectedly, a hand clamped on his shoulder. Caleb turned to see a handsome man smiling lopsidedly at him. "So you came to bear witness to this farce, did you?"

Caleb realized this gentleman was worse the wear for drink. "What do you mean, 'farce'? Who are you?" Caleb challenged.

"Oh, rather rude of me, chap, not to introduce myself first. Tyler Sinclair. I gather you're Caleb van der Rhys. Spitting image of your father, you know," Tyler awkwardly tried to correct his faux pas, with little success. Giving up the effort, he continued, "Surely you don't think it's love for the Dutchman that makes our pretty Camilla stand before the preacher, do you? Ha! More likely your father's prospects! You know, originally I'd planned to be elsewhere today. However, I couldn't bear not seeing the Langdons pull this one off!"

Caleb bristled. Whatever private thoughts he might entertain concerning Camilla, his protective instincts made him rise to her defense. "Sir, you seem to forget you speak of my father's bride."

"And it would serve you well if you remembered that fact yourself. Camilla is Regan's bride, not yours." Tyler seemed a bit unsteady on his feet and his color was ruddy.

Caleb paled. How many people suspected his connection with Camilla?

"Oho! Don't look so alarmed," Tyler soothed. "I've known our pretty, fair-haired sparrow too long not to know her tastes, Caleb." The musicians struck a chord. "If I'm not mistaken, here comes our little bird now on the arm of London's cockiest rooster!"

Caleb looked to the stairs where Tyler's attention was directed. Camilla came into view on Stephan's arm. She was a vision of purity and loveliness. For one insane moment, Caleb imagined he was the only other person in the room and that Camilla was walking hesitantly toward him. He imagined it was to him she came, wreathed in a smile of innocence. That her smile was for him, her eyes, her lips . . .

Camilla's gaze fell on the two men and for one instant she was frightened. Disregarding Caleb, she studied Tyler's features, trying to read his intentions. Would he dare hold to his threat and interrupt the wedding and declare publicly that she was already married, to him? For what seemed an eternity her heart stopped beating and she willed Tyler's eyes to meet hers. When they did she breathed a silent sigh of relief. There, instead of a burning resolution, was the familiar amused expression she had seen countless times. So, she assured herself, Tyler would keep her secret for as long as she wanted. The Dutchman would be hers. And so would his money.

If Sirena saw Camilla make her way down the stairs, she did not show it. She only knew Camilla looked adorably young and innocent in her froth of white lace. All else escaped her when she saw Regan take his place near the garden doors, looking trim and fit in a suit of royal blue with silver accents. His doublet was cut in military style and hugged his slender waist while it emphasized his broad shoulders. Breeches worn inside knee-high boots of soft pigskin revealed his well-muscled legs and his sheaf of near-white hair blazed against the dark of his garments. He looked more handsome than she ever remembered. It was only when he turned to look at her, and she saw the faint outline of the S-shaped scar on his cheek, that the irrevocable past flooded back to her. Regan was marrying Camilla. He would be lost to her forever.

Where was the delight she was to have anticipated in telling him she had married Stephan earlier that morning? Where was the victory? Hopelessly defeated, Sirena slumped upon her chair and was an unwilling witness to the event taking place. As Regan stood framed in the doorway leading to the garden, Sirena imagined he was reciting his vows for her. In her befuddled state it was she who wore the white gown, not Camilla. It was she who Regan looked down upon, swearing to love and to cherish. It was she who looked up at him adoringly, waiting, longing for that moment when they would be alone and he would take her in his arms and turn the world upside down with his kisses. And it was she who would welcome him to her, feel his heart beating against her mouth, his smooth, bronze skin against her hands. And when she opened herself to him, the world would become a distant place as they soared to the heavens with their love to guide them.

A woman sitting beside Sirena tapped her gently on the arm and silently offered her a handkerchief. "I always cry at weddings, too, my dear. That's why I brought several hankies along." Until that moment,

Sirena had no idea that her cheeks were streaked with tears.

Tyler and Caleb stood beside one another, each lost in his own thoughts. Several moments into the ceremony, just before the vows were sworn, Tyler nudged Caleb. "What would you say if I invited you to the nearest tavern to drink to the happy couple."

Caleb faced Tyler and saw his own misery reflected in the other man's eyes. "I'd say the first round was on me," he smiled weakly.

Together, to the servants' astonishment, they clapped arms across each other's shoulders and marched out the door.

The newly wedded couple was toasted and glasses lifted in their honor. Somebody pressed a glass into Sirena's hand and, before Stephan could retrieve it from her, the burnished liquid had found its way down her throat.

"Darling," Stephan cautioned, "you really will be quite ill if you take any more wine."

For answer, Sirena reached for a glass from a passing servant and glared at Stephan.

"Sirena," he said sternly, "it promises to be a very long day and, as father of the bride, I am duty-bound to stay until the last guest leaves. It will be quite late before we can be alone together." Even as he spoke, Sirena took another gulp from her glass and glared at Stephan with hostility.

"I can see I must make our happy announcement immediately, while you're still on your feet to accept the congratulations from well-wishers," he said through clenched teeth.

"Yes, do that, Stephan. It will be most interesting to note how our news is taken." Her tongue had difficulty forming the words and her speech sounded slurred and thick, even to herself.

Regan looked over Camilla's head toward Sirena. He had never seen her this way, and he felt a small tug of remorse that his marrying Camilla had spurred Sirena on to drink.

Camilla glanced up at her new husband and noticed his intense gaze directed at the other side of the room. Following his glance, she saw that Stephan had picked up a spoon and was ready to clink it against the side of his glass. "Come with me, Regan, I think Father has a little announcement to make. I nearly told you about it last night, but Father swore me to secrecy."

As Stephan clinked the silver spoon against the crystal glass to capture the guests' attention, Sirena saw Regan and Camilla come toward them. She was looking straight into Regan's eyes when Stephan made the announcement.

". . . and lucky man that I am, our lovely guest from Spain, Sirena Córdez, consented to be my bride. We were married early this morning."

At first, Regan didn't seem to comprehend the message in Stephan's words, then it hit him with full force. His face whitened, a terrible, ghastly hue. His lips compressed and the blue of his eyes became like chips of granite. While everyone gathered about Sirena and Stephan, she lost sight of Regan but could still feel his eyes on her and was aware of the hatred emanating from him.

The long day went on and on; Sirena was oblivious to what was going on around her. The wineglass in her hand always seemed empty and at every opportunity she helped herself to another. Regan kept his distance, dancing with Camilla or joining intimate little groups for conversation. Stephan was the most gracious of hosts, seeing everyone's glass was filled and that each guest had access to the buffet table. Later, when she would think of this day, Sirena would see it as a whirl of activity and grotesque smiles. The details would be hazy and she would never remember what was said either to her or by her, but she would forever remember the misery.

The room was dark and still, yet Regan was strangely ill at ease within its confines. It was a small chamber and undeniably girlish in its decor. The furniture was light and feminine; the bed barely large enough to hold the both of them. If he stretched out, his feet would touch the footboard. He realized his error in not insisting they spend their wedding night in his house on Lime Street among his more comfortable belongings. But he had acceded to Camilla's preferences, deciding she longed to take her first step into womanhood surrounded by her childhood possessions.

The strains of music coming from below was distracting as were the raised voices of the departing guests. From behind the discreetly placed screen in one corner of the room, he could hear the rustle of taffeta and the occasional splash of water as Camilla readied herself for bed. Poor child, he thought, she must be terrified. He would be as considerate of her as possible. He would take his time, initiate her into lovemaking as gently as he could. It wouldn't be difficult, he decided. Camilla didn't exactly inspire a heated passion in him.

A shadow appeared on the wall and Regan turned to its source. Camilla stepped from behind the screen. Her hair was free and loose about her shoulders like a silky, golden mantle, falling almost to her waist. It was then he noticed her nightdress. Long and full, sleeves coming to her wrists and neckline nearly up to her ears. Christ! Another inch of fabric and she could pass for a nun!

In spite of himself a vision of Sirena's naked, tawny splendor came to him. He almost had to shake his head to free himself of the haunting memory.

Regan motioned to a place on the bed beside him and Camilla coyly stepped forward, keeping her eyes downcast.

Tenderly, he took her into his arms, kissing her lightly, aware of her fragile framework. Wordlessly, he worked the buttons at the throat of her gown and slipped his hand inside against her warm skin.

Taking her cue from Regan, Camilla shyly undid the row of buttons and allowed the nightdress to slip off her shoulders. And when she came again into his arms, flesh touched flesh and Regan was aware of a building response in his loins.

Downstairs, Stephan was bringing Sirena her wrap, placing it around her shoulders and tucking it about her chin. "You mustn't take cold, darling," he whispered, leading her to the door. "The servants will take care of things here. We've had a long day and it's time we went home."

Sirena looked up at Stephan and wondered what he was talking about. *This* was his home! Like a blast of freezing air, she realized that she now shared her home with Stephan, everything she had was Stephan's. He was her husband! The wine she had consumed still made her thinking fuzzy. Just before he led her outside to the waiting carriage, Sirena turned and looked up the stairs. Regan was up there. With Camilla! Her bottle-green eyes flashed dangerously as she thought of what they were doing.

She actually had her foot on the bottom step when Stephan pulled her away. "Where are you going?" he asked harshly, startling her.

Suddenly she realized she had intended to climb the stairs and search out the room where Regan lay with Camilla. In her mind's eye she imagined she could see Regan's broad, muscular back as he leaned over his wife. She could see the back of his head where his light, silvery hair curled at the nape. How often had she tangled those errant curls through her fingers? How familiar the bronze skin was to her.

She would kill him! She would climb those stairs and search him out, and take the life from him as he had done to her.

Slowly, she sunk to the floor, tears streaming down her face, shoulders shuddering violently. Ultimately, she would take her own life because there was no life without Regan.

Someone had grabbed her arm and was dragging her to her feet, "Stand up," Stephan growled. "You're making a spectacle of yourself before the servants!" When she looked at him, his face was contorted into cruel lines. His lips curled in disgust. "I never knew you were a sot, Sirena. How did you manage to keep it hidden?" His tone was sarcastic and demeaning.

Sirena shrugged her arm out of his grasp. Head high, she walked out the door to the coach. She was silent during the short ride from Drury Lane to King Street. Stephan sat opposite her, glaring at her through the darkness.

Sirena's house was dark save for a few lights which

Frau Holtz had left burning. While Stephan turned to lock the door behind them with a proprietary hand, she tripped up the stairs, heading for her room. Just as she was opening the door to her suite, Stephan came silently up behind her, his hand grazing the surface of her arm.

"Your room is next to mine," Sirena said thickly. "I'm sure you'll find everything you need there."

"I'll join you shortly."

"Don't bother, I've a wicked headache. I need my rest. I'll see you in the morning." She tried to make her voice casual, but her throat was choked with apprehension. From Stephan's surly attitude she doubted he would conform to her wish to be left alone. Tonight and every night, Sirena thought with panic. The very idea of sharing a bed with Stephan was abhorrent to her.

"You won't dispose of me so easily, Sirena," he said bitterly. "You are *my* wife and this is now *my* house. I am lord here, and it is *my* wishes that will be considered." Roughly, he pushed her into the room and slammed the door shut.

Sirena turned to him, her fingers curling into talons. He recognized the expression in her eyes. "I wouldn't do anything foolish, like crying out, Sirena. You forget, you are my wife and none of the servants will interfere with our marital . . . harmony!"

"Perhaps your servants, but not mine!" she hissed. "Frau Holtz and Jacobus would run to my defense!"

"And they would lose their positions before morning. Is that what you want, Sirena darling?" His voice was heavy with threat. "Now prepare yourself for bed, I'll be in presently." With a last backward glance, Stephan walked through the connecting door between their rooms, leaving Sirena in a paralyzing dread.

If only she could think! Do something! How could she allow herself to be cowed by Stephan Langdon? Her head was buzzing loudly, her arms were too heavy to lift and her eyelids felt as though they were lined with gravel. Her mouth was dry and tasted sour. Her gaze fell on a silver tray bearing a decanter of brandy and two glasses. Hands shaking, she poured out two fingers of the amber liquid and sat down near her dressing table. Moments later, when Stephan returned, that was where he found her, asleep in her chair, the last drops of brandy spilling from the glass and down her skirt.

His hand closed fiercely on her arm and dragged her from the chair, flinging her to the floor, bringing her back to awareness. "Why aren't you ready for bed?" he growled.

Gasping for breath, Sirena looked up at him from the floor, her foggy vision and dulled senses rebelling against this assault.

"Get up, you wench! Take off those clothes!" Viciously, his fingers found the delicate fabric near her throat and tore it asunder. Staggering from the impact of his attack, Sirena stumbled backward. "Look at you! Staggering drunk! What do you think my friends will say when they discuss your disgusting behavior at my daughter's wedding? They'll laugh and think me a fool for taking a lush for a wife!"

Her hand lashed out and found his face, leaving a trailing imprint across his cheek. "Shut up, Stephan. You're as hysterical as a fishwife." Her tone was cold and deadly, causing Stephan to look at her in astonishment. "I don't have to explain my actions to you or anyone else! Now, get out of here and leave me alone. I'd sooner sleep in a nest of vipers than share a bed with you."

Stephan's eyes blazed, blood rushing to the surface of his face. As quick as thought, his hand flew out, knocking her on the jaw, sending her reeling across the room.

Then he was upon her, tearing away her garments, pinning her beneath his surprisingly strong body, flailing her, hitting, hurting, pulling her to the bed.

Sirena retaliated, punishing him with her fists, yanking at his hair, kicking out with her legs. But her movements were slow, hampered by the amount of wine she had consumed. She felt her energy ebb, knowing she was leaving herself victim to his violence.

And when he had divested her of the last shreds of her attire and her body was revealed to his eyes and his cloying touch, she heard a strange, alien sound floating to her ears. It was remote and distant, and it was with horror and defeat that she realized it was the sound of her own whimpering as Stephan forced himself between her thighs and pummeled her resisting flesh with the staff of his manhood.

Her resistance yielded to subjugation as she lay beneath him, repressing her instincts to fight him, overthrowing her defiance against his victory to become subservient and submissive. She hoped he would finish and be done with her, leaving her in isolation to lick her wounds like the wounded animal she was.

Regan turned on his side, away from the sleeping Camilla. His bride was a lovely girl and would have made any man look forward to the prospect of having her warm his bed each night. Any man who had never slept beside Sirena, he thought with chagrin. Camilla could never compete with the warm-skinned, fiery-natured Sirena. Camilla was a delight, a confection, with her bright hair and pink skin, but she definitely bored him. It was Sirena with her cloud of dark hair and wet luscious lips he wanted. He squeezed his eyes shut against the image of Sirena sharing Stephan's bed. The bitch! She had contrived to marry Stephan to prevent him from using the Langdon money to secure his business. Sirena always managed to get the upper hand somehow, regardless of what it cost her.

Unexpectedly, Regan felt the urge to turn over and grab Camilla by her shoulders and shake her till her eyes fell out of her head. She had known Stephan and Sirena were getting married that morning! She knew it and she hadn't told him! For once in her life Camilla had kept a secret, and it had to be the worse luck for him. If only she had told him about Stephan's wedding plans, he would have walked away from his marriage to Camilla, laughing his head off. For once he would have beaten Sirena at her own game! Would have, he thought sourly as Camilla's hand crawled over his shoulder and came to rest against his chest. He looked down at her hands and thought, There's no fool like an old fool! he snorted. "And she wasn't even a virgin."

Chapter Twenty-one

"Mevrouw, Mevrouw, come quick! Jacobus is having trouble keeping them out!" Frau Holtz cried hysterically. "Quick, before they break down the door!"

"Before who breaks down the door?" Sirena asked, raising her head from the pillows and then lowering it again as a surge of pain shot through her temples. "Please, Frau Holtz, lower your voice. Ooh, my head!"

"Mevrouw, come instantly, there is a line of creditors in the street. Each is waving a sheaf of bills for which they demand payment. Your husband's bills!" the housekeeper said sharply.

Sirena's sleepy eyes were suddenly wide and alert, the effects of wine and brandy forgotten. "There must be a mistake! Where is Stephan?" she asked, throwing her long lissome legs over the side of the bed.

"He left after he breakfasted. He said something about going to see a boy's school and he wouldn't return until the dinner hour. Hurry, Mevrouw, or they'll kill Jacobus to get into the house!"

"There must be some mistake!" Sirena exclaimed, again as she donned a demure dressing gown. Each time she moved, her muscles ached and she noticed several bruises on her arms. Adjusting the sleeves of her dressing gown so Frau Holtz's quick eye wouldn't notice, she pulled a brush through her long, dark hair, gathering it into a knot at the back of her head. She had some difficulty with the pins and the housekeeper came to her aid. "Frau Holtz, send one of the footmen for Tyler. Have him come here immediately."

The old housekeeper's all-encompassing eyes had already scanned the bedroom and settled on the torn and shredded gown Sirena had worn the day before.

Picking it up, she examined the wide rents in the fabric and then her gaze flew to Sirena. *"Vish!"* she snorted in disgust. "The man is a beast! How badly did he hurt you?" she demanded.

"Don't worry about me, Frau Holtz. Just be assured it will never happen again."

"*Ja,*" the Frau grumbled, "and just how do you think to accomplish that? He is your husband."

Sirena didn't want to discuss it. It was painful enough to bear this humiliation without having it talked about. "Please, Frau, send someone for Tyler."

After Frau Holtz had left her alone, Sirena inspected the damage done to her person. Her arms bore faint black-and-blue marks which would deepen in color as the day progressed. Her legs ached, the muscles of her inner thighs twinged each time she took a step.

Stephan had used her roughly and she would never forgive him for it! Had she had him within her sights at this moment, she would gladly run him through. And now these bill collectors.

She splashed water on her face and scrubbed her teeth with the rough side of the washcloth. She didn't ever remember feeling so terrible. The huge quantity of liquor combined with Stephan's treatment had left her sick and sore. No time to think of that at the moment; she dressed hurriedly, donning a day dress of light green with a paler lace edging. Stuffing her feet into slippers, she took a moment to compose herself before facing the growing crowd downstairs. Even from her room which was at the far side of the house, she could hear angry male voices.

Out in the hall, little Wren ran to Sirena and buried her face against her, a wild, frightened look in the child's eyes. "There now, Wren. There's nothing to be frightened of. Go back to your room and Frau Holtz will bring up a nice breakfast for you." In spite of her own apprehensions, Sirena managed to quiet the scared girl before leaving Wren in her room.

Bustling down the stairs, Sirena encountered an ashen-faced Jacobus. "Show the gentlemen into the library, one at a time, and we shall see what this is all about. Don't look so concerned, Jacobus, I'm certain it is a misunderstanding. When Sir Sinclair arrives, show him in to me right away."

Sirena had no sooner positioned herself behind the desk when the first creditor was admitted. She listened patiently, then slipped into fury as she was presented with a lengthy list of debts.

"Sir Langdon assured us they would be paid immediately upon your marriage."

Swiftly, she calculated the staggering amount and then leaned back in the chair. "How long have you extended credit to Sir Langdon?"

"It seems like forever, Lady Langdon," the merchant said sourly. "In truth, these bills are two years in arrears. Occasionally, when the dice are in the lordship's favor, he pays a small amount on the account."

Puzzled, she pressed her slender fingers to her throbbing temples. "Why was such extended credit allowed?"

The merchant shrugged. "It is usual to extend credit to the nobility. Considering your husband's affiliation with Baron Sinclair, every courtesy was extended him. Neither I, nor the others who are waiting to see you, had any desire to lose the Baron's patronage and, from time to time, the good lord would be generous and pay a grand portion of the account, such as he did last Christmas."

"I think I understand. I wonder if I might ask you to be patient for a short while longer. My solicitor is on his way here and the matter will be settled to your satisfaction. You have my word on it. If it wouldn't trouble you, would you convey this message to the others waiting outside?"

Sirena went into the kitchen where Frau Holtz was preparing a breakfast tray. Her mind was whirling. And she had thought Regan a bastard! Duped! Sirena Córdez van der Rhys had been duped! She had married a debt-ridden old man. Penniless! What a fool she had been. Regan. If she had married an impoverished nobleman, then Camilla was also without a farthing to her name. She threw her head back and laughed as she pictured an identical gathering of creditors lining Drury Lane outside Regan and Camilla's cozy love nest. They had both been fools, especially herself! There had been no reason to rush into marriage with Stephan to insure that Regan didn't avail himself of the Langdon fortune. Fortune! A fortune in bills!

Standing near the stove, drinking her morning coffee, Sirena could not force herself to meet Frau Holtz's eyes. "Would you care for more coffee, Mev . . . Lady Langdon?" the woman asked. Only the day before yesterday Stephan had asked why the housekeeper used the Dutch form of address. He made it clear he did not approve and cautioned that as soon as the wedding took place Frau Holtz was to use Sirena's correct title.

"No, thank you, Frau. Has Wren had her breakfast yet?" Sirena's eyes were tragic and Frau Holtz wondered what had transpired behind the closed bedroom door last night after she heard Sirena and Stephan return home.

"*Nein,* I bring it now. Poor *Liebchen,* terrified out of her wits. And you were going to see to it that she never had reason to be frightened again! Harmph!"

"Sirena! Sirena!" Tyler's anxious voice called her from the front of the house. Rushing through the door, she nearly knocked him over. All she needed to see was the look on his face and she knew it was all true.

"Why didn't you tell me!" she demanded, color suffusing her face.

"I tried to warn you, Sirena. Look, there's no need to go into that now. The first thing you must do is to settle these accounts and plan from there. Come, let's take care of this immediately."

By the noon hour all the creditors had been paid in full. They left the library, smiles on their faces, exchanging knowing winks over the fact that Sir Langdon had gotten better than he deserved when he married the beautiful Spaniard.

After they had departed, Sirena allowed herself to relax. An expression of rage was evident in her eyes and in the hard, firm line of her jaw.

"How could you allow me to marry Stephan knowing his circumstances?" she demanded of Tyler.

"I tried, Sirena; I really did. You would have no

part of what I was trying to tell you. And if I had come right out and proved to you that Stephan was living on credit, would it have made any difference?"

"Yes! You're damn right it would have made a difference. I wouldn't have married him. As it was, I only married him to stop Regan from getting his hands on the Langdon money! If I'd known there wasn't any, I would have warned Regan and the both of us could have avoided a terrible mistake." She shot her words out at him, her voice seething.

"Would you have? I don't think so, Sirena." Tyler's voice was calm, unruffled, and Sirena could have slapped him.

"What do you mean? Of course, I would have told him!" She advanced on Tyler. He saw in her the reason she had been named Sea Siren and understood the temper which enabled her to slay men. Sirena lifted her arm to strike him, strike anyone, anything.

He grasped her arm and forced her into a chair. "Listen to me: I don't believe a word you're saying and, if you stop to think on it, you'll realize I'm right. You wouldn't have told Regan! You would have let him marry Camilla and tie himself to her because you know he doesn't love her. Possibly, you even know he could *never* love her. You'd never take the chance he would find someone he could love! Camilla is a nice, safe little girl and no one knows better than you that she could never take your place as Regan's wife. No, Sirena, you wouldn't have told Regan under any circumstances. And as for marrying Stephan, what better way to insure your remaining, in some way, connected with Regan? You would have married Stephan if he'd been a pox-ridden, one-legged beggar. You went into this marriage with your eyes wide open and you can't place the blame on my head."

Sirena lowered her head in dejection. God help her, Tyler was right. She would have paid any price to insure further relations with Regan. She had to be a part of his life, even if it meant she played the role of his stepmother-in-law.

"I told you English law put the female at a distinct disadvantage. As much as I hate to admit it, you are at your husband's mercy. From the moment you uttered your vows, you became his chattel. I warned you and you thought you could outsmart him. Why else do you think I hurried to place the largest bulk of your inheritance into trusts? It was to keep Stephan's greedy hands off it. You are responsible for his debts and, right now, he is probably sweeping the city running up bills. That is if he isn't on that gambling ship frittering away your money. There is nothing you can do about it."

"You could have given me something to go on, Tyler. How could you have let this happen to me?" Sirena shouted angrily. "You betrayed me, Tyler, in spite of everything you say, and I mean to find out why!"

"I did try to warn you. You just said to take care of the disposal of your money. If it's any consolation to you, you did make the wise move when you had most of your holdings transferred to Caleb and your housekeeper and, upon your death, to van der Rhys. Stephan cannot touch those."

"What will happen now?" Sirena asked pathetically. "I hate him, Tyler. I hate him, and we've only been married twenty-four hours. The man is a beast!"

Tyler shrugged, pity welling up in his breast. Somehow, he couldn't tell her what fate the first Lady Langdon met. He didn't think she could bear it at this moment.

Sirena lifted her head and looked into Tyler's face. "You know something," she hissed. "What is it? Tell me, you must!"

"I can only tell you what happened to Camilla's mother."

"Tell me! Tyler, please, I must know!"

"I don't want to frighten you unnecessarily. It is only conjecture."

"If you won't tell me, I'll go to your mother, the Baroness, and inform her of the way her son betrayed me."

"Save your threats, Sirena. I'll tell you so perhaps you can prepare yourself somehow. Remember, I said it was only conjecture." Tyler's voice was firm and deep.

In the last few moments he had grown in Sirena's esteem. This was a new side to Tyler. It was a forceful character which she could respect. She admitted to herself that all he said about her was true, and he wouldn't be cowed by her threats to go to the Baroness. Now, when he spoke, she listened.

"Stephan Langdon is a very determined man. A man who wears two faces. There are those in my family who call him a cold and dangerous man. When Stephan married my Aunt Flora, his finances bordered on poverty. His own father was afflicted with the gambling vice and what was not lost on the tables he frittered away on get-rich-quick schemes which, I'm sorry to say, were not always on the white side of the law. I've heard she was near out of her mind for loving him, and, against her family's advice, she married him. Since she was of a gentle and sensitive nature, my grandfather feared for her health. It was the only reason he was induced to give his blessing to the marriage. In the end, Stephan had worked his way through my aunt's inheritance as well as Camilla's."

"It's not a pretty story," Sirena whispered.

"There's more," Tyler said sadly. "In the end, Aunt Flora could not bear the disgrace she felt she had brought down on the family. She became . . . ill. She spent her last days at Bedlam."

"Bedlam!" Sirena was shocked. She had heard of the infamous institution for the insane.

"I don't know if Aunt Flora actually lost her mind or if Stephan contrived to have her committed there. In England all that is necessary is for the husband to swear she is insane, bribe a physician and affix his signature to a document. She died there, Sirena."

"Good God! If what you say is true, Stephan is demented!"

"I believe so, Sirena. If you cross him, even once, you may find yourself in the same position. Especially when he learns he was outsmarted when you placed the bulk of your holdings into trusts."

"And Camilla, does she know all this?" Sirena asked, wondering how the girl could be so obviously devoted to a father who had had a hand in destroying her mother.

"I doubt it," Tyler said soberly. "She was very young at the time. Myself, I hadn't the heart to tell her what the family whispered about behind closed doors. There didn't seem any sense to it. Stephan has always doted on his daughter."

"And Regan? Does he know any of this?"

"No. Who would tell him? This is not something known outside the perimeters of my family. By the way, if it would make you feel any better, Regan finds himself in much the same position as yourself. Camilla's creditors are lined up outside the house on Drury Lane. I saw them on my way here. Fortunately, you are coming out in the clear; you have more than enough to carry you through. But van der Rhys is not in your position. He'll go under."

Sirena felt pity for Regan. Regardless of how he had hurt her, she had never wished this upon him. "Tyler, I want to thank you for your honesty and for straightening out the matter of the debts. I'll be very wary of Stephan and warn my most trusted servants to keep their eyes open."

"Sirena, have you looked at your employees since you married Stephan. I know the wedding only took place yesterday, but his own footmen and valet have already joined your staff. And a motley crew they are. It would not surprise me to learn they keep Stephan informed of your every action. Sirena, if he had little compunction about ridding himself of my aunt, a few trusted servants will make little difference. Be careful," he warned as he prepared to leave the house.

For the first time in her life, Sirena knew true terror. She had fought pirates, suffered at their hands, braved storms at sea and faced death, yet she had never been as terrified as she was at this moment. Her hands trembled as she paced the library, reviewing her situation and desperately trying to find a solution for it.

When Frau Holtz brought Sirena's luncheon tray, she found her mistress before the cold hearth. Sirena explained the situation quietly, her eyes dry as she made a pretense of nibbling at the food. "We must all be careful around Stephan until I find a way out of this mess. Have Jacobus go to the *Sea Spirit* and bring back Jan and Willem. Tell him they are to apply here for work. They are to ally themselves with Stephan's valet and the new footman. For now, I can think of nothing else."

"I could go to the Mynheer and tell him. I'll ask him to help you," Frau Holtz pleaded.

"Regan is in much the same position. No, Frau Holtz, I got myself into this predicament and I will have to get myself out. Just be cautious around the new servants and, whatever you do, don't cross swords with Stephan. Do whatever he says. Frau Holtz, how could I have been such an idiot? How could I have made such a dangerous mistake?"

"You did it because of the Mynheer," the old woman said dourly.

"Yes, because of Regan," Sirena said softly. "And now I'm worse off than I was before. If I had my hands on his neck right now, I would choke the life from his body and laugh while I'm doing it."

Frau Holtz was shocked. "You would do no such thing! You know you love him."

"Not Regan. I would cheerfully kill Stephan!"

"And I would help you," the Frau grimaced.

"Instead, I must play his game until I learn what his plans are. When he comes home for dinner, I'll behave as though nothing happened. I'll wait him out. If he mentions it, then I will behave as though it is an everyday occurrence to have bill collectors beating down the door. I'll not give him the satisfaction of knowing what hell he has put me through today. I'll play his game, Frau Holtz, and I'll beat him at it!"

Camilla met Stephan near the gangplank of the *Sea Siren*. "Up to your old vices, Father?" she asked sarcastically, lifting a finely arched eyebrow.

"Camilla, child, how much I've missed your voracious appetite at the breakfast table. I haven't been in your company since our weddings. How do you find married life?"

Camilla smiled. "Regan is wonderful, Father. Precisely as you said he would be. He barely allows me out of his sight." There was a sour note in her voice, but Stephan preferred not to hear it.

"The man must love you dearly; he can't bear to be separated from you."

"More that he worries I'll run up my accounts. Father, if you could have seen him the morning after the wedding you would have thought him a madman! He terrified me. I can't imagine that fire-breathing Spaniard you married was in a much better frame of mind!"

"Nonsense, Sirena knows her place. She didn't utter a word. She knows when to keep her mouth shut, that one."

"Do I hear a note of disenchantment in your voice, Father?" Camilla sent him a piercing look.

"Just call it straining at the bit. Marriage doesn't agree with me, I'm afraid," he sighed, brushing an imaginary speck from the front of his new brocade frock coat.

Camilla glanced down at his hand and saw that he waited for her to comment on a huge ruby set in diamonds glittering on his finger. Perversely, she clamped her mouth shut.

Camilla wondered if her father had disliked being married to her mother and just how far he had gone to rid himself of the encumbrance.

"Well, we did it, young lady," Stephan laughed jubilantly. "No more poverty, living off the charity of others, keeping up a front. Our credit has been restored, the riches of the world are open to us."

"Your credit has been restored, Father. Regan has closed all my accounts. Before I make any purchases, I am to clear it through him. God only knows what he'll say when he learns I purchased new draperies and carpets before the wedding. They should be delivered any day now, along with the new furniture." Camilla shuddered.

Stephan struck a pose of sympathy. "At the very least, dear daughter, the Dutchman won't allow you to starve. If I remember correctly, that always was your main concern."

Camilla's nose rose into the air. "It is much more than could be said for my own father," she retorted.

"You know, Camilla, there are times you remind me of your dear, departed mother. And let me say the resemblance is not flattering. Good-bye, darling, remember me to the Dutchman." He tapped her on the arm with his walking stick and turned to his carriage.

Caleb stood at the rail and watched Stephan depart, leaving Camilla to climb the gangplank. His heart hammered in his chest and his hand itched to bring her head close so he could run his fingers through her hair. His brown eyes narrowed as he saw her lift her eyes to meet his. This was wrong! Brutally wrong! Technically, Camilla was his stepmother. Over and over since the wedding, Caleb had agonized over the situation. His involvement with Camilla stung his conscience, made him sick with himself. But there was no help for it.

He was falling in love with her. She was so young, so sweet, so tender. Too tender to be at the mercy of Regan's rough hands. Even now, as he looked at her, he could see that something was desperately wrong.

"Caleb, oh Caleb. How glad I am to find you here!" Her voice was on the point of breaking into tears.

"Camilla, what's wrong? Tell me! Come into my cabin; we can talk in privacy there."

Meekly, Camilla allowed Caleb to lead her into his dim quarters. Tears dribbled down her cheeks and she pushed a fist to her face to wipe them away. The gesture was so like a child's that Caleb's heart turned over in his chest.

"Camilla, love, what's wrong?"

Suddenly, she threw herself into his arms, holding onto him for dear life. "Oh, Caleb! I'm so miserable! It's Regan! He's a madman!" she sobbed, hiccoughing to punctuate her words.

"What has he done to you?" Caleb demanded, remembering Regan's temper.

"He frightened me. Several merchants came to the house and asked payment on the accounts. Oh, Caleb, I'm such a foolish ninny. I have no head for figures at all. I assumed those bills were paid. In fact, I know they were. When Regan demanded I show him the paid receipts, I couldn't. I never received any."

Caleb fumed, imagining the scene. She was so sweet, so trusting. He could understand how easy it would be for an unscrupulous merchant to cheat her.

"Regan settled the accounts," she sobbed, "but now he won't let me out of his sight. He's horrid, I tell you! I didn't even have enough to pay the fare on the hack that brought me here. Thank goodness I met Father and he offered to pay it for me. Otherwise, I would have had to ask you." Camilla sniffled prettily and dabbed at her eyes while she watched Caleb covertly. She prayed he went for the bait. Although she had exaggerated greatly, Regan did insist on putting a halt to her spending.

"Little love, here, here, don't cry. Here," he said, pulling gold guineas out of his pocket and forcing them into her hand. "Keep this aside and use it for the hack fares. And if you need more, you must come to me, I insist. I won't have you being made a prisoner because of my father's penurious nature."

"No, no, I couldn't," Camilla protested, already opening her tiny reticule and dropping in the coins, liking the weight they created in the slim beaded bag.

She broke out into a new fit of tears and Caleb felt helpless. He gathered her close, all feelings of guilt dispelled. Camilla was only a child. Regan didn't deserve someone as sweet and innocent as she.

Camilla's arms tightened about him. "Oh, Caleb," she breathed softly, making the tiny hairs at the back of his neck prickle, "how I wish it was you who took me to wife. I need you, Caleb. I need you."

She offered him her lips and he took them greedily, feeling her fragile weight in his arms. He was overcome with emotions of love and protectiveness and desire. "Love me, Caleb," he heard her whisper breathlessly, "love me." Her mouth was warm against his, her arms twined around his neck, pulling him nearer.

Caleb reached down and swept her into his arms. He carried her to his bunk and she pulled him down beside her. The scent of her skin and the soft swell of her breasts exorcised all the mixed emotions of deception and hatred for his father. Camilla was here now and she needed him.

Lord Farrington adjusted his cravat and gave himself one last glance in the mirror. Satisfied he looked the part of a wealthy entrepreneur, he nimbly walked past Caleb's cabin, smiling knowingly because he knew Camilla Langdon was sharing the boy's bunk.

Aubrey nimbly jumped from the gangplank to the

ground. His destination was the haberdasher's, to choose a new wardrobe. The tailor, Mathias, would have a fit when he learned Lord Farrington was paying off his account. If things went according to plan, he would be able to have all his debts settled within a short time. "Thank God for young Caleb," he muttered to himself as he sauntered along Mincing Lane to White Chapel Street.

Aubrey was weary of living by his wits and robbing Peter to pay Paul. No, he corrected himself, cheating Peter to pay Paul. It never paid to lie to oneself. He had really fallen into the cream crock when he met Caleb van der Rhys. From now on, it would be cash for everything and peaceful, sleep-filled nights.

He turned the corner onto Philpot Lane and entered Mathias' haberdashery, a wide smile on his face, his purse in his hand. "Ah, Mathias," he beamed, "I've come to square my account. Get out your ledger before I change my mind."

The tailor looked puzzled. "But, my lord, your man settled it days ago. Have you forgotten? Look!" he said as he pulled a thick book from beneath the counter. "See, paid in full!"

"My man? What do you mean, 'my man'?" Lord Farrington questioned disagreeably. Before meeting Caleb and finding his fortune aboard the *Sea Siren*, the lord would have been most grateful for just such a misunderstanding. However, his fortunes had changed and he considered himself in control of his own affairs. This news was startling and somehow disquieting. Roughly he pulled the ledger from the man's hands and peered nearsightedly at the awkward script. "Where have you marked me? Show me."

"Right here, milord," the tailor said nervously, pointing to Farrington's name with a needle-scarred finger.

"I don't understand," Aubrey persisted, "I made no provision to settle my bill. Who was this man who said he served me?"

"I've no idea, milord. But a tough-looking thug he was. All crippled up or something. Couldn't seem to move too well. He just marched in here one day last week and said he had come to pay your bill and would

I please tally up the debt. I did so, not thinking anything amiss. I'd heard of your successful gaming house—"

"Stop blithering!" Farrington demanded. He was becoming exceedingly nervous about this whole transaction. Beads of perspiration were breaking out on his neck. He'd heard of this kind of thing before. Someone bent on destroying another could buy up all debts and hold that person accountable on demand. Visions of ruination blinded his vision. "Now tell me again. This man, did he tell you his name?"

"Blimey no, milord. I never thought to ask him! Say, you don't suppose someone is planning to put the crush on you..." No sooner were the words out of the tailor's mouth than he regretted them. "Crushing," the popular term applied to such an action, was a fearsome practice and he could see that Lord Farrington was well informed of the ultimate consequences. For a terrible moment, he thought Aubrey Farrington's eyes would bulge out of his head and the nobleman would suffer a stroke.

Lord Farrington felt the first stirrings of panic. "No, no, this is not the case," he insisted, visibly trying to compose himself. "How could I have forgotten something so important," he murmured. "Mathias, I've just remembered something I must do. I'll return in a few days' time and make my purchases... now that my account is clear."

"Anytime, milord," Mathias answered, looking after Aubrey as he hurried out the door.

Once again on White Chapel Street, Aubrey looked around him, his breathing ragged. He didn't know exactly what he expected to see. Business seemed to be going on as usual. No one was looking at him suspiciously or paying him any kind of attention at all. Yet fear crawled up his spine and his natural gambler's instinct told him something was devilishly wrong.

His suspicions were confirmed when the bootmaker and the barber also told him his accounts were settled. His fear was rapidly turning into blind panic when he entered the Blue Nose Pub and sought out a bookmaker named Hawkeye. Aubrey was in debt to Hawkeye for several thousand pounds. There were others who had extended Lord Farrington credit in like amounts. When Hawkeye raised his head and greeted Aubrey warmly, panic turned to terror. Even before the bookmaker said it, Aubrey knew that this account, too, had been paid and in his bones he knew *all* his debts had been taken care of.

Stumbling out of the Blue Nose, he walked blindly down White Chapel to the Boar's Tooth, where he found an empty table and ordered wine to quench his thirst and calm his shattered nerves.

He could be called to reimburse his so-called benefactor at any time. When that happened, even selling the *Sea Siren* and making off with Caleb's share wouldn't bail him out. It was a perfectly splendid means of ruining a man if someone had a mind to do it. The practice was legal, although not usual. The person buying up a man's debts was within his right to demand exorbitant interest on the loan. Aubrey had even heard of one-thousand-percent interest being upheld in the courts. Numbly, he shook his head and lowered it to the table. Just when everything was going along so well. He was pulling his affairs together. Young Caleb's ship and his brains were going to make them both rich. And now this.

A tall, swarthy man entered the pub. His eyes surveyed the room and came to rest on the drunken Lord Farrington. His eyes became slits and his cruel mouth curled into a smirk. Limping painfully, his left arm at his side at an awkward angle, the man seated himself and called for a jug of rum.

When he paid for his drink, he was not surprised to discover he had but a few shillings left. A few coins and a sheaf of paid receipts from Aubrey's accounts. He had existed on less and still lived, the man told himself. He would do it again and survive. Hadn't he survived that oily Spaniard's vicious tongue and underhanded ways? Bah! he spat. Chaezar Alvarez was long dead and, if what he heard was true, it was by the Sea Siren's hand. What a fool he had been to listen to Alvarez. He had been a respected pirate in those days, and somehow that bastard had lured him into becoming a part of his schemes. From the moment he had agreed, his life had changed. And all because of that woman! That bitch, the Sea Siren! He would gain his revenge on her if it took him the rest of his life!

He swallowed his rum and poured himself another. Twice, he had tried to kill her and twice he had failed. He had followed her for days and, when she was shopping at the Royal Exchange, he had stolen a hack and tried to run her down. Another time, at a masquerade party at her house, he had rigged the lantern over the dais to crash down on her and send her to her death in a crackle of flames. This, too, had failed. Now he wanted her out in the open sea, like before, only this time *he* would be the winner.

He poured another tot. He had almost given up hope of ever finding her. By sheer luck, he had heard of the folly, *Sea Siren,* and knew that wherever that ship was, she would be close by. How he had wrangled with one idea after another until, one night, it had come to him. The sweat in his armpits ran down his sides and his hair was plastered to his head. Even now, he could remember his excitement. The boy. Caleb. He would use the boy to draw her out. And the way to get to young van der Rhys was through Lord Farrington's debts. Then that living, breathing she-pirate would be his for the taking. All he had to do was be careful and play his cards the way he planned. He couldn't lose.

Another glass of rum, then another and his mind wandered as the pain in his arm eased to a dull ache. How long ago that had been when the bitch drove him against the rail and shouted, "En garde! En garde!" as she flexed her arm and brought up her cutlass and slashed at his weapon. His arm had flown backward and he was stunned with the force of the blow. He had recovered quickly and jabbed straight for the Siren's midsection. Nimbly, she had sidestepped his attack, her blade striking repeatedly. "How does it feel, Blackheart, to see your arm in tatters?" she had mocked. "Guard it well, for I will strike again and again until I lay it open to the bone!" She had feinted to the right, her cutlass finding its mark across his shoulder. The crack of shattering bone had brought cheers from the Siren's crew.

"Let me hear you beg, Blackheart!" the Siren had

demanded. "Shout for quarter and I'll throw you to the sea!"

"Never!" he had hissed through clenched teeth. The Siren had held the cutlass loosely in her hand as she watched his agonized face. "You have only one leg left to you. Surrender to me or you leave me no choice."

"Never!" he had spat, using his uninjured arm to lash out with his cutlass. He never saw the blade as it ripped his other leg from thigh to toe. The Siren had backed off. "You have only seconds to surrender." His weapon had thrust forward, aiming for her abdomen. In the instant of protecting herself, she had avoided his attack and her cutlass had parried and found its mark in the flesh of his belly and he had crumpled to the deck.

The pain had been unbearable but he had lived, lived to see another day, then another and another. She thought she had killed him, but he had survived. And he would continue to do so. At least until he saw her dead, the blood flowing from her wounds, wounds that he inflicted. But first, he would see her humiliated, tortured in both mind and body.

Even the rum he consumed could not dull the knifelike pain that shot across his gut. He doubled over and cursed the Sea Siren vehemently. Damn her soul. She would pay and pay with her life, he muttered through clenched teeth. When the stabbing sensation eased a trifle, he wiped at his perspiring brow and cursed again. If she made one mistake, she could make another. She had left him for dead, being so intent on van der Rhys. All women were idiots. If it hadn't been for the quick thinking of one of his old crew, he would be dead. Rolph had told him later how he laid in a near coma for weeks and then miraculously pulled through. He knew now that it was his vengeance that kept him alive. And it would keep him so till he killed the Sea Siren.

All his dastardly, insidious plans would not be in vain. Madame Córdez's little accidents would take on a new meaning now that he had Lord Farrington in his pocket. He would do whatever he was told or he would rot in Newgate.

Blackheart finished his whiskey and watched Aubrey reel drunkenly from the pub, a look of fear in his eyes. "You have good reason to be scared, my friend," he muttered as he followed Farrington.

Chapter Twenty-two

Sirena had awakened feeling well and rested. Sitting in her bedroom, sipping strong, hot coffee, she watched as Frau Holtz threw open the long windows to admit the fresh morning air and bright sunlight. Wren had accompanied the old housekeeper to help with the bed and just to be in her benefactor's company.

"Oh, Missy-ma'am, it's a beautiful day!" the child cried with exuberance, using with affection her adopted name for Sirena. "Would it be all right if I went to help Jacobus work in the garden?" she asked, looking at Sirena with adoring eyes. "I'll earn my keep so I can stay here with you," she added happily.

"Wren, there's no need for you to work in the garden unless you would like to. And," Sirena added sternly, "I don't want to hear any more about your earning your keep, is that understood? Frau Holtz and I love having you here."

"But, Missy-ma'am, I *have* to pay my way! My mum always taught me you can't take something for nothing!"

What was she to do with the child? She gathered the small, thin body close to her and looked at Frau Holtz. The old woman shook her head and smiled. She, too, adored the wide-eyed little girl.

"Instead of working in the garden with Jacobus, why don't you cut some of the flowers, and we'll arrange them in bowls to brighten the rooms? Go on now," she said when she saw Wren's eyes turn to the unmade bed, "I'll help Frau Holtz here." Sirena knew that Wren's main concern was assisting the German woman with her chores. Frau Holtz had told Sirena how often Wren insisted she sit down and put her feet up while the child continued with the work at hand. "Go on now, and remember to mind Jacobus."

Sirena watched the child skip away, a smile on her face. How beautiful this little urchin was and how she brought joy to her days. Eventually Wren would grow into a beautiful woman. The problem was, how could Sirena give her the best possible start in life? "Frau Holtz, what shall we do with Wren? I've taken her away from the only life she knew, and she's now my responsibility. In the short time she's been here, I've grown so attached to her. Just as you have. Don't deny it, I've seen the way you cuddle her every chance you get."

"*Ja,* Wren needs love and affection, and she gives it in return. If only she knew how she's brightened an old woman's life, she wouldn't be so obsessed with earning her keep, as she puts it." Frau Holtz plumped up the pillows on Sirena's bed and bent to the chore of straightening the sheets. The maid could tend to the keeping of Sirena's room, but the Frau wouldn't hear of it. She preferred to do it herself.

"Well, I guess that's part of our answer. We'll have to contrive small things for Wren to do so she'll feel useful and wanted. However, there's always the question of schooling. She's almost ten and has had no formal training."

"Ten!" Frau Holtz exclaimed. "She looks no more than seven or eight!"

"You would look the same, old friend, if you were left to fend for yourself on the streets of London and have occasional scraps for food. Do you see how she's blossomed with your good care? She needs someone to mother her, Frau Holtz, and you are that person. She loves you; I see it in those magnificent eyes of hers."

"Ach!" the Frau exclaimed, clearly flattered. "What do I know of raising a girl? The Mynheer was the only child I ever had a hand in raising and look at the way he's turned out! Bah!"

"Then you will learn to raise a little girl." Sirena's eyes followed Frau Holtz around the room and her gaze came to rest on the connecting door between her room and Stephan's. "Frau Holtz, have you seen my . . . husband this morning?"

The housekeeper's face became hostile and she answered with a note of venom in her voice. *"Ja!* I've seen him. He's in the library sipping whiskey and water. He has his feet on the desk and he looks like he's taken root there. I have to say it, Mevrouw, marrying that man was the biggest mistake of your whole life! He'll be the end of us all," she said doomfully. "I feel it in my bones!"

"I can't dispute you on that. But for the moment, at least, I must make the best of a bad situation."

"Your husband wishes your company at luncheon," the woman snapped. "I nearly forgot to tell you, *Lady* Langdon," she added pointedly.

Sirena felt her stomach churn. God in Heaven, what did he want now? Surely he wasn't going . . . he wouldn't, not in the full light of day! He revolts me! Sirena thought as she walked to the wide windows that opened out over the garden. He makes my flesh crawl. She couldn't help but remember how she had used the only weapon open to her. Immediately after their wedding night, Sirena had quickly learned that if she remained completely impassive, not moving a muscle, Stephan became impotent. It appeared his passions were directly proportional to the degree of her struggles. She had steeled herself against his demands; and even when he became enraged and hit her and treated her roughly, she would not fight back. Within a few moments Stephan would lose all interest in sex and would go back to his own room, cursing her. She wasn't certain which sickened her more, Stephan's aberration or her own passivity. How often, since their marriage, had she cursed the English system of law wherein a wife was a man's chattel? A man could beat his wife, kill her even, and the law would stand on his behalf.

What did he intend to do with her this afternoon? Once or twice he had brought home preposterous costumes. One of a serving wench, complete with laced stomacher and short, knee-length skirt, whose bodice left her breasts almost completely exposed. Another was of a Roman goddess which draped over one shoulder leaving half of her chest open to his salacious eyes. Each time she had hesitantly donned the costume. Each time she had remained cold and aloof, as unmoving as a statue, and no amount of his cruelty would draw a cry from her. Thankfully, so far he had left her in a rage of helplessness.

His unctuous voice, when he tried to make love to her and failed, sickened Sirena. When it happened the first time, she thought he would kill her, so angry was he with his own inability to perform. How many nights of his insidious torture was she to endure before she took matters into her own hands.

What was worse? The humiliating nights or his hate-filled eyes staring at her across the dinner table? His remarks of late had been frightening. The day before, at breakfast, he had watched her pour cream over her figs. "I never remember your using so much cream before, darling," he had drawled. "Doesn't it seem to you that your behavior is undergoing a change?"

"And what do you mean by that?"

"Oh, nothing really. It is only that I have noticed a change in you, Sirena. A radical change. And your fondness for the grape? Really, darling, you must pull yourself together."

"If you are referring to our wedding day, Stephan, I want to hear no more about it. I have never drowned my sorrows in wine and I doubt I ever will. But you must admit, darling," she added, using the same deprecating tone as he, "our wedding day was reason enough to drink!"

"Do you see what I mean, Sirena?" he pretended concern. "I can barely utter a word that you don't bite my head off."

"I'd like to *cut* your head off!"

"Tsk, tsk, control yourself, darling. I wouldn't like to see you do anything rash; Smythe and Rathbone might have to take you in hand." He was referring to his valet and footman, two brutal-looking scurves that Sirena wouldn't have had scrubbing the bilges on her ship.

"Did I ever tell you about the first Lady Langdon? Sad woman," he said smoothly, fingering a new diamond stickpin that he had purchased with Sirena's money. "It was pathetic. In the end I had to have her committed to Bedlam. For her own good, you understand."

Too angry to retort, Sirena left the table, cursing herself for the position she had placed herself in. She was also afraid for her life and she didn't like the feeling. She was no fool. One word from Stephan and these burly servants of his would have her in their clutches and that would be the end of her.

Her head began to ache as she thought of myriad wild schemes to leave this house and free herself from Stephan.

The luncheon hour arrived all too soon for Sirena. She had changed into a watermelon-colored day dress with crisp ruching around the modest neckline. Patting her hair into place, she descended the stairs to meet Stephan. Only one hour of his company and the remainder of the afternoon would see her free of him. Until evening, she thought, gulping, her mouth dry as sand. Not to think of that now, she chastised herself. Just take it hour by hour.

The table was set according to Frau Holtz's scrupulous standards. The white lace cloth was pressed faultlessly and the silver service gleamed with a high sheen. Stephan was already seated and digging with relish into his brisket when Sirena entered. He hadn't even lifted his head to acknowledge her.

Sitting opposite him, she watched him out of the corner of her eye. She felt she would choke on her food if she had to swallow another bite. When was he going to get to the point? She could tell by the set of his jaw there was something on his mind. She refused to meet his eyes and would not speak unless spoken to. Her heart fluttered madly and she wanted to strike out in order to slash his head from his body. How she hated him with a passion.

"Tell me, darling," he drawled, "how do you plan to spend the afternoon?"

"I thought I would go into town and see my dressmaker," she answered quietly.

"That will never do, darling. You must have your dressmaker come here. I don't want my wife strolling through the merchants for all the world to see. It's definitely not seemly," he cooed unctuously. "No, have your little seamstress come here. Sirena, I find it strange you haven't asked me how my affairs at the academy are going. Somehow, I thought you would show a bit more interest in your husband's activities. Especially since the whole idea can be attributed to your dear friend, Baron Sinclair."

Sirena could feel his eyes on her, waiting for her to placate him. Despising herself, she heard herself say, "How is the academy coming, Stephan?"

"The school will open within a fortnight. I have scheduled my classes for two afternoons a week. Only the sons of the best families will attend. The cost is prohibitive, quite expensive. I was quite impressed by the engraved plaque near the door with my name on it. Of course, the stipend is ridiculously small, no more than a pittance. But then, I have no need of money, do I, darling? I feel I am being more than gracious in accepting the appointment."

"Yes, it is generous of you, Stephan. Most befitting a man of your stature."

His pale gray eyes widened and then narrowed. It was difficult to tell what Sirena was thinking at any given moment. Bile rose in his throat when he considered she was mocking him for his ineptness in the bedroom. Yes, he decided, she was indeed. And his inability to perform was all her doing! Well, his little purchase this morning would change all that. "Sirena, I brought a present home for you. When you retire tonight, I want you to wear it for me."

Unable to restrain her tongue, Sirena lashed out, "Are we to again witness your impotence, Stephan? What did you conceive this time? I can barely wait to see what it is you think will stir your manhood!" She rose from the table, her emerald eyes glittering. "There is no device known to man that will bring life to a dead man, Stephan." Gathering her skirts, she stamped from the room, leaving him at the table, feeling the pinpoints of his glare stabbing her back.

At a sound from near the kitchen door, Stephan snapped his head around to see a large-eyed Wren standing there holding a relish dish. Apparently Frau Holtz had instructed her to bring it into the dining room. Blood rose to Stephan's face as he thought of what the child had overheard. The glare he fixed on her paralyzed her on the spot.

"Come here with that dish," he commanded. Still Wren didn't move. "Give it to me!" he commanded again, his voice louder and harsher.

Slowly Wren advanced. She didn't like Sir Stephan, not one bit. She had seen men of his ilk in the back alleys of London. Nasty men, men who beat the whores after using them. It was sufficient for Wren to know he was cruel to Sirena and that she was frightened of him to encourage Wren's dislike to bloom into hatred.

"Not over there, I can't reach it. Here," he instructed, taking pleasure from the child's apparent terror.

Wren did as she was told, carrying the relish dish carefully so as not to spill a drop of the pickling on the Frau's spotless carpet. Just as she neared him, Stephan reached out a hand and deliberately tipped the dish, spilling the sweet-sour juices down the front of Wren's apron. "Now see what you've done, you clumsy girl!"

Astonished, horrified, Wren stood helplessly by as the fluid dripped down onto the toes of her shoes. Choked with fear, she raised her eyes to her master, her childish pink mouth forming a soundless O. Stephan dragged her toward him and placed her between his knees. "Stupid girl," he scolded as he reached for his linen napkin and began to wipe the front of Wren's dress. "See what you've done to yourself!"

Wren was in severe distress. She wanted to cry out for Frau Holtz and explain that it wasn't her doing, but no words would come out of her throat. She didn't like the way the master had trapped her between his legs and was cleaning her clothes in light, long touches.

She didn't know exactly why his actions scared her so much, she only knew she wanted to run away from him, away from his white fingers and wine-scented breath. In the way of a child she stood firmly planted to one spot, determined not to turn toward him and aid him in his ministration.

Stephan gripped her arm and tried to force her to face him when Frau Holtz suddenly stepped into the room. Immediately, Stephan released her and pushed Wren away from him.

"Look what this nasty child has done!" he roared. "Get her out of my sight!" he commanded a bewildered Frau Holtz as he stood up from his chair and stomped toward the library.

Wren flew into the kitchen and out through the back door to the garden. Her cheeks were flushed red and her dark eyes welled with tears. She hated him! Hated him! He was the nasty one, not her. He was dirty! Tears streaked her cheeks and she thought of going to the Frau or to Sirena to tell them what had happened. But even as she formulated the words in her own mind she realized there was not much to tell them. Mayhap the master was right. Could it be she was really a nasty, clumsy child and that she was the bad one for even thinking for a moment that the master liked touching her?

Back in her room, trembling hands clutched at her sides, Sirena noticed the package on her bed and sent it sprawling to the floor with a sweep of her arm. Gold chains! Thick chains, thin chains.

She kicked at the half-opened parcel and one of the chains looped about her ankle. Sirena looked down at it and tried to shake herself free of it. She bent over and ripped it from around her foot and tossed it against the wall. An expression of hatred and loathing on her face, she gathered all the shining links and threw them under the bed, too revulsed to look at them and too frightened of Stephan to dispose of them.

"I'll take your present, Stephan darling, and rope it around your skinny neck, choking the life from your odious body!" she spat. "I'll watch your eyes pop from your head and laugh when your tongue swells and your face turns blue!"

The only other person in her life she could remember hating this way was the pirate captain, Dick Blackheart.

Blackheart! she thought. Rapist, murderer, kidnaper! On that day, long ago, when he had boarded her ship while it sailed to Java under the guise of being in distress, he had led a band of ruthless pirates who had used her brutally at will. Time and again they had used her, beat her, stripped Sirena of her will. She had become less than human, praying for death.

And then that final day, when her spirit and will to survive had been restored by Caleb, the cabin boy, and Blackheart had sent her to his quarters. Sirena's eyes narrowed and her chest rose with deep, heavy breaths. The memory came back to her in all its harsh reality. Her flesh had recoiled from what she knew Blackheart had planned for her. "You're mine now," he had growled. "The crew won't come near you again."

Sirena had backed away, dreading the touch of his pawlike, calloused hands. But there was no escaping his long arms which pulled her toward him, crushing her. With savage intent, he had wound his fingers in her sable curls and yanked her head back until she had thought her neck would snap. His thick, wet mouth had burned her throat where he kissed her, nipping at her tender flesh, making her recoil.

She had fought him, writhing to escape his grasp, but when she had been almost free, he caught her again and had flung her onto the bunk. He had stood over her, a lustful glitter in his eyes, his tongue wetting his viscous mouth. She had cowered on the bunk, apprehensive of his next move.

He had thrown himself atop her, his weight pushing her into the bedding. His intimate touch to her stiff, unyielding form had been light and seductive in its intent. His kisses to her unwilling mouth, throat and breasts had been fraught with suppressed frenzy.

Sirena had refused to allow him to take her without a struggle. His attempt at arousing her had been almost worse than the attacks she had suffered previously. At those times she had been used, nothing had been expected of her except as a receptacle for their lust. But this attack of Blackheart's had been a blatant effort to elicit a willing response from her. It had been an admission that she was alive, real, capable of choice. That the barbarian has assumed she could be enticed by his advances had added outrage to her already wounded dignity. She couldn't . . . *wouldn't* have allowed him to assume she might respond like a wanton to his insidious caresses.

"Get your filthy hands off me!" she had cried. "Leave me alone!" she had spat, pushing him away and wriggling out from under him.

The shock on his grizzly face had been almost comical.

Sirena had wrestled to her feet, her eyes flying to the door and its bolt. The helplessness of her situation had nearly rendered her insensible. In that moment Blackheart had pounced on her.

She had felt herself being forced to the floor, his weight knocking the breath from her body. She had lashed out at him blindly, her nails gouging the flesh on his cheekbones. He had cuffed her on the back of the head and then had pinioned her arms to her sides. Her struggles had been the minuscule protests of a flea biting a dog.

"So, there's spirit left in you yet," he had crowed exultantly. He had forced her arms above her head, holding them there with one powerful hand.

She had spit and snarled, twisting her head, trying to sink her teeth into his capturing arm. He had smashed his fist into her face, splitting the lower lip against her teeth, filling her mouth with blood. His knee had forced her legs apart; his free hand had touched her breasts, her stomach, between her thighs. His face had been directly above hers, and he had salaciously grinned down at her. She recoiled her head and sprayed his beast's face with spittle and blood.

"You can take me morning, noon and night!" she had spat out her words with revulsion and disgust, "but I'll never be yours. Never!"

"And I'll never be Stephan's either," she said aloud, the sound of her own voice breaking her from her reverie. She had hated Blackheart and ultimately had destroyed him. She was repulsed by Stephan, in some ways more than by Blackheart, and she would find her way to victory again. Slowly the tears rained down her face. Such brave words from such a frightened woman.

Throughout the remainder of the day, Sirena was distracted. Even Wren's cheerful chatter couldn't jar her loose from the thought of what was hidden beneath her bed. She was nervous as a cat. By the dinner hour she pleaded a headache so she wouldn't have to join her husband at the table.

Hour after hour she sat in her room, refusing the tray Frau Holtz had brought her. The old woman looked at her with puzzled, worried eyes, but did not question Sirena about her state of mind.

The downstairs clock chimed nine, then ten. With each melodious note, Sirena grew more feverish. Any minute now he could climb those stairs.

By eleven o'clock Sirena was in a state of near hysteria. She hoped, prayed, Stephan would retire soon. Anything, just to get it over with! Simply to know she could close her eyes in sleep and not have to think about him till the following day. Abruptly, there was a sound from the room adjoining hers.

Slowly, the connecting door opened and Stephan stood framed in the doorway, the light behind him, throwing his face into shadow. "Why aren't you dressed and waiting for me, Sirena? Didn't you like my gift?" His voice was low, deprecating.

Sirena's eyes flew to the bed where she had placed the chains. Earlier, after Frau Holtz had retired for the night, she had crept down on hands and knees and retrieved them from the darkness beneath, but could not find a good place to dispose of them.

"Ah, I see you have waited for me to dress you. How charming," he said, closing the door behind him. He wore a brocade robe and, when he walked past her, she could detect the sweet aroma of brandy. "Take off your clothes, darling. Let us see how you would look in bondage." Picking up one of the lengths, the links tinkled against each other.

"I said undress!" he menaced. "Shall I do it for you?"

Never taking her eyes from his, Sirena divested herself of her own attire and stood there in her chemise.

"Everything!"

Locking her stare with his, she peeled off her chemise and petticoats.

"Leave the stockings," he ordered. "I somehow like the feel of silk against my skin."

Almost completely naked, Sirena stood poised, ready for his next move.

Selecting a chain, Stephan walked over to her and draped it about her neck, crossing it between and under her breasts and fastening it at the back. Another length was draped around her waist and over her hips. On and on, he applied the cold, metal links until they were wound about her limbs. While he was doing this, Sirena stood with her arms outstretched, never flinching when he tugged at a coil and it cut into her flesh. For all the world she seemed a mannequin, moving only when told, posing however he directed, while her face was a study in passivity.

When he was finished, Stephan stepped back and admired his handiwork. "Beautiful," he murmured, the heat of his passions lighting his eyes. "Now come here to me!"

Hesitantly, she stepped forward, anticipating his next move. Roughly, he seized her by the chain looped about her waist and forced her to him. His lips found hers, pressing, hurting, while his hands covered her flesh, probing, seeking. Suddenly, he threw her away from him. "Bah! You're an icy woman, Sirena, and you need to be taught a lesson." His hand reached out and clubbed her on the side of her head. Unflinching, she readied herself for his next attack.

Stephan slipped his dressing gown to the floor. Beneath it he was naked as she knew he would be. Again, he reached for her, this time knocking her to the carpeted floor, his arm hovering over her, ready to strike again.

In spite of herself, Sirena flinched, throwing up her arms to ward off his blow. Again and again, he struck her, pulling her by the chains, pushing her lower to the floor, watching her feeble attempts to protect herself.

"And you think me not a man?" he demanded. "Look, look you bitch! Tell me I'm not a man!"

Slowly, she lifted her head, knowing what she would see. Stephan's slim, athletic body showed its supple strength and the object of his pride rose out from his body in masculine power.

"Now, let me hear you say I am more than a man! I am a god! Say it!" he demanded. "Say it! Stephan, you are more than a man, you are a god! Say it, you bitch!"

Unexpectedly, the whole situation seemed ridiculously funny. She, cowering on the floor covered only by numerous links of gold chain, and Stephan, standing naked as a jaybird before her, wearing only his dubious erection, demanding she tell him he was a god. A peal of laughter was born in her throat and bubbled forth. The sound filled the room and danced off the walls. Hearing it, she laughed again and again. Stephan loomed over her, hatred in his eyes, his fists clenched at his sides. Dropping her gaze, she noticed the effect her hysteria was having on his passion. Again, she allowed the sound of her laughter to ring out.

Stephan was enraged. "Laugh at me, will you, bitch?" He struck out with his fists, catching her in the fleshy part of her arm, in the lean section of mid-thigh. The more he punished her, the harder she laughed. She was beyond controlling herself and for one instant wondered if she were as insane as Stephan.

The longer and louder she laughed, the more limp Stephan became until his staff, which had caused him such pride, was completely flaccid.

Long after he had sent her one last ineffectual kick and stamped from the room into his own, slamming the door soundly behind him, Sirena remained on the floor, laughing till the tears came from her eyes and blinded the last few moments from her thoughts.

Chapter Twenty-three

The weeks passed with Sirena a virtual prisoner. She was watched over constantly. Beside Smythe and Rathbone, Stephan had added two more footmen who lived in the loft over the stables. Jan and Willem had joined the household, acting as gardener and stable hand. From time to time she would see them, and they would nod politely, but due to instructions from Frau Holtz and Jacobus, they were not, under any circumstances, to engage in conversation with her. It was important that they establish themselves as being in Stephan's employ and solidly faithful to him.

Invitation after invitation was sent back with Sir Langdon's regrets that his wife was not well enough to attend. Stephan was too tired after his arduous days at the academy and his many trips to the *Sea Siren* to be concerned about missing social engagements.

In one way Sirena felt relieved, because he no longer came to her room at night after the debacle with the golden chains and the ridiculous costumes ceased appearing on her bed. Still, she was afraid and the hackles on the back of her neck would rise every time Stephan came within range. By now, she told herself, his impotence was an embarrassment and he was finally going to leave her alone. For some reason this annoyed her almost as much as his pestering and violating her.

Day after tiresome day dragged by with Sirena doing little more than pacing from room to room or supervising a few informal lessons for Wren. Her eyes became haunted with deep hollows underneath. Even Tyler Sinclair had not come to see her recently, and she suspected Stephan was at the bottom of that.

She longed for the warm, easterly trade winds and for the sight of Regan's face. She knew she would have sold her soul to be free again, aboard the *Sea Spirit,* feeling the motion of the sea and the spindrift on her face. She prayed for a violent storm to purge her emotions, so she could run out into the garden and let the pelting rain wash down on her and the wind blow through her hair. She would drink it in, taste it, drown in it. And when the lightning streaked the sky, she would lift adoring hands and give thanks to be amidst the elements.

"No more. Never again," she said in a quiet, deadly voice. Slowly, she walked to the large wardrobe and flung the door open. She licked at her dry lips. She knew exactly where it was. All she had to do was reach in and draw out the rapier that had killed Dick Blackheart, the Hook, and wounded Regan.

Imperceptibly, her shoulders straightened and the muscles in her legs tensed. The feel of the blade in her hand was all she needed to remind herself of who and what she was. A killer of men, Regan had once called her. She frowned. Perhaps. But she was Sirena Córdez van der Rhys—her own woman. She would remain so till the day she died. What a pity Stephan Langdon didn't know that. Though, soon he would, she promised herself.

Tears shimmered in the sea-green eyes as she lifted them upward. She flexed her legs, brought up her arm and parried the weapon. She lashed out at the draperies and slashed them to ribbons. She attacked the coverlets and perforated them with knife sharp slashes. She thrust at the stout wood of the clothespress. Each time she pulled the rapier from the wood, she smiled. The Sea Siren was reborn!

Frau Holtz entered her room carrying a full load of bedding. Her watery eyes took in the shambles and she shivered, dropping her burden. "Mevrouw!" she whispered hoarsely. "What are you doing? God in Heaven, when your husband sees what you've done, we will all suffer!"

"And if a wager were placed as to who would come out first, where would you put your money, Frau?" Sirena asked as she flicked the rapier point in the air.

"Mevrouw, they hang people in this godless country. Jacobus has told me what the prisons are like. That man you married will have the lot of us locked up," she said. "If you can't think of yourself, think of Wren. The poor child is terrified of Sir Langdon as it is. He'll do away with the *Liebchen,* too!"

"Not if I kill him!"

"God in Heaven," Frau Holtz muttered. "And how do you plan to do that?"

"I'll take a page from his book and stalk him the way he does me. Tell Jacobus to go to the harbor and ready the ship. Stephan rarely ventures out into the gardens so he'll never miss him. Do it, Frau Holtz," she ordered coldly, "now!"

"They'll hang you by the neck," the old woman warned as she backed from the room.

Sirena shrugged. "First, they'll have to catch me. I don't think there is anyone on the face of the earth I hate more. I'll carve the manhood from Stephan's body and laugh while I do it. I've had enough!" she screamed. "Enough!" Without warning, she collapsed to the floor, her arms reaching out to her old friend.

Frau Holtz ran to her, holding her close, crooning to her as though she were a small child while heaving sobs shook Sirena's shoulders. The Frau knew that Sirena had vented her rage and there would be no need to send Jacobus to the ship. Sirena wasn't going anywhere.

Regan's head pounded as he looked at the figures in the thick ledgers. How Sirena must be laughing. Although, come to think of it, maybe not. She might have money to pay off Stephan's debts, but he was also gambling away her fortune; and, at the rate he was going, she would be impoverished fairly quickly.

He lit a cigar and swung his booted feet onto the desk. An aromatic puff of gray-blue smoke circled the room and came to settle around his head like a halo. A month, two at the most, and he would be finished. Figures didn't lie. Something had to be done soon. His small capital was dwindling alarmingly and, when he told Camilla to stint herself for a short while, she had laughed and said she would not be made the fool. In her new position as his wife she had to entertain and dress correctly. There was no point in arguing, so he was now controlling his anger with an effort. Before the day was over he would have to arrive at some sort of answer to his miserable affairs.

Groping in his desk, he opened some rum and drank thirstily. He thumped the bottle on the rough desk just as the door opened to his offices. "Dykstra! You son of a bitch, what are you doing here?" he said, jumping up and heartily clapping the Dutchman on the back. "Christ, I never thought to see your ugly face again. What brings you to England?"

Dykstra beamed good-naturedly. "You. I came to hand over the profits from the sale of your crops in Java. As yet, the plantation has no buyer, but all things in good time. It's a tidy amount and more will be coming shortly. Tell me," he laughed, "how much is left in that bottle and is there another handy. I feel a drink coming on."

"There's plenty more where this came from. Dykstra, do you remember the time I took you to the brothel back in Batavia. Do you remember how magnanimous I was in giving you the two 'virgins'?"

"Virgins, my ass," Dykstra guffawed. "You didn't fool me. Those were the two most experienced virgins I ever saw. They taught me a few things!"

Dykstra downed his rum and poured himself and Regan another hearty jolt. "What are these English women like?" he asked. "Are they as good as Clarice's women?"

Regan stood and leered down at his friend. "Dykstra, old friend, I hate to tell you this but here isn't a woman in the city who could hold a candle to the worst of Clarice's girls. They cover themselves with twenty-three layers of clothes and a man gets sorely tired trying to remove them." He grasped Dykstra's shoulder and leaned over. "They bat their eyes and swoon. Dead away," he said, throwing his arms wide and losing his balance and tumbling against the wall. He laughed drunkenly as Dykstra's eyes popped. "And," Regan said indignantly, "either they're too skinny or too fat. That's why they wear so much. So we men can't see what we're getting."

"Well, what are we going to do?" his friend asked

piteously. "I came all the way to this goddamn city knowing you would take care of me. I was hoping for a woman tonight."

"And you shall have one," Regan laughed. "I'll find you a woman if I have to waylay her husband for you. Nothing is too good for you, Dykstra," he said virtuously. "What kind do you want, old, young, skinny or fat?"

"One of each," Dykstra hiccoughed.

Regan pursed his lips together. "I know just the place," he said drunkenly. "My son, Caleb, is operating a gambling ship at the harbor, and I've seen some women that might appeal to you."

"We need another bottle," Dykstra mumbled.

"Whatever you want," Regan said, pulling the cork from another bottle and handing it to the captain. "Dykstra," he muttered, "if you had a real virgin, would you know what to do with her?"

"What kind of question is that?" Dykstra asked, slurring his words. "I had a virgin once in Sumatra. Hours, Regan, it took hours. But, by God, she was worth every minute of it," he said, sighing deeply.

"What happened to her?" Regan demanded as he took another pull from the bottle.

"You should ask, you bastard, you snatched her from me right under my very nose. You remember that dark-skinned beauty. The one who wore all the bangles. The one who pierced your ear! Now, do you remember?"

"That wasn't all she pierced," Regan mumbled as he slid half on and half off the chair. "I never forgave you for that. Look, I still have a scar from that damn hole in my ear," he said, fumbling with his earlobe.

"What's a bit of a scar between friends. I broke her in for you. You should thank me instead of grumbling," he said, slipping from his chair onto the floor.

Regan eyed his friend and grinned. "I'll forgive you for the virgin, but not for the damage to my ear. Is that all right with you?"

"Now that I think about it, she was a little too handy with that needle. How's your wife, you bastard?" Dykstra demanded, thumping Regan on the back.

"Don't ask and I won't have to lie," Regan laughed.

"The most beautiful woman I ever saw. You have luck up your ass, Regan," he groaned.

"You got it all wrong, Dykstra. I divorced Sirena. I married someone else. Her name is . . . is . . . What the hell is her name?"

"Whose name?"

"The woman I married."

"How the hell should I know? Right now, I can't remember my own. Maybe it's Polly?" he said, trying to bring the rum to his lips only to have it dribble down his chest.

Regan leaned over to look at the front of Dykstra's shirt. "You spilled good liquor, you bastard. What the hell kind of friend are you, anyway? You don't even know my own wife's name! Polly! It's as good as any," Regan laughed.

"I always liked Sirena," Dykstra said, punching Regan on the arm. "I think she's the most beautiful woman I've ever seen and you're the biggest goddam fool ever born. Come to think of it, I should punch your teeth out for the way you treated her. Maybe I will," he threatened, raising his arm only to find it too heavy. He let it fall back on the table.

Regan looked at his friend from beneath scowling brows. "You want to fight? Why? What did I do to you?"

"I like Sirena," Dykstra complained, "and you left her behind when you left Java. Christ, Regan, I thought she'd become a madwoman when she watched the tip of your tops'l drop over the horizon."

Suddenly Regan grew serious. "When was this?" he asked, trying to enunciate.

"The morning you sailed out of Batavia harbor. Sirena came riding up to the company office with her hair flying down her back. Ah, I've never seen a more beautiful woman."

"She came to the offices and what?" Regan pressed.

"She came riding down the wharf like the hounds of Hell were on her heels. She ran down the dock and into the office calling for you. I don't think I've ever seen a woman happier than she was at that moment. Cheeks all flushed and pink from the ride, the glow of love lighting her eyes . . . Christ, man! How could you leave her behind? When I told her you'd already gone I watched the destruction of a woman's heart. You really are a bastard, Regan."

Regan fought to clear his head so he could absorb Dykstra's words. Sirena *had* told him the truth. Heaven help him, what had he done? Blindly, he reached for the bottle and wrested it from Dykstra's hands.

"You're more than a bastard, Reg, you're the biggest idiot I've ever met! There can't be another woman as gorgeous as Sirena. Or is there, you old dog? Is Polly as beautiful?"

Regan shook his head. "No one is as stunning as Sirena," he said, lurching to his feet. "And do you know what, you son of a bitch, she said she's going to ruin me."

"Serves you right," the captain retorted, holding out his hand for Regan to help him to his feet. "Anybody with a scar on his ear doesn't deserve someone like Sirena. I hope she does split your gullet. I hate the name Polly. Parrots are named Polly."

"A bird, eh. Well, she doesn't eat like a bird. She eats like a . . . a wolf, and all she wants to do is spend money. Come on, old friend, it's time you met . . . what's her name. I'm going to take you home so we can sober up."

"I hope she eats you out of house and home and sends you right into the poorhouse."

Camilla donned her shawl in preparation for going out when the doorpull sounded. She opened the door and stood back, a look of shock on her finely wrought features. "You're crocked," she snapped. "Quickly, get inside before someone sees you," she said, grabbing Regan by the arm and pulling him into the foyer. "Who is this?" she demanded as she let her eyes fall on the staggering seaman at Regan's side.

"He's the one who told me your name," Regan laughed uproariously.

"Take him out of here before you embarrass the lot of us. Wherever you found him, take him there and leave him," she demanded imperiously. "I won't have two drunks in my house. This instant, Regan!" she said, stamping her foot.

Regan swiveled and almost lost his balance. "Did you hear what . . . she . . . said? I'm to take you all the way back to Batavia."

"What does she know?" Dykstra slurred as he reeled behind Regan to a large overstuffed chair. "What kind of brothel is this; there's no liquor. For shame," he leered at Camilla. "You'll never do any business this way. Is she the keeper of this establishment?" he asked Regan in a low whisper.

Regan shrugged. "Fetch my friend some rum," he ordered Camilla.

"Fetch it yourself," she snapped. "I've never been so ashamed."

Regan assumed his full height and wobbled slightly on his legs. "And how do you think I feel; here I bring my friend home and he thinks you run a whorehouse?" He wagged a finger under Camilla's nose and reached for her. Nimbly, she sidestepped his outflung arm and moved away.

"You're drunk," she hissed. "Father was right, you do love your rum!"

"Regan, you sly fox, you didn't tell me this was a father-daughter enterprise. How grand. Now where in the hell are the rum and women?" he asked, struggling to his feet.

"Get him out of here," Camilla said through clenched teeth.

"Captain Dykstra brought me money from Batavia. Do you still want me to take him out of here?" Regan demanded, his eyes narrowed. "Enough money to pay your bills for another month."

Camilla reconsidered for a moment. "All right," she acquiesced, "but have him back where he belongs before I get home. Enjoy your own soused company," she sniped as she closed the door behind her.

"You bastard," Dykstra shouted. "The only woman to be seen and you let her get out the door. Now, what are we going to do?" he cried pitifully.

Regan thumped his friend on the back and grinned. "No loss, she's not for the likes of you . . . or me. I think we should sleep off this drunk, Dykstra. I don't think either of us could take a woman in this condition. Come with me and I'll find you a bed."

"Speak for yourself, you son of a bitch," Dykstra shouted as he followed Regan. "You're burned out, an old man," he needled. "You lost a good and beautiful woman and you live in a house of ill repute run by a father and daughter. I never heard anything so disgusting in my whole life," he said piously. "Never."

"Just shut the hell up, Dykstra, and mind your own affairs. I'm not an old man and I'm not burned out. And I didn't lose Sirena. I can have her anytime I want her. All I have to do is snap my fingers and she'll come running."

"Ha! And what will Polly what's-her-name say to that?"

"Dykstra, didn't you learn anything. Any man whose had a hole in his ear is superior to all others. It's a sign of virility."

"Bastard, you made that up," Dykstra said, falling on the bed. He was asleep immediately. Regan leaned over, lost his balance and laid down next to his friend. Loud, erratic snores permeated the room for hours.

Lord Farrington amused himself by shuffling a pack of playing cards. His thoughts worked as quickly as his nimble fingers. A pall seemed to be settling over him, and it was an effort to quiet his racing mind. Who was torturing him this way? What could anyone want with him? For the first time in his gambler's life he had landed in a safe berth, and now he was about to be tossed into the swelling, churning sea.

A strong gust of wind came up and the cards scattered over the deck. Dropping to his knees, he noticed a slim pair of ankles boarding the ship. A foolish look on his face, he rose to acknowledge the young woman who asked for Caleb. With a mischievous smile, Farrington escorted her to Caleb's quarters. A haughty look about her, she thanked him and entered the room, carefully shutting the door in his face.

The lord smirked to himself. If the young rascal weren't careful, he would find out he bit off more than he could chew. The lovely thing with the ravishing ankles belonged to Caleb's father and somehow he didn't think Regan would take lightly to Caleb playing games with his wife.

Regan woke first, his mouth dry and his tongue cottony. He shook Dykstra out of his stupor, then called the servants to administer to them both. An hour later, they descended the steps in preparation for an evening aboard the *Sea Siren*.

"That was some bout we both had," Dykstra laughed. "I seem to remember getting here but not much else. Tell me, Regan, how is it that Caleb opened a gambling ship? And, I believe, you told me it was the infamous Siren's ship he is using."

Regan shrugged. "Bought it from a harbor master in Spain. I would think when the Siren retired from the seas she would have her ship in Cádiz and moved on to other interests."

Dykstra looked at Regan suspiciously, but said nothing.

"I've been toying with the idea of going into business with Caleb. I have something I want to talk over with you when we get aboard. I'm glad you came, my friend. I was at a low ebb when you walked through my office door. It's not a pretty story, but I need another ear for now. I would appreciate your unbiased opinion, Dykstra."

Captain Dykstra frowned. They had been friends for quite a number of years. It was obvious something was bothering Regan. Was he in some kind of financial trouble? He remembered the lightened look in Regan's eyes at the mention of the profits from the nutmeg crop. "Regan, I wanted to tell you something, but when we were in the offices, the rum made me forget. I can't swear to it, but I think I saw Dick Blackheart on the wharf when I debarked. He spotted me staring at him. He seemed as though he were defying me to acknowledge him. He walks with a stiff leg and his left arm is damaged, but his face is still as hateful as ever. I would swear that it was him. I figured to myself that after the Siren ran him through he made off somehow and managed to make his way back here to his homeland. Have you seen him or heard that he's about?"

Regan was stunned. "I saw the Siren kill him with my own eyes!"

"Did you see him die or did you see her injure him and toss him overboard?" Dykstra asked.

"Neither," Regan answered shortly. "Things were wild. The Siren was ordering her wounded and my own to be tended. I suppose he could have gotten off the ship. For both our sakes, I hope you're wrong, Dykstra."

"So do I," the captain mumbled to himself.

"Here we are. What do you think of her?" Regan said, pointing to the twinkling lanterns that outlined the ship in the hazy fog.

Captain Dykstra nodded. "An impressive sight. Did the boy do all of this on his own?" At Regan's affirmative nod, he fell in line to board the ship behind a long string of people chattering like magpies.

"I don't think my gut can take any more rum today; let's just head for the tables and see how our luck is running," Regan suggested. "What's your fancy, Dykstra, cards or dice?"

"I think I'll take a crack at the dice," the captain grinned.

"See that man at cards, the one who's scowling? He's Sirena's new husband," Regan said coolly. "He's also my father-in-law." Dykstra shot his friend a grim glance, but said nothing. "You can tell by the look on his face he's on a losing streak." What in the hell was going on, Regan wondered as he threw the dice and watched the tiny dots appear.

Midway through the evening, his pockets empty, Regan stepped back to study the milling gamblers as they tossed money on the round tables with gay abandon. Women dressed in their finest, their jewels sparkling in the glowing lamplight, squealed with delight at every toss of the dice or flick of the cards. He felt his eyes drawn time and again to Stephan Langdon. It seemed his luck had turned for the better. Regan noticed a deft movement of Stephan's. Caleb, who was standing behind Stephan, was obviously angry. He nodded his head slightly to Lord Farrington and moved away from the wild activity Stephan was creating. Regan grinned to himself. Langdon was a card cheat and Caleb had found him out and was about to inform the lord. It would be interesting to see what happened.

Captain Dykstra tired of the dice and sauntered over to Regan, a glass of wine in his hand. "How much did you lose?" he asked quietly.

"Enough," Regan answered curtly. "Watch," he said as Caleb walked over to Sir Stephan and whispered in his ear. Even in the dim light, Regan could see the man's eyes were alarmed and indignant. He laid down his hand, picked up his money and followed Caleb.

"What is it I'm supposed to be watching?" Dykstra asked.

"Caleb just caught a card cheat who happens to be my father-in-law and Sirena's new husband. It will be interesting to see how my son handles the situation."

"If he's smart, he'll give him a warning and let it be known that from this point on he's going to be observed sharply. I'll say one thing for you, Regan. Wherever you are, there's always some sort of trouble brewing. Do you think the boy can manage it or should we give him a hand?"

"For now, let's let him have his head. He's got his partner to help him if he runs into difficulty. If the boy doesn't panic, he'll be all right."

"I'll stake you to a game of faro," Dykstra said affably as he withdrew a sheaf of bills for Regan's inspection. "Keep your eyes out for a comely wench for me." Regan laughed as his eyes circled the room. He was glad Sirena wasn't in evidence. If word got back to her of Stephan's escapade, he wondered what she would do. A ripple of apprehension washed over him as he picked up the cards.

Stephan Langdon stood on the deck, his stance arrogant. "Whatever you called me out here for had better be important," he said coldly.

"Oh, it is," Lord Farrington said in exactly the same manner. "Cal caught you cheating with cards tucked in your sleeve."

"What a dastardly lie!"

"Then what do you call this?" Caleb demanded as he handed over two identical cards.

"How am I supposed to know. I could call you out for this humiliating experience."

"That won't be necessary", Lord Farrington said suavely. "From now on, one of us will be watching you every time you come here. We had no wish to embarrass you in front of your friends, that's why we asked you out on deck. The next time we will show no such courtesy, but will make an example of you in front of the others. This," he stated, "is just a friendly warning. It would be wise if you left now and didn't come back for a while. There might have been someone other than Cal who saw what you did."

"This is despicable," Stephan snarled. "You, sir, are a cur of the worst sort. Believe me, I will not forget this. A cheat indeed! I believe you maintain a crooked operation and are using me as an excuse to cover your own dastardly ways."

"Perhaps you would like to go inside and make that accusation in front of the rest of the patrons," Caleb said in a deadly voice. "Then we could retaliate with our charges against you. It was a foolish thing you did."

Stephan bristled and then looked into the cold faces of the partners. Whatever he was about to say remained unvoiced, and he left the ship.

"You have a good eye, Cal," Lord Farrington said, thumping Caleb on the back. "It was bound to happen sooner or later and this was as good a time as any. In the future, if Langdon comes here, one of us will have to keep a vigil over him. I've seen episodes where men were killed on the spot for cheating. Gambling," he said virtuously, "is an honorable profession. One does not cheat. Our venture is too new for us to have a scandal. Keep your eyes open, Cal, and keep me informed."

"Damn it to hell," Caleb muttered under his breath. Of all the men in the world it had to be Regan's father-in-law. How was he going to explain it to Camilla when he next saw her? His shoulders squared, he grinned in the dim light. He shrugged; he didn't have to explain anything he didn't want to. It was as simple as that.

Thoughts of Camilla were pleasant for the moment,

but before long a frown settled over his face. Bedding Regan's wife was something he couldn't come to terms with. When Regan came aboard this evening, he had felt so guilty he could not look at his father. What would Sirena say if she knew Stephan had been caught cheating at cards? Should he warn her or leave it alone? He decided to leave it alone. He would keep his promise not to interfere in either Regan's or Sirena's affairs.

Stephan stormed his way into the house and up the stairs to Sirena's room. Not bothering to knock, he thrust open the door and shouted for Sirena to get up and join him in the ballroom.

"Are you out of your mind?" Sirena snapped. "It's after midnight and I'm tired."

"I won't ask you again, my dear," Stephan said, leaning over the bed and leering down at her. "Now!" There was no mistaking the vicious mood he was in.

"Give me time to dress and I'll join you in a few moments," Sirena said, sliding from the bed.

"Your nightdress will do nicely. I'll be waiting for you, so don't tarry."

Sirena looked around wildly for some form of escape. What did he plan for her this time? Something must have happened aboard the gambling ship. Afraid to delay any longer, Sirena crept from the room and descended the stairs to meet Stephan. She watched in horror as he lit one candle after another till the immense room was bathed in yellow light. She drew in her breath when Stephan walked over to her and held out a rapier. "I'm going to teach you how to fence," he said in a calm, though bitter voice.

"At this time of night?" Sirena demanded incredulously.

Stephan ignored her as she grasped the rapier at the hilt, holding it loosely in her hand. "Listen to me carefully," Stephan said, flexing the thin blade above his head. "Fencing does not take any enormous strength. Anyone with normal reflexes and a relatively conditioned body can do it. Your coordination is very good, my dear, so I don't anticipate any great problem. As we progress with the lesson, you will see that you must have constant mental concentration as well as total body control. Actually, you could liken fencing to a game of chess but played at lightning speed. What makes fencing exciting is that one needs great intelligence to be masterful at it. Tactics are the brainwork of fencing, based on observation and analysis of your opponent, and wise choices of action against him."

Panic gripped Sirena. With the weapon in her hand and Stephan so close, she could easily slit his gullet. "Stephan, I could never learn this sport," she lied. "I'm a woman. Why are you making me do this?"

Again, he ignored her comments. "Courtesy is a word closely associated with the sport and is an integral part of the engagement. Each match is preceded by a salute and an acknowledgment of your opponent. Every fencer, no matter how good or bad, can learn something from his adversary, and one should never assume one will win. My old master told me fencing is a school of humility. I don't necessarily agree with him. I'm going to teach you to maintain control of your body. In the beginning your upper arm muscles and your inner thigh may become sore, but as we work out all of your muscles will loosen up and then there will be no problem."

"Stephan . . . I—"

"Bring your rapier up to touch mine and say, en garde!"

"But Stephan," Sirena protested, "don't we need some form of protective equipment. I really would rather not do this," she said in a trembling voice.

"You need have no fear, my dear. I shall not hurt you, and there is no way you could touch me, as inexperienced as you are. We will parry and thrust and do a few lunges and then we'll rest and go at it another day."

The next hour was a revelation for Sirena as she fumbled and moved awkwardly with the rapier, to Stephan's amusement. He knew his sport and it interested her to see where this charade would lead. She managed to handle herself well enough to keep his interest, yet awkwardly enough not to give herself away.

"Do you see what I mean about perfect coordination?" Stephan laughed as he flicked at her nightdress, exposing her rosy-tipped breasts.

"If you wanted to see my naked body, why didn't you just come to my room instead of this insidious cat-and-mouse game you're playing? You know that I can never hope to be a fencer and yet you want me to play with you." Suddenly, the tip of his blade was at her neck.

"I wouldn't move if I were you, my dear, nor would I speak. I am fully aware of the fact that I can see your body whenever I desire. You are here because I want you here. And you will do what I want when I want it. Is that understood?" The tip of the blade moved downward and pricked at her breast. "Answer me, Sirena, do you understand?"

"Yes, Stephan, I understand perfectly," Sirena said in a cool, calm voice, her eyes downcast.

"You can go back to bed now, my dear, unless, of course, you would like to join me in my chamber. Ah, I see by the revulsion in your eyes you have no desire to climb in my bed." He shrugged as he brought up the rapier and sliced downward across her naked breast. Sirena's eyes widened and then narrowed.

"You see, my dear, what a master of my craft I am. I didn't draw one drop of blood. All you have is a slight welt which will soon disappear. Good night, Sirena," he said, turning his back on her.

"Insufferable bastard," Sirena muttered under her breath as she left, the tatters of her sleeping gown trailing out behind her as she climbed the curving stairway.

Wren walked across the rear lawn humming softly to herself. The morning was bright, the air fresh and the sun glanced off Jacobus' brilliant blooms in a kaleidoscope of colors. Her pretty yellow ankle-length dress matched the marigolds for vibrancy and heightened her glossy curls and huge brown eyes.

Wren had removed her stockings and shoes, glancing cautiously around for signs of Frau Holtz, who was bent on teaching her to become a proper young miss. But Wren loved the feel of the icy morning dew creeping between her toes and the spongy earth giving beneath her slight weight.

When she had first come out to the garden she had searched for Jacobus, hoping he would let her help him cut fresh flowers for the house. The old man was nowhere in sight and Wren assumed he was lingering for a second cup of morning coffee with the Frau. It was just as well, the child smiled to herself; she loved having the garden all to herself. It had become her own private heaven. The green lawn, the gay flowers, the small summerhouse at the edge of the walled acreage, had been almost more than she could comprehend when she first explored the area. To her mind it was as large and sprawling as St. James' Park across the way and twice as beautiful. Raised in the slums and alleys. Wren drank in the beauty of nature and could feel it nurture her soul.

Humming a nonsensical tune and stopping occasionally to caress a velvety petal or bask in the fragrance of the rose hedges, she didn't notice a tall, silver-haired figure treading the path parallel to the one she was taking. Near the end of the rose hedge, where the paths merged, Wren walked blindly into Stephan's arms.

Her first impulse was to free herself from his grasp and run, run, as fast as her little legs could carry her. But Stephan had taken a firm hold of her bony shoulder and forced her to stand as she was. Panic seized Wren as she remembered the scene in the dining room not too many days ago, and the sound of her own heartbeat echoed in her ears.

"Such a pretty little girl in such a pretty garden," Stephan said softly. As he shifted his weight the gravel made a grating noise beneath his boots and Wren somehow knew beyond a doubt that the master had stalked her, walking on the spongy grass so she wouldn't hear his footsteps and race back into the house.

Stephan tipped her chin up to look down into her face. Stubbornly, Wren kept her gaze lowered. "Do I frighten you, child? You shouldn't be, I had a little girl like you, once. Now she's a grown woman and married. Camilla is her name."

Wren had never heard the master mention his daughter before and she became curious. "Was she pretty and did she wear pretty dresses?" she asked in a squeaky voice that seemed to please the master.

"Yes, she did. As a matter of fact, she once had a yellow dress almost exactly like yours." He touched the sleeve of Wren's garment, feeling the fine muslin with appreciation. "She was a good little girl, my Camilla. Are you a good little girl, Wren?"

Color suffused the child's features. "No sir," she answered softly, "I'm not."

Stephan was amused. "And why aren't you? Don't you have everything you could wish for?"

Wren shrugged her shoulders in a helpless gesture. The master had never spoken to her this way before and she wasn't certain how she should react. He seemed different this time. She wasn't scared of him. His voice was so low and gentle and she hoped he would tell her more about Camilla.

"Is it because I told you you were a nasty, clumsy girl, that you feel you are not good? I was angry that day, child. I didn't mean what I said. I even apologize for spilling the relish dish on you. There, are you happy now?" His fingers had crept up from the sleeve to her neck and he touched the tender skin behind her ear.

Wren shook her head. "No, that's not why. Here, see?" she said, poking forward a tiny foot. "I took off my stockings and shoes and Frau Holtz says a proper miss doesn't ever go barefoot. But I like the way the dew feels between my toes and at least I won't ruin my shoes."

"Yes, I see," Stephan answered, staring at her chubby foot with its pink button toes. "Frau Holtz is correct, Wren." He couldn't seem to take his eyes from her foot and Wren tucked it beneath the hem of her skirt, somehow embarrassed. All her life she had run the streets of London minus shoes and stockings, but nobody ever looked at her bare feet the way the master did.

"Where are your shoes and stockings?" he asked. Wren pointed to the beginning of the path where she had left them. "Be a good girl and run and get them.

I'll help you put them on. I always helped my Camilla with her shoe straps when she was a little girl. Just like you," he added, seeing interest light her eyes whenever he spoke of Camilla as a child.

Wren hesitated, but on the master's urgings, she ran back down the path on the narrow border of grass so the gravel wouldn't hurt her feet, which had lost their callouses since living in the big house. Almost at once she returned, carrying her soft kid slippers and white lisle stockings. "I can put them on myself," she said in a boast. "It took me a week to learn to work the lacings, but I can even do it in the dark now!"

"I used to help my little girl," Stephan sighed, "and then just like you she grew up and didn't need me anymore. A father misses being needed by his daughter. Did I ever tell you about the time Camilla was invited to her first party and she couldn't decide which of her lovely dresses she would wear? You see, her mother was dead and she came to me for help." As he spoke he led Wren to the bench at the end of the path and pressed her shoulder gently to make her sit. He bent on one knee and continued the story of Camilla and her party dress.

Mesmerized by the soft sound of his voice and by her curiosity about another little girl, Wren allowed him to take one of the stockings from her hand and slide it over her foot, all embarrassment gone. The master kept his gaze level with hers, his fingers working mechanically as he regaled her with his tale. But as she watched him something else became evident on his face. Wren was too young and inexperienced to put a name to it but her basic female instincts rebelled. The master seemed to be having trouble with his mouth, he kept wetting his lips with his tongue. All of a sudden, her stocking seemed to be giving him trouble; his fingers kept straying up the inside of her leg. Almost before she knew it, he had rolled her dress up past her knees and his fingers were fumbling and stroking the soft skin leading to her thighs.

Wren stared at him, no longer hearing his words. She knew his voice had become thick and he was stumbling over the phrases he was uttering. The flesh on her leg crawled and goose bumps broke out on her arms.

In her mind's eye she remembered sleeping in an alleyway when a doxie and a man were suddenly beside her. They had awakened her but she was wise enough not to utter a sound. The woman had been leaning against the wall of a building and the man's hands were roaming over her body. The couple had stepped off the street because they wanted to be out of sight. If they discovered Wren they would have cursed her and the man would have possibly hit her to chase her away. Wren hadn't wanted to go away. She had found a nice supply of old rags to make a soft bed and she was tired.

In the darkness Wren had seen the man press himself against the prostitute, she had heard his breathing become ragged. In the moonlight she had seen his face and the expression he wore was the same one the master was wearing now.

Just as Stephan's fingertips slid higher up her leg, Wren jumped off the bench and began to run for the house. She hadn't gone more than a few steps when Langdon grabbed her by the hair and dragged her backward. "Stupid little bitch! Come back here!"

"No!" Wren screamed, terrorized. Quick as a flash, she pushed and managed to knock him off balance. In order to keep himself from falling, Stephan released Wren's hair and swayed against the bench.

Without looking back, Wren tore for the house, leaving her shoes and stockings behind, not caring whether or not the Frau would scold her. This minute, she would dearly love to hear the housekeeper's voice, to feel her stocky arms go around her protectively. But When Wren reached the kitchen the Frau was nowhere to be seen. Glancing blindly over her shoulder, the child ran to the front of the house and up the stairs to her room, fighting back shudder after shudder of revulsion.

Chapter Twenty-four

As the days passed, Frau Holtz came to love the young girl placed in her care. At night she would tuck the child into her bed and tell stories of life in the Spice Islands.

"Frau Holtz, could you tell me the story about the Sea Witch again? It's my favorite. I don't mean to hurt your feelings, but you've told me the story of how you worked to plant the nutmeg trees seven times. Do you think someday I could grow up to be like the Sea Siren? I wonder where she is now, Frau Holtz. Do you think she's happy?"

"No, little one, I do not think she is happy where she is. The Sea Siren loved only one man and he chose not to return her love."

"What will happen to her, Frau Holtz?" Wren asked sadly.

"Only the Lord above knows, child, only the Lord above."

"She sounds so beautiful when you tell me about her. And the man she loved, he sounds so handsome. If there is a God, like you teach me there is, why doesn't He help the Sea Siren?"

"Perhaps because Heaven helps those who help themselves. I don't know, Wren," the old woman said, gathering the child close to hide her own tears. "I don't know. It is time for sleep," she told the child, patting her firmly on the rump and laying her against the snowy pillow. "It is you who will grow to be as beautiful as the Sea Siren. Already your cheeks have filled out and your hair shines to match the sparkle in your eyes. That is what proper living and happiness does. When you are older, you will find someone as handsome as the man the Sea Siren loved. But you will be luckier, *ja*. He will love you back."

"Oh, I hope so," Wren cried, throwing her arms around Frau Holtz. "But I must not keep taking all of this proper living and happiness for granted. I must help Missy-ma'am. I hope I dream of the Sea Siren tonight. Each time I do, she becomes more beautiful. Like Missy-ma'am. Good night, Frau Holtz, and thank you for the warm milk." Wren snuggled beneath the covers and whispered a few quick prayers the way Frau Holtz had taught her to do and was soon asleep.

Hours later, while the girl slept, a dark shadow crept into the room. Cautiously and stealthily, the figure walked to the window and drew the heavy curtain to block out the moonlight. Slowly, on cat feet, the tall figure moved toward the bed. Inch by inch, the coverlet was pulled back to reveal the petite body.

A sensuous smile crossed the face of the man who stared at her. He dropped to his knees and gathered her small form to him, jarring her awake. Quickly, he covered her mouth to prevent an outcry. "Not a word, do you understand? Keep silent."

Wren's eyes widened in fear and she pushed against him, trying to pry herself from his grasp. She hated him more than she ever hated anyone. He was so strong, too strong to break away from. And when she struggled, he laughed, low and menacingly.

His hands covered her body and he pressed his mouth to hers, rubbing his hands over her slim legs and trying to part them so he could steal his hands between her thighs. She wanted to die as his tongue found hers. She squirmed and tried to kick herself free of him. Unexpectedly, he released her and she rolled out of his reach.

"Remember, not a word of this to anyone. If you tell, Frau Holtz will find herself out of work and your precious Missy-ma'am will develop a limp," he threatened before departing just as quietly as he'd entered.

Wren gagged and threw up in the chamber pot, her shoulders heaving and arms trembling. She had lived on the streets long enough to know what his next step would be. She wanted to escape down the hall and throw herself into Missy-ma'am's arms and tell her what he did. But she couldn't. She remembered his heavy threat. Frau Holtz was too good to know how to watch out for herself. And Missy-ma'am. Beautiful Missy-ma'am. He would hurt her. Terribly.

For a moment she thought of running away, but she knew she couldn't. Frau Holtz and Sirena would suffer for it if she did.

Perhaps she could ask for a bolt on the door. Hugging her knees to her chest, the child pondered her problem. The housekeeper would want to know why she wanted a lock and what could she say? Perhaps she would say she was afraid of spooks. Yet, in her heart, she knew a lock could never keep the master out.

Caleb walked back through the crowds into the gaming parlor, saw Regan notice his return, and knew he could not escape his father's company. Regan was signaling him to pay his compliments to Captain Dykstra. The pleasant amenities over, Caleb joined them for a drink. In quiet tones he explained about Stephan's gambling methods and the warning he and Farrington had issued. "I know he's Camilla's father, but I couldn't allow him to continue his practices. We run a clean ship here, and we wouldn't want to sully our reputation. The question is, do you think Sirena should be told. He's bound to get himself into difficult straits and, perhaps, she should be warned. Also, he's lost fantastic sums of money, and I'm certain it is hers he's so generous with. What do you think?"

"Yes, definitely. Though, she probably already knows what effect Stephan is having on her finances. However, I shouldn't advise you what to do, Caleb, you're your own man. Whatever you think is right. Actually, I came here tonight to talk business. Do you have time to listen or should I return in the morning?"

Caleb cast a practiced eye around the room. "Now will be fine. Lord Farrington has matters well in hand. What is it?" he asked, his heart pounding in his chest. Surely Regan didn't know about Camilla coming to see him during the afternoon hours. Then he remembered Regan had said business, and Caleb sighed with relief.

"I want to invest in your enterprise. Captain Dykstra has come to England with profits from the nutmeg crop in Java and I don't like to keep reinvesting in my own venture. Whatever terms you decide upon, I would find most agreeable. Do you have to consult with Aubrey Farrington, or can we keep this between ourselves?"

"Between us," Caleb answered. "It would be part of my share." How could he refuse? He couldn't. Because of his guilt over Camilla, Caleb would have to compromise. "Of course, I would only agree if you consented to a binding agreement that the shares be sold back to me and no one else."

Regan smiled at Caleb. His son was a level-headed businessman and he was proud of him. "Of course," he readily agreed. "Actually, I hesitated to ask you, but there is nowhere else to turn. Your ship would be a wise investment to earn some ready capital. I hate to admit it, son, but I'm nearly wiped out."

"And without Sirena's help," Caleb couldn't help adding. Somehow it gave him pleasure to see the wounded look in Regan's eyes. "I agree. I'll arrive at the figures tonight after closing. Aubrey will be told, naturally; I feel it only fair. I'll stop by your offices in the morning on my way to see Sirena."

"Sounds fine to me," Regan smiled. "Caleb, Dykstra here has a yen for a—"

Caleb laughed and pointed a finger. "She's been waiting for somebody like you to come along. Tell her I said to give you a drink on the house." Dykstra grinned and sauntered over to a voluptuous serving maid who was eyeing him openly.

"Now that Dykstra has been taken care of, I think I'll go home. I have a bride waiting for me," Regan laughed. "Keep Dykstra here and see that he gets to my office in the morning." He clapped Caleb soundly on the back and left.

Caleb stared after him with tortured eyes. What would Regan do if he ever discovered that he and Camilla . . . He swallowed hard and began to make his rounds, stopping to talk to various patrons and having a drink here and refusing one there.

A few quick rolls of the dice and he found himself near Lord Farrington. He drew Aubrey into a secluded corner and quickly explained that he had agreed to sell Regan shares into the business.

Farrington didn't take the news well. An angry spark lit the depths of his eyes and his body tensed.

"He's my father and the shares I sell him won't have any effect on your profits. As a matter of fact, your share will improve in that we have more working capital to help us reap higher profits. It's my ship and my money, don't make me remind you of that again," Caleb said coldly.

"And does he pay you for these shares by the use of his wife?" Aubrey muttered to himself as he watched Caleb's retreating back. "We'll just see about that!" Every gambler kept an ace in the hole and sweet Camilla would be just that!

Caleb deposited a bleary-eyed, satisfied Captain Dykstra at Regan's office the following morning. He winked at his father and pointed a thumb at Dykstra. "He'll never be able to say I wasn't hospitable."

"That you were, boy. That you were," Captain Dykstra smiled.

"Here," Caleb said, extending a slip of paper to Regan. "I worked out an informal agreement. If you have no revisions to suggest, sign it and bring your investment to the ship. I spoke to Lord Farrington and, while he was less than enthusiastic, he had no other choice than to accept it. With the money you invest, we can seal off a portion of the quarterdeck and buy more equipment. More space, more equipment, and we can raise the limit of patrons we take on every night." Caleb held out his hand and his father shook it.

Later, Caleb rang Sirena's front doorbell and was surprised when she answered it herself. Her face lit up and she hugged him soundly. "How nice of you to come, Caleb." Her expression sobered instantly. "Is something wrong, did something happen?"

"No. Everything is fine. Sirena, where can we talk undisturbed?"

Sirena frowned, but ushered him ahead of her into the library. She closed the door and waited expectantly.

Caleb was blunt and to the point. "Your husband is losing vast amounts of money, and I suspect it is yours. Last evening, I caught him cheating. I discreetly brought him out on deck and, with the help of Lord Farrington, properly dressed him down. I don't know if we made an impression. It was our intention to put the fear of God into him. Instead, he became downright nasty. The reason I came here was to ask if I should allow him to patronize the ship. I'm almost certain he will continue his swindling methods and it could be dangerous. I can't keep my eye on him every moment. One of these days someone else will realize what he's doing and call him out. It's bad for business and I may have to take extreme measures. I wouldn't want anything to come between us, Sirena. Whatever you decide should be done, I will abide by it."

"There's no decision to make, Caleb. There's nothing I can do. Let him continue as he is. Their damn English laws are not made for the likes of me. I should be so lucky to have someone challenge Stephan out and kill him for me. I really don't want to discuss it. I do, however, appreciate your coming here. I might not approve of what you've made of the *Rana,* but I also know a gift is a gift and I do wish you well. I love you, Caleb, and whatever makes you happy will make me happy. Please believe that." The library doors opened and Frau Holtz and Wren entered. The old woman's eyes lit up and she clutched Caleb to her stout bosom.

Sirena glanced at Wren, whose eyes were as large as saucers and full of disbelief. "Come here, Wren, there's someone I want you to meet. This man is very dear to me and he comes from the Spice Islands the same as I do. His name is Caleb and he is Mynheer van der Rhys' son."

"We were just coming in to show you Wren's new dress," Frau Holtz explained the intrusion. "Pink is her color, *ja?*"

Wren was staring at Caleb. Oblivious of her frock,

she slowly moved toward him and softly asked, "Do you know the story of the Sea Siren?" Her amber eyes lit like tapering candle flames.

Caleb laughed, his strong, white teeth catching the light. "I know the story very well. She was a beautiful lady." He took a step closer and dropped to his knee. "I think she was almost as beautiful as you are," he said, taking her hand and bringing it to his lips. His smiling eyes sobered as he looked into Wren's.

When she spoke, it was quietly and her words startled Frau Holtz and Sirena both. "I hope the man the Sea Siren loved looked like you."

Caleb temporarily tore his gaze from Wren and looked at Sirena. After a brief period he whispered, "I hope he looked like me. I would be proud to have someone like the Sea Siren love me."

Wren giggled. "When I grow up, I'm going to be like the Sea Siren, then I can . . ." she hesitated. "Will you wait for me to grow up?"

Caleb laughed and suddenly became serious. "I very well may do that."

"Caleb, this is my ward, Wren," Sirena said, putting her arm around the girl's shoulders. "Soon she'll be off to school and, when she returns, she will be a proper young woman." Wren couldn't seem to take her eyes off Caleb, and the young man seemed to share her fascination.

Sirena's gaze sought Frau Holtz's. He doesn't know it yet, Sirena thought, but he's looking at his destiny. Wren is Caleb's future.

"It's time for Wren's lessons, Frau Holtz," Sirena said softly. "I want to be alone with Caleb for a bit." She smiled at her "little brother," who seemed intrigued with the bright-eyed youngster in her frothy pink dress.

"*Ja*, the lessons," Frau Holtz murmured as she drew an unwilling Wren along with her.

"Caleb, can you stay and have lunch with me? It's been so long since we have spoken."

"I'll stay a while longer, but I must refuse your invitation for lunch. Sirena, did you know Captain Dykstra is here? Regan brought him to the ship last night. Sit down, there's something I must tell you."

Sirena could feel the tension in him and her own nerves grew taut. "Of course, I should have realized you wouldn't come all the way to tell me about Stephan. You could have handled that yourself; you didn't need my opinion. I'm not stupid, Caleb."

"I know you aren't. That's why I came today. And you're right, I could have decided what to do with Stephan on my own and you need never have known. You taught me too well, Sirena."

"Get on with it, Caleb. Whatever it is must be important."

"As I told you, my father came to the ship last night. He told me his business is failing and he is in difficult straits. Most of his capital is tied up and he needs money now or his business will go under."

"And he managed this all by himself," Sirena said in amazement. "Are you telling me he has only himself to blame?" She laughed. "What makes you think his business affairs interest me? I couldn't care less."

"You can't deceive me, Sirena. Right now, you're delighted Regan is going bankrupt. The money he took from you has brought him no luck, and you're glad. Once again, you've proven yourself victorious. Is your victory bitter or sweet?"

Sirena leaned over and looked Caleb square in the eyes. "I did teach you well, little brother. Believe what you will; I love Regan and always will. I'm not a whole woman without him. I've lost him and I've nothing left except bitterness and humiliation. Now, why have you come here to give me this information?"

"So you'll understand why I allowed Father to buy shares in the gambling folly. I dropped off the agreement this morning." He watched anxiously for some sign of her anger, but instead saw sadness. "I felt I owed you an explanation. I wanted you to hear it from me and not someone else. Least of all, from your . . . from Stephan."

"I think it's time you left, Caleb," Sirena said, standing and moving to the door.

"Tell me you understand, Sirena," Caleb pleaded, his face young and boyish in his apprehension.

"I understand, Caleb. I understand you are doing what you swore you would not do. Take sides. I don't think I can forgive you. You've compromised yourself, and I think I know why. It's because of Camilla." Caleb was about to deny her accusation, but she raised her hand to silence him. "Yes, I saw the two of you together the night of your grand opening. You've been sleeping with her, haven't you?" she questioned rhetorically.

Caleb was stunned and his lean jaw trembled slightly. He became a boy again in her presence. He tried to defend his actions, but Sirena held up her hand again.

"Somehow, Caleb, I thought there was one small portion of you that belonged to me. In many ways I felt we were bound to each other by an invisible cord from those days long ago when we risked life and limb to right a wrong. I've misjudged both you and Regan, and for that I'm sorry. I don't know who has hurt me more. I've had all I can take from the van der Rhys men. Good-bye, Caleb, and good fortune." She turned on her heel and stalked from the room. Moments later, she was running, tears streaming down her cheeks. She felt as though a part of her heart had been cut away.

An hour before Stephan was due home, Sirena sought out Frau Holtz in the kitchens. She drew her aside and whispered to her. "In a fortnight, Frau Holtz, I want to leave this house. I want you to seek Jacobus out and get word to the men. Little by little, so no one will notice, I want our things taken to the ship—in the dead of night if necessary. There must be no mistakes to make Stephan suspicious. We're going back to Batavia. Tomorrow, I will pen off a note to Tyler and Wren is to deliver it after Stephan leaves for the academy. Do you think you can handle this in secrecy, Frau Holtz?"

The old eyes lit up happily. "*Ja*, Mevrouw. I can take care of it. What about the child, is she to come with us?" she asked anxiously.

"But of course, there is no one else to look after her. I plan to take you all to Batavia and make certain that you are settled there."

The Frau grew agitated. "And you, Mevrouw, where are you going?"

"I have a yen to see America. Perhaps I'll go there, or perhaps I'll just sail the ship till I see someplace that takes my fancy. I don't belong anywhere anymore, Frau Holtz."

"The Mynheer, what of the Mynheer?"

"What about him?" Sirena snapped. "That part of my life is over. It was over back in Batavia. I acted the fool. When something is over, it's over. I should have realized this before. Regan doesn't belong to me; Caleb doesn't belong to me. I'm alone. Father and son have struck up an alliance and that is as it should be. There is no room in either of their lives for me. It would appear that you and the crew, as well as Wren, are saddled with me."

Chapter Twenty-five

Stephan, in a lighthearted mood, talked endlessly through lunch. Sirena couldn't have cared less. She allowed him to drone on and on, listening with half an ear. She tried to be amicable to Stephan since he currently left her totally to herself.

"And what have you planned for the next few days, Sirena?" he asked, nibbling on his lamb chop.

"Whatever could I have planned, Stephan? I haven't left the house in weeks." Although she tried to keep her voice level, even she heard the note of contempt which crept into it.

"Ah, then you have none. Good. I've organized a little outing for us. I'll expect you to be ready in approximately half an hour."

"Where are we going? I must know so I can wear something suitable."

"What you have on will be fine, darling," he said in

his most unctuous voice. "It is only a short carriage ride, nothing more."

"I don't think so today, darling," she imitated his tone. "I have a violent headache coming on—"

Stephan threw his flatware against a china plate, creating a loud clattering sound. "I said I would expect you in half an hour. You have no choice, Sirena. Go prepare yourself!"

Sirena watched the muscles work in his jaw and his lips compress. God, how she hated him. "And I told you, I don't care to go." Her voice was level and strong, meeting his in challenge.

Stephan took his attention away from her and continued eating his lunch. She knew he wasn't finished with her and she waited for his next move. "Sirena, darling, have you noticed any of your jewelry missing? I was looking for my gold timepiece this morning and it was nowhere to be found. I wondered if you, too, were missing any valuables. How long did you say your stoic Frau Holtz worked for you?"

Sirena gasped. He wouldn't! In her heart she knew he could and would. It wouldn't be the first time an employer had accused a servant of thievery and had the poor unfortunate sent to prison. "It won't work, Stephan. I would swear to Frau Holtz's innocence. Your accusation won't hold water."

"Ah, darling, you women are so loyal, so sentimental. The courts would see at first glance that you would forgive your servant of so many years almost anything. Especially when you protested the poor woman was getting on in her years. But I'm afraid, darling, the judicial system is not based on sentimentality and, as master of this house, it is my word that would stand."

Sirena sprang up from her place at the table. Thank heaven she would only have to endure another two weeks of this insanity. By then, the *Sea Spirit* would be ready to sail them back to Batavia.

"Where are you going, darling? You haven't finished your lunch?"

"I'm going to prepare myself, as you requested, Stephan!" she retorted hotly, feeling his cold glare as she turned from the room.

In the coach, Sirena stared silently out the window. Jacobus had not been in sight when the carriage had been brought around to the front drive. At the reins was Stephan's own driver. Rathbone acted as footman. The day was bright. Early summer had warmed the air and the people of London were taking advantage of the fine weather. The busy streets were more crowded than usual, and from several pubs the sounds of minstrels' music wafted out into the open.

The coach was following a direct route to the outskirts of the city, and Sirena wondered where Stephan was taking her. He had given his instructions to the driver after she had climbed into the coach, so their destination was still a mystery. Out, past Charing Cross, along the Pall Mall to Whetstone Park on the High Holborn. The driver took a sharp left onto Gray's Inn Lane and Sirena looked at Stephan with puzzlement. They were nearly out of the city.

"If you're wondering, darling, we're nearly at Codpiece Row at Clerkenwell Green." He watched her face carefully to see if his words held any meaning for her. She turned him a blank look and Stephan smiled.

The carriage pulled up outside the gates of a dark gray, stone building and, in the ironwork over the gate was the sign, *Bethlehem Royal Hospital*. As the coach drove under the high arch, Sirena craned her neck to read the plaque. When she looked back at Stephan, she saw his amused grin. She was horrified, terrified. Bedlam!

She sprang to her feet, knocking her head on the cab's roof, striking with her hands, seeking to gouge out his eyes.

Stephan defended himself by grabbing Sirena roughly and slamming her against the seat, pinning her arms to her sides.

"Control yourself, darling, else they will think you mad and take you from me to pen you in a cage." His breath was hot against her cheek.

"Let go of me! You're the madman! There's not a soul in all Bedlam more crazed than you!"

"Control yourself!" he ordered. "We only came for a visit. That is all, I promise you. I often come here of an afternoon to take in the sights. It's an inexpensive form of amusement. Many do it. Only a ha'penny and you're admitted into another world." He laughed, the sound cruel and maniacal in the confines of the coach.

Presently, the vehicle pulled up at the heavy, iron-bound doors, and when they entered, Sirena noticed the only latch was on the outside. A guard admitted them and smiled at Stephan with recognition. So, it was true, the bastard did come here to entertain himself by watching the pathetic, soul-less creatures.

Stephan tugged a linen square from his vest pocket and held it to his nose. She saw him hand several coins over to the guard, and she thought she saw the glint of a gold guinea.

The odor was putrid. Sirena was assaulted by the stench of rotting fruit and human waste. Down the dark passage Stephan led her, the smell becoming more fetid with each step. The guard stopped to lift his neck cloth over his mouth and nostrils. When he saw the expression on Sirena's face, he laughed coarsely. "You'll soon get used to it."

As they descended into the bowels of Bedlam, the stories she had heard about the place accosted her mind. She heard that if the lunatics became too quiet, retreating into a world of their own, the guards would tease, starve, prod and abuse them until they were unmanageable. Only in a wild, tormented state would they draw a paying audience of peasants and gentlefolk who came to sightsee.

As Stephan held her tightly by the arm, Sirena came to believe every rumor she had ever heard about the infamous Bedlam. She heard the shrieks and moans of the patients. The gruntings, growlings, ravings, rantings were awful, but worst of all was the deadly silence of some of the cells they passed. In these cells the poor creatures sat, contaminated by their own filth; vacant-eyed hollow shells of people who used to live within healthy bodies.

As she was led past a tiny, thin window cut into the stone wall, Sirena realized they were going even further below ground. The smells were even more acrid and horrible, if that was possible. The stench made the air rank, pinching her nostrils and causing her to choke for breath.

"How do you like it here, darling?" When Stephan received no answer, he continued. "No one likes it at first, but some learn to live very well here. Provided, of course, they have someone on the outside to insure they are cared for by supplementing the guards' income."

Sirena was silent, closing her eyes against the cubicles on either side of her, keeping her gaze straight ahead, dreading each step she took.

Stephan veered off to the right, dragging her with him. "This way, Sirena. There's something I want you to see." Down the corridor and through double bolted doors, which the guard opened, Sirena stood in the entrance to a high-ceilinged room furnished with peculiar-looking items. At first her befuddled mind couldn't conceive any use for them, but then as Stephan pointed out several fine points—leather straps, canvas jackets, muffs and handcuffs, chains and dousing buckets—she felt herself retch.

A chair, solid and built low to the floor, was equipped with manacles and straps to tie the victim firmly. Thankfully, none of these torture devices was in use, but as Stephan described them, Sirena realized he had come to see their effect on some human wretch.

Unable to stand it another moment, Sirena pleaded, "Please, can we go now?"

"Go?" Stephan asked, taking his pocket watch from his waistcoat. "Yes, it is time to go. Guard!"

Gratefully, Sirena stayed close to Stephan, trying to hurry his steps.

"There is something else I thought would interest you. It is over here," he said, pulling her arm. "Come."

Unwillingly, Sirena followed, hoping that if she gave him no resistance he would take her out of here. They stopped before a dank cell. "This is where the first Lady Langdon spent her last days." His eyes pierced hers for a reaction.

Suddenly, his hands were clasped around her wrists, holding her firmly. Before she realized what was happening, the guard's key was clanging against the iron bars. "Stephan! No! Stephan, you can't! Stephan, please!" she shrieked.

Her cries resounded throughout the cell block, stirring the inmates and causing them to echo her screams. "This is madness! Stephan!"

Rough hands threw her into the blackness at the rear of the cell. Before she could recover her footing, the door shut with a clank of finality, and the last thing she saw was Stephan's face before he sauntered away.

In one section of the cell straw matting rustled, and when Sirena's eyes became accustomed to the dark she realized she had been placed with three other prisoners. There was no telling how long these women had been confined, but from the looks of them she ventured to guess it had been quite some time since they had seen the light of day or had a breath of fresh air.

They were emaciated creatures, bathed in their own filth, ragged and pest-ridden. Her flesh crawled and she prayed that she would be removed immediately or else lose her mind in short order. They watched her shrewdly, and one of them began to laugh shrilly, cowering in the corner like a primitive animal as she scrutinized Sirena with hate-filled eyes.

Sirena backed away, taking up a position in the single unoccupied corner. The dim light cast by the torch in the corridor allowed her to survey the surroundings; stone walls sweating with the damp, dirt floor strewn with filth and excreta, and a moldy hay heap, soaked with urine that served as a bed. Pitifully, she wondered how long it would be before she, too, succumbed to these conditions. Every nerve in her body was taut.

Without warning, she was jumped upon and had her thin capelet seized. Another inmate, apparently the oldest, knocked the wind from Sirena in addition to stripping the slippers from her feet.

The third followed her cellmates' example and tore at Sirena's gown, ripping it from her shoulders, while emitting half-human sounds.

Sirena tensed and stood her ground and, as if by some unspoken command or understanding, they all came at her together. She found herself fighting for her life.

They scratched and beat her, and pulled her hair. She swung, cracking one of them hard on the head. The inmate whimpered like a whipped dog and skulked away. But, the other two persisted. Sirena swung out again, knocking another of them backward, hearing the breath escape in a loud whoosh. The last, being denied the protection of her cellmates, merely retreated. Sirena stood in the center of the cell, glaring at them, ready to defend herself further if need be.

Silently, she advanced on each in turn, taking back the garments they had ripped from her. They made no protest, seeming to respect her strength. Sirena supposed they had not expected to find that she was stronger than they. She only hoped they wouldn't try to overpower her again.

It was many hours later when the wardens brought slops and water. Sirena could hear the banging of the small grids through which stale bread, soaked in an unidentifiable gravy, and wooden mugs of water were passed. Sirena's companions had also heard the commotion the meal hour had created and, even as she watched them, they slavered in expectation of their ration.

Hour after hour Sirena huddled against a wall, not daring to sleep or move lest she incite another assault. A sole desire burned through Sirena's being—to get out of this lunatic asylum and run as far away as possible.

Again the guards delivered rations. Again came howls and shrieks, and the awful sound of iron scraping against iron. When she saw the bowls of thin gruel passed to her cellmates, she realized it must be morning. She had spent the entire day and night staring into the dark, her eyes constantly returning to the dim flare of the torch in the corridor. Her body ached; chills racked her spine and still she sat, quietly, silently, praying for a divine miracle to release her from this place.

Wondering how Stephan explained her absence to Frau Holtz, Sirena realized with a feeble ray of hope that Stephan could not leave her here. He could not! The sightseers! Instantly, she calculated on her fingers.

Tomorrow was Saturday! Curiosity-seekers would be coming to pay their ha'penny. Surely, someone would recognize her. Surely, she could promise to pay someone to bring a message to Frau Holtz. Jan and Willem! They would get her out! Somehow they must!

Then a fatal tremor of fear shook her. Why should anyone believe her when she told them who she was? They would see she was locked in an asylum for the insane! It was hopeless!

Sirena shut her eyes, sensing the three madwomen were watching her, waiting for their chance to attack again and steal her clothing—strip her naked if possible. She did not care. Nothing mattered. Let them kill her. Death would be a welcome visitor compared to living out the rest of her days in Bedlam.

When the key sounded in the lock, she did not even hear it. Suddenly, a bright light blinded her, and strong hands gripped her arms, pulling her to her feet. A voice she recognized and would hate for the rest of her life spoke. "Have you had enough, Sirena, darling? Will you come home and be a good, obedient, little wife or shall I leave you here for another day or so?"

Sirena hung her head in complete dejection and humiliation. She would be his slave.

"Come along, then. Don't be offended, but may I say you sorely need a bath! I hesitate to ride in the same carriage with you. Really, Sirena, you must learn to take better care of yourself, else you'll drive me to the arms of another woman." He chuckled, loud and harsh. It had the familiar ring of the lunatic laughter she had heard during the night.

Later, gratefully at home among her own things, Frau Holtz bathed her and put her to bed. The old woman had tears in her eyes but was lovingly silent. And when Sirena at last fell into an uneasy sleep, it was the Frau's arms about her that chased away the nightmares which came to taunt her.

Time and again, Stephan would waken Sirena and insist she go through the intricate fencing maneuvers. Endless nights would pass in sleeplessness, waiting for him to drag her out of bed and down the long staircase into the ballroom. It seemed to the dispirited Sirena that whenever she waited in anticipation of him he would not come. Yet, no sooner would she close her eyes in exhausted sleep than Stephan would be beside her, pulling her from the bed, stating it was time for another lesson.

Sirena never objected beyond a grimace. She remembered Bedlam all too well. Telling her that a husband reigned supreme was not enough for Stephan. He had shown her. She remembered his perfidiousness and was powerless against it.

She spent her days pacing her suite in distraction. Indecision was her downfall. She found it impossible to choose between an egg for breakfast or sweet rolls. The choice of which gown to wear was completely beyond her ken. This terrifying hold Stephan had over her left her confused and tearful. Sirena was totally demoralized, confused and disoriented.

Frau Holtz, who had never seen Sirena this way, not even when a captive of Chaezar Alvarez, was at a total loss for an answer. She knew what Stephan had done to Sirena. She knew the effect being imprisoned in Bedlam had on her mistress, and the old housekeeper decided patience and loving care would bring Sirena out of this state of malaise. Even Wren had difficulty breaking through Sirena's depression and rarely was able to draw a word from her benefactress.

The *Sea Spirit* was nearly ready to sail, but when Frau Holtz related this to Sirena, the green eyes became distracted. Each time the Frau tried arousing Sirena's interest in escaping with Wren and the crew, Sirena would burst into tears and wring her hands in pitiful helplessness. She feared Stephan would find her and place her in Bedlam. At last the Frau desisted, feeling she was doing more harm than good by forcing Sirena to a decision.

One night Stephan had come for Sirena, bringing along a pair of breeches and a boy's shirt for her to wear. Obedient to his wishes, Sirena had donned them and they had become her regular costume for the lessons Stephan pressed on her. The breeches were tight, hugging her hips and thighs like a second skin, and the shirt was far too small and could not be laced over her ample breasts. Soft, lisle stockings and flat-heeled, kid slippers completed the costume.

Sirena had stood in the center of the ballroom waiting for his first move of offense. The night was warm and he had opened the long windows which looked out over the parklike front drive and into the street. Occasionally the clatter of carriage wheels on the cobblestones could be heard along with a "Yah!" from an impatient driver to a recalcitrant horse.

For a moment Sirena stared outside, a winsome expression lining her face. Angry, Stephan made a sudden move to catch her attention and tossed her the rapier. "Don't look so stupidly toward the window, darling. You'll have me thinking you'd rather be out there instead of in here with me. Now take your stance!" he ordered harshly, the light in the room glancing off his eyes, giving them a hard, silvery appearance.

Resignedly, Sirena tightened her hand around the hilt of the weapon and knew again a fierce compulsion to pierce his heart. She would enjoy seeing the life flow from his body and onto the shining floor.

"That's the spark I want to see in your eyes," Stephan cooed, "the fire of a winner. I hope you'll be worth the effort tonight. You haven't been putting to use all I've taught you."

Wordlessly, Sirena glared at him and with a toss of her head to throw her gleaming dark tresses over her shoulder, she made the first thrust, hoping to catch Stephan off guard. But he was too much the master, too quick. His reflexes were superb and he was ready for her. "You've forgotten to say 'en garde!' darling," he said condescendingly. "If I didn't know better, I'd think you meant to kill me!" His feeble attempt at humor seemed to please him and he threw back his head and laughed, all the while keeping a careful eye on her.

With the gesture he exposed the flesh of his throat and Sirena could almost feel the tip of her rapier slitting his neck in two. Several more times Stephan drew her into a parry and Sirena defended herself admirably. "So, it would seem these lessons have been serving you well, darling. Your agility impresses me."

Feinting to the left, but striking to her right side, the hilts of their weapons meshed and locked. Before Stephan could force her arm down, Sirena was ready for him and made an upward slice. Her weapon was free and she swiftly touched his midsection with the protected point.

Stephan seemed startled and pressed another attack. Sirena realized he was trying to discover if it was mere luck on her part or if she had become a truly able student. Wisely, she allowed him the advantage this time, smiling to herself that the master of fencing had a flaw after all.

Time and again he pressed her into the same position, repeatedly she allowed him the win. But her heart was beating rapidly and a small feeling of triumph sizzled through her veins. It had been worth being dragged from bed, she thought. Stephan was becoming too sure of himself, too certain of the win. By keeping alert she was learning his habitual reactions to her actions. Reactions which could prove fatal to him if she ever sought his life. For the first time in weeks, Sirena knew hope.

The session over, Sirena pleaded thirst. While he was putting his prized weapons back in their rack on the wall of his study, Sirena went into the kitchen. What she had learned during the lesson had exhilarated her and she knew it would be difficult to fall asleep. Perhaps warm milk would help.

While she was waiting for the liquid to heat, she turned and was surprised to see Wren sitting at the table munching on a thick slice of cake. "What are you doing here at this hour? You should have been asleep hours ago."

Wren's wide, amber eyes took in Sirena's strange attire, but she said nothing. "I couldn't sleep and I was hungry." She would never tell Sirena how she had been hiding in various places so the master would not find her in her bed.

The fine hairs on the back of Sirena's neck seemed to rise when she saw a shadow near the doorway. Stephan! Carefully, she poured the milk into a heavy mug and sat down beside the child.

Stephan stepped into the kitchen, a smile on his

face. Sirena saw the reflection of fear in Wren's eyes and something in her became alive again. The girl dropped her cake on the floor and drew her breath in what sounded to Sirena like a stifled sob.

"You're a nasty piece of baggage," Stephan sneered as he stood over Wren. "Were you born in a pigsty? You dropped your cake, now pick it up and eat it!"

"No, Wren, I'll cut you another piece," Sirena said quietly. Both Wren and Stephan seemed shocked that Sirena had spoken; she had been silent for so long.

"No, Missy-ma'am, it's all right," the child said in a strange voice as she stuffed the cake into her mouth.

Sirena looked from the trembling child to Stephan and frowned. Wren was petrified. Was it Stephan who terrified her? Wren finished the cake and licked her lips. Sirena pushed the warm milk toward her and told her to finish it and go to bed. Round eyes pleaded with Sirena. "What is it, Wren? What's wrong? Did you have a bad dream? Is something troubling you? Come, finish your drink and you can sleep in my room tonight. We'll talk until you fall asleep." The relief on Wren's face stirred all of Sirena's maternal instincts.

Stephan stepped closer to the girl, looming over her, his bulk throwing Wren into shadow. The child cowered, trembling and shaking so violently it was impossible for her to hold the cup in her hands.

Oh, dear God, no, Sirena thought to herself. It couldn't be. He wouldn't. Not this beautiful, sweet child! Her emerald eyes became like frozen chips of ice when she stared into Stephan's mocking, pale eyes. "Good night, Stephan," she said with all of her old authority. "Come, Wren."

"It's not fitting for a child her age to sleep in your bed," Stephan said coldly. "Take her to her own room."

"Go to hell, Stephan," Sirena spat as she took Wren's arm and led her from the kitchen. Sirena seemed to stand straighter; her shoulders were drawn back and her head held high. Stephan might be able to threaten her and reduce her to a cowering imbecile, but he would never do that to Wren. Not while there was life left in Sirena's body; she would never allow it.

"Did you hear me, darling Sirena," he snarled. "Take the girl to her own room."

Sirena turned and was beside him before he could blink. "And did you hear me, Stephan. I said go to hell. Wren comes with me!" She allowed her hand to slip over the scrubbed kitchen table top and grasped the handle of a stout carving knife. With a lightning movement, the blade was at his jugular. "Tell me again where Wren will sleep tonight and then tell me where I said you were to go. Speak, my husband," she said menacingly, pressing the tip of the knife into his neck. Droplets of bright red blood dripped down into his collar. Imperceptibly, she moved the blade, almost making a circle around his throat. She laughed, the sound eerie and chilling. "I'm waiting, Stephan."

Malevolent hatred spewed from his pale eyes as he murdered her time and time again in the confines of his mind.

Slowly, Sirena backed off, the carving knife held in front of her. "Sleep well, Stephan. You may not have many nights left to you. I want to kill you as much as you want to kill me. Which of us will realize his goal?" she whispered before she left the room.

Stephan fingered his neck and wiped at the blood on his fingers. For the first time in his life, he knew fear of a woman. He would have to get rid of her sooner than he had thought. There was something about her, something about the way she moved and the way she had handled the weapon. He wondered why she was so clumsy and inept with the rapier. A musing look settled on his features as he cut himself a piece of cake.

It was a bleak, rainy day, and the lamps in the office couldn't seem to dissolve the gloom. Tyler Sinclair's eyes ached from the strain of looking through his finely scripted legal papers. Time and again his gaze went to the window and the fog that eddied around the treetops. He stood and walked to the window, longing for a day of warm sunshine to make him feel energetic. What was wrong with him? Why was he acting this way when he had mountains of work to do? It was Camilla. It was because he had seen her aboard the *Sea Siren* the night before with van der Rhys, and the encounter had left him with unbidden pangs of jealousy.

He knew she was married, unhappily so from the appearance of things. But that wasn't the cause of his jealousy. No, it was because she was apparently having an affair with Cal. If anyone knew Camilla, it was himself. It was too late for him to do anything now. For some reason, he was always after the fact. Was it because secretly he wanted it that way? No responsibilities, no ties.

His thoughts ran to Sirena and he blanched at what he supposed were her circumstances. She had not been seen out of the house since she married Stephan. An uneasy feeling settled itself between his shoulder blades and he made a move to return to his desk and the work waiting for him. A sparrow, flying blind, crashed against the window and fell to the ground. Startled, Tyler felt the bird's pain and flinched. Was that what he was doing, flying blind? Of course it was. It was what he had always done when things threatened to get the best of him.

Before he could change his mind, he reached for his coat and threw it over his shoulder as he left the office. He would go to Camilla and settle it all. He wanted her. He could no longer deny it. And, by all that was holy, he would have her.

Tyler was admitted to the house on Drury Lane and shown into the parlor while a maid went to announce him. When she returned, she asked him to wait, the mistress would be down shortly and would he care for tea. Tyler declined, he wasn't here for tea. As soon as the servant left the room, Tyler bounded up the stairs, calling Camilla's name.

"In here, Tyler," she answered languidly from her nest in a high bed surrounded by frilly, fluffy pillows. "How shocking! What would Regan say if he found you here? He might take it into his head to call you out," she answered her own question.

"Would he call you out if he knew you were bedding his own son?" Tyler demanded harshly.

"How dare you make such an accusation? What

right have you to storm in here and say things like that to me? I won't listen," she put her hands to her ears.

"You're damn well going to listen to me whether you like it or not," Tyler shouted as he leaned over the bed and pulled her hands away from her ears. "This isn't van der Rhys you're talking to. Remember, Camilla, I knew you a long time ago and, if my mouth should ever decide to flap, then you could find yourself in some pretty dire straits. Why," he said ominously, "you know they still stone adulteresses."

"You can't frighten me, Tyler. You would have as much to lose as I would."

"True, but then I don't care anymore and you do. I'm a man and you're a woman and that makes a big difference."

"What do you want; why are you here? I'll have Regan pay you back the money you advanced me. I'll see to it today."

"That's not what I want."

Camilla giggled. "Are you saying you want me? How gallant! I was always fond of you, Tyler, you know that. I even married you. That should prove something to you."

"It proves something, all right. It proves you married me for what you thought you could get. You and your father both thought my parents would relent about my inheriting if I married before I was twenty-five. When they didn't, you left me, convincing me you would wait for me. You lied, Camilla. You always lie. I know you for exactly what you are."

"And you still want me? That doesn't say much for you, does it, Tyler?" Her voice became soft; there was a shine in her pansy eyes and a tear fell on her cheek. "You know the worst about me and you still want me." She reached up and her delicate white hands pulled his head down to hers. "Come here, Tyler, let me hold you close."

"Why couldn't you have waited just a little longer?" he groaned as she brought her lips to his.

Camilla drew out of his embrace and looked into his eyes. Her breathing was loud in the silence of the room. "I couldn't wait, Tyler. I want it now. You're no good for me. We both know it. You loathed coming here, I can see it in your eyes. In your own way, you're the most honorable man I've ever known. You hate yourself for wanting me. We both agreed to forget our marriage; no one needed to know, we told each other. We were free."

"You mean you were free of me to hook another fish on your line," he muttered. "You're right about one thing, though. I do hate myself for loving you. If you can bed van der Rhys and his son, then you can spread the wealth a little further. For me, Camilla," he said in a husky tone, finding her lips with his own. "I need you, Camilla. I'll always need you."

His hands slipped the nightdress from her shoulders and soon they were naked together, beside one another, his eyes devouring the purity of her form and the silkiness of her skin. Gently, he ran his fingers through her wealth of golden hair. How he loved the satin feel against his hands and cheek. For a time he held her tight, simply enjoying the nearness of her. He felt her breasts grow taut with desire, and he drew in his breath, relishing the clean, sweet smell of her.

Camilla stretched out, leaning closer to him, the warmth of his body seeping into hers as she pressed her slimness against him. Shivering with his hot breath on her neck, she answered his light, teasing kisses and offered him her throat, her breasts. His hands were practiced and sensual and they moved over her, caressing each curve. She found herself moving to the rhythm he initiated and felt herself take wing and soar. All the forgotten sensations coursed through her as she brought her hands down his back, feeling the strength of his muscles and the smoothness of his skin.

She felt her buttocks being lifted slightly as he began a series of sensual thrusts. Frenzied, she arched her back to meet each wave of passion. Lightning and thunder rolled across the sky as she burst internally time and time again till she didn't know if the storm outside her window could excel the tumult within her.

An eternity later Tyler leaned on one elbow and looked deeply into Camilla's eyes. "Tell me you've enjoyed anyone more than me. Tell me you haven't missed my caresses and my arms holding you. You're mine, Camilla. You belong to me," he groaned as he buried his face between her breasts.

Camilla stroked his dark head. "You know I've never found anyone like you, Tyler. I still love you, will always love you. But I can't go hungry! I won't! There are other things I want from life, Tyler. Things you can't give me, can never give me if your parents disinherit you. If I could have those and you, too, I'd go with you in a moment."

Tyler's head jerked upright. "Do you mean that? Is it only wealth that stands between us? I'll give you everything you've ever dreamed of, Camilla." His voice was low and steady; she believed every word he said. As she crushed his head to her breast, she wished she could be a different kind of person. She wished she could tell him money be damned, the only thing that mattered was being with him. But she wasn't strong enough, she just couldn't do it.

Tyler's fingers wound through her blond hair. "I'll have you yet, Camilla; do you know that?"

For answer, she lifted his head and brought her mouth to his. "Make love to me, Tyler. Again and again," she whispered throatily.

When Sirena awoke that morning, she felt better than she had in weeks. She remembered exactly where she was and what had transpired between herself and Stephan the night before. She was herself again; she had stood up to Stephan; he could bully and threaten her no more. Turning over, she felt Wren's slight, warm body beside hers. God, when she thought of what could have happened to the child. Why hadn't she or Frau Holtz been aware of what the little girl was suffering?

She looked down at the sweet sleeping face and silently begged forgiveness. How in heaven could she have been so incredibly foolish? She knew what kind of man Stephan was, she knew he was bordering on the insane. Poor little Wren, when Stephan couldn't satisfy himself by torturing his wife, he had turned his terrifying tactics on her.

That was all behind them now. All Sirena had to do was keep her wits about her and she could leave it all behind. She would tell Frau Holtz this morning that she would adhere to her plan to leave England. Two more days and she, Wren and Frau Holtz would be free of Stephan Langdon.

Sirena climbed from the bed, careful not to waken the child. She dressed quietly and, in her mind, listed which belongings she would take with her when the *Sea Spirit* sailed out of port.

Could she leave without seeing Regan for one last time? She must. She faced in her heart she would never see him again. When they found her gone, Caleb would tell Regan of his visit to her. Tears stung her eyes when she thought of Caleb.

Her head began to ache and she rubbed cologne on her temples in an effort to abate the pounding. There were things to be done but she didn't think she had the energy or the stamina. She had been her own prisoner since Stephan had brought her back from Bedlam. She had been unable to conduct even the most mundane affairs of everyday living. She hadn't been eating correctly, sending the trays back to the kitchen barely touched. She was weak and much too thin. But, last night had changed all of that. Stephan had robbed her of the will to fight for herself, but he hadn't counted on her deep, maternal feelings for Wren and didn't know she would fight like a tigress protecting her cub.

Sirena descended the stairs to the dining room and made short work of her breakfast. She would need every bit of strength. She was relieved Stephan had left early for his classes at the academy but she knew he would join her for luncheon. He wouldn't want the happenings of the night before to reinforce her will if he could possibly help it.

No sooner had she finished her meal when she heard the sound of the doorpull and a few moments later Frau Holtz ushered Tyler Sinclair into the dining room. She saw the old woman, who as yet knew nothing of the events of the night before, look at her empty plate with pleased amazement.

Sirena's face brightened. "Tyler, how nice of you to come and see me, in spite of my husband's orders to the contrary. What a miserable day to visit, though.

I don't know how you English abide this weather. Even in summer the fog rolls in and cloaks the city for days at a time."

"I suppose I'm accustomed to it. When you don't know anything else, it is easy to live with."

"You should visit the Spice Islands, Tyler. You would love it there and never want to leave. Warm, gentle breezes the whole year through, sparkling clear blue water. Smiling, happy people. Slow, easy living. A peaceful atmosphere to live in. Do yourself a favor, visit the East Indies someday. You'll never want to leave."

"Sirena, I came here to talk to you about a matter of importance. To me," he amended. "Listen and don't interrupt before you make a decision. I need money, Sirena. A lot of it."

Sirena's face fell into perplexed lines. She never remembered hearing Tyler sound so serious and, as she listened to him, her expression became incredulous.

"If you help me," Tyler said, "I can promise you a clear road back to Regan. Don't ask me how I can make such a promise, but believe me when I tell you it is so. At the same time I will take care of your current husband so that he never bothers you again."

"Tyler, what is it? How can you make me such rash promises? Are you in some sort of trouble?" Her eyes were large and full of shock at his desperate words and at the wild look he projected. "Tell me," she said softly.

"I don't know how to ask you this," Tyler hedged.

"Just say it, Tyler," Sirena said impatiently.

Tyler blurted, "I want us to go to sea and be partners. I want us to sail the seas and be pirates. That's the only way I can get enough money for what I . . . Will you do it, Sirena? Believe me, I wouldn't ask if there was any other choice open to me."

Sirena's mind raced. "Are you saying . . . do you expect me . . . Tyler, that's piracy!" she said virtuously. "Outright thievery!"

"Exactly!" Tyler beamed. "I knew you would understand. Will you do it?"

Sirena's mind continued to race. "Tell me why and then I'll let you know my answer. You know, Tyler, piracy is not a matter to take lightly. You could hang by the neck if you're caught and then what good would all the monies and cargoes be to you. I, for one, have no desire to be executed."

"Don't you want Regan back?" Tyler asked, his eyes moist and pleading.

"And if I agree to your plan, then you can guarantee that?" She shook her head. "If I get Regan back, if it's meant to be, then I will do it myself. I do appreciate your offer, but I fail to see how you can help me," Sirena said sarcastically.

"Sirena, I give you my word."

"Tyler, what do you take me for? Piracy is a dangerous business. I told you I have no wish to hang by the neck."

"You miss the sea; you hate your husband and you're in fear of him and you want Regan. If you do as I ask, then you will have everything you want. Help me," he pleaded.

Sirena was torn by the look in the man's eyes. She ached to give him some form of comfort. "If you would just tell me why, then—"

"I can't tell you, that's the problem. I've never begged for anything in my life, but I am now. You're the only person who can help me."

"There's no need for you to grovel, Tyler. I'll help you, but not for the reasons you suggest. I'm leaving here in two days to take my housekeeper and crew back to Batavia. If you wish to sail with us, it will be your chance to see the Spice Islands. If we should come across any prosperous ships along the way . . . well . . . ," she shrugged.

Tyler wrapped his arms around her and kissed her soundly on the cheek. "I knew you would help me. I just knew it. Stephan, does he know?"

"Of course not, and you must not give away our secret in any way."

"Never!" Tyler yelled, outraged that she would suggest such a thing.

"Good. Take your baggage to the ship and be ready to sail at midnight the day after tomorrow. If you aren't on board at that time, we'll sail without you."

"I'll be there, have no fear. Thank you, Sirena. But, Regan . . ."

"That's over and done with. Don't mention his name or bring him up to me again," Sirena said coldly.

"Whatever you say," Tyler agreed happily as he made his preparations to leave. "I think you just saved my life, lovely lady."

"Don't count on it, Tyler. This could well be the beginning of the end of your life. And no recriminations later. I warned you, remember that."

Chapter Twenty-six

In his coach on his way home from the academy, Stephan Landgon passed Drury Lane and he thought about his daughter, Camilla. He was going to return home for luncheon but the prospect of seeing Sirena was far from attractive. He hadn't yet decided what to do about her sudden about-face into the old self-confidence and he was loath to have her get the better of him once more before he decided on a course of action. He should have taken the knife away from her last night and cut out her heart with it. He blanched, his ashen features a mask of consternation and fear. He knew in his heart he could never have taken the weapon out of her hand; she would have killed him with it first. His fingers sought the small wound on his neck and he remembered the feel of the sharp point held there. Wherever had she learned that unpleasant and dangerous tactic?

Rapping on the roof of the cab with the head of his walking stick, Stephan commanded his driver's attention, and gave directions to his former abode on Drury Lane. Rather than going home, he would join Camilla for lunch.

Several minutes later, Stephan disembarked, carrying his cane at a jaunty angle. He lifted the brass knocker and let it fall several times, annoyed and impatient with the servant's tardiness in answering. He must speak to Camilla about that. When the door was finally opened by a flighty young maid with frizzy brown hair, he gave her a searing look and demanded to see his daughter.

In a flurry of activity and nervousness, the trembling maidservant showed him directly to the dining room where Camilla was enjoying a solitary meal. When she saw her father enter, she pointed to a place opposite her with her fork and continued eating.

"Really, Camilla, must you eat like a little cannibal? It is most unbecoming."

Camilla shot him a venomous glance. They had never really repaired their disagreement of the night she had met Caleb. Her hostility for Stephan lay just beneath the surface of her civility. "At least I can't complain of not getting enough to eat, which is more than I could say when I looked to you for my welfare." She pushed a sweet roll to her mouth and took an enormous bite, filling her cheeks like a greedy squirrel.

"Aren't you going to invite me to luncheon?" Stephan complained. "I was about to join my lovely wife when I decided it had been too long since I had you to myself."

Camilla picked up the small silver bell resting near her plate and shook it. The tinkling sound brought a maid from the kitchen. "Service for my father," she ordered. "Are there any more brandied peaches in the kitchen?"

Stephan snorted indignantly as he watched Camilla tear into her broiled trout. "Where have you been, daughter?" he asked after he had been served. "I swear it's been days since I've seen you."

"If you mean you haven't seen me aboard your favorite gambling folly, that's right. You haven't. I've been there but you haven't been able to pick your eyes off the faro table long enough to see me."

"Don't sound so peeved, Camilla. It's not becoming. Besides, faro is a game of concentration, and I must admit I've been taking a trouncing lately. If I don't keep my wits about me, I'll lose my shirt."

Camilla stopped chewing long enough to say, "Perhaps you will be asked to remove your shirt before anyone will play against you, father. Even cheating doesn't seem to insure your winning."

"So, it would appear you still visit your young admirer. Caleb van der Rhys, isn't it? You're hardly the one to talk about scruples. Has it ever occurred to you your relationship with that young man is nearly incestuous? You *are* his stepmother. Really, darling," he used the unctuous voice Camilla hated, "your behavior is not motherly, no, not motherly at all. Tsk, tsk," he shook his head.

Camilla threw her flatware down on her plate. She was sick of his supercilious, superior attitude. "And just how is it a mother behaves? I wouldn't know, Father, since you saw to it *my* mother was taken from me. All these years I suspected; I even heard whispers among the relatives and from Tyler, but I never believed it. I believe it now! You killed my own mother! You had her sent to Bedlam and she died there!" Once into her tirade, Camilla found it difficult to control herself. She hadn't known she was going to say this. She hadn't even known she had harbored these feelings toward Stephan until the words were finally out.

"I didn't kill your mother," Stephan hastened to explain. "She died of an illness in the Bethlehem Royal Hospital. She was very ill." His face flushed and he stammered. He had never known Camilla was aware of her mother's fate much less that he had been the cause of it.

"So, Bethlehem Royal Hospital, is it now? Do you think it sounds better than what it really is, Bedlam? Why even the name is synonomous with insanity. My mother was not a lunatic!" she screamed. "Mother was sick and dispirited, she had given up hope. *You* drove her to madness in the end. You did!"

Stephan stepped around the table and clutched his daughter by the arms. "Hush your mouth, Camilla," he hissed. "Do you want the servants to hear?"

"I don't care if the whole world hears me!" she bellowed, standing up and wrestling free of his grasp. "You killed her!"

Stephan struck her full force in the face and Camilla reeled, holding her hand to her injury. Her tone low and venomous, she spat, "I despise you! Do you know that? I hate you! I hate you for what you've done to me all these years. First, you took my mother away and then you convinced me to desert my marriage to Tyler. Then you offered me like a piece of goods to any oncomers who were rich enough to interest you. You sold me to Regan, into a loveless marriage. And now you dare to chastise me for finding a little diversion with Caleb. Well, it's over, Father. It's finally over. You've had too much influence over my life. I did things I never wanted to do because you told me to do them. I don't like the woman I am, Father, and I mean to change! And when I do, it will go the worse for you. I promise you that!"

Stephan staggered backward. Camilla had never spoken this way to him. She had always acquiesced to his wishes. They had been more than father and daughter, they had been partners. It was all true what she said, but to hear her say it with such hatred rocked the foundations of his life.

"And I'll tell you another thing, Father," she spat the word as though it were a disease. "I plan to right situations. For one thing, I'm going to tell Regan exactly what we did to him, how we lured him into marrying me. If my guess is right, he'll be relieved to be rid of me. And then I'm going to Tyler on bended knee and beg him to take me back. I don't care if he's rich or poor, I love him; I've always loved him." She waited for her words to sink in. She picked up Stephan's hat and walking stick from the sideboard where he had put them and handed them to him. "And may I tell you, Father, when word reaches the Baron and Baroness of how great a part you took in this whole sordid affair, I hesitate to think of what the Baron will do. You may have married a rich wife and have money to burn, but it won't get you into polite society."

Stephan was nearly out of his head with rage. "You would do that, wouldn't you? Bitch!" he cried, raising his walking stick over his head to strike her down.

Camilla stood up to him unflinchingly, waiting for

the blow to fall. But when Stephan saw the resolve in her face, he seemed to crumble like a dry leaf in a wind. His shoulders sagged and he looked suddenly older by twenty years.

"Go on, hit me! If it was good enough for my mother, it is good enough for me!" Stephan lowered his arm, the cane falling from his hand. "Get out of here and never come back!" she hissed. "And if you should pass me on the street, don't even glance my way! You're dead to me; I have no father!"

Camilla stepped lightly aboard the *Sea Siren,* delicately lifting her skirts to keep them from dragging in the soapy water being used to swab the decks. She avoided the neatly coiled rigging lines and hurried to Caleb's cabin. What she had to tell him was very important, and she couldn't lose her nerve. It was never easy to admit you were wrong.

She tapped lightly on the solid cabin door and Caleb answered it. He was in the process of shaving and still had lather on half his face. He smiled and bade her enter and went back to his mirror, stroking the straight razor over his face in smooth, practiced motions.

"Caleb, I've come to talk to you," Camilla said, trying for his attention.

"Talk away, I'm listening." He drew his mouth over to the side in a comical way and continued shaving.

"I'm afraid I've come to say good-bye, Caleb." Her voice was soft and so girlish, at times Caleb found it difficult to believe she was a grown woman.

Caleb's throat constricted. Did she mean, could she mean, Regan had found them out? "This is so sudden, Camilla. What brought this about?" he asked, fearing the worst.

"If you mean has Regan discovered us, no. And he will never know." Imperceptibly, Caleb's muscles relaxed.

"Then you must have some other reason—"

"Yes, yes I do," she blurted. "It's because it's wrong. Everything in my life has been wrong and I mean to set it straight. I've wronged you, Caleb, and

I've wronged Regan. I don't think I ever loved either of you. I . . . I love someone else and have for a long time. Since I was a child, really. I'm going to make a life with him and I only thank God he still wants me." She was nearly in tears, but they weren't the winsome, pathetic tears he had seen her shed in the past. These belonged to a woman . . . a happy woman.

Caleb felt as though a great burden had been lifted from his shoulders. His conscience had been more than twinging him and he found it difficult to be in Regan's company. He would never really be absolved of the sin of bedding his father's wife, but he would try to make it up to Regan in every way he knew how.

"Do you plan to explain this to Regan?" he asked, coming near her and taking her hand in his. "What do you think he'll say? A divorce is difficult to obtain under English law, Camilla. Do you plan to desert him?"

"No . . . no," Camilla flushed. "You don't understand, Caleb. Those times I came crying to you that Regan was beastly . . . well, it really wasn't true. Regan and I . . . we used each other. We never loved each other and I'm certain he'll be glad to be rid of me." She sobbed brokenly into her glove, but she persisted. Her tears were actually more from relief of at last telling the truth than from a broken heart. "As far as a divorce is concerned . . . it won't be necessary. You see, Caleb," she said, raising her pansy eyes to level with his, "I was already married when I married Regan. I'm counting on his being a gentleman about it."

Married! Caleb's eyes widened and he jumped to his feet. "Married!" he echoed his thoughts. "Were you crazy to try a stunt like that on my father! He could have snapped you in two with his bare hands!"

"I know!" Camilla cried hysterically.

"God, Camilla, I hate to think what he would do to you if he really loved you!"

"I know, I know!" she repeated, nodding her head, her brilliant yellow curls dancing.

"And about us? What was that farce? I thought you loved me!"

"Oh I did, Caleb, truly, please believe that," she

raised her eyes imploringly. "I never meant to hurt you; it's just that I love someone else more. I never have to pretend with him, he knows me exactly for what I am and, wonder of wonders, he loves me in spite of it all. Please try to understand, Caleb."

Camilla was genuinely distressed and Caleb's heart went out to her. He patted her hand soothingly, murmuring words of encouragement. After all, he could be generous about this whole thing, couldn't he? Think of what a pickle he'd be in if Camilla had decided it was Caleb she couldn't live without! "There, there, darling, don't cry. I'm certain my father will do whatever is right. If it is as you say, Regan will be more than generous about it all, I'm certain of it. Now, can you tell me who this lucky man is?"

Camilla smiled brightly and whispered, "He's the most wonderful man on this earth, Caleb, and perhaps you know him. It's Tyler Sinclair," she beamed.

Caleb laughed. Tyler Sinclair! He laughed till the tears came to his eyes. He found it ridiculously funny that Camilla should think Tyler more a man than Regan! Suddenly, he sobered. Obviously, Camilla also thought Tyler more a man than himself!

An ominous undercurrent of excitement crept around the main room aboard the *Sea Siren*. Caleb felt it; Aubrey Farrington was aware of it and Stephan Langdon knew it also. Professional gamblers milled about, their eyes sharp, their shoulders squared as though they were marching into battle.

A chill washed over Caleb as his glance went back and forth between Regan and Langdon and then to the gamblers who were making ready to play. Purses of coins and gold guineas were placed on the green baize tabletop. Satisfied with their surroundings, they had placed themselves at the same table where Stephan was gambling recklessly against the house.

Farrington withdrew some silver from his pocket and worked his way through the crowd. His eyes sought Regan's as Regan, too, inched past the guests. Stephan stood, his money in his hand, oblivious to everything except the stacks of silver in the center of the table. If he knew he was playing against professionals, he gave no sign.

It was close to midnight when Stephan looked up from his dwindling supply of cash and noticed Regan and Aubrey Farrington. He glanced at his nearly depleted hoard and licked his dry lips. Out of the corner of his eyes he saw Caleb walk from the table. His thoughts raced. It was now getting to be a matter of principle. He would not leave empty-handed. At best, he had another hour of play. His son-in-law was a fool and Farrington was little better. What could they do to him in a room full of guests? They had their reputation to think of. They knew as well as he that a scene would be regrettable.

He was nervous and jittery. The scenes with Camilla that afternoon and Sirena the night before had left him strained and an eerie foreboding haunted him. He must get his emotions under control if he were to pull off any tricks. If his hands shook, he would drop the cards and he would be finished.

He played listlessly for a while, his thoughts conflicting with his better judgment. Did he dare try the card in his sleeve? He looked furtively at Regan and Farrington. They knew. If he had any brains left to him, he should leave, but his sickness for a gamble overruled his better judgment.

Worms of fear crawled around Lord Farrington's belly as he concentrated on Stephan Langdon. Why did that fool have to pick tonight of all nights to try his tricks? These were professionals he was playing against. They played with a vengeance and their eyes were as sharp as axes. Farrington knew the blade would fall within minutes.

Damn, didn't he have enough troubles with that scurve Blackheart breathing down his neck? The man was a monster. He must leave the gaming room to get back to his cabin to see what the swarthy seaman wanted this time. Deftly, he withdrew his round, gold timepiece and the sickening sensation moved to his throat. Almost an hour had gone by since he had taken Blackheart to his cabin with the promise he would return shortly. How long would the scurve wait? Would he come into the gaming parlor and make a scene? What was he to do? Caleb, where was Caleb? He lifted his long-fingered, aristocratic hand and tried to catch Caleb's attention.

The young man was greeting a new arrival, appreciating the deep cut of her neckline and smiling wickedly. Damn! Cal would be of no use to him. The young man had other thoughts on his mind at the moment. Regan then. It was time he did something to earn his share in the *Sea Siren*. Let him handle it. He didn't give a damn if the gamblers killed Langdon. "It's my own neck I'm worried about," he whispered to himself. Blackheart wasn't going to wait much longer.

Carefully, he inched his way between a small cluster of murmuring women, unmindful of the gaiety at the other tables and the soft, sensual music in the background. And that was another thing; why in the name of God did Cal insist on music? Everything was bothering him. Now, the sounds of the gaming tables and the music hit him full force as he came abreast of van der Rhys. He would have to shout or signal Regan so he would move from his position beside Langdon.

Just as he was about to tap Regan on the shoulder, Stephan Langdon doubled over, his face a mask of pain. Play stopped while the dealer looked around for help. Regan, who was closest to Stephan, reached out to grasp his arm, fearing a seizure of some sort, when Stephan straightened, a grim look on his face. "It's nothing," he said huskily. "Let's resume play." He tossed his cards down and pandemonium broke loose.

"Asinine fool! That trick is as old as my grandmother," one of the players growled.

Farrington hissed in Regan's ear, "I thought you were watching him!"

All play in the room ceased. The soft music came to a tinny halt as Caleb, a murderous look on his face, approached the card table.

"Cheat!"

"Liar!"

"Double-cheating scurve!"

"Unhand me, you lout," Stephan shouted, fear in

his eyes. "Unhand me this instant or I'll call you out," he threatened.

Two of the gamblers grasped an arm and literally dragged him to the nearest exit. The taller of the two, his face sharp and hateful, shouted so that everyone could hear him. "Then call me out, in front of everyone."

Fear snaked its way to Langdon's throat, making it impossible for him to speak. If he did as the gambler wanted, the gambler would have the choice of the dueling weapons. Christ, what if he chose pistols! He licked at dry lips and tried to squirm loose.

"Do it," Regan said harshly. "You have no other choice. If you don't, by this time tomorrow, you'll be a dead man, and you know what I say is the truth. Not only is it your honor but it is also your life. Decide now, before some of these gentlemen take matters into their own hands."

Stephan Langdon swallowed hard and nodded. The viselike hold on his arms loosened and the sharp-faced man smiled. "Pistols at dawn. Name your second."

Stephan looked around the room and could sense hostility and animosity. Guilty of cheating at cards. He was ruined. He pointed a trembling finger at Regan who immediately backed off a step and felt murder rage in him. He, too, had no other choice. He nodded curtly at the circle of gamblers and made as if to leave. A gambler brought up a pistol from his belt and flourished it in the air. "One of my men will escort you home and watch your house. We wouldn't want you to lose your way."

Regan shrugged. The only thought he could cope with at the moment was if Stephan were dead, Sirena would be a free woman. Now, why in the name of God should that thought enter his head and why should it bother him? He watched as Langdon and the gambler left the ship amid catcalls and raucous shouts of "Cheat!"

For the first time in his life the urbane Aubrey Farrington was out of his depth as he looked to Caleb to bring order to the salon. Regan was no use; he was following Stephan and the gambler.

Caleb spoke soothingly as he made a motion with his hand for the music to resume. He winked roguishly at the ladies and grinned at the men as he shrugged helplessly. His attitude clearly said these minor upsets were bound to happen.

Within moments the room was as before with wine flowing freely, compliments of the house.

Caleb walked on deck, his hands clenched at his sides, the sweat pouring off his face. If he were a gambling man, he wouldn't give a farthing for Langdon's chances of living to see another sunset. What would Sirena say when she found out? How would she hold up her head as the wife of a man caught cheating at cards? Somebody must warn her. He couldn't leave the ship. Would Langdon himself tell her? Not likely. No man wants to be made a fool in front of his wife. Then who? Regan? No, that would be like pouring salt in an open wound. Sinclair. He was the one to tell Sirena. After all, he was her solicitor.

Caleb returned to his cabin and scrawled a brief message. He handed it to a cabin boy with instructions to deliver it to Sinclair's house with all speed. Poor Sirena. Why did she have to be beset by so many traumatic problems? Would she ever attain the normal life everyone else took for granted?

The water was choppy as it slapped against the sides of the *Sea Siren,* and the vessel rocked slightly as Caleb stood in the dark at the rail. Whispers reached him and he spun about. There seemed to be an urgent malevolence in the hushed words filtering to him. He strained to hear and, at the same time moved closer to the ladder where he surmised the voices were coming from. Lord Farrington and another man. The second voice was familiar; he had heard it somewhere before. He frowned but was unable to distinguish the words because of the rough slap of water against the hull.

Something teased at his memory but would not surface. He knew in his gut he had heard that harsh, evil whisper, but where? And why was Lord Farrington hiding in the dark like a criminal? What was the distinguished lord up to? It must be something not quite legal, he thought to himself, otherwise why did he need an out-of-the-way place to discuss his business. He had been jittery of late. Caleb had not failed to see how assiduously he counted the monies at the end of the night and the grim, tight line around his mouth when he pocketed his share. Always the look was in his eyes that it wasn't enough. Something was wrong. The hackles on the back of Caleb's neck rose as he heard the words, "kill . . . suffered enough . . . my right . . . you have no other choice if you want to live."

Caleb withdrew further into the shadows as the figures emerged from their hiding place. Damn, he could only see the other man's back. He limped and his arm seemed to hang lamely at his side. Caleb scowled and knew the set of the head and height, as well as the voice, were familiar. Who was he and where had he seen him? Why was he threatening Lord Farrington? This was his ship and he deserved to know what was going on. As soon as the man left, he would go to Aubrey and demand answers. If Aubrey were in trouble, perhaps he could help him.

On catlike feet Caleb walked to the hatchway and waited for the crippled man to descend the gangplank. He moved and grasped Farrington by the arm. "Who was that?" he demanded harshly. "I want to know what's going on and I want to know now."

Lord Farrington turned, a look of fear on his face. "A small matter, Cal, and one that need not concern you," he said, trying to force a light note into his voice.

"I've heard that voice and seen that man somewhere and, if I'm not mistaken, he can mean only trouble. Are you in some financial difficulty, Aubrey? Perhaps I can help. We have a good thing going here; we're both becoming prosperous and I wouldn't want anything to jeopardize our business venture. Let me help you."

Aubrey clapped Caleb on the shoulder, his face all smiles. "Cal, my boy, it's a matter of personal . . . let's just say it concerns a lady and her good name."

"You're lying, Aubrey. I'm not going to ask you again. If you won't accept my help, the least you owe me for what we have going together is honesty."

"You won't leave it alone, will you?" Aubrey said coldly. "I told you it's a personal matter. I wonder how quick you would be to confess to me of your affair with your father's wife if I were to press for details? Ah, I see that my statement has hit home. I have no wish to discuss your affairs nor mine with you. The matter is ended."

Aubrey Farrington watched Caleb walk away, his face stony and hard. His own face wore a hate-filled look at the position he was in. He felt like fiddle strings were being stretched throughout his whole gut.

When Regan shook the fair-haired Camilla awake, she rolled over and murmured sleepily, "Not to—"

"—night, I have a raging headache," Regan finished for her. "It isn't your body I desire but I must tell you something. Wake up, you must listen to me. Your father was caught cheating tonight on the *Sea Siren* and one of the gamblers called him out. There's to be a duel at dawn. Are you listening to me, Camilla? Dawn is just a few hours away. I'm going to be your father's second. The weapons are pistols and we both know that rapiers are your father's strong point."

Camilla sat up in bed, her hair tousled as though she were having a restless night. The eyes she turned to Regan were deep violet and there was something he had never seen in them before. If he had been forced to put a name to it, he would have to call it maturity. He had expected a tearful scene full of recriminations. Not this quiet, pensive girl.

Camilla waited for Regan's words to sink in to her consciousness. She waited to feel the guilt of Stephan's and her last parting. Her father could be killed and yet the grief and concern would not come.

"Stephan is a fool," Regan said as kindly as he could. "This isn't the first time he was caught cheating on the *Sea Siren*. He was given a warning and this time it was professional gamblers who caught him at it. Now, every man in London who ever lost a farthing to your father will be certain he was cheated. Even if somehow Stephan manages to come through this duel, which is unlikely, he's a ruined man."

"He has nobody to blame save himself," Camilla said quietly. "I've warned him time and again. When you do something that hurts others, eventually you have to pay for it. Father is just beginning to pay."

Was this Camilla speaking? Regan asked himself. Before his eyes she had changed; for the first time Regan found himself liking his bride.

"I'm only sorry you became involved in this, Regan. I wouldn't like to see anything happen to you. You're a good man." Tears welled up in her large eyes and spilled down her cheeks. Regan traced the path of one salty drop with his fingertip. Yes, Camilla had definitely changed. Before tonight her tears had always been for herself and had taken the form of childish tantrums. These were the tears of a woman. The tears of regret.

"I'll have to be leaving, Camilla," he said softly.

"Take care of yourself, Regan. Father isn't worth one drop of your blood."

He left the room, closing the door behind him. "I'll be damned!" he swore lightly, finding his way to the stairs.

Sirena stirred fitfully in her sleep, dreaming she heard Mikel calling for her. Even in her dreams she knew it couldn't be Mikel. Her son was dead, his tiny bones rotting in Javanese soil.

She moved again and curled herself into a tight ball for warmth. It was no use; she was awake so she might as well get up and get another light cover. The moment her bare feet touched the floor, she clearly heard the soft mewing sound. She hadn't been dreaming! It must be the cook's cat. She would have to find him and return him to the kitchen before he woke the whole house.

Quickly picking up a dressing gown and slipping her feet into her mules, she grasped the lamp firmly and entered the hallway. The lamp cast flickering shadows on the high walls and ceiling. "Here kitty, here kitty," she called, peering into dark corners. At the top of the stairway she stopped and listened. Cats didn't hiccough!

The light held high, the front of her robe clutched

in her hand, she raced down the stairs and into the library. She was shocked by the sight that met her eyes. Wren stood with her back to the cold hearth, clutching her nightgown close to her, while Stephan was trying to forcibly strip it from her.

A bellow of rage burst out of Sirena as she threw the smoking lantern at Stephan and watched it roll into the depths of the fireplace. "Run, Wren!" she screamed as Stephan retreated into a corner near the desk, shock on his face at having been caught in the act. He was stunned by the force of the blow from the lamp as it glanced the side of his head, and he rocked precariously on the balls of his feet as he brought Sirena into his line of vision. Sirena emitted a bloodcurdling call for Frau Holtz, never taking her eyes from the most loathsome creature on the face of the earth.

His eyes hate-filled, a sneer on his thin lips, Stephan advanced on Sirena, his intent clear. Wren cried a warning as Frau Holtz rushed into the room and took in the scene. She gathered the child to her and, with one swift motion, had one of the crossed rapiers off its wall brackets and tossed it to Sirena. "Do it, Mevrouw. He doesn't deserve to live," she menaced viciously. "Do it!"

Sirena needed no second urging. She hefted the thin blade to test its flexibility and nicked the air. She backed off as Stephan stopped short, an evil smile on his face. Sirena took that moment to shed her negligée and slice at the nightdress till it hung in tatters high above her knees.

When she next looked at him, Stephan had armed himself with the second rapier. As he sliced the air, Sirena kicked off her slippers and crouched low, flexing her knees. "En garde!" she threatened softly as she advanced, bending her knees, and the tip of her rapier scraped Stephan's cheek.

Scarlet beads dripped onto the snowy ruffle at his throat. He blinked, unable to believe his eyes. He had lost the advantage he might have gained when Sirena advanced and parried, her weapon finding its mark time and again. "I'll kill you for what you tried to do to this child!" she exclaimed, lunging toward him and bringing up the rapier till it cut his upper arm.

Stephan stepped backward and Sirena lunged again, her aim sure as she brought up the rapier with all possible force, jarring the weapon from Stephan's grasp. He reached out to grasp the hilt with his left hand. In that moment Sirena knocked the weapon to the floor and drove him to the wall till he cried out, his eyes bulging with fear.

"Don't kill me," he cried brokenly, "don't kill me!"

Sirena was beyond hearing, beyond caring as she coldly and mercilessly advanced, one step and then two, till she was inches from him. Her green eyes were glazed and all she could hear were the whimpers of a child. She thrust the blade into her husband's chest and watched his mouth fall open. Blood and crimson gore gushed forth. Savagely, she pulled the rapier free and wiped it across his shoulder. He reached out for her arm, but fell within inches of her bare legs.

The deadly implement dropped from Sirena's hold as she clasped her head, tears welling in her eyes. Frau Holtz gathered her in a comforting embrace. "You could do no less, Mevrouw. Vermin the likes of him deserves to die."

Wren came to Sirena and hugged her waist. "Missy-ma'am, he didn't . . . I'm all right now, truly I am," she assured.

Sirena staggered over to the softness of Stephan's favorite chair and lowered herself into it. Frau Holtz poured her a tot of rum and Sirena gulped at the liquor as it seared her throat.

"Did I kill him?" she asked in a quivering voice.

"*Ja.* It is finished."

"Frau Holtz . . . what will happen to me if . . . I'll go to prison for this. I'll be hanged!" she cried brokenly. "He deserved to die for what he did, but no one will ever believe me."

"*Nein!*" Frau Holtz said harshly. "No one will ever know and neither Wren nor I will ever tell. Is that right, child?"

Wren inched closer to Sirena. "I love you, Missy-ma'am. I loved the Sea Siren ever since the day the

Frau first told me about her. I'll do whatever you say. I'll never tell."

"We bury him, Mevrouw. Who is to say why or where the likes of him disappeared? Men disappear every day. Doesn't he haunt those dockside pubs? Who is to say he did not meet his end at the hands of a criminal? *Ja*, we bury him like the trash he is. I go get Jacobus."

"All the blood! There's too much blood!" Sirena said in a dazed voice. "We can't have his servants clean it. We have to do it ourselves. Get a pail of water and some soap, Frau Holtz. I'll clean it myself."

"We're going to need more than one pail of water," Frau Holtz said grimly as she left the room with a parting shout to Wren to get dressed.

Wren wrapped her arms about Sirena and kissed her lightly on the cheek. "I'll be right back. You sit here and don't move. We're going to help you."

Sirena nodded, her mind whirling. She couldn't think. All that blood. It was like a river. She would be executed for this crime. People with Stephan's standing didn't do things like he did. They wouldn't believe her.

Frau Holtz came back into the room dragging a drunken Jacobus beside her, an empty bucket in her other hand. "Look!" she yelled, "he's as drunk as sin. He won't be of any use to us. We'll have to do it ourselves."

"We have to get rid of the body. This fool," she said, jabbing a finger at Jacobus, "is no good to either of us. We'll have to bury the body ourselves."

"Where? Where will it be safe, Frau Holtz? When Stephan doesn't make his daily rounds, someone will come looking for him. How long before someone thinks he met with foul play? The first place they'll come is here. We can't bury him."

"A piece at a time. In different places," Frau Holtz babbled.

Sirena blanched and gulped. "For some stray dog to dig up. No, it won't work."

"The ship. Take him to sea and toss him overboard."

"Toss who overboard?" Jacobus asked drunkenly.

"First, we have to get him on board. Good thinking,

Frau Holtz. Yes, that's what we'll do. Think," she said, pressing her hands to her temples. "A barrel. We'll have to stuff him in a barrel and load it into the carriage. It's the only way. Oh, God, I can't believe I'm doing this."

"The Mynheer. I'll fetch the Mynheer," Frau Holtz cried excitedly.

Sirena's head jerked upright. "You'll do no such thing. If Regan were to know about this, he would toss me over the side with his father-in-law. No. Not a soul is to know, save us. We'll manage, Frau Holtz. Fetch a barrel and see if there isn't something you can do about sobering up Jacobus. While you're doing that, I'll get dressed. When Wren returns, send her to the stables to waken the groom and have him ready the coach. We're going to have to move quickly as it will be dawn soon. Hurry, Frau Holtz."

Within the hour, working fast and furious, Sirena had dressed as had Frau Holtz, and Stephan's body was tightly fitted into a wooden stave barrel and the lid nailed shut. It was a grisly business but there was no one else to help. Jan and Willem had left the house nearly a fortnight ago to prepare the *Sea Spirit* for sailing. It was simply thought by Stephan that they had run off for a better position.

Stephan's valet, Smythe, and the footman, Rathbone, were still in the household staff. Smythe's room was at the far end of the house near the garden and Rathbone's was over the stable. Something would have to be done about them. Although, apparently, neither of them had overheard the commotion because they hadn't come anywhere near the library.

The sounds of furious knocking set Sirena's teeth on edge. Who, in their right mind, would be rapping on the door at this hour of the night? Cautiously, she walked into the foyer and peeped through the heavy draperies. Her eyes widened. Tyler Sinclair. Something was obviously wrong. Something must have happened to Regan. Quickly, she opened the door and dared him with her facial expression to reveal the bad news, whatever it was.

"Sirena, what are you doing up at this hour of the

night? I fully expected to have to stand here for hours till someone came to let me in. There's something I must tell you, so, please, sit down and let me get you a drink. You're going to need it when you hear what I have to say."

"Tell me, is it . . . is it Regan?"

"It has nothing to do with him. It's Stephan. He was caught cheating this evening on the *Sea Siren.* Caleb sent me a note that I should come and tell you. He was called out and they're to duel tomorrow at dawn. Actually today, since dawn is but an hour away. Regan is Stephan's second."

"Did you say at dawn?"

"Yes. Pistols were the gambler's choice. There's not much hope for Stephan, Sirena. If it had been rapiers, I would have put my money on Stephan—" Tyler stopped in mid-speech. Sirena had sat down on a seat and was laughing! She laughed until the tears streamed down her cheeks and Tyler thought she would choke to death.

Frau Holtz ran into the foyer, her eyes frightened and confused. When she saw Tyler she stepped backward, the pails she carried slipping from her hands and falling soundlessly on the thick carpet.

Sirena managed to gain control of herself and grasped Tyler by the arm. "Come with us, Tyler, there's something you must see." She led him into the library and pointed.

Tyler walked to the container and looked inside, expecting to see it full of jewels and gold; plunder of the Sea Siren. When the enormity of what he beheld hit him, he gulped and swayed dizzily.

"We're taking the barrel and its contents to sea. Nail the lid shut for us, Tyler. We don't have much time. If you're coming with us, this is it. You won't have the opportunity again."

"Oh my God!" Tyler exclaimed hoarsely as Sirena pressed the hammer into his hand.

"Nail it shut, Tyler!" she commanded. Woodenly, Tyler took the tool and the nails which were offered by a silent and stern Frau Holtz. He squeezed his eyes shut as he banged the first nail and his thumb along with it.

"Has Jacobus readied the carriage?" Sirena asked of the Frau.

"Ja," the old woman nodded.

"Do you want to come along with me or will you stay in London with Wren?" Sirena asked, already knowing what her answer would be.

"We go! The child has already taken what is most necessary and put it in the carriage. She waits outside with Jacobus."

Sirena smiled and fondly clasped her loyal friend's sturdy hand. "I will see to the child's welfare and yours," Sirena promised. "But I think it best that you and Wren should go to Spain for the time being. I will join you when I'm sure things are safe. For now, take some of my jewels; it will tide you over till I can get cash to you."

Sirena looked at Tyler, who had just finished his gruesome task. "I've been thinking. What should be done about the servants? And Stephan's valet and footman, Smythe and Rathbone?"

"Don't worry about them. The cook and housemaids will go to my mother to complain their mistress skipped off without paying them their wages and, to keep peace, mother will pay them. As for those ruffians Stephan hired, they'll make off with anything of value in the house. They won't want to be running to the law. They don't have loyalty to anyone or anything. Besides, what they'll manage to steal from here would be twenty times what they could earn in a lifetime of fetching and carrying for the gentry."

"All right. Now, please roll the barrel through to the kitchen and Jacobus will help you get it into the carriage. Hurry, we've only half an hour before dawn. Someone is bound to come looking for Stephan when he doesn't appear for the duel."

"What's this?" Jacobus cried happily as he saw Tyler rolling the impromptu casket out the kitchen door. As he hurried to lend a hand, he asked jubilantly, "Booty for the crew?"

"It goes over the side as soon as we make open water," Sirena said coolly. "This booty you wouldn't want, my friend."

In the dark of the coach Sirena looked out the window. "Tyler, did you notice that man standing outside the courtyard? Have you ever seen him before?"

Tyler's face whitened and he leaned toward Sirena to look out her window. "Yes, I know who he is. He's one of the gamblers sent by the man who was to face Stephan in a duel. He's there watching to see that Stephan doesn't try to get away."

"Well, I suppose his suspicions aren't aroused, otherwise he would have made an effort to stop us. To all intents and purposes he still thinks Stephan is in the house."

"Yes, and a lucky thing for all of us," Tyler breathed.

Through the streets of London Jacobus drove the horse team, wildly and recklessly. As they approached the wharf he slowed the animals. Wren squealed and grasped Frau Holtz for support as the coach came to a jarring halt and Tyler opened the door for them to exit. Jacobus raced to the ship on his skinny bandy legs and, within minutes, all hands were aboard. The anchor was hoisted and the ship ready to sail. The first faint glimmer of dawn was showing when the copper-bottomed ship slid from her berth in search of open water.

Regan pounded on the door with a vengeance. Where the hell was Stephan Langdon? Why wasn't someone answering the damned door? His eyes sought those of the gambler who was waiting patiently.

"He's in there. I saw him go in and he didn't come out. Break down the door," he said flatly.

Regan tried the handle and was surprised to find it unlocked. Cautiously, he entered the mansion. Lamps were lit and smoking everywhere. He shouted for Stephan and was not surprised when he didn't answer. Something was wrong; Regan could sense it instinctively. He picked up one of the lamps and walked around the ground floor, his eyes alert. When he entered the library the sight made him draw in his breath.

The floor was still wet from the scrubbing Frau Holtz had given it, and he only needed to see the carelessly tossed rapiers on the desk to become suspicious. Upon closer examination, he found bloodstains on the draperies and dark vermillion specks spattered on several papers strewn on the desk.

His booted foot slipped. Bending over, he picked up a thick nail. Frowning, he let his eyes circle the room. The library even held the metallic smell of blood.

A knot of fear settled in his gut as he raced through the first-floor rooms. All were empty. His search of the second floor convinced him that Sirena and Stephan had done battle.

A growing sinking feeling crept through Regan. Stephan was a master of fencing. His reputation was known far and wide. Sirena had grown weak being out of practice. Stephan had the advantage. Sirena! Sirena! his mind cried. Anger and vengeance filled his chest and constricted his heart. He would kill Stephan with his own bare hands if Langdon had harmed one hair on Sirena's head! The thought of Sirena inert, slain, brought shudders up his spine.

Through one room and into another, Regan searched. Hoping, yet dreading to find Sirena. At last he came upon her bedroom and his eyes fell on the tattered nightdress and negligée tossed carelessly on the floor. Relief flooded him. From the condition of the nightdress he knew Sirena had been wearing it when she faced off Stephan. If Stephan had killed her he wouldn't have removed her clothes and left them here on the floor as evidence. No, his mind raced. He broke into a smile. It was the other way around after all. Sirena had killed Stephan.

Killed him and ran. But where was the body? He looked blankly at the nail still in his palm. This piece of evidence was undoubtedly linked to the missing corpse. Sirena must be riding out to sea already.

He should have known better. What a fool he had been to think for one moment that Stephan had slain Sirena. Sirena would always live to fight another day. Sirena would always survive, with Regan or without him. The thought gnawed at him and caused him pain.

Regan descended the steps slowly, coming to stand next to the gambler who waited outside the door. "He's gone. There isn't anyone in the house except a cook and a servant. Check for yourself."

"I saw no one leave this house except two women,

a child, a young man, and a bandy-legged coachman. I know what Langdon looks like and he wasn't with them," the gambler said.

"Look for yourself and if you find him, fetch me at my office. I need some sleep, so if you'll excuse me."

"He won't get away with this. He's hiding, the coward. I'll find him," the man threatened.

"You do that," Regan answered coldly, turning up his collar against the damp morning air and turning his back on the house on King Street. If he didn't miss his guess, a storm was brewing and London would feel the force of it before noon. Just the kind of weather Sirena loved, reveled in. It occurred to Regan that Sirena didn't need to wait for storms to happen; she created them for herself.

Chapter Twenty-seven

The copper-bottomed *Sea Spirit* sliced through the churning swells as if bound for hell. Sirena stood near the bow, her feet firmly planted against the heaving deck. Soon, she would take the wheel and command her ship.

Her eyes flicked sideways to the barrel lashed to the foremast. In a short while it would be time to hoist it overboard. Stephan deserved no more than that. He was scum, a scourge against humanity. She didn't regret that he was dead; she only regretted she had been the one to kill him. At one time she had sworn that she would never take another life and she had reneged on that promise. There was no recourse open to her except to live with it just as she had learned to live with the other tribulations of her life.

Her emerald eyes searched the open waters for a sign of another vessel. The horizon was clear; no mastheads jutted sharply from the faraway line where sea met sky. A squall was heading in on the *Sea Spirit* from the northeast and would engulf them within the hour. Time enough for her to take the wheel. At the proper moment Jacobus would drill holes in the sides of the wooden stave barrel and it would be tossed into the sea. No prayers would be said for this burial.

The wind began to lift, billowing the canvas and lifting Sirena's long, dark hair and whipping it about her face. The squall had moved in quicker than she expected and she heard Jan issuing orders for all unneeded hands to go below decks. Sirena waited, feeling her spirits lift along with the bowsprit, loving the salt tang on her face, exhilarated by the force of the elements.

Taking her place at the wheel, the wind howled in the rigging as she steered the *Sea Spirit* under her close-reefed sails.

Gigantic swells, whipped into curly white combers by the gale, rolled in continuously from the north. Spindrift flew in flakes stinging her face as she fought the wheel.

The holocaust demanded her full attention. Hands gripping the slick, stout steering mechanism, which was nearly as tall as she, Sirena stood erect, and brazened nature. Lightning flashed, illuminating the dark, spectral clouds scudding across the sky. Rain had not yet begun to pelt the decks, but it was out there, waiting. Making ready for the onslaught, she lashed herself to the wheel.

Minutes seemed hours and hours eternities. The storm raged in full fury. Sirena was blinded by the savage downpour, but she kept the ship true to its heading. Her body was battered by the elements; her hair beat against her face and twisted about her neck like insistent, strangling fingers. When physical strength began to fail, an iron determination to survive became her mainstay. Nothing could stop her. Not Stephan's death, not Regan's rejection, not Caleb's siding with his father against her. Nothing. She would survive by her own wits and determination just as she had always done.

Tyler Sinclair fought his way across the deck with Willem. Their hands grasped lines and rigging as they struggled against the wind. Gaining the bow, they flanked the barrel, Stephan Langdon's cylindrical coffin, and struggled to tip it on its side. For a moment the vessel got away from them and Tyler imagined Stephan's body pushing out against the wooden staves and escaping the container. A horrific vision flashed through his mind as brightly and as instantly as the sudden lightning. He could almost see the body sliding on the decks, propelled by the wind and rain; almost giving it life. Gasping, taking in a mouthful of rain, Tyler choked, and grasped the barrel more firmly. Stephan Langdon would not haunt this ship! Not if he, Tyler, had to drown to make certain of it.

Willem grunted from the weight, his body fighting the strain and the elements. Turn by turn, they rolled the barrel to the rail, cursing the weather and their own clumsiness. Soaked through to the skin, the deluge plastering their hair to their heads in dark slabs, they hefted one side of the cask and tipped it upright. Without a final prayer or ceremony, the barrel went over the side and Stephan Langdon rested in the watery depths amid the crashing waves and the thundering sky. Ominous and deadly were the elements and a fitting graveyard for one who had been both. Sirena shouted for Tyler to go below; the deck of the *Sea Spirit* in a storm was no place for a landlubber.

The ship heaved with the force of the swells, the masts groaned with the weight of the saturated rigging. Rhythmically, the *Sea Spirit* rose and fell as she rode the turbulent waves. Sirena guided the vessel from the trough to the crest of each swell. For moments she would balance dizzily on the crest, then plunge steeply into the next trough. Each time she rode up onto the next crest, she became buoyant and invincible.

The weather held as the *Sea Spirit* and the crew made headway into Waterford's port. Under Frau Holtz's protests about being halfway around the world in Java, Sirena consented that she and Wren should return to Cádiz and set up residence in the Valdez house on Via Arpa.

Preparations were underway, packing, letter-writing and instructions that Frau Holtz should contact Señor

Arroya immediately upon arriving. The Frau and Wren might have several weeks' delay in booking passage on a ship bound for Cádiz so plans were made for Tyler to go to Waterford with the Frau and Wren and visit several acquaintances he had there. He was certain they would see to their welfare until passage could be secured to Cádiz.

Tears glistened in the elderly woman's eyes as she descended the ladder to solid ground on Waterford's wharf. Wren threw her arms around Sirena, stifling the sobs which choked her. Sirena forced herself to remain composed and quickly kissed the young girl on the cheek with the promise to see her soon.

"Mevrouw," Frau Holtz called from quayside, "when will we see you in Cádiz?" When Sirena did not reply, the housekeeper reached out an arm in entreaty. The iron-gray head shook as she read the expression in Sirena's eyes. The Frau said nothing, turning with Wren and following Tyler to the harbor master's office.

Sadness pricked Sirena's sea-green eyes. You know me too well, Frau Holtz, she cried silently. Thank you for turning away. If you hadn't, I would have leaped over the rail after you. *Vaya con Dios,* good friend.

She started for her cabin, barking several orders at her crew to lay in stores and fresh water. They would sail out on the evening tide. The crew hastened to do her bidding. To a man, they agreed the only thing in this world they could not stand was to see tears in their Capitana's eyes.

Shortly before sundown, Sirena awoke from her brief nap. She ate sparingly of the food Jacobus set before her and then went out on deck. Tyler was just returning from the city.

When he climbed aboard, he went directly to Sirena, answering her unspoken question. "The Frau and Wren have been settled in with friends of my family. They're delighted to have them. It's been some while since they had a child to pamper. There's a ship leaving for Cádiz within the week, but I preferred them to sail on the packet leaving ten days from now. I thought you would want them to be among missionaries going to Africa, rather than take a chance on their traveling with a motley crew of mercenaries."

"Thank you, Tyler, it is exactly as I would wish." Her voice was low and husky. "We sail on the evening tide. Three hours should see us out of Irish waters."

It would be none too soon for Tyler, who remembered, even if Sirena did not, that English law reigned supreme here in Ireland and they would be just as subject to English justice as they would have been in London.

Shortly before nine o'clock the *Sea Spirit* slid out of her berth. The sea was calm and the fugitives followed the path of the Moon.

Late that night Tyler came on deck and, to his surprise, found Sirena leaning over the stern, watching the wake created by the ship's rudder. He had been hoping for an opportunity to talk with her and was glad to find her alone.

"Sirena," he called softly, interrupting her thoughts. She turned to face him, and from the glint in her eyes he could see she had been weeping.

"What is it, Tyler? It's very late, I thought you would be bunked down."

"I wanted to discuss that little arrangement we made. I've decided it was unfair of me to ask you to embark on a career of piracy. I've changed my mind; I don't think I could go through with it. That last time, it wasn't our fault Regan's ship was sunk. We really did nothing more than salvage the cargo from going down with her.

Sirena smiled. "I thought you would see it that way, Tyler. In fact, I was certain you would."

"Then we can go back and get Frau Holtz and little Wren!"

"No, Tyler, that is the one thing we cannot do. I don't want them associated with me until I know I am clear of what I did to Stephan. They're safer sailing to Cádiz without me. As for you, you can always go back to London after we reach Spain. Who knows, Tyler, luck may be with you and you will cross paths with pirates? They are one breed of fish I consider fair game. You may have your fortune yet."

The *Sea Spirit* rode her southern course, and shortly before twilight a few days later, a cry was raised from the crew. "Sail ho!"

"Where away?" Sirena answered, rushing out onto the deck from her cabin near the stern.

"Breaking the horizon coming from the west," came the reply.

"Keep to course, and as she runs in, tell me what flag she wears."

As Sirena and the seamen kept their eyes peeled to the west, they cursed the darkness which was rapidly falling, obscuring the arrival except for its outline against the blackening sky.

"Man the guns," Sirena said softly, "I don't like the looks of her. Let her pass unmolested, but ready yourselves."

As Tyler peered, his eyes focused on a pinpoint of light coming from the bow lantern of the distant ship. He was apprehensive. Sirena had warned that pirates and soldiers of fortune peppered the well-traveled shipping lanes, seeking easy victims. Jan had loaded the starboard gun and the wind blew a haze of powder Tyler's way, burning his eyes and stinging his nostrils.

Coughing and sputtering, he moved upwind of the gun and concentrated on the western horizon.

Sirena and her crew were tense. They, too, were aware that this spectral vessel could be manned by pirates. Silence fell over the crew and Jacobus made a last tour of the ship to be certain no lanterns were lit, giving away their positions.

The sky was totally black now. Just as the darkness shrouded the oncoming ship from the *Sea Spirit*, so was the sleek, copper-bottomed brig hidden from it.

They could feel the presence of the other ship even though they could not see it. Jacobus studied the sky, hoping for the stars to light the scene, yet dreading that they might, and reveal the *Sea Spirit*'s position. Sirena changed course to southeasterly, hoping to outrun the pursuer.

All eyes fastened to the west and, suddenly, they saw a flare not a quarter of a mile away. A lamp was being held aloft and circling to starboard. The mystery ship had found the winds to her advantage and had gained on the *Sea Spirit* more quickly than they could have imagined. The ship was so close that Sirena could almost make out the features of the seaman who signaled with the lamp.

"They signal to heel to starboard!" she said incredulously. "They expect us to give up without a fight!"

Just as she uttered the words, the mystery ship's port gun fired, blazing red and fiery gold. "She attacks us! Jan! Fire the starboard gun!"

Feeling his way to light the fuse, Jan struck the flint and kept his eyes directed away from the flare to keep from losing his night vision. He found the fuse and lit it, the small red glow travelling up the wire. The *Sea Spirit* rocked from the recoil of the cannon. Quicker than the eye could follow, the ball shot, shuddering the opposing vessel's hull and splitting her timbers on the port side.

Feverishly, Jan reloaded with Jacobus' help; the cannon was ready to fire again within moments.

"Fire!" Sirena commanded, not wanting to lose the advantage. A deafening roar ripped through the night and an inky black smoke billowed upward.

"Dead on its mark," Willem called direly.

The other ship, which was now identifiable as a galleon, limped to starboard, away from the *Sea Spirit.*

"They run like mice!" Jan cheered, his voice shrill with excitement. Suddenly, he ran down the deck to the wheel to Sirena. "Capitana . . . the ship . . ."

"It was a good shot, Jan, you have a keen eye."

"Look," Jan said, pointing his long arm at the floundering galleon. "Look at her flag!"

Sirena studied the foremast, now illuminated by the flames shooting from her deck. The flag of England! And flying just below it was the Monarch's crown. The King's ship!

"Capitana, we attacked the King's galleon. We'll have to make a run for it!"

"Too late," Willem cried. "Look who's coming up behind her!" he shouted incredulously.

"Merciful God!" Sirena cried. "We can't outrun two; they'll hem us in."

Tyler groaned aloud as he brought his hands up to his head. The enormity of the situation hit him and he thought he would retch.

Sirena had no time for Tyler now. She pushed him

out of her way and stepped closer to the rail for a better look. "The galleon is floundering, but she can be shored up. She's hit well above the water line."

"She wasn't signaling to *us* to heel to starboard," Jan said, "she was signaling to her escort. She probably didn't even see us when she fired her gun."

"Capitana," Willem directed, "go to your cabin and change your clothes. We don't need more trouble than we can handle. Hurry!" he instructed hoarsely.

When Sirena returned on deck, the two vessels had sidled in close to the *Sea Spirit* and the order was being called for her men to stand back and make way for the boarding party.

A tall officer in the King's navy led his men aboard from the jolly. He was a striking man in his gold braid and high boots. "Who captains this oddity of the seas?" he demanded. "Present the ship's papers."

Jan handed the officer the documents and Sirena moistened her dry lips and was about to speak when Tyler stepped forward and spoke. "I am the captain," he said imperiously.

"He lies," Willem said, shouldering Jacobus and Jan out of his way. "I am the captain."

"Liars, the lot of them, nothing more than scurves," Jacobus protested as he maneuvered his way to stand directly next to the naval officer. "There is only one captain aboard the *Sea Spirit* and it's me!"

Jan smiled wickedly. "A man of your intelligence will certainly know these sea rats are not fit to command a jolly boat. I am the captain."

"Enough!" roared the officer. "Next you'll be telling me the woman is the captain."

"That's exactly who I am," Sirena said coolly. "I gave the order to fire upon the galleon and I will take the consequences. My men merely followed orders. If you'll examine the papers, you'll see this ship belongs to Sirena Magdelena Esthera Córdez. Langdon," she added as an afterthought.

"Madame, as owner of this ship, do you have any idea of the position you are now in?" the English lieutenant asked.

"I only know," Sirena said coolly, seeing the admiration for her in the officer's eyes, "that the English galleon came upon us in the dark. We saw a lantern signal to heel to starboard and then a shot was fired. Naturally, we thought ourselves under attack and we retaliated in kind. It was not until we saw her escort that we realized our error."

"An expensive error," the Englishman said with courtliness.

"I agree. Naturally, I will pay for the damages, and ask her captain and your King to please accept my apologies."

"Dear lady, there will be no need for that. You can extend your apologies in person. It is said His Majesty tours Newgate prison once a year. You will have ample time to prepare your speech. My men will board your vessel and escort you to London where you will be incarcerated until your trial."

He gave the order for Sirena and her crew to be placed in the hold till they reached London. Only Tyler protested weakly as he was dragged over the deck and dumped unceremoniously through the hatch.

Sirena and her crew spent eight dark days in the hold of the *Sea Spirit* as the ship made headway through the Atlantic, retracing her wake to London. Several times each day they were brought up on deck to breathe the fresh air and to eat their meals. At these times they were under close guard by Lieutenant Fenner, who now captained the brig.

In deference to her sex, Sirena was allowed the privacy of her cabin several times a day for her personal needs and to change clothes as necessary. Often, when strolling out on deck, she would find her way to the wheel where Fenner stood watch. She found him to be a pleasant young man with a deep sense of duty, and when he went on at length with admiring comments on the *Sea Spirit,* Sirena found herself liking him in spite of the fact she was his prisoner.

One blustery day, when the cliffs of Dover were rising starkly out of the horizon, she questioned, "What do you think will become of my crew, Lieutenant? It was an honest error on our part, firing at the King's galleon."

Fenner smiled at her with sadness in his eyes. Over

the past few days he had come to recognize she was a remarkable woman. She had kept her head while most women would have become hysterical, screaming banshees. And she was beautiful in spite of the deep sadness he saw in her bottle-green eyes. "I can't answer that question for you, Lady Langdon. I can only suggest you bring whatever money you have at hand. You will need it in Newgate in order to insure that you are treated in a humane manner. I can't, in all conscience, hold out any hope to you. The King takes a dim view of piracy unless, of course, it is his navy which commits it to his profit."

"You're an honest man, Lieutenant Fenner," Sirena said warmly. She liked this red-headed man with the twinkling, blue eyes. He was the kind of individual she would like to serve on her ship. When she turned away, Fenner touched her arm lightly.

"When my men searched your ship, no money was found. Was there any? I wouldn't put it past some of these swabbies to filch it."

"No, there wasn't any," Sirena said truthfully. Every available farthing was given to Frau Holtz when they had docked in Waterford. "I have come from a business appointment in Ireland and, I am sorry to say, was returning empty-handed. The supplies for the galley and some new rigging emptied my coffers."

Fenner looked genuinely concerned. "I haven't much, but what I have is yours," he offered.

"Thank you, but—"

"Please take it. You will need it until your family comes to your aid. Please," he implored.

"On one condition," she smiled, "that you call me Sirena. I can't possibly borrow money from anyone who calls me Lady Langdon."

"Please, Sirena, you can repay me if you wish when you gain your release. I'll give it to you in the morning, before docking. It's only a few pounds, but it may help."

On the eighth day Sirena, Tyler and the crew were in the hold when they heard the hull scrape against the berth. They knew they had arrived in London. Through the broadside they could hear voices and the commotion on the dock. It was only moments later that the hatch opened, and Lieutenant Fenner stood looking down at them. "Come on up, men. Sirena, if you'd care to repair to the privacy of your cabin before going ashore, I'll understand."

Sirena mutely nodded her head. Since bedding down last night, the crew had become silent, afraid to voice their apprehensions. She herself had barely uttered a word except to beg their forgiveness for dumping them in the middle of this mess. They had all been so gracious, swearing to her that it hadn't been her fault. Tyler was especially vocal, insisting she not take the blame for any part of it.

Up on deck, Lieutenant Fenner led her to her cabin. He was quiet and Sirena could see he was very concerned. He, at least, believed it all to be a horrible mistake. Before entering her cabin, she threw a glance at the busy wharf. London. And she had hoped never to see it again.

Throughout the long days at sea, Sirena and her crew had concocted a feasible story concerning Stephan. He had been washed overboard at sea. Their time of departure would coincide with the squall that was certain to be reported and there was no one to refute their tale. Still, Sirena was terrified that someone would know she had been responsible for Stephan's death. There were the servants, Smythe and Rathbone, and what about Camilla? Surely, owing to her closeness to her father, she would demand an inquiry.

"You will have to hurry, Sirena," Lieutenant Fenner broke in on her thoughts. "In a few moments the carriage will be here to transport you to Newgate. Your men will ride in a cart, but I didn't want to see you ridiculed through the city streets and tormented by urchins. I've hired a coach for you. One of my officers will accompany you while I make out my report to the Commissioner of Navies. Trust my report will be in your favor."

Sirena thanked him and stepped into the dim cabin. The first thing she saw was a small cache of coins that Fenner had left for her.

The young officer in the carriage with her seemed embarrassed by her presence. He kept watching her covertly while pretending to look out the window. Sirena had made a small neat bundle of clothes to take to Newgate with her when Lieutenant Fenner stopped her. "They won't allow you to keep it, Sirena, and someone might try to murder you for it. It's best to leave it here."

She had looked at him blankly. What kind of place was this Newgate prison? "My ship—"

"The *Sea Spirit* will be seen to, I promise you. And when you return, she'll be here waiting for you. Goodbye, Sirena, I hope we meet again someday under different circumstances."

"So do I," she assured him, taking his hand, almost loathing to let it go for it represented the world she knew and not the place she was going to.

The hack took its course along Thames Street. The same route she and Frau Holtz had driven how many months ago when she had first arrived in London. They were nearing the corner of St. Dunstan's Hill where Regan's offices were. She remembered how she had first glimpsed his sign and how she had looked back at it, searing its location into her brain. Now, as the carriage wheels took her past it, she slumped in a corner, not daring to glance out for fear she would see him and call out to him, begging him to help her. It was too late. Where had she heard that? Had Regan told her that? "It's too late, Sirena," she could hear his voice as he growled the words.

Through the city she rested her head against the seat back, her eyes closed, refusing to look at the passing people, refusing to acknowledge they were free to walk the streets while she was on her way to prison.

She only opened her eyes again when the carriage stopped and she was aware the escort was climbing down from the hack. He extended his hand to help her, but she refused it. She would manage on her own. This was something she had to face alone and she would go the last few steps of it exactly that way. Alone.

Gray granite, rising several stories high and displaying iron bars where windows should have been, ran around the perimeter of the yard. She thought of the Bethlehem Royal Hospital where Stephan had had her incarcerated for a day, and felt the old terror begin. Then she squared her shoulders.

The cells on Condemned Row were dark, dank and incredibly filthy. Straw rushes lined the dirt floor and the solitary window was set high in the wall. Even if one could climb to it, it was too sharply cut and too narrow to permit escape. Sirena sat on a low, scarred stool, staring at the heavy chains they had placed about her wrists and ankles. They were encrusted with rust and the bright orange flecks rubbed off and stained her skin. Following Lieutenant Fenner's suggestion she had dressed warmly, and she blessed him for the advice. The light of day and the warmth of sunshine had never seen the inside of Newgate prison. A solitary candle, no greater than an inch in length, burned feebly, unable to penetrate the dark. Vaguely, Sirena wondered what she would do when the candle gutted itself and she was left in darkness.

A jangle of keys clanking together reached her ears and when she picked up her head, a tall woman with forbidding features was entering her cell. She had voluminous breasts which hung down onto her belly and her dark, bombazine dress was grease-stained with large wet circles showing under her arms. Her hair was caught up at the back with greasy strings hanging over her face. Her shoes were stout and she wore an apron of an indeterminate color. "I'm the jailor's wife!" she announced harshly. "I've come to see if ye've enough to pay yer way out o' Condemned Row."

When Sirena looked at her blankly, the woman exclaimed, "Lor', ye're a stupid one! Have you any money to pay garnish?"

Wisely, Sirena asked her how much money she would need if indeed she did have any.

"Come now, me fine lady, you've not been brought 'ere for bein' a debtor. Ye've committed a crime against the Crown! Surely, ye've a few pounds ta make yer stay 'ere more pleasurable."

"How much!" Sirena demanded.

"Two pound ten," the jailor's wife spit, having no patience for the uppity likes of Sirena.

"And what will it buy me?"

"For one thing, yer ladyship, it'll get ye out o' Condemned Row while ye wait yer trial. Fer another, the conditions are much improved on the other side o' the prison. Fer another thing, ye'll 'ave fresh water and yer biscuits won't be wormy. An' ye'll have a bed ta sleep in 'stead o' 'ay on a dirt floor."

Sirena only needed to hear about the bed and she stood and fumbled beneath her skirts to retrieve the price the woman asked.

"Oh, an fer another shillin' yer chains and braces will be a lot lighter, I promise ye that."

Aghast at such practices, Sirena dug beneath her skirts once more to find the shilling. Thank the Lord for Lieutenant Fenner's generosity.

As Sirena walked along behind the jailor's wife, she asked, "Have you heard when my trial will be held?" Her voice echoed off the high ceilings and tunnel-like corridors.

"If'n yer lucky, it'll be before yer money runs out," the woman laughed harshly.

She showed Sirena into a cell with two other women. Her chains and braces were exchanged for lighter ones, but she didn't think they were that much lighter to cost her a full shilling. Suddenly, she laughed, seeing the humor of the situation. Here she was worrying about a shilling when she had thousands, hundreds of thousands, but she could not get her hands on any of it. Tyler, who controlled her money and investments, was also a prisoner.

Before the jailor's wife left the cell, after depositing a leaky pail of foul water beside her, Sirena asked, "How can I get a letter out of here?"

"It'll cost ye six shillings and two more for the paper and five more for the quill."

"How much for the ink," Sirena asked tersely, lifting her skirts to find the little medicine pouch where her hoard was kept.

"We'll have none o' yer lip!" the woman scowled. "If'n ye wants ta write a letter, say so!" Her eyes glittered greedily as she looked at the coins in Sirena's palm.

"On second thought, you'll be paid after I receive the paper and quill. And ink!" Sirena demanded.

"Tosh! Ain't she the fine and mighty one?" a voice from behind her taunted. "Who does she think she is? Braggin' 'ow she can read and write! It ain't proper somehow, her bein' 'ere in Newgate an' all!"

"Oh, shut up, Nell, leave her alone. Don't you remember how it was on your first day in this pest hole!" another voice commanded. While the tone was harsh, the diction was perfect, and there was a quality about it that suggested the woman was used to commanding servants. Sirena turned and saw a willowy redhead with the blackest eyes she had ever seen. When she smiled her thanks, the redhead smiled back. "See here, sweetheart, what are you in for?"

"It's all a misunderstanding," Sirena began to explain when she saw she had the attention of the jailor's wife and the woman named Nell. She snapped her mouth shut, not wanting to discuss her affairs in their presence.

"Certainly, what else could it be. My name is Theodora, Theo to my friends." Theo looked up and her eyes fell on the jailor's wife. "Well, why are you standing around gawking? Surely, there are others in this hell hole you can filch for a pail of sour water. Get on with you! And don't forget to bring the lady her paper and quill, you want her money don't you?"

The slattern turned and locked the cell behind her. Theo's haughty tone and commanding nature had moved the woman into action. Then she turned about and pressed her face up against the bars. "An, why am I doin' yer biddin', yer ladyship? Yer the one who's the prisoner!" She broke out into raucous peals of laughter as she walked the length of the corridor, her keys jingling loudly at her waist.

"What a hag that one is," Theo said to Sirena, "I've seen whores peppered with disease who looked better than her."

"If'n she's a 'ag, imagine what her 'usband looks like," Nell interjected. It appeared she didn't want to alienate herself from her cellmates, and it was bound to happen if Theo took a liking to the new girl and she were to keep taunting her.

"So, Newgate's a novel experience for you, is it? You didn't tell us your name," Theo said, pulling her dark green cloak about her to keep the hem from dragging on the floor.

"Sirena."

"Well, Sirena, how did you know enough to dress warmly? Most of the new ones come in here dressed according to the weather. Seeing it is summer I would have to think this isn't your first visit to Newgate."

"But it is," Sirena protested. "A . . . a friend warned me to dress warmly."

"Did your friend tell you anything else?" Theo looked at Sirena with interest, scrutinizing her attire and listening carefully to the way she spoke and watching her mannerisms.

"He told me I'd have to pay garnish."

"And so right he was!" Nell agreed. "Lord only knows what'll 'appen to me in a week's time. Me money's near gone an' I 'aven't enough fer a drink o' water."

Sirena pointed to the leaking pail the jailor's wife had left her. "Help yourself. You might as well drink it before it all seeps out."

"You mean to tell me that shrew didn't tell you for a pence more you could have a pail that doesn't leak? Really, Sirena, the conditions here become more intolerable each time I come. Here, if you pour it into my pail, we'll manage to save what's left of it."

Sirena hobbled over to Theo's supply, carrying her own leaking pail, and carefully poured the water in.

"I can see you're new here. That could have been a very costly oversight on your part if it were anyone but me you were dealing with. It could have meant you your week's water. But it won't. I believe in share and share alike. That's the reason I'm here in the first place."

When Sirena looked at her questioningly, Theo explained. "I'm a prostitute, Sirena, when I can't find work at my real vocation, which is the stage. I'm a first-rate actress."

Nell started to giggle, nervously pulling at her straggly brown hair and biting her fingernails past the quick. "Act somethin' fer us, Theo. G'on. She's the most bee-you-ti-ful lady I ever seen when she play-acts."

Sirena smiled. "How long have you two been here."

"This time?" Theo asked. "Oh, we've been together nigh onto three months now. Nell here was quite worried about her children at first, but she's over that now, aren't you, Nell?"

Nell's bottom lip began to tremble. "I imagine they're dead and gone by now, right, Theo? No sense wonderin' and worryin' about them. They've passed on ta their reward, 'aven't they, Theo?"

"You bet they have, old Nell. And a damnsight better than this world it is, believe me. Now, don't you feel better since you don't pull your hair out and scream half the day and night calling for them?" Theo glanced at Sirena and her eyes said that Nell was near to the breaking point when Theo finally convinced her that she was worrying herself into Bedlam for nothing. The cruelty of Theo's words were actually a kindness to keep Nell's body and soul together.

"Well, Theo, don't ye think we should tell our Sirena 'ow to get along here in Newgate? You tell her, Theo, ye know I loves the sound o' yer voice."

Sirena wrote her letter to Baroness Sinclair, omitting the details, telling her only how she and Tyler managed to get themselves locked in Newgate. She was confident the Baron would exert his influence to see to their release as soon as possible.

The jailor's wife came by to see them each morning, trying to induce them to spend their last farthing on this luxury or that. Theo, Nell and Sirena were quite fortunate as prisoners in Newgate went. Since they were being held for specific crimes, they were closed out of the Lady Debtors' Ward, and since they were not hardened criminals, they were spared Condemned Row.

Nell had been arrested for stealing food for her starving children. She had already had her day in court and had been sentenced to two years in prison. Both Theo and Sirena knew Nell would never outlive her sentence.

Theo had been a prostitute in one of the most expensive bordellos in London. Her crime had been holding back on her madam. In retaliation, her employer claimed she caught Theo stealing, and since the madam had more money to bribe the officials to seeing matters her way than Theo, the courts had sentenced her to six months and the confiscation of all her personal property which the madam promptly bought at auction at a ridiculously low price.

Theo's education of Sirena about the intricacies and intimacies of Newgate was thorough and dramatically told. Even Nell was mesmerized by the sound of Theo's voice and her gesticulations.

Sirena learned how fortunate she was not to be located in the Lady Debtors' Wards where overcrowding was so severe fifty or sixty women were assigned to the same quarters. As there was bedding for only twenty or so, it was impossible for everyone to sleep at the same time. Eating utensils were at a premium and had to be shared.

Theo had suggested to Sirena that she use her supply of water for washing only, pointing out the algae and specks of sewage floating on its oily surface. "It is much better to spend a few shillings for ale or mead, Sirena, than find yourself sick with dysentery," she advised.

Twice a day they were permitted to go into the yard for a breath of air and on their way they were permitted to empty their slop jars. Since on their way to the cistern, they had to pass the long row of cells where condemned men waited for the gallows, it was not a part of the day any of them enjoyed. Not even getting outside in the sunshine was incentive enough to go through that narrow corridor where the prisoners would hoot their approval and shout obscenities while they stretched their arms between the bars reaching and clutching for an unguarded breast or buttock.

Just the day before Nell had found herself in an inmate's clutches, and his rough handling before a guard could beat his hands off her with his bull's pizzle, a leather weapon for commanding discipline, caused Nell to spill the contents of her slop jar down the front of her already filthy gown.

While beating off the prisoner's hands, the guard had succeeded in belting poor Nell several times with his club, leaving her with a bruised arm and a blackened eye. But the worst of it was when Nell had been compelled to clean the mess, leaving her to the tauntings and ravings of the men.

Theo, whose protective instincts toward Nell were admirable, if not wise, had stood her ground and wrenched the bull's pizzle away from the guard and beat him over the head with it several times. "Watch who you are swinging at!" she had ordered, throwing a haughty look at the inmates, freezing their lecherous leers on their faces. Since the episode, which Theo paid dearly for with nearly the last of her cache to keep from being thrown in Condemned Row, she was known as the Duchess by the men throughout the ward. Where before she had been able to pass their cells with only the usual taunts and groping hands, the men were now more determined than ever to get her into their clutches.

Nell's dress had been ruined beyond repair. There simply wasn't enough water to wash the offal from the already too thin and worn fabric, even if soap had been available. Generously, Sirena had offered Nell several of her petticoats and Theo contributed the waist-length long-sleeved jacket right off her own back. Nell was delighted to be wearing something so fine as Theo's jacket and she preened and sported it for all to see.

The jailor's wife came to their cell and breathlessly asked if they would care to attend a party given by a gentleman in the Tap Room. Her eyes avoided Nell, whom she knew would not please the gentleman. Nell had become more than gaunt; she was taking on the macabre look of a skeleton and the skin was stretched tightly over her cheekbones. She had developed a hacking cough and several times Theo and Sirena had seen blood in her spittle, although Nell tried to keep it carefully hidden. "There's food aplenty and enough wine to float a ship. Seein' as 'ow ye two are the closest things to ladies here in Newgate at the present moment, when they asked for some female companionship, naturally, I thought o' ye."

"And how much did they pay you?" Theo demanded. "How much will you kick back to us if we do go?"

The stout woman bared her blackened teeth and menaced at Theo, "If'n the party of gentlemen ain't ter your likin', I can have it arranged fer ye to spend a day with the condemned men."

Theo knew she was beaten; the threat would be made good. Standing her ground, Theo took another tack. "And what about poor Nell here? She could do with a good meal and a healthy tot of wine."

"As I said, the gentlemen were looking for presentable females, and that one," she said, jabbing her thumb in Nell's direction, "ain't no more than a bag o' bones! Now, are ye comin' or ain't ye?"

Theo was not about to give up so easily; she suspected the jailor's wife had received a handsome sum for providing quality ladies and would be loath to return it. "What's a bit of food and a tankard of wine compared to what you have already profited? Surely, poor Nell will hardly be noticed among the crowd. Sirena and I will go gladly if Nell comes with us. Else you'll find yourself dragging a couple of slatterns from the Debtors' Ward and you know it."

The woman's eyes glittered as brightly as the coins she had tucked beneath her apron. "Well, come along then, they'll be waitin' fer ye."

Sirena looked at Theo questioningly. "Lots of well-to-do gentlemen find themselves in an unfortunate position, Sirena," the black-eyed redhead explained. Just because they are prisoners doesn't necessarily mean their social life is past. Come along, I assure you it is only our company they seek, nothing more. The food is usually sent in so you won't be eating this prison slop. Come along, Nell. Here, let me straighten your hair a bit," Theo clucked over Nell and used her own comb to untangle the snarls in her dingy brown hair.

"There's no time fer that!" the jailor's wife protested. "Who's gonna look at her anyhow?"

"Nell likes to look pretty, don't you, Nell? It will only take a minute." The woman stood watching Theo's ministrations while she tapped her foot impatiently. "There, all done, doesn't she look nice, Sirena?"

Nell looked at Sirena hopefully, waiting for her answer. "As pretty as I've ever seen her," Sirena answered smiling, extending her hand for Nell to take.

"Harrumph! Who'd ever think the likes o' you would take yerself on a full-grown baby?" the wardeness sneered at Theo. "Well, enjoy 'er. From the looks o' 'er, she hasn't got much time left ta 'er!"

Nell glanced quickly at Sirena, fear narrowing her eyes which now seemed too big for her face. "Don't listen to her, Nell. She's only jealous. She knows how fashionable it is to be thin," Sirena assured. The wardeness had uttered her own secret thought but it was cruelty to have Nell hear it.

The high rate of mortality in Newgate was a well-known fact. It wasn't the first time Sirena wanted to take the wardeness' keys and stuff them down her throat.

The Tap Room was thick with smoke. The wood burning in the fireplace must have been damp because it was giving off white vapor and a heavy choking aroma. Combined with the pipes which many in the prison smoked, believing tobacco warded off many diseases, the atmosphere was stifling and gloomy. The long benches set near the planked tables were filled with people, mostly men. They were eating heartily and taking great gulps from their tankards.

Sirena's mouth began to water as she noticed the fare; crisply done briskets and haunches of lamb and pork, and bowls of fresh fruit! How long had it been since she'd sunk her teeth into an orange? She hadn't realized how much she hated the moldy bread and charity meat the prison served until now.

Theo led Nell over to a far table and sat her down. Then she filled a plate with an assortment of meat and picked up a whole bowl of fruit and set it in front of her. She filled several tankards of wine and lined them up in a row, directing Nell to eat and drink as much as she could hold and to fill the front of her jacket with everything that would fit. Especially the fruit.

Sirena found herself holding a tankard of wine that someone had thrust into her hand and she sipped at its coolness, relishing the flavor after weeks of bitter ale and stale mead.

"We might as well dig in and fill our bellies, Sirena. There's no telling when we'll be this fortunate again," Theo said, dragging Sirena over to the table.

Several of the men moved over to make room for them, putting their arms around the women familiarly. Sirena felt herself stiffen. There was a certain price she would never pay to fill her belly.

Theo made short work of them by fixing her freezing Duchess stare on them till they removed their arms. "I've no objection to your company, gentlemen," she said politely, "only you must remember a hungry girl does not make for pleasant company." She then turned back to her plate and signaled for Sirena to do the same.

After Sirena had eaten, swearing it to be the most delicious food she had ever put to her mouth, she was in the process of draining her tankard when she heard a familiar voice.

When she turned to the voice, she found Tyler at the head of the table, coaxing his companions to eat well else the jailor and his wife will sell the food in Condemned Row the next day. From his proprietorial manner Sirena knew he was the host of this affair. She narrowed her eyes to peer through the smoke. No wonder she hadn't recognized him. A full, dark beard had grown on his face and his hair was longer and curlier than before coming to Newgate. In spite of her pleasure at seeing him, she wondered where he had gotten the money to host such an expensive affair. Had the Baron and Baroness somehow come to his aid? Had they received her letter? Why hadn't she heard from them herself?

Dropping her meat back on the plate and wiping her greasy hands on the petticoat beneath her skirt, she stood away from the table and walked over to him. "Tyler?"

She caught him in mid-laugh and his eyes were shocked to hear her voice. "Sirena!" Quickly he rose from his bench and led her over to a quiet corner. "How are you? How are you faring?"

"Not as well as you are, Tyler. Where did you get the money to afford this little party? I thought we hadn't a farthing left between you, me and the whole crew? I thought we gave it all to Frau Holtz?"

Tyler lowered his eyes in shame, not able to meet her penetrating gaze. Then a thought occurred to him. "And where did you find enough money to keep you looking so well all these weeks?"

"Lieutenant Fenner gave me his last ha'penny, that's where. I felt guilty enough taking it too, until he assured me a woman needed it more than a man did," she said reprovingly. "Have you heard anything about when we come to trial? When I first arrived, I penned off a letter to your parents, thinking you wouldn't have any money to pay the bribe to have a missive sent out of this Godawful place. I can see how wrong I was."

"I could have told you my parents have left the city for the Netherlands. A cousin of my mother is getting married and—"

"Spare me!" Sirena held up her hand. "Tyler, what are we going to do? We'll die in this place before they hear our trial and, even then, we may not be released."

"It will all be taken care of, Sirena," he assured. "I've seen to it."

"Seen to it? How?"

Again Tyler seemed hesitant to meet her gaze. "I . . . I sent a letter to Regan." Seeing the anger rise in her, he hastened to explain, "Actually I sent it to him in care of Whipple. I had to do it! I knew you never would and I had to sign your name!" he said, telling more than he intended.

"Sign my name! You stupid lout! You knew Regan would be the last person in this world I would ask for help! Tyler, I could cheerfully kill you!" To emphasize her words, she kicked out and struck him in the shins with the toe of her shoe.

Tyler hopped around on one foot holding the other up in his hands. "Please, Sirena, listen to me. It was our sole hope! And it's some time since I sent the last one. I'm praying this letter got through to him!"

"You sent more than one! With my name on it, so he thinks I'm the one begging him for his help?" Again she kicked him, this time on the other leg.

"Sirena, forgive me," Tyler cried out in pain, "it was the only thing I could do! Forgive me."

Sirena stood with hands on hips, glaring at him through slitted eyes. "How much money have you, Tyler?" she demanded.

"I don't know—" he began.

"Don't lie to me, Tyler. How much money have you left after this gay affair you arranged for tonight? You'd better tell me else I'll spread the word you've tucked a fortune away up inside your bowels and there's not a man here who wouldn't be glad to slit your gullet just to see if I tell the truth."

Tyler was horrified. "You'd do that?"

"Damn right I would. Now, how much have you?"

"I . . . I'm not really certain, but whatever it is, it's yours. Honestly, Sirena, I wasn't trying to hold out on you. It's just that I hadn't the chance to give it to you. Ask Jan and Willem and the rest of the crew. I divided everything I had between all of us."

Sirena believed him and immediately warmed to him. She had been deeply worried how her men were faring here in Newgate. Now that she knew they each had a bit of money to pay their easement, she was grateful to Tyler. "You did that? You shared with the crew? Then you must forgive me, Tyler. Still, my small cache is running dangerously low. How much can you spare?"

"I've forty pounds left—"

"Forty pounds! Are you certain you didn't steal the Frau's purse when you took her to your friend's house in Waterford? Forty pounds left! And how much did you share with the crew?"

Tyler winced. "They each received fifteen."

Sirena was relieved. She herself had come to Newgate with eight pounds and she had been sharing with Theo and Nell. Her men would do quite well.

"Keep fifteen for yourself, Tyler; give me the rest. I've Theo and Nell to look after, now give it to me."

Tyler pulled off his boot and fished in the lining for the amount she asked, a sheepish grin on his face.

"When was the last letter you sent to Regan?"

"A couple of days ago; with any luck we'll be hearing from him soon. I gave it to a man just being released from the Men's Debtors' Ward. I'd done him several favors and he promised he would see that Regan received it."

"Go back to your party, Tyler. I've got a great deal to think about. For one thing, I have to decide just how I'm going to face Regan when he discovers where I am and why."

After Sirena and her two friends left the party, Tyler discovered he wasn't having a good time. The wine flowed generously, the food was more than ample, and quite delicious compared to prison fare, the company was jolly, and yet his mood became blacker and blacker. Sirena was unhappy with the letter he had written to Regan. He had seen it in her eyes, heard it in her voice. Damn! he cursed himself. The woman had had more than enough to bear without his interference. He swore again, cursing his own impotence in arranging to have himself and Sirena along with her crew released from Newgate. The Baron and Baroness were off on their travels and were of no help to him. For the first time the name Sinclair was without influence.

Newgate was a horror to Tyler. He had come to the gray-walled prison several times when a client had found himself in sorry straits and even at those times the atmosphere was rank and he would hurry through the transaction and rush for the outer gates where he would take deep heavy breaths to clear his lungs of the putrid odors from inside. He remembered the first time he had been summoned to Newgate; sweat broke out on his brow and he could feel his armpits become damp and sticky. He had thought to himself then that he would rather die than ever be confined in that awful place.

Yet here he was, acting jolly and paying his easement, making the best of the situation. He had wondered how Sirena was faring and from the look of her he saw she was getting along well enough. Sirena always would, he thought. She was a special breed, strong and confident, seeing even the worst of times through to the end.

Back in his small, square cell along with three other men, Tyler lay on his bed of moldy straw and made a silent prayer that Regan would receive his letter and act on it. Even the money he had given Sirena didn't guarantee she wouldn't come down with a fatal disease; or that he was immune from disease, for that matter. Money didn't protect one from the sudden bloody flux and the death that followed.

Turning on his side, away from his cellmates, Tyler brought a picture of Camilla into his mind. Throughout these past long days and nights it was her face that brought him the strength to go on. A new resolve had taken hold inside him. He knew now, without a doubt, that if he should ever gain his release from Newgate, he would stand tall and strong and confess everything to Regan. Camilla was his, Tyler's, wife and nothing save death would keep her from him. The days of the weak, vacillating youth were over, and in their stead was an assured, determined man, willing to take the risks necessary to gain that which he most wanted in life. Camilla.

Each time Sirena heard the jangle of keys at the wardeness' waist jingling through the halls, she held her breath expectantly, waiting for an answer to Tyler's letters to Regan.

Each day passed slowly as she adhered to her routine. The money she had extracted from Tyler went to use buying worn, although clean, coverlets for the bare mattresses for herself, Nell and Theo. She had also spent four shillings for a bottle of spirits of turpentine to chase away the body lice that made them scratch and itch with unbearable regularity. The turpentine burned their skin and left an oily film of acrid stink but it seemed to do the job and they were grateful. They even rinsed their hair in the vile solution and they prayed they would not be forced to shave their heads as so many of the women did to rid themselves of the vermin. With scrupulous fine combing and daily doses, the problem seemed to be resolved.

The turpentine, however beneficial, was an irritant to Nell's weakened lungs. She coughed and spat and was generally weaker, dark hollows showing beneath her too-large eyes.

Nell lay feverish in the center of her narrow pallet,

coughing and retching. That day when she had emptied her slop pail in the free-flowing cistern, one of the other inmates jostled her. Whether by accident or on purpose, the results were the same. Nell fell into the cistern, gasping and hollering and taking in great mouthfuls of filth-strewn water. It took three guards to hoist her out while Theo berated them for their slowness. Sirena had run back to their cell to retrieve a thin coverlet to wrap around the shivering Nell.

With her newfound fortune from Tyler, Sirena induced the wardeness to bring her dry clothing for Nell, throwing out the wet and stinking petticoats and underwear. Nell would not hear of tossing Theo's jacket into the rubbish and insisted that when she felt better she would wash it and it would be as good as new. It was one among many things which showed Nell's hero-worship of Theo.

Sitting outside in the yard, the hot summer sun beating down upon her did little to warm the ailing Nell. Theo watched her with worried eyes, tugging at her coverlet, tucking it high under her chin, making clucking, motherly sounds. Theo's morals may have been lacking but never her devotion to the poor, wretched creature who was her cellmate.

Now, as Nell lay shivering and coughing, Theo crooned to her, wiping her fevered brow with cool water and heaping blanket after blanket upon her thin, wasted form.

Sirena dug into her petticoat again and paid the jailor's wife for a small brazier and several bricks which they heated over the flame and tucked around Nell. When the wardeness looked down at their patient, she clicked her tongue and shook her head. Theo turned venomously on the woman, pushing her out of the cell, cursing and calling her names. Sirena realized how important Nell's survival was to Theo. If the thin, wasted woman who was racked with choking cough could survive, there was hope for the healthy, snap-eyed Theo.

Through the night and well into morning, Theo and Sirena alternated caring for Nell. When dawn was breaking over the high, gray walls of Newgate, Nell gave up the ghost, her filmy eyes looking adoringly at

Theo, silently thanking her for all she had done these past months.

The fiery-haired Theo gently released Nell's bone-thin hand and placed a last kiss on her sunken cheek. Then she and Sirena sat quietly saying their silent prayers for poor Nell, wondering who in the whole of Newgate prison would pray when death finally came to them.

Chapter Twenty-eight

Caleb stood on the deck of the gambling folly, the old feeling of being hemmed in nagging at him. It was time to close up the *Sea Siren,* repaint her hull, re-outfit her decks and change her name back to *Rana.* He wanted to take to sea again. He'd had enough. There were other things in life besides money. He would last out the winter here in London, then take on a crew and set sail in early spring. He considered going back to Batavia but thought how lonely he would be there without Regan or Sirena. No, he would see if he could secure a letter of marque from the King and set out for America.

Sirena herself had made off for parts unknown. Probably to Cádiz, Caleb thought. Even Regan, when Caleb questioned him, didn't seem to know where she had gone. It was well known that Stephan Langdon had run off from the duel with the gambler, and when Caleb had asked Regan if Sirena had left with Stephan, Regan had an unreadable expression on his face and said, "In a manner of speaking. I suppose you could say that." Then he had snapped his mouth shut and refused to say any more on the subject.

Another subject for secrecy was Regan's marriage to Camilla. Caleb knew that Regan had moved into the room behind his office on Saint Dunstan's Hill, but he hadn't given his son any explanation of the move. Caleb shrugged. When Camilla thought the time was right, she would tell Regan. He wondered how his father would take the news.

Caleb knew dissolving his business would come as a blow to Lord Farrington, but then he would hand over all the gambling equipment to him and help him get started somewhere else. The *Rana* was a seagoing ship and Caleb was glad he hadn't let Aubrey talk him into opening her hull and expanding their business dockside.

A frown pulled Caleb's mouth downward. Aubrey had been behaving very strangely as of late. Several times in the past weeks he had seemed about to confide in Caleb, but at the last minute he would clamp his lips shut and stride away. In the past month he had gone from morose to belligerent to outright hostile. Caleb didn't know what sort of trouble the lord could be in. Profits from the *Sea Siren* had skyrocketed and he had little opportunity to gamble since he put in long hours aboard the ship. Whatever it was, Caleb had no patience for coddling the ageing aristocrat. It was time Caleb got on with his life and his future, and adventure lay just over the horizon.

Caleb flexed his muscles, trying to work loose the knots of tension in his back. An ominous feeling kept wrapping him in a cloak of depression and uneasiness. His brown eyes flashed as he heard the bone crack in his back. The muscles in his chest rippled and his biceps bulged through the fine lawn of his white shirt. He threw back his head and twisted his neck to work loose the knots that were settling between his shoulders. But the ominous feeling wouldn't leave him. Should he try to talk to Aubrey again, would it do any good? No, he told himself. Aubrey was saying only what he had to say and counting his money with a vengeance. No, it was too late for talk. He would have to wait it out as Sirena had. Waiting was like a game except this time Caleb didn't know who the other players were.

Aubrey Farrington watched Caleb, a haunted look in his eye. If anyone could give Blackheart a run for his money, it would be Cal. He owed Cal more than he could ever repay and it bothered him when Cal repeatedly asked if he could help. How many more times would he have to turn on the young man? Cal could deal with the hatred and vengeance Blackheart dealt him if he were given an opportunity. If he could in some way warn him, caution him that . . . "I value my own shiftless life too much to take a chance on warning him," Farrington muttered to himself. Cal had the strength of youth on his side, plus a keen eye and sharp reflexes while he, Aubrey, was old and getting older by the moment. He no longer had the wit, the expertise to get himself out of a scrape.

His throat worked convulsively as he was hit by a thought too horrible to put into words. What if Blackheart didn't keep his promise and killed him? What if the swarthy seaman sneaked up on him after he overpowered Caleb and comandeered the ship. He wouldn't put anything past that scurve. If there were only some way he could absent himself when the event happened, he would be safe. He could hide out; he had plenty of money.

Aubrey looked skyward and felt the knots tighten in his stomach. Twelve hours more and it would be the end. The end of him and the end of Cal. What would Regan van der Rhys do when it was all over? He would bellow like a wild animal and unleash his animal strength. Wherever Aubrey went he would have to be sure that he was safe from Blackheart as well as Regan. Would he ever have a peaceful night's sleep again?

Caleb watched a seagull take flight and soar upward. He marveled at the incredible wing spread and the slow, effortless glide of the bird. He wanted to be like that—free, free to go where he wanted, do what he wanted with no ties, no binds. He watched a moment longer as the bird swooped and dipped his way into the thick, gray mist hovering overhead. Did the gull fly by instinct; did he depend on others to get what he wanted or did he do it alone? How would he find his way in the thick fog? Gut instinct, he told himself. The same gut instinct that was telling him something was going to happen, and happen soon.

If he had the sense he was born with he should up

anchor now, this minute, and sail as far away as he could. Nobody mattered to him. Not Regan, not Sirena, and certainly not the yellow-haired Camilla. He grimaced ruefully. Somewhere, someplace there was a woman who would belong to him. All he had to do was find her.

An hour before the gaming rooms were to open, Aubrey Farrington sought out Caleb and complained of severe stomach cramps. "You'll have to manage alone for a while, Cal, I have to go into town and seek out a physician. The pain is becoming unbearable," he mumbled as he grasped his stomach and wobbled back and forth over the deck.

"Of course, I can manage," Caleb said quietly. He was completely aware of the fact that Aubrey would not meet his eyes. Now, why did he want to absent himself from the *Sea Siren* this night? Damn, and Regan had said he had a pressing business engagement. Something was in the wind; and Aubrey exuded fear as though it were a tangible thing. "You better hurry before the pain gets any worse and you can't make it to the doctor."

Farrington stood up, forgetting about his stomach for a moment. "Cal . . . I . . . good luck."

"Do I need good luck to run the games tonight? What makes this evening any different from the other nights?" Caleb asked sarcastically.

"Not . . . nothing. It was just a figure of speech. I hate to leave you alone. Tonight should be a big night." In more ways than one, he muttered to himself as he scampered down the gangplank. He turned once and waved a hand wanly. "Good luck and Godspeed, young Cal," he said softly.

That evening Caleb wandered among the gaming tables and was aware of the undercurrent of charged emotions. He looked around and could find nothing to explain the feverish gambling and the reckless atmosphere. Satisfied that all was running smoothly, he walked out to the deck and stood stock-still. Even here in the stillness, the uneasy feeling wouldn't leave him.

Quietly, he called over two of the deckhands and told them to search the ship. When he was asked what they were to look for, Caleb shrugged and replied if they found it they would know. He frowned and strode to his cabin and withdrew a stiletto from his heavy sea chest. He unbuttoned his waistcoat with the intention of slipping it in the band of his trousers. Then he changed his mind and buttoned his waistcoat and slipped the blade up his sleeve. Deftly, he secured the ruffled cuff at his wrist and moved his hand back and forth. Warily, he walked back to the deck and knew that he could do no more for the moment. Whatever was going to happen would happen.

One of the deckhands returned to Caleb's side, a puzzled look on his face. "We found nothing but wet footprints on the stern deck. Someone was here and one step ahead of us. We circled the deck but could not lay hands on the intruder. The anchor chain is loose and ready, as if the order to up anchor were due any second. It's been freshly oiled, within hours, would be my guess." Caleb nodded to show he understood and told the men to go back to their duties. So, he was right. Another hour and the ship would be empty. All the gaming patrons and serving help gone. Then he would be alone with the unknown force who moved on his ship, unseen and unheard.

When the last of the kitchen help exited the ship, Caleb sprinted to his cabin and tore off his waistcoat and removed his shoes. He rolled his trousers up to his knees and, on catlike feet, moved out again to the deck. He knew the ship like the back of his hand so he had the advantage. Quietly, he extinguished each of the smoking lanterns until the *Sea Siren* was in total darkness. "Come and get me, you bastard," Caleb whispered to the stillness around him.

Stealthily, he stalked the ship, his eyes wary and alert till he came to a stop near the anchor chain. His bare foot told him the deckhand spoke the truth. Fresh grease and used lavishly.

Crouching low, he moved like a hunted animal, his teeth bared for whatever was to come.

When he felt the prick of a blade in his broad back, he was stunned. "If you move even one muscle the knife will go through your ribs." The voice was cold, deadly and familiar. The same voice that spoke with

Farrington in his cabin and whispered hoarsely on deck. "Your ship is surrounded with my men and there is no hope of escape for you. I speak the truth so do nothing rash. It's a wise man who knows when to surrender. And it's a wise man who returns to fight another day. I am the living proof of that statement. Light a lantern," he called to a figure that hovered nearby. When the lantern was lit and hanging, Caleb was told to turn around.

Caleb's eyes bulged as he backed off a step. "Blackheart!"

"Yes, Dick Blackheart at your service," the hate-filled voice sneered. "As you can see, I've lived to return another day to fight. Only my quarrel isn't with you. You, my fine young man are the bait."

"You scurve! I saw the Sea Siren kill you with my own eyes. How did you survive?" Caleb demanded harshly.

"Does it matter? A murderous attack it was. There isn't a day that goes by when my body doesn't ache with pain. In truth, I'd be better off dead. Now, it's my turn. An eye for an eye, my fine feathered friend. Very just, wouldn't you say?"

"You're a fool, Blackheart, if you think holding me will help you. Help you to do what?"

"To draw out the Sea Siren. Why else would I be here? And you're wrong, I'm not the fool, it is you who are the fool."

"The Sea Siren is dead, haven't you heard?" Caleb lied.

"The Sea Siren is very much alive and living in England. I've been watching her for months and your little lies do not bother me. I've been waiting and biding my time for a long while. You won't cheat me. I'm sailing this ship out onto open water and then a message will be sent to her. A message that you will write so that she'll know it's no trick. She'll come to your aid. And if for some reason you aren't important to her, she'll come after me to finish the job she left undone."

"You'll have to cut off my hands before I write any messages for you," Caleb said coldly.

"That, too, can be arranged. I can also manage to have an accident befall your father, the lovely Sea Siren's husband, or should I say ex-husband. You see," he sneered, "there is little I don't know. Make no mistake, you'll write the message if you want to see your father continue with his good life."

Caleb's shoulders slumped. He had to play for time until he could figure out what his next move should be. How many men did the damn cutthroat have with him? Were they as savage as he was? If he could just get the bastard alone, he would run him through the first chance he got.

As if reading Caleb's thoughts, Blackheart laughed evilly. "Don't think for one moment I'll leave you alone or that both of us will be alone together. I can no longer use a weapon to defend myself, thanks to your Sea Siren. I give only one warning and let this be it. One false move, one trick, and your father will have a knife in him. Do you understand what I just said? If your father dies it will be because of you. His death will rest on your shoulders. I want to hear you say you understand."

"Yes, I understand what you said, damn your eyes. You win. This time, but the day will come when you—"

"Enough! Lead the way to your cabin so you can write a message to the infamous Sea Siren. You know it was the name of your gaming parlor that led me to you. And to her," Blackheart laughed. "It was talked about on the docks weeks before you actually opened. Now, move! And while you're in a writing mood, you will also pen off a message to Regan van der Rhys. Just in case the Siren has any qualms about coming to help you, your father will bring pressure to bear, even if he has to kidnap her. He'll move heaven and earth to save his own flesh and blood."

Caleb moistened his lips and felt something die within him. The cutthroat spoke the truth. Caleb would do as he was told, for now. At the moment, he had no other choice.

Inside the dimly lit cabin, Blackheart tossed Caleb a quill and told him to write. "And," he said menacingly, "I can read well enough to know if you write what you're told. So no tricks!"

Sirena:

Dick Blackheart has comandeered the Rana *and says he will kill me if you don't join us at Pelee in the Caribbean. Blackheart is very much alive and means every word he says.*

Caleb

"Now write one to your father; only this time let it say, if *Sirena* doesn't join us at Pelee . . ."

Caleb looked up at Blackheart. "You know this ship hasn't seen open water since before opening the folly. Her caulking is dry and the equipment is too heavy for her top decks—"

"Shut up and write! Do you think me a fool? It's a small matter to take her down the river to Portsmouth where she'll be careened. We've plenty of time, young Caleb. All is ready and awaiting our arrival."

Regan was just closing the door of his office when Camilla disembarked from the carriage parked on the corner of Thames Street and Saint Dunstan's Hill. When she saw him, she lifted her tiny gloved hand in signal for him to wait for her. Regan sighed; he had hoped to avoid a long, tearful scene with his bride caused by his leaving the house on Drury Lane.

Resigning himself to the fact that this moment was inevitable, Regan took several steps toward her. She seemed extremely overwrought, and Regan's thoughts flew to Stephan. He himself had seen to it that everyone thought Langdon escaped London to avoid the duel with the gambler.

"Regan, Regan," Camilla called. "I'm so grateful I found you here. Please, I must talk to you! Please," she implored, her pansy-colored eyes searching his.

Resolutely, Regan fished for his keys in his pocket and turned back to the office door. In a moment he had the lamps lit and he placed himself at the desk opposite his wife.

"I think I should warn you, Camilla. I'm not in the mood for a long-drawn-out scene. Can you get to the point? If it's about me returning to the house on Drury

Lane, forget it. It's over, Camilla. It was a nice try, but it's over."

Camilla shook her head, her yellow curls bobbing on her head. "No, no, that's not why I'm here. Actually, if you hadn't left, I would have had to. Regan, I came here for your help."

"How much do you want," Regan said crassly, reaching for his pocket.

"No, I don't need money. You were very generous, thank you. First of all, I came to tell you something and then I want you to help me. Only, I don't know where to begin," she faltered. "It's such a long, involved story."

Regan had never seen Camilla like this. And she wasn't crying in an hysterical tantrum; she seemed truly in distress. "Start at the beginning, Camilla, I've all night. I was on my way to see Caleb to tell him I could give him a hand after all. Originally, I had a business appointment, but that was canceled. Just take a deep breath and start from the beginning."

Camilla stared at Regan wide-eyed. She had never known him to be so patient with her. Perhaps telling him would be easier than she had thought. "Regan, a long time ago I met Tyler Sinclair . . ."

Regan listened incredulously to Camilla's sordid tale. She spared no detail, telling him how she and Stephan had contrived to lure him into marriage for the sake of his money. She told him how Stephan had worked on Sirena to the same end. But, most of all, she told him how she had never stopped loving Tyler and that she would love him if he were a penniless pauper living at the Haymarket.

The further she progressed with her story, the wider the grin on Regan's face got. At the end they found themselves laughing together over the way each had expected the other to bring a fortune to the marriage.

Regan supposed he should be incensed at how he was duped, but he was so relieved to know their marriage had never been legal and binding, he graciously assured her he would never press charges. Then Camilla's eyes filled with tears again. "And that's why I've come to you, Regan, to explain everything and to beseech your help. Tyler is missing! He's not anywhere in the city. I've even checked with the Baroness' staff and they all assured me that Tyler did not sail to the Netherlands with his parents. Why, the housekeeper saw them off herself!"

"Where do you think he could be?" Regan asked. He was willing to bet Tyler had somehow implicated himself in Stephan's killing and had fled London with Sirena.

"I have no idea! And that's why I'm beginning to panic. Regan, Tyler would never just leave the city this way, without a good-bye or anything. No, he's in trouble, I know it, I just know it!"

Regan was moved by Camilla's tears. Reaching over his desk, he patted her hand comfortingly. "There, there, don't cry. It won't help us find Tyler."

"Us?" Camilla asked querulously. "Does that mean you'll help me?"

"It does. Now, can you tell me where his office clerk lives? Perhaps I'll pay the young man a visit." Regan lifted his timepiece from his waistcoat pocket and studied it. Caleb would just have to do without him tonight.

Sirena combed her hair idly, watching Theo out of the corner of her eye. It had been two days since they had come and dragged poor Nell's body out of their cell. Theo was already showing the effects of Nell's death. She hadn't combed her hair or washed her face. Her hands were gray and grimy and there was a thin line of black forming beneath her nails. The healthy pallor of her skin now looked sickly and green and there were hollows in her cheeks because she had refused all food.

Sirena understood Theo's depression. Nell's death had proven her own mortality to her. "Theo, please have a sip of mead, and there's still a bit of meat left from this afternoon's meal. Take it before you waste away."

Theo looked at Sirena vacantly, shaking her head in refusal. "I don't think I could get it down, Sirena. Thank you." Even her voice lacked its usual vibrance.

"Are you going to sit there and waste away till they come to drag you out by your heels?" Sirena had lost all patience. Her tone was harder than she intended.

Theo looked up at her, a sneer turning down the corners of her wide, full mouth. "What do you know?"

"I know enough to survive! Do you think Nell is the first woman to die in this stinking place? Now shape up, Theo, before they bring out the death cart for you!"

"What if they do? It will happen sooner or later. None of us has a chance here, including you, Sirena."

"No. I won't believe to that. Listen to me, Theo, I've gone through hell many times. There were moments I thought it was the end for me. But it wasn't, because I wouldn't allow it!" There was a spark in Theo's black eyes and Sirena knew she had captured her curiosity. Theo looked at her the same way Nell had looked at Theo when she waited to hear some bawdy fantastic tale of life in an exclusive bordello. Or for Theo to regale them with tales of the theater, which was prohibited to women at that time in London. Theo's stories had kept them alive, including Sirena. Now it was Sirena's turn to repay the favor.

"What kind of hell could you know about? It's clear from your manner of speaking and everything else about you that you were born with a silver spoon in your mouth!"

"Perhaps I was. And I'm wealthy to this day. But I'm not talking about money, I'm talking about living! I fought for my life. I know how easy it is to have that feeble flame flicked out, Theo, and I'm not about to help it extinguish itself. I wanted to live; I want to live now and always will. When my time comes, I won't give up easily, I can promise you that."

Theo brushed the hair out of her eyes and Sirena tossed her the comb. "Now, if you fix yourself up a bit, I might be induced to tell you a story." Theo ran the comb through her hair, pulling at the snarls and tangles which matted near the ends. Her eyes never left Sirena's face, waiting for her next words. Sirena had always been very closemouthed about herself, answering even the most basic questions with a yes or no.

"Tell me, Theo," Sirena began, "have you ever heard the tale of the Sea Siren?"

Chapter Twenty-nine

The jailor's wife was announced by the jingling of her keys and the sound of her voice. Sirena and Theo looked at each other in puzzlement. Instead of the harsh cursing which usually preceded the woman's arrival, her tone was soft and womanly, almost coy as she giggled over something someone had said.

"What has gotten into that hag?" Theo questioned.

"It almost sounds as though she's flirting, doesn't it?" Sirena smiled. Suddenly, she jumped from the bed and straightened her skirts and rubbed her face to bring color into her cheeks. Regan. It had to be him. She had seen him have that effect on hundreds of women. Then she heard a deep, booming voice and knew she had been right.

A moment more and he stood outside her cell looking well and fit. She stepped sideways, sliding into a shadow to hide her appearance. "Sirena? Where are you?" he asked.

"She's in there all right, sir," the wardeness said coyly, looking at his fine, strong build and sheaf of near-white hair with interest. "Mayhap she doesn't want ye ta see what's become o' 'er 'ere in Newgate."

Sirena stepped forward. "Regan. I'm glad you've come."

"Can you open the door for me?" he asked the wardeness, his clear, blue eyes smiling down at her. The jailor's wife pushed her greasy hanks of hair from her face and preened, took the keys from about her waist and opened the cell door.

"If'n ye be needin' anythin', just call. Me name is Myrtle."

"I'll do that, Myrtle," Regan said softly, flattering her with his notice.

Theo scrutinized this tall, blond man who had captured the heart of the infamous Sea Siren. Seeing him, she could understand why Sirena had sailed the seas from Batavia in search of him; why she had been willing to move heaven and earth to make him love her again. As the snap-eyed redhead saw the way Regan was looking at Sirena, she knew that whatever lengths Sirena had gone to to make Regan love her again it had all been in vain. To Theo's wise and knowing eyes, it was apparent Regan had never stopped loving Sirena.

Regan stepped close to Sirena, and his hands wanted to reach out to brush away the pain he saw in her eyes. "I've come to take you home, Sirena."

"Would you like me to step out?" Theo asked, not wanting to intrude on this reunion.

"No, Theo, that won't be necessary. There's nothing Regan can say to me you can't hear. Is there, Regan?" Sirena said, her eyes flashing.

Regan turned and looked at Theo for the first time. "I suppose not. I've come to take Sirena home."

"Home?" Sirena asked querulously. "Where's home? I have no home, Regan."

"Look, I haven't come to argue. I'm taking you out of this place. Now, if there's anything you have to bring with you, get it and come along."

"Not until I explain a few things," Sirena protested. "I didn't send you the letter you obviously received, Tyler did."

"I know that. The signature was obviously not by your hand and who else, aside from Tyler, would realize I could be contacted through his clerk? Now, don't carry on, Sirena." Regan bristled. "Let it be enough that matters have been resolved and the King and captain of the galleon accept your apologies and restitution. The thieves, they squeezed out ten times the amount over what the actual damages were."

"And my crew? Tyler?"

"All has been taken care of, they were released several hours ago. I sent all of them, except Tyler, to your ship to make ready to sail. Tyler has sworn never to set foot on another ship."

"Are you telling me I've been banished from England? Little I care, Regan, this country has nothing to offer me."

"You haven't been banished, not at all. But I need the *Sea Spirit*, Sirena, mine are all at sea, and I need your crew, but most of all I need you. Caleb needs you." Regan's expression was grave and somber and there was a deep hurt in his eyes, turning them cloudy. "I received a message, and when I went by your house on King Street, you'd also received one. Your past has come back to haunt you, Sirena, only this time it affects the innocent. I'll read it to you," Regan said, reaching in his coat and withdrawing the letter in Caleb's handwriting.

When she heard what it said, Sirena remained passive, her eyes downcast. "Did you hear what this letter said?" Regan demanded.

"I heard and I'm thinking what I should do. Caleb is *your* son, Regan, not mine. You do recall the day you pointed that out to me, don't you?"

Regan cringed as though he had been struck by a blow. "Yes, I remember, but I also remember the circumstances. I was angry then and I didn't mean what I said!"

Regan looked into her eyes and wanted to gather her close, to ease away her anguish for those long ago memories. He wanted to make right the wrongs he had done her. The misunderstandings between them. "You forget, Sirena, Mikel was also my son." His voice, while quiet, resounded throughout the cell and sounded hollow to his own ears.

"Yes, he was your son, Regan, and contrary to what you think, Caleb is more than a son to me. Between Caleb and myself there is a bond stronger than a woman giving birth to a child. When I call Caleb 'little brother,' it means more than that, much more. I'll find Caleb and I'll help free him from the monster who holds him captive. But I do it for Caleb, not for you, Regan."

"Then let it be for Caleb. That is more than I have a right to ask. Hurry, have you everything?"

Theo rushed to Sirena and threw her arms around her neck. "Good-bye, Sirena, good luck. Think of me sometimes."

Sirena held Theo close and looked into Regan's eyes. "Isn't there some way . . . could you . . . ?"

Regan stepped over to the cell door. "Myrtle! Myrtle! Where are you, sweetheart. Come here, I've got something for you!"

The wardeness pranced down the corridor and opened the door to the cell. Her face was flushed and she seemed flustered. How long had it been since a handsome gentleman like Regan called her sweetheart? "What can I be doin' fer ye, sir?"

"Myrtle, darling, I seem to have run into a problem and I know you can help me out of it. This stubborn woman here," he said, pointing to Sirena, "has vowed to spend her last days here in Newgate rather than leave her friend behind. You don't suppose we can come up with something between the two of us, do you?"

"D' ye want me ta use me bull's pizzle on her?" she asked, delighted with the notion.

"Only if it must come to that," Regan hastened to say. "Look here, darling, surely you can find some use for this," he said, pulling forth a purse heavy with coins. "Last time I looked there was two hundred pounds in there. Now, if by some chance you could say that Theo had . . . er . . . passed on during the night, that money could be yours and none the wiser."

Myrtle's fascination with the purse almost made her slaver. Looking up at Regan, she smiled her black-toothed smile. "Well, as it happens, sir, there was a poor lass from the Debtor's side who met 'er maker durin' the night. It would seem the poor little thin' had no family ta claim 'er. Who's ta say it weren't Theo 'ere?"

"No one. I'm certain," Regan assured, pressing the purse into her hand. "Of course, we will be wanting to leave at once. Can it be arranged?"

"If'n she was to wear that one's cloak and pull the hood over her 'ead ta 'ide that fiery 'air o' 'ers. I'll walk ye out to the gates myself, sir. It's time I 'ad me a breath o' fresh air!"

Theo seemed dazed by her good fortune. She was constantly thanking Regan and Sirena for getting her out of Newgate. There was a new life in her black eyes and her cheeks were tinged with pink. In the carriage Sirena wrote a note to Tyler and handed it to Theo. "Now, promise me you'll take this to the address on the back. His name is Sir Tyler Payne Sinclair, Esquire. He's my business manager. I've told him to give you a thousand pounds, Theo. All I want in return is your promise never to put yourself in such straits as to land in Newgate again."

"A thousand pounds! Lor' wha' a lass couldn't do wi' a thousand pounds!" Suddenly, she clapped her hand over her mouth and looked at Sirena, who began laughing till tears formed in her eyes. In her excitement, Theo had slipped back into her native cockney and had given herself away.

"When you said what a marvelous actress you were, Theo, I didn't half realize how truthful you were being. Oh, if those slobs in Newgate could only know the refined and articulate girl they called the 'Duchess' was really a cockney."

"And if they had known," Theo said, slipping back into her Duchess role, "do you think they would have respected me? Oh, no, they would have torn my hair out!"

After the final kisses good-bye and good wishes and promises to stay in touch with Tyler, who could keep them in contact with one another, Theo climbed from the coach. "You've given me a new start on life, Regan, and I won't forget it. If there's ever anything I can do for you, let me know."

When they were alone, Sirena looked at Regan. "That was a wonderful thing you did for Theo, Regan. I know how careful you've had to be with your money and realize how generous you were."

"It was only money, Sirena. You can't put a price on life." His voice was somber and serious as though he were remembering something painful. Then he brightened. "The two hundred pounds was a lot easier to give than that kiss to Myrtle whan we reached the gate. God! What a hag!"

Regan and Sirena laughed. The first laugh they'd shared together since before Mikel had died. It felt good and natural, as though all the awful events since that time had never happened. When Regan reached out and touched Sirena's hand, she clasped it as they thought again of the smitten, black-toothed Myrtle.

Tyler Payne Sinclair stepped lightly out of the carriage that brought him to Camilla's house on Drury Lane. He smoothed the hair at his temples and frowned when he saw how pale his hand was in the bright sunlight. Prison pallor. Even with paying easement for better food and larger portions, Tyler's clothes were too large by several sizes. He was self-conscious of the way his frock coat sagged over his chest.

Earlier that day, Regan had come to Newgate to see him. He had explained in detail the restitution necessary to resolve the upset with the King and captain of the galleon the *Sea Spirit* had damaged. He had also told him of Camilla's confession to him and that he held no malice toward either of them. Regan was greatly relieved to be free of a loveless marriage and wished them both well. Tyler expected to hear him say that Camilla and Tyler deserved each other, but he hadn't. Before leaving, Regan explained that he hadn't told Camilla of Stephan's death, he was leaving that chore to Tyler. Wordlessly, there was a communication between the two men that Sirena would not be implicated in Stephan's death.

Tyler stepped up the wide tiled stairs to the front door and lifted the brass knocker. He was prepared to announce himself to the servant answering the door when the solid mahogany panel flew open and there stood Camilla. For what seemed an eternity they stared at each other, each drinking in the sight of the other. Tyler could see faint purple smudges beneath her blue eyes and her long dark lashes were moist and spiked as though she had been crying.

Camilla noticed immediately the weight Tyler had lost and his pallor, and her heart went out to him. "Tyler!" she breathed, hardly more than a whisper. Her knees felt shaky and she nearly tumbled into his waiting arms.

He was overcome with the sight of her, the feel of her in his arms, the sweet clean fragrance emanating from her silky yellow curls. And when his mouth touched hers he savored the taste of her, reveling in the fact that her mouth sought his just as eagerly.

Camilla pulled Tyler into the house, closing the door behind her and leaning against it for support. "I thought you were dead," she whispered tonelessly, her distress showing in her eyes. "I thought I would never have the chance to tell you how much you meant to me; how much I love you."

Suddenly she was in his arms again and he soothed her tears and quieted her, holding her fast, swearing he would never leave her again, never let her go.

When at last their torrent of emotions was under control, Tyler led Camilla into the drawing room, seating her gently on the settee and sitting down beside her. "Camilla, sweetheart, there's something I must tell you."

She looked at him, her huge eyes holding puzzlement and fear. "You've come to tell me about father, haven't you?" she said softly. "Then tell me, Tyler, quickly, before I lose my courage."

"Stephan is dead, sweetheart. I . . . I saw him go over the side during a storm." His voice was gentle, consoling.

"You saw him go over the side? Side of what?" Camilla persisted.

"Your father was running away from a duel, Camilla. Frightened, he learned of a ship in the harbor which was sailing to Ireland. I had gone to the house on King Street just as he was preparing to leave. He begged me, pleaded with me, to accompany him so I could introduce him to family friends in Waterford. I did. That first day out a storm came up quite unexpectedly. Stephan . . . went over the rail. He's dead, Camilla." Tyler scrutinized her face for sign of emotion.

"I'm glad he's dead, Tyler," Camilla said in a barely audible voice. "He can't hurt anyone again. He was my father but I'd always suspected what connection he had in my mother's death. When I learned the truth, I wanted nothing more to do with him. I suppose what I'm feeling right now is regret for the man I thought he was; not for the man he truly was. Camilla's eyes cleared and the corners of her mouth lifted hesitantly in a smile. "All that matters to me, Tyler, is that we can be together."

His arms tightened about her, drawing her to him, pressing her close. Camilla offered herself to him, reveling in his embrace, feeling his love nourish her soul. There would never be another man for her. Only Tyler. Always Tyler.

Sirena leaned against the quarterdeck rail, watching her crew lay in stores. Regan had calculated that the journey to the Caribbean would take roughly fifty days, providing they were lucky and caught the easterlies. Jacobus was directing Jan where to put the crates of live chickens they would need for their voyage and the pig for a change of diet. Salted meat and grains were hauled on board by the sackful, along with numerous casks of fresh water in which a limestone had been dropped to keep it sweet.

As Sirena surveyed all the activity going on around her, she scowled. Regan, who was testing the rigging and had jumped the last few feet to the deck, observed her. "What's troubling you, Sirena? Have you thought of something we've forgotten?"

Sirena looked up distractedly. "I was just wondering when Blackheart found the time to lay in the stores needed to make a journey of this length. Even calculating the time from when he left, doesn't it seem like a terribly long way to go just to avenge himself on me?"

Regan's eyes widened. "I should have thought of it myself. I see what you mean. Where are your charts?"

"In the cabin," Sirena said, starting for the sterncastle.

Regan peered over the charts. "Pelee," he murmured, drawing lines and calculating routes. "It's just as you suspected, Sirena. The quickest way to Pelee is along this route; all the others go round about the Caribbean Isles. Blackheart knows we wouldn't waste time weaving in and out of these islands, so he's pretty certain of which course we would take. Even if he miscalculated us, he'd still catch up to us in Pelee."

Sirena was excited. "And knowing our course, he could come up behind us while we're at sea! Blackheart never meant to sail all the way to the Caribbean to pay a debt owed."

"That's right. Unless I miss my guess, he'll be waiting for us right here," the point of his quill stabbed the map just at the cliffs of Dover. "There's plenty of places to take cover around the western side. We'd sail right out on top of him and never see him until it was too late. That bastard is only four days away, not sixty!"

Suddenly Regan sobered. "Sirena, I don't want you to come with us. Now that we've uncovered his most likely plan, I think the men and myself can handle it."

"I thought you wanted me to come. That's what you said yesterday in Newgate."

"I know what I said, but that was because I wanted the best crew available, the best possible seamen, the most courageous fighters. You, Sirena are all those things. I wanted the best and I asked you." His voice grew gruff, as though embarrassed by admitting these things.

"And have I changed since then? Am I less an able-bodied seaman? Am I not a courageous fighter? Don't say any more, Regan, I go with you."

"No! You will stay here in London. I've made up my mind and I'll hear no more about it."

"You seem to forget, Mynheer van der Rhys. This is *my* ship and *I* give the orders. Either I go with you or you find another ship and another crew. That is final." The heat of her temper blazed in her cheeks and lit her eyes from within. Regan stared down at her and she backed away.

"You also seem to forget that you're a married man!" Before he could say a word in protest, she turned and went out on deck.

The evening tide rose with the moon and the *Sea Spirit*'s moorings and broadsides groaned with pleasure at her release from the quay. Sirena stood on board, watching Regan take the wheel, guiding her ship down the Thames to its mouth. Regan's hands were firm on the spokes and his eyes peered ahead watching for small craft and buoys marking the channel. The sight of him standing there nearly took her breath away. He handled the ship the way he handled a woman, the way he had handled her, with concentration and a gentle touch.

The moonlight reflected off his hair in a silvery halo. The fine white lawn and billowing sleeves of his shirt fluttered in the breeze, his breeches hugged his firm muscular thighs and the pigskin boots he wore gave him an air of the military. He hasn't changed, Sirena thought. He's as handsome as when I first met him. The expanse of his chest which showed in the gap at the neck of his shirt had whitened from lack of exposure to the sun; but his strong capable hands and his face still held traces of a bronzed tan. He still exuded that healthy strength, that feeling of being at one with the elements.

He had not tried to speak with her since she had stormed out of the cabin that afternoon and she wondered what he had been about to say when she turned her back on him. Perhaps it was time they stopped this game-playing and spoke what was on their minds. To hell with the fact he was married to Camilla. She loved him; she had always loved him; that would never change. She had allowed pride to come between them and she had sworn it would never happen again, but it had and there was no retreating. What mattered was the present, and Sirena didn't want to face possible death without having told him that she loved him still. The past was past and it could only rear its ugly head if they allowed it. Now, with the prospect of meeting Blackheart again, she realized how precious life was and how much the prospect of confronting that scurve frightened her.

She had been pushing it down since Regan had come to Newgate and told her about Caleb. She was frightened of Blackheart. Facing him would be another open confrontation and she didn't think she could defend herself against him. Too much blood had flowed past the tip of her rapier. She didn't know if she could kill again and, with Blackheart, it would come to kill or be killed.

The *Sea Spirit* slid through the dark water and Sirena was looking at London's rooftops against the night sky. She had admitted her worst fears to herself and was better for it.

The hour was late, and when she looked toward the wheel, Willem mastered the ship. The thought of going back to her cabin did not appeal to her. She wanted to see the stars in the sky and feel the breeze on her cheeks. Her feet found their nimble way past the coils of rigging and marine equipment to the bow. The *Sea Spirit*'s bowsprit was painted white and reached out over the water as though it were pointing a path to the brightest star. She leaned over the rail and felt the salt tang wet her cheeks, or was it tears? The night was silent and clear as they glided free of London into the wider channel. Suddenly, she was aware of someone behind her. Sirena turned and looked up into his beloved face. His arms came around her, holding her tightly. She pressed her face against the place where his shirt came away and felt his hard chest beneath her lips. She answered his embrace and her love overflowed.

In his embrace she was safe. She could hide behind his strength until her own courage was restored. His arms protected her, sheltered her from the world. His solid virility shielded her from the unknown and became a haven where she could revive her flagging will and brace herself against the terror of things to come.

"Tell me," he said, his voice warm and gentle.

"I'm afraid," were the only words she spoke, yet he understood.

He lifted her off her feet and took her to the place where the bowsprit rose out of the scrubbed deck. He sat, leaning against the rail, cradling her as though she were a small child. He did not speak, yet offered her his protection. Long into the night he held her, loving her.

She felt his caring in his touch, in the tender way his lips rested against her brow and in his silent comprehension. She had never loved him more than she did at this moment, when they watched the stars blink at them from the heavens, leading them onward, together.

The Moon made its graceful arc across the sky and Sirena nestled against his chest, feeling as though she were an extension of him. His arms kept her warm, his fingers making tiny, soothing circles on the flesh of her arm. This is the way it feels to be reborn, regenerated, she thought silently. This is where I begin and end, here with Regan. Out there, somewhere, my fate awaits me, but for the moment I am here, with my love, sheltered by his love.

If they slept, she did not know it, and if they moved, she was not aware of it. On through the night he held her, letting his love flow into her, asking for nothing, save her acceptance of him. Giving her all he had to offer. And when the sky began to light he pressed his lips against her ear and whispered, "And now, my love, let me tell you about my marriage to Camilla."

She let him tell her, listening silently. And when he was through, a smile brighter than the new sun upon the glistening waters lit her face and she found her peace.

The next two days were an idyll. The crew attended to their chores in quiet respect of Regan and Sirena's newfound love. The days were bright and joyous, a balm to the soul. And the nights were long and silent and they passed them in each other's arms, renewing their passions and feeding their desires. It was their last night wrapped in their snug little world. Tomorrow, dawn, would show them the chalk-white cliffs of Dover and the brutal power of Blackheart.

Regan joined Sirena in their cabin where she was brushing her lustrous black hair. Her arms were lifted to her head, revealing the outline of her proud breasts beneath her nightshirt. The lamp cast its yellow light onto her face, polishing her skin with buff tones of ivory.

He had never known her to be more beautiful. Her features were calm and serene; her eyes were aglow with her love for him. Wordlessly, he took the brush from her hand and smoothed her sable curls with his palm, feeling the silky strands between his fingers and thinking her hair was like the sea itself. Dark and curling and glowing with a light of its own.

When she turned to him it was to offer her lips and body in tribute to their love. There was a hint of desperation in her kiss and the way her arms wound around his neck, as though she would never let him go. Her emotions found an answering response in Regan and his mouth took hers greedily. Unable to satisfy his need for her, Sirena's fears for the future echoed in the core of him.

They were both aware what the confrontation with Blackheart could mean. Death was eternal, a forever loss, and it was looming out there, beyond the world they had created for themselves. Both were aware of the havoc and destruction which threatened their bliss. But they still had tonight and their bodies could comfort and be comforted and their rapture could ease their hearts.

She separated from him and Regan looked down adoringly at her. It was as though he were trying to memorize her features, her lips, her eyes, the classic tilt of her nose. Tenderly they silently agreed to commit this moment to memory, to have it, to cherish it whatever the fates might bring. Their hands reached out for one another, softly touching, sweetly caressing; hair, cheeks, lips. Rediscovering the wonders of each other, those intimate, beautiful differences which made them unique. The turn of a lip, the tilt of an eye, the soft, velvety feel of an earlobe. They were like children discovering a world of glorious wonder.

Tenderly, so tenderly, Regan removed her nightshirt, touching his lips to those soft, mysterious places near the back of her neck and the crease where her arm rested against her breast. His mouth lingered, giving and taking pleasure and love.

Her hands sought the skin of his back beneath his shirt and luxuriated in his warmth. He shrugged out of his shirt, freeing himself for her touch. Her mouth covered the place where his neck joined with his shoulders and she was aware of the shudder of delight and anticipation which coursed through him. A tear fell from her eye and rained down her cheek. Seeing it, Regan kissed it away, tasting the saltiness of it, as though it had come from the sea. And he knew and understood though not a word passed between them that her fingers and lips were committing him to memory. That her lips and eyes were devouring him in tiny pieces, so that if the fates should be cruel and if she were the only one to survive, she would be able to close her eyes and see him again as he was now; remember the feel of him, the taste of him, and live again this last night of bittersweet love.

Regan moved away from her and when they touched again he was naked just as she was. Magic spun a web and cloaked them from the world. They were two in love as none before and none after would ever be. And when his hands slid down her body, it was to adore her, worship her, take her with him to newfound heights, where passions of the flesh became a gift to the gods.

She offered herself to him, her body a shrine on the altar of their love. Never had their love been so pure and untainted, untarnished by the misunderstandings that had always loomed between them. They were one in body and heart. As they lay in each other's embrace, their desires sated, they knew they had the strength to face what must be confronted.

Sirena's eyes were bright and clear, unclouded by the apprehensions which had haunted her. She would face Blackheart with courage and valor. She had the world now, and the stars in the heavens. She had it all. Regan loved her.

Chapter Thirty

Regan and Sirena stood together near the wheel, their eyes turned toward starboard as the high cliffs of Dover loomed in the distance. The early-morning sun cast a golden light over their chalk-white surfaces and they seemed like sentinels guarding the gateway to the Atlantic.

Regan's arm slipped around Sirena's waist, his hand warm and confident against her bare midriff. She turned to smile up into his eyes. She was ready to face anything, anyone. She was restored.

The current and the tide complemented the winds and the *Sea Spirit* sailed toward the end of land as if the ship knew that beyond the soaring cliffs she would find open water. Regan and Sirena found themselves holding their breaths. If their instincts were correct, Blackheart would be hiding on the westerly side of the jutting cliffs. It would be only moments before they gained free water and they waited expectantly to see the *Rana* slide out of hiding and follow them out of the channel.

Sirena's prayers echoed Regan's. Dear God, let Caleb be alive and well.

Ten minutes out into the Atlantic and a cry was heard, "Sail ho!"

Regan and Sirena had seen it also and he looked to her to give the order. "Loosen sail!" her voice rang out, strong and sure and unwavering.

"A kiss for luck, sweetheart," Regan murmured, finding her lips with his. "This is your show, Sirena, give him hell!"

The sleek, three-masted frigate was coming about. "Heel to starboard and make ready to come alongside!" she ordered her crew. "Willem, to the wheel! Jacobus, down below!"

The old man was about to protest, but saw the determination in her eyes and realized it was useless. Coffee mugs clattering, he went toward the galley, closing the door behind him.

"Regan, look! There he is! Jan, hand me the spyglass." Their attention was focused on the *Rana*'s mizzenmast. Lifting the lens to her eye, she focused on a figure secured there with his arms stretched behind him to encompass the thick, sturdy beam.

"I see him, Regan. Here, look. He's alive!"

Regan took the glass from her. She saw some of the tension go out of his shoulders and the lines of his mouth relaxed. "So he is, the young cub. Thank God for that." Regan trained the glass on the oncoming ship. "I count six crewmen and old Blackheart himself. Good Lord, Sirena, have you seen him?"

He handed her the glass. "There, on the quarterdeck."

Sirena focused on the *Rana*'s quarterdeck. She gasped when she saw Blackheart hobble across the deck, one leg dragging behind him, his left arm held at an awkward angle. "No wonder he wants to kill me. He's maimed beyond all help, Regan, and I did it to him." She allowed the hand holding the spyglass to fall to her side. Her eyes clouded over.

Regan took her by the shoulders. "I won't have you punishing yourself for what's become of that scurve. He should have died long ago when you found him among my crew. He's an evil man, Sirena, and never forget what he did to you. Never. Remember your uncle and your sister and what he did to them! You can never go back, Sirena, only ahead, and it has come down to either you or him!"

Regan's words awakened a long-dormant portion of her memory. She thought of the man Blackheart had once been, strong and powerful and evil. Only the evil remained. She had once thought herself rid of the stain he had put upon her; she had thought that part of her life over, dead along with Blackheart himself. But it wasn't; it could never be as long as he drew breath. But how could he fight in his present condition? It would be worse than murder.

Seeing Caleb stretched on the mast strengthened her resolve. Caleb. He was the reason she had survived the ordeal with Blackheart's crew. Caleb. He had nursed her back to health. He had instilled in her a will to survive. He had witnessed her debasement with eyes older than time itself and his compassion and understanding had seen her through the most terrible trial of her life. Sirena lifted the glass to her eye again. Caleb was still strapped to the mizzenmast, struggling against his bonds. She remembered another time she had seen him strapped there, with the flesh of his back exposed and taking a cruel lashing at Blackheart's hands. And the boy had not cried out. That was the most terrible part of it all. His silence and his wordless suffering.

And that last day flashed through Sirena's memory, when her spirit and will to survive had been restored and Blackheart sent her to his cabin. Her eyes narrowed and her chest rose with deep, heavy breaths. That was the final straw and she would never forget or forgive him. Her skin had had a crawling sensation for what she knew he would do to her. "You're mine now," he had growled. "The crew won't come near you again."

Sirena had backed away, dreading the touch of his pawlike callused hands. But there was no escaping his long arms which pulled her toward him, crushing her. With savage intent, he had wound his fingers in her sable curls and yanked her head back until she had thought her neck would snap. His thick, wet mouth had burned her throat where he kissed her, nipping at her tender flesh, making her recoil.

"Sirena!" She had been so lost in her thoughts the sound of Regan's voice startled her, making her jump. She had retreated so far into the past and with such concentration she had not even been aware that the *Rana* had pulled alongside, dangerously close. Blackheart had left a scarce ten feet between the hulls and the two ships rose and fell together on the swells like lovers in the throes of passion.

Her green eyes flashed and skimmed the decks of the *Rana,* the hunted searching for the hunter.

"Sirena!" came a hoarse cry from the deck of the sterncastle. "Are you ready to feel the point of my blade?" Blackheart hobbled crablike across the deck, his once great height diminished by his maiming. She could see him clearly now, his face a feral mask of vengeance, a fire of insanity banked in his eyes.

"How do you like the popinjay I've secured to the mizzenmast? Have you come to watch me carve his guts from his body? I told him you would come! I knew you would!"

"So I have," she called back, her voice, strong and clear, rang out over the water. "And now that I am here, what is your next move?"

"Don't you know?" he laughed. "Can't you guess? Shall I come to you or will you come to me?"

"Stay there! It is fitting I end it where it all began—on the *Rana!*"

Regan looked hesitant when she asked him to heel

into the *Rana* and throw a plank between the rails. Her finely muscled legs found their footing and she stepped lightly and quickly across the plank and leaped onto the deck of the *Rana*. She avoided Caleb's eyes, not wanting to see what she would find there. She had expected Regan to follow her, but when she quickly looked about, he was nowhere in sight.

"Come and get me, Blackheart," she beckoned with her rapier. "Let's get it done with. Or don't you have the guts? Did I kill at least that in you?" Sirena brazened.

"As you can see, I'm not quite the man I was. So, I have come prepared to even the odds."

"Sirena!" Caleb cried. "Watch out. He has a pistol!"

Sirena rapidly sidestepped as the ball whizzed past her ear and soared out to open water. Blackheart stood holding the smoking weapon.

"Would you have me believe you would end this so quickly? After all these years of planning, that you would merely point your gun and finish it? And what would you do with the remainder of your life?" she asked. "What would be your reason for living?"

Her alert eye saw his hand tremble. She knew that he, too, had thought of this. Once the Sea Siren was dead, Blackheart might just as well follow her corpse into the sea. All the purpose to his life would be swallowed beneath the swells.

His good right arm reached into his belts and withdrew another pistol, and she heard the click as his thumb brought back the hammer to cock it. He laughed, a wicked, menacing laugh. "Your cutlass will do you little good, Siren! You won't get close enough to me to use it! I mean to shoot you dead where you stand. I should have spilled your blood along with the rest of the crew when I first set foot aboard this vessel so long ago. I was a whole man then, and I had other appetites as you must well remember. But I'm as good as dead now, with what you've left me. And the dead belong with the dead, Sea Siren. It will be you and me for the rest of eternity!" He threw back his head and laughed, taking his eyes off her for that one second.

Like a flash of lightning, she closed the distance between them, holding her cutlass out before her, ready to sever his arm from his shoulder if he raised the pistol in her direction again.

Blackheart recovered and waved his arm, menacing her with his weapon. "I've got a good shot left in me, Siren, and you're going to have it." He leveled his arm, directing the barrel straight at her; she could see his finger playing with the trigger, seemingly reluctant to have it done with.

Was this how it was going to end? she thought wildly. Here on the deck of the *Rana* without a chance to defend herself? At least she had given him that . . . a chance.

Over the rail of the sterncastle a figure climbed. Regan! He dripped seawater on the deck, his hair was plastered to his face. That's why she hadn't seen him after she boarded. He had gone overboard and swam to the *Rana*'s stern, taking the dangerous climb up the anchor chain and halyards.

Blackheart saw her attention focus on a point behind him, and turning, he saw Regan approach and fired. The sharp, crackling sound rang out over the waters.

Sirena acted instantly on impulse to finish Blackheart. He had dared to attack Regan. No one, not the Devil himself would be permitted to harm the man she loved! All reluctance because of Blackheart's disabilities was dispelled. In three long leaps she covered the distance between herself and the pirate. Her cutlass found its way between his ribs as he moved to face her.

She watched the expression on his face pass from hate to incredulity. Blackheart sank to his knees, clutching his chest. Blood bubbled up in a froth on his lips and drenched the deck red.

He lay crumpled on the boards, more dead than alive. His mouth worked with difficulty as he tried to utter his last earthly words. Stepping close to him, Sirena watched his hand reach out to grasp her boot. His grip was loose, no strength in his meaty, pawlike hand. He breathed harshly, choking and sputtering on his own blood. "You should have finished it the first time. And now it is done."

Sirena backed away, pulling her ankle free of his

hand. It was a full moment before she realized Blackheart was at last dead.

Regan came to stand beside her as they turned to face the commotion behind them. The crew of the *Sea Spirit* had come aboard the *Rana,* blades and pistols drawn. Blackheart's men, having no stomach for a fight, agreed to come peacefully.

Together, Regan and Sirena went to the mizzenmast where Caleb was still held by his bindings. Taking the dagger from his belt, Regan cut his son free and clasped him tightly. No words were necessary. In tacit understanding they clapped one another on the back, the way men do at times to express strong emotion. Caleb turned to Sirena, a sheepish grin on his face. Instantly she was in his arms, both forgiving and being forgiven for the anger that had been between them.

Blackheart's scurves were escorted across the plank to the *Sea Spirit* and Jan offered Sirena a jaunty salute.

"Capitana!" Willem called from the quarterdeck. "Shall I toss him over the side?" he asked, pointing to Blackheart's inert form.

Sirena's eyes fell to the body near Willem's feet. Her eyes became cloudy and her expression sober. Her eyes flashed spars of green lightning and her voice was stern and crisp. "Give him a decent burial, Willem. Take him aboard the *Sea Spirit* and have Jacobus prepare him for the sea. And when you say a prayer for his soul say it at the top of your voices. Perhaps it will serve to remind God's angels that once he had a soul."

Jacobus smiled toothlessly and called from the deck, "Can we go to Cádiz, now? Wilhelmina will be worried about me!"

"Who?" Sirena called, her eyes puzzled.

"Wilhelmina!" he answered. "Frau Holtz!"

"Is he serious?" Regan laughed. "Could it be Frau Holtz has found the love of her life?"

"It must be," Sirena answered, her face glowing with happiness, "even I didn't know her first name. If she's told it to Jacobus it must be true love."

The crew wrestled with Blackheart's body, taking it to the *Sea Spirit* to prepare it for burial. Sirena's quick eye saw Caleb follow the men, and then remove the stout board bridging the distance between the two ships. "Caleb!" Sirena called. "Where are you going?"

"I thought you and Regan could take the *Rana* back to port! You don't need me! I'll sail with the crew. Do you think you can handle it or should we tow you in?"

"We'll handle it, son! Won't we, Sirena?" Regan asked, his voice husky with emotion.

For answer, Sirena smiled up at him, her eyes saying what his heart needed to hear. Caleb beamed across the distance. Somehow, somewhere, Regan and Sirena had found each other again. Their being together was as good and natural as the wind in the sails and the spindrift misting in the air.

"Where to, Capitana?" Jan called.

Sirena looked up at Regan, waiting for his answer. Her emerald-green eyes revealing all he needed to know. She would follow him anywhere in this world or the next. He was her world.

"Back to London to clear up our business and then to Cádiz!" Regan called back. "Caleb tells me there's a new addition to our family. A little girl with dark hair and laughing eyes! Then we'll catch the trades and sail back to Java. Back home!"

Arm in arm, Sirena and Regan entered the captain's cabin. His hand lifted her face to his and he gazed lovingly at her beautiful face. As their lips found each other's, they knew with silent understanding that here, aboard the *Rana*, they had discovered their love. Here they would find it again.

In Regan's arms, protected by his love, Sirena's world became whole again. She was his woman; he belonged to her. Here she could feel his outpouring of love for her; and she returned it. Regan's arms tightened, pressing her closer, holding her as though he would never let her go; giving Sirena her reason for being. She would always be happy here; wanting, needing, loving to be here, in his captive embrace.